AETERNUM SAGA
J.C. KING

NO PLACE FOR US

Dedicated to:
Our many friends and family who never let us quit &
provided the support necessary to reach for the stars.

"Thank you" are two very small words for how much everyone has blessed us
through this journey.

And to Jennifer, Abbie, Jessica, TW Hurst, Kelly & Maria who gave us valuable
insight.

*—Readers can find character bios, pictures of locations, author insights,
chats about the book, and more on the author and book page—*

https://www.facebook.com/profile.php?id=61572704312258

Chapter One

F or at least the fifth time this morning William glanced over at the two men lying across from him. One was a scoundrel to be sure. He knew it from his first chance encounter with him at the port since two able bodied crew members had to be forcibly enlisted to carry him aboard, such was the state of his drunken stupor. A condition which did not improve favorably with his lack of intoxication either, for when the port had worked its way out of his system, it was instead replaced by the worst conversation befitting a man. Most definitely nothing a gentleman would have uttered in even the most chaste of companies, let alone in an open crowd of strangers.

Thankfully, most of his vernacular was entirely in French so it was easy enough to ignore once he had been placed in the hold of the ship. Not utterly removed from the crew, but most definitely away from the paying passengers. A place exclusively reserved for the worst of offenders, or at least that was what William had been told by the crew since he had no real experience concerning these matters. From their very colorful descriptions of the conditions below, just days of having to live down there with an unknown number of rats, rancid seawater up to your knees and thick darkness would do its job of moral remediation quite sufficiently. Or so he hoped.

Well, he surely had time to wait and see. The *Endeavour* had only left England three days earlier bound for Philadelphia. A journey that was predicted to take them anywhere from six weeks, if the weather held true, to months if misfortune befell them. A fact which William had optimistically expected would land them somewhere in the middle.

Now that the Colonies had officially claimed their independence, he had found that he was rather looking forward to the new opportunities and atmosphere such a nation could provide. Anything would be better than living in the shadow of other men far more qualified than he for the rest of his life—feeling adequate but systematically overlooked. For far too long he had dutifully served alongside his father in his surgery without complaint, but William was ready for a change of scenery now or rather, for an aspiring physician, a chance to hang up a sign of his very own.

"Doctor William Harvey Wells," he imagined it would proclaim in neatly painted white letters outside his office door in some rural town or city of distinction. At the moment, he did not have a preference which. Given his unique training and experience under London's most prominent surgeon, he was confident he would be successful anywhere he went. He was sure of it. But first, he had chosen to pay for his passage with temporary servitude as a ship's apprentice doctor on the *Endeavour*. A ship built for the delivery of merchant goods more than people, but capable none-the-less.

Thankfully, despite his initial reservations against it, his father had arranged this novel chance for William to escape his life in England and venture abroad while he was still young. His mother, on the other hand, had intended him to do nothing of the sort, as her one goal in life, it seemed, was for him to marry a woman of noble standing and rise up together with her in society. Maybe he could also have a few grandchildren along the way to carry on the family line, should he be so disposed.

This one point alone was the only thing William would have been happy to endure as he had always loved doting on his brother's children, but his learned father had known his son far too well to subject him to such a life as the rest entailed.

"A man has to make his own way in the world, my dear. You know as well as I that it is not our place to stop him," his father had reasoned quite efficiently with William's mother as the two of them ate their last meal together back in London before his trip.

"Yes, but why all the way in the Americas, dear? Could he not find somewhere more suitable here in England? Those people are surrounded by savages they say." She had then repeatedly blotted the side of her eyes to dry her tears, and it warmed William's heart to think back on the scene and know that in the end, they had at least left on the most amicable of terms.

Sitting below deck in his cabin only days after their departure, William could still feel the warm hug she had given him at the port and his promise to faithfully write them both as soon as humanly possible. As much as he loved the home in which he was raised, he respectfully no longer wished to be a part of the world he had been born into. And so, it was time to discover just who he was when all of that had been stripped away. Whatever that may be underneath.

The man with the curly brown hair and rough appearance groaned beside him, bringing him suddenly back to his present duties.

With a steady hand, garnered by years of experience, William wrung out the muslin rag lying in the bowl next to him and took a few steps over to the man's bunk to bathe his forehead. "This should cool you off a bit, sir." He tried to comfort the man and checked for a rash or any other signs that would predict just what the man was suffering from. The mysterious fever-like condition that had begun just two days prior had not abated in the slightest since he arrived. Moreover, witnessing his increasing deterioration with each passing hour, caused fresh concern to rise within William once more at the speed at which the man's ailment was progressing.

"Charlotte..." The man murmured her name twice before adding more sorrowfully, "must... sorry."

Though no other symptom presented itself, the man with the olive complexion seemed to sleep fitfully as if in a strange trance, soaking the tan cotton shirt he wore in obvious sweat. Yet more concerning than the fever was the fact that his skin was also growing colder and greyer to the touch instead of the expected pink flush the doctor was accustomed to seeing.

Whatever the true nature of his ailment may be, it had left the new apprentice utterly stupefied and uncertain about his qualifications after all, as his diagnosis continued to elude him.

"You should rest, sir. You will be just fine. You'll see." William attempted to reassure him though deep down he was unsure if this was a lie he would need to confess at a later date, for just the day before they had buried a woman at sea. Someone who had died of something else altogether, or so said the more learned ship's doctor, Doctor Clarke, but a sad fact just the same.

Gratefully, her name had not been Charlotte, but she was no doubt important to someone, somewhere. And yet, even though he had never met the man in his care, who resembled a Spaniard more than an Englishman, he was sure, whoever this person was he was calling out to, she was equally special to him as he had not stopped saying her name since his arrival below.

The other man in the bunk above him, the tall Frenchman that had just arrived from his stay in the hold, watched everything transpiring beneath him with an air of curiosity mixed with an equal dose of casual indifference. "At least he has someone who will miss him when he is gone." He looked away and over at the wall once more as if suddenly now bored with the conversation at hand. "I dare say, not everyone is that lucky."

"Luck may not have anything to do with it, sir," William replied shortly but remained professional. Though in truth, he did not particularly care for the man and his lack of manners to those he encountered, he still felt compelled to make civil conversation with him as he would with any other patient he might meet. "Are you feeling any better today?"

"My... Oh, how do you say it? ... head is still... ummm, what is the word? ...pounding? And I feel so... cold. You would not happen to have a... another blanket?" The man with the long hair that was neatly tied back with a black satin ribbon managed to reply in broken English layered with an especially thick French accent.

"Sorry, no, but I will see if the captain will loan me another from the cargo." William reached over and then handed up to him a mug of mulled cider from the table beside him that he had poured earlier. "This is probably not what you are used to, but it will help you get your strength back as I assume no one properly fed you down below."

"Quite." The man took the drink without reservation and smelled it tentatively first before taking a sip and wincing in disgust. "What I'm used to..." He chuckled, then started coughing uncontrollably before taking in a rather large gulp of air before continuing. "... is definitely far from this um... I don't even know what to call it precisely."

"Me, neither." William chuckled politely. "But it's the best we have, so drink up."

Without another word, the man lifted his eyebrows just once before also raising his glass slightly in his direction. "Sante, or to your health, as you would say it."

"Well, it would not hurt, that's for sure." William tied his light blonde hair back into a neat ponytail behind him to keep it out of his way as he set back to work flipping through the pages of his notes.

Just then, the door to his quarters opened suddenly and in ducked Doctor Clarke through the tiny doorway followed by two men carrying yet another sick passenger.

To his surprise, however, William instantly recognized him as the young-looking minister that had been excitedly speaking with as many passengers of the ship as possible since his boarding. From piecing together the bits of several conversations he had overheard in passing, he had been able to gather that the minister's story was not that much unlike his own in many regards. The man's leaders had intended for him to begin a prominent parish in England, but despite the sensibility of that decision, he had begged them instead for a placement in the Americas.

Reluctantly, they had agreed and paid his fare, provided he worked for at least one year in some school that was being established just outside of Philadelphia. Their gracious decision was most likely meant as a high honor for someone in his position, which obviously made him more than thrilled to relay the story again and again to anyone who would listen. In fact, most of the paying passengers had already heard it at least once, but of course, all were patient to let him tell it again regardless, seeing as he was such an amiable fellow. As William was quickly learning, distractions were few on board a ship like theirs and interesting conversations were in even shorter supply.

"Nearly fell off the ship, this one." Doctor Clarke shook his head casually as if things like almost dying were a natural, daily occurrence. "One of those do-gooder womenfolk bound for the Colonies saw him stumbling near the port side and before she could call for help, he had nearly tipped head over heels clear over the lower railing. The sea would have claimed him for sure had it not been for her quick thinking and a few well-placed lads up on deck."

"Any idea what is wrong with him?" William queried as he prepared the hanging bunk under the Frenchman and readied the necessary supplies to treat the new arrival. "You can put him here, please."

The sailors obeyed in an obvious huff and roughly dropped into the suspended rope bed the man who was dressed in the short collared white shirt, brown pants and tight overcoat of a typical minister of their day.

"Will that be all?" One of the men asked Doctor Clarke gruffly before following his companions out the door and into the corridor outside as the cabin was quickly becoming crowded.

"Yes," the elder doctor answered him casually. "I'll call for you later should we have need to dispose of a body."

"As you wish." The leader of the group nodded back to him apathetically and climbed the stairs to his right, back to his work above.

"Speaking of dying, isn't it about time you took a break for your dinner?" Doctor Clarke prompted the young apprentice with seemingly little concern for

5

the infirmed men collecting around them. "You won't last the voyage if you keep up this pace. Doctors need to eat, too."

"No, thank you, sir." William shook his head respectfully and swallowed back the bile threatening to make an appearance. "I'm not hungry, truly."

Doctor Clarke shrugged and the whole conversation made William wonder if perhaps the casual disregard his mentor had shown to the suffering men was simply the older doctor's seasoned practice to dismiss outright the severity of any illness, no matter how a patient might appear to the naked eye. Or maybe this was yet another thing the older physician had seen amongst his many voyages to make it more commonplace to him, though William had never encountered whatever they were suffering from once. As young as he was, surely there were countless illnesses that were still unbeknownst to him as his medical knowledge had been mainly restricted to those ailments that often plagued the sick on land and never those at sea. Either way, three men ill in just three days' time seemed more troubling to William than whether or not he had eaten his supper.

His father had often said that his son tended to spend far too much time on the what ifs and whys and not enough on the actual medicine, but he couldn't help the nagging feeling deep down in the pit of his stomach that he was on the verge of something strangely unusual, as the facts were simply not adding up for him as they usually did.

Feeling a deep responsibility for these men once again, the very thought of leaving them in their hour of need felt quite literally impossible. "The porter offered me some stew earlier. I still have it here if you would like some." William felt his insides turn over another time with the swaying of the ship as he nodded in the direction of the barely touched bowl on the table between them.

Not impressed by his lack of compliance to his obvious hint of a command, the older doctor eyed his food on the table with scrutinized judgement as if debating whether or not it was still safe enough to eat.

"I'm sorry, I just haven't had the stomach to finish it, but I am sure there is a fresh serving to be had in the galley if you are interested. Though I'd steer clear of the biscuits if I were you." His nose wrinkled and his stomach flipped the other way just remembering the weevils he had encountered that had already firmly established themselves happily within the layers of flour.

"You'll get used to it." Doctor Clarke observed the room lazily from one man in his bunk to the next to at least appear to demonstrate to his new apprentice that he was still cognizant of their condition. "By the time we are almost to the Americas you'll think those biscuits are cake in disguise."

William shook his head and smiled, incredulous at the mere suggestion of such a fallacy. "Respectfully, I doubt it, sir."

"You'll see." Doctor Clarke nodded knowingly. "Well, if you have a mind to stay with them, I'll be on my way then, but I'll be back to relieve you at first watch."

"First watch or last watch, I'd just as soon keep my place here if it's all the same to you?" William requested, wishing once more he had never left the stability of solid land.

"Haven't gotten your sea legs yet, eh, son?"

"I'm afraid not. It's embarrassing, but it's true," William admitted, though he secretly hoped the man would not continue the conversation further. It was taking far too much of his concentration already to keep whatever food he had managed to consume today in its proper place.

"So, it would appear. Well, see that you tell the captain when or if you need the crew's help tonight." He advised reluctantly before leaving William alone once more with his patients.

Elated to be no longer under the man's critical gaze, William sighed after his departure, feeling ineffective and small. Learning to be a doctor under his father's watchful eye had been hard enough but struggling to prove himself to a complete stranger when he already felt ill from the ever-shifting waves felt crippling.

For the briefest of moments, he allowed the feeling of inadequacy and uncertainty to wash over him once more. *Was he wrong to have thought he was ready?* He second-guessed his abilities yet another time before turning his focus back to the men beside him who were quite obviously in much more need of attention than his vague insecurities.

"Now, let's see what seems to be ailing you, Mr. Beckett." William started to untie the starched collar of his newest patient but stopped when he noticed a small collection of pooled blood near the left side of the man's neck. Beneath the many layers of folded cotton fabric lay a nearly half-inch incision that was still clearly visible to the naked eye though the rather unusual wound had already begun to show signs of clotting.

"Did you cut yourself when you fell, sir? By the depth of this it appears possibly superficial in nature, or at the very least it does not appear to have resulted from some kind of blade or other instrument," he deduced aloud, "and then there is the unusual shape?"

"Did you stumble up on deck? Did you bow too low? Did God strike you down?" The Frenchman mocked the young doctor's professional evaluations from above. "Ah, the frail English."

"Let's not forget. You are here, too," William retorted sarcastically as he glanced up over the edge of the bunk above him with rising indignation building at the overly formal-dressed deckhand.

"Ah, but why?" The French sailor rolled his eyes impertinently as if toying with the man's intellect. "Oh, and you did not happen to see a rather worse for wear chapeau upon the deck after I arrived? It appears to have regrettably gone missing along with your country's manners, it seems."

"No, though by the way you arrived, you should be grateful that was all you lost in the chaos." William shook his head disdainfully and ignored him, refusing to engage further while he cleaned out the minister's wound. "Vile man," he muttered under his breath after finishing his task, and waited in the silence that followed for his temper to lessen to a more cordial level before asking in a tone that he sincerely hoped was not filled with the contempt he was now feeling, "Are you even sick?"

"Define... sick. My symptoms are so... I lack the proper words..." The Frenchman did not comment further but instead continued with an incessant humming of some unfamiliar tune, no doubt popular in his part of the world.

"I don't have the energy for you right now." William mentally chose to momentarily ignore the man's antics again and focused instead on spending the remainder of the evening tending to the Spanish man and the young minister. The Frenchman obviously needed none of his attention medically, but he appeared to be harmless company for the present, maybe even helpful should one of the men become more violent in his sleep. Still, if he persisted in his facade beyond the fleeting patience of those around him, William would simply let the elder doctor take care of him then.

The hours passed, and as they did, he began to feel even more defeated by the fact that his efforts were accomplishing little of anything beneficial whatsoever. Yet, it was well after midnight when his role as a healer suddenly paused, and his focus unexpectedly turned to something infinitely far more pressing.

The mighty vessel, that had been casually swaying from side to side from the natural passing of the waves for days, now began to violently list to one side as if suddenly plunging down a great chasm of some kind before shifting in the opposite direction to compensate. Then, like a tremendous cannon that had just been discharged somewhere beneath his room, the world around him began to quake in reaction to it, casting the contents on his bed onto the floor in total disarray.

"Land's sake! What on earth is going on out there?" William rose instinctively to retrieve his journal and the leather satchel his father had given him upon his departure from off the floor but soon regretted it. In the dipping motion that followed thereafter, all of the other furnishings in the room that had not otherwise been stowed away were carried sideways with the table as it slid from one area of the cabin clear over to the other, taking the two chairs and William along with them.

"Hold on!" The Frenchman reached down a protective arm to the man below, seizing the young doctor by the arm securely and holding him upright in his place.

"Thank you, but I think I can manage from here." William shrugged off the necessity of his help and reached out instinctively to anything solid around him that would give him purchase but only ended up clinging tightly to the bed frames mounted on the wall beside him. "Still, I'm obliged for your quick thinking all the same," he replied to the man sincerely while inspecting the condition of his patients in the swinging bunks who were obviously fairing far better than himself.

It was at that moment that a loud groan echoed throughout the various corridors of the ship causing him even greater alarm than the tremendous listing. With a loud shriek, the vessel all around him cried out as if the very boards of the hull were now screaming in agony against the strain placed upon them.

"All hands to the ready!" The quartermaster shouted from just outside his door before adding in an even sterner voice, "All passengers to your cabins immediately!"

Hearing the intensity within the man's voice, William and the Frenchman exchanged worried glances at the chaos ensuing just outside their cabin, attempting to vaguely prepare themselves for what might transpire next.

They did not have to wait long.

In the time that it took for William to secure the candle and the dishes that had fallen onto the floor back to their position on the dislocated table, the door to their own cabin flew open, hitting its back against the wall behind it with a loud thud. "You, Frenchie! On your feet!" The quartermaster commanded in a voice that would make anyone obey instantly, no matter what their occupation.

The Frenchman, however, was neither amused nor motivated whatsoever by the command. On the contrary, he seemed rebelliously resistant to comply in any way as he got out of bed as slowly as he could possibly manage before standing up to his full height to challenge him, his head touching the edges of the ceiling where he stood. "*Qui? Moi?*"

"Qui... what? I don't care. Like it or not, you are coming with me," the quartermaster demanded as the tell-tale sound of boots clambering up the stairs behind him sounded.

"What is happening, sir? Can I be of use?" William offered timidly though he was not especially sure he would know what to do if the man agreed.

"Looks like the beginning of a hurricane, son. But at this point, I'll take any man I can get so, come with me both of you." The quartermaster handed William his overcoat that had also fallen onto the floor by the door and motioned with his hand for the two men to follow him.

"Have you ever sailed before?" The Frenchman cast a wary glance back at him, certain he knew far more than the man who appeared more advanced than him in age, but in nothing more besides medicine.

"No, you?" William followed after him and closed the door behind them securely.

The man did not reply but only shook his head mournfully at the ineptness of his companion as the two men climbed the worn, wooden stairs behind the quartermaster before being instantly met with a curtain of heavy rain upon their backs. Harsh wind gusts struck their gaze as they flew across the deck before them, pummeling fiercely against their bodies as William tried to follow the quartermaster as obediently as he could manage but fell forward onto the deck more than once as the ship dove headlong down yet another steep wave crest after another.

Just like in the cabin below, on each occasion, a steady hand caught the back of his overcoat like a vise and held on firmly, keeping his cargo safely upon the deck.

Grateful beyond words for the saving action, William swung around instinctively to thank his rescuer only to find the Frenchman steadfastly holding onto one of the ropes anchored to the deck with one hand and William's coat with the other. "Thank you, again!" William shouted appreciatively over the roaring wind.

"*De Rien*!" He released his grip on William only to continue busying himself with tying the rope at his feet into two large loops. "Put this around your waist!"

William obeyed without question as the Frenchman did the same.

"Our fates will be the same, you and I." The tall man wiped the running water from off his face and pulled back his black hair that had entirely loosed itself in the ensuing storm into a makeshift knot. "Now, stay close or we are both finished!" He instructed briefly as he momentarily abandoned his efforts of assisting the other sailors and focused his strength instead on remaining vertical on the deck.

"Wonderful," William muttered, but since the other man clearly had more sense than he did in these matters, he followed his lead blindly. From the sheer power of the torrent attacking the ship, he was sure if a man were to go overboard in these kinds of conditions, no rescue of any kind would be attempted. And once lost at sea, it was either God or Davy Jones that would certainly meet him at the bottom of this watery grave, not the cherubic-like angels and fairy nymphs of the myths and legends he had read as a child.

Following the quartermaster's directions to the letter, the two men spent the next hour at least loosening and tightening the rigging for the three sails before hauling bucket after bucket of water out of the hold in a vain attempt to lessen the ocean within that was collecting more rapidly than they could expel it.

When that wasn't enough, they began ridding the ship of any cargo they could spare to part with, including many of the belongings of their fellow passengers. Still, despite emptying the vessel of at least half of its load, their efforts appeared fruitless as the ship sank lower on the waterline towards certain destruction.

"We'll have to turn back!" The quartermaster called over the crashing waves to the captain behind the wheel. "It's no use! Got six feet of water below the bilge line and rising fast!"

What?! William shook his head in disbelief at what he had just heard. *Were they really turning back?* He could not believe his ears. *Hadn't they only just left?*

The captain scowled with the same thoughts in mind and then nodded seriously before yelling back, "Hard to Starboard! Into the wind, lads!"

The ship's wood timbers almost shrieked in disapproval this time as the captain guided the ship back towards land. With the worst of the hurricane's gale behind them now, wave after wave caught the vessel broadside in its attempt to turn. Before William knew how to react, another sudden rush of water spilled over the rails towards him, hurtling both he and the Frenchman across the deck and into the air, yet surprisingly, they did not fall overboard with the rushing stream as William had expected. On the contrary, as they flew past the center mast on their way to the railing, the thick, hemp rope the Frenchman had so wisely secured around them snapped hard against their bodies, knocking the wind out of both of them completely.

"Argh!" William gasped as he hit the deck and held onto his sore stomach.

The Frenchman only uttered what sounded more like a disgruntled curse.

By the grace of Providence, and who knows what else, they were at least safely still on board but had now found themselves hopelessly entangled around the largest mast of the ship.

"*De Rien... De Rien...* I know!" The man waved his hand dismissively as he struggled to find his footing once more on the ever-shifting deck. "I think we have satisfied the quartermaster's quota of danger for one day! Wouldn't you agree?"

"Definitely!" William called back. "It would be madness to remain! I'm going below!"

"*D'accord!*" He stumbled after him, knowing that neither of their efforts were going to change the course of the events unfolding above.

From the severity of the storm and the damage it had already caused to their ship, it would take a sheer miracle if they made it back to land, let alone survived long enough to talk about it.

What's more, not a single sailor stopped them as they retreated.

They had more important things to worry about, like surviving the night.

Chapter Two

November 24th, 1792

D octor Clarke met the two thoroughly soaked men outside door as they were coming down from the deck to the lower level of the ship, lifting his face up slightly to reveal a rather sheepish look at the sight of them. So odd was his expression in fact that it reminded William entirely of the many times either he, or his brother Robert, would steal a fresh biscuit from the cooling pan in the kitchen before their cook could catch them. A singularly pleasant memory by his recollections, yet on the man's face before him, it seemed to bear something a bit more sinister in nature. "Ah, you have both returned safe and sound, I see. Should I presume that everything is now under control up above?"

"Not exactly. Actually, the captain says we are turning back, sir," William informed him breathlessly after being thrown down the last two steps on his way back down to the infirmary.

"Turning around?" Doctor Clarke's voice betrayed a thin hint of alarm mixed with confusion. "That can't be possible."

"Well, it is. It's hell up there!" William replied, though admittedly a bit more dramatically than he probably should have, given his position underneath the man's authority.

"A good day to die from the looks of things," the Frenchman philosophized morosely while trying to wring out the water from his finely tailored brocade vest and sagging cravat. "Just not so much for me, I hope." He tilted his head in a muted question towards the waiting bunk inside, hoping to avoid another excursion above or below that would only result in more danger or continued dampness.

"Go on." Doctor Clarke admitted his entry. "It appears there is not much <u>any</u> of us can do up there when the winds and the sky have turned against us. Better remain below where it is safe for now. No doubt they'll have need of you both later."

"Have you seen many storms in your travels?" William took two steps into the cabin after the other man and tried to make small talk to distract himself from the ever-present queasiness that kept overtaking him as the ship rocked back and forth incessantly.

"A few, though none as fierce and as fast as this one appears to be," Doctor Clarke replied though he was not entirely focused on the conversation at hand as he kept casting a sideways glance back down the corridor to his right frequently as if expecting someone else to possibly pass by.

"*Il va vomir, monsieur,*" the Frenchman casually chortled from his bunk to his right in partial amusement mixed with the very least bit of concern for the young doctor as watching the man's struggle in life was quickly becoming his new favorite pastime. "He is... um, green. I think that is how you say it?"

"Seriously, again?" Doctor Clarke took a step closer to the door, away from any possible contact from what was to follow.

"I'm fine... really..." William tried to say, but as if on cue with the finishing of the man's prophesy of his imminent demise and his adamant refusal thereafter, his stomach obeyed in violent fashion all over the newly polished shoes at his feet. "Fantastic." William spat the remnants of the remaining liquid twice into the pile before stretching slowly upwards to stand upright and collected himself once more in front of the man.

"Agreed." The Frenchman pinched his nose mockingly. "You couldn't have done that up on deck?"

"*D'accord.*" William nodded wearily as he wiped his mouth with the back of his sleeve before drawing in a very long and somewhat shaky breath. "That would have been infinitely better in comparison, I suppose. But then again, no one times these kinds of things, do they?"

With a reproving glance, Doctor Clarke eyed the mess on the floor next to his bunk for the night and regretted his decision once again to take on such a clearly inept apprentice so late in the year. In truth, he had only agreed to teach the young man what he knew as a personal favor to the captain, but with each passing experience with the lad it was starting to feel like more work than what it would be worth in extra pay. "See that you clean this up immediately, then send the Frenchman back up on deck later when he is dry. The captain won't approve of us sheltering the likes of him indefinitely when he really should be working."

"The likes of him?" William questioned curiously and cast the Frenchman another puzzled look as if trying to see the harm in the man other than his ill-portrayed manners.

"Yes, haven't you ever heard the term 'conscription', son?" Doctor Clarke inclined his head to one side and squinted one eye.

"I'm afraid not," William declined honestly but felt equally embarrassed by his lack of knowledge on the subject. As seasoned as his current teacher may be, Doctor Clarke's continual harsh tone of condescension towards everyone, including his patients, was beginning to unsettle him greatly.

"Well, I suppose if you are going to work on a ship, it's high time you learned the way the system works in regard to scum like him."

"Scum?" William glanced over at the Frenchman again, but the man appeared entirely disinterested in the conversation altogether as he focused his attention instead on examining the cleanliness of his nails with great care.

"Riffraff, scum, you can use whatever term you like, though they all apply equally." He leaned his back against the door casually and folded his arms across his chest. "You see, William, when an English vessel needs new recruits, but none are to be had for pay, they just <u>happen</u> to find many willing souls in taverns and gambling dens alike." He paused before placing his hand on the other side of his mouth, as if disclosing a trade secret just to William himself. "With one free drink and a quick thump on the head it is done, and lo and behold, the ship's captain is the proud owner of a new recruit."

Startled at the abhorrent revelation, William flinched away from the man, his eyes wide-open in astonishment. "You mean to tell me that this man has essentially been kidnapped?"

From the bunk to his left a light chortle sounded at William's naivety on the subject followed only by a hand gesture from the Frenchman as he raised his eyebrows towards William as if to clearly say, "Now, you see."

"Noooo..." Doctor Clarke shook his head casually, then leaned in closer still to William so that the very breath of the coarse man could be felt upon his face. "To kidnap someone would be a crime, right, my boy?"

For a moment, William stood rigid in shock and moral disgust at being an accessory to such an action. "So, if he is essentially our prisoner, when will he be freed?"

"Come his return trip back from the America's, I suppose—provided he survives that long," Doctor Clarke affirmed without the least bit of concern as to the fate of one man over another. "The King is nothing if not gracious to his... um... new subjects." He chuckled but then added in a darker, more foreboding tone, "Though, I think he might make an exception in his case, being French and all."

"*Ou pour toi...*" The Frenchman cursed lowly an accusatory challenge at the audacity of the doctor and those with whom he was employed by on the ship, knowing full-well from his last statement about William that the man by the doorway completely understood his vernacular. Though from the short time that he had been given to become acquainted with the man, he had quickly assessed that there was not a single redeeming quality he felt the older doctor still possessed.

In his estimation, he had now seen at least five other men like him before in his lifetime. Men who clearly displayed only the keenest of pleasures in bringing pain to others—the total opposite, he surmised, of his would-be apprentice. But then again, evil always did love company, and who knows how long the younger doctor would be able to maintain his morals under such a tutor.

"You understand more than you let on, don't you, lad?" The doctor accused him frankly, calling his bluff with narrowed eyes that seemed to bore into him from across the room.

"As you say... I am no longer a... guest on your fair island." He sneered right back, begging the man now for an altercation. Beyond a doubt, just by the man's obviously bulkier physique, he knew he would most definitely lose, but he felt incredibly certain by the look on the man's face just now as he leered at him from the open doorway that he would enjoy every minute of it all the same.

For the better part of half a minute, the two men glared each other down, measuring the other's thoughts disdainfully before the older doctor surprisingly withdrew his challenge altogether and suddenly threw his hand up to dismiss the subject and the man in question. "It isn't for us to say anyhow, Mr. Wells. He should be proud to be part of His Majesty's service. Besides, the captain makes the decisions on this ship. Just be sure not to cross him and send that poor excuse of a sailor over there up on deck before dawn," the doctor commanded from the doorway. "Oh, and keep an eye on Mr. Smith, too. I don't think he will make it through the night at this rate."

"Yes, sir." William obeyed remotely, feeling naively disillusioned and confused by the most recent conversation.

Had he just unknowingly become a part of a criminal act by keeping the Frenchman here against his will? Worse yet, how could he continue to serve in this position knowing full-well what the captain was capable of doing or would do once more if ever the need arose again?

Satisfied at last that he had instructed the lad enough for one night, the older doctor left William to tend to his patients in peace, though definitely not in quiet, as the ship and everything in it continued its argument against the waves just as it had since earlier that morning.

Yet despite all of William's care and attention throughout the day, the minister continued to worsen, much in the same fashion as the Spaniard lying next to him had done just the day before. His much fairer skin, though slightly less mottled in texture, had also taken on the most peculiar, albeit now familiar gray pallor, and the inexplicable profuse sweating had already begun to commence. Though, if William were to be honest, the most intriguing fact of all concerning his care was that the wound on the young man's neck had almost completely healed itself in the twelve hours that had passed since his arrival. Much faster than any wound in his experience should have been able to accomplish as he could barely find its mark other than a small, raised line where the bloodied incision used to be.

As for Mr. Smith, the older man with the calloused hands from obvious daily labor, William had not seen any improvement in his symptoms whatsoever. Though upon further examination, the apprentice could find no wound like that of the preacher's on his body other than a small scar that ran along the lower edge of his jawline. By William's careful estimation, it was most definitely similar in size and shape to that of the other man's, but in a way, it also looked much older in its presentment and not from a recent injury at all. Yet at this point in his care, since nothing else made any sense directly pointing towards a possible diagnosis, the slight mark could also not be ruled out as to the plausible cause.

Though if William were to be more honest, the most worrisome symptom in both of their care was the concerning fact that Mr. Smith had regrettably ceased his murmured pleas altogether after midnight as he fell quite suddenly into an almost deathlike slumber. So much so, that had the doctor not been able to plainly observe the slightest rising and falling movement of his chest, in all other aspects he would have assumed that his poor soul had already ceased from its earthly struggle as Doctor Clarke had previously foretold.

"You must hold on for a little longer, my friend. The ship has turned back to England, so you will be home soon if we can make it," William encouraged him with a yawn as he had now been awake for almost a full day's time. "Be strong for Charlotte, and for me... please. I'm not ready to lose another patient just yet." He patted his arm remotely and fell into his own bunk across from the men, feeling totally spent from the day's activities and lack of lasting nutrition.

"Will you watch Mr. Beckett and Mr. Smith for an hour, please?" William barely mumbled to the Frenchman as he closed his eyes, hoping to find just a few moments of peaceful rest.

"I will, though I am not sure what good it will do. One of them is almost gone as it is," the tall man on the upper bunk answered him plainly, but William truly did not register his reply for he had already begun fading off to welcomed sleep.

And sleep he did, though unfortunately for him it was not the slumber he had initially desired, for it was filled with the very vivid imaginations of what might have transpired with the Frenchman at some shady tavern along the port's busy street. Like the minister and the Spaniard before him, William tossed back and forth throughout his dreams trying to defend the man against his would-be attackers only to be awakened with a start thereafter by a loud thud inside the infirmary after what felt like only seconds, though several hours had already passed.

Freshly alarmed by the noise and the darkness now enveloping his quarters all around him, he looked over at the three bunks across the way and rubbed his eyes twice to clear the sleep away from them.

Without the light from the now extinguished candle on the other side of the room, the shadows crawling across the floor seemed to move of their own accord along the walls within the darkened room and over to the door across from his bed.

Uncertain of what he was truly seeing, William reached for a nearby candle to light it and peered harder into the darkness beyond. To his great relief, nothing in the room appeared unusually amiss whatsoever. The minister was still restlessly tossing, just like he had been doing for the past day, murmuring something about being terribly cold and shivering. The older man beside him was still alive, though he continued to lay very still, and the Frenchman...

Wait! Where was the Frenchman? Was the thud from someone who had come to take him back up to work on deck?

Impossible! He would have heard his passing or at least been awakened by the light in the outer corridor when they opened the door to fetch him.

Still... William felt an uneasiness overtake him by his unexpected absence and knew he would not be able to rest further unless he found out for sure. Reaching over wearily, he fought against his body's desire to remain and snatched up his overcoat dutifully as he slid both arms into it and leaned over to secure his newly purchased boots, the ones his father informed him 'no seaman worth his salt would be without'. Yet they were not where he had left them carefully below his bunk. With the movement of the ship during his sleep, they had displaced themselves entirely and were now lying sideways in a large puddle of water upon the floor.

"The ship **is** sinking!" William's eyes grew instantly wide with alarm as he jumped into action. "I'll be right back!" He said to the men in his care though he expected no audible reply from either of them in their condition. Nor would they probably care that he was leaving, he supposed, but he made the polite gesture anyways—compelled more by his instilled manners than by actual logic.

With increasing panic rising within his chest with every step, he left the room urgently and entered the chaotic scene unfolding just outside his door. Below deck: men were shouting, women were crying, and items were floating everywhere the eye could see. In truth, nothing was as it should be, nor had it ever occurred in this manner previously during the voyage thus far. Yet once he arrived on the upper deck, he could plainly see that the storm was still raging on just as furiously as it had done hours earlier, only this time the ship was now struggling to crest a mighty wave before plunging down steeply into the trough of another one as it listed quite heavily to one side.

Peering through the driving rain for any sign of the Frenchman working in the vicinity, William turned his face instinctively into the wind just as a strong northeasterly gust pressed hard against his back. High above him, an eerie form of darkness that matched that of his room below, enveloped the landscape all around, obscuring the ocean as well as the sky as it cast its doom upon all who existed within it.

For a moment, it frightened William to his core to witness such intensity and power from something so entirely beyond his control. In fact, the fear that gripped his heart in that moment scared him beyond even contemplating his fragile mortality for at no other point in his life had he felt so insignificant than he did right now with the driving rain pelting him incessantly with such force that he could barely endure it.

With a shaky hand, he pulled his soaked hair back away from his face and fought valiantly just to remain standing amidst the gale. There was nothing left for him to do but watch powerlessly as the waves crashed again and again against the railings, spraying him with each blow until he was quite thoroughly soaked to the skin as before and half-blinded by the salty mist. Nevertheless, he decided once and for all that he would not give in to his fears and return below, even if it took everything in him to keep his balance and footing against the onslaught of oceanic forces.

Surveying the empty deck before him, for the first time in his life, William was suddenly uncertain as to what to do next. From what he could see, not a single member of the crew was still at their posts... not the quartermaster... not the captain, nor any other of the lower members of the crew to speak of save one solitary man who appeared to be almost certainly tied to the helm itself.

Had everyone else been cast overboard while he slept or were they all below repairing the damage to their vessel?

Either way, he wouldn't find the answers he sought standing there exposed to the elements. Determined anew to find the foreign prisoner, the young doctor steadied each of his movements deliberately as he took one step after the other in his journey around to the side of the quarterdeck in search of anyone who could explain what had happened to the man, but he encountered no one. Oddly enough, not a single solitary soul remained on the second, upper deck as well as the first. It was almost as if the storm was controlling the fate of the Endeavor now and not the men who commanded it.

When he had finally reached the beginning of the second platform on his way over to the following section, he thought he saw off in the distance what appeared to be the shadowed form of the older doctor with another man standing close beside him near the stern of the boat. Yet try as he might, it was still too hard to see exactly what was transpiring between them from his position so far away.

"Doctor Clarke!" He called out to the man, but his voice was quickly drowned out by the next crashing wave. Undeterred by his foiled attempt, he pressed onward and refused to yield.

"*Demon*!" He thought he heard one of the men shout but the strangeness of the word in the wind made him certain he must have been mistaken.

Stopping to view them better, he continued to watch them both in increasing horror from his position as they struggled violently back and forth until one of the men suddenly fell in a crumpled heap upon the deck.

Afraid he might be too late by his lack of ability to traverse the ship; William quickened his pace but stopped abruptly when he noticed a rope tied fast to the railing on his right as he passed. As if in fear of a repeat of the day's earlier occurrence, he wrapped it securely around his center, just like the Frenchman had done for him prior, before continuing onward.

"Doctor Clarke?" William called over the roaring surf and storm and reached for the railing to steady himself through the rushing water.

Hearing his labored approach, the man standing over the fallen mass on the deck turned to face him in movements almost too fast for William to fully comprehend. The figure who he had seen fighting was indeed the older doctor, but something was wrong, too. A red splash of color was now clearly visible on his face as it dripped down from the spray on his chin and onto the deck below, leaving behind small watercolor stains wherever it touched.

"Sir, are you injured?" William rubbed the salty spray out of his eyes, as if trying to make sense of what he thought he was seeing.

"*Satan*! Run!" The man on the ground warned him in rasping gasps, then fell silent once more, no longer trying to defend himself against the man now towering above him.

Caring nothing for his own safety, William rushed to his side to assess his condition.

The man who was injured was most definitely the Frenchman, though his neck and hands were both thoroughly covered in fresh blood that was now mingling with the sea water rushing over him.

"He is hurt!" William cast a glance up at the man above him before trying to mechanically stop the bleeding. "What happened? Did he fight you?" William reasoned as he searched for the explanation that continued to elude him, choosing rather to think well of the doctor by assuming the kidnapped man had attempted some kind of foolish escape while he had been asleep. Though where he had hoped to flee in the middle of the vast ocean was totally beyond his comprehension.

"Leave him," Doctor Clarke replied before wiping his mouth off with the back of his sleeve as if the action would erase the image already burned into William's memory. "He is expendable."

William's mind raced feverishly with this nonsensical reply before suddenly putting together all the confusing pieces. "Expendable? Wait! You have been doing this!"

Doctor Clarke smiled almost regally before answering in a manner as if he were chastising the young apprentice in his studies. "But, of course, you silly boy. Why else do you think those men have been suffering down below? Though honestly, if you had not been fussing over them for days, they would have already been buried at sea like the rest and not mothered by a skinny whelp of a surgeon like you. There was never a moment to..."

"But, why? ...that woman... the Frenchman. Who else?" William's face flushed with anger at being cruelly used once again on this doomed voyage.

"Maybe you, too," Doctor Clarke challenged him impatiently, then reached down and abruptly seized William by the shirt, heaving him fully upright before the man could find his footing upon the boards.

Suddenly certain he would end up like the victim at his feet, William fought back with every ounce of his worth, yet he was clearly no match for the bigger man who gripped him tightly. Growing up in a world of privilege, William had never once been given the opportunity to defend himself physically. His was the world of forbidden duels and carefully laid verbal critiques, not fists and knives or whatever other instrument the older doctor had chosen to murder his victims with on the ship. But none of that mattered now. William's sole thought at this moment and every second thereafter was centered on only one thing—survival.

Thrashing this way and that against him, William struggled as best as he could to free himself from his captor but in just a few short movements he found himself being choked from behind with nothing else within his reach with which to fight. Regrettably, just like the man lying on the deck at his feet, it was becoming increasingly apparent that his first real fight was quickly proving it could also be his last.

Then, as if the situation could not deteriorate any farther, in an instant of torturous agony, a hot searing pain shot through him as if he was being branded by an iron on the side of his neck, followed by an almost inescapable sensation that he could no longer breathe. Just like in any other bloodletting ritual he had attended with his father, William felt the warmth of his fleeting lifeforce spread all the way down to his toes despite the cold rain washing down his hair into his face, as it soaked through his clothes.

Desperate now to be free of his personal hell, he kicked once or twice backwards feebly at the man to stop his attack, but the agonizing pain continued until he began to feel dizzy and lightheaded by the overall ordeal. Yet, it was at that very moment, between what felt like life or death, that another towering wave came suddenly crashing over the two fighting men with such voracity that it displaced everything in its path including the two combatants.

Gasping for the air his lungs so fervently needed, William fell hard against the deck. "Agh!" He cried out in pain and coughed as he mentally assessed his faculties for any lasting injury. Grateful that there appeared to be none at the moment beyond the sizable cut towards the back of his neck that was now throbbing incessantly, he tried to exhale fully but stopped when a sharp pain within his chest brought him up short. His ribs appeared to still be intact, but his battered lungs were now screaming out in agony against the burning saltwater he had just consumed.

Instinctively, he lifted his head through the pain and searched for the Frenchman before managing to grasp the bloodied man's arm tightly as he felt the rope flex around his smaller waist once more. Then, seeing the rushing water head towards them again from the opposite side of the ship, William braced himself against it, attempting to shield the other man from the crashing wave as it washed over the two of them instantly, pressing them hard against the wooden railing like rags upon a table, wiping it clean.

The man beside him only groaned in response to the beating and it almost matched perfectly the haunting moan that echoed next from deep within the ship below them, reverberating the wooden planks upon which they lay.

"What... was... that?" The Frenchman gasped when he could at last draw in a full breath.

"I'm not sure." William shook his head twice to clear away the fog-like confusion that was beginning to build within it before steadying himself on his feet and realizing with fresh horror that the sound they had just heard was coming from the very hull of the ship. "We need to move! Now!" He shouted as he used his remaining strength to lift the semi-conscious Frenchman upright before securing an arm beneath his shoulder for support.

"I can't." The man panted back his reply, his head barely able to lift itself, much less his feet.

"You must, or we will both perish here and now!" William ordered and began the process of dragging the man towards the lower half of the second deck.

"Where... where is he?" The man cast a shaky glance back over his shoulder, as if needing to remind himself once again that they were indeed still alone.

"Doctor Clark? I don't know, and I don't care!" William gave the same wary look behind him and was cautiously relieved to see that the culprit, Doctor Clarke, was no longer anywhere to be found. It was almost as if the sea, with all of its justice and mercy, had simply reached out and claimed him as its own—a point which seemed vaguely justifiable given the current circumstances.

"You know, if we keep meeting like this, you are going to have to eventually tell me your name, friend." William struggled to haul the two of them and the heavy, wet rope towards the safety of the lower deck.

"Emile," the Frenchman said, though William could tell, it took much of his strength to speak it. "Emile Deschamps."

"William Wells," he introduced, heavily out of breath, as well, but continued taking step after agonizing step towards safety.

"You learn fast." Emile chuckled lightly and touched the rope responsible for their survival.

"I had a good teacher." William smiled and untied it when they had reached the door to the lower cabins.

"I hope not." Emile raised his eyebrows, but both of them fully comprehended his hidden meaning about Doctor Clarke.

"Can you walk on your own, now?" William asked as he examined the wound on Emile's neck to make sure it did not need to be bound.

"Not yet. Just leave me here a moment." Emile dropped to the deck by the open door and rested his back against the wood panels of the structure, grateful for some stability at last.

"The ship is sinking, Emile. I have got to get the other men below or they'll drown where they are."

"They will most likely drown, anyways." Emile tried to reason with the man but could not continue further as he lacked the energy for such a complicated moral discussion.

"Maybe, but just like you, they are my responsibility." William confessed, feeling an overwhelming bond forming with the man he had only met days earlier.

"Go, then." He nodded in understanding but chose to remain steadfastly where he sat. "...and *Merci*, William."

"*De Rien*," William replied simply, though no expression of gratitude was ever needed on his part.

With no time to lose, William rushed below deck and lifted the more incapacitated of the men onto his shoulders before taking him up the short steps and placing him next to Emile. Then, as quickly as he had done with the first man, he returned dutifully once more below for the minister and his scant belongings, cautiously optimistic about their chances of survival.

With all four men finally up on deck, William surveyed his surroundings closer and tried his best to form a plan as to what to do next. Their options were most definitely limited and, on the whole, entirely undesirable, but whatever he finally decided upon, he knew they needed to move fast to secure it before nothing else remained.

"You're bleeding," Emile interrupted his planning by pointing weakly up to William's neck, then dropping his hand just as limply back upon his lap.

Startled, William felt the severity of the wound with his fingertips and winced at the pain that shot through his body in doing so. "It's just a cut from when we hit the railing, I think." He wiped his hand off on the length of his wet sleeve, then continued. "It's not important. Look! I see a small craft over there that might hold us all." William pointed to the tightly secured rowboat on the far side of the ship that was meant for ferrying a few passengers ashore once at port.

"If this big ship cannot handle those waves, what do you think that tiny skiff is going to do?" Emile rebuked him incredulously as he had no intention of volunteering to go on a suicide mission by getting into that small of a boat in this violent of a storm. "You'll kill us all that way for sure!"

"It's the only thing we have left, I'm afraid, and we had better take it before there is no chance at all. Now, please help me with these two. I'll cut the ropes once we are inside if the ship sinks. If not, we will only suffer from being drenched further by this Godforsaken rain. I should think it would be a small price to pay for possible salvation, Emile." William defiantly instructed as if begging the other man on the deck to question him in the slightest.

"As you wish." Emile spat out the seawater that had been splashing against his mouth from the quarterdeck above. "I guess it is a good day to die after all."

"Oh, stop being so dramatic and get up already." William picked up the heavier of the two men first and worked steadily through the rain until all four of them were now safely inside the lifeboat. "I will need your help to make sure they remain in the rowboat once we cut the ropes!" William commanded over the roaring wind that now threatened to drown him out each time he spoke.

"Pardon me for saying this, but dead men don't particularly care where they are laid, William!" Emile quipped back sarcastically before taking his place at the other end opposite of William.

"Just the same! I mean to get us all home to our families, one way or another!" William called back and arranged the minister so that his body could lay parallel to the other man between him and Emile.

"Your home or mine?" Emile ducked his head to escape at least some of the wind's abrasive pummeling before wrapping his arms tightly around his body to control some of the racking tremors.

"Does it matter really?"

"At this point... no!" Emile shouted back over the roar.

For almost thirty minutes, William sat shivering in his seat at the head of the rowboat as he struggled to stay upright. From time to time, he could feel his body sway slightly as he began experiencing the effects of his injury the longer he was stagnant, but each time it did, something inside of him pushed himself to remain incomprehensibly coherent. From everything he had learned over the years in treating his patients, William was painfully aware that should he remain in this condition much longer, exposed to the elements as they were, he was not entirely sure he would still be conscious when the ship began to sink, much less have the strength necessary to row them all to safety when he was needed most. However, he had to at least try... even if that meant his life over theirs, which in the bigger picture of things, who knew if any of them would survive the night at this rate, much less the storm.

Then, in the moment that he felt his body finally drifting off mentally at last, a sudden flash of lightning struck the mast in the center of the ship beside them, causing it to burst into a swarm of a thousand exploding splinters. With a jolt and a moan that sent shivers up William's spine, the keel groaned loudly next in response to the now gaping hole that had been created by the massive timber before the ship beneath them began rapidly descending downward, plunging everything around it into the deep.

Fresh adrenaline coursed through him once more, pushing him into action as he immediately cut his side of the rope before tossing his blade quickly over to Emile when the rope on his side stuck in the pulley above. "Emile, NOW!" He shouted and trusted that the man on the other side of the boat was coherent enough to do the same.

As soon as the blade hit his hand, Emile swung around awkwardly and sawed at the fibers with all his might before managing to complete his task mere seconds later. "Hold on!" Emile yelled as he gripped both sides of the boat to brace himself for the horrifying impact and certain destruction, yet his fears were greatly unrealized. With a splash not unlike any of the waves that had hit the ship previously, the vessel connected instead with one of them and they watched gratefully as it thrust them farther away from the larger vessel like they were riding upon the current's mighty crest. A feat beyond anything that either of them could have ever accomplished on their own.

"Now Row! Row like your life is depending on it!" William shouted to Emile and grabbed one of the larger oars stored safely near his feet to steer the vessel with it.

Together, the Frenchman and the doctor fought as hard as they could to guide the boat away from the ship and the pull of the currents that threatened to drag them under, knowing that if they did not, they would not survive. While behind them, a chaotic scene unfolded as men and women jumped over the railings and clung to various pieces of cargo or wood from the ship. From their unique vantage point, it appeared as if the very sea itself had turned into a mass of humanity and nature as the waves ate some of them up like a huge, horrible fish while others struggled until they found something buoyant enough to hold them afloat as best as possible.

Feeling a great sense of despair for the perishing passengers, William felt compelled many times over to return for as many survivors as he could possibly manage to save but he did not move once to intervene. Sad as the reality of the situation unfolding was, he knew there was no way could save them all, and so he did what he must. He looked away from the scene entirely, stealing within himself, as his father had once taught him how to do, to block out their cries so that he could focus on the men that he could save. For some unknown reason beyond his comprehension, Providence had placed each of them in his care making him feel solely responsible for their survival.

Remorseful, but also firmly resolved that he had made the right decision, he glanced back at the tragic scene once more before forcing himself to row onwards towards what he hoped would be land. And row, he did, well into the night, against the wind and the rain that threatened more than once to overturn their vessel and cast them all into the deep along with Doctor Clarke, but William refused to relent even once. At this point, it was a test of wills between them and the ocean, and though the odds were most decidedly stacked against them, he was determined to win—whatever the personal cost.

Quite obviously more injured than himself, Emile contributed as he was able, and together they managed to keep the vessel afloat by taking turns rowing throughout the day and well into the evening hours. Yet by the time night fell at last upon their vessel once more, both men were utterly spent and ready to be done with the hellish nightmare that had befallen them. It had been hours since either of them had seen anything of the ship or its passengers and still no land was in sight though the waves had calmed considerably the farther they had moved away from it.

At last, with very little strength remaining, they both collapsed across the back of their seats in total exhaustion, letting the ocean drag the four of them wherever it willed. The mighty Poseidon had finally won the battle, like he knew that he would, and as incapacitated as they were in that moment, they had ceased to be able to make a conscious action of rebellion against him.

Across several miles of open ocean, the waves happily dragged their beaten vessel back to land, like a defeated child under his master's watchful gaze. Still the vessel defiantly refused to comply, and within just a few hours, William and Emile were both awakened once more by the awful realization that their small savior was now being pummeled not by the rough waves of the ocean, but instead against a rocky cove.

Fearing their certain destruction, they used their oars to steer around the largest of these stoney guardians and were rewarded miraculously when the boat finally felt the bottom of its keel find firm purchase upon the sand. Relieved and more than a bit worse for wear, they climbed out of the boat, then attempted to pull it higher up on shore, knowing the rougher surf would only drag it back out to sea with the tide if they did not. Then, with the last of their strength remaining, William and Emile carried each of the incapacitated men higher up upon the beach, away from the pounding surf, before collapsing next to each other in overwhelming fatigue.

"Well, we didn't die, my friend." William gasped each word out as he struggled to take in enough air for the next, his head pounding from his injuries in the fight and the shock of the journey. The adrenaline that had once been flowing freely through his veins had regrettably vanished hours ago, leaving in its wake an overbearing chill that seemed to grip his every muscle so tightly he felt as if his very bones were about to break. In fact, so intense were the tremors now that it was all that he could do to keep his teeth from chattering violently against each other as he spoke.

"The way I am feeling right now, I rather wish we <u>had</u> perished at sea." Emile rolled over onto his side to vomit up some of the excess seawater he had swallowed along their journey.

"Agreed." William turned his head weakly to look over at the other men lying next to him but refused to move any other part of his body, feeling a great sense of atonement for accomplishing at least something noble after all that Doctor Clarke had blamed him for in their survival. "At least we are all safe."

"For now..." Emile laid himself prone upon his back once more and faced upwards letting the rain wash away the rest of the salt from his face and clothing.

"For now," William agreed breathlessly and drifted off to blessed unconsciousness.

Chapter Three

November 26th, 1792

"Wake up, please, sir," a man's voice urged over the noise of the incessant pelting of the rain upon the sand.

As if in a horrible nightmare-like dream, William felt someone shake him roughly several times but could not produce enough energy to move anything in response. "Go... a-way." He resisted with his arm draped firmly over his eyes to shield them from the constant water and throbbing pain transpiring within his head. With thud after deafening thud, his heart now matched his head in its drum-like pounding within his ears much like the rhythm of the waves beside him.

"We will have to carry him," another voice spoke, only this one he recognized vaguely as being that of the preacher on the *Endeavour*.

Every muscle in William's body felt as stiff as the oar he had rowed with for hours, but hearing the man's voice, and knowing he most certainly survived, brought him at least the smallest sliver of joy, even if he could not move at all to express it.

"One... Two..." With a jolt upwards his body lifted and the motion of it sent surges of fresh pain throughout his body.

"Just let me die here!" William groaned in agony though he did not have the strength to struggle against them.

"Not today, sir," the first man commanded, over the sound of crunching sand beneath his feet.

"You know…" The other man drew in a quick breath. "For someone so thin, he sure is heavy."

He could hear the preacher remark under the repeated drumming noise as he swayed back and forth within their arms. His world spinning with the movement it created.

"Oh, I don't know," the other man stated in a distinctly Spanish influenced accent though oddly enough, also highly muted by a more southern, English dialect. "The taller man was much worse, and definitely more volatile. Could you even understand what he was trying to say?"

"Not a word, I'm afraid," the other man answered just as quickly.

Emile? William's thoughts remained scattered, but vaguely cognizant that his companion was still with him.

"True." Struggling under his side of the load, the preacher sounded vaguely overwhelmed, yet enduring the torture dutifully, anyways.

Straining under their second load of the day, the two men succeeded in carrying the young doctor a good twenty feet up from the shoreline and into the mouth of a sheltering cave, before they laid him directly next to the other man they had found earlier on the beach.

The beach where they had awakened before dawn had appeared utterly desolate of vegetation near the water's edge, surrounded on all sides by a waist-high wall of dark grey boulders along the upper edge next to a line of thicker pines. Nothing like the flat beaches they were accustomed to back in England with their tall cliff-like walls and soft sand. This was more of a craggy wasteland that had resulted from years of uneven erosion of the nearby mountain.

"We should probably try to pull the boat farther up on shore too!" The younger man yelled over the howl outside, not especially eager to go back out into the blowing rain. "If we don't, the waves may take it altogether!"

"You're assuming we are going to need it again!" The other man shouted in return.

"I don't know if we will or not, but I would hate to lose what little resources we have left at the present!"

"Agreed!" The Spaniard simply nodded and ran with him back through the storm to the water's edge.

Working together, with a few coordinated heaves and pushes through the rising surf, they managed to bring the boat a good ten feet up the bank to its final resting place upon a taller outcropping of rocks before turning it over to secure it.

"That should do it." The more fit of the two men determined as he drew both of his hands through his lengthened curls to lessen the heavy weight of the water accumulating upon them as he ran back to the cave's small entrance.

"You wouldn't happen to know how to fish, would you?" The preacher asked as he dusted the wet sand from off his palms, though distractedly missing the rather thick layer of sand that was still coating his wet pant legs below.

The other man merely shook his head and laughed lightly at the foolish suggestion. "I think you will find that we lack both bait and pole, sir. Besides, most people of my acquaintance do not fish in the middle of a thunderstorm, at least not sane people."

"Of course, you're right," the preacher replied, smiling for the first time since he had awakened earlier that dismal morning on the beach. "But we could at least try to find something to eat while we still have light. There must be something edible nearby."

The man across from him tilted his head to one side, then squinted one eye shut to peer over at him. "Got any other bright ideas?"

"A few." He paced awkwardly, uncertain if the man in front of him would be amenable to what he was about to suggest. "I hate to even mention going out again in that mess, but when we were running up here just now, I did see what appeared to be some kind of tide pools beyond those boulders over there." He pointed to the dark rocks directly east of the cave's entrance. "We may yet be able to find some edible sea life in them if we can manage to be quick enough to catch them, or perhaps some small crustaceans might even have been collected there over time."

Peering in the direction to which he had pointed, his companion pursed his lips once in obvious deliberation, then answered, "It wouldn't hurt to look, I suppose, seeing as we are already soaked to the skin anyways. At this point, we can't get any more wet."

"My thoughts precisely." The preacher nodded in resolution, then stepped out of the cave confidently into the blowing wind once more as he made his way skillfully over to the tidepools while all the while trying his best to remain closer to the somewhat dry ridge of beach that the projected ledge from the cave beside them created. Cascading waterfalls and small streams escaped from off the top of it every few feet, causing them more than once to navigate closer to the rough walls that clawed at their coats and snagged at their skin to avoid their currents, but at long last they reached the small pools beyond and the possibility they provided.

"I can't see anything in all this rain!" The older man admitted in frustration, trying his best to peer through the ripples on the surface the rain created for anything that appeared remotely edible.

"No? There's a feast here, my friend!" The preacher rejoiced happily as he took off his well-soaked vest to carry the large handfuls of clams that he had already pulled out from within the shallow edge of the pool. "Do you think ten or twelve will be enough for the two of us?"

"Yes, but those would be better cooked, I should think. I've never tried them raw," the man with the slightly olive complexion suggested while trying to contain a shivering tremor that was now spreading throughout his entire body.

Eager to be out of the elements and back into the protection of the cave, he raised one hand over his eyes to peruse the woods nearby. "I think I can see an area over there that has some smaller pieces of wood that might still be dry, or at least I hope so. Do you think you could secure some of them if I go back to start a fire?"

"You can do that?" His companion looked pleasantly surprised by his stroke of good fortune, for if God had seen fit to deposit him on this deserted island, at least He had decided to give him an added blessing of such a resourceful fellow.

The other man nodded with an air of confidence and pointed to the area down the stretch of protected wall where the bleached limbs lay nestled under a much larger pile of logs. "Give me the clams. I'll go prepare an area by the others. It won't be much, but it will at least keep us warm, I hope."

"Alright." Without further discussion on the matter, the preacher handed over their collected meal and climbed obediently up the small, mounded ridge to recover the dry wood. He intended on carrying back as much of it as he possibly could so as to not have to go back out in the driving rain. As a rule, he was not normally one given to complain, no matter what the circumstances, but after working for the past hour in these rather dismal conditions hauling in the two men, he felt justifiably opinioned that he had endured quite enough of being wet for one day maybe two if the weather did not change dramatically soon.

The two parted ways, each setting off to their appointed task of survival. The preacher scurrying towards the tree line beyond, and the older of the two men dodging the waterfalls once more as he traveled along the path until he was safe in the protection of the cave.

"Blessed rain!" He pulled back his longer curls that had been flung into his face by the gusting wind and breathed out a long, exhaled sigh that culminated in a quick shiver that passed its way through the entire length of his being. "What I'd give for a woolen blanket and dry clothes right about now." He paused and squinted his eyes to survey as much of the cave as he possibly could in the dim light pouring in from the opening. Satisfied by what he saw in the distance, he trudged farther back into the far recesses of the cave determined to find what he required to create the necessary fire bundle—the key to sustaining a flame no matter what the conditions he might experience. It wasn't going to be easy, but then again as he had learned on many occasions in the past, most things worth having rarely were, and in situations like the one he was in now, fire was more than necessary, it was vital.

When at last he reached the back wall and its ragged shelves of various shales and sharp outcroppings, he stopped and listened to the faint tapping of the rainwater that fell from the ceiling to ascertain in which direction he should look first. "It would be a miracle if anything in this wretched place is dry at all right now," he scoffed pessimistically, then stooped down to scan the nooks and crannies along the mid-section of the cave.

Unfortunately, he had been right, painfully so. There wasn't much around him that wasn't already thoroughly soaked from the rain or the moisture from the tide and completely covered in decaying sludge. However, in a very small pocket at his eye level, he spied something at last that made his heart sing. There, tucked away from the elements, he discovered the smallest piece of flint, some decaying bark scrapings, and a sizable handful of Spanish moss.

Excited beyond words, he snatched them up and tucked the precious cargo within the folds of his shirt, afraid that they would moisten further in the salty sea air if he were to carry them otherwise. Then, near the area where the two men lay, he saw at least two clumps of sun-bleached foliage tucked partially under the sand that might prove to work nicely, as well. In all, it wasn't much to speak of, but perhaps with a little coaxing, he would be successful. Or at least, it was worth a try.

Feeling more confident about the task placed before him than when he had first entered the cave, he set to work diligently digging a small hole in the sand with both of his hands far enough away from the men who were sleeping so as not to burn them, but close enough to emanate a good bit of warmth in their direction, as well. The pit itself would not be much to look at by any stretch of the imagination, but the fire it would contain could provide at least some small measure towards their survival. "If I can get it started that is..." He said hesitantly under his breath and arranged his collected treasures into a small bundle in the center of the pit.

"My! You _are_ handy!" The younger man exclaimed as he entered the cave once more in awe of everything the man had been able to accomplish in the short time that he was away. "I would not have even known the first thing to do, let alone how to get a fire actually started."

"Then how do you stay warm at home?" The Spaniard held his hair back from his face as he tilted his head close to the sand base and blew ever so gently on the glowing embers he had created from his knife and the flint that he brought from the back of the cave.

"I'm afraid that task has always been given to one of my pupils back home," the preacher admitted sheepishly.

"Hmmppf," the man scoffed quietly in subtle judgement before adding, "I suppose I know fire better than most being a blacksmith and all. Been lighting the forge for as long as I can remember." A small flame grew to life before him, causing him to raise one eyebrow in exultation and smile at the blessedness of the dancing light. It had been close to twenty years since he had first been given his initial instruction as an apprentice, yet the delight of the simple creation had never once waned for him.

"That is truly astounding! Miraculous even!" The preacher's eyes were filled with a complete admiration for the man and his obvious talents.

"It's a fire, not an act of God, man." The man on the ground moved quickly to add one small twig after another, then paused momentarily as the action brought back to him a familiar memory of his family. His sons loved to make little pyres of small twigs along the dirt floor of his forge while he worked, each taking turns to see whose flames grew the tallest.

"Well, maybe not but I am grateful for it just the same, and for you." The man across from him fumbled for the right words after the older man's harsh criticism.

"No thanks needed. Though to tell you the truth, I haven't made a fire this way for many years. Still, I suppose not everyone can manage it without learning first." He dusted off the sand from his hands and added more kindling to the growing flames. "When I started my apprenticeship back in Portsmouth, all I needed was for someone to give me a stick and some shavings and I could get a flame burning quicker than my master could collect his tools."

"Do you have a family back home?" The preacher removed several articles of his damp clothing to wring the excess water out of them, in the hopes that doing so would allow them to dry faster.

"Yes, my wife, Charlotte and two boys that pester their momma a bit more than help her most days." He chuckled at the recent memory of his two sons running around the house playing pirates before continuing. "Jedidiah will turn eight this fall, and Elijah just finished his fifth year, though right now they are both trying to eat us out of house and home, I think. They have a knack for playing in the ashes, too. Or at least that is what my wife calls it. I guess they are much like their papa in that regard." He paused and looked out at the storm in reflection.

"Have you been married long then?" The younger man kept the small talk going, afraid of the awkwardness within him the silence always created.

"Seems like forever on somedays like today... others, not so much." He added a few of the larger sticks and even a hand-sized branch to the fire before removing his chocolate brown vest and coat to drape them on the pile of logs the younger man had placed nearby. "Though I'm careful not to say any of that in front of her to be sure or she might refuse me my supper."

The two men laughed together lightly at the simplicity of the statement and stopped their conversation momentarily to truly appreciate the joy the fire was bringing to them on the otherwise overcast day.

"Still, all things considered, we are glad we have each other, which is more than most people can boast. And what about you?" The older man smiled up at him as he stoked the fire and arranged the now reddening coals skillfully around a flat rock that had been placed therein to cook their meal.

"A bachelor still, I am afraid," the younger man replied, then tried to pull back his tawny brown hair into a more manageable, albeit quite shorter ponytail behind. "Fact is, I have been a bit too preoccupied with the Lord's work for anything like that to occur."

"You should make the time," his companion advised and added their collected food to the flat stone one at a time before eyeing the man across from him skeptically. The young man illuminated by the growing flames looked barely old enough to be beginning a trade, much less be engaged as a leader of an entire congregation. "How old are you, anyways?"

"I just turned twenty-two this past October. I know that seems rather young compared to the three of you, but I assure you that I am just as eager to work as the next man." He smiled back rather humbly.

The man in front of him only shook his head in growing amusement. "That is a full year younger than when I was married," he said as he half-grinned up at him out of the corner of his mouth. "I've put on ten years since. But still, I suppose, you will find a woman someday, just don't make her wait too long."

"Understood. I'm Nathanael Beckett, by the way." He tried to appear as reassuring as possible before stretching out his hand formally in front of him to the other man, paying attention to avoid the rising fire.

"Sebastian Smith." The older man only nodded back but did not engage in any further contact with the stranger before him, choosing rather to focus on the coals of the fire in front of him than in making new friends, however amiable they may be at the present. For more years than he could count, it had been his experience that strangers rarely meant what they said, and those in the higher social classes, like the man across from him, were normally the most untrustworthy of all.

Sensing the tension suddenly shift again between them, Nathanael retracted his hand awkwardly and rubbed them together twice to dust off any further sand that had accumulated on them. Then, as if with greater caution he added further, "I hope you do not feel like this is a further intrusion, sir, but Smith? Is that your Christian name, perhaps?"

Sebastian smiled politely at the man's keen attention but waited for the expected prejudice against him to follow, much like what had been done to him for most of his life. "Christian or otherwise, it is the name that I go by back home. Where my forge and shop are, Sebastian Fabbri seems to scare away most of the customers. So, to keep my family from starving, I go by my trade name instead."

"Ah, I see." Nathanael nodded, grasping his meaning finally. "Some people can hold unnecessary prejudices. Not myself, mind you, but some people, yes."

"And especially so when there is talk of a war with Spain on the horizon," Sebastian said flatly as if testing Nathanael's position on English politics, as well.

"I wouldn't know, truly, Mr. Fabbri," Nathanael admitted honestly. "My parish is fairly removed from anywhere that would hear news such as that. I haven't lived my life under a stone entirely, of course, but I have learned where not to put my oar in so to speak."

"Wise." Sebastian nodded thoughtfully, approving of the man's choice to use his true name without the least bit of contempt.

The two men fell into an uncomfortable silence once more as they attempted to warm their hands near the fire, but in the end, only grimaced together in collective dismay.

"It is funny," Sebastian remarked more to himself than to the man beside him. "My whole life I have strained beneath the oppressive weight the heat from the burning hearth created, even winced as I felt the scorching flames lick the very skin on my hands somedays when I wasn't quick enough to avoid them, and yet in this moment, I cannot even sense a fraction of its warmth though I am mere inches away from it."

"I was just thinking the same thing. Odd, isn't it?" Nathanael agreed, then turned away, distracted once more by another flash of lightning as it arched across the sky, highlighting the swaying sparce pines that were staunchly clinging near the opening of the cave. "What do you make of the other men we found?"

"One of them is dressed far too well to have been on a sea voyage at all." Sebastian looked over to study Emile more intently. "I'd say a gentleman maybe, but the way in which he spoke was anything but."

"Perhaps," Nathanael walked over and checked to see if William's health had improved at all now that he was out of the horrendous conditions outside. The man's clothing, as meager but finely tailored as they appeared, still clung to him as if thick with sweat and not from the storm's drenching power. "Can you hear me, sir?"

With a jolt, William grabbed the man's hand frantically, utterly surprising Nathanael, who was not the least bit prepared for his semi-alert and desperate state. "Are we safe?" William asked urgently with a tinge of panic in his voice, his eyes deeply bloodshot as they stared back at Nathanael with a sudden urgency and terror as if he had been reliving some horrendous dream countless times over during the length of Nathanael's casual conversation with Sebastian.

"I think so, Friend." Nathanael moved William's hand back down to his chest reassuringly and patted it once to comfort him. "You can rest, now."

William's body appeared to relax at his command, but only slightly. "Emile needs help." He weakly motioned with his other hand to the man next to him. "Is he breathing?"

Sebastian raised his eyebrows just once as he peered over at the man from his position by the fire. "I think so, though I can't be sure."

"Can you check?" Nathanael asked politely, not wanting to leave William's side.

Feeling a bit put out to be obliged to be any nearer to the disagreeable man once more, Sebastian stepped through the mostly dry sand begrudgingly, then stooped next to Emile to examine him more closely before placing his ear upon his chest when he saw no movement through the multiple wet layers. "Yes, and I can still hear a faint heartbeat, but he is quite literally trembling from head to toe."

"Perhaps we should try to dry some of his clothes by the fire," Nathanael suggested but continued to feel ill at ease not knowing what the right thing was to do in this kind of situation.

"Fine," Sebastian muttered with great reluctance and began unbuttoning just a small portion of the man's vest as he attempted to remove at least some of the chilling attire covering him for the man appeared to be wearing at least four overly soaked layers from his fancy blouse to his brocade vest and thick overcoat. All of which seemed to have been created with very fine workmanship indeed, much too expensive for anything Sebastian might have been able to afford or even the preacher by his side. Yet for all his efforts, he did not accomplish much.

At the first hint of a touch, the man on the ground threw himself instinctively at Sebastian in an attack, reacting violently as he viciously lunged at him repeatedly and snatched at the hands on his buttons. "Hand's off, you demon! SWINE!" Emile fought him wildly in his delirium. "*Arrête... arrête*, stop, I say!"

"He is harmless, I promise you." William tried to apologize for him, but his voice sounded fragile even in his own ears. "A vile fool at times," he smiled at the memory of their first encounter, "...but harmless."

"I'll have to take your word on that, sir," Sebastian grunted in opposition as he continued to try to stop Emile's forceful wrestling while all the while assuring the man repeatedly that there was no Satan or devil or whatever else the man was trying to say to him in French.

"Emile, stop... please." William reached over clumsily before placing a hand on Emile's shoulder to calm him down. "No one will hurt you here, I promise."

Feeling the reassurance from the man beside him, the two men struggled less intensely for a few moments longer before Emile eventually exhausted himself and gave up entirely, collapsing once more into a fitful rest.

"Thank you, sir." Sebastian breathed in and out deeply to catch his breath.

"Is there anything I can do for you?" Nathanael folded his tan tweeded coat in half before carefully placing it under the doctor's head and neck for support.

"You wouldn't happen to have an extra blanket over there, by any chance? I'm freezing," William complained as he fidgeted on the ground, wrapping his arms around himself ineffectively again and again in an attempt to draw in more warmth.

"I'm afraid not, but we could move you closer to the fire if you like."

William shook his head, and his teeth began to chatter loudly. "I d-don't th-think... it wou-would help-p."

Nathanael and Sebastian exchanged worried glances at the increasing deterioration of the man's condition, uncertain what to do next.

"Could you tell me your name at least?" Nathanael pressed him a little more seeing that he was already slowly fading back into unconsciousness. He wasn't sure just what exactly he was going do with it once it was spoken, but he surmised that if the worse possibility should ever come to pass, it would be nice to have a name to notify his next of kin.

"William Wells, ship's.... doctor," William mumbled back before finally trailing off into a fitful sleep once more.

"Ship's doctor!" Sebastian appeared taken aback by the immensity of what that might mean. *What all had happened to the ship while they were unconscious? For if the ship was truly still intact, neither the doctor, nor any other member of the crew would be here with them.* He surmised mentally but dared not utter his assumptions out loud in case doing so might upset his other companion. "Do you remember him at all from the ship?" Sebastian inquired while studying the face of the man he failed to recognize at all.

"Just a few chance encounters here and there, an amiable fellow for the most part though a bit shy in temper," Nathanael replied as he stood up and began to pace nervously.

"Hmmm." Sebastian rubbed the half-stubble of a beard that had been beginning to form along his jawline and walked back to his place by the fire. "Come to think of it, I can't remember a single detail after the first day of our trip." He shook his head to dislodge the fog that was keeping his memories from him. "I do remember boarding rather early on that Thursday morning. Charlotte and the boys had seen me off at the port and had even packed me a lunch complete with two of her wonderful ratafia cakes."

"Ratafia cakes?" Nathanael took a seat next to him near the fire. "What are those?"

Sebastian closed his eyes as if savoring the remembrance. "They are a wonderful mix of oranges and apricots all blended into a small biscuit-like circle. You might call it a scone in your world, though it is nowhere near as dry I assure you."

"Sounds absolutely wonderful right about now." Nathanael licked his lips unconsciously in response.

"They are. Anyways, when the ship finally set sail, I took my meal down below deck and decided to eat it in the cargo area as there was a great deal of commotion up on deck with everyone finding their lodgings and such. And then...," he paused as he tried to remember again any other detail about his trip, "nothing. It is almost as if the entire voyage never happened at all."

"Strange." Nathanael appeared equally puzzled. "I, too, came on board that Thursday, though I spent much of my time the first day with several of the other passengers. On the second day though, I remember escorting one of the young ladies from the Miller group around the deck since the weather was somewhat agreeable at the time. A Miss Margaret Caldwell, if I remember correctly. Anyways, we had decided to watch the sunset off the stern as Doctor Clarke and the captain had suggested at lunch. I thought that maybe I might even discuss a little philosophy with her, if she was so disposed. Yet, the rest is a blank—a total, and incomprehensible blank."

"Philosophy? Really? I don't wonder now why you aren't married yet." Sebastian chuckled lightly with a shake of his head. "No woman wants to discuss philosophy, man."

Nathanael smiled, too, then admitted, "You're probably right. Come to think of it, she did try to change the subject a few times throughout our conversation."

"Of course she did." Sebastian only laughed more before trying to compose himself once more. "So, what do you think happened to the ship?" He looked out of the cave and to the ocean beyond that was now glistening here and there along the horizon by the escaping sporadic rays of late morning.

"I haven't the foggiest of notions," Nathanael remarked simply. "I do not even remember getting into that rowboat."

"Me, neither." Sebastian frowned. "Do you think they put us in there?"

"Possibly." Nathanael pondered on that thought. "But why?"

"I have no earthly idea." Sebastian sighed. "Well, we are here now, and if we want to survive, we had better make the most of our breakfast. And when we are done, we can take some of that collected rainwater that has been falling off the ridge over there to the men. I don't know just what is ailing them, but with their chills, that usually means fever, and fever means they need liquids more than food," Sebastian instructed. "Or at least that is what my Charlotte always says."

"You wouldn't rather try to head farther inland to find a doctor in a town nearby?" Nathanael looked almost scared at the prospect of losing one of the men due to his own negligence of care.

"Absolutely not!" Sebastian answered quite forcefully, then repented of it instantly when he recognized the hurt it produced on Nathanael's face. "Listen, we could be anywhere in the world right now. And who might we find? The French? They will at least be civil to us, maybe even take that madman off our hands. God bless them. They can have him. Or possibly even the Spanish? I might get by enough to solicit their help given my heritage, but you will not, neither will the doctor." He shook his head. "Or what about someone else?"

Nathanael gulped at the very real possibility of headhunters, tribesmen or even worse, pirates that could possibly await them just a few hundred yards inland. "Agreed. Besides, it's probably more important to remain here to take care of William and Emile, right?"

"Right." Sebastian nodded. "For the moment, we will stick together until they are more stable, or at least well enough to travel. Then, we will all form a plan as to what our next steps will be. For the present," he motioned again to the food cooking above the flames, "*Buen provecho*, or as they say it in England, we should eat."

The two men sampled the various items eagerly in silence until the meal was thoroughly finished and the last shell discarded, not wanting to waste a single morsel of the food the ocean had provided.

"It does not taste like anything I have ever eaten before, but then again, it is not horrible either." Nathanael tried to remain positive about the meal even though he was beginning to feel a tad bit queasy by the whole experience.

"Not horrible? I'll admit that it does lack flavor." Sebastian laughed as he added, "But maybe try not to say that to your girl when she makes you her first supper, alright?"

Nathanael joined him in his laughter, and it felt oddly good, despite all that they had been through, to be enjoying something once more.

"I'll be sure to remember that if I ever find one brave enough to make it all the way to marriage." He brushed off the sand from his hands once more and made his way over to the still reclining William. With some fresh water in hand, he placed a filled shell of it just below his mouth. "William? Do you think you can drink some of this?" Nathanael encouraged.

William leaned forward slightly to obey but coughed back more than he drank as he attempted to swallow it. "Ugh, it's ra-rancid."

Nathanael smelled the water carefully but found nothing amiss more than a strange seaweed-like odor. "Try to sip some more anyways. You need to keep your strength up."

William obeyed dutifully and took another gulp of the liquid before wrinkling his nose and pulling back away from it in disgust. "It... really is.. quite awful, s-sir."

Nathanael shrugged to Sebastian and tried a sip of the water before spitting it out forcefully into the sand beside him. "He's right. It tastes worse than the clams."

"How... is... Em-m-m-ile?" William looked wearily over at the Frenchman at his side.

Sebastian shook Emile's shoulder twice, bracing himself for his attack once more, but the Frenchman did not stir in the slightest. The only sounds he uttered now were a faint groaning that passed his lips every few moments like a child's whimpered cry, more than a man's last breath. "He is still alive, sir. Though he probably wishes he wasn't right about now."

"I under-st-stand com-plet--ly." William gritted his teeth to control his chattering as he spoke, his jaw becoming almost rigid with the effort.

"We had better stay close tonight," Sebastian advised solemnly.

"In case either of them needs, um, last rites?" questioned Nathanael.

Sebastian nodded in understanding.

"I hope those are not for me," William said weakly.

"I pray not, but one must always be prepared." Nathanael folded his hands to pray next to William's body. The good Lord had brought the young doctor safe thus far. He would ask God to continue to do so again.

Content to be with his own thoughts instead, Sebastian left the preacher to his prayers and sat back down in the shadows at the mouth of the cave. "That leaves me to take the first watch. Just come and get me if I'm needed."

"I will, and thank you, Sebastian," Nathanael said simply before adding, "for your counsel and the fire."

Sebastian nodded and returned his gaze outward.

The two men remained in that position for the duration of the entire day. With little else to do, their thoughts occupied their minds through it, until the coals of the fire began to grow quite cold, reminding them once more of the impending night that lay ahead of them.

Chapter Four

November 27th, 1792

"If we are to remain here another night, I had best go find more fuel for the fire," Sebastian said as he leaned over and picked up the last stick lying near the pit, eyeing it speculatively after he had awakened. "This here is the very last piece from what you brought in yesterday and when it is gone, we will need much denser wood if we want our fire to last the rest of the day, not to mention the night." The older man eyed the tree line outside the cave once more and shook his head, dreading going back out into the inclement weather. Not a minute had passed since he had awakened on the beach that the sky had ceased to overflow with its incessant moisture.

"I think there should still be plenty of driftwood over there by the pile I went to yesterday," Nathanael defended, confused as to the need to search for new resources. "Couldn't we just use that?"

Sebastian shook his head slowly and pursed his lips not wanting to hurt the other man's feelings with his naivety. "Though it is certainly true that bleached twigs such as these are in high supply near the shore and sufficient to get a fire going, I'm afraid that the majority of them will be wet all the way through like a sponge after last night's deluge," Sebastian declared with a toss of the stick into the small fire. The glow of it instantly turned the red flames blue from the salt it contained.

"Then what do you propose?" Nathanael rose and walked over to where the other man stood, eager to be of assistance.

"Well, I've been surveying that area just beyond for the past few hours." He pointed to a part of the beach just east of the cave where several trees had formed a tightly knit burrow of sorts. "And I think I have spied out several fallen logs that might serve our needs quite nicely since neither of us possesses an axe of any kind. Though it would surely come in handy if we did." The way he spoke was calm and distant this morning, almost like he was talking more to himself than to the companion sitting next to him.

"Will that be enough?" Nathanael dusted the sand off his hands once more, not wanting to appear vulnerable in front of the man, but the texture of the grit upon them was setting his nerves on constant alert.

"Let's hope so." Sebastian put on his short, brown overcoat over his shirt to protect at least part of his attire from being drenched in his task. "If I can haul them over here quickly enough that the rain won't soak them entirely, that should suffice. Then, with even better luck, I'll be able to find some smaller branches that are readily available near the edge. The important thing is to bring back as much as we can now so it can hopefully dry out further in here."

"I see. Would you like me to help you, or go see what I can find for our supper?" Nathanael offered trying his best to remain positive under the circumstances.

"Food would be nice, thank you. I'm starved." Sebastian gave him what he felt was an appreciative look.

Feeling elated that he could be useful in this smallest of tasks, Nathanael agreed. "Me, too."

The two men left the cave once more to their separate hunts in the lightly drizzling precipitation, and it was not a full hour before Sebastian had managed to bring in a rather large assortment of two-foot-long logs the width of a man's leg and a few others for smaller kindling—not a huge pile like the one he always kept at the ready near his forge, but enough to last them sufficiently for the time being.

Nathanael too had been victorious as he had discovered at least a handful of snails for each of them, two pockets full of berries in various varieties and some wild onions that had grown neatly tucked into the rocky crags just farther up the hill.

"Wonderful!" Sebastian exclaimed. "You certainly know how to forage well enough for a preacher—an essential skill for any man."

"Yes, though I do find it funny in a way." Nathanael took off his wet overcoat and shook the moisture out of his lightly brown hair that was just long enough to touch his collar.

"Why?" Sebastian set down the rest of his cargo and dusted off his sleeves before doing the same.

"Just the Sunday before we left, I preached a sermon on Lydia who was, as you might know, a seller of purple," Nathanael replied simply.

Sebastian raised his left eyebrow and shook his head in confusion. "Did Lydia possibly teach you how to cook these well enough so that they don't taste horrible, too? Because that would be pretty helpful right about now"

Nathanael laughed lightly at the absurdity of such a question and handed him a portion of the berries to eat. "Not unless I lived over 1700 years ago, and in Israel."

"Oh, I see." Sebastian busied himself with the fire while snacking here and there on the delicious fruit. "A Bible story then... I grew up hearing many of those tales from the monk who raised me, but I have yet to find anything as practical as a hammer in my hand and a good piece of steel to shape."

Nathanael smiled genuinely at the familiar judgement but went right on with his story, unperturbed by the man's lack of interest in his faith. "Well, I don't know if you realize this but, in those times, people would often collect hundreds of snails, much like these, and by crushing them up, they could create and sell a very vivid purple dye—dye only the rich could afford to pay handsomely for, of course." Nathanael put the snails and onions on the flat stone next to the fire and watched them as they were roasted by the coals—sizzling and popping as the water was smoked out of them. "To Lydia, they were more than just food for the body. They were income for both her and Paul, the missionary."

"Are you a missionary, then?" Sebastian asked, trying to better understand this odd man and his reasons for getting on a boat headed all the way to the Americas.

"Not in that sense of the word, no. I admit, I did once feel like I was led to reach a new kind of people. People who may possibly have never even heard about our Lord, but alas, God has clearly seemed to have decided otherwise."

"But you said you had pupils that started your fires. How long were you a teacher?"

Nathanael shook his head before answering politely, "Just a year or two after seminary. For the majority of my life, my father was a professor of theology at a very small school back in England. I learned most of what I know from him, I suppose. But being a preacher is a rather new profession for me you could say. Or at least it was going to be in the new world. My fellow bishops have been training me diligently for the past three years in the hopes that I would make a fine preacher. They were so invested in me in fact, that they gave me the overseeing of a choice parish church in Northern England where I could have been quite comfortable the rest of my days should I have been willing to remain. From what they had told me, some vicar had left that church months earlier and for quite some time they had not been able to fill his position. For them, my decision to reach all of God's children was the perfect solution to their vacancy."

Sebastian pushed the cooked snails and onions out of the fire with a stick before choosing one of them to eat. "Then why didn't you take it? A stable income for life sounds like every man's dream." He popped a small onion into his mouth after it had cooled, then frowned for it also tasted like absolutely nothing at all. Yet at least even that disappointing fact was an improvement over the putrid flavored water and the clams. "In Portsmouth there is no chance that my sons will ever amount to anything more than being a poor blacksmith or some other negligible trade, and that is not the life I want for them or my family. It's a hard way to live for anyone and one most men cannot endure under that constant strain even without the added prejudice."

"By your own struggles, I feel now as if I have been entirely foolish in my desire to leave in the first place. I had nothing from which I was escaping, and only everything to gain by remaining," Nathanael admitted, seemingly affected by the man's plight. "Is that why you left? To make a better life for your family?"

Sebastian's face grew grimmer, and yet still tinged with the slightest bit of hope as he stared into the fire. "I only did what any father in my place might do. I made the decision to find my own fate in America. I was actually on my way to Philadelphia when we left, endeavoring to establish a home for myself and them—a place free to be a Fabbri or a Smith. Or so I am told." Sebastian distractedly placed a larger log onto the fire and used one of the longer sticks to build up the coals against it. Fresh steam from the escaping water within its fibers mixed with the white tendrils of smoke as it rose upwards from the action. It filled the cave immediately with something vaguely familiar and almost inviting—the wonderful aroma of fellowship at Yuletide.

Nathanael nodded and gingerly sampled some of the food himself, still extremely hesitant to eat anything after his last attempt. "Yours is a far nobler reason than mine any day. Though I expect many young men of my age are bound to crave a little more adventure in their lives rather than their economic stability."

"Most definitely a young man's dream," Sebastian responded wisely.

"Yes, so my bishops have reminded me many times over, but I have lived my whole life in the same town where I knew every house, hill and street. As foolish as it may be, I felt it was time I did something more with my life—something infinitely more meaningful. Or at least, that was what I was trying to do."

46

"Now that is one thing to which I can relate, friend." Sebastian threw the last of the shells and greens that were left over into the fire and watched as the flames consumed them heartily. "Well, we had best try to rest while we can today. Tomorrow will be here soon enough, I'm afraid. Perhaps then this infernal storm will finally end, and we can start forming some kind of plan as to how we can get back home to our families."

"Agreed, but if it's all the same to you, I'd prefer to keep the first vigil this afternoon with the men," Nathanael offered cautiously as he sat down next to the two, now still, companions they had been tending to all night. "I'm certain my presence will do nothing to aid in their recovery, but with their declining condition, I am hesitant to leave them unattended."

"Suit yourself." Sebastian put several logs, in a layered manner, within the firepit and curled up with his back to them to keep warm. Or at least try to, for nothing so far had worked to stop the cold chill that crept up his back constantly since yesterday morning.

"Rest easy, my friend. I shall comfort your soul at the very least." Nathanael attempted to reassure William by patting his arm before closing his eyes to pray and recite aloud several of the longer passages of Scripture he had memorized years ago. When he had motivated himself to learn the lengthier passages back in seminary, he had not the foggiest notion how calming and essential they would be for his future. Countless times over the years they had brought him comfort and hopefully would do the same for the others today.

With his voice strong and steady by the faith behind the words, Nathanael replayed precisely the poetic phrases of Psalm twenty through twenty-four perfectly throughout the long hours of the afternoon. The words, as simple and as heartfelt as the day David had first penned them, spoke now to Nathanael's very soul, as well. And as they did, the hours passed by not in panicked desperation about their situation, but in contented hope as they lulled the men within the cave above the rhythmic music of the waves and softly cooing wind without.

The world that had once seemed so terrifying and foreign to all of them became peaceful once more as they lay there upon the sand, their minds soothed by the atmosphere the weather created. And yet, if the four of them had been there under any other circumstances, they might have even enjoyed it, but they were not.

Then, as the rich hues of the following sunrise arrived and passed and the new day beckoned, it brought along with it the increasing despair that greeted all mariners lost at sea. The sad realization that William and Emile might not survive their ordeal after all, for though the rains themselves had thankfully ceased shortly after daybreak, the skies above had still remained overcast and gloomy as if they were also in a state of perpetual limbo—merely waiting for the next decision. Yet, Sebastian and Nathanael could make none. The dutiful compassion they held towards the other men would not allow them to leave them behind, and as fragile as their state was now, they could not take them with them either. Their only hope now was a peaceful resolution in death or a miraculous recovery—no matter how long that may take.

So, with little else than a hopeful anticipation, they waited. They prayed. They watched. They contemplated what they might do next. They discussed whatever topics men talk about when they are trying not to talk about the very thing that is on both of their minds. In fact, for the past two days since their arrival, they had followed this numbing cycle of obligation, hoping for an equally positive outcome—the one they would have wanted if their situations had been reversed. But as depressing as it was quickly becoming, the grim reality of their failure stared back at them hauntingly with every passing hour for despite all their attentive efforts to the contrary, somewhere around lunch both men took a decidedly drastic turn for the worse as the pallor of their skin faded to a deathly gray one right after the other, and their breathing slipped farther towards a deathly form of quiet. So much so, that Nathanael was almost afraid to accept it and be forced to inform Sebastian of the sad news that they had indeed perished. Or more lamentably, that their next task might not be in gathering supper after all, but in digging a shallow grave, a job neither of them relished no matter the necessity.

Yet Nathanael hesitated further, unwilling to consent to the truth staring back at him for several hours more, as if prayerfully hoping that he was possibly wrong in his assumptions or that something extraordinarily miraculous might still transpire here in this cave beyond the return of their normal complexion, but it did not. In the end, he was regrettably compelled to resign himself to facing the facts as they were. William and Emile were most certainly on the edge of eternity as they were no longer stirring, nor responding to any of his motivating questions whatsoever.

"Sebastian?" Nathanael asked as he walked over to the man who was now staring out of the mouth of the cave at the dim sunset approaching along the horizon.

"Hmm?" Sebastian looked back at him briefly, inviting him over with a wave of his hand. "Something on your mind?"

"I think it is time that we start making some decisions regarding Emile." Nathanael tried to say the words without emotion, but his voice still faltered uncontrollably. Since the day he had helped his mother bury his father, he had never once been very good with death, no matter who it was that was dying. A true deficit for a member of the clergy he was told, but one he could not simply hide like so many of his peers.

"And William?" Sebastian added as he absentmindedly rubbed his thumb across the smoothness of the rock wall beside him. "Do you think there is still hope for him?"

"I really couldn't say." Nathanael shook his head. "They both look much better overall in some ways, and their breathing has leveled out considerably, but I doubt they can last much longer without any sustenance to speak of. It has been over two days as it is already."

"Do you think the same thing happened to us?" Sebastian asked thoughtfully while squinting slightly as the sun's deep red and orange rays slid just below the horizon into the rich blues and deep purple of twilight. "I mean, maybe that is why we were all together in the first place, and why we can't remember anything from our time on the ship."

"Perhaps." Nathanael swallowed hard at the frightening possibility while all the while fighting back the nagging certainty that he too had been so incapacitated that he still could not recall a single detail of it.

"Or perhaps we are still just trying to sleep you blubbering idiots!" Emile groaned dramatically as he lay with both his arms wrapped firmly across his face and down to his ears to block out the irritating noise.

Shocked beyond the means of expression, the preacher practically jumped back and collided with the wall beside them as if he had encountered some kind of specter or angel, though either would have been less surprising in this moment and far less unsettling.

"You're awake," Sebastian noted begrudgingly, a little less enthusiastically inclined than Nathanael due to his last encounter with the disagreeable man.

"So, it would appear," Emile countered right back, equally terse in his delivery towards the man.

"Well, he seems delightful," Sebastian added more quietly to the preacher beside him, though at the moment, he could not have cared less if the man had overheard him or not.

"Has the fever left you completely, sir?" Nathanael asked politely but was still not convinced enough of the man's goodwill or earthly presence to venture any closer to his position by the fire.

"I've stopped shivering finally if that is what you mean." Emile snorted, but still did not move an inch from his prone position.

49

"Well, that answers that question," Sebastian quipped sarcastically. "No grave for Emile."

"And William?" Nathanael countered hopefully.

The man beside Emile who looked only slightly older than the preacher across from him sighed heavily before answering with a moan, "Feeling slightly improved, though still a bit weak, thank you." William sat up slowly, taking great pains to shake the sand from out of his disheveled blonde hair and pulled his body closer to the fire for more warmth. "You can ignore Emile. He's an acquired taste, I assure you." William shot Emile a tired look, then waited until the man looked up at him from under his arm. "You are grateful, are you not?"

"Delighted..." Emile's voice came back louder still but altogether muffled greatly under his protecting arms.

"Well, at least your English seems to have improved considerably." William shook his head with humor at the apparent ruse the man had created on the ship.

"You assume there was ever a problem with it in the first place, *Monsieur*." Emile quipped right back at him. "After what they did, I was not about to make their lives any easier by my compliance. That much was certain."

"On that we can both agree without reservation. In my opinion, Doctor Clarke deserved every ounce of the impertinence you exuded, maybe even more." William chuckled, then looked over at the two men at the mouth of the cave. "Have we been unconscious long?"

"Only a few days at most, if you count from the day we found you." Sebastian crossed his arms before leaning back on the cave's wall to take in the unfolding scene before him.

"I'm sorry to be so direct, gentlemen, but to whom do I give thanks for our survival? Though I did care for both of you on the ship, I have never been formally introduced." William stretched his arms in front of him and flexed his stiff fingers and muscles to further loosen them for everything felt strangely stiff and rigid from his days spent lying on the sand.

"Nathanael Beckett," Nathanael remarked quite happily and walked over to offer his hand cordially out to William. "And that is Mr. Sebastian Smith."

With definite approval, Sebastian smiled slightly at the adept way in which the man guarded his secret, feeling justly rebuked for judging the man so quickly.

"It is a pleasure to finally make your acquaintance, gentlemen." William took his hand readily and cast another reproving glance back at the reclining Frenchman who was quite clearly still choosing to ignore them. "Emile, could you at least try to be social, please?" William chided him sternly though he knew from his recent experience that the man would not take offense since it was

50

coming from him. Someone of doubtful authority would have been a different matter entirely, as William had seen with the quartermaster and with Doctor Clarke. But from someone the man respected, Emile always appeared placidly cordial.

With a labored sigh as if being tortured to do so, Emile stood lazily to his feet and almost trudged like a rebuked child over to where the other two men sat by the fire. "*Bonsoir...* or as you English say it, good evening." He made a slight bow of deference towards the group. "Emile Bastien of the family Deschamps."

Sebastian leaned forward slightly from off the wall and joined the group. "Glad to see your manners have improved. You were quite the madman yesterday."

"Indeed." Emile sniffed and lifted his head as if slightly offended by the man's disparaging remark. "And you are the man beneath my bunk who cried out incessantly for some woman named Charlotte. Your wife, I'm assuming?"

"Yes," Sebastian answered though he could tell already that he did not particularly care for the man across from him, nor did he like him even speaking his wife's name so flippantly. "She resides in Portsmouth, sir."

"I'm sincerely glad to hear it. Though I doubted it, I was afraid she might have been among the other passengers when the boat went down." William tried to change the subject before the temperature between the two men rose even higher. "We lost almost seventy souls that day to my recollection."

"That many!" Nathanael exclaimed, looking vastly affected by the sheer magnitude of the tragedy.

"I wish I was wrong. Emile and I could only fit the two of you in our boat in the state that you were in when we saw it was sinking. How or if the rest survived, I know not." William continued to try to warm his hands near the outside edge of the fire but furrowed his brow repeatedly with the futility of the action. "It took us almost two nights to row here, wherever that may be."

"Have you seen anyone else from the ship?" Emile asked tentatively. "Maybe even a fairly robust man, about my height, with a full head of black hair and matching beard?"

William cast a quick glance up at Emile, concerned at what he might be insinuating by his line of questioning.

"No." Sebastian shook his head. "Was he a friend of yours?"

"Certainly not!" William and Emile said immediately almost in unison, then both appeared to equally roll their eyes as if in hidden conversation between the two.

Sebastian and Nathanael each lifted their heads in turn at their harsh declaration, their eyes suddenly much more focused as to the reasoning.

"My apologies." William cleared his throat to dispel the awkwardness that had followed quickly thereafter. "Though not to change the subject, but why are my hands still so cold?" He probed discreetly as he tried in vain yet another time to warm his hands by the fire.

"One of many confusing questions, sir." Sebastian stoked the fire to a higher intensity, then placed his hand just above one of the brightest flames as if to demonstrate his point. "As a blacksmith, my mind knows this should be most definitely searing my flesh, yet I feel..." He turned his hand over to reveal not even a mark of smoke upon the palm placed near the flame. "...nothing. Not even a single hair has been singed upon its surface."

"And our food appears to lack any taste whatsoever, or so it seems," Nathanael added with a slight shrug not wanting to elaborate further on the unpleasant subject.

"Now that, I remember." William wrinkled his nose at the memory of the offered water.

"I promise you, William. I was not trying to poison you," Nathanael pleaded earnestly, appalled that he might have caused some kind of offence so early on in their acquaintance.

"I never thought it for a second... truly." William tried to reassure him kindly and stood up to stretch his legs.

"And the eyes?" Emile pointed towards William at last, drawing the rest of the group's attention to the strange coloring his irises now held. "We will definitely draw someone's undivided attention if we stay as we are today."

Nathanael looked at Emile and William in turn as if just now noticing this change in his companions for they had both indeed carried a much paler color than which most people of their acquaintance possessed. In truth, they were not too stark of a difference that someone might be overly curious about them as a whole until they were much closer. Yet still the color was markedly different enough to pause with concern. "Um, you wouldn't happen to remember what you called out earlier, would you, Mr. Deschamps?"

"*Satan.... demon?*" Emile half-closed his eyes as if relishing his newfound identity. "Ah, dear father, I'm afraid you will find what I am about to divulge to you is the most difficult information of all."

Nathanael looked intensely puzzled at the man for he could not think of anything that would cause a change such as this to a man's physical appearance.

"I'm sorry to say, on your account, that we all have become that which is typically destroyed by most of <u>your</u> kind." Emile taunted him mercilessly. "Though others throughout history have worshiped and even revered their granted immortality as a blessing from the gods."

"Enough, Emile. You don't need to upset the man to prove your point." William tried to intervene by moving between the men before shooting Emile a condescending look. "It is a lot to take in, and you know it. I'm still having a hard time wrapping my mind around everything that has happened myself."

"As you wish." Emile closed his eyes and smiled a huge cat-like grin in response, obviously enjoying himself at last, though regrettably at the other man's expense.

"Father…" William began to speak but was interrupted quickly by the man across from him.

"Preacher Beckett," Nathanael corrected him quickly but humbly, not wanting to confuse the man as to his chosen religion.

"My apologies again." William started to pace behind them as he thought about the right way to explain what had transpired on the ship. "What I am about to relay to both of you is something out of those tales most mothers tell their children before bedtime." He paused while carefully choosing his words so as not to upset either of them unnecessarily. "Yet, I can assure you, from everything Emile and I witnessed before the sinking, that I believe it is as true as the Bible is to you and others in your profession."

"Go on," Sebastian urged. "What do you <u>think</u> has happened to us?"

William took a deep breath, then began to relay the whole terrible sequence of events that transpired since they had all encountered the dreadful Doctor Clarke—everything from the men being nursed in William's cabin, to the awful realization that the man in question was the real reason why they were all here in the first place. At the very last, he explained slowly his basic knowledge on the subject from the various medical journals he had read in the past so as to provide a more logical context to the conversation. "Though I have never once treated an individual with this particular form of ailment, nor do I profess to know more than the most basic of lore belonging to such individuals, it is my firm opinion that the doctor has infected the four of us with some form of vampirism. Or at least everything points in that general direction."

"So, you think we have all become like this evil doctor?" Sebastian looked as stunned as the rest of them felt. "Impossible." He spat the word out incredulously, but everything on his face spoke quite the opposite.

William looked out of the cave and to the open ocean beyond and added almost in total agreement, "I wish it were."

"For the French, the vampire is almost romantically renowned, desired even," Emile stated fluidly as if he alone was quite visibly proud of what he had become.

"They would..." Sebastian muttered under his breath and rolled his eyes at the man who seemed far less concerned about his present reality or his future.

In the next moment, Nathanael, who had been sitting there quietly for the majority of the discussion, sucked in a deep breath, utterly aghast by everything transpiring around him. "This... is... it's quite... how can I be? No! ...impossible." He stuttered through a myriad of sentence fragments, too overwhelmed to form a coherent thought completely.

Feeling sorry for the man, William stepped closer and placed a comforting hand on his shoulder to calm his trembling further. "I know and I understand, Mr. Beckett, but I'm afraid that the facts cannot be otherwise. All of us have changed into something far different than what the Lord had ever intended, and we must make our own peace with that one way or the other."

For a moment, each man appeared to retreat deep within his own thoughts, all that is except for Emile, who seemed perfectly content to close his eyes and smirk as if he were remembering a particularly fond memory or a delicious meal.

"I am not sure what to even say, William?" Nathanael seemed the most affected out of everyone. "I mean... I don't <u>feel</u> any different other than being most definitely starving, but we haven't exactly had much to eat since we arrived. Are you sure you are not mistaken in this?"

"I am sure. You even had a cut along your neck when they brought you into the infirmary." William motioned with his finger along his own neck to represent what he had seen. "If you feel just above your collar, you will see that the slightly circular scar is still visible. Sebastian has one, too, though his is closer to the back of his neck."

"And you?" Sebastian stared back at William as if the entire reality he was now forced to endure were solely his fault. "You say you had no idea this doctor was killing people? How is that even possible? You're a doctor, too, aren't you?"

To everyone's surprise, it was Emile now who forcefully spoke up next, defending William firmly as he could see from the tortured expression that his friend now wore that he was still struggling inwardly with his part in the whole terrible ordeal. "It's all true. I was with William for the majority of our voyage and thought no differently of his employer besides the fact that he was most certainly some kind of a sadist in his bedside manner. Moreover, Doctor Clarke bit William when he was trying to save me from the man. When he was trying to save us all."

His eyes flashed with increasing irritation at the indignation of any suggestion that William bore any guilt whatsoever on the matter.

As if still entirely within his own world, Nathanael traced the raised line slowly along his jaw several times, then spoke softly in utter disillusionment, "Then I am now one of the cursed, an outcast from God's perfect design, just like those King James discussed in his Daemonologie."

"I don't think any of this is His design, Nathanael. But here we are just the same." William worried for the man and all the ramifications their change would entail upon his life, upon all their lives, for though he may not be a man of faith, he was still well-read enough on the matter to know the weight of their damnation as most faiths presented it.

Emile only raised his head aloofly as he leaned back and stretched his limbs upwards, obviously bored with the lengthiness of the conversation, more than the topic. "If you will excuse me, Gentlemen. I believe I would like to go for a slight... walk. It appears that I have been dormant for far too long." He stepped around the preacher before patting the top of his head in a mockingly playful gesture. "I'd put on my favorite *chapeaux* and tails if I had them, William, but alas, I do not." He smirked with great amusement at the playful thought, then waltzed smoothly towards the mouth of the cave past Sebastian.

"Fine, but don't go too far, please," William instructed, pushing down a sense of great skepticism about the actions of his newest companion. "We will need to make some decisions as to where we will go next as I don't plan on living the rest of my life out in this cave."

Emile only smiled patronizingly back at him. "I should think, not." Then, tipping his head slightly to one side in acknowledgement of William's request he started his stroll down the moonlit beach like he was on some kind of a restful vacation.

William and Sebastian shook their heads in unison at his display and continued to reflect heavily about their situation by the fire.

"Do you think he will stay close?" Sebastian finally eyed William from across the cave in front of him, obviously referring to the Frenchman who had just left.

"I hope so, though I sincerely doubt it," William answered honestly. "He was a prisoner when I met him."

"A prisoner?" Nathanael's voice raised an octave in response. "Is he dangerous?"

"Not at all, I assure you." William waved his hand and chuckled heartily at the mere suggestion. "He was not a prisoner by fault, but rather by conscription."

"I see. Well, I had better keep an eye on him then," Sebastian offered begrudgingly. "From that smirk on his face, I don't trust a thing that man says." He placed both hands upon his thighs and heaved himself upwards from his crouching position in front of the fire before turning around and walking resolutely towards the ocean.

"You are probably right," William replied.

"I think I need a minute, too." Nathanael walked out of the cave and in the opposite direction of Emile, too stunned and tormented to speak further to anyone.

"I think we all do." William sighed and held his hands close to the fire once more, grateful that he was still alive, but increasingly uncertain as to what all of that now meant.

Chapter Five

November 28th, 1792

S ebastian treaded heavily away from the cave through the thick sand that pulled at his boots with every step and headed directly into the darkness beyond, towards the restless ocean in front of him. Oh, how he wanted to walk straight into that midnight blue surf right now and just let it swallow him whole. Then again, maybe that would be what was best for all of them—a quick and respectful death.

But no! If there truly was a God, why would He have allowed him to become this... thing... this aberration of humanity that had been forced upon him whether he wanted it or not? And he most definitely did not. How could he ever hope to support his family in this state? Or even contemplate for a moment the thought of exposing his sons, not to mention Charlotte, to such danger? It was inconceivable! And yet, how would they survive without him?

His thoughts warred against each other back and forth within him like crashing waves, allowing each to wash over the other again and again with increasing ferocity as if dragging bits and pieces of himself further out to sea. Yet, despite the crushing weight now placed upon his very chest, if he truly loved them the way he always professed, there had to be a way, no matter what his cruel change of fate!

"But how?" He whispered quietly in desperation through his teeth, then jolted when he looked up and realized it had been quite some time since he had last seen Emile walking near the shadows of the forest. With fresh concern welling up within him, he scanned the shoreline quickly one more time from one side to the other, the tide pools beyond the cave, the woods and the shaded ledge nearby, wanting to give the man at least the smallest benefit of a doubt. But no, he was right in his first assumption, as if there were any reason under the sun that he would not have been. No one was on the beach now except himself. Not even the preacher who had retreated to the safety of the cave hours ago. In fact, the only thing that even hinted at the possibility of civilization was a faint outline of smoke that rose from somewhere to the east, just above the line of firs and thick pines. The same direction, in fact, that Emile had been walking earlier.

"Selfish Frenchman," Sebastian muttered angrily at himself for his negligence and distraction, then stormed back across the wet sand to tell the others. "Emile has left us." He furiously snatched up his dry vest by the fire and started buttoning it up quickly.

"Wait... what?!" William rushed to the opening of the cave from where Sebastian had just entered, as if needing to verify for himself the truth of his words. "I was afraid something like this might happen!"

"Well, it has," Sebastian fumed inwardly at Emile's sheer lack of regard towards the rest of the group. "It figures. That sorry excuse of a man was given a chance to live another day, and now he might get us all killed."

"Us?" Nathanael squeaked. "How so?"

"If he does anything rash, someone is bound to come looking for where he came from, and I, for one, would rather be on the offensive any day than sitting here waiting for trouble to find me." William grabbed his tailored overcoat and slid both arms into the sleeves, uncertain if they would be returning to this cave tonight or ever again.

"Where do you think he will go first?" Sebastian asked as he used the side of his boot to douse the embers of the fire with the sand from around it.

"First place he can find a ship home, I expect. But I wouldn't put it past him to look for some um, sustenance first..." William politely let the rest of his sentence drop off, but the rest of the group certainly knew to what he was alluding.

"Then we had better make sure that he doesn't," Sebastian replied in a tone that reminded William very much of his father. The one solely reserved for the scolding of one of his children.

"My thoughts precisely," William added and then turned to face Nathanael. "As much as I regret asking this of you, given your position in the church and all, but you should probably come along with us, as we may need your help."

"Me?" Nathanael protested in shock. "But I wouldn't know the first thing about stopping a vampire."

"I have no idea either, Preacher, but for the sake of those he might prey upon, we have to at least try." William tried his best to persuade him with logic before ushering his new acquaintance hurriedly out after Sebastian.

Together, the three men formed a rather ragtag looking group, as they ran up the shore into the woods and towards the light they could still imperceptibly make out on the horizon ahead of them. To their surprise and grateful relief, the village was thankfully, not a far distance from the beach after all, and as they drew nearer still, the sharp outlines of a well-populated port city came into view. One not as grand as the one from which they had sailed, but sizable enough to dock several ships within its harbor.

A populated group of Mediterranean style homes lay on the edge of the coarse tree line, standing out from the others in their whitewashed exteriors and richly hued terracotta tiles. Immediately next to them were several other more simply built structures, most likely for the working class by the various items lying beside their walls and within their courtyards. However, despite the approaching sunrise, most of the windows still remained dark, except for a few who were just beginning to show the first activities of the early morning, as mothers were busily baking bread for the fast. Tables within were soon to be carefully set, and men readying their tools and fires for a day's work. Nothing at all seemed terribly amiss, and yet something deep inside of the visiting men knew Emile was here somewhere and from his previous comments, up to no good.

"Do you think he is close by?" Nathanael whispered loudly to William at his side.

"I hope so. Or at least I can't imagine he has boarded a ship back to France already." William eyed the ships docked below and the lack of activity near them before following Sebastian's lead into town. "Come on. We should search the village first, then we can look down by the docks."

Nathanael pursed his lips nervously several times in hesitation, deliberating whether or not to continue, but in the end decided to keep close to the men in front of him as the three strangers walked as inconspicuously as they could manage through the streets that were thankfully, still mostly empty for this time of day.

Clinging strictly to the shadows of the cobblestone lane to escape suspicion, they watched as several men approached them and passed by on their way down to the ships held at port. Yet to their great relief, none of the group even took notice of the strangers, as if three men traipsing along at this hour was quite a common occurrence. Then again, in a busy port such as this, maybe it was. Maybe it was just the three of them that were on edge this morning as they watched everything and anything they encountered, as if there might be some hidden danger lurking around every corner. It appeared so, for the other group of men were far too busy laughing boisterously about some girl they had just seen down at the corner.

"Did you see Rebecca today?" One of the men elbowed the other next to him who was stouter and obviously, the clear leader of their group.

"Still as crazy as ever, that one," another man remarked.

"Doesn't have the good sense God gave her, poor girl," another judged callously.

"She missed the day they gave that out, I'm afraid." They all laughed and continued on their way. "Still, she should know better than to sleep on the corner like that."

The demeaning conversation of the men carried on down the street before they stepped into a building at the edge of town when everything fell silent once more.

William listened intently to the ensuing silence and squinted his eyes as they adjusted to the changing light around him. By all accounts they felt dry and irritated from the added light of approaching morning, not entirely debilitating per say, but still slightly more painful than a nagging distraction. As for the task ahead of him, there were no other noises to be heard except for that of the ocean hitting the piers down below. Not a single thing seemed out of place, except for maybe themselves, of course.

"Anything at all?" Sebastian's gaze followed up and down the street as well, as he too was searching for some clue to their misplaced companion's location.

William shook his head in frustration but then stopped abruptly when he thought he had picked up the smallest hint of a whimpering cry coming from the end of the alley to his right. *Was that Rebecca or Emile?*

"This way, I think." He motioned with the tilt of his head.

The others trailed behind him, creating an almost human-like wall as they ventured down the passageway, each staggered a few feet behind the other. With building apprehension, they stepped carefully past house after house before pausing suddenly in turn as each of them picked up the most intoxicating scent they had ever smelled in all their lives. A smell so tantalizing that the aromatic quality of it felt almost alive as it reached out to them with an odor that held onto each man with a nearly tangible pull. Much more powerful than the lure of any food they had ever eaten and most definitely, twice as desirous.

The smell, whatever it was, begged them to draw closer with an enticement much like that of a siren as she tempted besotted sailors to their doom upon the rocks. In an instant their hearts beat wildly within them in response and triggered a sharpening of their recently deadened senses.

"What is that?" Nathanael asked quietly though his voice held also an audible tremble to it that mimicked that which all the men were now experiencing. "Make it stop!" He turned away from the others in horror and whimpered childishly as if begging for his very life against it.

"Nathanael, I can't..." William snapped his head back and forth, quickly trying to force away the control that it had over him and seized the young man by his shoulder with his other hand to ground him by his mere presence. "Can you go on?"

"No!" Nathanael shook his head convulsively and clenched his eyes tightly shut, his legs completely paralyzed as he pressed both of his hands upon the sides of his temples to contain the pounding pulse the scent had created within his skull. "I can barely breathe, let alone walk, William!" He gasped, effectively debilitated where he stood in the middle of the path, fighting against the temptation that threatened to crumple him under its weight.

"Fine. Just wait here, then. We'll handle this." Sebastian guided Nathanael into the shadows gently but did not delay long enough for his further consent. Instead, he struggled against his own demons to press onward with William towards the uncertain darkness beyond with great irritation at the necessity of their excursion. "This is all my fault entirely," Sebastian muttered, disgusted with his failure once more. "I should have kept a better eye on him."

"I don't think anyone is to blame. He was going to leave anyway. It was only a matter of when," William replied shortly back, clearly trying to hold his breath in-between sentences to avoid taking in any more than necessary of the attractive odor still wafting through the alleyway.

"It's blood, isn't it?" **Sebast**ian asked coldly, his voice holding the faintest hint of something more than merely anger—the tiniest tinge of desire.

"Definitely," William replied quickly as it didn't take a great deal of intelligence on his part to recognize what he had encountered probably countless times over in his father's practice. Though never before had it ever affected him quite in this way nor caused him as much discomfort and enticement all at the same time.

The silence around them closed in tighter still as the two of them soldiered on, barely going ten more paces into the darkness before a dim figure moved ever so slightly in front of them. So slowly in fact that it appeared as if the two individuals were molded into one in the dim light of the morning. Not unlike the vision William had seen of Doctor Clarke before the shipwreck, the face of a young girl came out from the distorted mass and looked back at them with empty eyes. Her slender body, as small and diminutive as that of any woman they might have met back at home, lay lifeless on the street before them with a man hovering over her—an unfortunately familiar man.

"Emile," Sebastian hissed and strode over to him angrily. "What have you done?" He clenched his hand upon his shoulder gruffly and pulled him away from his victim as he placed himself between them. "Don't you think of anyone but yourself?"

Almost poised for an all-out altercation between them, Emile swung around to answer, but Sebastian never heard his explanation. At that same moment, a man fully covered from his head to his knees in a thick, black cloak stepped forward from the darkness behind them and placed a white cloth quickly over Emile's mouth.

Unwilling to yield to anyone so easily, Emile struggled against him for several moments more as he fought for his freedom but in the end, fell helplessly limp at his feet. Dangerously similar in many ways to the girl he had just killed.

"Pick up your man," the cloaked figure commanded Sebastian curtly with little emotion regarding him or their reason for being there in the first place. "We can't leave him here."

Sebastian obeyed immediately, wrapping one of Emile's arms around his shoulders before calling Nathanael over to support the other.

William, on the other hand, instinctively bent down and checked the woman's pulse to confirm what he had already suspected. "She's dead, I'm afraid."

"Very fortunate for her," the cloaked figure replied in a thick Italian accent as he reached down and lovingly cradled the poor, young girl in his arms before lifting her easily. "Now, follow me if you wish to live."

William stared back at him in confusion, but without another word, the mysterious figure took off into the woods beyond the town without even looking back.

Still reeling from the ordeal and with no other options laid out before them, the three men followed warily as the cloaked figure guided the group up the mountain and through a labyrinth of stone walls until, at last, they came upon the large wooden door of a medieval style castle.

"Inside," the cloaked figure demanded once more as if he were their master and not a complete stranger. "Quickly, if you please."

Without further hesitation, they obeyed yet again. After all, by the mere association with this murdering stranger, they stood accused in his eyes just as much as he for they had been unsuccessful in stopping his abhorrent crime. Their only hope now was to pray that whoever this man was, he would be more merciful to them than Emile had been with the young woman.

"Now, bolt the door behind you, sir. The villagers are nothing if not overly curious, and rightly so when those in their midst disappear like this young child did tonight." The man delicately laid the dead girl down upon the carved bench within the shaded inner courtyard.

"What will become of her, sir?" Nathanael looked compassionately at her now ashen face, saddened by the loss of someone so young for she looked barely a few years younger than himself.

In a quick motion that startled the preacher beside him, the older man threw back his hood to reveal a robust gentleman of at least 60 years stature complete with silver hair that curled into loose ringlets down his slightly covered neck. "If you would be so kind as to assist me, she can be buried within my own humble cemetery, and no one will be the wiser for this transgression."

"I should think it would be the least that we could do under the circumstances," Sebastian said honorably, grateful for the man's understanding in this matter.

"Wisely spoken." William joined him and removed his outer coat and vest, feeling guilty on behalf of his companion for his deeds. A part of him wanted to outright condemn Emile for taking the life of someone who was obviously too helpless to defend herself. And yet, the other, darker half of himself now, couldn't stop thinking of doing the exact same thing. Or really, anything that would cease the pounding that would not be abated within his brain.

"If it's all the same with the two of you, I'd much prefer to wait over here and keep an eye on Emile." Nathanael shrank farther away from the dead body and over to the still unconscious man now sprawled out on the entryway floor. "Just in case he should wake up."

"Understandable under the circumstances." The older man acknowledged his choice simply but did not judge him. Instead, he turned to the other men and instructed them kindly, "We will need to hurry though as the morning will be here soon, and with it the sun," he cautioned as the men quickly set to work digging the necessary grave at the base of a large stone within the outer courtyard before placing the young lady inside.

"The sun?" William asked their host curiously sometime later, seemingly perplexed by the strangeness of the statement. "Why should that matter?" He placed the last shovel of dirt from the pile back on top of the grave and patted it down firmly.

"It matters a great deal, I'm afraid. Have you not noticed the burning sensation that it causes on your skin or the harshness of its glare to your vision?"

The three men each looked in puzzlement at the other in turn before shaking their heads politely.

"We haven't had the opportunity as of yet, I'm afraid. We were shipwrecked on the other side of the island during the storm but have spent the majority of that time since in a cave near the beach," Sebastian explained as he put his outer garments back on one by one, then leaned their shovels against the stone wall beside the grave for safe keeping.

"I see." The older man walked over to William before lifting the young doctor's chin to scrutinize the exact coloring of his eyes. "How new are you? From the looks of your eyes, you can't be more than a few days old, three at most for the color has almost returned completely for two of your other companions."

"It has been longer for Sebastian and Nathanael. Though possibly much less than a day for the man over there and myself." William pointed his thumb in the direction of Emile who was still slumped rather unceremoniously as if hastily discarded during their gruesome task.

"You know what we are, don't you?" Sebastian eyed the man skeptically, realization dawning on him for the first time since they had arrived.

"Yes," he replied just as simply.

"And you are not afraid of us?" Nathanael asked timidly from his corner.

"Should I be?" His one eyebrow lifted.

The men all looked at each other and then back at Emile before shaking their heads and saying in unison, "No."

"Well then, have you not noticed any other changes?" The man asked plainly before ushering the group back to the safety of the inner courtyard and hallway, away from the rays that had begun to pour over the top of the tall walls around them.

"A few, but mostly in our temperaments and strength," Nathanael replied honestly while trying to avoid some of the more unpleasant details. No one, least of all him, wanted to remember the awful headache, unrelenting chills and unquenchable thirst that vividly plagued him again and again in his dreams, nor the way everything he ate made him feel completely nauseated.

"Truthfully, sir, I think you will find us all very much at your mercy. Only Emile here seems to be enjoying this new fate." Sebastian stamped the extra dirt from off his boots, saying what everyone else in the group was probably already thinking.

"Yes, well, the irises are the biggest give away for a vampire in the first twelve hours after he has changed. For some reason, the color fades quite dramatically during the process of transition, then returns just as quickly. Because of this foundational change, you will now be acutely aware of all light and movement in the dark, yet sensitive to even the slightest amount of true sunlight by day." The older man motioned for them to follow him down the long stone hallway to a larger inner chamber. "The sensitivity will pass somewhat in time, and the original color will return as promised."

"That is at least comforting that something will return to normal in all of this," Nathanael's voice gave away how much he was still clinging to those last shreds of hope that all of what he had become could still possibly be reversed, if not erased forever from his mind.

"Normal will become a somewhat relative term I am afraid for what you will experience in your new future. Despite what you may suspect, you will indeed be able to still go out into the sunlight. You will just need to take some necessary precautions... like for example, covering your skin as much as possible if there are no clouds and so forth. Given your new form, you are not necessarily a creature of the night, but you will have to be studiously mindful of the day."

"Why is that?" William asked as he was becoming entirely intrigued by this line of thinking, drawn by the deductive reasoning and research that instantly appealed to him in every form of conversation.

"Sadly, our skin does not rejuvenate as other things do when they heal. Once burned it will restore eventually, but there will forever remain a mark, a scar of remembrance if you will. So, unless you wish to be marred for all of eternity, it is important to remain vigilant in keeping yourself from injury in that regard." Now inside, the older man removed his cloak and hung it over the back of his chair at the head of a long table. "Sit... please."

The men all did as he requested, and as they took their seats, a small woman entered the room and curtsied, taking no notice of them whatsoever as she focused her attention instead in the direction of her master.

"Would you please us bring five cups of tea, Hannah?" He requested politely. "It has been a cold night, and I am sure our guests could use something to warm their spirits."

"It will just be a minute, sir." She nodded obediently and left to prepare the beverage.

"So, are you implying that we are immortal then?" Sebastian asked curiously once the woman was out of earshot while endeavoring not to make eye contact with anyone else at the table. His focus instead was on the examination of the tapestries and artifacts lining the walls of the large room, searching in vain for a distraction great enough to pull him away from the rising resentment that was being triggered at every word that was being spoken. For the majority of his life, he had never been a man who much enjoyed the company of one, let alone four complete strangers at one given time. Now, adding to that the necessity of trying to be graciously hospitable, as well, only grated on his nerves almost as much as the reality of his current situation.

"Immortal..." The word fell like a lead weight from Nathanael's lips thereafter as if suddenly fully grasping the awful truth—an actuality none of the others had fully contemplated as of yet.

The older man at the head of the table tilted his head as he reflected upon the veracity of this important fact. "Oh, we can still die, let me assure you on that account. Many of us have." He paused before adding more congenially, "I'm sorry. Where are my manners? Let me introduce myself. My name is Señor Moretti, and your wayward vessel has reached the *Iles de Sanguinaires.*"

Chapter Six

November 29th, 1792

N athanael's head swam madly as if in a fog as he struggled to fully take in everything that was being said to him in this horrible nightmare. "The Iles de what?"

"Iles de Sanguinaires," Emile interrupted rudely while entering the room unannounced, his head held defiantly aloof and distant as if to rebuke the men gathered for his rude treatment and obvious dismissal. And yet, though he put up a good front, a noticeably unsteady sway still lingered in his stance from his recent rise from unconsciousness.

"Yes." Nathanael nodded. "But what does that mean?"

"The Bloody Isles," Emile translated easily as he fixed the lace precisely on the cuff of his sleeve before walking over to the empty chair next to Sebastian. Then, upon judging the man's dark demeanor towards him as he drew closer, changed his mind suddenly and took the seat next to William, instead.

"Welcome," Señor Moretti greeted him in a manner befitting a kind host as if nothing out of the ordinary had transpired in the village below. "Though I expect you would prefer something along the lines of Bienvenue, n'est pas?"

Emile nodded respectfully in his direction, clearly impressed by the welcome he had received from at least one person in the room.

"The name seems rather ironic given our current circumstances; don't you agree?" Sebastian remarked sarcastically, ceasing to guard his tone in a moment of sheer incredulity. "Did you name it or someone else?"

Their host merely laughed and the joy of it felt almost discordant to the overall mood of the conversation. "No, no... it is actually the name given to this whole group of islands due to the purple light that you no doubt have noticed along the rocks here just before sunset. However, others throughout history have also speculated that the designation originated from the flowers which are grown more inland. You see, when they first bloom, they have the most unusual shade of pink but as time passes and autumn arrives, they change to a bright red, thus the blood connotation. Though now that you mention it, I do see your point." He chuckled lightly once more. "It is rather ironic."

"Have you lived here long?" William asked as he admired the hand-masoned white and tan stone walls around him that reflected the candlelight beautifully. "From the looks of this castle, your family must have been here for generations."

"Generations, yes, but not all mine. I spent my youth apprenticing in Florence under someone you will no doubt have heard of but have not had the pleasure of meeting in your lifetime, nor many others before you."

"Really? Who was that?" Nathanael's curious nature returned momentarily.

"Does the name Da Vinci seem familiar to any of you?"

A collective gasp of astonishment filled the room as all the men seemed taken aback for an instant and stared in blank shock at his startling revelation.

"Da Vinci?" William shook his head incredulously but refused to accept the possibility. "But that was over two hundred years ago."

"Three to my recollection, but then again, after the first hundred or so years, time starts to matter very little."

With the swing of the wooden door adjacent to their room, Hannah returned just then with the tea and gave a cup and saucer to her host before she dutifully placed the tray with the remaining steaming cups in the center of the table without so much as making eye contact with any of them before curtsying and walking back out of the room just as quickly as she had entered.

Emile's eyes alone traced her passage, greedily watching her like a man lusting after a prize before picking up one of the cups and smiling covetously. "She doesn't mind her employer?" He asked slyly, clearly wanting something more than just tea at the moment.

Señor Moretti motioned for the rest of the group to select their refreshment from the tray as well and paused to answer him pointedly, his tone changing dramatically in its delivery than any way in which he had spoken before. "She does not know her employer, Monsieur, and while we are discussing that point, let me also make one thing crystal clear to all of you." His eyes bore down hard on Emile directly. "While you remain on my island, you are my guest, and as such, no matter what your... desires might be... you will follow my rules to the letter. Comprenez-vous?" He demanded authoritatively in French knowing full-well Emile was the only man sitting at the table who needed such a warning.

"But of course," Emile complied amiably, but in no way were any of the men at the table assured of his sincerity. "I would never..."

"Hold your tongue please, Emile." William turned his head and hushed him firmly, attempting to discreetly cut off whatever ludicrous statement he was about to make. "We just finished cleaning up your last mess. I'd very much like to not do so again."

"As you wish." Emile raised his eyebrows once in irritated response but did not reply further on the subject. He was not a child, and despite the fact that William might have saved his life twice upon the ship, friend or otherwise, there was no need for such condescension from the man.

"And what exactly are your rules?" Sebastian asked cautiously while also mentally exploring his limited options. "Should we choose to remain that is."

The older man acknowledged his question with a simple nod before calmly taking a sip of his tea and continuing along the same lines where he had left off previously. "Simply this, if we do not bother them." He nodded in the direction of the village. "They will not bother us. I am sure all of you can value the importance of that kind of arrangement."

The group nodded soberly at his simple explanation, all that is except for Emile. A few even took a sip of their tea. The majority tried not to spit it back out.

"Learning to eat again is most definitely a practiced skill." Señor Moretti laughed again lightly. "I forget how difficult it was for me when I first changed. I had a hard time stomaching anything other than well... you know... for probably months, if not a solid year."

"Is that why everything tastes so horrible?" Nathanael asked as he smelled his tea once more before carefully setting it far away from him...very far away, too nauseated to have it placed any closer.

"When people like us turn, they lose much of their ability to taste and to feel the temperature around them while their other senses are being developed or rather heightened such as their sight, smell and hearing. It is almost as if the body is readjusting itself, so to speak, to another method of living. Your heart still beats as it should. Your lungs still expand and take in air. But everything else is shifting to a new order of priority."

"That explains a great deal. And why her um... blood was so appealing." William rubbed his temple thoughtfully, trying to forget the sensation it had caused, while also struggling to comprehend the complexity of his new form compared to what he knew as a physician. "So, let me see if I am understanding this correctly, is it only human blood that we will find enticing, or will any form of the liquid create a response?"

"It depends on the vampire, I suppose," Señor Moretti replied flatly. "Normal food will sustain you for a short period of time if no other blood can be had, but eventually you will need to find real nutrition if you want to survive."

"How long will it sustain us?" Nathanael spoke up curiously.

"A week, maybe less if it is more vegetable based. Though I haven't tested my own parameters in a very long time," Señor Moretti answered as honestly as possible without the least bit of reservation.

"And how exactly were you created?" Sebastian asked quietly as if finally realizing the mutual plight of their gracious host.

"Created?" Señor Moretti cocked his head at the confusing terminology, then nodded in final understanding. "Ah, I myself was turned by mistake actually. A careless action on my part if I were to be completely honest, but in simplistic origin, it was by the blood of a centuries old vial placed within the pages of a somewhat vintage looking book, something akin to those found around the times of Martin Luther's predecessors I should imagine."

William's eyebrows lifted in surprise. "How was that even possible?"

"It sounds fantastical, I agree, but my dear sir, as you will soon discover, most things usually are where our kind are concerned. You see, I have always been a researcher of sorts. History, politics, philosophy, science, it all draws my curiosity with the same weight. Yet on this one particular night so many nights ago, I came across a rather strange looking volume of theology tucked neatly inside an old chest in a local monastery."

"How did they come by such a fatal manuscript?" Nathanael asked, though he could well believe such an item could exist as he had grown up accustomed to the vast libraries at his father's university and personal study. To him, finding an old volume of forgotten lore was not only entirely possible, but it was also highly probable, like a long-lost treasure from some pirate or explorer. In fact, it was quite easily his favorite pastime whenever he travelled to delve into undisturbed libraries in search of misplaced gems of knowledge.

"It was a gift, I suppose, as most things are in those types of itinerant ministries, though I could never be for certain exactly. All I could ever find out was that it had been given to them anonymously by someone on his way to the Americas around the time of their European colonization."

Emile and William exchanged a knowing glance of suspicion as to the author before focusing politely again on their host.

"It is really of no matter how they came into the ownership of it but suffice it to say upon opening its pages I soon discovered the author's more sinister intent." Señor Moretti raised his hand to show the small scar that ran down the very center of his palm. "I opened the book. The vial fell, and I instinctively tried to catch it before the priceless artifact smashed onto the floor. Yet it was too late, for it and for me. In the end, I only succeeded in injuring myself in the process, and thus, began my journey towards immortality. A rather rough beginning at that, for there was no one then to direct me in the matter or to help me in avoiding some of the more dangerous pitfalls of our existence."

"So, after you changed," Nathanael stammered for the politest way of asking his question while also feeling totally inadequate in the face of the new path that now lay before him. "Were you able to return to your old life?"

William's heart ached witnessing the growing fear and disillusionment on the man's face. "Nathanael, I don't think going back to the way things were is truly possible for any of us right now. You can see that, can't you?"

"Actually, that is not entirely correct either, sir," Señor Moretti contradicted him politely before he drank more of his tea. "The eye color will change back shortly depending on your nutritional consumption and overall constitution, though I may also add that the young doctor is also correct to another degree. You are a physician, are you not?"

"Yes, my father has a practice in London, though I was serving for a time as an apprentice on a ship to the Americas when this happened."

"To the Americas?" Señor Moretti questioned, pondering the mathematical possibility of four men becoming vampires on one trip alone. "All of you?"

Three of the men nodded soberly. Emile alone chose only to raise one eyebrow and sip his tea from his saucer without flinching, mumbling his rebuttal of their host's conclusion quite sourly, "I was a guest. And your fair King owes me a new chapeau, Doctor Wells. My head has been barren long enough, I should think."

William shook his head and smirked in amusement while listening to Emile's muttered complaints against his teacup. "It's true. Emile was impressed into service, for lack of a better term. And you are right. If you can manage to behave yourself for one day put together, I might be able to see about finding you a new one. Though you will most likely need to wait until we reach the mainland for it, as I doubt there are any adequate shops here in town."

"Hmpf... behave myself indeed. I doubt there is anything up to my standards, that is for certain." Emile smiled right back, enjoying the playful banter between them immensely. On the whole, it had been quite some time since he had found someone as agreeable and intriguing as the young doctor, and it almost pained him to consider being rid of the man shortly. "The last one was actually…"

"Enough already, you two!" Exasperated and fed up with the pointless rabbit trail the conversation had suddenly taken, Sebastian rudely pushed back his chair and stood to his full height, totally disengaged from forming any kind of bond with those around him. With the mounting weight of his failure pressing down upon him, he cared very little right now about Emile's stupid hat or how the man had been so incredibly inconvenienced by the loss of it, nor did he want to entertain a single thought about whatever struggle the young preacher seemed to be having. Anything the man might fear about his sorry little existence would be nothing in comparison to the magnitude of the decision he was facing in his own life right now. Three innocent lives were depending on him alone for their survival and wasting his time on meaningless conversation only irritated him even more to listen to it. "So, let me see if I understand this correctly. For 300 years you have remained here, in this castle, doing nothing? Who does that?"

Stunned into silence by his sudden outburst, each man pondered upon what the agitated man might say next as the entire room fell to an uncomfortable hush around him. Then, when the quiet seemed to grow to an almost breaking point, Sebastian suddenly fixed his gaze once more upon his host, only this time it was not the stare of a welcomed guest, but that of a truly hardened skeptic.

"Pardon my bluntness in saying this, sir, but in all this civility and opulence you have offered us, your story seems more like the actions of someone who is either incredibly out of touch with reality or is clearly insane. Either way, I don't see the difference or how it relates to any of us. Not to mention, why aren't the rest of you more upset? From what you have told us, we have basically been turned into literal monsters and here we all are sipping tea?" Sebastian fumed, though by the clenching and re-clenching of his fists at his side, William could tell that the man was just trying to keep a firm hand of control on whatever it was he was fighting against, which at the moment, seemed to be all of them.

"Huh… speak for yourself," Emile muttered sarcastically at the insinuation, but his dark gaze never left the man across from him as if daring the man once again towards an actual fight.

"Don't push me, sir. I am warning you," Sebastian challenged him right back, both men seemingly poised in almost relished tension on the matter.

"Sebastian, please. Señor Moretti is not our enemy here, and neither is Emile." William tried to respectfully reason and calm the man further, feeling ashamed by his companion's outburst given the immense generosity and latitude their host had already demonstrated towards them. One day, the two men, who were like oil and water to each other, might come to actual blows, William was almost sure of it, but today would not be that day, nor would doing so in front of their host be acceptable either—at least not while he could stop it.

Sebastian refused his counsel and shook his head at William's overly simplistic view of things. "No. He is one of us, too, right? As if that makes everything so much better." The frustration on his face had now been joined with a single tear that was now coursing down the left side of his cheek, his voice breaking on every word that was thick with the emotion he was feeling, "How does a man leave everything behind as if none of that mattered anymore... as if no one else existed that he cared about? What do we say to our families, our friends? Surely someone will wonder what has happened to us. Or are we to simply forget they ever meant anything to us in the first place. I don't think I can do that no matter what I've become. Not today... not ever. It would be like abandoning them since I am clearly not dead."

Señor Moretti smiled patiently at the man before nodding in the most sympathetic way possible, his expression full of empathy for the choices the man was facing. "It has not been without difficulty, I can assure you, but I do have a few distractions to speak of, hobbies mostly. And I have managed to keep a small business of sorts back in the village, which is how I discovered the four of you tonight. But no, friend, there are no easy answers for the questions plaguing your mind right now, only a vague acceptance of what you can and cannot do. Only you can determine how far you are willing to push yourself for those that you love and what sacrifices you are willing to make on their behalf."

"But how did you even know we were there tonight?" Nathanael asked. "We could have been anyone in that alley?"

"Well," Señor Moretti tried his best to answer the man next to him as carefully as possible so as not to upset Sebastian any further. "I was on my way home when I smelled your friend's conquest. That, and I felt all of your presence there."

"Felt our presence?" William asked inquisitively unsure what the man was referring to.

"It is something rather unique that you will discover in time. In fact, every vampire seems to have an innate ability to sense the presence of another of its kind should they cross paths," Señor Moretti explained simply.

"Is that why you have chosen to remain alone then?" Nathanael inquired, though part of him dreaded the expected response.

"Partially. Though, the draw to human blood is merely one of the main reasons why I have kept so secluded over the years. I have learned that, for myself alone, it is... easier... to abstain from that sort of human companionship and temptation than to fall under its spell once again. Besides, I did not have a living family to speak of before I turned so there was little keeping me anywhere at the time. Not that I desired the company of others much before then either. As a rule, I tended to prefer a life of solitude in my youth, as well as afterwards. But yes, people do come to me from time to time when they have a need for advice or some other medical treatment that the doctor in town is unable to provide. It is not the life I had envisioned living once upon a time, but I do try to contribute to the people in this world when I can, and as I hope to do for all of you."

"What were you planning on doing before, if I may be so bold?" Nathanael asked curiously.

"I wanted to be a mapmaker actually, maybe even sail the great oceans and explore some of the recently discovered lands and spices. At the time, it was all very enticing to me. New worlds and people were being encountered daily, and I wanted more than anything to be a part of it, too. Imagine with me if you will, sailing across the seas with men like Columbus and Magellan? Or, plotting out the very lines of our Earth today. I could have been writing the history you have only read about. It would have been amazing." He paused as if remembering his days from long ago, then with a small smile crossing his lips he continued as if content once more in his chosen path. "Instead, I now spend my hours unveiling new truths that have long been hidden to mankind and sailing through the seas of philosophy. That and occasionally hosting guests like yourself who have managed to cross my path in one way or the other," Señor Moretti answered honestly.

"Is that our new world, too?" Sebastian turned to face him directly, a look of despair filling his eyes as his carefully protected world and dreams shattered one by one at the possibility. "A life filled with everything except companionship, our desires forfeited?"

"For some..." He paused, then added more encouragingly, "But not for all."

The room around him hushed once more as each of the men looked down at the table in front of them in intense contemplation of everything that had just been explained.

"There are only two ways that I know of to return to the world in which you are familiar. One, your young friend has so easily demonstrated for you." He glanced over at Emile quickly, but did not mention him by name. "Feed on the weak. Challenge the system. Embrace the creature you have become. It is easy. It is efficient, but it is also dangerous."

"And the other?" Nathanael asked more timidly, completely assured within his own mind that he would choose any path right now other than the one he had just witnessed tonight.

"Live simply but live the life you have chosen to live with honor and discretion. This will not be an easy road for any of you, not by any means. There will be concessions, changes, necessary sacrifices, but in doing so you will also find something infinitely far more valuable than momentary lust."

"And what, pray tell, is that?" Emile asked as if he were finally interested in the conversation at hand.

"Courage, enlightenment, a greater purpose even." Señor Moretti tried to speak as optimistically as possible. "Something we can all appreciate, don't you agree?"

"Sir, I know I have behaved poorly tonight, and I sincerely apologize for my harsh words, but from where we are all sitting, none of that seems even remotely possible?" Sebastian countered as if in a challenge though he meant it only as a means of creating a direct plan for himself and the others. Something undeniably tangible with which to hold onto on this slippery slope of disappointment.

"It will be difficult; I'll not lie and say otherwise... but it is not impossible. I am living testament to that fact, as are many others that live among you today, undetected."

"Undetected? Wait, how many others are there like us?" It was William's turn to be shocked, though if he were to be totally honest, it also made him feel oddly grateful, all at the same time.

"Many, though I have not personally spoken with another vampire in well over thirty years. Yet, I would wager that by now there must be at least a hundred, if not more. They do exist and walk among the living as casually as you or I are sitting at this table right now. You may have even entertained one during your lifetime already and had not the slightest inclination of his or her existence."

"And you don't feed on others at all then?" Nathanael added in welcomed disbelief at the possibility before him.

"Not in that sense of the term, no. Since being trained as a doctor since, I have a ready supply of all the blood that I have ever needed to survive."

"How?" William asked, very much intrigued.

"Consider this for a moment if you will? Exactly how many times have you or your father been asked at a patient's side to perform a bloodletting? A ritualistic cleansing of a patient's overabundance of humors as we used to call it back in my day and in yours."

"Hundreds in my lifetime alone, quite possibly. Why?" It was then that the realization finally dawned on him. "Ohhhh, I see. You save the collected blood, don't you?"

Señor Moretti nodded and smiled at William's excellent intellect, albeit slower time necessary for deliberation. "Yes. People expect the doctor to perform the task, but no one asks what becomes of that life-giving liquid when it is done. I am certain most patients assume it is simply disposed of, which it is, except that I simply store it away in a small container for future use and no one is ever the wiser for it." He looked over at Emile who was now only half-listening at this point in the conversation, distracted instead by the piano that sat across the room behind his host.

"But not all of us have access to that sort of thing..." Sebastian cringed inwardly at the possibility of draining another human of their life blood, yet his mouth began watering just thinking about it yet again.

"Or would want to," Nathanael added in obvious, shared disgust though both men knew the temptation was the very thing they craved presently, despite their aversion mentally.

"Oh, you will want to," Señor Moretti assured him, remembering his own first feeble attempt at satisfying his hunger. In the beginning, he had acted much like the Frenchman and sought only the easiest of conquests until he had learned the very real importance of restraint. "Gentlemen, as I have mentioned, you are not the first of your kind who have crossed my threshold. Many before you have come. Some have stayed... for a time, which I hope each of you will, while others have left to pick up the pieces of whatever lives they have chosen to live. They could be your neighbor, your grocer, even your physician." He winked playfully over at William. "Either way, you must each make the choice yourself as to what you will do with the answer of just one question. One question that will become the motivation for all your endeavors hereafter."

"Really? What question might that be?" Emile leaned in closer, somewhat intrigued though little else in this conversation had piqued even the remotest interest for him. Polite though it may be, the whole discussion felt rather like an annoying buzzing within his ears than useful information at this rate.

"Do you want to live forever, gentlemen?" Señor Moretti stated simply without any added persuasion in either direction. With the formality of the conversation seemingly completed, he rose from his chair and pushed it in once more. "It is late, or rather early, let us all rest for the day, and we can discuss this again more at length over supper."

The men all rose and mimicked the action of their host, each paying careful attention to leave the room in the same condition as when they had arrived.

"And in regard to my housekeeper, Hannah," Señor Moretti motioned for the others to follow him. "You might also have noticed that she is blind, so you need not fear discovery here."

"Convenient." Emile smiled and felt the rush of bloodlust rise within him once more like the most excellent of sensations before his host stopped abruptly in front of him.

"Indeed, Monsieur." Señor Moretti studied him intently as if judging the risk of allowing him to remain. "But I challenge you not to test me in this area, sir. I may seem quite amiable on the surface, but Hannah is more than my servant, she is also my ward, and as such, under my express protection. Do we understand each other fully at last?"

Justly rebuked, though no further word was spoken, Emile nodded towards his host with an expression of obedient compliance, or at least on this point alone. The rest he would decide upon later, much later, when he could finally be rid of this group and on his way back to France. Vampire or not, it was becoming clearer to him by the second that he had spent far too much of his life obeying all the rules he had been given. In his estimation, it was high time for a little... fun, and he knew just the place to find it. He always did.

Señor Moretti's eyes narrowed slightly as if he had just read the man's lurid thoughts, but he did not press the subject further. With renewed peace of mind about his guest, he led the way down a hallway and up a winding set of stairs to several upper rooms within the castle.

Stopping outside the various doors as he passed, he paused and gracefully opened each of them in turn before bidding his guest a peaceful respite—first for Sebastian, who only grumbled a goodnight back to him, then for Nathanael, who looked like he was about to collapse from the strain of the day, and at last, for William, the only one of the group who seemed to be rationally moderate in his thinking at the moment.

"Things will look better after some rest, doctor," Señor Moretti encouraged him warmly, hoping to offer the man more insight into their condition when he was more settled in his transition.

"I doubt that very highly, but I thank you for your hospitality all the same." William politely replied as he sat down on the single bed within the room and placed his head wearily within his palms. "Will the throbbing ever stop?"

"In time, though I will bring you up something that will help keep it at bay momentarily," Señor Moretti replied. "Physician, take the time to heal thyself. Sleep and be at peace. It is the only thing required of you at the present."

William nodded and laid out on the bed, clothes and all, too exhausted mentally and physically to do more.

Señor Moretti smiled quickly and closed the door behind him before heading down to the last room in the corridor, the one normally reserved for Thomas, Hannah's beau from the village when he had occasion to have need of it. "The young doctor is especially weary tonight it appears. He is the newest of you all, is he not?" Señor Moretti inquired thoughtfully as they walked side by side.

"Only slightly more so than myself, but yes," Emile replied nonchalantly. "Though his condition could be more attributed to the fact that he does tend to take on far more responsibility than is absolutely necessary."

"So, it would appear," Señor Moretti answered. "Yet, that probably cannot be helped, given his position as a healer."

"Perhaps." Emile grimaced as he realized again that he held an inexplicably deep connection with the man he had only just met weeks earlier.

Señor Moretti nodded in understanding, then placed one arm across the opening to Emile's room to bar his entry as he studied the man before him once more, looking directly into the man's eyes as he judged what kind of a man he truly was inside. "I know this will mean very little to you at the present, but I have actually met several men like you over the years."

"I'm sure you have." Emile smirked with an air of selfish defiance as if he needed to give no explanation whatsoever for his actions, either here or otherwise.

"Hmm..." His host lightly chuckled at his open audacity, remembering his own tendency to do so at times. "And I expect you have decided upon your own plans without the company of the others."

"You assess correctly." Emile refused to yield his position in any way.

"Then let me say one thing only before you leave, and that will be all I will impress upon you thereafter." Señor Moretti touched Emile's shoulder gently in a gesture of intended friendship. "I do not judge your choice. It is the freedom of a man to choose his own direction no matter his immortality. Yet, I also fear that the path you enter will not be entirely what you have envisioned either. Though I know from personal experience that you must try it just the same."

"High talk for a man who has spent the last 300 years as a prisoner... isolated in a lonely castle... on some secluded island. You say you are free, but really, you are still... just a prisoner," Emile scoffed as he rebuked him with haughty consternation. "I'm done being a captive of my own life."

"But sir, that is my choice, and if that makes me a prisoner, so be it. Monsieur?"

"Emile Bastien of the family Deschamps."

Señor Moretti removed his arm from the doorway to allow him entry. "*Monsieur* Deschamps, as a matter of parting kindness, I like to bestow upon each of my visitors a gift in exchange for something of greater value in return."

Instantly skeptical, yet still cautiously intrigued at the same time, Emile raised one eyebrow in question. "A gift? It has been my experience that most gifts do not come with strings attached."

"I am inclined to agree with you once again. None-the-less, on your way out you will find a small box already waiting for you on the piano below. No doubt you saw it during our discussion earlier?"

Emile nodded. "It is a beautiful instrument, created by Louis Bas of Villeneuve-lès-Avignon, was it not?"

"But, of course. You know your instruments well." Señor Moretti replied easily, clearly impressed.

"How could I not? It was one of Bach's favorites."

"Perhaps you will play it for me sometime."

"Perhaps," Emile tilted his head respectfully. "If I ever return..."

"Yes, well, in the burgundy box on its top, you will find 1,000£, a handkerchief, and a small bottle of Ether. Use them all sparingly, and they may help you with your new start in the world. It is my gift."

"That is incredibly generous, sir." Emile felt genuinely surprised by the gesture but true to his nature, fell immediately cynical thereafter. "Then what, pray tell, do you want in exchange? My eternal servitude? No, thank you."

"Oh, nothing so unnecessary, as I am sure you will soon discover." Señor Moretti waved a dismissive hand to dissuade his suspicion further. "I only ask that you return one year from tomorrow, if you are so indisposed, and share just a bit of the life you have created for yourself. Consider it a trade if you will if the word isn't far too inaccurate."

"D'accord." Emile nodded in final agreement and entered the provided room before turning back to him and adding politely, "Will you give Doctor Wells my regards this evening as I doubt I shall see him again before I leave?"

"You two seem to have some history together, do you not?"

"Yes." Emile nodded respectfully. "I owe him a debt."

"Debts can be difficult to live under, but if leaving is your wish, I bid you Bonne chance, au revoir, à bientôt... until we meet again. May this new world be everything you hope it will be." Señor Moretti wished him well warmly and closed the door, leaving behind it a very puzzled and still deliberating Emile.

Señor Moretti closed his eyes. It had been over 300 years since his own journey began and despite all his efforts, nothing about this exchange had ever seemed to change. As grateful as he was for the new company after such a very long period of solitude, the whole experience left him feeling disheartened and yet encouraged all at the same time.

With a long sigh, he hung his head in remorse at Emile's most certain failure before looking back down the hallway at the other rooms behind him. "Perhaps this time it will be different," he mused hopefully and walked with his hands clasped casually behind his back to his study downstairs to retrieve some blood for William. The necessary liquid would cure the bulk of the symptoms the man was experiencing but it would do nothing for his own palpable dread toward the possible events yet to come.

"Perhaps..." He whispered almost in prayer and closed his eyes for a moment to reflect deeply.

Chapter Seven

December 15th, 1792

William sat down on the edge of the bench in the library that looked like it held one of the most extensive collections of books that he had ever seen and glanced over curiously at several of the framed paintings on the wall next to him before settling on one in particular. The woman in the image could have been any of a number of his acquaintances back in London. Dressed in a simple, European gown, smiling sweetly, she stared back at him, inviting his scrutiny and his adoration.

Who was she—someone's mother or sister perhaps? Or maybe a betrothed? With little other details in the painting itself, he could not tell anything about her besides her calm exterior and angelic air. Did it really matter? With a drawn-out sigh he returned his gaze back out the window and towards the inviting ocean beyond. The same tumultuous waters his father was no doubt viewing as he received word of the shipwreck.

Imagining the hurt and shock his father would soon be experiencing at his apparent demise, the expression on his face shifted to one of intense guilt. The grief he must be going through right now as a parent was surely a tremendous burden for anyone to endure, making his own crippling troubles pale in comparison. In fact, for the first time since he had awakened in the cave, he finally permitted his mind to contemplate the path that truly lay before him.

Feeling more than a little overwhelmed by the entire situation he was now a part of, he laid the book he had been trying to read distractedly on top of his short collared blue overcoat that rested on the stone bench beside him before wondering aloud. "Can it really be as easy as simply choosing a path and taking it? To just return to England like none of this horrible nightmare ever happened in the first place?" He looked at the ocean once more and stood up, eager to work out the anxiety spreading across his skin like a thousand needles teasing at the surface.

At the moment, there were no ready answers for the myriad of questions that were constantly plaguing his brain. The best he could do was incessantly pace the large room as he slowly paused more than once to ask question after following question in inward deliberation. *What should I do next? Return to Father's surgery?* He threw his head back and blew out a long exhale of frustration. "Inconceivable. And yet, as humiliating as that might be, what other option do I have?"

At 28 years old he had thought himself more than ready to take on the world, maybe even enjoy a small taste of adventure if it presented itself, but as he was today, he felt more like a man beginning primer school than the accomplished figure that left England weeks ago. When he had stepped aboard that ship, blonde hair tied back into a neat ponytail, neatly cut attire and polished boots, he thought he was prepared for everything he might encounter. Certainly, he was not overly strong like the deckhands that roamed up and down the passageway, nor had he ever been. His profession required him to search journals instead of jungles. But "Everything has a purpose," or at least that was what his father had recited to him countless times over during a difficult diagnosis. So, with that being assumed, William knew even in this, he could trust that for whatever reason Providence had for bestowing on him this, albeit dangerous quality, he would have need of it somewhere... somehow.

"Just not here... and not to get what I want right now..." He mused darkly thinking of the one thing he wanted more than anything else at that moment, another taste of what Emile had consumed so freely when they had found him.

"If I am going to survive at all, I must figure out how to control this first," he vowed resolutely and began the process of resigning himself to the inevitable as little else presented itself as a possibility to him at this point as a vagabond amongst vagabonds.

Yet try as he might, his brain ached incessantly attempting to envision it. After all his ridiculous rantings about starting his own practice after completing his university training, he could not force himself to welcome the possibility of going back into his former existence with his father no matter the ease of which it would be to do so—not only for his father's sake, but also for his own. His parents would, of course, quite happily accept him back into their society, but his decision to establish a life outside of his father's influence and provisions had still not changed in that regard, despite his recent transformation otherwise.

But how? Where? There has to still be a way. But what? And with whom? The questions played themselves out within his mind, constantly swirling like the waters beyond as they searched for the answers that eluded him.

Without a word or forwarding information of any kind, Emile had chosen to leave weeks ago and even though William would not have wished his friend to remain where he was not content, he had often missed his lighthearted company and playful banter since his departure. And Sebastian would not be a suitable companion either, for he was far more concerned with escaping his failure than in creating any kind of a new future for his family with him in it. That left Nathanael, the timid preacher who seemed more like an insecure younger brother to him than a cherished acquaintance or mentor. *Would he be willing to go back to England and begin afresh? Possibly... with help.* The man seemed perpetually eager to jump into anything that would put him back on the road to his former life... *as if that were even possible.*

William shook his head again as he tried to discern his next steps, rubbing his hands against the other repeatedly in front of him in intense concentration. *And what kind of life would this new form provide me anyways? Is it a benefit or a curse like Nathanael views it? Or is it simply a disability that needs to be overcome like everything else and not something that will rule my every thought and decision thereafter?* Sadly, there was only one way in which for him to find out... and that would require him taking a leap of faith or at least leaving the safety of this castle.

Thankfully, the throbbing sensation of his transition had finally ceased after his first sample of Señor Moretti's emergency supply. However, more troubling than the physical manifestations of his body's new nutritional requirements was the fact that his mind had been made no clearer by the many revelations and questions that had emerged following his host's complex explanations. The smallest of deliberations now held an absolute plethora of possible answers—too many to contemplate in one given setting, yet all were important factors that had to be considered before he acted.

For years he had always prided himself on the way that his thoughts were consistently based on a logical progression of facts, but standing here today, he was quickly discovering that they were more a muddy mixture of emotion and indecision now than actually scientifically inclined. *Other vampires among us? That seems so incredibly impossible. Or is it?*

Sighing, he walked over to the tall candelabra positioned closely near the far wall and blew out the last of the candles one by one that had been illuminating the lingering shadows of the chamber. The muted rays of the early morning sunshine now filtering through the glass window to his left cast long streaks of radiant light upon the stone floor at his feet.

Morbidly curious to test just one of his theories, he reached his hand timidly into them and turned it over, expecting to feel the burn Señor Moretti had described, but nothing transpired beyond a warm glow upon the upper layer of his skin. Though possibly hot in nature, the light did not even produce the slightest increase in temperature on his forever cold hands.

"Hmmm." William studied the phenomenon carefully before surmising audibly as if he were conducting a very thorough experiment. "Perhaps, the thickness of the glass in these windows decreases the intensity enough to not cause me any damage, or at least not at this time of the day. Or maybe it is the clouds diffusing its force," he debated, then stopped when a polite knock sounded discreetly on the old, wooden door, interrupting his scientific examinations and calling his attention back to his world of far more troubling questions.

"Enter," William said formally and took his seat once more, then regretted the tone in which he had replied. High societal manners were hard to forget once they had been learned but forget them, he must, if he were even contemplating living a more conventional life outside of London proper.

With a slight creak, the door swung softly on its hinges and William watched as Nathanael poked his head just within the opening of the doorway and inquired, "I'm not disturbing you, am I?"

"Never." William motioned for Nathanael to join him with a smile that finally felt genuine enough to display. "I was only sitting here considering possibilities, if you will."

"I won't beg you to divulge the particulars, though it is probably the very same contemplations that are on all of our minds." Nathanael moved the navy-blue coat over slightly and took his seat next to him on the bench. "Robinson Crusoe?" He held the book up slightly to view the cover, his curiosity piqued.

"An old favorite," William added with just a hint of embarrassment. "But stories of shipwrecks and survival aside, I sometimes find that reading distracts me when my mind is feeling rather... um... complicated."

"Yes, well, on that we can both agree. But what I really came to tell you was that I have finally gotten a reply from my bishops back in England." Nathanael set the book back down upon its place on top of William's coat carefully.

"That soon?" William raised his eyebrows. "I only managed to send a quick correspondence to my family yesterday. Knowing my mother, she was probably in a faint when the news of the shipwreck reached them."

"Then it was probably most prudent on your part that you did, though I have no such relations to notify at this time. As for my elders, it seems our host has very excellent connections both on the continent and abroad."

William nodded in agreement. "His help <u>has been</u> inexhaustible. I shudder to think what might have become of us had Emile not run into town that day."

"Yes, Emile may demonstrate more than a few narcissistic tendencies, but given the right encouragement, I think he may still be quite useful under God's direction. If he is ever willing that is as no man can be forced to change his ways, no matter the necessity."

"That is very gracious to say, all things considered." William laughed at the positive light the minister placed on Emile's rather colorful character.

"Well, I have found that in my profession it helps to remain optimistic about those I encounter." Nathanael smiled slightly. "Like so many other things, people usually turn out to surprise you in the end."

"So, you have chosen to remain faithful to your beliefs despite all that God has allowed to happen to you? Even if most people may view our kind as something evil?" William prodded deeper, testing further the man's recent resolve out of amiable curiosity and not malice.

"I admit, the thought of our immortality has certainly caused a great deal of struggle in my spiritual walk these past few days, undeniably so. And still, even though I have not fully comprehended the various complexities of what I have become or how it will affect my ministry in the future, I find myself still believing that if this path is truly what God has intended for me, then who am I to tell Him otherwise. Why, even Job, from the Old Testament, found himself in a fairly similar predicament, though arguably not as dire. God allowed Satan to take away all his possessions, health and even his family from him, but Job still chose to trust that God had a plan in it all. Should I do any less? Besides, the men in the Bible did live quite long lives, too. Some even to upwards of 900 years, yet only one of them did not die."

"Really? Who?" William tilted his head towards him, becoming keenly interested in the topic, or rather any matter that might distract his mind from the impending choices before him that still needed to be made.

"Well, for starters, the prophet Elijah never tasted death because God took him up in a glorious chariot of fire." Nathanael looked upwards as if visualizing the story as some majestic play or another such production. "But come to think of it," he paused. "There <u>was</u> one more man, too."

"Go on. I am interested now." William turned to face him, fully invested now in his story.

Feeling more at ease in the man's presence than with any of the others, Nathanael leaned against the tall, wooden bookcase behind him. "His name was Enoch, and it was said that he grew so holy, or close to God, that he simply walked up to Heaven <u>with</u> God."

"Well, I doubt any of us wants to attempt a chariot of fire any time soon." William tilted his head and smirked at the insanely ludicrous thought and they both laughed together in earnest humor of the mere suggestion.

"Nor am I close enough, within a fraction of the sense of the word, to say that I have reached the holiness necessary to walk up to Heaven with God either," Nathanael admitted honestly.

"But you might one day." William tried his best to encourage him even a little, enjoying the budding camaraderie existing between them. Looking at him today in a new light, he realized that perhaps he had been wrong about him after all. His only younger siblings were two girls almost five years younger than he was and they sincerely lacked his current companion's wealth of conversation and were most definitely far more self-focused overall.

"If I am given 900 years, perhaps... maybe. Though I highly doubt it," Nathanael admitted humbly.

"You never know." William raised one eyebrow and tilted his head in his direction. "You still have plenty of time..." He let the sentence drop off as the realization of such a concept overwhelmed him again just to speak it. "We all do, it would seem."

"Quite," Nathanael replied just as quietly as he seemed equally affected by the notion.

For several long and quiet moments thereafter, they sat collectively silent in mutual reflection before William finally cleared his throat to dispel his darker thoughts and inquire once more, "And your bishops? What did their message say?"

"They want me to accept the same position they offered me before our little excursion on the Endeavor. However, things being as they are, I am hesitant to even contemplate such a thing. My previous school in Worcester is far too populated a position and necessitates quite a transparent life spent in constant supervision by the congregation as well as from those attending the school there."

"I see." William nodded in great understanding. "So, what will you do then?"

"Well, there is one other option they have afforded me. But although it is one they have yielded to rather reluctantly, I feel it is also the option for which I am the most inclined to accept due to my requirements." Nathanael fingered the material of Williams overcoat absentmindedly, focusing on the comforting sensation the soft fabric between his fingertips afforded.

"Really, what alternative is that?"

"A more remote parish that has been long empty by the previous tenant. They have not given me all the particulars concerning it precisely, nor do I care to know why the man left, but I do feel that this could possibly be the place where I am to reinvent myself," Nathanael explained before adding hesitantly, "If I can manage it, that is."

"Remote, you say. How remote?" William's eyes narrowed, considering the possibility along with him.

"It would be somewhere in the northern territories of England, if I understood them correctly. Somewhere that I can still do the Lord's work yet remain entirely unnoticed by anyone outside of my most singular scope of service—obscure, yet modest in all other areas of consideration."

"No more mission work for you then?"

"Not in that sense of the term, no." Nathanael stood and faced the window, attempting to shield his guilt-ridden emotions entirely from the other man's view. "I think God has punished me enough for my lack of obedience and humility in that area. Wouldn't you agree?"

As if trying very hard inwardly not to say what he really felt on the matter, William shook his head at the absurdity of the statement before countering incredulously, "You think he has punished us all then?"

Nathanael touched the thick glass with one finger and traced the folds in the glass along one edge for several moments before answering just as matter-of-factly, "Perhaps."

"Nathanael, I can see that you plainly feel very passionately about your faith, but do you really think there is a God above that is issuing penalties on His frail human subjects like a father with spoiled children?" William tried to reason with the man who he felt was as loyal to his convictions as he was disillusioned. "Is it not easier to think He has created this Earth, with all its fascinations, for us to simply manage and discover it?"

"That is a very Deistic view of things, my friend. One held by many in the Americas, like their Benjamin Franklin, in fact. An incredibly intelligent man like yourself, but for all his vast knowledge, in my scope of belief, he is still equally lost."

"Lost?" William shook his head before grimacing at some of his points. "You can't be lost if someone knows where you are. That is only logical."

"Yes, but logic will only get a man so far, William." Nathanael rubbed his still cold hands together to warm them out of habit. "My personal belief is that every man must realize deep down that he has done many things wrong in his life that need amendment. And as such, that amendment can only be given by someone who has not committed the same."

"So, everyone is doomed then. Is that what you mean?" William tried to reason with him gently. "That seems rather harsh for a loving God."

"I do see why you might think that. It is a point of view that I have heard on many other occasions. Though undoubtedly, I would say that although God does love His children, He cannot allow their sin where He resides in Heaven. So, He did the only thing He could do to remedy the situation. He sent someone to take that punishment for His children." Nathanael chose his words slowly and carefully as if weighing them out cautiously as he spoke them.

"Ah... Jesus. Yes, I have heard this story many times in my life—the humble Savior if I remember correctly. My grandmother used to tell me that He was a man who died for the sins of the world. A man who rose again so that all men could have eternal life. Did I get it right?"

"Yes, a man... but also God, William. That is why He was the only one who could do it."

"It still all sounds like dizzying logic to me." William joined him at the window. "But if that is what you believe, my friend, I will not dissuade you from it. Every man must have some truth to cling to in this life or he will go mad searching for its existence. I have science. You have your God."

"Indeed." Nathanael smiled back at him, as patient with the man as with others who doubted his faith.

"Have you decided if you will accept the position then?" William asked, hoping he had not offended the man too severely.

"Yes, I think I will." Nathanael tucked the loose strands of hair that had fallen forward into his face behind his right ear and looked over at the man beside him, curious as to why he was asking. "But unfortunately, they would like me in place by Christmas if I can manage it, so that leaves me precious little time to travel."

"And how will you... um, survive there?" William asked him with even greater interest.

With a shake of his head, Nathanael left his place by the window and began to pace nervously around the center of the large room, deliberating his next course of action. "I have been giving that a great deal of thought, as well. Unlike our friend, Emile, I cannot even fathom living in such a way that would put other people in danger of eternal damnation, nor can I perform the necessary bloodletting Señor

Moretti has suggested without great suspicion, either. So, I suppose that leaves me with only one other alternative. Abstinence has always been a part of many a church's religious protocol, so perhaps I will try that if I am able. It won't be easy by any means, but maybe by feeding on small animals if I must between fasts or..."

"Emile probably would have suggested snacking on the church mice if he were here," William interrupted him with a sarcastic quip before suddenly realizing with a light chuckle the negative impact the man's dark humor had already made on him.

"Not funny, William. I was being serious." Nathanael tried to look authentically offended, but the expression on his face only humored William even more.

"I'm sorry, Nathanael... truly." William stepped forward and interrupted him in his path midway across the room by gently placing one hand upon his forearm in reassurance, suddenly resolved in his own course at last. "I have also been giving my return much consideration, and though I know my position would be assured on another boat, I simply cannot go back to sea as that would only place me in the same unfortunate circumstances in which we found ourselves. And I'll not become another Doctor Clarke, even if it was the last choice in all the world available to me. Not to mention the irritating fact that I apparently lack the wherewithal to withstand seasickness it appears. Despite all the new physical benefits we now possess, I highly doubt it has cured me of that." He walked abruptly over to the bench he had been sitting on and picked up his jacket before putting it on in one swift, determined motion. "So, as you see, I am much like yourself in that regard. Vampirism aside, I am also a man whose future is entrapped by his physical limitations."

Nathanael nodded, grateful for his openness in sharing his struggles. "Then what will you do?"

"I suppose that leaves me with few other options except to simply use what little savings I have left to start a practice of my own or maybe an apothecary in a small town in England until I can control my urges. I've helped my father do it before, though on a much grander scale to be sure. Still, I do not think it will take long to make it a successful venture, and in turn, perhaps I can help us both."

"Both?" Nathanael looked up and cast him a glance that was almost overflowing with hopeful desperation.

With a smile of genuine contentment finally, William turned back to face the man with a look of renewed peace at his decision. "Nathanael, the four of us entered this journey together, so it would seem that Providence would like us to continue that acquaintance." William looked over once more at the painting resting on the wall, then back at the man beside him with an expression of true support. "You will not be alone, no matter what you decide."

"I never was," Nathanael reassured himself again almost in a whisper before adding a much louder reply to William, "I'd be indebted to you, if you do."

William nodded but not in any way that would provoke a feeling of gratitude from the man. He was merely satisfied to earn the joy of his friendship than make the man's life even more complicated than it already was. "Shall we tell our host that we will be leaving then?"

"Of course." Nathanael's mood had now improved considerably since his arrival to William's quarters. "Though I fear I should warn you that my bishops have said the village may be a tad bit more obscure than what you may have been accustomed to."

"How remote is it?" William placed the book he had been reading carefully back up on the shelf from where he had retrieved it before clasping the handle to his door and holding out his hand to direct Nathanael to pass through before him.

"How do you feel about Wakefield?" Nathanael asked timidly, hoping the doctor would not suddenly change his mind at the revelation.

"Cold," William stated flatly, then grinned.

"Then we should both blend right in." Nathanael smiled, too, and the two men laughed in unison as they descended the stairs together while excitely making plans for their upcoming trip.

Yet upon reaching the great hall of the castle, however, they found their benevolent host seated casually at the piano while playing a flowing piece of music that echoed along the sides of the hall as they passed. The room itself was large enough for two rooms put together, illuminated only by several rectangular windows high above that cast light down the white stone walls with the perfect amount of ambiance and warmth. Certainly, enough to brighten the whole room, but not enough to cause them any distress. It reminded William very much of how the inside of a cathedral might appear given the perfect light.

Sebastian, on the other hand, was a whirlwind of ferocious energy on the other side of the room. Quite the opposite of the music being played as he paced the floor back and forth in front of the large fireplace with heavy, deliberate steps as if creating a strange sort of dance with his sharp movements and gestures. From his sulking expression to the jerking motions of his arms as he deliberated mentally and ran his fingers furtively through his wavy curls, he exuded a tense form of restlessness in every definition of the term.

Like the others, Sebastian knew full-well that he had options, but nothing he felt he could even contemplate undertaking without incredible distress to someone involved. As a father, his duty would forever be to their provision first, no matter what the strife or pain it would cause him to do so. But with no income coming in anymore from his shop back in Portsmouth, they were now counting on him more than ever for their very survival. Something he felt utterly ill-equipped now to remedy. The sheer fact alone that he was just remaining here day after day like he was, doing nothing to alleviate their possible suffering, only made him feel like he was continuously letting them down with every idle hour. And that betrayal maddened him most of all, almost to the point that he felt like a caged bear before the gladiators awaiting its final fight.

From across the room, William could see the fresh guilt wash over his new companion countless times over as he stared into the fire and looked as if he were on the edge of a complete breakdown emotionally. The man had obviously made countless promises to his family about their new life in America. To fail them now when they needed him the most was probably more than devastating, it was unthinkable.

"Has he been like that all day again?" William asked the man at the piano while shaking his head back and forth slowly in remorse. "I'd say he will wear himself out with worry, but I am afraid that is not possible, anymore."

"Quite right." Señor Moretti looked over his shoulder at Sebastian who had stopped pacing several minutes ago but still remained fixed in his position like a rigid statue, his back towards the group. "But he could wear out my rug."

They all laughed quietly at the notion. Though it was most certainly true that nothing about their situation in general was at all funny, they had not lost all sense of humor entirely.

"So, you both have made a decision then?" Señor Moretti began to softly play another piece more familiar to Nathanael than the last. Something that was far more slow and melodic as it progressed on through the scripted pages, but also faintly haunting when the chords lingered.

"A rather interesting choice," Nathanael noted the poignancy of the selection from Mozart's recent publication almost a decade earlier.

"My attempt to soothe the savage beast." Señor Moretti smiled wryly before tipping his head in Sebastian's direction. "Though I doubt a mere Sonata will do much good at this point."

"Better that than his Turkish March, I suppose. We might all be terribly agitated after that piece," William added sarcastically.

"I can hear you both, you know," Sebastian growled as he gripped both hands like a vise upon the mantle above the ornate fireplace. "I can hear... everything!" His fingers flexed as the muscles along them tightened. "My mind knows that the world should be quiet, but it is almost as if it will not accept that fact. The buzzing of the flames on the candles. The faint wind running up the chimney. The incessant tinging that the hammer makes on each string of that piano you so love to play. It is all quite literally deafening!" He plopped down with a huff into the large chair beside him, too irritated to stand any longer.

"Patience, my young friend," Señor Moretti soothed. "It will pass in time."

Sebastian only scowled helplessly back at him. "So, you say..."

"Um," Nathanael cleared his throat quietly and tried to express his sincerest gratitude as a means of changing the focus off Sebastian. "I did want to thank you for your help with my bishops, sir."

"Oh," Señor Moretti inclined his head towards the piano in subtle acknowledgement but continued on in his playing. "So, you will accept one of their offers?"

"Yes, the latter," Nathanael answered respectfully.

"And you, dear doctor? By the look on your face and animated conversation coming in here just now, should I assume that you will be joining him?"

"Since it has worked so well for you and others in the past, I will begin as you have and try to relieve some of the burden on Nathanael, as well. Perhaps together, we will fare better than alone." It was then that William walked carefully over to Sebastian and paused before placing a comforting hand upon his shoulder. "You can join us if you wish. I cannot say that we will be the company that you are used to, but we will certainly try to ease some of that weight you are quite obviously being flattened under. "And..." he leaned in closer to see his expression more clearly before adding further, "You will at least be closer to your family living in England."

Sebastian looked up respectfully at the gesture before a shadow immediately fell over his face once more. "That would probably make it worse, but I thank you anyways."

William patted his shoulder. "Please consider writing me then at the very least."

"Why?" The man appeared entirely disinterested in the senseless occupation.

"Let's just say for my own personal assurance that you will not resort to anything rash. Will you promise me that?"

"I will," the man replied firmly. "Writing may be all I will be able to do here, watching from afar, while others accomplish what I cannot. Sadly, you would think that I should be used to it as that is all I have ever done in this world it seems."

Nathanael's heart felt broken for the man to watch his increasing melancholy and despair. "Is there not anything you would consider that would make things better for you and your family?"

"Not unless you are in the miracle business yourself," Sebastian added wryly.

"Um, not even close." Nathanael chuckled lightly at the idea.

Señor Moretti knew then that the time for his departing gift had finally arrived. As he had done on so many occasions before, he rose from the piano, picked up the three boxes that had been laid precisely beside him on the shelf, and made his way over to the men with great care. "Perhaps, now that you all have made your decision, I may be of further assistance in that regard."

Surprised, William turned to give him his full attention. "But you have already helped us so much already, Señor Moretti. We couldn't possible accept more."

"It is nothing beyond that which any man would do under the circumstances. Are we not to provide food and shelter to those who are in need?" He waved off the intensity of the gratitude as he continued, "There is one gift I have yet to give each of you. The same that was given to your friend, Emile, on the night that he decided to leave. One of which I bestow upon every man or woman that has inadvertently become one of my special guests."

Sebastian looked swiftly up in his direction but still remained silent as if seizing desperately onto whatever last shred of hope he was being offered.

"Living in this castle has been a bit isolating, as Sebastian and Emile have both clearly surmised earlier, but it has not been without its benefits, too." Señor Moretti placed one ornately carved wooden box into the hands of each man in turn. "It has allowed me the chance to study and seek out ways to benefit those around me. And..." He paused. "It has provided me the opportunity to invest in the lives of countless others." He nodded, indicating his wish for them to open their boxes.

"What?! It is a king's ransom! A year's salary many times over for a man in my position." Nathanael gasped audibly, realizing the immense wealth contained within.

"Some might say so." Señor Moretti walked over to the fire and picked up the poker to stoke it higher. "Yet, it also contains the means with which to begin your new life. Should you wish to invest it."

"And the liquid?" William held the amber glass bottle up to the light and examined it closer.

"Ether."

"Ether?" Nathanael queried, his nose wrinkling in puzzlement at such a gift. "What is that?"

"Not everyone chooses to feed as others do, and in this point, I feel that I should explain, for all of you were bitten were you not?"

The three men nodded soberly.

"And the young girl in the village was also bitten, was she not?"

A horrified look fell instantly upon Nathanael's face. "Did Emile condemn that poor child to a life as a vampire, too? And we... we just..." He began stammering helplessly as he recollected their first day at the castle.

"...buried her," Sebastian finished before adding, "Will she come back to life then?"

"No," William answered for Señor Moretti. "Doctor Clarke, himself boasted as much to me that the reason why you two are here today is because I would not stop trying to treat you. My efforts to heal you kept him from finishing his intentions."

"Precisely," Señor Moretti agreed, obviously very pleased with William's intellect on the matter. "It has been my experience that to be fully changed into a vampire, one must have been bitten and yet <u>not</u> die of natural causes thereafter. The vampire's transformative venom, whether by physical contact directly or through the transfer of his blood to another, allows his victim to forever remain in a state of immortal limbo—neither dead, nor alive. If a victim were to be bitten and then succumb to some kind of physical injury before that transition has taken place, or if the vampire were to drain them entirely, then he or she would most certainly die and not be grated immortality after all."

"So, we all <u>could have</u> died on the ship with everyone else." Sebastian looked down at his hands and contemplated morosely the possibility.

"Would that have been your wish?" William glanced over at him, suddenly concerned as to what the man might think about his earlier decisions on the ship.

"Yes!" Sebastian immediately replied, then thought the better of it and added quieter still, "No...of course not. Though alive as all of us may appear to be, I feel that in many ways a part of me did die that day on the ship."

"I'm so very sorry, Sebastian." William felt deep regret rise within him once more, uncertain if he could ever forgive himself for the part he played in their demise.

"Please, William, none of us blame you for anything." Sebastian moved quickly to dissuade him on the matter.

"You don't have to. I blame myself." William bit his lip and closed his eyes remembering the look on Doctor Clarke's face as he stood over Emile. It was quite easily the singular moment that forever haunted his thoughts every time he closed his eyes. It was the only thing stronger than the searing, phantom pain he felt any time he but touched the skin where he had been bitten by the man.

"You were only doing what anyone else in your situation might have done. There is no way you could have known the outcome at the time." Sebastian continued, unwilling to allow the man to assume the responsibility any longer for his actions or lack thereof, as he could see now that he had been entirely wrong to think so once upon a time.

"Actually, Sebastian, what William did to save us is <u>exactly</u> what the two of us did for them, as well." Nathanael swallowed hard as he recalled how they had cared for Emile and William during their illness after the shipwreck, both men refusing to leave them as long as any hope remained. "If we had let them die, they would not be vampires today either. So, in the end, we are all responsible."

William nodded, then lifted his head to stare at each man in turn. "Still, you have no idea how much I wish I could take away the pain it is causing you both."

"It's not your fault," Sebastian offered freely. "Despite how everything has turned out, I am actually glad you were <u>on</u> that ship. None of us would be here if you had not been."

"But the ether?" Nathanael awkwardly brought Señor Moretti's attention back to the original vein of questioning.

"Yes, well. The ether is there should you choose to feed as I have done, by bloodletting or in a more discreet way of satisfying your fast. If you use it sparingly, your victim will be none the wiser, and you will have achieved a sense of control in your otherwise... restricted life. It will take some time to learn how to do it properly, but it is essential if you are to remain unnoticed by the world at large."

Without a moment of hesitation, Nathanael handed his bottle over to William and waited for the man to accept it. "I would not even know where to begin with such a thing. The very idea of seducing some poor soul for my own pleasure would be beyond anything I can comprehend."

"I will teach you," William whispered quietly so that Nathanael only might hear him.

"I'd rather die," Nathanael whispered back tersely.

"You can't." Sebastian brooded before laying his box on the table next to him as if it contained nothing of consequence.

"You <u>can</u>," Señor Moretti corrected him gently. "And why Sebastian are you still so utterly downcast!" He threw his arms up in animated fashion and began walking around the room.

"Because I feel so trapped!" Sebastian finally burst out as he wrung his hands, his frustration spilling over once again. "For the first time in my life, I was finally doing something that had the potential of changing my family's future, but just like every other time before, it has all been taken away... again."

"Then stop the cycle, my dear Sebastian. Become the man they need you to be!"

"How?" His eyes scrutinized him but not in defiance or anger, but as one truly seeking a solution but struggling to find one. "I can't go back to them, not like this. If I injured even one of them, I would never forgive myself."

"Alright, then if you have decided that you cannot, use this money in your place. Invest it in taking care of your wife and sons from afar."

"And when it is gone?" Sebastian countered logically.

"Provide more. Why even yesterday I learned that the men down at port are looking for someone with your particular skills to help repair the many ships that dock there. You're Spanish even. You will fit right in. You know the language. You look the part. I'd be surprised if anyone even notices anything amiss about you besides the fact that you are not as open as the rest of those who work around you."

"I could probably use my christened name," he replied in a dead tone though his expression was beginning to show definite signs of starting to take an interest in Señor Moretti's idea or at least the merit of the plan before him.

"Use any name you choose." Señor Moretti seemed utterly energized by the man's meager acceptance. "Live with me as long as you like."

"You would not mind the company?" Sebastian felt hesitant to be a further burden on his gracious host.

"I should think I would welcome it! These walls, as sturdy as they are, make terrible company, and they don't know how to play chess," Señor Moretti replied. "Tell anyone who asks that we have a familiar acquaintance back in Italy—make something up. I am certain that given enough time, you will find that the darkness you think is threatening to swallow you whole, is actually just the moment before bursting through a brilliant tunnel of light."

"...of life," Sebastian quietly corrected him for the word felt far more fitting.

"Yes!" William agreed eagerly and stepped closer. "It is not the life you imagined for your future, but it is a life you can live, and live well, Sebastian."

Sebastian nodded his head in agreement, then stood up with the rest of them. "It is all agreed then." He smiled for the first time in the past two weeks. "Should you wish to visit or write, gentlemen, you shall find Sebastian Fabbri, cousin to the family of Moretti, working down at the port."

Overjoyed at the positive step the man had just taken, Nathanael and William each hugged him in turn despite his tense body language against it.

"We will try to communicate as often as we can," Nathanael promised him excitedly.

"And I am happy to be of service, should your family ever have need of it. You have but to ask, and I will go," William also pledged faithfully.

"Thank you, I am sure that will be extremely helpful." Señor Moretti couldn't help but smile at the scene unfolding before him. "And now, let us partake in some more fitting nourishment before your journey."

The three men nodded in understanding.

"William, will you take some of my supply with you as you may need it for your travels back home," Señor Moretti offered.

"Only enough to see us to England. From there, we will begin again."

"Wisely, spoken." Señor Moretti placed his arm around William and guided them all into his inner study.

Chapter Eight

December 25th, 1792

C hristmas day in Wakefield was shaping up to be as mild and cheerful as any Christmas Nathanael had ever remembered back home, which had surprised him greatly. Since the northern cities were generally accepted to be quite a bit more frigid than closer to London, he had half-expected Wakefield to have an even frostier atmosphere when he arrived. Yet, from what he had experienced thus far, this winter had greeted the residents here with an albeit weaker entry with only one or two truly cold nights to speak of. Still, it was only the end of December and thankfully, a rather thick snowfall had arrived just in time for Christmas Eve morning and had continued well into the night, blanketing the countryside in a fresh layer of downy white snow.

"Christmas morning..." Nathanael smiled once more. What a joyous day it had truly been, and it had only just begun! Why just the night before he and William had spent their entire evening casually resting by the fireside, exchanging stories and memories from their childhood, and singing together familiar Christmas carols. If the philosophers were right, and music was indeed the means to heal a man's soul, then the two weary travelers had most certainly found it to be true. With each new song and chorus they sang, they soon discovered a unique joy in the experience that exceeded all of the fears and doubts they had experienced on their journey from Señor Moretti's to Wakefield, England.

Keeping with tradition, they had respectfully decided to wait until Christmas morning to open their presents to each other and the few others from William's family, but much to their mutual disappointment, William had been called away before the break of day on a necessary visit to a patient.

"No matter." Nathanael hugged his plain woolen coat tighter around his body for added warmth even though he knew quite assuredly that it would provide none. "He'll be back by supper, I am sure." He surmised optimistically for that was what the younger doctor had typically done, unless his patient warranted much more extensive care, but normally, that was not the case.

Even the message from Mr. Gabe Summerfield this morning did not seem to worry William too greatly. "A simple sprain of some kind over at the mill during their festivities last night," William had explained as he wrapped his blue overcoat over his black vest and neatly pressed white shirt before donning his all-too-familiar now shorter black cloak. "I shan't be long. You'll see. And you had better not open a single present without me or I will be severely cross with you."

Nathanael smiled at his remembrance of William's chastising expression, like that of a scolding father, and contemplated his friend's upcoming reaction to the small item neatly wrapped for him by the fireplace.

It was not much in terms of worth, a poem dedicated to the young man's efforts as a doctor and a tiny hand-carved boat to sit upon his shelf—one that bore the resemblance of the *Endeavour* herself, but it was still a gift, and one he had spent the last few days feverishly carving.

Had two weeks really passed by so quickly? Nathanael contemplated with fresh amazement.

Children squealed with delight beside him, interrupting his scattered thoughts as they slid down the hills and skated on nearby patches of ice. Merriment in every form of the word seemed to be practically everywhere around him. So much so, that he himself was feeling a special kind of warmth within his heart that he knew only God himself could have given.

As Señor Moretti had so accurately predicted, the physical warmth of his hands had never quite returned to its previous level, but the lack of proper circulation was one of the few deficits he was managing to deal with quite easily. On most occasions, he had found it convenient enough to don his favorite gloves or periodically warm his hands over a flame before a necessary handshake or otherwise.

Yet controlling the errant thoughts of his mind was another matter entirely. In ever need of daily distractions, he had been extremely grateful this morning that Christmas day had finally arrived with all its joy and blessings. Yet though it did not fall upon a Sunday per say, his parishioners would still be arriving slightly after ten this morning for the customary Christmas service. New in his position as he was, he was still as excited as ever to see them again for it was only his second service, and one he had planned for greatly. In fact, he had spent the good part of that week arranging all the decorations and details of his sermon to the minutest degree, reveling in the joy it had brought him each day in doing so.

Nathanael drew in a deep breath of the crisp, winter air and coughed slightly as it constricted the muscles in the back of his throat. Standing outside in the frosty weather today, he had to admit that whether it was the chillier climate, the holiday, or his newfound purpose in life, he had never felt so at peace with the world around him, hopeful even. Both of which felt rather odd given his most decidedly hopeless condition.

"Life surely seems so short and yet also infinitely long, doesn't it?" He frowned as he contemplated the complexity of his eternal situation once more before pushing the dark thoughts back into the farthest regions of his mind as he passed a large field beside him on his walk to the church. The view of the now snow-covered countryside around him caused him to pause for just a moment to take it all in.

Today, he decided resolutely, *was not the day to be entertaining that sort of melancholy. After all, had he not countless things for which to be thankful?*

Like William for example. Upon their arrival two weeks ago, the young doctor had set to work most diligently in beginning his practice out of a small store near the eastern edge of the town. The tall, greyish-blue building just on the other side of the river had once been that of a local veterinarian and blessings beyond blessings, the man had even left behind much of his belongings when he passed away last summer, including several key pieces of furniture and various accessories.

This two-story edifice was the perfect place for the two of them in every way, affording William exactly what he needed in every facet and feature. With the much-desired open space below for his apothecary and medical practice, the men could use the second floor above for their lodging. In truth, there was nothing more that they lacked. In fact, it included countless boxes of tools, jars and other necessities William might need should his practice ever go in a more surgical direction—which Nathanael sincerely hoped it would not. He would, of course, support the man in whatever endeavor he should undertake, but he was quite certain he was not ready to withstand that kind of temptation just yet. Someday perhaps, when he was more stable and adjusted, but most certainly not for a while.

Their humble lodgings above were indeed a very modest space for them both, and Nathanael much preferred the simplicity of it over the rather ornately decorated rooms at Señor Moretti's. With a room each, complete with: a simple bed, a rocking chair, a braided rug that lay on top of an excellently finished dark wooden floorboards, two rather thick tan curtains that hung across the single window to the side of each bed along the outer wall, and a table placed to the right of the room's center from which they could sup. It was the perfect place for each of them to study or work should the need arise.

For the present, William had been content to focus his practice more on providing care for the simpler remedies of his profession like powders for headaches, ointments for rheumatism, elixirs for the stomach, and all other sorts of remedies for maladies Nathanael wouldn't have a hope of remembering even if he tried. Including, but not also limited to, the occasional sick call whenever a villager might have a fever or something else far more serious in nature and they could not seek other care. Yet, despite the fact that William appeared utterly at ease with the complexities of his profession, Nathanael could tell that deep down the man was working very hard to hide how his affliction was also limiting him.

On more than one occasion he had seen the man practically storm back into the shop and up to his room without a single explanation as to why. Not that he especially needed him to bear his soul to him every time he faltered. Still, it would have been nice to know that he was not alone in this melancholy world of theirs. In addition, there were at least two other separate moments he had noticed just this week alone where the man's hands visibly shook when he tried to hang up his cloak after a day of work.

Thankfully, there was another doctor in town, Doctor Josiah Hadleigh, but gratefully, he did not seem to mind the new visitors whatsoever. William was clearly not his competition. Quite the contrary, the elder doctor relished the chance to be able to have long discussions with William after a night's work. For what doctor wouldn't want to impart upon others his many years of wisdom concerning local herbs and their medicinal uses?

Since his arrival, William had been able to convince the man of his desire to study the human circulatory system as his namesake had done and the more seasoned doctor had been only too happy to help guide him along in his endeavors. This explanation was not entirely false on William's part for he was genuinely interested in the topic to some degree, just not to the extent to which he alluded.

This particular area of fluid study had provided the perfect ruse for the two men's covert, dietary needs. And as an added favor, Doctor Hadleigh had chosen to periodically provide William with samples for his 'study' or directed William as to where he might find other individuals who might be equally as eager to help, provided a small token of monetary appreciation, of course.

As they were reminded by the fellow doctor, winter could be fairly difficult for the families in these small village towns, so the inducement of a certain, though small, cashflow would aid them immensely. Though most decidedly, for the two of them, it was a small price to pay for anonymity and security.

Almost to the tree-lined ridge of the opposite side of town now, Nathanael began humming a familiar Christmas hymn as he walked farther along his way to the small stone church that lay beyond the western part of the village. The stone foundation itself had been built well before the 16th Century, but none of the building's construction bore the more austere qualities as those in the more populated sections of the country. For starters, it lacked many of the beautifully ornate, stained-glass windows that churches of his acquaintance contained, but it mattered not in the slightest to him on that account. He much preferred the distorted and wavelike leaded glass and divided windowpanes to that of the fanciful pictures decorating cathedral walls. He always had.

With an added spring in his step, he rounded the corner and as he began to the climb up the short flight of stone steps to the courtyard above, he distinctly made out a familiar tune being played inside the chapel itself. The melodious notes of a well-known Christmas favorite came flowing out to him into the Chapel's small garden, now completely dormant with its covering of white snow, red cardinals and other birds alike.

Joy to the World, the Lord is come!
Let Earth receive her King;
Let every heart prepare Him room,
And heaven and nature sing,
And heaven and nature sing,

What an utterly wonderful reminder of everything God has still blessed me with in this life, he mused as he strode up to the door and threw it open wide. "And heaven and heaven and nature sing!" He sang boldly the repeated line, though regrettably slightly out of tune on the last note as he had never had any formal music training, nor could he hope to match the glory of the music being played.

"Oh," the young lady in the starched white dress behind the pianoforte exclaimed politely and stopped her playing immediately. "You startled me, sir."

"My sincerest apologies, Miss Summerfield." Nathanael hung his overcoat and long brown cloak upon the wooden peg opposite the door and turned to face her with the biggest grin he had worn in months. "I simply could not help myself given such angelic inducement."

The girl smiled back at him timidly. "Now you are just teasing me." She rearranged the music nervously on her instrument before selecting another more traditional tune and began to practice softly once more.

"Would it offend you terribly if I was not?" Nathanael gave the girl a playful wink from the back pew.

"No, but if you tease me like that again in front of my father, he might just get ideas and make you join us for Christmas dinner." The girl smiled sweetly but continued playing the music in front of her.

"Sounds like an absolutely capital idea, though one I would need to refuse on this singular occasion for I already have plans with a dear friend of mine."

"Another young lady, I suppose." She looked up at him demurely before adding in a teasing tone, "Should we be concerned so soon? You've only just arrived to have formed such a definite attachment of that kind."

Her playful conversation without the least bit of insecurity delighted him more than the music itself. Shy as he was, he found that he rather liked this form of innocent banter compared to the medical conversations he had been having with William as of late, and coming from someone as beautiful as she, made it doubly enjoyable.

"Certainly nothing of that kind, I assure you." He made his way down the center aisle, paying careful attention to adjust each of the garlands at the end of every row so that they were hanging just so. "The friend is a very recent acquaintance of mine. He owns the new apothecary shop on the other side of town over by the tavern. No doubt you have seen it?"

"It would be hard to miss. Though you have made it look much nicer than it has in years."

"Thank you." Nathanael beamed proudly. "Perhaps I can introduce you to him when he arrives."

"I'd be only too delighted, sir." She finished her tune and stood up from the piano to secure her seat in one of the closer pews for the service. "Would you like me to play for all of the congregational pieces this morning or just the first and the last?"

"The latter, if you, please. I believe continuing as we have done in the past service would be best. In other words, playing only for the opening and closing numbers will be sufficient. We don't want to give them too much of Heaven in one day, do we?"

The girl blushed and shook her head with a smile.

Upon his arrival, it had been the largest blessing of all to find such an accomplished player as she in his congregation for most churches survived on the musical abilities of their leaders alone. As he had discovered in the previous service, he had but to give her the name of any given tune in their hymnbook and she had been able to play it simply by memory. And thankfully, the congregation followed her more tuneful rendition than his own as he often found himself singing terribly off key no matter how hard he tried to remain on the pitch.

In addition to her musical ability, he had also discovered a wonderful wit that matched his own. A young lady who seemed very much at ease with his position and her ability to augment it. Truly a rare gem indeed given the fact that most women of her caliber and age were far too focused on monetary support to satisfy their security within a marriage. As a rule, he had no such funds either before, nor would he hope to have so in the future, as the livelihood of all preachers was entirely tied to the benevolence of their congregations, not their own pocketbooks.

Nevertheless, he was reticent to form any kind of a romantic attachment with anyone at the present. After all, he had only just arrived and a delicate relationship such as that took time. And time, he felt the apathy rising within him once more at the remembrance of Señor Moretti's explanation, was the one thing he knew he would have in the largest of quantities no matter the romantic opportunities.

Focusing his attention back on the young lady's previous statement, he pondered once more her gracious offer of hospitality, reconsidering his response. *It would be rude of him or at the very least discourteous to refuse her invitation outright,* he concluded simply as if he needed a rational excuse to be in her company.

"Miss Summerfield, if you are so disposed, please do inform your father that if he is graciously inclined to provide a meal for this humble preacher, I would be most happy to join your family on any other given day that he wishes. Moreover, I have heard from many that your mother is quite the accomplished cook in our area of the country."

Miss Summerfield blushed once more. "She will be quite happy to know that you think so highly of her."

And of you. He couldn't help but add mentally and looked away as he felt a rush of emotion warm him from his head down to his toes most unexpectedly, something far beyond his normal response to anything these days.

Embarrassed by the flush he felt certain must be obviously present on his cheeks, he cleared his throat and went behind the altar of the church to retrieve his more formal attire and begin his ritualistic time of quiet reflection and prayer before the service.

It was true that he had written quite literally hundreds of sermons both in seminary and afterwards, but not one of them had created within him as much angst as he was now experiencing. Why even just reading God's Word this week had caused him an increasing amount of anxiety that could not be quelled by partaking in any amount of appeasement—blood or otherwise. It had all started back on that awful day at the castle, and since then he had found it increasingly difficult to compose even a short devotional, let alone focus on what God was trying to speak through Him.

Though it was this last point that worried him more than he cared to admit. It was one thing to feel lost physically and at odds with mankind all around him. It was quite another to feel estranged from his God, the only person that truly mattered to him at all.

Could he no longer communicate with God now? He pondered the thought more deeply in prayer, then let out a short sigh when he felt as if nothing, but the walls were listening.

Please, I need to know, God. Do you still hear the prayers of people like me—people displaced from your perfect timeline and plan? Nathanael waited but he did not receive an audible reply whether in his heart or otherwise, and this disturbed him even more. *Have you forsaken me after all?*

The silence continued until noises beyond the room intensified, notifying him of his arriving congregation. There was simply not enough time this morning for this kind of dissertational conversation, and he knew it. Resolved to proceed ahead in faith alone, he placed both hands flat upon the cover of his Bible and bowed his head lower still in abject humility. Then, when he finally felt some semblance of peace return to him, he took in a deep cleansing breath and prayed with renewed conviction. *Until you show me otherwise, God, I will continue to serve you as best as I am able.*

With a jolt, he felt his nerves and pulse instinctively quicken once more in opposition to that vow, but he fought even more to bolster his efforts to calm them. These involuntary reactions may have been given the power to overtake his focus whenever they sensed he was around people no matter the time of day or dietary fulfillment, but he refused to let them control him completely.

"Wretched man that I am!" He cursed aloud in frustration before whispering under his breath a calming yet determined prayer, "Lord, give me strength for today... this very moment... I beg you. I can't do this alone."

With shaking hands, he clasped them once more firmly together above the candle on the table to warm them to a more normal temperature before plastering on the most convincing smile he could manage. Feeling more self-assured, he stood and opened wide the side door into the courtyard with great exuberance as he began the process of greeting all of those who had arrived for the service.

In truth, he need not have worried about the sermon at all. Just as they had always done in the past, the words flowed easily through him and out to the waiting ears of each in the crowd. Some of the people smiled, others nodded, a few slept, okay, more than a few, but it was to be expected. No preacher or orator ever thrilled all his attendees. So, why should he be any different?

Miss Summerfield led the congregation as she played the beginning notes from "Hark the Herald Angels Sing," and everyone joined her happily, even those who had stopped their slumber. It was almost as if the very sound of her music had aroused them into a new life and attention.

Hail the heave'n born Prince Of Peace! Hail the Son of Righteousness?
Light and life to all He brings, ris'n with healing in His wings.
Mild He lays His glory by, born that man no more may die.
Born to raise the sons of Earth, born to give them second birth.
Hark! the herald angels sing, "Glory to the newborn King!

Nathanael smiled as he sang along. God <u>was</u> good, and He was present always—even today. He just had to keep remembering that.

The singing ceased and with it the music ended as abruptly as it had begun. Knowing the timing of the service was already drawing quite late for their afternoon meal, Nathanael prayed and exclaimed happily to the crowd his salutation, "Merry Christmas to one and all!"

The congregation echoed back his sentiment, and then began to dutifully disperse, ready for the day's continued festivities.

Exhausted but elated once more for yet another victory, Nathanael moved to the back of the chapel and shook every hand of each family passing by him at the door, thirty in all. They were a healthy flock and very accepting of their new preacher for the last minister had left so suddenly that it had taken the bishops several months to find their replacement in Nathanael.

Though no one would say specifically as to why the last clergy had left, Nathanael was led to believe it had something to do with the weather not being suitable for his old bones or some sort of utter nonsense to his way of thinking. In the end, the reason truly did not matter, and in all other aspects of the employment, Nathanael had found his current post to be quite suitable, enjoyable even.

"Merry Christmas, Preacher Beckett!" William called as he bounded up the stone steps two at a time towards the church as the last family left. "Fine weather for caroling later I should think, or do they not do that this far north?" He was still smartly dressed in his nicest blue overcoat, ruffled ivory blouse, and neatly tailored black pants. And though he had been hard at work for the past six hours at least, not a single item of his wardrobe betrayed that fact, nor that he had no doubt slept even less.

"I believe many of the younger members of our town do plan on singing, though I am unsure how many wealthy homes they will encounter here in order to receive their figgy pudding." Nathanael embraced his friend warmly.

"They only need one." William slapped his friend on the back and laughed. "Never cared for figs myself, but that did not keep me away from the caroling every Christmas back in London. Besides," he winked, "it was a great way to meet the young ladies."

Nathanael chuckled, too. "Scandalous, dear William! You really were a rascal growing up, weren't you?" He led the way to the side door of his private study and opened it for his friend to pass inside before him.

"I had an older brother to keep up with and two younger sisters to annoy incessantly." William plopped down unceremoniously into the nearest chair and put one leg over the other comfortably. "Here. I brought along one of your presents." He placed the smartly wrapped package on Nathanael's desk.

"Why?" Nathanael passed him on his left on his way to the other side of the room.

"Mostly because it belongs here more than at home," William admitted sheepishly.

"Oh?" Nathanael removed his robe, taking the time to carefully hang it up in its place before picking up the present and opening it excitedly, then in turn, looking back at him utterly perplexed. "A book?" Nathanael flipped it over twice to view the carefully designed linen cover.

"Oh, not just any book, fair Nathanael. A book about you!" He laughed and motioned for Nathanael to open it to the title page.

"The Vicar Of Wakefield," Nathanael read aloud with great puzzlement.

"It is very popular in all of the neighboring towns, though I will admit freely that from what the bookseller told me of the plot, the storyline does not fit you personally, but the very title does capture your attention, does it not?"

"It does." Nathanael's brow creased.

"He said that it is a true story written by the man himself, though he made his brother promise not to print it for at least two years after his departure."

"He probably wanted to get out of town first." Nathanael respectfully placed the book on the shelf behind him with his other scant, but cherished belongings. "I thank you for the gift, though you will need to forgive me. I'm afraid your presents are still back at home."

"I did not expect anything in return." William moved his hand from side to side dismissively. "To tell you the truth, I only picked this one up on a whim while passing a store the other day. I thought you might find it interesting at the very least or entertaining at most."

"I do."

"Shall we dine then?" William leaned in closer and added quite casually while opening his leather satchel that he carried with him to all his patient visits, the one he had rescued before he left the Endeavor.

Shocked that William would suggest something so brazenly dangerous in public, Nathanael sat back in his chair quickly, in momentary surprise, before whispering quietly so that only William would be able to hear, "Not in the Lord's house, Doctor Wells!"

William immediately burst out laughing. So much so, that Nathanael feared the man might quite literally fall out of his chair from all his mirth. "I wish you could see your face just now, Nathanael! Sebastian was right when he said you tended to take things a bit more literally than the rest of us." William's eyes sparkled with amusement though they both knew exactly what Nathanael had thought he had meant.

"I'm sorry, William, for the misunderstanding." Nathanael looked down, feeling slightly embarrassed before joining his friend in his merriment. "I am assuming you have you heard from Mr. Smith then?" He shook his head at the necessary correction. "Pardon me, I mean, Mr. Fabbri. It has not been that long since our departure."

"Why it arrived just yesterday, in fact." William pulled a small envelope out of his bag that he had begun retrieving earlier and closed it. "I was saving his letter to share over our lunch as I thought it might lighten both of our spirits hearing from a friend, no matter the distance between us." William handed him the envelope to inspect, then added further, "And I hope you don't mind, but on the way over here I ordered a meal to be prepared for us down at the local tavern."

"Then by all means. Let us partake," Nathanael agreed easily though part of him had secretly wished William had chosen a less public place to endure their daily form of torture.

Closing the door to the study behind them and depositing the key underneath the carefully stacked tower of old hymnals beside it, Nathanael and William walked to the back of the church where Nathanael put his simple brown overcoat back on top of his bishop's collared white shirt and wool pants. Though he certainly had the savings now to upgrade the few pieces of clothing he had been gifted, doing so at such a time as this felt frivolous and wholly unnecessary. Besides, having abandoned his previous aspirations, he had every intention of saving every farthing of that sum and using it for a worthy cause should the need ever arise. Or at least that was his current plan.

The yearly stipend from his elders was sufficient enough to replace his lost wardrobe from the wreck with secondhand attire and that suited him fine. A mended hole here and there were nothing compared to how so many others in this world were suffering. Nor would he want to flaunt any form of wealth among a congregation as poor as this one appeared to be.

The two men put on their necessary cloaks before exiting the door and happily conversed through the ankle-deep snow, slowly taking in the beauty and amusement of the day before enjoying a splendid conversation over a Christmas lunch and memories both new and old alike at the village tavern. Then, when the sun had eventually set and their conversation had been exhausted, they retired contentedly to William's apothecary, feeling utterly satisfied with their circumstances and God's providential placement of their lives.

"Do you think Sebastian is having a merry Christmas?" Nathanael asked William before he closed the door of the shop behind them, delighting in the soft ringing of the bell positioned just above the door to herald all who entered therein.

"I hope so." William looked upwards and shrugged. "Though I don't know how happy anyone can truly be when they are away like he is from those he loves. I know for myself that even though I do not wish to work in London, I do find that I miss my family's company very much today. Yet, I will also admit, that my sister-in-law's children would probably be driving us all batty right about now as they have quite the knack of asking enough questions to overwhelm both the body, soul <u>and</u> mind."

Nathanael chuckled at the picture and the corners of his mouth turned upwards in hope. "My prayer is that he can find some way to be with them soon... for their sake."

"And for his." William nodded in agreement.

"Have you heard anything further regarding Emile?"

William shook his head with a hint of disappointment. "I am not sure if that makes me grateful or even more concerned that there are no troubling rumors coming out of France as of yet. From my brief acquaintance with the man, I was certain he would be at the center of something rather raucous by now."

"They <u>are</u> in the middle of a great political turmoil with the monarchy trying to flee Paris after all. I would think that anything Emile could do would pale in comparison to all of that," Nathanael added but then cocked his head with concern. "You don't think Emile is wrapped up in it, too, do you?"

"If Emile is Emile, he is probably enjoying every minute of the rebellion, I am afraid," William surmised with a mischievous smile. "Though I doubt he is in any actual danger. He is more the kind to cause it than to be wrapped up in it."

The two men nodded their heads in uniformed agreement.

"Oh, I almost forgot!" Nathanael walked over to the hastily hung stockings by the small fireplace and retrieved the gift he had intended for William. "I made this for you."

"For me?" William unwrapped the small carving and marveled at its accuracy. "Did you carve this yourself?"

"Yes. It helps me to focus on something other than well, you know," Nathanael admitted rather reluctantly.

"It's fine work, Nathanael—very fine work indeed," William complimented him freely as he began to untie the rolled parchment before Nathanael stopped him by placing his hand upon the scroll.

"Maybe read that one later. I'm afraid I might be a bit too embarrassed if you were to read it in front of me now."

"If you prefer." William tucked the scroll into his lower pocket and began climbing the stairs upwards with the other man following close behind. "I'm glad we came here Nathanael. Sincerely."

"I am, too," Nathanael replied warmly. "Merry Christmas, William."

"Merry Christmas, Nathanael." William raised one hand in salutation and closed the door to his room behind him.

Feeling that same sense of peace wash over him once more, Nathanael dressed himself for the night and knelt beside his bed as was his customary practice.

"Father, I thank you for Christmas, and for sending your Son to this Earth, today on this most holy of days. Thank you for your provision monetarily and in giving me this parish. Please guide me to lead them in the way you wish me to do. Protect them from those who would take advantage of them." He paused, breathing in and out heavily, before beginning again. "Protect them from... me, dear Lord.

Shepherd Emile from his own actions and help Sebastian as he seeks to be a father to his family from afar. And dear Lord, thank you for Señor Moretti. I know that you are using him mightily, far more than even <u>he</u> realizes. Bless him for that, please." Nathanael paused and thought about his friend in the other room next to him, the last on his rather long list of requests tonight before adding warmly, "Lord, you know how incredibly grateful I am for this friend you have given me—the man who gives more sacrificially to others than anyone else I know. Please help him as he cares for your children here on this Earth, but most of all, cause him to see <u>You</u> all around him. Help me be who you have called me to be, your example here on Earth. Amen"

He rose contentedly and blew out the candle.

Chapter Nine

January 1st, 1793

E mile stepped out of the hired carriage and into the busiest portion of the Rue de St Antoine one lazy afternoon on the first day of 1793. Since his arrival shortly before Christmas, the snows of winter had been barking upon Paris' door, promising an uncommonly frigid season with every gust of wind that pummeled across his back as he walked. It was almost as if the arrival of the new year had also announced the imminent return of everything Emile despised most about the season and not the proclamation of good things to come.

Yet despite his feelings about the cold conditions outside, all along the street as he passed, merchants were out in droves, haggling this way and that outside their establishments for their livelihood while assuring that any man could buy anything he wanted to possess here given the right price.

"Well, almost anything," Emile said with a smirk as a rather beautiful young lady in a dark blue and white woolen coat that matched the color of the sky at twilight passed by on his right. As crowded as the street was to traverse across it without bumping into many other individuals along the way, she appeared to be equally struggling under the burden of carrying a somewhat awkward and heavy-looking metal pail packed to the brim with various brushes and dirty rags alike.

Poor girl. Emile felt momentarily sympathetic towards her plight, then held his thin coat closer to his body as a gust of wind passed directly between them at that moment on its path westward.

Briefly startled, while also clearly partly annoyed by the unexpected attack, the young woman with the unusually shaded strawberry blonde hair clutched at the fraying fabric with the hand that held one of the pails in a vain attempt to manage both her trappings and the inability to keep her buttonless coat closed against it. The fruitless attempt, however, did nothing to stop her coverings from flapping helplessly in the wind in its desire to escape its owner entirely.

"Ugh!" Her brow furrowed in frustration momentarily before her expression changed once again to one of joy as if someone had hit the poor girl on the head with a magical wand of some kind. *"C'est la vie, monsieur.* You win." She set her pails down and threw her arms open wide to the wind and embraced the happiness it brought her in doing so.

Then again... maybe she has a touch of madness. Emile smiled broadly, then tried to hide it behind his other hand. Instantly intrigued by her *laissez-faire* attitude about the whole situation and the lightness that had filled him in watching her enjoy her moment of unexpected delight, he took her in fully from head to toe before raising both eyebrows up and down in most definite approval. She was lovely... absolutely breathtaking, even under all of those dismal layers.

Then, as if in response to another stimuli altogether, his heart quickened and his mouth watered reflexively, contemplating seriously what he might do if he had her alone for just a few minutes, then thought the better of it. "Focus." He calmed his racing thoughts away from pursuing her further and continued towards the tavern at the end of the street, but not before stopping at least one time more to give her a second glance from behind.

There was definitely something oddly enticing about the woman, make no mistake, but what it was, was nothing he could readily put a finger on at that moment. Or at least not anything to warrant the flirtatious distraction she would no doubt bring should he pause to speak with her. Still, she was not the reason why he had gone through all the effort to come here today. Why he had uncharacteristically found himself dressed the same as those with whom he was seeking.

From everything that he had heard only the night before; this tavern in particular was rumored to be the place to witness the passionate speeches given by those hailing themselves as patriots of the Assembly. Rebels, in his mind, that served no useful purpose but to cause further trouble for the already beleaguered country, and now, more importantly, to him. Yet despite what his feelings might be on the subject, he also could not ignore what was possibly transpiring around him any longer. When men like Robespierre spoke, the people listened and worse yet, acted.

Just four years earlier, a mob had stormed the Bastille and emptied it of all its prisoners. Peasants mostly from what Emile had heard, and admittedly they were probably individuals who did not belong in the prison in the first place. Yet those same citizens were now calling for the execution of the King, as if that were the only solution they would be willing to accept at this juncture in time. In every tavern conversation and public corner Emile encountered, many were the cries of the country for the new National Assembly while other more unfortunate citizens simply wanted the justice so long refused to the common people.

With a healthy disbelief, mixed with a bit of incredulity, he had skeptically chosen to watch the events unfold from afar like a falling deck of cards and wondered if everything that was transpiring would ever affect him personally. It was part of the reason why he had journeyed to England in the first place last November. That, and the fact that he was simply bored with an unfortunately clingy conquest he had made at the time. The reason made little difference to him at the present. The girl was happily married now, and he wished her all the better for it. He had no need for such a conventional institution such as marriage today or any day as long as he could cajole and charm people into getting what he wanted.

In fact, some poor soul had accused him once of being a master manipulator of his life and those around him, but despite how hard he had tried, he failed to see the truth of it. To his mind, he was simply good at getting whatever it was he wanted, unlike everyone else.

But Paris was a second home to him, a city ablaze with some form of passion or another for centuries. That was precisely why he had returned here after the shipwreck. After all, it was the city of true culture and the finest the world had to offer, was it not? And who did not enjoy a good party or the opera from time to time? He did. He almost breathed in the atmosphere his opulent lifestyle provided daily. For not only did it thrill him as before, but even more so now in his new persona, as he liked to call it.

Seeing the world around him through these new eyes, he relished the chance to grace every formal occasion, or at least he had when he first arrived. And then there were the various social responsibilities. Ones where gentlemen, like himself, preyed upon available debutantes and marchionesses for their hand in marriage, or at the very least for him, a piece of their more sizable fortunes. These more intimate events were far less formal and all of them were a thrilling game now to Emile. Or to put it plainly, they were delightfully enticing... and in more ways than a gentleman would dare to admit.

Yet, stepping out on the overcast street today he had found himself on quite a different mission altogether. One that was fraught with far more danger than he would care to experience on any given day. Why only the night before last, one of his closest acquaintances had not returned home from the card game he had hosted. Something which, in itself, would not have troubled him too terribly for Jonathan had often enjoyed a dalliance or two down at *Madame* Jeannette's after a long night at cards, especially when he had been winning. But, when his overly dramatic sister had banged upon his door quite early the next morning, he had scarcely had the time to dress properly to receive her, such was the state of her panic and persistent pleas.

And so, feeling more than a little personally obligated thereafter to investigate his sudden disappearance, he had dutifully made a few discreet inquiries near the man's home and at some other establishments he was less reticent to name in search of where he might have gone. All had pointed to the fact that he had been taken by citizens of the French National Assembly. And where he was held, one could only assume, was no doubt tied to these new revolutionary speakers down at the tavern.

Determined once again to be done with his errand and occupied with more pleasant diversions like the woman in the street perhaps, Emile strode confidently through the open doorway and up to the tavern's counter knowing precisely what to expect in this kind of a place for he had frequented many such locations along his travels back home. Most were excellent places for pleasant conversation and a good drink or two, others were the perfect way to disappear and find oneself sitting in the hull of a ship bound for the Americas or any other such port of service—too drunk to resist until it was too late.

Emile frowned, unsettled by the notion of rubbing elbows with the unpredictable rabble. He wanted nothing more right now than to ask the bartender for a bottle of his best wine no matter what the cost but thought the better of it given the clientele already assembled around him. Doing so would only arouse their instant suspicion of his noble position and in turn, deprive him of his true purpose.

"May I help you?" The man behind the counter welcomed him warmly, stepping away briefly from the conversation he was just enjoying.

"What would you suggest for someone who is... um, thirsty?" Emile asked politely while skipping all the necessary pleasantries normally involved in such a greeting in his social circles.

"Well, I don't know. You look like a man that might prefer something a little stronger than the cider most people 'round here can afford." The stout man who looked equally as shrewd as he was observant threw a white linen cloth over his shoulder casually while measuring him up from his position.

"You would be correct." Emile angled his head in agreement slightly. "But only when I have been as blessed at cards as I was last night, sir."

"Well, in that case, I've got a solid ale that was brought in just this morning."

"That would be excellent." Emile paid a little more than the meager fare requested of him, and a tall mug of the yellow-brown liquid was placed swiftly before him. "*Merci.*"

"You don't look like you are from around here, friend." The man continued the conversation while drying one of the newly washed pitchers from the stack waiting for him in the sink. "New in town, are you?"

"Only just." Emile tried to hide the austereness of his speech by keeping his conversation brief, not wanting to give his identity away completely as he sipped respectfully on the drink he was given. Truthfully speaking, he had lived in France for the majority of his life and in Paris proper for almost a year, but he had never once set foot in this particular part of the city until he had arrived three months ago. Yet now, the winding and transecting streets of merchants and patrons alike were more like his hidden playground than a casual place within the city in which to visit.

"Don't talk much, eh?" The man prodded further.

"Occasionally." Emile placed the finished glass gently down upon the counter before chancing a redirection towards the reason for which he had originally come. "Actually, I was told I could hear news of the new Assembly here."

With a stern look and a slight inclination of his head towards the men on the other side of the room, the man put down the pitcher he was holding and instantly leaned in closer to Emile, obviously on the offensive. "That so. And who might have told you that? No one in these parts that's for sure. I don't know if you have noticed, but as a rule, we don't take kindly to strangers sticking their noses in where they don't belong around here."

Emile smiled and narrowed his eyes slightly, partially amused by the man's veiled attempt at a threat while also vaguely trying his best to disguise his intense stare on the man's pulsing jugular. "A girl I met last night might have said something along those lines, but perhaps I was mistaken. I usually am, or so she says."

"A girl!" The man laughed raucously, the tenor of his voice elevating to a higher level. "Hear that, gentlemen?" He drew in the other men sitting closely nearby even more. "A girl told him to come here."

Obeying his signal, the men all joined their host at once, but their laughter was anything but full of merriment. Moreover, from the way in which they were now watching Emile's every move, they looked more like a pack of hungry wolves waiting to attack their prey than commonfolk stopping by for a cheerful pint of ale. Prey they should most definitely know better than to attack where he was concerned.

"Does she have a name, this girl of yours?" One of the men jeered while drawing closer to his flank.

Emile ignored his question momentarily and played with the rim of his mug with only one of his fingers on his right hand, clearly entertained by the chaotic turn of events. "I'm sorry to disappoint you, gentlemen, but where I am from, I was taught that a true man does not kiss and tell."

The bartender and the men really burst into amusement now but then relaxed as if they had finally accepted his story as the truth.

"Now, that's a fact!" One of them laughed.

"Sweet whispers in the night," another echoed from across the bar to his right.

"Something like that, yes," Emile replied, though he did not disclose any more details.

"Well, you are out of luck I am afraid. No one like that is scheduled to be here tonight. Though you could try down the street. I hear some of Robespierre's men like to frequent the inn on the corner from time to time," the bartender offered freely, no longer concerned about the man's hidden intentions.

"*Merci*, once again." Emile left a considerably large tip for his assistance and walked towards the door, but not before eyeing the men from the side to make sure he was not being followed. The almost annoyingly necessary action had never been something he had casually done in the past, but rather something he had learned to mimic carefully since the attack on him back in England. Like being burned by fire and subsequently forever scarred by an attentiveness to the heat of the flame it produced, a man had but to make that mistake only once to forever remember to be diligently cautious thereafter.

Content that the men were otherwise engaged for the present, he left the tavern and stepped back out onto the front porch to take in the view before him once more. In his brief absence, the young lady had quite obviously went on her way to wherever it was that she was working for the day, and Emile was partly glad that she had. As tantalizingly attractive as she might be in both disposition and appearance, he found that for once, he actually preferred to leave a bit of mystery concerning the woman in question for the time being.

117

Nevertheless, that did not also mean that he was fulfilled yet either. The conversation in the tavern had left him experiencing the same strange pent-up frustration that had lingered after a dinner party a few nights ago. The kind of sensation that made you feel like something was uncharacteristically off, or at the very least wanting. But as he stared down the street and back up it once more, everything around him spoke only of commerce and industry, nothing of the revolutionary movement obviously brewing underneath. And yet, the invisible perception of danger was building there under the very stones of the street just the same. It was almost as if the air around him quite literally pulsed with its growing intensity more than in the collecting fluffs of white flakes upon the surfaces of the city.

Were his friends correct in their rumors about the nobility being taken from their homes in the middle of the night? Surely none of the merchants here seemed to intend any harm to come to those who so bountifully supplied their daily welfare. But how could he deny the possibility when three of those in his inner circle had most unceremoniously disappeared in just the last month alone, leaving behind their wives and children to wonder what had become of them. The news from his sources said that an announcement would be made soon regarding the National Assembly, and he for one wanted to be there to hear it and judge the danger for himself. Like in any game of cards, it was drawing time to find out whether he needed to close out and run or raise the stakes even higher to remain where he loved and stand his ground.

With a renewed determination, Emile continued towards the direction of the inn that the man at the tavern had indicated, hopeful once again in his quest.

"Can you spare a sol, sir?" A child who was rubbing his hands together to fend away the biting chill interrupted his travels as he begged from a nearby corner of a more dismally looking establishment. Small as he was, he looked almost as pathetic as the rest of the rabble gathered around the various alleyways on Emile's journeys to *Madame* Jeannette's.

Emile stopped briefly and fished out a small coin from his upper pocket before placing it into the blind child's hand and waiting patiently for him to accept it. "What do they call you, Boy?" He asked with deep respect for the plight of the child beside him.

"Lucien, sir." The boy felt all sides of the coin to identify it before exclaiming excitedly. "A whole liard! Oh, thank you, sir."

"It is most freely given." Emile dusted off the collected snow on top of the step beside him and sat down next to the boy who could not have been much older than seven. "Do you happen to know what your name means?"

The boy shook his head from side to side slowly but did not seem the least bit bothered by the conversation with the stranger.

"It means light, young one." Emile tapped the young child on the head affectionately and stood up before looking back down the street.

Standing here, in the midst of the so-called new National Assembly itself, he began to see a whole new Paris come alive before him. From the silversmith to the cabinet maker, shop after shop was quite literally stuffed to the brim with unsold goods and every street filled with beggars and salesmen alike trying to scrape together whatever living was available to them in these most impoverished of times.

Feeling more than a bit rebuked by his rude behavior earlier, he thought back to the beautiful woman from the street who was no doubt a part of this world given her threadbare attire and cumbersome load and chastised himself for not offering to at least carry it part of the way for her. *Why had he let her struggle so when it would have cost him literally nothing to be of assistance? Was it pride? Disinterest?*

"Definitely not disinterest," Emile mused and smiled once again at the charming way in which the woman had embraced her struggle like someone who was dancing with the wind. "And most definitely a little mad, but then again, who isn't?"

And yet, distractions aside, here was humanity, too, in its rawest form and people like himself had been turning a blind eye to them for centuries. For a brief moment, he felt almost sad for the blind beggar boy beside him and for the rest of their harsh state of existence, but in the next moment a humorous thought crossed his mind, too, drawing him towards more pleasant reflections. "Well, as the fair Marie Antionette said, 'Let them eat cake then.'"

Though he knew full-well that the woman, as vain as she was, had indeed meant her statement to be taken in far less than the derogatory manner in which it had been repeated to her subjects, the sentiment it displayed still felt rather appropriate to him standing here. Life was too short indeed to be bothering himself with the momentary trifles of this world. If Señor Moretti was correct, they would pass long before he would, so to concern himself much more than necessary with their plight seemed almost ludicrous, if not pointless.

"Speaking of cake..." His mouth watered once more at the memory of his last conquest and pulled him towards where he knew it would be satisfied. Despite his best of intentions otherwise to delay his meals as long as possible, he was hungry, and that meant he needed to feed, and soon... just not on cake... and not on the girl in the street either for that matter. Whoever the woman was, he needed her to remain far away from him today. Or at least safely outside his realm of temptation until he could figure out just what it was about her that intrigued him so. As a rule, people like her did not cross his path often, nor did he especially desire to end someone so... so.... Emile shook his head, his brow furrowing in several places. He actually had no idea just how to describe her. Not yet anyways. There <u>was</u> a word, certainly. A perfectly precise term that encapsulated everything that she truly was, but try as he might, it eluded him completely today.

In its place, the irritating frustration returned. No longer feeling the least bit philosophical, he began walking towards an establishment he knew only too well on the opposite side of town. Down towards where even the blind boy would fear to tread after dark. One, only a few of his noble acquaintances would dare admit frequenting, though many did—the local brothel. *Madame* Jeannette was sure to have some yummy strumpet he could feast upon, if not in the literal sense of the word. That would be too risky in broad daylight. But at nightfall, all was a different story, and <u>no one</u> missed one of <u>those</u> girls, no matter what part of the city they were from.

Chapter Ten

February 1st, 1793

S ebastian wiped his brow for the fifth time that morning purely out of habit. Since daybreak, he had been working under the heat of the forge with little pause for rest, knowing that his labor would continue until after sunset with his given list of tasks. To his greatest surprise, establishing himself as a blacksmith down at the port had probably been the easiest thing that had ever transpired in his not quite 33 years of age. Much simpler than it had actually been back in Portsmouth, not that he was complaining.

Señor Moretti had also been correct about the very real demand for tradesmen back in town. They were so desperate for his services, in fact, that when Sebastian met the master of the port outside his office shortly after Christmas, he had not even been given a moment to recite the excellent soliloquy he had prepared so diligently the night before should anyone be curious about his background and work history. It was almost as if not a single man he encountered held any concern whatsoever about where he was from, nor even thought to ask. To them, he was just like any other able-bodied, excellently trained blacksmith and in the Port master's opinion, "...sent from God himself."

"Indeed, if that were even so?" Sebastian shook his head and smiled at the rare turn of events that had befallen him. "If I had known that all I needed to do was move here, I probably wouldn't have troubled myself with that ticket all the way to the Americas."

With an equally heavy heart, he thought back to his time working as an apprentice under his master near Portsmouth. At the age of 12 he had been sent to work in a trade like many others his age, an opportunity most lads relished as a path to security in manhood, but one an orphaned boy like himself would never have been given in most circumstances.

With no family, no home, and quite literally no other relations willing enough to pay for his daily needs, the monk at the small monastery who had practically raised him since the age of four was the only person he knew who could have arranged and paid the fee on his behalf to begin his apprenticeship. What that man had seen in him; he never did understand. And to this day, though he never fully comprehended the reasoning behind all the how's and the why's of that fateful decision, he knew that he was forever grateful for the chance he had been given to improve his situation, however small.

And improve he did. As the months turned into years, from dawn until well after the setting of the sun, he worked steadily doing whatever task was required of him. Like a stone rolling down a very steep hill, he diligently completed nearly any task requested of him, provided he had the ability to do so, from stoking the fire every morning to hauling heavy coal from the docks before he retired for the night. It all took respectful thoroughness and grateful devotion, and with them, he was beyond dedicated to his master. It was probably one of the chief reasons why he had even remotely prospered where others in his position had not.

Yet the only thing he could not improve upon through effort or sheer fortitude alone was the color of his skin. When it finally came time to start his own blacksmith shop at the age of twenty, he naively thought that this would be but the first step towards the life he had always longed for, a life where he could stand on his own two feet and make his way in the world. And by all accounts, he had done everything he had been instructed to do for its success. He had built his forge in a prominent location, accessible to many forms of trade by the port so the work should have been fairly steady, but sadly, it was not. Instead, he had only struggled more and more with each successive year just to make ends meet, getting by on the meager tasks that the poor or the desperate could afford to hire him to complete.

It was not until he changed his name from Fabbri to Smith that his business started to improve dramatically, but never to the same level as others in his position. In the end, he had been compelled to resign himself to the frustrating fact that although many people needed the work done, few were willing to have a Spaniard do it for them. It simply made no difference to the world at large that he was far more English now than he was Spanish, having spent a lifetime in the same country as those who were soliciting his services. His skin quite literally told a different story than his speech, one in which he could not escape from no matter his desire to do so many times over.

However, there <u>was</u> one ray of sunshine in his sad tale whenever he told it. A beautiful girl who was one of only a handful of people who did not appear to hold his heritage against him. Charlotte, the fair-skinned daughter of a local dairy farmer just up the hill from his shop, brought him his milk every other morning and stayed usually an hour or two to chat while he worked. An immigrant from Ireland, herself, she was as sassy as she was a no-nonsense kind of a girl, but most of all he simply loved the way that she made him laugh at himself when he was taking things far too seriously. She had "the light of the Irish in her," as she always loved to say to him, and he would agree, for it made her golden hazel eyes, the color of poured honey, sparkle like the ocean and were just as vast in their depth.

After they wed, their two boys had thankfully inherited their mother's wit and personality, and not his more melancholy demeanor, but unfortunately they had also inherited his Spanish complexion, which had caused them more than a few issues in their schooling already. Even at their young age, local boys already tended to tease them mercilessly about their tanned skin and curly brown hair and though Sebastian tried to shelter them as best as possible when these incidents began, Charlotte had been right in refusing his efforts at every turn.

"She is always right." Sebastian smiled once more as he put down his hammer and stood for a minute to enjoy the view of the ocean waves breaking against the manmade seawall in front of him. "And she would love it here." He sighed quickly, then shook his head to dispel that aching thought before opening her letter to read it once more. Only a week old, the paper was already well-smudged and crinkled on the corners from repeated reading, but he did not care. The inside held her heart within, and as lonely as he was becoming with each passing day without her in it, he hung on every written word like they were feeding his very soul.

At William's suggestion, he <u>had</u> managed to compose a brief letter to his family back home, informing them of his well-being to remove any of their fears upon hearing the news of their shipwreck. However, despite what he had wanted to write, there wasn't much else he could say regarding his future plans, his situation being as it was. Deep down, he knew that Charlotte deserved the truth, as horrible as it may be, but the last thing he wanted to do right now was give her too many specifics. Despite being hundreds of miles away from him, she was the one thing that was still holding him together at this point, and he needed that connection desperately. Or rather, her love was the single ray of sunshine in the darkness that threatened to envelope him completely if he let it.

And so, like a man trying to hide a secret sin, he chose rather to keep it simple and tell her only that: he had been taken to a friendly shore, that he was currently working for his passage to the Americas and that he would be leaving shortly. Well, the first two points were absolutely true. The last was a necessary lie to dissuade her from coming to where he was for he knew that she would if given the opportunity. And it <u>was</u> his plan after all to live in the Americas as soon as he was able. He just did not know how soon that would be.

Given Señor Moretti's overly generous gift, he had also felt it prudent to send another letter to the agent in Philadelphia with whom he had been corresponding for several months before his departure. Only this time he inquired as to whether or not the man still had the small home and 50 acres available just outside the city proper. The price in November had been 100 acres of land for fifteen pounds ten shillings or the small home and 50 acres for the same, which had been desired, but far too steep a price for his meager income at the time. Yet with his recent influx of wealth, he had realized that this idea of his for a life in America was no longer a distant dream, but rather a very real possibility. And in truth, the best use of the gift that he could think possible at the present.

Owning the land would not only benefit his family's situation now, but it would also give his sons the same status as gentlemen maintained in England and according to what he had read, they would also be afforded the right to vote in the constitutional elections when they were of age. In truth, it was everything he had wanted for them in life but could not give them personally, or maybe... it was just a fresh start for all of them. A way in which his children could become successful no matter what the path in life they chose to follow. In fact, of all the many ways he could have thought to spend the money on his family, this was the most exciting prospect of all, and one he did not intend on passing up.

The remainder of Señor Moretti's gift he would undoubtedly use on their passage fee and whatever else was left would be sent in installments to his wife and sons after their arrival. Not a single shilling would be squandered or saved for himself. After all, at this point, he had little need for any physical comfort in the opulence in which he was living at the present. And should he learn how to become less of a danger to his family in time, he would simply work for his passage then, either before leaving or on the ship itself.

Yet, all of that was a far too distant dream for him at the present. Today, his only focus was to create nails, a lot of them, for the ship being built directly to his right. Tomorrow would be tomorrow, complete with problems all its own as Mark so appropriately put it in the Bible. And despite how overpowering those issues might seem at the present, he would simply have to face those then.

"Hey, Smithy!" A burly man called up to him from the boardwalk below. "Do you think you will have time to fix the wheel rims for the wagon before lunch?"

With a nod, Sebastian carefully folded the letter he had been reading into quarters and answered, "I'll get right on it now actually. I was just trying to finish up some of these nails for the men first."

"Thank you. Be sure to deliver them to Pascale as soon as they are ready."

In sudden frustration, Sebastian squinted at the bright landscape while looking out of his covered area and judged his need for safety. The sun was especially strong today for the beginning of February, but then again, the winter sun usually <u>was</u> always brighter by far than the summer's. And yet, though holding none of its penetrating heat, that also did not mean that it would not burn him just as badly.

For over a month, Sebastian had faithfully heeded the warnings he had been given, while paying the strictest of attention regarding his actions during the day, but at times like these, his mind raced nervously to create possible excuses and replies. Anything that would sound remotely plausible without sounding utterly ridiculous. "Um, I am not sure I can take the time to deliver them myself as I have a large order that also needs to be done quickly. Think you have a man that can do it for me? Either that or I can drop them off on my way home for supper if they can wait."

"Might be able to send Thomas your way after lunch if you think they will be done in half an hours' time." The man rubbed his chin where a definite two-day stubble remained while searching for a mutual solution.

Sebastian nodded once more, immediately grateful for the man's flexibility. He knew in order to meet the new guidelines specified, that he would have to work even faster to complete it, but with little other choice presenting itself, he would just have to diligently push himself to do so. Hammering through his list of tasks always made him feel more productive and useful anyways and, in a way, empowered—far different than the way he felt upon his arrival. Yet another thing for which he could be thankful.

Like a man driven by determination alone, Sebastian battered the anvil steadily throughout the entire afternoon without rest, and well into the latter part of the day as he worked to finish the order of nails he was given. Sebastian knew more than anyone that the shipbuilder's needed them for their work in the morning, even if most of the men had already ceased their labor hours earlier. But working in this single-minded way was nothing new to Sebastian. He had often kept his forge fires blazing until well after suppertime if not later back home, despite the frown it usually produced on his wife's face or his need for penitent apologies thereafter. It was just something that was a part of who he was, and Charlotte knew it. What's more, she had lovingly accepted it for the most part... or at least most days she did for she knew that once he started a task, he simply would not be able to rest until he knew that the job had been done and done right. That was all there was to it.

Sebastian stretched his limbs upward to work out the kinks in his back from leaning over slightly all day and felt a bit more fatigued than he had remembered feeling in weeks. With no one holding him to any particular schedule he had steadily tackled more projects than he might have done so at home just to keep his mind focused on other things. "Still, I have to go home sometime, I suppose." He sighed as he finally allowed the coals in the fire to die down to a dull grey and lifted the bellows high above to their place of rest. Then, he lined up every tool of his trade, one after the other, along the short brick wall to his right in methodical fashion, before hanging up his long leather apron on its peg close beside.

"There. Everything is as it should be now," he said with great satisfaction and pride as he stood in the silence for just a moment to take in the scene before him. With a smile and a nod, he turned to leave thereafter, contentment filling his every step.

For the most part, the village and its inhabitants had already retired to their homes for the evening, much like the morning he had first strode into town with William. All that is except for a solitary young man who was still waiting for him half-way up the cobblestone street with a small satchel slung over his left shoulder and three letters in hand.

"You're out pretty late, Thomas." Sebastian greeted him casually as he drew nearer.

"Well, you're a popular person today, Mr. Fabbri." The youth, who he guessed could not have been much older than seventeen or eighteen, handed him the letters carefully. "I have never had the pleasure of seeing one all the way from the Americas. Do you have family there, sir?"

Sebastian shook his head as he rubbed the back of his neck with his soot covered hands. "Not at this time, Thomas, but maybe someday." He politely took the envelopes offered to him without even glancing at the inscriptions and tried to deflect the young man's interest in them and his personal life.

"It must be exciting though," he replied, trying to make the small talk last long enough to see the contents of the unopened letters.

Sebastian smiled warmly at the boy's eagerness to please and tucked the objects of his curiosity into his inner pocket before answering as honestly as he possibly could. "It is probably some notice from the shipping company regarding my lost

126

belongings." He continued in his walk down the street towards home, but the young man only joined him in his steady pace, still in animated conversation.

"Were you in the Great Storm I heard about?" He whistled at the immensity of the thought. "They say it destroyed nearly half of the ships in the English navy, not to mention countless other merchant and sea vessels. Was it bad? Of course it was bad. But you survived! How did you survive?" He prattled on without seeming the need to come up for air in-between sentences. It all reminded Sebastian very much of the endless questions his youngest, Elijah, would ask him every day when he returned home from work after being away from him all day.

Was it hard work today? Did you burn himself? Did you have a lot of orders? What did the baker say at lunch? Did he send home any fresh bread? Can you read me a story again before bed—the one about the conquerors? Can I marry Mama when I am older? Will you teach me to work the fire just like you, Papa?

The questions always fell out of the boy, much like a cascading waterfall from the moment he walked in the door to the second he sat down and pulled the young child onto his lap before supper. And never once had he lost his temper in their quantity or silliness of topic, and though he may never hear them spoken again by his son in this lifetime, he knew that for tonight, he was simply glad to have been given just a little piece of his world back once more to enjoy.

Feeling amusement rise within him again at the memory, he decided to tease Thomas just a little regarding his own questions. "Yes, the storm was mighty indeed. It was almost as if the Great Poseidon in all his fury had stirred up the depths and had thrown them into the very sky."

The youth's eyes grew large at the depiction. "Then how did you survive, if I may ask?" He added in wonder and reverent awe.

"By riding those massive waves on a door from my ship." Sebastian tried to keep as serious an expression as he could manage given the playful nature of the story even though every word of it was false. He had actually been unconscious for nearly every minute of his voyage on the Endeavor, as well as for the shipwreck and their miraculous deliverance afterwards. "With these bare hands, I tied an old rope to the front of it and used it like a simple sled. Then, with the wind on my back to guide me, I sailed right up on shore and here I am."

Thomas pondered the image he described for a minute or two in great seriousness, like a scholar contemplating the very meaning of life, before crinkling his face up in total disbelief. "I think you are telling me a falsehood, Mr. Fabbri."

Sebastian smiled and tried his best to contain the laughter that wanted to escape at such a fanciful tale. "Maybe I am, son." He tapped the young man's shoulder lightly before tipping his head. "Or maybe I am not. The point is, how would you know?"

"I suppose it doesn't matter, really." Thomas smiled and shrugged his shoulders at the man across from him, not caring a bit whether or not the story was true. "Sure, is a nice tale either way."

"That it is, Thomas. Oh, were you able to deliver those rims to Pascale, today?"

Thomas nodded quickly. "It was he who gave me your mail. Just came off the ship it did."

"I am much indebted to you for bringing it all this way, and for waiting for me." Sebastian put a grateful hand on the boy's shoulder and gave it a light squeeze. "Now, I must be off. Señor Moretti was probably expecting me hours ago. Will I see you tomorrow? I might have a few tasks you can do for some extra coin if you have the notion to earn it."

"Yes, sir. You can count on me!" Thomas affirmed excitedly and took off running in a different direction with other letters to deliver in his hand.

Sebastian grinned once again at his willingness to please and started his trek back up the mountain to the castle. Yet as late as he was in his arrival, when he finally reached the front gate, he collided quite unexpectedly into a departing Hannah.

"Beggin your pardon, sir," she for bumping into him accidentally. "In my haste to be off, I did not hear you coming."

"The fault was mine entirely, I assure you." Sebastian rehung the blue shawl back across her shoulder that had fallen slightly in the collision. "Are you heading home for the night?"

"Yes, sir. The Master has already eaten and left instructions that I was to leave your portion in the Great Hall."

"That is more than sufficient, Hannah. I am sorry I was so late to have caused the trouble in the first place. As you know, I am very thankful for all that you do for us." He held the gate open for her so she could pass through it without difficulty. "Would you like assistance in getting to your home? It is awfully dark tonight."

Hannah giggled slightly at the absurdity of the gesture and refused him outright. "But sir, it is <u>always</u> dark for me. Why would the time of day or season make any matter."

Justly rebuked, Sebastian chuckled, as well. "Correct, as always, fair lady."

Hannah giggled once more like a young schoolgirl and not the woman of 20 that she was. "Fair lady... how funny, Mr. Fabbri. The next thing you will be saying is that I live in a magical castle and a prince in shining armor is coming to rescue me one day."

"Well, you never know... anything can happen," Sebastian replied humorously.

"Oh, you go on. Your dinner is already cold." She laughed and repeated his words over and over again happily as she walked along. "Fair lady, indeed. Ha ha ha... a prince ... ha ha ha... more like a frog, no doubt, if one were to come knocking on my door."

"Goodnight and thank you, Hannah," Sebastian called after her, watching as long as he could over her as she made her way down to the safety of her cabin.

"Goodnight." Her reply was carried with the wind back to him as she continued on her way down the worn pathway that led to her small cottage about halfway to the village.

She herself did not choose to live within the town's borders either. Like others who had similarly been born blind, her birth had been met with much scrutiny and declarations as to whether or not this malady had been brought on by some form of witchcraft or evil omen. Even the religious leaders of the village had also taken it upon themselves to question her parents quite thoroughly as if needing to ascertain if some form of sin had occurred which might have brought her condition into existence.

There had been none, of course, but to make her situation even worse, Señor Moretti had told Sebastian that twenty years ago there just so happened to be a lunar eclipse on the night of her birth. With the red-hued moon high overhead, the healers and skeptics in the town went wild with speculations and prophecies, whipping other gullible villagers along with them into an absolute frenzy of gossip and conjecture.

Through it all, her parents protected her as best as they could from them. They still loved their child deeply but had not been strong enough physically or financially to navigate around the terrifying rumors cast upon their only child. After all, what hope did Hannah have for a life in the village where everyone she met only saw her as a harbinger of Satan himself or some other such nonsense.

Seizing their last ray of hope for a possible future for her, they did the only thing they could think of and chose instead to leave poor Hannah at the door of the castle above in hopes that someone there might be able to help their poor child.

Señor Moretti was no faith healer, nor was he any form of medicinal shaman. And Hannah's parents knew that he could not restore to their child her sight, but what he could do was offer her a place to grow in safety or grant her a living when she was of age, and protection from the harsh views of those around her. For Hannah's parents, that was enough. He was her means of salvation here on Earth, and now fully grown, Hannah was utterly devoted to him for the kindness so freely bestowed upon her.

Sebastian bolted the large wooden door behind him like he had done on his first arrival months ago and folded his light cloak in half before setting it carefully down on the bench directly next to the door. With a burning curiosity that had plagued him since Thomas had first mentioned the letter, he withdrew the three envelopes carefully and thumbed each of them in turn. *God be praised*, one was from his love, Charlotte. Another was from the ever-faithful William, no doubt filled with his depictions of life back in Wakefield. While the last was a rather professionally inscribed envelope from Philadelphia, the obvious object of Thomas' earlier curiosity. Excitement surged through him once more at the mere sight of it, prodding him as he opened the latter first, eager to read its contents

Dear Sir,

It does my heart well to hear of your good fortune and not of your demise on that dreaded voyage. The house and land in question is, in fact, still available, and I have taken the necessary steps to purchase it in your good name, as well as put a hold on all adjacent land until you have replied to this letter. All that remains now is for you to sign the enclosed documents and have them witnessed by an official in your country of choice.

In the meantime, I will make all the necessary arrangements on your behalf to secure not only the house, but also most of its contents for the use of your wonderful wife and two children. The estate has been left fallow for at least two years, and so you will most certainly have much work ahead of you upon your arrival.

The previous tenant was of an elderly nature and has gone on to live with her children in Virginia already. As such, if you are so disposed, she is of the mind to complete this sale at your earliest convenience.

Should you have any questions regarding this transaction, please do not hesitate to contact me directly.

Your Humble Servant,
Mr. Ezekial Davis Esq.

Sebastian's heart leapt with excitement at the news. Impatient to reply as quickly as possible so as not to lose this rare opportunity, he strode up the stairs two at a time to his room and immediately set to work on his reply. If Thomas or the port master were available at the registrar in the morning, he would sign the official documents then, and with luck, have them sailing on the next tide.

Taking his seat at the familiar writing desk in his room, he pulled out the necessary items from the small drawer and dipped the quill into the inkwell to pen a brief note to attach with them before signing his official name at the bottom of his return letter.

Dear Sir,

Thank you for your prompt reply and efforts on behalf of my family and myself. I will indeed take the house, and the 50 acres originally requested, but I would like to also make one small change. Please go ahead and secure for purchase the full one hundred acres. If the land is as fruitful as you claim, I should think that it will be a wise investment to have the whole instead of separating it. The necessary retainer will be sent to you directly with the other documents you requested.

In the second, I realize that this may seem an equally unusual request, but would you please put all official documents in the names of: Charlotte Erin Fabbri-Smith, Jedidiah Mateo Fabbri and Elijah Michael Fabbri. Since they will be arriving before I am able, I wish them to be able to do all things necessary with the least bit of inconvenience possible in my absence.

With gratitude,
Sebastian Fabbri-Smith

With a sense of deep satisfaction, he placed the pen within the inkwell once more and cast his glance heavenward. "Thank you, for your provision, again and again." He kissed his two right fingertips then held them up in a form of religious respect, before a soft knock sounded on the door next to him. "Come in."

The heavy door opened slightly, just wide enough for his host to peek his head through. "Pardon the interruption, but when I saw that your meal had still not been eaten, I grew a bit concerned for you, dear Sebastian." Señor Moretti bent his head as he stared back at him inquisitively at seeing the man's newest correspondence on the table before him. "Good news, I hope."

"The best as far as my family is concerned, though it is only due to your generosity, of course. Which I thank you for once again for none of this would be possible without your provision." Sebastian handed him the letter and documents without reservation for his perusal.

Señor Moretti's face tried to remain positive and yet hopeful, as he read over the folded documents that he had been handed, very much desiring his new guest to remain with him just a little bit longer. As a rule, he had so few visitors as it was, and for some unknown reason, he felt particularly responsible for this group of newcomers though he had never felt so of anyone else in the past. "So, does this letter mean you will leave us soon?"

"No, not unless I have completely worn out my welcome here." Sebastian raised his eyebrows questioningly at his host.

"Far from it. May I?" Señor Moretti petitioned for his permission to enter.

"It is your castle, after all," he replied respectfully, leaning back in his chair and folding his arms casually across his chest.

Señor Moretti smiled at his simple answer. "Just the same." He took a seat in the large wooden chair that had been placed beside the only window in the room, affording the occupier a marvelous view of the entire island and the sea beyond.

Like a man who might stand for hours admiring a foreign painting at some museum back home, Sebastian studied him. From his position and posture across the room, he could have easily been mistaken for King Claudius in Hamlet or any number of royal dignitaries given his regal form and suave mannerisms. Nevertheless, with all the talent that he possessed, he had chosen to remain here in obscurity reading over his many texts and parchments in peace.

"Please pardon me for asking this, but what is it exactly that you study every day and night without fail. Given the time spent on your endeavors, you are no doubt a master of many subjects by now."

Señor Moretti beamed with approval at his keen observation, then flexed his fingertips into a triangle in front of him. "A master of some, yes, but a mere student in others. Why, take the famous Albucasis for example. He is known as the father of modern surgery while also having invented well over 200 tools. Many of which are still used to this day. Though admittedly, some could very well use some alteration and perfecting to make them more applicable. Yet this accomplishment is altogether remarkable all the same."

"200 of them! That does seem fairly impressive. I have less than twenty in my shop and most of those are finer files and instruments for specific tasks like in making swords or more specialized pieces." Sebastian stretched out and crossed his legs in front of him to give the man his fullest attention.

"Throughout the centuries, mankind has forever been in the pursuit of that which betters his surroundings, Sebastian. From Da Vinci to dare I say, Doctor Joseph Guillotin over in Paris, they have both desired a better world than the one in which they currently belong. Though with the latter, one could argue that his abilities do not stretch towards the realm of enhancement, but rather to its extermination. Yet I have read recently that even he feels very strongly that his device will provide quite the opposite effect on its victims by giving them a quick and painless means of death as opposed to the more garish methods of his predecessors." Señor Moretti stood at this point and began walking around the room as he spoke. "A rare moment of mercy in the madness, I suppose you could say."

"So, you are merely looking for a needle in a haystack, it appears." Sebastian tried not to seem overly simplistic in his cynicism, but he couldn't help it.

"No, and yet, yes." Señor Moretti laughed lightly. "For myself, I lean a bit more towards an increased enlightenment in my studies. Despite the restrictions placed upon beings like ourselves, I mean to leave a positive mark on this world in every way possible. So much so, that I refuse to allow the mere trifles of our physical limitations dissuade me as to what I might hope to accomplish in my lifetime, however long that may be."

Sebastian listened to the man intently like a student gleaning knowledge from a learned professor. "So, instead of traveling or working in some form of profession you have instead decided to devote your life to your studies."

"In a small sense of the word. Rather, I have chosen to use my days perfecting those things which have been discovered before me, while also consistently learning from those who have arrived thereafter." He paused. "Like my newest experimentation with the concepts set forth by *Monsieur* Jan Baptiste Denyshas. He is the scholar who has so wonderfully perfected the person-to-person blood transfusion over a century ago. Still, in all those years that have followed, we have yet to fully understand the large scope of its capabilities or find ways to avoid its fatal deficits. It is to something along those lines that I have been hoping to discuss with you more at length soon, not today mind you, but soon."

"I'm sorry, but I am afraid that William might be far better suited for that conversation than I, sir. My head began to spin when you first spoke of surgical instruments," Sebastian admitted sheepishly.

"Perhaps, but my research involves your participation in some regards."

"Really? How so?" Sebastian nearly choked on the word. "There is nothing impressive about me, nor have I accomplished much of anything in my life worthy of putting into any of your books."

"You sell yourself far too short, as you are well aware, but it is my hope that one day I will be able to change that which we have become or at least allow us a path to a more normal form of existence." Señor Moretti stopped pacing and placed one hand on Sebastian's shoulder. "Not a cure, mind you, but a treatment that would permit us to be less of who we are and more of what we long to be."

"Mortal?"

"Or something very much like it for a time," Señor Moretti said with a tilt of his head back and forth.

"But how is something like that even possible?" Sebastian asked in total bewilderment.

"Well, if you must know, since just before your arrival, I have been experimenting with the transfusion process of my own blood and that of some of the blood that has been received via the process William and I spoke of before. For a mortal, to do what I am proposing would result in a less than favorable outcome, but for myself, I have noticed a considerable change to my dietary needs and sensitivities thereafter. Though mind you, it is in no way a cure. The transformation itself has only lasted for a few hours the first time and a half a day in the second, but it is at the very least, considerable progress indeed," his host finished explaining.

"Any relief from what I am would be more than I would have dreamt possible." Sebastian's eyes lit up with hopeful anticipation.

"Yes, well... you will need to be patient for the moment as I do not as of yet, understand the full scope of my endeavors, but I hope to have more promising news by the month's end after many... many more tests," Señor Moretti assured him with an encouraging smile. "Now, you must at least try to eat your dinner. Hannah spent a great deal of time today making it precisely the way she thought you would like it. Though she has not the slightest clue as to our hidden identity, she understands, at least remotely, our dietary aversions and has become quite good at adjusting her recipes to accommodate them."

"As you have said, she is always so very kind." Sebastian smiled appreciatively before adding, "I'll join you directly downstairs in a minute. I just want to finish up a few things first. Then, maybe we can play another game of chess, if you are willing."

"That would be delightful, of course. Perhaps this time you may even win." Señor Moretti cast him a sideways glance and winked.

"Maybe, though I sincerely doubt it," Sebastian replied. "You're the master here. I am but your apprentice."

"We shall see." Señor Moretti merely shook his head at Sebastian's playful remark and exited the room before shutting the door quietly behind him.

Feeling a bit more encouraged by the possibilities mentioned in his conversation with his host, Sebastian opened Charlotte's letter next before leaning casually back in his chair to read it.

My dearest Sebastian,

Has it really been almost two months since I last kissed your lips in farewell? I know this time apart is expected, but try as I might to ignore it, I still find that our bed is so cold without you in it. Of course, your two sons have often kept me company in your absence with excuses about their nightmares regarding your recent absence and shipwreck, but it is not the same, as I am sure you know. Their little hands reach out to me in their dreams, especially young Elijah who misses you terribly, but they do nothing to quell the overwhelming desire I carry with me to have you wrap your arms around me once more.

Life here is progressing on much as it always has. Chores, school, and keeping up with your sons fills the majority of my waking hours. I do believe Jedidiah is a full notch taller on the wall by now and is doing his best to be the man of the house while you are away. Elijah has learned to read considerably well under his extra tutelage, too, and that of their very strict schoolmaster, Father Benedict. I believe you will find yourself quite proud when you next meet with his ability to read circles around the other children. Or rather, earnestly delighted with both of your handsome sons who steal my heart away every morning when I look into their faces and see you, my dearest Bash.

When <u>will</u> we meet again, my love? Soon? I hope so.

I pray every night for your safe return to us, and that you will carry our love with you wherever your travels may take you. Please send us word when you are finally settled in America at last, so that we may know where we are to join you.

Would this Christmas be too soon for a hoped reunion? I pray not. Though I think I pray more that I can make it that long without you than I do about the possible dangers that might befall all of us along the way. In this time apart, I have quickly discovered that though I have always thought myself to be a fairly independent woman and strong of mind when it comes to moments of deep stress and turmoil about me, sadly, I am not. In my weakness, I have plainly seen how much I need <u>you</u>, more than I have ever needed a comfortable life for us financially. I love you, my stubborn husband, and I support you for wanting to make it all possible for us, but nothing in all this great Earth can ever replace the man that you are to this family. You are as essential as the air that I breathe and twice as desired.

Missing you beyond measure with all my love and devotion,
Your Charlotte

Overwhelmed by the depth of the words written, he pressed the paper against his lips and tried to hold back the sobs that had been threatening to escape every time his family entered his thoughts, which was quite often. This eternal, emotional separation was certainly far worse than any form of physical death he might have endured, as not being able to be close to her was, in itself, regulated torture.

Sebastian held her letter close to him a moment longer with a feeling of being so close to embracing her very soul and yet so utterly removed at the same time allowing it to drive the ache deeper within him of his desperation to hold them once more. What sheer relief it would be to sense for just a moment the touch of her hand upon his cheek or to hear the soft whisper of her words of love upon her lips. All of it would have been heavenly tonight over the crisp coldness of the parchment between his fingertips.

Closing his eyes, he fought back in earnest against the unbearable pain and rawness of his loss that almost broke his resolve entirely to remain. Their ultimate safety was worth far more than whatever agony he had to endure today or every day if it meant protecting them. It had to be.

Like a secret obsession kept by the vilest of criminals, his mind had almost daily returned with the utmost of precision to the memory of Emile hunched over the lifeless form of that girl. In fact, the enticing image had been quite literally seared into his brain like a hot iron from his fire that branded him as "dangerous" right alongside the Frenchman for though he had not laid an actual finger on her, he could still almost taste the lust he felt towards Emile's prize through the memory.

He was not a saint, nor was he likely to ever be so. As such, he knew beyond a shadow of a doubt that if their roles had been reversed, and if he had no one else to live for, he might have ravaged her, as well, for he wanted her blood even now with the same dark desire that drove his anger at craving it. It would have been so incredibly easy... so deliciously enticing to seduce her into compliance and submission with just a few softly spoken words. His mouth watered at the wonderful possibility and his fists clenched instinctively in reaction to it afterwards.

Sebastian shook his head to dispel the temptation once more, he needed no more assurance tonight to convince himself of the very real threat he would be placing upon his family should he return to them as he was... a vampire. Determination alone would not safeguard them from what he wanted more than their love, and the truth of that stole his very breath away, drawing him closer to a deeper depression than ever before. First and foremost, he was a vampire now. His place as a husband and as a father was second to that fact now, and like it or not, he needed to accept that truth as horrible as it was before he could even hope to conquer the former.

Resigning himself now more than ever, that nothing in Heaven or Earth would ever stand in the way of that goal, he nodded to himself remotely as he thought it and stood up from his desk before he tucked the last of his letters into the top pocket of his vest. The letter from William would no doubt hold news of those he cared for in his practice there and some unusual anecdotes about the young preacher rooming with him. Possibly even something about his own personal struggles as the man had strangely chosen him alone in which to divulge them.

The physician's letters were quickly becoming like a written confession of his temptations and near failings as he shared his darkest thoughts with him, hoping, he supposed, that in doing so he would in turn instill some shred of hope that his friend reading was also more man than monster. Which was in a way comforting to know that they at least had that in common. But William had been also wrong, too. As uplifting as his continued friendship was, the rather lurid details written in a rather cryptic fashion had often left him a bit too desirous to partake with him in them. Still, he welcomed his letters for they were yet another steady constant in his new life of change.

At least this piece of the outside world he would enjoy reading over his supper, and perhaps, if his host was so disposed, he might also share a bit of the more mundane details with Señor Moretti. The penitent confession of the truths they both shared would forever remain just between them—and of course, sacredly secure.

Chapter Eleven

February 7th, 1793

T he woman's laughter from the night before still rang in Emile's ears, or quite possibly, it was the effects of the rather strong wine *Madame* Jeannette had chosen to serve, but either way Emile still felt rather full and satisfied with himself like a cat who had pleasantly slept all day in his favorite spot in the sun. And yet, just like that cat, he was also always poised to spring at the slightest hint of danger whenever necessary.

"Emile, my friend!" A man dressed in lace and frills from his head to his knees called from the other room of his spacious apartment, "Come join us. We need another man for whist."

Feeling suddenly obligated to play the host since it <u>was</u> his gathering after all, Emile lazily rose from his comfortable settee near the entrance to his apartment, adjusted the folds in his now crumpled vest and pretended to look both utterly amused and completely disinterested at the same time as he sat himself down at the table before the fire. "But, of course, Henri. It would be my pleasure. And perhaps in doing so, I can hope to win back a bit of what you took from me the other night."

"Not a chance, you shark." Henri hit him playfully on the arm with his pair of silk gloves. "Your money is already safely stored away in my vault at Versailles and not even the King himself, may he rest his soul, will make me part with it."

The two ladies on either side of him at the table giggled in response but only one of them flirted with Emile outright.

"We shall see..." Feeling rather impish at Henri's refusal, Emile leaned his head towards one of them and raised his eyebrows teasingly. "Then I shall simply have to deprive you of some other kind of riches." He kissed the hand of the attractive woman sitting directly next to him, causing her to smile in response.

"You fiend! You wouldn't dare!" The man gasped in mock accusation.

"For a woman as beautiful as Madeleine, how could I refuse the temptation?" Emile's eyes drew the woman in closer to his web like a carefully positioned spider, waiting for his next meal.

The lips of the woman beside him suddenly froze as she seemed paralyzed for the briefest of moments before he released her from his gaze, allowing her to blush and fan herself nervously.

Emile had always been a bit of a charmer, a harmless player if you will, but as a vampire, he had quickly discovered that he had also been granted an unusual effect on the inhibitions of all women he encountered, whether they could help it or not. In fact, just the mere movement of his hand across their skin, or the chance eye contact from across the room would hold his victim quite incapacitated, and yet also openly eager to receive his advances, whatever they may be.

And still, however useful the new ability may have seemed on the surface, it also made it almost too easy for him to get what he wanted most, and at times if he would admit it... made him feel bored with the game it spoiled. Lost was the thrill of the momentary gesture, the flush of anticipation, and the regret of dismissal. In its place instead was the hunt, the capture, the conquest, the empty trophy if you will.

"Careful, Emile or I will tell Angelique that you have been flirting with me." The young lady beside him continued to fan herself, but nodded her head audaciously towards a brilliant, raven-haired beauty standing by the window beyond.

"Ah, my Achilles heel, *madame*. You strike me down with your arrows." He feigned the necessary expression of personal injury and played another card on the table in front of him.

"Quite so. And when pray tell are you going to take her for yourself and stop flirting with my wife, sir?" Henri placed one of his cards down after him, followed by a similar action from the others. "I have heard talk that her father and brother, Jonathan, were both taken by those Jacobian rebels from the Assembly last month. Denounced they were, or so they call it. Next thing we know, they will be coming after the likes of us."

Emile felt the hairs on the back of his neck stand straight up at the man's accuracy like hearing an ill-spoken prophecy of things to come, though the man himself seemed to have no inkling as to the truthfulness of it. From all appearances otherwise, the majority of the group seemed visibly apathetic to the darker details of the conversation and yet also focused on the inconvenience of it all the same.

"I'm afraid that I cannot entertain such an idea as marriage at the moment, my dear Henri. You know as well as I that both of our financial affairs are... oh, how can I say this appropriately given the current company?" He placed his last card down on the table to complete the set and continued, "In a bit of a flux due to our recently changing environment. None of us can hope to marry anyone without also guaranteeing them the lifestyle they so justly deserve. It wouldn't be fair," Emile declared earnestly though every word that he had just uttered was a bold-faced lie. Yet, also thankfully for him, everyone at this party knew nothing of the kind.

The truth of the matter was that his family fortune had been in ruins for nearly half a century now, bolstered only by profitable marriages and shrewd business alliances alike. Yet, no one, other than the closest of his acquaintances, like Jonathan, knew of it. As a gentleman of social standing, he was almost required to attend the parties given by others and entertain those same guests at his in-town apartments whether he was financially able or not. It was the kind of life that he had accepted along with his position in society.

Even as a young boy, he had known his place, and he had learned to play his part well. Still, he had accepted long ago that his only hope for a more permanent financial survival was to marry and to marry well. Either that or gracefully accept the demise of his societal fortune and stature like all the others who had come before him.

His father's estate, which had once been the envy of the countryside, now lay desolate and empty. A mere shell of its former glory and sadly, a perfect depiction of the state of his own bank account until most recently.

In his desperation to keep all his family's troubles hidden, he had even tried travelling to England in search of a fresh start or quite possibly a new venture into society there. But that idea had only ended in quite a disarray when he had no sooner set foot on shore than he was quite forcibly kidnapped by the Endeavor's crew and thrust into her service on the very next ship out of port. Worse yet, he had lost his favorite hat. The one his father had given him just before he had passed, and the loss of it had bothered him much more than the rude manner in which he had been accosted or rather... imprisoned.

Once freed from his floating cell, Señor Moretti's overly generous gift had granted him the needed capital to return to the life he had once known and loved in France, or so he presumed, as he had no intention of ever setting foot back on William's horrid island again, hat or no hat. Nevertheless, the only thing the gift did not grant him was the knowledge of how long that money would last in the current lifestyle of his choice, for it was disappearing quite rapidly at his rate of spending.

"And that is the last trick, m*onsieur*!" Madeleine cheered triumphantly. "I win!"

"Bravo!" The rest of the table clapped their hands politely in her triumph.

"Well played, my dear," Henri politely congratulated her. "Shall we go again?"

"Not with me, I am afraid." Emile excused himself. "As you have so dutifully reminded me, a fair damsel awaits my attention."

"You cad!" Henri smirked knowing his friend's true motivations concerning the woman. "Though I believe you will still find her most certainly worse for company."

"You would be too if your brother disappeared before he ever made it home," Emile answered a little more honestly than Henri would have preferred for the man immediately displayed a grimace much like someone who had just smelled the foulest of cheese at the market. Then again, he probably had servants who purchased those things for him. A definite luxury considering the tumultuous times they were now enduring.

"Ladies..." Emile inclined his head out of respect to the women at the table and bowed slightly before standing up and making his way over to where the tall woman by the window was quietly standing, her back purposefully facing everyone else in the party.

"Do you like my view?" He opened the conversation amiably hoping to diffuse whatever storm was already brewing behind her brown eyes.

"It is tolerable, I suppose." Angelique attempted to show utter disinterest, but wasn't fooling anyone in the room, least of all Emile.

"Come, come, now. Why are we so glum tonight?" He used one finger to slightly lift her chin so that he could look directly into her eyes that almost matched her long curly hair in perfect shade and color for though her hair was truly a raven black it also held a bronzed glow upon its surface. Indeed, it was one of the few things about the woman that mesmerized him each time that he saw it. From any position in the room, he could appreciate the way that the light could shift across her hair and change its hue from darkness as black as ink to liquid metal ringlets. In truth, it was fascinating to behold. And the way she always styled it half-up and half-publicly displayed assured him that she invited his adoration just as much as she wanted his attention. Like a true fisher of men, it was her lure, and she knew it.

"I am sure half of Paris has already heard of my family's misfortune with the rabble by now, *monsieur*." Angelique turned away, looking as if she were completely heartbroken.

"Maybe not. I dare say that not everyone in this room is as informed on the subject as the two of us appear to be." Emile looked out the window towards the Bastille off in the distance, then back at the woman beside him, attempting to see the true reason for her sadness.

"Mark my words, if this new Assembly continues its endeavors, the rest of you will be next." She stifled a soft sob with the back of her hand, but her eyes told a completely different story as they were brimming over now not with the expected sadness for someone in her type of situation, but with a fevered rage.

Sensing that she was drawing some of the room's attention once more, Emile quickly provided his embroidered handkerchief, the one he always kept for occasions such as this and leaned in closer to whisper softly. "Now, now, dry those tears, *Mademoiselle* Toussaint. It cannot all be as bad as you say."

"You are correct, *Monsieur* Deschamps." She held her head high once more and stepped slightly away to leave a definite space between them, refusing outright to take the offered token. "It is <u>much</u> worse."

"How could it possibly be worse?" Emile tried his best not to react physically or otherwise to the drama the woman was exuding with every sentence she spoke, but it drained him mentally to do so—his patience clearly wearing thin, as always.

"If they have their way, we could <u>all</u> be sent to the dreaded guillotine just for being... us." She began to softly whimper once more, milking the moment for all that it was worth.

Emile rolled his eyes and tried his best not to react outwardly. *How utterly dramatic and pointless!* He thought before letting out a long sigh.

When she had come to him asking for his help in finding Jonathan, he had assumed at first that the woman was sincerely worried for her brother and his welfare, as was he. Yet her performance tonight spoke only of her own concern toward her personal safety than her actual devotion to her family. In fact, until her brother had disappeared, she had never once given her brother a second thought. So, why she was now openly expressing a deep devotion to his memory in front of a room full of acquaintances only proved his point further.

"My dear, if the fair citizens of this country of ours were to rise up against all of the nobility, where would it leave them? Poverty. There would be no one left to buy their goods, govern them and in turn, add a bit of culture to their otherwise uncivilized lives. Besides, I doubt any of them want to return to those days in the dark ages or worse," Emile reassured her politely, hoping it would bring an end to her hideous display.

"You mock me, sir, but I can verifiably tell you it is a very real possibility, and one I fear will come true in a very short time given the Assembly's current desperation," Angelique defended hotly.

With another roll of his eyes, Emile now realized that he had already grown tired of this conversation before it had even begun. "Angelique, is there anything I might be able to do to assist you in this hour of need?" He offered the obligatory olive branch, hoping beyond description that she would refuse his help just like she had done his handkerchief.

"You could try to rescue them," she countered flatly and tossed the bulk of her curls over one shoulder in bold rebellion.

Emile couldn't help himself as he chuckled lightly at the sheer stupidity of her idea but managed to retain a cordial display of decorum. "If only that were possible, mademoiselle, but you know these rebels. They must have their justice, however disorganized it is in the delivery. Besides, I doubt they will keep either Jonathan or your father for more than a few more weeks, let alone condemn them to an actual execution. This is all probably some sort of ruse to solicit empathy to their cause than an actual sentence."

"You obviously have not heard what has been happening there." Angelique's gaze bore down on him with fire and indignation at his perceived foolishness.

"Oh?" Emile tried to look surprised.

"Ask your friends at the table. They will tell you."

"As you wish then." Emile reached for her hand and kissed it politely before retreating eagerly, grateful that the woman had finally provided for him the best excuse possible to leave. Given her insincerity, he had no desire to disclose to her, either now or later, that he had already traced her brother's steps back to the Bastille weeks ago where the fair citizens of Paris were quite obviously keeping them both. Nor did he have the energy tonight to explain to her that he knew much more about this new Assembly than he casually let on. Information that he feared the majority in this room would be most obviously oblivious of.

Like the consummate actress that she was, Angelique crossed her arms as he left but did not move to follow him, choosing rather to maintain her position, staring out the second-floor window in silent defiance of the rest of the people gathered there.

Thoroughly bored now with everything transpiring around him, Emile did not inquire about such absurdities with those remaining at the party. Due to the uncertainty of the times, the others barely left their homes for social gatherings now, let alone walked the streets of Paris itself like he had done earlier today. These people in attendance knew nothing of what the common man was doing besides what time he was bringing their milk and bread, and even then, that detail was probably relegated to a litany of servants beneath them.

No, he would need to get the information he required regarding Jonathan and his father's release from a more reliable source. Perhaps possibly, someone who lived where the working classes lived, and not at their places of employment where they were less likely to talk to anyone that resembled him, or rather someone not within their particular station.

After giving instructions to his butler to see his guests out promptly at nine o'clock, he left the occupied room with his animated guests and crossed over to his quarters at the end of the hall before shutting the door firmly behind him.

Emile was thoroughly exhausted once more but the alarm that Angelique's comments had given him still clutched at his thoughts.

Were the citizens truly capable of mass murder?

Impossible.

Or was it?

Unfortunately, there was only one way to find out.

And he knew just the person he needed to talk to.

Chapter Twelve

February 15th, 1793

"You shouldn't be so solemn all the time. You know that right?" Elsie Summerfield, the young pianist, admonished Nathanael as she kneaded the dough on the worn, wooden counter in front of him.

"Me? Solemn?" Nathanael pulled himself from his deep retrospection as he sat watching her work. His face was covered by a look of utter astonishment for he had never seen himself in that manner, or at least not before the events of last November. "Whatever do you mean?"

Elsie shook her head and laughed at his expression outright because it reminded her very much of one her loyal dog might have made at the foot of her bed in the morning as he waited patiently for her to get up. "I can't believe you need me to remind you of something you have read probably a million times over by now."

"What is that, pray tell?" Nathanael handed her another pan in which to place the next loaf of bread but continued to admire her handiwork like a dutiful student.

"Well, for starters, 'Rejoice evermore. Count it all joy.' Why the word "joy" itself is listed over 160 times in the Bible, I believe. Or at least that is how many I have counted so far." She wiped the back of her hand across the side of her face to remove a tickling piece of her red hair but in doing so only managed to leave a white streak of flour upon the top line of her cheek instead.

Ever trying to be of assistance to someone in distress, Nathanael quickly took out his faded handkerchief and reached forward with one hand to wipe it away for her. "You seem... to have a bit of... um, something on your cheek." He stammered for the right words, but his nervousness at being so close to the young lady took over his ability to speak soundly.

"Really?" She looked up at him in confusion before using her other hand to try to brush away whatever it was he was seeing. Yet, without a looking glass of any kind, she only managed to succeed in making the situation far worse.

"Nevermind, you know what? You should just leave it. The flour suits you anyways." Nathanael chuckled at her pointless struggle and took his seat across from her once more on one of the high stools gathered on the other side.

Elsie rolled her eyes as she blew sideways out of her mouth to dispel it, mildly frustrated by the sudden burst of attention, but only ended up looking even more endearing in Nathanael's opinion. In the end she chose to resort to using the clean, bottom half of her apron to wipe her entire face when the previous action made her long front bangs tickle her nose horribly. "Now, you've done it? I'll never get my work done at this rate."

"My dear lady, I have not the faintest idea of what you mean." Nathanael raised both of his hands up apologetically. "Here I sit. How could I possibly be to blame?"

Squinting her eyes in playful determination now, she threw the flour covered towel from the counter directly at him and hit him square in the middle of his chest. Like an arrow aimed true to its target, it collided with his tan shirt in dramatic fashion, resulting in a fantastic cloud of white dust that flew everywhere around him with the impact.

"Ugh! I think you have mortally wounded me, Miss Summerfield!" Nathanael coughed repeatedly through the dust the assault created in a vain struggle to clear his lungs while all the while still waving the cloud away with the very rag with which he had been attacked like some form of surrender. Much like the flour that had tormented Elisie upon her face, this futile action on his part only managed to make the situation he was facing infinitely worse and soon the entire area was engulfed in a thick haze of fine dust, the morning sunbeams shifting to accentuate the tiny particles as they floated by.

"Oh, Mr. Beckett, stop. I beg you." Elsie covered her mouth and giggled incessantly unable to control her laughter at his distress and mayhem.

Upon hearing the unusual commotion from just outside while churning the butter, Mrs. Summerfield entered the room quite unexpectedly and gasped audibly at the scene. "Land's sake what a mess!"

"I'm sorry, Mrs. Summerfield. I'm afraid I got a bit carried away helping your daughter." Nathanael rolled the offending rag into a ball quickly at her entrance and hid it safely behind his back in one quick motion, fearing that Elsie would receive a portion of the blame and be reprimanded.

"It's no use trying to hide it or sweet talk me now, Preacher. I already done seen you waving the white flag," she chided him most sternly and picked up the worn-out broom beside the door before handing it to him promptly. "Now, see to this mess immediately or there will be no visiting during work hours in the future. As much as I love your preaching, I'll not have you creating more distraction than absolutely necessary, no matter the blessing your presence here gives me or anyone else in my family." She eyed the girl critically who hastily took the hint and went back to her work.

"Yes, ma'am." He obeyed immediately, feeling rightly rebuked by the woman who seemed more like his parent than his parishioner on any given day. After all, it wouldn't be right to make more work for the woman, or the young lady who was already endlessly giving on the behalf of others. Never before in all his life had he met such a gentle soul as Elsie Summerfield, and as such, he simply could not stop marveling at her goodness no matter how much he had tried to keep his thoughts distracted otherwise.

And so, Nathanael swept, while also constantly stealing long glances up at the girl who was trying diligently to finish up her baking. From the corner of the room by the front door to the hand-crafted wooden chair that held Mr. Summerfield's Bible and a finely sewn patchwork quilt, he made his way around to the front of the counter before continuing his labor throughout the entire room beyond, sweeping up all the misplaced flour into a small, white pile.

"Stop." The girl blushed at the focused attention he kept giving, resulting in a light pink glow to coat the top of each of her cheeks that almost blended in perfectly with her tiny freckles.

"Stop what?" Nathanael teased lightly back, flicking his eyebrows up just once quickly like a petulant child. "I'm merely sweeping, Miss Summerfield."

"Oh, you know exactly what I mean," she said with a huff that sounded more like a sigh than frustration as she pushed past him sweetly and placed several risen loaves into the hearth to bake.

"Are you certain?" Nathanael looked up at her innocently still admiring her from afar. "As far as I can see, I am just doing what I was told." He watched her move across the room and took in the humble nature in which she approached everything in the world around her. From the hours of baking six days of the week to the subsequent time she spent delivering all of the goods to various taverns and markets, she did everything with an air of someone who genuinely desired to serve others and not of one being compelled to work in any way. Yet he knew from the many conversations that he had enjoyed with her father, that without her help, the family would most definitely be suffering.

"You are quite aware that you mean to distract me, dear preacher. Now move along to the chapel and study or I will never finish at this rate." She shooed him out of the kitchen and then out the front door without saying another word on the subject.

"As you wish, but may I see you again, tomorrow?" Nathanael pleaded, desirous of whatever time the young woman could afford him daily.

"Not unless I finish all this baking for the tavern first. They have asked for twice as many rolls as normal this week, but I need to have them done by tomorrow's dinner. Now off with you before I get cross." Elsie smiled to reassure the man of her favor, knowing there was nothing the man could ever do that would vex her to that extent.

Nathanael took the hint and reached for her hand to kiss it lightly before leaving and smiled. "I'll be sure to stop by around six then."

"If I finish," she warned him yet again with a wag of her finger before retreating inside the kitchen to complete her chores.

~   ~   ~   ~   ~

With a feeling of deep affection, Nathanael smiled at the memory from what seemed like ages ago and picked up the small loaf of bread that lay on his desk beside his now studiously filled journal.

The months since Christmas had passed by like none he had ever encountered before in his life—full of promise, pleasure and yet also centered most strangely on a period of intense inner deliberation. Like any other preacher of his day, Nathanael had spent the majority of his time busying himself either in the meditation of Scripture, writing sermons, or by taking the time to visit at least several of the weak and infirmed among his flock every week. And yet in all of this, he had also managed to quite skillfully squeeze in not one, but four wonderful suppers with the family of Miss Elsie Summerfield since. A fact which comforted him greatly as William was often away on house calls many evenings, which only left his mind much too available for the darker thoughts the silence always brought along with it.

Nathanael would not go as far as to say that he felt utterly dependent on the man for anything other than nutrition. Yet there was also something else about their current living situation that had bothered him greatly for although he had always lived alone at the school before, the deafening quality of the silence and lack of focused occupation in his free time now unnerved him more than he cared to admit. In fact, if he were to explain it more properly, he might go as far as to say that the two of them were completely opposite in their daily routines and yet also so very similar in everything else that truly mattered.

As affable as William always was with everyone else that he met each day on his visits with his patients and Doctor Hadleigh, his friend was quite the opposite in his free time—seeking the calmness that the quiet brought him to rejuvenate his energy for yet another day. A most peculiar fact indeed seeing that not a single night had gone by this week where the man had not been totally content to pass his evening reading the overly dense medical journals that his father kept sending him or in writing letters to his friends and family both here and abroad.

But Nathanael knew that he needed something altogether different than books and journals to occupy his mind after studying for hours on end at the chapel every day. When he finished his work that was performed in the solitude of his chambers, he always found himself craving the input from physical people to fill his silence in the evenings... or rather something more tangible in nature to distract him from seeking what he should not. A series of more animated discussions perhaps, but other than passing his evenings down at the tavern with those in whom he held very little in common, there was no other place where it could be had.

In the beginning, returning to all the things with which he had become so accustomed to for the past two years had felt oddly comforting. In fact, other than some of the more unpleasant aspects of his survival, it was almost as if the whole horrible shipwreck and its aftermath had never actually happened. And yet, because of a certain piano player, he was now realizing that there was also something fundamentally lacking in the very core of his being that he had not felt for a very long time, something Sebastian had admonished him to at least consider... tangible love. It had been years since he had enjoyed the warmth and devotion of his parents' love. Nor, as he had so correctly told Sebastian, had he ever felt compelled to seek a wife throughout his many years of study. Yet, as nice as that thought might be to him now, that did not also mean that such a thing was correct for him to pursue in this newly created form either.

In the past, he had always felt more drawn to the belief that Paul and others in the Bible held in desiring to give their lives wholeheartedly and solely to God's work as Moses had suggested in Deuteronomy. And yet, given his newly formed infatuation with the lovely Miss Summerfield, he was quickly realizing just how essential each day that connection with her was becoming, almost painfully so.

But still, should he be leading her on towards something that most assuredly would not be in her best interest if she knew the whole truth about him? The conflicting thought had played itself repeatedly within his distracted mind for weeks following the Christmas service as he had laid down at night as if just the very act of reasoning it out would bring about a satisfying solution. Unfortunately, it did not. On the contrary, the overly critical and exhaustive mental deliberations had only made him feel even more uncertain about what to do next than the day before and noticeably wearier than he would have been otherwise due to the inner struggle.

"Enough." He had finally decided one morning as he threw the covers off in built-up frustration at the feeling of the all too familiar now prickles on his skin, like goosebumps running down both his arms and legs. "I will simply have to choose something, or I will go mad this way," he resolved, then added with even more dedication, "Surely, this is merely a test, a distraction if you will, from my greater purpose." Nathanael concluded firmly about the young woman and resolved once and for all to fight against the pull that drew him towards the girl and away from everything that he thought would bring him the desired stability and peace of mind in his life.

In its first conception, the plan that had begun weeks ago had been a brilliant resolution on his part, but as he soon discovered after many failed attempts, it was far more difficult to achieve in practice than in purpose. Beginning with his duties at church, he chose to engage just enough with Miss Summerfield so as to proceed through the weekly service with only a congenial relationship with the young lady, much like anyone else in his flock, and nothing more.

On the surface this action had seemed completely logical and conceivably easy to accomplish, yet as each Sunday passed, he quickly discovered that such an abusive action was utterly impossible. Her submissive spirit to his newly dismissive manner, entirely disarmed him at every turn and left him feeling indelibly smitten even more by the congenial character of the young lady for not once had she rebuked or questioned him concerning the change of his countenance towards her, nor had she treated him any differently because of it.

Still, having these new, albeit pleasant, emotions thriving within him at any given moment had only furthered to bolster the uneasy balance of his nature towards accepting her. In many ways, it was almost as if he were in a constant war, if you will, between what he wanted as a man, and what was right regarding her presence in his life, given his current occupation. So much so, that he purposed to try a different strategy altogether, only this time, something that he felt had a tad bit more ability to succeed—distraction. If he wanted to re-establish his desire to focus solely on his Savior, he would simply need to redirect his attention towards other things. Seeking to avoid this pleasant temptation, he did what most men might do in his situation. He chose to make a few, albeit necessary, changes to alleviate that discomfort by replacing his desire for companionship with another occupation entirely.

Like a man obsessed with the task before him, day after day he chose to feverishly pour himself into his work, spending every waking minute of his time either in studying or in memorizing Scripture. Yet night after night he still found that he fell asleep fitfully, dreaming of a certain Elsie Summerfield whether he wanted to or not. The entire never-ending cycle of futility was maddening, and yet altogether pleasant, too, until he woke-up that is, feeling unfilled and alone once more, with no one he could talk to about it as William would often have already left for the day.

Was he causing more damage to himself and to Elsie, by continuing to avoid his feelings concerning her? Nathanael had reasoned just this morning, while trying to swallow the last of his eggs and bacon that he had managed to finally learn how to cook, though truthfully with only sporadic success. And trying was a good word for that action, too, as he had been attempting to force himself each day to eat a little more of the offending staples of humanity as if building up a resistance to the repulsion of them. Though if he were to be completely honest, most likely anyone would have found themselves enduring the difficulty of eating his hastily concocted breakfast as it was today for the normally yellow scrambled eggs were a rather odd shade of light brown and the bacon had been most definitely blackened out of existence. It was cooked, yes, and scarcely edible, but certainly less than desirable to look at.

With a sigh of definite defeat, Nathanael scraped the bits of blackened bacon that remained in the bottom of the pan into the trash and pouted, "Elsie wouldn't have served her family charcoal on a plate."

"Thankfully not, or the rest of us would starve down at the tavern." William laughed lightly as he bound down the stairs beside him while buttoning his freshly pressed shirt all the way up to his neck. "Is it sunny today?" He grabbed his hooded cloak beside the door as a precaution before tying the clasp at his neck securely.

"Not that I have seen. Why? Do you have another patient today?" Nathanael inquired as he leaned back casually against the counter behind him and glanced out the window to affirm the weather correctly. "Yup, not a ray in the sky, so far."

"Good, but no, I was just going over to Doctor Hadleigh's this morning to learn more about his herbs. Though I wish it had decided to rain today. It would have made my visit a bit easier to maneuver without all these necessary layers. Still, perhaps I can get in a short conversation before the sun makes its way out of the cloud bank that rolled in yesterday." William slid his satchel over his head easily and smiled. "So, have you finally decided to stop avoiding Miss Summerfield already?"

A look of total shock passed over Nathanael's face at the blatant honesty his friend always displayed to him before he tried to answer. "What?"

William shook his head at Nathanael's characteristically surprised expression and waited patiently for his endearing friend to recover.

At first, Nathanael didn't know what to say. As a rule, he understood that William never meant to be nosy regarding his affairs in any way, but the man could not possibly escape the fact that hardly anyone in a town as small as theirs could have missed the well-choreographed dance he and Elsie had been performing as of late. "William, you know as well as I that she is far too kind of a person to continue to be led along by me."

With a look that spoke only of his continued friendship, William ignored his comment of self-defamation once again and grabbed a rather thick slice of wheat bread from the counter before spreading a thin layer of honey on one side as he folded it in half. "Then don't lead her along. Seems like a logical solution."

Feeling suddenly exhausted by the struggle he had been enduring for weeks, Nathanael hung his head in response to the simplicity in which William always viewed things. "I'm sorry, but I fear that I am much too indecisive of a man to simply walk away like I know that I should. In a way, just daring to consider her as a possible mate makes me think I am finally starting to truly understand Sebastian's dilemma after all."

"Please..." William rolled his eyes at him dramatically and took another bite of his breakfast, fearing that he now had two brooding vampires on his hands. "Sebastian has his own opinions and, trust me when I say that they are completely unfounded, Nathanael. Besides, you'll have to decide one way or the other about this sometime, and it might as well be sooner than later for both your sakes. Or do you want to spend the rest of eternity stubbornly sulking in some far away castle like a monk or some other such nonsense?"

"Of course not," he agreed almost reluctantly and decided once and for all to let go of his preconceived prejudices concerning their relationship for the time being. "But seriously, William... how does it feel to be right all the time?"

"Perfectly normal, why?" William tried to chuckle, but his mouth was still partially full of bread and sticky honey.

"Goodness. I'm sorry I asked." He handed his friend the linen napkin from the counter to clean up the crumbs that had spilled out onto his clean shirt. "Though I must say, why on earth you waste perfectly good honey on something you cannot even taste is beyond me?" Nathanael swiped his finger across the top of the jar and sampled just a drop of the golden substance to reassess his opinion on the subject. "Though I suppose it does tastes like something sweet, if you like that sort of thing, but that is it."

"It's just a habit I have, I guess." William shrugged innocently but mostly ignored his friend's melancholy opinion altogether. "Well, I must be off. Will I see you at supper or will you be at the Summerfield's tonight?"

"I'm not certain as of yet." Nathanael looked out the window towards the Summerfield home and pondered that thought quickly. "Today is market day so I am not sure if they will have time for company."

"Alright. If I don't see you when I return, I will assume you are otherwise engaged."

"That sounds reasonable." Nathanael nodded back distractedly and watched as his friend bid him a short goodbye with a wave of his hand and a sticky smile.

"What am I going to do God?" He waited for an audible answer to his overwhelming dilemma concerning Elsie then felt the justifiable shame wash over him immediately for not consulting with Him sooner.

"I'm so sorry, God. I've been so distracted by trying to figure all this out by myself that I forgot what should have been the most important step," he apologized audibly, then like a penitent child, took a moment to lean his head down upon his arms on top of the counter and prayed most fervently to the only person who truly knew what was best for him. "God, if Elsie is what you want for my life... or rather, what would be best for me as I serve you here on this Earth... then, please either allow it to be or close the door entirely. I am so tired of using my own logic to accomplish what only You can do. I beg only that you let it be Your decision alone and not mine to make for my wisdom on this and so much more is severely lacking. As always, I thank You for Your continued guidance and grace, dear Father. Amen," he pleaded in prayer knowing that on many other occasions in his life God had either blessed his decisions or had put a stop to them altogether. He would simply have to trust Him to do so again where Elsie Summerfield was concerned.

And yet, though the decision had been finally made, his feeling of insecurity did not totally diminish. Much like everything else in his life now, this path for the future was no longer planned out in a neatly arranged order of events. Instead, it was as blank as the next page in his journal, and that fact alone unnerved him as much as it thrilled him.

With a lighter heart and a clearer direction, Nathanael threw on his brown cloak that rested on its peg next to the door and made his way over to the chapel on the other side of town. Once inside, he entered through his study door and locked it behind him, intending to spend the morning researching something Elsie had told him the other day.

On his desk within lay his Bible, which was already opened to I Thessalonians, his favorite quill pen and a recently baked loaf of bread. The same kind incidentally as the one he had helped Elsie to create the other day.

"What a wonderful surprise. She must have stopped by on the way to the market." Nathanael sighed pleasantly, as he remembered the visit they had enjoyed weeks before and smiled at the memory. Funny as it was, he doubted that in all his life he would ever look at flour in quite the same way, nor feel any less love for the woman who had formed it.

"Focus, Nathanael," he rebuked himself sternly while removing his coat and took his seat behind the desk, remembering the prayer he had uttered just that morning. Because of Elsie's recent admonition during the flour incident, or so he had started to humorously call it, he had decided to spend his time this morning delving deeper into his cherished text to see if what she had said was true. After several hours, and a plethora of page turning thereafter, he was pleasantly surprised to discover that not only was she right, but there were also many other wonderful analogies that could be made regarding it.

Pleased again beyond measure by his progress and the wonderful truths that he found therein, he penned the verses down eagerly into his outline and closed his journal with a smile before he stood up and admired the view outside of his window, satisfied with his sermon at last. The landscape which so often greeted him here was always exactly what he needed on any given day as he studied, dependably pleasant and calm with none of the more irritating distractions like what William's incessantly ticking clock gave. No, God's abundantly diverse creation with all its variations, constantly arrived in colorful splendor with its red and brown brilliantly colored cardinals searching for berries beneath the holly trees, and squirrels foraging for winter chestnuts. It was precisely what he required daily to help him focus on the task God had prepared for him and not on the many things his body craved most of all. Yet today, it also afforded him a view of Miss Summerfield.

Like a man lost in awe, he watched her a moment longer as she made her way up the street, basket in hand, returning from her deliveries. Her cheeks reddened from the robust exercise; she was a beautiful sight to behold as her face shone with the joy of the winter sunlight and something more within her.

With a shy smile, she waved at him as she passed, and the very sight of her made him blush with anticipation of their next conversation.

Hoping to encourage her, as well, he smiled just a little in response before lifting a hand timidly to acknowledge her salutation and forced himself once more to measure his wildly, pounding heart to a more normal cadence.

In truth, the young lady was as talented as she was stunning. In fact, she was... well... everything he could have ever wanted in a wife, if that was indeed what God had intended for him. And yet, though he was not as romantically inclined as those men in the books and journals he had sometimes read out of sheer diversion, he most certainly could not refute the attraction he felt towards her the moment he saw her at the pianoforte last Christmas nor the countless moments thereafter. Just watching her here today, he was also forced to finally admit that she was steadily becoming his sole purpose for survival. And if he were to be completely honest, the most wonderful thing in all his existence. So much so, that he was tempted more than once since he arrived today to go over to her home and invite her to take a stroll unaccompanied with him after dinner tonight but thought the better of it. Not only because he did not fully trust himself as a vampire, but also more importantly because he did not trust himself as a man.

That last thought hung itself longer within his head more than it probably should have, given his position. Feeling a bit divinely rebuked for the second time today, he immediately pulled it back and focused instead on the more uplifting or rather platonic events of their outing just last week.

If he was going to make this courtship between them a success, he needed to keep everything, including his more human emotions, in their proper place. William had been right, as he so often was, that a life devoid of human attachment was obviously not what God had intended for him. Though his only problem now was how he would ever navigate that delicate balance between both of his worlds, the darkness and the light, and whether or not he would ultimately be successful.

Nathanael took his seat once more behind his neatly organized desk and opened his journal, a fresh quill in hand.

Journal Entry for February 15th
In the time that I have spent with the Summerfield family, I have quickly discovered that the Summerfields are a delightful household with ten little ones of various ages, all with hair as orange as cooked carrots mixed with the deep redness of a summer tomato. Elsie is, of course, the most highly favored child, being the oldest with only one other daughter to speak of, but the rest of the boys can usually be found running around playfully within the outer yard or managing to get into mischief on any given day.

Elsie's father, Gabe, the muscled patriarch of the family, maintains the threshing and millworks near the center of town, which provides ample funds for his ever-burgeoning debts and family. While Elsie, on the other hand, spends the good part of her day practicing her music and helping her mother with the baked goods they sell at market.

Nathanael closed his journal with satisfaction and sat at his desk awhile longer pondering the words he had just written therein and wondered how many other people throughout the course of time had collected their thoughts in such a way. Many had no doubt probably included far more entertaining details about their lives and many adventures, but his journal was different. In his musings, he felt more content to merely keep to the factual aspects of life than in the overinflation of the reality of his achievements.

Though he was also fairly more certain, whether plain or otherwise, that anything he recorded thereafter regarding his relationship with Miss Summerfield would scarcely do justice to the beautiful lady he was coming to admire with each passing day. And yet, if he were to somehow write that truth down, he felt like he would be betraying that delicate balance existing between them more than dutifully recording a piece of living history. Which in the end, the conflicting turmoil of indecision regarding her inclusion, almost made him feel more connected to his human side in a way, and not wholly given to the darkness... at least not yet.

And perhaps there was something else he needed to consider. Perhaps Elsie was also right about him, too. Maybe he was given to a great deal of solemness in his life right now. He hadn't thought so in the past. But then again, wasn't a bit of seriousness where matters of the heart were concerned prudent? He hoped so, though only time would tell.

And time... as Nathanael knew only too well, was the one thing he had in the largest of quantities.

Chapter Thirteen

February 22nd, 1793

"You mean you have never built a snowman before?" Elsie's younger brother stared up at Nathanael in obvious incredulity, not wanting to be entirely disrespectful of the man but was still completely confused as to how someone could be as old as he and not enjoy one of the simplest of things winter had to offer.

"No, I haven't. I never really liked playing outside as a child." Nathanael wrinkled his nose at the idea before hugging his arms tightly around his woolen coat for added warmth.

"Whyever not?" The young boy, not much older than twelve, continued his interrogation while busily pushing a large mound of snow over and over on itself to increase it in size.

"I suppose for the main reason that I'm not overly fond of everything that resides in it like bugs and dirt, and well, you get the idea. For the most part, I much prefer my books over nature any day no matter what form it is supplied, snow and all," Nathanael answered him sincerely. "Do you like to read, Michael?" He tried to find something in common with the boy because he knew it would please Elsie that he was interested in the members of her family, too.

"Nah." The boy shoved the ball one more time and stopped since it now reached up to the middle of his thighs. "Only what I have to do in school. You know how it is."

"It's important to go to school. Isn't that right, Mr. Beckett?" Elsie prompted him as she pulled both her woolen mittens farther up on her wrists to protect her delicate skin from the exposure of the cold.

"Why, yes!" Nathanael agreed readily. "A man must prove himself in all his ways if he is to achieve true greatness. Or at least that is what they taught me in seminary. Which is a very high level of school for those wishing to enter the ministry, Michael. Not unlike a finishing school in that regard, but more specialized in the area of theology, and incidentally, only for men," he explained to the boy hoping to draw his interest further on the subject.

Still not convinced in the least bit towards continuing on in his education, the boy squinted one eye shut and eyed Nathanael harshly. "There is nothing great about working at a mill which is probably what I will be doing every day next year so I might as well stop wasting my time with books now."

Elsie frowned at his pessimistic assessment of his future life but kept silent as she bent over to pick up the next portion of the snowman.

"Here, let me assist." Nathanael walked over to her quickly and lifted one side of the heavy mass with her.

"Just put it on top here," the boy instructed in a tone as if he were the supervisor of a great building plan.

Half-waddling sideways under the heavy load, the two adults carried it over to the larger bottom and placed it gently on top, steadying it while the younger lad secured it with extra packing around the base.

"Michael, you know that Papa said you did not have to work at the mill." Elsie began rolling another snowball but stopped when it was only half the size as the one before. "Besides, if Papa's work doesn't thrill you, maybe you might want to try a different type of apprenticeship. There are plenty in town to be had, like carpentry for example since you seem to be so interested in building things."

"Maybe." The boy picked up the ball with a shrug and answered matter-of-factly something that sounded more like an excuse than an actual opinion, "We can't all be talented like you Elsie. Some of us just need to be content at being mediocre."

"Oh, Michael." Elsie sighed. "That is just a sad view of things, and you know it." She dusted the excess snow from off her gloves and frowned at the boy.

Nathanael watched the exchange between the siblings and pondered awhile on their unique relationship. In his own family he had never been blessed with brothers or sisters to speak of. It had always been just the three of them at the table discussing life and philosophy until in his late teens when his father died. Then, it was just the two of them at the market and farming tasks before his mother also succumbed just a year later, joining her husband in the grassy knoll beside the stone church.

Many had said that her death was because of a heart condition that had plagued her for years, but he knew the real reason and though it had most certainly involved her heart, it was not in the way any of them had envisioned. She had simply missed his father too greatly for her heart to remain on this Earth without him.

At the end it was just himself as he sailed off to new adventures, trying to live out the life his parents and he had always imagined. The trip they would have been quite excited to take together with their son had they been given the chance.

"Noone should ever be content with being just average, Michael," Nathanael said quietly as he tried to quell the lump forming in his throat at the tender memories from long ago. "Or at least that was something along the lines of what my father used to say to me when I made similar statements."

"What was he like? Your father." Elsie placed her mittens in her pocket and reached over to lay a comforting hand on Nathanael's arm, grateful for his added wisdom.

"Oh, he was someone most men would probably pass on the street and never give another glance, I suppose. Not that he was bothered by that fact in the least. He actually much preferred his life of quiet existence and the contentedness that surrounded that simple anonymity."

"Sounds like someone else I know." She smiled, then asked another question since this was the first time he had really opened up about his past since they had met. "Was he a preacher like yourself?"

"No, actually he was a teacher at a university when I was younger, though I think he much preferred the life of a country schoolmaster more during in my teen years."

"Oh, was he your teacher, then?" Elsie looked up at him in curious admiration.

"He tried; God bless his soul." Nathanael chucked remembering the struggle his father had endured while attempting to instruct him. "Though I am sure over the years that he wished I had retained more than I exhibited many times over. Truth be told, I didn't like school all that much as a 12-year-old either. Math was always entirely far too complicated for me to grasp and the Greek philosophers' logic equally dizzying. But I loved other kinds of books, so I think that encouraged him to keep trying, even when he was forced to hunt for me in the hidden stacks of books at the university's library."

Elsie's brother smiled up at him at his honest revelation and continued his work solidifying the snow figure next to the tree. "What made you change your mind then about school?"

"When he died, I realized how much I wanted to be just like him. Life is funny that way, I guess." Nathanael stamped his foot to dislodge the snow from it, but also more importantly, to distract himself from his more emotional thoughts.

Watching his struggle to maintain his composure, Elsie's hand tightened on his sleeve. "You don't have to tell me anymore if it is uncomfortable for you to do so."

"Oh, no. Please, it is truly nice to speak of them once more, Miss Summerfield. I haven't had the chance to do so in almost four years." He smiled before looking up into her green eyes and placed his right hand on top of her own. "I had just forgotten how much I missed them, I suppose."

With a jolt, the girl's eyes widened in response to his touch, forgetting their previous conversation entirely. "Land's sake alive, Preacher! Your hands are like ice today!"

Instantly frightened by his carless mistake, Nathanael immediately retreated his hand back inside his pocket in alarm and began uttering the most convincing excuse he could manage to deter her curiosity, "I'm sorry, it must be from working with the snow just now. I've always been a bit cold-natured to begin with, and when I forget to wear my gloves, it only makes the situation worse. But not to worry, Miss. They will soon be right as rain."

Like the experienced mother that she was, Elsie did not seem overly convinced of his pathetic explanation and chose instead to extend her pocketed mittens out to him, forcing his complied obedience with the motion. "Just put these on. You won't be able to help me later if you can't feel your fingers."

"Later? Do we have plans?" Nathanael put them on appreciatively and rubbed the palms of the wool mittens together to increase their warmth from the friction they created. Though from recent experience, he knew that the repeated action would only change the temperature of his hands slightly by doing so, yet the motion as his hands slid over the other in turn did help to distract him from the anxiety he was now feeling by his negligence.

"I was rather hoping we might try practicing that duet together again today. The one we were working on for Pasha." Elsie placed a small pebble in each of the places for the snowman's eyes and mouth.

"You play the piano, too, sir?" The boy exclaimed again, more in surprise than in admiration. "I thought that was for girls."

Nathanael chuckled at his honesty once more. "Oh, I don't know if it is for any such distinction, though admittedly I am nowhere near as talented as your sister," he affirmed before adding truthfully, "Elsie is trying to teach me how to play, though I am still a terrible student in this subject, as well."

The boy nodded, then stood back to admire his work. "Looks about right."

Nathanael glanced over at Elsie and swiftly leaned in closer to whisper in her ear his agreement to her brother's reply. "As do you."

The girl blushed once more at his favorable comment, then playfully batted him away in polite response. "You best be heading home now, Michael. I believe it is almost time to milk the cows."

"Aww, so soon?" The boy did not seem the least bit interested in returning home when so much fun was being held elsewhere.

"Yes." Elsie gave him an admonishing smile, then added, "I'll be home presently to help you feed them after Nathanael's lesson."

"Alright," Michael replied without further complaint and waved back at the couple when he was halfway down the road, checking to make sure the two were still watching him as if he might suddenly make an unexpected detour of some kind.

With a grin and a slightly raised hand, Nathanael waved back at him, then offered his companion his arm, which she took most readily. "Did you know that you are incredibly good with children, too?"

"Well, I should hope that I ought to be by now with eight brothers and a sister to care for." Elsie walked slowly along the path beside him but fell quiet and withdrawn as if something was weighing heavily on her mind.

"Did I say something wrong?" Nathanael glanced over at her and prodded respectfully, slightly alarmed by the change, for she was normally never this reticent.

"Oh, it's nothing." The girl tried to seem unaffected while focusing instead on other items in the scenery on the opposite side of him to distract herself from whatever it was that was sincerely bothering her.

Unconvinced or rather unwilling to let the moment pass, Nathanael brought them to a slow stop just outside the outer stone wall of the church cemetery and turned himself directly to face her. "What is it, Elsie? Surely you know by now that nothing you could ever say would upset me in the slightest."

With great hesitation, Elsie held back her question a few moments longer, then bit her lower lip a few times before quietly asking just one question with even greater deliberation, "I know this is probably far too early to ask such a thing, but by any chance, were you hoping to have a house full of children someday?"

Nathanael's eyes widened with surprise at her intimate question for he had never truly given the subject much thought, nor had he ever envisioned himself as a father. Though on the other hand, as appealing as such a union as theirs would be, he was also struck by the sheer fact that he had regrettably not even stopped long enough to give the proper consideration as to what a marriage like theirs would even entail, especially given his rather unique limitations now.

Misinterpreting his startled reaction and most definite pause thereafter, Elsie quickly retracted her question, looking more hurt by his response than in the acceptance of his already assumed answer. "I'm sorry. I should not have been so bold to have asked it of you. Please forgive me." She deftly managed to diffuse the apparent impropriety of her question and started to walk once more without him towards the chapel door at a quicker pace than before, trying to put as much distance between herself and her embarrassment as possible.

Fresh guilt at watching her leave so unceremoniously washed over him immediately for his obvious misstep. Like a man grasping for a rope for his survival, he reached forward to catch her, seizing her hand gently to stop her escape and holding it tightly within his own before responding with a genuineness that begged to flow out of him. "Miss Summerfield, please do not mistake my silence in any way as my disapproval of you or the topic in question. I simply had never contemplated such a question before." He finished and watched her body relax as he looked down upon her worried face.

"But do you want any children, Nathanael?" She maintained her position a good two feet away from him as society demanded of any young woman no matter her marital intentions.

Seeing her lingering doubt remaining, he took two careful steps closer to her, desiring merely to reassure her of her erroneous assumption but also fearing that if he remained any farther away from her his heart might quite literally break watching her suffer like she was. "Though I do suppose that children are most certainly a wonderful blessing for most families, Elsie. I am afraid I lack... oh, how do I say this correctly? Um, the necessary temperament and patience... for what all of that would entail." He skillfully crafted his reply for the majority of it was true. Being an only child himself, he had never once wanted a large family to speak of, nor any children for that matter, even before his transition. And now with the situation being as it was, he had fully accepted the fact that he would never have any children of his own, at least not in the conventional way.

He rubbed the fingers of her hand within his mittened glove and waited for her disapproval. Yet despite his initial fears that such an explanation would make her even more despaired, Elsie seemed entirely at ease with his response, happy even.

Which only made the overabundant joy of her countenance worry him even more than the previous question. "I'm sorry, but you will have to pardon <u>me</u> this time for asking this, but most women of my acquaintance would be utterly mortified by such a declaration. Yet <u>you</u> smile?" Nathanael's brow furrowed slightly in the puzzlement of it all.

"Then let us be content to say that we are much the same you and I and leave it at that, shall we?" Elsie drew closer to him still before placing her warm hand upon his wind-burnt cheek.

With a sigh of relief, Nathanael felt an authentic smile appear once more before taking her hand and kissing her fingers gently, reveling in the softness of her skin against his lips. "And you truly would not mind it being just the two of us and nothing more for all eternity?"

With an equally satisfied smile, Elsie shook her head. "Most definitely not. I should think that I have raised enough children already for at least two lifetimes. As much as I love my family dearly, I for one am ready for some peace and quiet."

The two laughed lightly together in mutual understanding and continued on their way to the chapel before stepping inside and closing the door behind them.

"Would you like me to hang your coat up for you?" Nathanael offered as he removed the gifted mittens from before and held them out to her.

With a shake of her head, she took them and placed them safely within her coat pockets once more before answering, "No, thank you. I am still a bit chilly. And, though I would love to play the piano for hours upon hours on end, I can't stay long. Mother <u>is</u> expecting me to help with dinner, and I did just promise Michael that I would help him with his chores."

"Oh, yes, of course. Then, do we still have time to practice at least once?"

"Definitely." She started to walk down the aisle, then stopped abruptly and turned to look at him from the center of the church. "As long as we are asking uncomfortable questions today, may I ask another?"

Without looking up, Nathanael shrugged and answered her quickly without thinking, feeling completely at ease now with the trust building between them, "I don't see why not."

Elsie bit her lip once more and, unlike her normally quiet manner, almost blurted out the most startling question he could have ever imagined her asking, "Can you see us marrying someday, Nathanael? Not now, mind you. That would be completely sudden and to be honest, a bit too soon to even consider, but someday? Maybe?"

The question brought him up short and forced him to finally evaluate the weight of the decision before him. *Was such a thing as marriage even possible for*

William or himself? Or did being doomed to a spiritual and Earthly damnation also mean that he was cursed to a life of eternal abstinence, too? More importantly, was he being selfish to even consider this possibility or was this yet another test to see if he was truly trusting God concerning her?

As the days had passed since he had prayed for God's direction, he had waited patiently for God to guide him otherwise concerning her, but as he did, he had found that his affection for her had not waned in the slightest. On the contrary, it had only grown stronger and deeper like a well-planted flower that had been finally allowed its chance to flourish within the right soil, with few of the concerns that had plagued him in the very beginning. Still, lacking any Divine leadership in either direction, he had simply been content to enjoy her company for the present than to think about all the problems and complexities such a union brought along with it. Yet with the question finally asked today, he was uncertain as to whether or not he should pursue this relationship at all, or how to answer Miss Summerfield in general regarding it.

Slightly stunned once more, he stared back at her from the last pew and cleared his throat nervously, almost wincing at the crack in his voice as he replied, "I admit freely that the thought has crossed my mind at least more than once since I arrived, but I am afraid I cannot provide the answer you seek, at least not yet."

Appearing slightly stunned by his suddenly anxious reply, Elsie nodded twice in stoic acceptance but thankfully did not press him further on the subject. "I understand." As if the topic of conversation were suddenly closed, she mechanically turned around and continued over to the piano forte, seemingly restored to her normal disposition of quiet servitude. Yet also more importantly, far from the playful and honest transformation he had seen only moments earlier.

Feeling more than a little bit apprehensive by the abrupt change and disappointed countenance, Nathanael approached the instrument timidly, unsure as to what his next response should be.

Elsie, on the other hand, did not acknowledge his presence whatsoever, but simply patted the seat next to her in silent repose, waiting patiently for his compliant acceptance.

Nathanael walked around the bench and sat directly to her left, unsure what else to do when the woman clearly wanted nothing more than to forget she had ever spoken. "Elsie..."

Still unwilling to converse further, Elsie placed the three pieces of music on the stand in front of them and closed her eyes to collect herself once more, obviously focused only now on the lesson at hand.

Nathanael did the same, though albeit more hesitantly, and as they had done on so many other lessons in the past, the two methodically laid their hands upon the piano in unison and attempted to play the selected piece though both of them made mistake after mistake upon the keys before they had even finished half of the first page.

"Elsie, stop, please." With a deep sigh of defeat mixed with an equal share of painful regret for having inadvertently hurt her feelings, Nathanael finally put his hands gently on top of hers and held them there above the keys.

Her eyes followed his hands and up his arms until they reached his eyes, her own brimming over with a wellspring of emotions that she had been carefully concealing. "I should never have presumed so much. I just thought that…"

"Oh, Elsie…" He closed his hands around hers and pulled them closer to his chest. "You need never apologize to me for anything, least of all this. Though I realize now that my answer was not what it should have been. I never intended to hurt you so." He lifted her chin slightly higher and leaned in so close to her that he could almost touch his forehead against her own. "I want you to share with me your dreams and your struggles. Your honesty helps our relationship grow. As a man, the only thing my mind wants to do right now is take you into my arms and never let you leave. But please also understand, that as a preacher, I must set that aside and wait on God's direction first in decisions like these, nothing more, nothing less. A commitment to marriage is not mine alone to make, no matter how I might feel about the very beautiful woman sitting beside me at this piano."

"And if He says no?" A tear slid down the opposite side of her cheek before she finally closed her eyes to hide the overwhelming emotions that she felt were far too soon to be experiencing.

"Oh, Elsie, how could our God in Heaven ever refuse me, you?" Nathanael reached up and gently brushed away the liquid from one of her cheeks with his thumb. "No good thing will He withhold to them which walk uprightly, true?" He tried to be as encouraging as possible without helplessly giving in to the desire he wanted most of all in this moment—to kiss the soft lips in front of him and stop them from quivering. "We must have faith in that and trust Him for the rest. Agreed?"

Elsie smiled and looked away from him at last, composing herself with a deep breath in and out, then asked, "Shall we try this again?"

Nathanael nodded and released her hands reluctantly at last.

With renewed peace, they played through the next two pages of the composition with far fewer issues than before. Each playing off the others' successes and failures to create a continuous melody.

Yet it was at the moment when they both reached almost the end of the score that the door, in the back of the chapel, hit the wall with an audible thud suddenly interrupting them. It's echo shattering the peaceful setting and their stolen moment of solitude.

As if sensing an unseen danger approaching, Nathanael's senses heightened instantly as he gripped the woman beside him in reactive protection, his arms enfolding her easily within them.

"You will never believe the letter I have just received!" William strode through the door next and over to the back of the pews just within, his face utterly contorted though only with the slightest flush of color on his cheeks. Moreover, with every step he took therein, there was also a fire and fury dancing within his eyes that now matched the irritation Nathanael felt at the unwelcomed disruption.

"William?" Nathanael released Elsie immediately, so as to protect her honor, and stood up in front of her in response not knowing what his friend's intentions were for he had never seen him in such a state. "Is something the matter?"

Equally, momentarily startled by his friend's response, William glanced up at the young lady at the piano as if finally noticing her for the first time. "Oh! My sincerest apologies for the outburst, Miss Summerfield. I did not mean to frighten you."

"Doctor Wells," she acknowledged his presence kindly. "If you have ever visited my home, sir, you would know that I am quite accustomed to such displays of enigmatic energy. In fact, they are almost expected." She smiled sweetly and closed the lid of the piano without a second thought.

"Yes, well…" William stammered, feeling instantly at odds with himself for his rude behavior while still incensed by the purpose of his initial mission.

"Here, let me escort you out." Nathanael politely side-stepped his friend in the center aisle while walking her to the door in the back.

Feeling out of place from the peculiarity of his arrival, William bowed slightly in her direction as she passed giving her the deference one in her position should deserve. "I'm so sorry, Nathanael. I should have looked before I spoke."

Not wishing to cause a further scene, Nathanael only raised his hand to pause his apology but did not address William directly. "May I come by tomorrow?" Nathanael focused on Elsie instead.

"You would be most welcome any time, Mr. Beckett, you know that," she added graciously.

Placing the outer door between William's view and Miss Summerfield, he leaned in and kissed the top of her hand briefly in farewell and watched her leave before turning back to face his friend with an almost irritated look of disapproval at the sudden intrusion. "Is it from Emile?" Nathanael guessed randomly as no one else in William's life had seemed to bring out the same emotional reaction in him as that man always did. In fact, for the past two months, not one word had been written about anything in the French chronicles except for that which was occurring in the social upheaval there, which assured them of only one thing, Emile was at least not being conspicuous enough to warrant a mob's attention.

"No." William shook his head in fevered rage. "I wish it had been a letter from that pompous man. That would have been a sheer delight compared to this letter. Though it is also true that on board our ship he found a unique delight in being a thorn in my side, he has never once made my blood boil as it does now! Quite the opposite, in fact. Compared to this, Emile was merely a comical nuisance."

Alarmed even more so, Nathanael drew closer to his friend and took the offered letter William was holding out before beginning to scan the contents suspiciously.

My Dearest Son,

It was with great joy that I received your letters these past few months. Once again, your mother has asked me to tell you that hearing you had survived that dreaded wreck has brought a great joy back to her heart that I feared would grip her unto death. As you might expect from her exuberant remarks made thereafter, no parent ever intends to outlive their child, so your safety was highly cherished... by both of us.

The papers are still talking all about it to this day. They are calling it a storm similar to that of the "The Great Storm" of 1701. Though sadly, I do not think that anyone knows the exact count of those who perished at sea that day as so many ships were lost, including your own fair vessel. But I digress...

The true purpose of my letter is to pass on to you a message from one of your acquaintances from that ship. You remember a Doctor Malcom Clarke, don't you? Of course, you do. Well, I saw him the other day near the port in London while I was returning to visit a patient in the most bizarre of semi-fevered states. The young man, not barely older than yourself, William, had all the appearances of one who was suffering from severe dehydration coupled with a rather bizarre form of acute blood loss.

I am sad to report that though I tried my best to treat him, I learned the next day from Doctor Clarke that the lad had expired sometime in the night.

I know you will understand this when I say that it is always hard as a doctor when you lose a patient, but to lose one under such mysterious circumstances and equally strange diagnosis was quite disturbing to me. So much so, that I have taken to consulting my many journals, seeking out ways that I might be able to help others should this particular presentation of symptoms ever occur again. If you have any insight into this condition, I would most heartily welcome it as it has bothered me greatly to this day even considering it.

Your brother and sisters send you their love and hope that you will at least visit by Pasha so that we may spend one more holiday together as a family. You will try to come, won't you?

Oh, before I forget, I must also pass along a brief message from Doctor Clarke, as well. When I told him about your practice in Wakefield, he kindly asked me to send you his regards and said he will see you again soon. I am not precisely sure what he may have meant by that, but I am sending it along as he said it, anyways.

Are you planning another trip to the Americas? I pray not. Whether or not I support you in whatever location you should decide to set up your practice thereafter, I fear that your mother may not survive another stressful journey like that so soon.

Please write back as soon as is most convenient.

Your devoted father,

Doctor Joseph Wells

Having completed the reading of the letter, Nathanael looked up at his friend, his eyes opened wide with astonishment, not at the letter itself per say, but more out of sheer disbelief at how William was reacting to it, for though William gripped his hands firmly together in front of him they still physically shook with a temper threatening to burst through at any given moment. "William... please... be composed. It's just a letter, not a challenge," he warned softly as he attempted to soothe his friend's demeanor, suddenly extremely grateful that he had sent Elsie home when he did.

"I was so sure that he had perished on the ship!" William finally exploded, releasing much of the energy that had been carried along with him from wherever he had just come.

Nathanael moved around the chapel quickly as he closed the outer doors securely shut to avoid any possibility of listening ears, sensing the conversation would be taking a more vocal turn at last. "So, Doctor Clarke is in London now it would appear. That is quite unexpected." He chose his words very carefully not wanting to upset his friend any further.

"Yes! And did you read what my father says? The man is up to his old habits again, Nathanael. He is killing people! People like Emile! Like Sebastian!"

William paced wildly up and down the center aisle, letting his voice echo freely against the walls without any caution.

"People like you and me," Nathanael added calmly.

"Yes, people like me." William gritted his teeth together so tightly the words barely escaped his lips.

"Then what can we do?" Nathanael bit his lower lip, worried about what the next possible action might be that William might suggest. The last time William had been this angry, he had forced him to accompany him on a suicide mission to capture Emile. One that had ultimately culminated in him having to participate in an untimely burial. "It is not like there is an army that can be hired to stop every marauding vampire that chooses to live as they were created, William. Though we may think ourselves more righteous in how we choose to live otherwise, is it just to condemn his actions simply because he is obeying his innate nature? Where should we draw the line where morality is concerned?"

"That seems like a rather strange point of view, coming from you, Preacher, but it is also far easier to say such a thing when you do not know the victims," William replied disdainfully before suddenly grabbing Nathanael tightly by the lapel on both sides, his fists clenched by his increasing desperation. "Don't you see? He is in London, Nathanael. My London, Nathanael."

"Yes," Nathanael spoke slowly and nodded downward, not understanding his fervor fully as of yet. "And we are all vampires because of him, but how should that knowledge move me to action? I had to make my peace months ago with what I had become. I see no reason to rehash old wounds that can never be mended now."

William let him go instantly and turned around to pace, his voice holding less anger now. Instead, it was replaced by the emotion most expected from a revelation such as this. "This is so much bigger than the four of us, Nathanael. Doctor Clarke knows all about me. He even knows my family. What is to stop him from taking his revenge on me by hurting one of them?"

"But why do you think he would take revenge on you at all, William? You barely knew the man a week," Nathanael stated the obvious, still completely confused as to why William might think such a thing.

"Because of what he said as he was trying to kill Emile on the ship that day. He said I was a witness to his crimes," William explained, then shook his head at his friend's innocence on the subject.

"I see." Nathanael clasped his hands behind his back and thought deeply about the story before him. "And you think that is enough for him to seek out your family, too?"

"Truthfully... I don't know, but fear can be a powerful thing, too. If he thinks I will divulge his secrets to anyone of authority and endanger his current lifestyle, he may act on it. Yet there is also one other thing to consider—his anger. Though I doubt he knows if any of the rest of you survived the shipwreck or not, he was absolutely livid with me on the ship for saving both you and Sebastian. If he were to discover that you now existed as vampires, there is no telling how he might react because of it. The moment the wave washed him overboard was the last time I saw him alive, or as much as any of us are now. So, we can probably assume that my father's innocent mentioning of my miraculous survival probably triggered this current confrontation and nothing more, or why else, do you suppose, he would he send me such a message?"

"Saying he will see you again is not exactly a threat of revenge, William." Nathanael tried to reason with him further.

"True, but you were not there when he was trying to kill me, Nathanael. You did not see the look of pure unadulterated hatred in his eyes for both for me and Emile. I'll never forget it. Besides, even if the threat is intended for me alone, I could not bear it if he were to kill a member of my family when...when..."

"When you could do something about it." Nathanael embraced his friend kindly before drawing in a long breath and exhaling the words he knew William needed to hear most of all, "Then of course, you must go."

William pulled back, looking speechless and grateful all at the same time. "But do you think you can survive a few weeks without me?"

"Of course, William." Nathanael rolled his eyes at the man's overprotectiveness. "I have actually been giving that a great deal of thought since we first arrived last December should the occasion ever occur. As useless as I may appear on the surface, I am not wholly devoid of resources. Though at the moment, I think I would prefer to try something along the lines of what my Savior once did in the wilderness. It shouldn't be that difficult to do the same as I have fasted many before when I was younger. It is altogether different now in this form, I freely admit, but the overlying principle of the matter should still remain the same no matter where the nutrition comes from." He tried to give William the calm assurance that he needed to proceed on his journey without feeling an obligation to him in any way.

"But that was food, Nathanael. And you are not God." William shook his head at the cracks he saw in his friend's simple logic, but did not discourage him in any way.

"True on both accounts." Nathanael's brows lifted again before he sighed. "Look, I am not naïve enough to think that this will not be a difficult task. It always is. But with the Lord's help, I will endeavor to see it through until you return. You are returning, right?"

"Most definitely. There is truly nowhere else I would rather be, Nathanael Beckett." William sat down finally in the brown pew beside him, exhausted by the emotions of his argument. "Please do use at least half of the supply we keep here for emergencies. I'll take the rest with me for the journey. I am sure I can manage something in London once I am there."

"Seems fairly sensible." Nathanael rubbed his fingers absentmindedly on the smooth wood on the back of the pew next to him.

"And I won't stay long, Nathanael. I promise. Only long enough to be sure that my family is safe and to discourage Doctor Clarke from ever contacting any one of us ever again." William's face filled with a furious determination once again.

"Thou shalt not kill, Doctor Wells," Nathanael replied out of rhetorical habit.

William laughed, though it was not his usual lighthearted laughter mixed with merriment. This expression sounded, much darker instead, and far more menacing. "God made his decision about me when the ship went down, Nathanael, and I will do what I must in London."

Nathanael nodded with folded hands. "I understand, and I do not judge you for it."

William's eyes cooled considerably at his simple affirmation, and his playful smile returned once more. "I have learned that you, of all people, would not."

"When will you leave? Today?"

"Yes, immediately even, as there is a stage departing in a quarter of an hour." William stood and began walking towards the door.

"Then you must go and prepare at once. When you return, you will find me here studying, most likely," Nathanael assured him.

"And I will return, Nathanael. I give you, my word." William stopped to pledge faithfully.

"Then I wish you His blessings on your quest and God speed, my friend." Nathanael tried to give him his most reassuring smile in return—the one he gave his congregation when he was attempting to comfort them about something important. "Oh, and one last thing..." Nathanael called after him.

"Yes?" William turned around at the gate.

"Be sure to leave that bottle from Señor Moretti on the table in your room... just in case I have need of it. I am not sure what on earth I will do should it become necessary, but it might be nice to have it just the same."

William cast him a skeptical glance of incredulity at the very idea he was insinuating before calling back to him as he walked away, "You shan't have need of it, I assure you. I will be back sooner than you think!"

With a heavy heart filled with a sudden anxiousness that refused to be quieted, Nathanael held one hand up in farewell. "I hope so, dear William. I hope so."

Chapter Fourteen

February 23rd, 1793

The candles flickered in the white tiled room as Emile sat in his bath enjoying his rather splendid view from the small window to his left. Everything within its panes danced with light and color like a palette of one of those artists down by the Seine. Night had fallen, and with it the moon had brilliantly taken over for the sun in painting its cool beams along the scenery before him. Flickering lights danced like gypsies in the stained-glass windows over Notre Dame, its gargoyles appropriately poised high above the buttresses to protect its patrons from hidden dangers, like himself.

"Sanctuary indeed," Emile grumbled sarcastically and took a sip of his wine, needing something to numb him from the dismal activities of the day. From his inquiries into yet another one of his friend's disappearances to his meeting with his solicitor, nothing whatsoever had gone well for him at all today, which only frustrated him more when he had returned home empty-handed.

Closing his eyes to focus better on relaxing away the lingering irritation that remained, he thought back to the days of his youth when things were far simpler. For years he had joyfully spent his afternoons playing with his elder brother within the trees of his family's estate or running off to create some kind of adventure with him. For two rambunctious boys, his family home had always been a place of safety, protection and dependability as a child. I guess he could say it was his own personal form of sanctuary of sorts at the time, but not now. Today it was more likely to be full of ghosts and memories than shelter of any kind.

"Poor boy, how did Gabriel never catch on to my tricks?" He muttered humorously with a smirk and took another sip of his wine.

More than once, he had helpfully placed a ladder for the two of them to climb skyward within those majestic giants, only to mercilessly leave his terrified, older brother behind, clinging feebly to a higher limb. Oh, his mother had made sure that the servants were always called sometime later for his brother's repeated rescue, and he <u>had</u> been punished for it many times over by his father, but never very severely.

His father, though normally stricter with his brother than with himself, was an extremely perceptive man by nature and as such, he had seen right through his trickeries and schemes to the man he might become one day and did his best to prevent it. Maybe that was why he admired him so, and William, too, now that he thought of it. The doctor, through no fault of his own, tended to act just like his father in many ways when he rebuked him. And though his admonishment never stung as much as his father's had, Emile had learned to see the value of it. In truth, a part of him even missed his former companion. Yet not enough to return to England or wherever the good doctor had finally chosen to take up residence.

His mother, on the other hand, was nothing at all like his father. She often referred to her youngest son lovingly as her petulant child and spoiled him outright. Beyond reasonable consideration for someone who should have clearly known better, she saw no purpose in scolding him for things that any other boy his age might do. After all, his tricks were usually harmless in nature, or so she saw them at the time, and poor Gabriel had suffered relentlessly for years because of it.

Yet by his early teens none of that mattered anymore. The family's fortune had been terribly mismanaged by unfortunate investments and within a few months' time, they had all been forced to make drastic concessions just to retain ownership of their home. Gone were the servants, the parties, the friends, and the furniture. All that remained were the four of them and a very loyal servant of his father who Emile doubted had ever received any form of payment for his services whatsoever for the man was more of a friend and advisor to his father than he was ever a servant. His mother, bless her soul, had even learned to cook during those turbulent times, though most of her creations were far less appetizing than anything he had eaten since becoming a vampire.

"Mother." Emile shook his head and sighed at the fond memories. "Well, at least she tried. Which is more than I can say for you, dear sir," Emile rebuked himself sharply, feeling the sting of his imminent failure once more.

Why just that morning he had taken full stock of his activities and recent expenditures and found them shockingly shrinking. By all accounts it appeared, quite disappointingly, that he was down to his last two months of rent and expenses. And as such, that meant that if he wished to remain in Paris, he was going to have to either find someone suitable to marry or move on to where more promising prospects awaited him. Neither of which sounded like anything he was desirous to do at the present. Still, he had been here before, and just like then, he would find some way to rise up from the ashes. He always had, though this time he felt less inclined to do so than ever before.

Self-loathing was something he had grown well-accustomed to over the years as he navigated through disappointment after disappointment in his personal life. Oh, he had tried many avenues of lifestyle, endeavoring to regain his family's fortune, yet he had accomplished nothing in the way of financial fortitude—quite the opposite in fact. His life in Paris before his transition had been meant to be his rebirth into society, much like the introduction of available ladies were to the courting season. Yet it was never the joyous thing he had expected, as each glowing opportunity that crossed his path only ended somehow in a disaster of dramatic proportions.

Secretly, he had hoped that this pattern of incessant self-destruction would have passed along with his mortality as he now had been given the proper funds and inner passion to possess life fully, but it had not because here he was yet again. It was almost as if his curse of familial defeat had followed him wherever he went. So much so, that he doubted now if he would ever be able to escape it fully no matter which course he chose.

With a sigh, he sank deeper beneath the surface of the hot water and thought about how nice it would be to completely disappear from his life altogether and start over as someone new—to be another kind of person altogether perhaps. Someone far more worthy of the name and title he was born with, despite a possibly lower level of existence.

That was what Gabriel had chosen to do when he left for Austria though Emile had rebuked him harshly for it at the time. With the death of his parents only months earlier from the dreaded influenza, he had felt like Gabriel was abandoning him, too, and true to his callously selfish patten, he had behaved most rudely towards him for leaving him so helplessly behind.

"Money isn't everything, Emile. You must rise above your status in here..." Gabriel pointed to his chest and smiled. "In your heart," he added quietly and hugged him goodbye that day. In truth, it was a wonderful sentiment to say, yet though his words were simply spoken, deep down, the elder brother had hoped to instill within Emile much more than a mere cliché of parting wisdom. He wanted to give him a glimpse of a truth he himself had discovered, but he could not. The seeds of bitterness against him had held his means of personal salvation safely away from Emile's heart, hardening him against receiving it fully at the time.

After all these years, he knew now that his brother had been right. All Emile wanted today was to leave all this silliness behind him and become someone his father would have been proud to call his son. *But how? How does someone achieve the impossible in the midst of certain failure?*

Lying there, uselessly taking up valuable resources he could no longer afford to waste, he felt as cold inside as he did without, and no amount of wine or time spent soaking in this tub would ever change that. Nor could any amount of water wash away the destructive habits that had deeply rooted themselves into the very fibers of his being. No, those things were going to have to be plucked out one by one, root and all, to be rid of them.

"What's the use... I'm afraid it would take a miracle to change me now." Emile shook his head at the truth of his statement and closed his eyes until a polite knock sounded on the bathroom door, diverting his introspections as it drew him closer to reality.

"Enter," Emile called back nonchalantly, not bothering to even prepare himself for who might be entering.

"Begging your pardon, *monsieur*, but a young lady has arrived to speak with the master of the house." The manservant bowed politely.

"Formal or common, Gustave?" Emile finished his wine and set the glass down on the table beside the tub.

"Quite common, I am afraid. Should I ask her to leave? It is getting rather late." He picked up the empty glass and held out a long towel to his master in case he had need of it.

"No," Emile replied hurriedly and took the offered towel. "Tell her to wait, please. Whoever it is, I will meet with her directly. And you may leave for the night, Gustave. It appears I will not be needing supper after all."

"*Merci.*" The servant left, and Emile busied himself with quickly putting on the many layers of his wardrobe, each as equally important to him as the next.

A short, ten minutes later, Emile emerged from his chambers, perfectly composed and resplendent, ready to greet his unexpected guest but instead, was pleasantly surprised by who awaited him at the end of the large rectangular room. "Ah, it is you!"

The girl on the other side of the room swung around and practically jumped from the seat she had been occupying as if the man at the opposite end had shouted a callous accusation at her, which was quite obviously what the young lady must have been accustomed to for no other woman of his acquaintance would have behaved as thus. "Yes, sir, though begging your pardon, but I don't believe I have made your acquaintance as of yet."

With a pleased smile, Emile closed the door behind him and took in the understatedly dressed, but still tantalizingly beautiful woman who still drew him with such intense curiosity that he could hardly make himself wait to meet her. "It is I who must apologize to you, m*ademoiselle*, for I fear I may have startled you in my greeting," he pleaded genuinely. "It's just that you <u>do</u> very much resemble a young woman I saw in the street the other day, a very beautiful one I might add," he complimented her freely, hoping that in doing so, the young lady would begin to finally relax.

"Just one among many, *monsieur*, I am sure." The girl cast a quick glance around the very spacious, but more importantly, empty of occupants apartment and then back to the man in front of her. "Still, I think I would have remembered seeing someone like you."

"Well, I must admit, you were a bit preoccupied at the time," he answered easily knowing that the man she saw that day had most definitely looked nothing like he did right now.

"I normally am most days." She fidgeted with something concealed in the palm of her hands, then added as she slid it back into the pocket of her dress, "My apologies, *monsieur*."

Feeling more than a bit self-assured of himself and his ability to get what he wanted most, he sized her up once more as he had done on the street before walking slowly in her direction so as to avoid frightening her further and spark any need for her to escape. "I fear I must make a further confession to you tonight as I <u>have</u> been looking for you quite diligently since that day. I even inquired as to your whereabouts with one of my compatriots downtown. Understandably, she thought I was crazy to request a conversation with some random girl I had passed by on the street ... but secretly... I <u>had</u> hoped she would be successful in locating you."

"I'm flattered to be sure, but I am afraid I don't know what you mean as I am not especially hard to find." She looked down at the floor once more, obviously embarrassed to be in the man's apartment, then added more truthfully, "It might be more accurate to say that your confidant found me through a mutual acquaintance. *Madame* Jeannette is a friend of my fathers, for lack of a better explanation, though I personally have no association with the woman or her...um, colorful establishment." The girl tucked the loose strands from her mostly tied back hair behind her ears and continued uneasily. "In fact, it was she who told me to come here directly after I was finished with my last house and since she assured me it would be worth my while, I came, nothing more. Do you need me to clean your apartment for you? My clients say I do fine work at a fair price."

"Oh, I require nothing so mundane, I assure you." Emile carefully placed one hand politely around the back of her waist and guided her slowly into the small sitting room that had already been fully illuminated from when he had been in there reading earlier. "I had the place cleaned only just this week, actually."

"I see." The girl now visibly shook with anxiety, unable to hide the stress she was under in just being there.

Noticing her tremors, Emile effortlessly played the generous host, as he had on so many other occasions before, though never in this way, and never with a woman as compelling as her in this house. "Are you cold? Or hungry, perhaps? I could send for something to eat if you prefer or build up the fire. It has diminished considerably since I was in here last."

The girl jerked her head up and down quickly in response, then wrapped both of her arms tightly around her center refusing to make eye contact with him still. "Both... I'm sorry, but it is getting rather late. If you could just let me know how I can assist you, I can be on my way home." She paused and swallowed hard before saying something that she thought might add a bit of caution to the man, "I'll be missed."

"I'm sure you would." Emile eyed her hungrily but remained at a polite distance. *Madame* Jeannette had often sent a "gift" his way in appreciation for his overly generous patronage at her establishment, but this time she had truly outdone herself. Finding a specifically requested working girl amidst hundreds on the Rue de St Antoine must have taken her the better part of a day at least, if not two. "Why don't we first chat here by the fire where it is warmer. It will only take a moment." His voice was as soft as velvet, soothing the girl's nerves as he spoke until he could hear the very slow and rhythmic pattern of her breathing return back to its normal form of cadence. "You have nothing to fear here."

The words flowed like honey from his lips coaxing her closer to what he ultimately desired, but in the back of his mind somewhere they also issued to him the firmest of warnings. This woman was different, unique enough to warrant her preservation. *But why?*

Every fiber of his being wanted her more than he had ever wanted any other woman he had ever encountered, as a vampire or otherwise, and the truth of that fact struck him with an even greater need to protect her in some way from his darker self. It was almost as if his distracted mind was experiencing an inward battle against its own basest desires and truest necessities. Which side would ultimately win he did not know, but whichever way it was decided, he knew he must have her for himself alone, and that meant she must stay.

"I... I... should really be going." The girl glanced up at him, then paused as she tried helplessly to pull her eyes away from the dashing man who looked at her in a way no man had ever done so before. Yet try as she might, she could not bring herself to unlock her gaze from his own. Whatever his true intentions, something inside of her curiously wanted to understand what lay beneath the surface of his facade almost as much as he obviously wanted her compliance. His almost purple shaded eyes, the color of rich velvet, implored her to venture further and reached down deeper still as they delved inwardly towards a place she normally kept hidden from all others.

"Do you really have to leave so soon? We've only just met," he replied warmly and took the rather improper opportunity to run his soft fingertips down the length of her cheek to the hollow of her neck, clearly displaying his less than honorable intentions to the woman. "You must at least give me your name." He kept his statements brief, his movements irresistibly inviting.

"Em-ma," she said slowly and deliberately, elongating each syllable as she tried to control her racing thoughts. "Emma Larose."

"Mmm..." He slid very gracefully behind her and breathed in deeply the faint scent of lavender in her golden hair that resembled something closer to the color of a morning sunrise or a bubbling glass of pink champagne, both equally stunning and entirely mesmerizing. "The name suits you," his voice came back sweetly with just a hint of something more alluring.

"They... they say on the streets that you only like... um, certain women." The girl turned around slowly to face him at last and bit the center edge of her lower lip to steady its quiver before releasing it just as quickly. "Is that why I'm here?"

"Possibly." Emile caressed the side of her neck with the back of his fingers gently to calm her nerves further and leaned in to kiss her forehead just once, then when he saw no resistance to his advances, he did so once again, only this time on the side of her cheek. "It depends on you, really," he whispered softly, the coolness of his touch sending a new wave of shivers throughout her body.

Without meaning to, Emma unconsciously drew in a sharp breath to dispel them but did not pull away. "I'm... I'm not sure if I should stay." As alert as she had been when she had entered, she now found that she could not finish her sentences properly, nor could she manage to fashion a coherent thought through to its finality. "I'm not the kind of girl that you want, sir. I'm no one, or so everyone tells me." She turned her face away from him and to the side composing herself once more as she stared into the fire, away from the man who was most definitely from a station far above her own. Try as she might, she could not bring herself to see what this man saw in her to have made her worth searching for so diligently. "Surely you can find better elsewhere, someone more suited to your... um, style."

"I highly doubt it." Emile took her hand in his and caressed her fingertips wanting, oddly enough, to be whatever it was she needed him to be in that moment to have her unconditionally accept him. "Is that so hard to believe?"

"Yes, actually." Emma laughed lightly at the absurdity of his comment, then shook her head disappointingly. "People like me do not attract people like you, sir—not for the right reasons anyways." She chanced another glance up at him and wished she had not, for the look of desire she had previously seen filling his eyes had now been replaced with that of guilt. "You see, I was right." She frowned, but her lip quivered more like she was on the verge of releasing tears at the discovery.

Emile released her hand, justly rebuked at her accurate assessment, but as soon as he did so his heart ached because of its absence. Her insignificant distance away from him after his initial closeness was almost crushing him beneath its weight to experience it and not act immediately to prevent it.

He realized then what it was about her that had drawn him originally to her. She was light itself, or as close to it as he had seen in years. What's more, she had a pureness of spirit about her that made him want to be near her. A singularly enticing quality that begged him to drink in just a portion of that goodness as it held him gratefully captive. *Was she the answer to his earlier question? His means to personal , perhaps?* "What if I were to say there was something more I desired? Some other reason why I needed you to come here tonight than what you assumed. Would it make a difference?" He tried to speak slowly, but the sudden rush of realization quickened him with the anxiety of her possible flight.

"Well, I suppose that all depends on the reason," she said politely, but Emile could tell that she was most definitely still open to his advances for if she was not, she would have simply refused him outright and left.

Breathing a sigh of relief, Emile resisted the urge to pull her immediately closer to himself and compel her into complete submission to him as he turned her face back to him and studied her features intently, searching for the miracle he hoped existed in her. "I wish I could tell you what you want to hear, but I can't. The truth is..." He sighed quietly and attempted to express what he was feeling as genuinely as possible. "Until this moment, I have never wanted anyone as much as I want you right now and though that makes me a terrible person, I fear the judgement of that fact is far more hurtful in your eyes than it has ever been in the eyes of others." The corners of Emile's gaze narrowed as he studied her, confused as to why he was so indecisive now about this most singular of women.

"What is it that you think I want to hear?" Emma fingered the lapel of his outer jacket, suddenly wanting him very much to draw as near as possible to her.

"The assurance that it is I who is most unworthy of you, of course." He paused and stroked the side of her cheek with the back of his fingers desiring more than anything to convince her of his utmost regard and devotion and not merely his physical attraction. "In fact, I doubt that there is any status here on Earth that could raise me high enough to reach you, Miss Larose."

"And if I wish to go?" Emma asked quietly, knowing that leaving him after such a declaration would probably wound her almost as much as it would him at this point.

"Then I will do nothing to stop you, though I very much hope you will choose to stay." He went a step further and lowered his personal defenses as much as he dared. "Despite your initial fears as to my dubious character, I'll not force you to do anything here, Miss Larose. The decision will always be yours to make, and yours alone." He pulled his gaze away from her for just a moment to allow her the opportunity to decide once and for all under her own capacities and not be influenced in any way by his abilities. If she was meant to be truly his, he wanted her to submit freely and not because his powers compelled her to do so.

His honest sincerity at last lowered her resistance even more to him and removed the last impediments of her refusal. In the soft light of the room around her, she felt intoxicated and almost unable to think a single thought clearly under his spell, and she reveled in it. In fact, she loved every blessed second of it, if she were to be totally honest. For far too long she had been the last thing on someone's mind when it came to kindness and love, to the point that she felt almost invisible to everyone around her. But here, the very thing she had forever dreamt of possessing was standing right across from her, literally begging for her to take it with the same yearning desire that she was feeling as, well. "Then answer me this one thing, and I'll stay."

"Name it." Emile's eyes danced with the anticipation of the challenge.

"Why do you want me?" She stated the question that seemed to encompass them all—both his internal struggle and the one existing between them physically, for truly, at the end of the day, it was the only one that mattered.

Conflicted as to the proper response, Emile replayed her last question over and over again within his mind for a suitable reply, struggling to restrain his increasing desires while all the while fighting back each and every one of them until there was nothing left but a genuine love for the woman in front of him. "Because you, my dear, are simply..." He paused but gave in at last as he kissed her deeply until he was almost certain he would not be able to stop. "Exquisite," his voice whispered fervently in triumph as his mind finally realized the defining word that had eluded him for months. "And undeniably... wanted," he added resolutely as he traced his right thumb slowly across the lips he had just kissed and contemplated how long he could plausibly withstand waiting to do so again.

"Yes," she said breathlessly the one word he had been longing to hear since she had entered his apartment this evening.

That was all it took. With a sigh, she melted reflexively into his arms and with very little effort at all, he scooped up her delicate frame and carried her towards his awaiting room.

At the very least he would not be alone tonight, and with any luck, she would be alive tomorrow to enjoy the breakfast he made.

"Or become it," he mused darkly with a smirk, though he very much yearned for the first. After all, it would be a disgrace to waste such utter perfection as she, and he knew it.

Yet, it was at that moment, as he crossed the threshold from one room to the other, that he fully comprehended the gravity of the loss that would lay before him should he fail. It would take quite literally everything he possessed to not devour her completely like he desired, but he would try for her sake. From all he had witnessed both tonight and before, he knew beyond a shadow of a doubt that she would be worth every minute of delightful pain it would cause him to do so, and yet, despite what she might think otherwise, she already owned his soul entirely.

He had won, as he knew that he would, but more surprisingly, this time the triumph did not dissipate for it had also been accompanied by just one more thing—hopeful anticipation.

Chapter Fifteen

February 25th, 1793

A mere three days after he had left Nathanael, William found himself in front of an all too familiar set of doors—ones he had seen maybe a thousand times during his lifetime, possibly more. Yet today, the thought of opening even one of them felt staggering to contemplate, for though he had left on amicable terms with his parents last November, he had not seen them since his departure and subsequent shipwreck. Nor was he entirely certain beyond a shadow of a doubt that he had sufficiently tamed the temptation within himself to risk such an encounter so soon.

Still, if I can manage to treat my patients back in Wakefield without incident, surely, I can spend a few days with my family with equal success, William surmised and began to pace nervously back and forth upon the short porch, contemplating a myriad of possible conversations and explanations he might use to justify his unexpected arrival, trying to settle on just one direction of discussion before he entered.

Since it was still quite early in the morning, there was a good chance his mother would not even be awake as of yet, much less on the bottom floor to greet him. Nor would his sisters be alert at this hour as they much preferred to sleep late. That left his father as his first probable point of contact as he would no doubt be in the dining room consuming his breakfast before leaving for his regular house calls.

Definitely far more ideal to encounter him first than Mother's overwhelming conversation any day, William deduced mentally, then felt slightly rebuked at his disparaging opinion of her. Moreover, though it was true that William's father did have an office downtown where he occasionally met his more routine patients and performed various procedures, Mondays were the day he made his visits around town and helped at the infirmary down by the docks. In many ways, it was much like the routine William had also adopted in Wakefield, minus the office downtown, of course. When he was not in his apothecary or tending to those patients Doctor Hadleigh was too overloaded to treat, he was travelling to other neighboring villages to assist there if he was able or researching whatever lore he could find on what they had become.

To date, the majority of what he had encountered came from Middle Eastern legends of beings who devoured the blood of their victims entirely and were often times condemned to be buried upside down. Those decidedly morbid tales focused heavily on the creature being unable to exist under the sun's powerful exposure in any way, forcing those who had been infected by the curse to walk the night for their prey. These darker shadows of men seemed to have issues with blessed water and other religious effigies like crosses or even mirrors, too, but William knew that Nathanael had never experienced any problems to speak of regarding his faith in that way, nor had he or the others been especially affected by much else besides their undesired cravings and impulsive thoughts. And yes, the sensitivity to the sun's exposure was a definite nuisance in his life, but nothing so substantial that it could not also be carefully averted when the need arose.

Moreover, the cryptic stories coming out of France and Germany had a more romantic flavor to them, referring to the vampire's need to feed more as a means of seduction than actual thirst. This in itself was partially true as William was continually drawn back to the memory of Emile's first kill in the street almost as much as his companion. That most singular of temptations had an almost lustful quality to its pull, much stronger than any desire he had ever felt towards a woman and far more difficult to ignore when the object of his longing was within reach, as it was every day by someone simply walking past him on the street.

There was also a rare illness he discovered that caused blisters and hallucinations that resulted in the patient coughing up blood much like the way patients with the King's Touch suffered. However, this was not the least bit similar to their condition either as William had been delighted to discover that he had never been ill a single day since his transformation. Though it was still a mystery to him as to why that particular blessing occurred, it did however mean that whatever their composition was now, their bodies could no longer be touched by any form of ailment of that nature.

Standing up straighter and lifting his chin a bit higher still to regain the posture he had been trained to use, he grasped the handle of the large door and pushed it open, expecting to be greeted by Jared, the head butler or even one of the maids. Though strangely enough, despite his initial apprehension about who he might encounter first within, the house matched the porch without perfectly in its sparseness. No one in his father's employ arrived promptly to take his coat and hat, nor announce his presence to whoever was presently at home. In fact, not a single servant was busy pattering about with the fires as he had expected, nor could William make out any scent from a cooked meal either though the time was clearly after eight. From the floorboards to the walls with the ornately hung paintings, everything within his gaze was bizarrely still and deathly quiet, alarmingly so.

Freshly concerned by the uncharacteristic calm, William closed the door cautiously behind him and waited for his senses to pick up any trace of danger, but there was still nothing.

Where is everyone? William thought quickly, but didn't dare speak as of yet as he walked slowly, but purposefully around the main staircase to the right and made his way to the small dining room where his father should have been seated.

The room where everyone gathered for their meals was also shockingly empty. Not a candle was lit, nor a servant present. Only the remnants of a bowl of fruit remained in the center of the table under the large chandelier, with nothing of the normally carefully arranged trays of food the room usually contained.

Was he too late? Was Doctor Clarke's veiled threat merely the precursor of his new waking nightmare? William's breath caught within his chest at the thought, almost choking him as he contemplated the possibility.

Almost panicked now, William rushed back towards the stairs and began to climb them two at a time to the second level where his parents and siblings maintained their rooms. His older brother, who had married several years ago, had moved several streets over shortly thereafter. So, at least he should have been safe, but his two younger sisters still resided at home and from his experience, would normally be still in their rooms at this hour unless compelled to awaken for an earlier caller.

By all accounts, he could not imagine a single reason as to why the evil doctor would react so violently without provocation against any of them, but the facts staring him straight in the face remained. Nothing was as it should be and now, he was more assured than ever that he had made the right decision by returning home when he did.

Pausing to peer carefully over the lip of the floor above, he stopped at the middle landing halfway up to the second level and waited as he spied out if there was indeed danger present before proceeding further. William was not a fool to think that he alone could save his family from certain catastrophe should Doctor Clarke be waiting for him up above, but there was no sense playing into the Doctor's hand senselessly if he could help it either.

For almost a full minute, William remained on the landing and measured his racing heart as he contemplated his next move before his thoughts were suddenly interrupted once more by the closing of a door at the end of the long hall. From the direction of where his parents' room lay, someone was most definitely walking in his direction, and quite quickly by the sound of the approaching footsteps.

Still not entirely certain as to what he should do, William stood his ground, preparing himself for whoever he might encounter, be it Doctor Clarke or a member of his immediate family.

One after the other, the steps drew closer still until at last William was greeted with a sight that made his heart sing with relief and joy at last. "Father!" William exclaimed, unable to control his enthusiasm at seeing him unscathed and climbed the rest of the stairs up to him.

"Glory be, and saints alive! William!" The elder doctor embraced his son warmly. "I had no idea you were coming!"

Taking in the moment that he had dreamt of for months; William almost did not want to let go of his tight embrace. To his dismay, it had been almost four months since they had last seen each other and sadly, there might be another such stretch of time if not more under their current situation. But for William today, to give up even a single moment to drink in his father's tangible love felt wasteful, if not debilitating to even contemplate. "I only decided to come a few days ago when I received your letter. Where is everyone?"

True to his ever-observant ways, William's father held a finger up to his lips to quiet him and motioned for his son to follow him back downstairs.

William obeyed without question and when they had finally walked through the dining room and into the empty kitchen, William's father finally began his long-awaited explanation, "Have you had any illness up in Wakefield recently? A slight catarrh, aches, chills, or high fevers present among any of your patients?"

"No, why? Is something amiss here?" William folded his arms across his chest and leaned his back against the kitchen counter casually.

"Well, it is spreading like wildfire here. It laid up two of our staff this week alone. As for the rest, I wisely gave them permission to remain at home for the time being. I dare say, I think we can manage a week or two on our own and be no worse for wear, or at least I hope so. Your mother, however, is not so convinced, as you might imagine." William's father reached inside the cupboard and pulled out a cup and saucer, some tea and the other items he would need to make it. "Care for some breakfast, William? I had Mr. Thompson pay me in various breads and marmalades thinking it would help us out in the kitchen as well as be a blessing to him."

"That sounds like a fair enough trade under the circumstances." William picked up one of the twisted sticks of bread from the basket in the center of the counter and sampled it. "Mmmm, this has cinnamon in it, Father, your favorite, if I am not much mistaken."

"Is that so..." William's father picked one up for himself and sampled it, as well. "Quite wonderful, indeed. I'll have to order more in the future."

"Then I suppose it looks like Mr. Thompson might have had a dual purpose in his trade." William chuckled lightly and continued chewing, grateful that at least the spice gave the bread some kind of flavor.

"Maybe so." His father also laughed, then wiped the excess crumbs from off his face and hands. "So, what do we owe this unexpected pleasure? Not that I am complaining in the slightest. I relish <u>any</u> opportunity where I get to see my youngest son, but I thought your work in Wakefield was keeping you quite busy these days. Too busy to even stop by when you first arrived." He raised his eyebrows just a little with intended hidden meaning.

William swallowed the rest of his breakfast and tried to think quickly of an adequate excuse as it was indeed quite rude of him to not have at least reassured them both of an upcoming visit after such an ordeal. "I'm sorry, truly I am. As I said before, my new friend, Mr. Beckett needed to arrive in time to prepare for his first service and then I just got so preoccupied with my work starting up the apothecary and all that it totally slipped my mind."

William's father studied him seriously for several moments as if pondering on everything he had just said and then smiled. "I understand full-well the demands of a doctor's life. So does your mother, but do not think you will be able to escape so quickly once she has set eyes on you today."

"I suppose not." William shook his head and smiled. "It really is <u>so</u> good to see you once more. I feel like an ocean of eternity has happened since I left. There is so much to tell you. So much I want to share now that I don't have to write it all out in volume form."

"And I can't wait to hear it all, every last word of it in fact." William's father's face shifted then to one of hesitancy. "But... I do have to be off, I'm afraid. With this recent epidemic, there is a list of patients for me that is a mile long most days.

Far too many for just the few of us in town to assist. Care to lend a hand, or are you otherwise engaged during your stay?"

"Of course, I would love to help, just as long as I can run one errand before I do. It is part of the reason why I came in the first place. Once I stop by the docks and make a few inquiries at the shipping office this morning, my time is yours." William followed his father through the maze of rooms and out the front door, grateful that the sky was severely cloudy and foreboding today so that he would not need to lift the hood of his cloak for protection. It was a casual enough habit of his now whenever he left his home every day, that few of the people noticed in Wakefield, but his father, on the other hand, would surely question.

"Checking on your old master, Doctor Clarke?" Doctor Wells placed his top hat upon his head and closed the door behind him.

"Something like that, yes. Have you seen him since you wrote me?" William waited for his father at the front fence gate and walked beside him as they headed south towards the port.

"Now that you mention it, I have not. Though it was all a rather odd affair from the very beginning, and I don't mind saying it, William. Nothing about that poor young man's death has made any sense to me at all and as you know, I hate unfinished business." He guided the two of them down the various streets, pointing out new businesses and people to William as they passed. Despite the early morning hour, there were still many people they encountered who were busy at their craft or on their way to some form of work, making his father cautiously optimistic that the worst of the epidemic might possibly be reaching a decline.

"I am afraid that this is where we shall part, son. I need to see to Miss Harriet and her sister before heading over to the Taylor family before lunch. Will I see you in time to catch a quick bite down at Simpson's Tavern?" His father stopped at the crossroads between two streets and pointed down the length of one of them to indicate the direction in which he was headed.

"Do they still serve those delicious sandwiches you love?" William countered and waited for his reply.

"Would I be going there otherwise?" William's father laughed again lightly.

"I suppose not." William smiled, too. "Shall we say noon, maybe a tad bit earlier? Whoever arrives last has to pick up the tab?" He teased his father with the one thing both of them struggled to maintain—their sense of punctuality.

"Done and done. Best of luck at the shipping offices." He waved at William and made his way up the street to his first patient of the day.

With a heavy heart, William watched him leave and felt a part of him long to go after him. As obediently compliant as he had always seemed in the past working alongside him, he realized now that for years he had not truly appreciated the strength and diligent care of the man in front of him. Moreover, now that he had gained some much-needed perspective and a healthy dose of reality, he found himself longing to glean as much as he possibly could from him in the time he had left. Soon enough, all he would have of his father were his fond memories and he knew it. Which only made squandering even a single day on a pointless pursuit that took away from that reality, fruitless, yet he knew he must go anyways. If for no other reason than to reassure himself that there would be many more such days in his future.

"I must make sure Doctor Clarke is safely out of the picture and out of their lives." William grimaced and walked the rest of the way to the port, seeking out the small wooden building at the end of the row of ships where the master at port would be working. With luck, the man would know something about Doctor Clarke's whereabouts, or with an even greater mixed blessing, he would encounter him personally there. What he would say or do to the man if or when that moment occurred, he had no earthly idea, but he had travelled all this way to do so, and there was no way he would return to Wakefield emptyhanded now.

Reaching for the handle and opening the roughly constructed door before ducking to enter the rudimentary structure with the last remnants of whitewash still clinging to its grain, William walked up to the counter where a man a bit older than himself stood. Seeing no other patrons on the premises or gathering outside for that matter, William cleared his throat to alert the man of his presence as the giant of a man appeared entirely distracted though nothing was in front of him occupying his focus.

"Can I help you?" He spoke finally, but his speech appeared somewhat slurred in its delivery as if the man were intoxicated or otherwise impaired.

"I'm not sure that you can." William's eyes narrowed as he studied his tone and overall appearance more closely. The weather outside <u>had</u> been especially chilly this morning being as it was still late February, yet the man standing in front of him was profusely sweating, his hair matted with moisture about his temples, all the way down to the loose-fitting cotton blouse that was tied haphazardly about his neck. "Are you feeling alright, sir?"

The man swayed on his feet for just a second and gripped the counter in front of him to steady himself. "I'm f--… I'm f--…" He tried again and again to speak the two words he needed to utter for his dutiful response.

"No, you are not fine, sir. In fact, you are probably about to…" William never finished his sentence fully for at that same awful moment, the man across from him crumpled to the floor, hitting his head in the process on the sharp edge of the wooden counter beside him.

Like the rush of a hot breeze from an open hearth, the smell of the man's escaping blood hit William with a force he had yet to grow accustomed to experiencing. In front of Nathanael, he had pretended that the nutritional sustenance both of them craved had little effect on his senses in order to calm the man's more timid disposition, but his deception was anything but the truth. In many ways he was just like Emile in his desire to ravage half the countryside when he was hungry, but unlike his more impulsive friend, William had the necessary conviction to force himself to restrain... or at least so far. Today was another matter entirely.

Kneeling down instinctively next to the man who had just collapsed, he carefully examined the cut along the side of his head and touched the edges to see how deep it truly was. Clearly superficial by his estimation, and thankfully so, but one that would most definitely be felt for weeks to come.

William looked down then at the blood collecting along the man's temple and felt his mouth water in response to the thing he craved most. Then, like a thief scanning his surroundings to ascertain if he were truly safe to proceed with his crime, William glanced around him once more to judge his environment better. From all that he could see as he examined the room, the shipping office was completely devoid of windows of any kind with no other rooms to speak of save a small closet-type area in the far-left corner, no doubt a hidden bedroom of some kind.

The small building meant for conducting the processing of tickets and mail intended for the ships at port was just that. One big room, with a long counter, several cubbies for correspondence and tickets, an area that contained bags of grain waiting to be picked up and a large, braided rug upon which he now knelt beside. In fact, should he decide to proceed with what he had never once dared to do before, not a single person would witness anything that might transpire here, save the man who lay unconscious on the floor—no one, except maybe himself and God above, if He truly existed as his friend so staunchly believed. And better yet, no one would suspect him of doing anything either. He was a doctor after all, and the man was already clearly sick, though at the moment, not fatally.

With a shaking hand that begged him to proceed as far as he dared without any caution whatsoever, he raised his fingers to his lips first and savored the small amount of blood they held, almost smiling at the remembrance for it was the freshest he had ever experienced since his transition. In fact, in every way and description, it was simply delicious, far more so than the collected blood he normally endured and definitely immensely more fulfilling.

Nevertheless, despite the euphoric sensation the blood created once it passed his lips, that was all he could allow himself to experience. Feeling suddenly guilty once more for even sampling just a taste of the forbidden opportunity, he wiped the scant remnants of the blood from off his fingers onto the man's unbuttoned jacket and drew in a breath to steady his racing heart. What fantastical delight it would have been to simply reach down and taste some more. Or even more recklessly, to take all of what he wanted most in all the world as if it were entirely his prerogative to do so like Emile, but he could not.

Isn't that what I am made for after all, to seize whatever I want so easily as if enjoying the various pleasures of life? Or is my world still only filled with dutiful responsibilities? The darker side of his mind rationalized against the decision he had made but lost as it knew it would.

With a groan, the man on the floor next to him, loudly silenced the remaining evil lurking within, distracting William just enough from succumbing to his temptation and allowing him the opportunity to force himself back to the task at hand. "Sir, can you hear me?"

"I can, so please stop shouting." The man reached up his hand to hold his throbbing head and tried to sit up.

William smiled at the man's unhindered humor under the circumstances and supported him. "Do you have a bunk nearby where you can retire?"

The man nodded slowly, but still did not move. "Just over there." He pointed to the small room in back with a shaking hand.

"Then let me help you over to it." William stood and lifted the man easily from off the floor, grateful once again that his transformation had at least one positive feature, increased strength. In his old life, he would never have been able to help lift the man himself for he looked to be a full six inches taller and at least a foot wider though most of him felt trim and muscular like Sebastian.

No doubt from spending much time hauling cargo or working on board one of these nearby vessels, he surmised as he aided him.

Without another word, the two men trudged along together across the room with William leading and the other man leaning heavily upon the one arm that was draped over William's shoulder. When at last they had reached his small bed against the wall within, William helped him to it and covered the man with all of the blankets available to him. Then, reaching within his satchel he pulled out some of the powder he used for fevers and poured a small amount into the mug beside the bed and added water. "I'll need you to sip this a few times now if you can. The rest you can finish as you are able." He lifted the man's head and neck and guided him to the cup.

"I thank you most kindly, sir. I am assuming you are a doctor?" He took a few more sips, then held his hand up to stop.

William obediently set the cup aside and allowed the man to recline. "I am. Though I actually came here looking for Doctor Clarke. Is he still working around port?" William inquired carefully as he did not want to upset the man in his condition by forcing him to consider his patron's needs over his own health.

"Doctor Clarke was commissioned on the Defiance two weeks ago. She set sail last Monday," the man in the bed answered clearly, his mind becoming more alert by the minute.

"I thought that ship was burnt accidentally almost a century ago?" William's mind raced to recollect the various facts concerning the ship's demise as he was certain he had remembered reading something about its unfortunate history during his preparations for his trip on the Endeavor. At the time, he had read anything he could get his hands on concerning the port in London, shipping routes, cargo, etc., all in an effort to impress his new employer and make his trip more successful. The only thing he had not studied was how to identify a killer—something that in hindsight might have proven to be infinitely far more useful where Doctor Clarke was concerned.

"They rebuilt her years ago. She is on her way to the Colonies as we speak." The man looked over at William, then added, "I'm James Morgan, by the way."

"Doctor William Wells," William smiled, then cocked his head slightly. "I thought sailors were a superstitious lot. Don't they mind sailing on such a fateful ship?"

"We are... normally... but when there are few others to be had, a ship is just a ship." The man closed his eyes for a moment and William could tell the sedative was kicking in.

"I can see your point. Well then, if you can assure me that you will remain here resting in my absence, I will come by later to check on you this afternoon. Would you mind if I brought you some soup?" William offered.

"Mind? I would love some," Mr. Morgan replied.

"Good, then I will bring a bowl of it upon my return. Until then, I want you to get plenty of rest. I will put a note on the door that any customers needing help should return tomorrow." William stood and made his way back to the counter to draw up a sign, then carefully hung it on the outer handle of the door. Then, scanning the length of the long pier before he left, he spied a man he recognized as the purser from the shipping company he had signed up with last November and made his way over to him.

"Ahoy, Matthew! Fancy seeing you out here. Don't you normally prefer to be working inside?" William reached his hand out and clasped the one offered quite happily to him in return.

"William Wells! You survived!" Matthew's face shone with the true delight it was to see that he had not perished at sea after all. "Where on earth have you been hiding all this time?"

"Marooned on an island for a month, then in Wakefield until recently. Did many others survive? I was afraid that all hands perished when it went down." William casually gave just enough information to satisfy the man's curiosity and yet also compel him to offer more in return.

"Only about twenty, counting yourself, from your vessel..."

And three more if he knew about Emile, Sebastian and Nathanael, William mentally added.

"As it turned out, some of the survivors were able to stay adrift long enough until another boat happened upon them. It was nothing short of a miraculous story I am told, but since you were there, you probably know more than I." Matthew closed his ledger and crossed his hands on top of it. "I can't tell you how glad I am to see you."

"Me, too." William chuckled lightly. "Say, you wouldn't happen to know if my old master was among those survivors?" He prodded again easily, wanting to reverify the information he had been given just in case his newest patient's mental state had been confused by any of the more pertinent details.

"Doctor Malcom Clarke?" Matthew opened his book and ran a finger down the side of a page near the center of the book. "Yes, I do believe he was. See..." He pointed to the line in the book that gave the list of all those who had been rescued and who had perished.

William scanned the length of it quickly, his eyes focusing instantly on three of the names in the perished column, then picking out the one of more concern in the saved column. "Do you know where I might find him now? I would like to pass on my regards while I am in town."

Matthew shook his head solemnly. "I'm afraid you just missed him by a week. He was commissioned on the Defiance on its way to the Colonies. I signed the orders myself." He showed William another page with the ship's manifest and crew with his nemesis clearly printed underneath.

A part of William that had been painfully rigid since he had received his father's letter began to relax. "And you are sure he was on board?" He pressed more seriously, knowing that he needed to solidify in his mind once and for all that his family was indeed safe.

"I saw him board the ship myself before I left for the day. They were supposed to shove off at high tide. I don't know how much surer you can get, William. Unless you think he jumped ship thereafter? But who would do such a thing after going through all the trouble to leave?" Matthew laughed.

"I suppose you're correct." William joined him in his lighthearted mirth. "Well, I best go get some lunch for Mr. Morgan at the shipping office. He collapsed when I was in there a minute ago."

"Oh, I'm sorry to hear it. Should I send for someone to tend him?" Matthew stood and walked about the small table he had been occupying near one of the gangplanks.

"No, I gave him something for the fever, but I <u>would</u> tell the rest of the men to steer clear if they don't want whatever it is he has," William warned him sternly, hoping to avoid an even worse situation.

"Rest assured, I will spread the word immediately." The man walked with William over to the main street before stopping when William spoke up.

"Oh, and you can make one adjustment to your ledgers, too, by the way. Mr. Nathanael Beckett is alive and well," William offered for he knew that his father already had knowledge of the man's existence, so it was hardly a secret that needed to be kept. As for the others, he doubted that Sebastian wanted his whereabouts proclaimed, nor would the shipping company care what might have become of a recently conscripted Frenchman.

"I will certainly change the record promptly. Thank you, William," Matthew promised. "Will I see you before you leave town?"

"Possibly," William offered, then headed back up the street to the tavern to meet his father.

Chapter Sixteen

February 27th, 1793

Emile sat in the chair opposite the bed and watched as Emma slept, contentedly taking in every aspect of her delicate form from a distance. For hours, he had tried his best to fall asleep next to her but when he finally managed to drift off, he had only awakened an hour later, maybe two, drenched in a heavy sweat as his body fought against the steady pull he felt towards satisfying his hunger.

In the worst of circumstances, he had lasted over a week without his normal form of nourishment with very minimal side effects other than a slight headache and an abnormally faster heart rate, but on the whole, nothing had affected him as much as this. Which was in itself odd as his last meal had been more than enough to meet his normal requirements. But then again, he was not usually in the presence of someone so irresistible day in and day out, at least not in this way, and the added stress upon his body was taking its toll in more ways than one for he had never once perspired since the moment of his transition and in the span of one night he had changed his shirt twice.

Shaking his head, he licked his lips unconsciously, contemplating more deeply the rich delight it would be to simply taste just a single drop of her blood to stop his systematic torture. How he longed desperately to place his lips ever so gently upon her neck in such a way that she would scarcely even feel that he had bitten her. Really, anything she would be willing to offer him would suffice to quell the yearning he felt towards it more than any physical desire he had ever experienced before.

Yet despite how much his body wanted what she possessed, he still could not compel himself to move any closer to her. To do so would mean certain death for her, and a lifetime of regret for him, though no other woman in his existence had made him believe so. *What was it about this unique woman that made his mind utterly malfunction this week just being near her? Or what power did she possess over him that helplessly bound his body, mind and soul to her without ever asking him to do so?*

As far as he was concerned, she was perfection itself without a single thing he would ever change about her besides maybe the annoying fact that the woman occupied a bit too much of his bed. *Was that why he could not take her now?* Offering the woman more room before she pushed him completely off of the bed, was entirely something he could easily accommodate, but stealing her last breath was not. Just the thought of that plausible possibility made his throat constrict in panic for a world without her in it felt devoid of the very air he needed to sustain life.

Emile closed his eyes to steady his nerves once more and composed himself back to the state in which he normally remained, then opened them and waited for his eyes to adjust to the dim light in the room around him again. In the short time that he had been refocusing, Emma had rolled over onto her side towards him so that her head now rested comfortably on the pillow, the side of her neck entirely bare and exposed to his view as if openly taunting him. Narrowing his gaze further on the object of his every thought, he traced the contours of her neck until his eyes rested on the vein just below her jaw. For several long moments he allowed himself to be helplessly mesmerized by the rhythmic pulsations across her fair skin, his mouth watering reflexively when they shifted cadence in her sleep.

"Emi....mmm..." Emma murmured something in her sleep, but from where he was seated it sounded less like his name and more like the low hum of a lullaby he had heard as a child than an actual word.

Smiling in renewed adoration, he rose to his feet and stepped quietly over to her before sitting gently on the bed beside her in wonder. *Is this what love feels like?* His mind asked peacefully, welcoming him to agree with its assumption. In truth, he had only known the woman intimately for a few days, but in that time, her gentle acceptance and genuine care for him had changed him far more than most people could have done if given years.

Emile reached over and drew a portion of her strawberry blonde hair towards the side of her face and left his hand there, drinking in the closeness it afforded him by the warmth she emanated. If he did not truly love her as all other men professed so freely at this point, he at the very least adored her. For how could he not? He was a vampire after all, not a fool, and Emma was absolutely priceless.

As if hearing his thoughts spoken aloud, the woman in the bed smiled and opened her eyes. "Good morning, love."

"I'm so sorry. Did I wake you?" Emile brought his hand down and rested it on top of her own on the sheets.

Emma shook her head but just lay there admiring him in the same way he had been admiring her.

"I need to step out this morning for a few hours to tend to some things. Can you stay until I return?" He asked her tentatively while lightly tracing the back of her fingers with one hand. "I promise, I won't be long."

"I would, but I should really think about working sometime this week, Emile. My family will starve if I don't." Emma sat up hesitantly and ran her hand along the side of his head, her fingers playing with the rich, dark brown locks that hung far past his shoulders.

"You know as well as I that if you keep doing that neither of us will be going anywhere today." Emile's eyes turned darker as he struggled against his desire to continue where their last rendezvous had left off. "Unless that is your wish, as well?" He waited patiently for a response, then chose to kiss her lightly instead, endeavoring to respect whatever boundaries she placed for him as he knew that all it would take on his part was a brief moment of intentional redirection in his gaze, and she be powerless to resist anything he might ask of her.

"You are all I will ever desire, *Monsieur* Deschamps." Emma pulled him closer and kissed him deeper still, then released him. "But to answer your question, yes, I will return by supper if that is what you want."

"What I want?" Emile drew back dramatically from her, suddenly surprised. "Do you think you can be replaced so easily, Miss Larose?"

"I know I can. I am sure there are quite literally hundreds of women you can choose from if you really wanted to do so," she admitted honestly and pulled the covers up higher to stay warm. "I don't profess to know much on the subject of whatever this is we are going to call it between us, but I imagine that most men in this type of situation, handle the decision the same way as they do the other things in their lives."

"And how, pray tell, do we do things, as men, that is?" Emile half-chuckled at her correct assessment but remained playfully intrigued at what her unique interpretation or perspective might be.

197

Emma didn't elaborate further but rather her face became more worried than he had ever seen it as she looked away suddenly, too afraid to speak at all on the subject anymore.

Thinking that she might have been slightly embarrassed to continue her elaboration on such an intimate topic, he walked around the bed to the other side where she was facing and lay down next to her, holding her in his close embrace once more. "You're afraid I will discard you when I have finally finished getting everything I want from you. Does that sound about right?" He said plainly, then waited until he felt her nod the cheek that was pressed against his shirt.

"Oh Emma..." Emile sighed. "If you only knew how much of that callous statement is false, you would never be afraid again."

"But it is true of most men, is it not?" Emma asked quietly.

Emile pondered the question deeply and also his response before carefully choosing his words one by one. "It was most certainly true of me before I met you, Emma. I won't deny that. But no, not all men are like that. Some truly do love and value the people they are with enough to devote their entire lives to only them. I know my mother and father did and they were very happy until their deaths. Others too, I suppose."

Emma lay motionless in his arms, breathing slowly in and out for almost ten minutes but Emile knew she had not fallen back asleep. He had listened to her breathing long enough to know that and much more about the woman he was growing to care for more and more by the minute.

"Emile..." Emma finally said quietly, her voice barely above a whisper.

"Hmm..." He replied in the same calm tone, wishing he could capture this moment in time for the rest of eternity.

"I'll come back as long as you want me," she promised faithfully.

Emile's heart wanted to burst with the joy of her declaration, but a part of him also remained highly skeptical of anyone being so devoted to his needs alone. "Are you certain? I can't promise that I won't hurt you, too, in the end."

"I know, but you have already shown me more love than anyone has ever given me in my entire life and for now, that is enough," she said simply.

"For now." Emile again felt the rise of a deep cynicism grow.

Emma ignored his added comment, choosing rather to push away from him and get dressed. Their conversation on the topic was concluded for the moment. The day growing later still. "I need to clean at least four houses today to make up for what I missed yesterday. If I hurry, I think I can be back in time for supper, but please don't think the worst of me if I am late." She slipped her dress over her head and tied the long ties on either side behind her back quickly.

Emile watched her dress lazily, wishing he could do something to alleviate the struggle he had placed upon her by his recent distractions, but financially he was in no position to do so. In fact, that was one of his errands this morning, actually. Because of her service, he owed *Madame* Jeannette a small token of his appreciation for finding Emma, and the woman always appreciated prompt payment.

As a rule, she cared very little about what he might do in her establishment or without just as long as she was paid handsomely for the trouble involved. "I won't give it a second thought if you do not think the same of me." He cast a glance back at her while dressing as well, checking to see if her reaction matched his own. It did, and so he carried on in placing the many layers of his attire on top of the other and within a short time, the two of them were respectably presentable—ready to start their day in two completely different worlds after bidding each other farewell.

With a light snowfall still coming down, Emile made his way through the milling crowds of people along the river Seine, admiring the various artists' works, past the cathedral with its colorful windows and over to the seedier side of town where Madame Jeannette's brothel lay. A few of the more expensive offerings the establishment had available were already outside attempting to lure in their prospective marks out of the bitter cold, but for once he had no desire to give any of them a second glance. As far as he was concerned, he had everything he could ever want in Emma which meant his nights with these ladies were at an end.

"*Monsieur* Deschamps, what an unexpected pleasure!" *Madame* Jeannette greeted him warmly just inside the large parlor that contained several benches for relaxed conversations as well as a large staircase that led up to the second level balcony for the rooms above. "I trust Miss Larose found you safe and sound the other night."

From his position near the large settee by the doorway, Emile eyed the woman seriously and flicked his eyebrows up just once in acknowledgement. "Yes, Miss Larose and I enjoyed a delightful supper. Thank you for sending her." Emile placed a small pouch within her palm and waited as she bounced it just once to judge its worth and smiled. "She mentioned that you know her father?" He pried slightly into Emma's unfortunate story without her permission.

"I'm afraid I do not discuss the business of my clients with others. A fact which you no doubt can appreciate, sir," she said casually, noting the marked tenseness of the man in front of her as she spoke. "Can I offer you the usual upstairs? Or were you looking for something a bit more discreet? Something dispensable, perhaps." She eyed him carefully as if already suspecting his true nature though no one else of his acquaintance had.

"Discreet would be more appropriate for the present. What did you have in mind?" He studied her like a man arranges his cards in a game of high stakes, then placed a single silver coin more within her palm and waited patiently.

"We both know exactly what you need, *monsieur*, and Miss Larose will not be able to satisfy that particular desire—not yet anyways, I suspect. Though I am sure it is none of my concern to speculate further about your business with her, sir, but I believe you will find what you seek today in the room over there." She angled her head to the right and towards the area near the back of the brothel. "Please be sure to leave the room tidy this time. It is terribly inconvenient to straighten up afterwards." She left the veiled hint in the air and waved her hand in the direction of the room.

"But of course." Emile tipped his hat and walked down the long hallway before rapping his knuckles lightly on the door at the end, the only one that appeared to be shut for the rest lay open and empty, as if to allow anyone who might pass them to peruse the contents without restriction.

"Come in," a quiet voice echoed back to him so faintly from within that he almost did not hear it loudly enough to respond.

Feeling as if he were suddenly intruding, Emile entered the room quietly and stopped before closing the door with a soft click of the lock, taking in the haggard-looking woman who stood on the opposite side of the room. From all outward appearances she had most definitely been living on the streets for quite some time, if not the majority of her life, as her hands and feet were heavily soiled, and her clothes were tattered in so many places they were beyond repair. "*Madame?*" He tried to speak, but the very sight of such abject poverty made him pause.

The woman, who was probably well into her late thirties, did not say anything in response, but rather turned back towards the only light in the room, a large fireplace that was already thickly blazing upwards within, warming the room to an almost cozy temperature, even to him.

"May I at least ask you your name?" He walked over to her and waited, the desire to feed becoming stronger with every minute that was passing.

"I am no one worthy of such attention, sir. Take what you will," she said sadly, then held her head up higher, inviting him closer by the movement.

"For once, I am sincerely sorry, Miss." Emile stepped around to face her with his back to the fire and saw the fresh tears sliding down the woman's face. With great care, he placed both of his hands on the sides of her cheeks and drew her gaze

200

to his own, watching as the pupils dilated, then froze, her mouth parting slightly in response. He knew then she was under his spell. He could do whatever it was he desired now, and she would not cry out, though a part of him wished that she would, if only to save her from this certain death at his hands.

Suddenly filled with a conviction he had never experienced before, Emile flinched away, almost ready to leave the room entirely to seek out someone else less vulnerable, then gave in as he threw his head back with a groan and released the hold he had been maintaining so diligently for the past few days—freeing himself to his basest of desires at last. Like a spoiled child, he fed slowly, wanting to draw out his fulfillment for as long as he possibly could manage though he had never succeeded in doing so before.

In the past he often preferred to take what he wanted quickly as if his prey might escape his grasp if he did not, but today it was different. In this moment of stolen solitude, he was calm, methodical, greedily temperate in every movement. Choosing to honor her in just a small way, he made her life count for something in the end for she had allowed him to experience a level of satisfaction beyond anything he had ever contemplated—something he had never even thought possible.

And so it was that when she had finally breathed her last, and the final drop of her blood had been enjoyed, Emile placed her carefully upon the bed within and sat down next to her to compose himself for the task to come. Never before had he felt so at peace after such an experience and the thought of that almost frightened him. Deep down, he knew that there was nothing in the woman's blood that was in any way different than any other he had tasted elsewhere. Yet, the truth of what it had meant to him was equally haunting, for during the time that he had spent feeding on her, his mind thought only of Emma—of what she would taste like, feel like, be like if he were to have her so completely. The trance of his misplaced reality held him captive then as much as it did now in his memory.

Reaching down a slightly unsteady hand, he pulled out his pocket watch before glancing down at the time. Nearly three hours had passed since he had left his apartment, and he had little to show for it. He was satisfied, yes, undeniably so, but the price this woman had paid to grant him that satisfaction felt equally wasteful to consider it.

With an almost heavy hesitance, he glanced back at the woman's face as if doing so would erase the guilt he now felt about his actions and his heart sunk. For the first time since he had become a vampire, he considered the origins of the meal he had just consumed. What her life must have been like before she came to such a lowly and desperate place such as this. Or to whom she belonged as everyone who walked this Earth must have had someone for whom they might be missed. Would Emma also end up like her one day in the current life that she was now living, working her fingers to the bone day after day for little in return? Or was there some other way to prevent all of that for her? A way to rescue her from the horrors the darker side of her existence threatened to consume her with? Or perhaps most important of all, were his selfish actions drawing her closer to that abyss as she compromised herself and her integrity for his carnal desires?

And then there was the body. *Madame* Jeannette had been most direct in her request, and he was not about to refuse her in this now. The very fact alone that she had offered the girl up so freely, meant that she obviously knew his secret above all others and not only nurtured it, but also dutifully protected it. It would be wrong, if not dangerous, to cross her in this simple request as after all, it was the least he could do under the circumstances.

Closing his eyes, he prepared himself for the task ahead and then lifted the woman's body carefully, draping his cloak over her still form as he left out the back door and made his way down several overlooked alleys before he found a small, obscured corner within which he could place her for the time being. It wasn't as respectable a place as he might have preferred but someone was bound to come upon her in the weeks to follow and think that she had most likely frozen to death in the cold given her poor state and lack of outer attire. By then he would be long gone, and more importantly, *Madame* Jeannette would not be implicated in any way.

Emile turned around and walked back to the main street, taking in the busy scene once more like he had on a previous occasion when he had been searching for news on Jonathan. The same merchants that had been present then were still out haggling their goods to anyone who passed, minus a certain young woman who was no doubt carrying her dirty pails in a different part of the city today.

There was even the same beggar boy on the corner on the other side of the street. "Lucien," he thought he remembered him calling himself. But from his recollection, that boy had been blind and this one, though slightly shorter, appeared to not have the least bit of difficulty in seeing the people around him. *Had he been fooled initially?* He didn't think so, but still...

Emile studied him from a distance as his curiosity piqued. The boy absolutely resembled the other child in many ways, but as he watched this one's bravado from across the way, he could not help but smile. He was a charmer to be sure, a definite player of men as he cajoled and moved silkily from one passerby to the next. Yet there was also one more thing that this boy did that few others but Emile noticed. As an unsuspecting man or woman stopped to take notice of the poor specimen on the corner, the young boy also took the silent opportunity to peruse their pockets before slipping whatever he found therein quietly into his own. In all, the whole action took merely seconds to perform, but the reward was no doubt worth it.

Emile had seen enough. Taking great care to avoid colliding with any of the passing people, he stepped through the meandering crowd until he stood in front of the boy once more and asked, "Have you seen Lucien around? I was hoping to inquire as to his health." Emile greeted the new boy warmly, hoping that he would at least know of his whereabouts if not more.

"Lucien can't beg on this corner today, sir. Caught the Grippe he did, but don't worry, I can help you if you need something. What's your pleasure?" The young boy offered freely, ready to comply in whatever task might be presented.

Instantly concerned about the boy in question, Emile lifted his head and studied the new boy carefully searching for a way he could bestow on him some honest coin for his service. "You wouldn't happen to have some recent news of this new Assembly by any chance? Something more than what is in print?"

"Of course!" The boy's eyes quickly lit up at the prospect of easy money. "But it will cost you for something like that. Nothing in life is free, or so they say," he piped back happily working Emile like a seasoned card shark.

"What's your name, son?" Emile asked casually, playing his part with ease.

"What's yours?" He countered right back in the same manner and tone.

Intrigued by the lad's audacity and mimicked flattery, Emile lifted an eyebrow and replied without hesitation, "Emile should be sufficient for now." Then, he waved his hand in the boy's direction for his own while making sure to keep a respectable distance, or at least more than an arm's length away from the child.

"Michel." The boy crossed his arms across his chest firmly.

"Well, Michel, how about I treat you to some lunch? You can tell me all I might need to know where it is warm." Emile pointed to the tavern on the other side of the street and waited for the boy to accept.

"Fair enough, though I can tell you now that it might have been better to have just given me a few sous as I am pretty hungry."

"I am sure you are." Emile smiled quickly and watched as Michel picked up his few possessions from the step behind him and joined him as they walked over to the tavern and stepped inside, taking their seats close to the fireplace on the opposite side of the room from the door by which they had entered.

In no time at all, they had both warmed up considerably and a fresh bowl of soup was brought to the table, complete with a large basket of bread and a small mug of warm coffee for Emile.

Seizing his opportunity to consume whatever was in front of him instantly, Michel pocketed several of the rolls within the basket somewhere deep inside his tattered coat, then slurped happily on the warm tomato soup. "This soup is sure good. You certain you don't want some?"

Emile shook his head and thought back disappointingly to the woman he had just left on the street. "No, thank you. I've already eaten my fill earlier. And you? When was the last time you had a square meal to speak of?"

The boy couldn't help his overly abundant laughter next at the very idea. His eyes squinting shut when he did so. "You are probably the funniest man I have met this month, sir."

"No doubt." Emile drummed his fingers on the table like he was playing a particular piece of music with just one of his hands and waited patiently for the boy to finish his meal before pressing him further. In truth, he did not have to wait long though for almost as quickly as the food had been placed upon the table, Michel had gulped it down just as fast and now sat across from him, absentmindedly tearing away small pieces of the remaining loaf of bread in front of him.

"The Assembly?" Emile prompted once more.

"Oh, yeah." The boy chuckled. "Robespierre's men said last week that there would be trials soon. 'People need to pay for what they have done to us Citizens.' Or at least that was what they had shouted or something close enough to it. Maybe they will even give them the same punishment as the King if they have to," Michel replied seriously as if repeating what he had heard most recently.

"You did not happen to hear any names in that particular conversation, did you?" Emile pressed him further.

"Why? You 'fraid your name's on that list?" The boy crossed his arms defiantly, ready to jump to his feet and escape at the drop of a hat if needed.

"Not a chance." Emile shook his head and tried not to laugh at the picture of the scene before him. This boy was more like himself than he wanted to admit and seeing it in child form only made him pity his own mother more. "But I do have a friend that seems to have found himself in a bit of a predicament over in the Bastille. By what you have heard, do you think there is a possibility that they will let him out soon?"

"Not likely." The boy shrugged and ate a few more bites of the bread. "Might be best to say your farewells now on his account. He's a goner for sure."

Emile frowned in response for he had sensed for quite some time that the foreboding truth of that reality was quickly approaching whether he liked it or not. "I understand, though I think I will still hold out a bit of hope for the time being. Who knows, maybe someone will be merciful to him in the end."

As if in complete incredulity now at his last statement, the boy cocked his head and looked at him momentarily like he was a true madman. "Now I <u>know</u> you are crazy."

"I've been called worse." Emile paid the staff the price of the meal and motioned for the two of them to leave. Michel complied respectfully, at least at first. Once out on the street, however, he became another child completely as he suddenly fell against Emile in an overly emotional gesture of gratitude, hugging him at his waist and crying out most conspicuously to the crowd like a true man of his craft. "Oh, thank you, sir!"

Emile grimaced at the obviously dramatic display, then stopped short as he felt the hot rush of a warm hand close to his chest. With a movement so fast that the boy scarcely saw it, Emile grasped the child's small fist firmly within his own and withdrew it from the inside of his coat, his eyes dark and penetrating merely a foot away from his face.

"There is nothing you want in there Michel but danger." He stared the boy down, the bloodlust rising ever so slightly with the beating of his heart at his necessary response.

"What danger? You don't scare me." The boy defiantly refused him again and struggled to get the man to release his hand.

Unable to help himself, Emile smirked wickedly in response to his struggle and slowly shook his head from side to side just once in either direction. "You might as well stop fighting me. I'll let you go when you hand me back my watch," he said cooly, not budging in the slightest on his hold of the boy.

Knowing he was trapped with no hope of escape; Michel released the watch concealed within his palm and allowed it to fall into Emile's waiting hand. "That would have paid for a week's worth of lunches, maybe two," Michel grumbled sourly back at him, extremely put out by the man's refusal of his ill-gotten treasure.

"I'm sure it would have, but most people prefer to be asked first." For the briefest of moments, Emile stared down at the boy, partially indignant that the boy had used him in such a fashion after his kindness towards him and also slightly fascinated by his blatant audacity. "If you knew what was best for you, you'd know to leave people like me alone."

"I don't know what you mean, sir. People like you don't care about people like me. Remember?" The boy lifted his head higher still challenging him toe to toe. "But they will soon enough. You'll see. Just like with your friend. We will make you listen."

"I hope for his sake that you are wrong." Emile felt the guilt wash over him once more at his unconscious participation in the boy's struggle, then cocked his head and smiled quite ruefully at the sudden realization. "You don't even know Lucien, do you, boy?"

"Lucien, who?" The boy grinned wickedly and threw a taunting glance back over his shoulder knowing he had gotten his way at last.

"Indeed."

Today was full of firsts it seemed. Emile had never once been on this side of a scheme before in his life. On the contrary, he was always the one who played with his target, the controller who manipulated all the conversations around him, not the one taken in by such manipulation. To be on the other end of such a thing, felt interestingly bizarre, confusing even.

Had he done something kind by treating this boy to a simple meal, or had he just opened the door to yet another of his newly discovered weaknesses?

"Here." He unhooked the pocket watch from its chain and tossed it to the boy who caught it easily. "Make sure you get what it's worth or I'll come looking for you, and see that Lucien gets a portion of it, too. You owe him that much."

With a jolt, the boy's eyes widened, justifiably so, at the man's sudden generosity before he turned back towards him, instantly skeptical. "I bet you will just call the *Comite* when I leave and have them arrest me like a common thief."

"Aren't you?" Emile looked down his nose judgmentally for just a second, then tilted his head in denial. "But no. I will not. Call it a gift for services rendered as your conversation today was quite enlightening."

"Thank you." The boy smiled proudly at the intended compliment, tucked the watch deep within his pants pocket, no doubt next to the four rolls of bread, and turned to leave.

Emile couldn't help but watch him as he left, hoping that whatever the boy's fate, he had made some small difference for him, yet also knowing there was little else he could do. The world in which they lived was filled with hundreds of people in the same position as Lucien and Michel and the woman in the street, and there was not enough money in his bank accounts alone to help them all.

"Maybe one day." Emile sighed at the sad realization and was about to leave, as well, but stopped when the boy who had just left paused about ten feet away and turned back to him to call out. "And Mister?"

"Yes," Emile said respectfully this time, giving the boy the deference of civility he so rightly deserved.

"Lucien is my brother. I take care of him, and he takes care of me," Michel said proudly.

"As it should be. Tell him it is from the man who told him about his name. He'll understand," Emile replied simply.

The boy nodded and ran away at a quick pace back to the place from which Emile had just come.

With the day drawing closer to supper, Emile headed back to his apartment, certain that whatever he would encounter tonight would be far less complicated emotionally than what he had just experienced away.

Chapter Seventeen

March 1st, 1793

"You've left your queen unguarded once more," Señor Moretti cautioned Sebastian from across the board, already accustomed to the manner in which his opponent played. With little other entertainment to speak of, they had been playing this game nearly every night since the young man had begun working down at the docks in the hopes of offering him some form of distraction after a long day of work. And yet, despite the countless hours of playing, Sebastain was no closer to winning today than he had been almost three months ago.

"I don't understand why this keeps happening." Sebastian picked up his rook and held it aloft over the board before placing it back upon the square from whence it came, unsure as to what move he should make next.

"Have you considered that perhaps your thoughts might be elsewhere tonight?" Señor Moretti watched the man silently as he struggled and furrowed his brow again and again in concentration.

Sebastian moved the rook two spaces forward and into a position in front of his king. "I know to what you are insinuating, and yes, they are <u>always</u> somewhere else. But what I want to know is what kind of strategy are you using to defeat me at every turn? There <u>has</u> to be something I am doing wrong."

Señor Moretti leaned back in his chair and flexed his fingers into a triangle in front of him. "I'm afraid that life is very much like this game of chess, my friend. There are always going to be challenging obstacles and enemies all around us." He leaned in closer and moved his knight to another position that would, in time, capture Sebastian's unprotected rook. "What we need to learn first is how to anticipate those moves from the pieces that will cause us the most harm. Yes, as in the game of chess, some of your pawns will have to be sacrificed, or set aside for a time, but they will still be necessary to the overall strategy of your game."

"And what do you think is the most important piece I should be worried about... in chess that is?" Sebastian played with a pawn within his hand before picking up his bishop and sliding it in front of his king to protect him.

"Oh, Sebastian..." Señor Moretti sighed and placed his hand over his face to hide his smile which he knew full-well would only infuriate the man across from him more.

"What?" Sebastian studied the board to see what he had done wrong, but from his angle, nothing appeared in danger.

"Check and mate." Señor Moretti moved his queen into place, then picked up his tea and took a sip. "The queen may seem to be only secondary to the place of the king in worth, but she is undoubtedly a most formidable foe to all on the chess board. In many such scenarios, losing the queen quite often means certain ruin for her king as there are few other pieces on the board who can match her abilities."

"I see what you are trying to allude to here." Sebastian replaced all his pieces back upon the board and motioned for Señor Moretti to do the same. "Charlotte is my queen. Is that what you are trying to say?"

"Perhaps..." The corners of Señor Moretti's mouth turned upwards slightly at the man's increasing perceptiveness. "But honestly, I was most certainly only speaking about chess... this time."

"Hmmmm...." Sebastian looked at him sideways skeptically and grunted. "The day that you are not referencing something else philosophically will be the day I finally beat you in chess."

"Oh?" Señor Moretti laughed. "Confident are we at last?"

"Not in the least." Sebastian studied his various black pieces before selecting one and moving it carefully into a new position, a move that incidentally, he had not tried previously. "I think we have time for another game before we retire tonight."

Señor Moretti nodded and did the same with his first pawn on the left. "Didn't you say before supper that you needed to write another letter to William?"

"It can wait until later." Sebastian brushed off the importance of the letter and tried this time to place his full attention onto the game. "Charlotte says the boys have caught some kind of strange cold that is going around the school. A lot of the other boys in the town are sick as well and have missed almost a week of instruction already, but Elijah only took ill when she wrote her letter five days ago. I am sure he is on the mend by now, or at least I hope so."

"And so, you are hoping William might be able to check on them?" Señor Moretti moved his bishop all the way to the middle of the board and took Sebastian's unprotected pawn. "I believe he is still in London if his letter the other day is accurate. Something about investigating a loose end of some kind, though I have no idea what would be so important as to drag him all the way there on such an errand."

"A loose end?" Sebastian raised his pawn before looking up at Señor Moretti with even greater interest. "Did he say what the loose end was?"

"Just something about a man who visited his family. Someone from his past, I believe, but do not concern yourself too unnecessarily in that regard. He has assured me that the issue has been resolved quite satisfactorily for the present." Señor Moretti dismissed the worry just as casually as it had been raised.

"I see." Sebastian was instantly suspicious about the simplicity with which William had described his dilemma as his letters to him were always quite detailed and thorough in nature even concerning the plainest of things. "And he didn't say who?" He pressed his mentor further, not feeling at ease with the entire conversation given his location so far from home.

"Nor what." Señor Moretti studied the board, then motioned again to his competitor. "It is still your move, sir."

Sebastian's eyes narrowed as he placed the piece in his hand carefully on the board and looked up at Señor Moretti to judge his reaction before removing his hand.

Señor Moretti only laughed. "You will receive no help from me, young man! You must win on your own merit or die trying."

Sebastian suddenly froze, unable to move as an unexpected thought struck him deeply.

"What's the matter? Did I say something wrong?" Señor Moretti noticed the change in the man immediately and moved to delay his reaction.

"I was just thinking about which piece to move and couldn't help but notice that some of our friends are represented here on the board, as well."

"Go on," Señor Moretti encouraged him, suddenly intrigued about what words of wisdom Sebastian might skillfully divulge for he knew him to be of an excellent intellect, all things considered.

"Well, the rook is most definitely William for no other piece on the board offers the stability that it represents. For all the faults that the man claims that he has, the doctor has proved time and time again to be a strengthening force to those around him both in his professional and personal life. At great cost to himself, he saved us from the sinking ship, even defended that Frenchman against Doctor Clarke, though I most certainly wouldn't have, and is even now trying to help Nathanael over in Wakefield."

"Yes, I think that would be a fitting description for our Doctor Wells. He is predictable and constant, making his moves in a straight line as if directly connected to his unchanging character. That would leave the next piece as the easiest to delegate out of all of them. Preacher Beckett is most obviously the bishop since he is the only one of the four of you to display such genuine spiritual convictions and piety."

"I concur. Though I was raised by a Catholic monk, I am nowhere near as devoted as Nathanael seems to be. The whole time they were here I don't think I heard the man ever <u>not</u> talk about God in some way during a conversation. It was maddening each time he did it as I could not believe how skillfully it was done. And I mean that in a good way, truly." Sebastian looked more closely at his bishop piece before placing it back upon the board where it belonged. "And if I am open to it, I should think there is much I can learn from his piece, too."

"I know you will, given the proper time and temperament. It is usually those with the strongest faith that motivate our own to even greater heights, I believe." He paused as if contemplating the next piece before his eyes glistened over with increasing humor. "So, which piece do you think represents your most favorite of companions?"

Sebastian rolled his eyes. "I'd give him the jester piece if there was one, but sadly, there is not. Though if either of us were to ask him here today, he would most likely select the king so he could rule us all."

Señor Moretti clicked his tongue in disapproval. "You barely know the man enough to make such judgements against his character, Sebastian."

Sebastian looked down and studied the fire next to him. As much as this conversation had initially intrigued him, he was beginning to tire of it. This time of inner reflection only made the irritation he had felt on the beach begin rising within him once more. How many times had the scene of looking up from the sand and seeing literally no one flashed across his mind whenever he was feeling frustrated with a particular piece of metal? A hundred? "I know enough. If Emile cared anything at all about the rest of us, he would have never left here like he did."

"As a matter of fact, I spoke with Emile myself before he left. He had his reasons for leaving much like William and Nathanael did," Señor Moretti divulged. "Despite what you might think, he did not leave like a thief in the night as you suppose."

"Then you also know that I am right." Sebastian continued on in his line of judgement. "Honorable men do not abandon others, no matter their reasoning or intentions."

Señor Moretti only shook his head. "Emile is the knight not because he is honorable, but because he is noble. Honor does not make one noble, just as nobility does not make a man honorable. Take me for example."

Sebastian looked up at him once more in puzzlement.

"Do you think that I am honorable?"

"Yes! A thousand times over, sir!" The man exclaimed quickly.

"And yet, if you had met me three hundred years ago you might have thought the same of me as you do of Emile," Señor Moretti admitted. "I was not always as wise as I am now, nor did I make the best decisions in the beginning. And despite how much it pains me to admit it to you today, I even killed people, Sebastian. Not many, but enough to leave their scars forever with me."

Sebastian nodded his head in understanding. "So, you are of the opinion that Emile will do the same someday? That he will unexpectedly surprise us into being a changed man because deep down, he honestly wants to do what is right?"

"It is possible." Señor Moretti handed him his knight from across the board. "There is a very good reason why the knight is the hardest figure to fight against on the chess board. It is because the very manner in which he moves may seem unpredictable and erratic, but he also must follow a set course. Sound like anyone else that we know?"

"You never cease to amaze me, sir." Sebastian smiled. "Then since you already said that Charlotte is the queen, I know you are probably going to say that I am the king. Sadly, that is the piece with the least amount of power and the greatest need of defense. I'm sorry, but that sounds far more pathetic from this side of the board than it does regal."

"Pathetic? Honestly, Sebastian! I have never met a man so determined towards self-degradation than you always seem to be." Señor Moretti chastised him firmly. "The king can also represent leadership and protection and though you do not lead this group of friends you have joined, whether by fate or by chance, you do lead your family. I have seen you work harder than any man I have ever known, and for what? Your own personal gain? No, you have been doing it all for them, or so you say."

Sebastian curled up the left side of his mouth and tried to smile. "Truthfully, sir, I feel more like a pawn that is needed to be sacrificed to protect everyone else behind them."

"That is merely your perspective." Señor Moretti turned the chess board around so that Sebastian now viewed the game from the viewpoint of the white pieces. "When you flip the angle from which you look, the pieces take on a whole new meaning, do they not? Though I think we can both agree that whether you are a king, or a pawn, is entirely up to you. Both pieces on the board serve a very similar style of moving and function, yet the king is the only one the queen and every other piece on the board cares about in the end. It is their mission to help protect him, not the other way around."

Sebastian studied the board from his current direction then slid the white pawn over to capture the black pawn next to it. "Let's try it this way just once. I'd like to see if I do any better from this side."

"Suit thyself." Señor Moretti moved his rook to capture the white pawn Sebastian had just moved. "But it will matter not which side you play from if you continue to use the same strategy. Either way, you will still lose."

"I know." Sebastian boldly moved his rook to swiftly capture Señor Moretti's. "Perhaps I will try fighting on the offensive this time and not always running around trying to merely defend myself at every turn."

Señor Moretti began to say something additionally prophetic but stopped as he considered the move Sebastian had just made. "A very excellent suggestion, indeed, as long as you remember the first rule of chess."

"I know, I know..." Sebastian rolled his eyes and smiled. "Never leave your queen unguarded."

"Precisely!" Señor Moretti exclaimed before moving his queen into a position halfway across the board. "On guard, Sebastian! I am coming for you!"

The two men chuckled lightly at the playful antic.

Chapter Eighteen

Journal Entry for March 2nd
Day 10 of my fast

*F*asting as a... well, it begs not to be written down here, has been infinitely more complicated than anything I have ever endured as a human. For starters, as a man, I was always loathe to even be around food during my fast for fear of the temptation it would bring to quit my most worthy of endeavors.

I would even go so far as to utterly not permit myself to walk down the very road by the bakers or some other such culinary establishment, nor would I keep food of any kind within the premises of my home. Yet in my current state, that form of diligent aversion is not entirely possible when the very people for which I am called to minister unto are also the main sources of my enticement—my very real temptation, for I have never wanted something as much in my life as I have wanted this. A mere drop alone would have lasted me for days if I had been given it during my darkest longings when we first arrived in Wakefield.

In the recent past, this internal draw towards needing a physical substitute for sustenance had been carefully kept at bay by supplementing with what William had been faithfully supplying. But with my friend now in London, and the last of my emergency supply running out tomorrow, I fear that I will soon begin to feel especially panicked about the very real possibility of my imminent failure, or rather what that would mean for both of us should I not be strong enough to endure until his return.

Or to compare it to something a bit more mundane, any man who has been given to the necessity to drink, a break away from his strike of abstinence would be most inconvenient. A nuisance even, to his family and friends who have worked so diligently towards his perfected state. Though his fall back into sin would no doubt be equally disappointing, they would still choose to rally around him and begin again to safeguard his security against another such demise. Why? Because, quite obviously, alcohol is the devil's potion and quickly ruins both men and women alike with its destructive powers.

And yet, breaking from my own pledge could prove most fatal to not only the unfortunate victim, but also my very soul.

Since my change, I have come to a rather uneasy settlement of terms with the fact that perhaps God has chosen to place me on a very different spiritual timeline than His own. And though I do not understand His reasoning for this decision, I am forced to accept it as easily as I accept my own cursed fate as a sinner. This in itself has been far from easy, as the previous entries in this journal can attest, but even in this most dissident of states, I can honestly say that I have found the spiritual struggle to be equally rewarding as I strive to help others as best as I can in my current means of existence, no matter the eternal destination for myself.

My heavenly condition aside, I have determined once and for all to live my life in His service and obey His every commandment, highest of those being those ten given to Moses on top of Mount Sinai. Yet even in this determination, I fear my faith will not be truly tested until such time as I am no longer supported by my stored means of obedience. And so, I will savor my last vestige of security at breakfast tomorrow and pray that the Lord will sustain me thereafter.

On a small, positive note, Sebastian has written us a letter that arrived just this morning. Besides the usual light banter about Señor Moretti and the villagers below, he communicates that he has sent correspondence to his contact in the Americas. Though he does not go into all the particulars, I am encouraged by the hopeful countenance of his recent letter. Perhaps, this will be a means of rejoining his family quite soon, or at least that has been my prayer these past few months.

My conversations with Miss Summerfield have also progressed in a very positive direction. Over the summer, I am to tutor two of her older brothers in Biblical Theology, a topic for which I feel keenly connected to given my current occupation and recent experience with the school back in Worchester.

In exchange for their lessons, Miss Summerfield has agreed to continue to teach me on the piano forte. A decision, I am sure, that will draw much more effort on her part than mine with theology. Though one never knows. Perhaps, I will learn to be a good student, after all. For who could help being so with such a delightful teacher!

We are to enjoy a lovely stroll tonight if the weather is not too inclement as it has been raining for the better part of a week already. I do hope it will stop for it has been almost two weeks since we were last alone together without at least one of her siblings under foot.

I do not have a firm answer as of yet to her most recent question of marriage, but I do feel more inclined than ever to explore that possibility with her in the future. Who knows whether or not this time of careful introspection and physical denial is but a preparation for our future.

Only time will tell...

And I for one am looking most forward to those answers.

~   ~   ~   ~   ~

Nathanael leaned heavily upon the arms of his small wooden chair as he thought back to the day before, pondering once again what he might want to include in his daily journal entry for so much had transpired since his last entry a week ago that it would take him most of the day to record it if he tried. Yet he also knew that despite what he might wish to write, less might be far more desirable under the current circumstances.

For the most part, the day of his weekly outing with Miss Summerfield, had begun much like any other Thursday, complete with a light breakfast of his favorite item—cinnamon toast and a mug of warm coffee. It was not, of course, what he truly wanted, but it was at least the one thing he could stand to consume any time he craved something other than blood. Gratefully, as unworthy a substitute as one might imagine it to be, the meager meal still remained as the single most delight left in his otherwise unpalatable world of food choices.

The stored blood he had so carefully rationed since William had departed had been emptied six days ago, making him slightly more anxious with each passing day when the post arrived and there was yet no letter from William informing him of his return. Still, he felt somewhat assured at the moment that his body was adjusting to his fast reasonably well as he had only experienced a few unpleasant side effects as of yet, and not any of the more worrisome threats to others that he had half-expected by now.

Maybe all his fears regarding their safety were totally unfounded after all. Perhaps what he perceived as his weaknesses in being a vampire were really just mental insecurities that he had allowed to take a much stronger hold than what they deserved. Maybe... and yet, just the thought right now of finding someone to drink from made his mouth water contemplating it.

Nathanael shut the cover of his journal with a loud thud and closed his eyes, refusing to give in to his repeated, waking nightmare. *"Elsie..."* He forced his mind to focus on far more stable things like their picnic yesterday and the conversation he had also endured with her father.

For weeks, Mr. Gabe Summerfield had been pestering him after church for a moment to speak with him, but in his learned adeptness, Nathanael had managed to sidestep his request at every turn, creating more than one excuse as to why he could not do so. The man had understood at first for he knew the young preacher had many such responsibilities among his flock, but after the third such delay, he had chosen to corner Nathanael before the service, pinning him down verbally as to his intent.

~   ~   ~   ~   ~

"I would like an opportunity with you, Preacher, before the service begins, if you, please." Mr. Summerfield took off his hat and held it respectfully within his hands near the back of the church.

Having nowhere else to which he could flee, Nathanael paused and slowly turned around to face him, racking his brain quickly for a truthful reason as to why he could not remain. "How can I be of service, sir? Did you need some help down at the mill today?" He offered distractedly, knowing that the man had little need of his services in that regard, nor would he know what to do if he had chosen to ask.

"No." Mr. Summerfield shook his head and nodded it slightly after towards his daughter who was already up front taking her seat at the piano forte. "It's about my Elsie," he stated plainly, never a man who preferred a rather lengthy explanation.

"She is a wonderful blessing to our services, sir. I am extremely grateful to you that you provided such an excellent education for her over the years. You should know that we would be hopelessly lost every Sunday without her careful direction," Nathanael complimented her easily, knowing full-well that her ability to play music was not what Mr. Summerfield had intended to speak about at all.

"She is a gift. And speaking of gifts… what might you be expecting regarding a dowry should the time ever come to it? I don't have much to offer with nine other children under foot, but I would like to set something by her to see that she is wed proper and all," the man spoke humbly and thoughtfully, measuring each of his words with the others until he had said his peace.

Nathanael was sure his mouth must have remained open for several seconds for the man across from him had patiently waited for his response and then chuckled lightly when he did not.

"I suspect you have at least considered the possibility, Mr. Beckett, or you would not be entertaining my daughter so often as of late," Mr. Summerfield stated the obvious once more and waited a bit longer.

"Um, yes." Suddenly finding his voice once again, Nathanael cleared his throat and tried to speak, but his answer came back at a slightly higher pitch than he had ever intended, "I do not require anything to marry your daughter where a monetary blessing is concerned. The Lord has taken care of me throughout the years, and I know He will continue to do so afterwards if we should be so blessed. However, if you wish to leave a small stipend for her in trust with you, should she ever need it in the future, that would be entirely acceptable. Though again, it is not necessary, but I am sure she would look upon it most favorably." He managed to say, then exhaled slowly to calm the racing of his heart that the conversation or his lack of nutrition had created.

"Then you have my blessing, Mr. Beckett. You have but to ask her when you are ready as I do not wish to ever stand in the way of one of my children's happiness. From what I can tell, you are a good man, and our Elsie clearly favors you, so that is enough for me." He gave his permission freely and held out his hand for Nathanael to accept it and seal the agreement.

With a start, Nathanael looked down at the offered object, suddenly aware of the magnitude of what it would mean if he were to accept it and forced himself to consider the choice fully before doing so. He had asked God months ago to stop him from pursuing after her if she was not His will for his life and to date, no blockade or negative event had transpired between them, not even a single disagreement verbally or false step concerning his more impractical desires had occurred, which made him cautiously optimistic that he was indeed on the right path for the two of them.

And then there was Elsie herself. There was no one else in all the world that made him happier than she did right now, and he was certain that if he looked anywhere else in this wide world for someone better, there never would be. As far as he was aware, their eventual union would simply be just another joyous step along God's path for his life and not something he should be afraid of.

"I promise to love her as much as you do, sir, maybe more." Nathanael grinned widely as he reached out his hand and clasped Mr. Summerfield's in return, finally deciding upon the answer to the question that had been bothering him since he had arrived.

Mr. Summerfield also smiled, the corners of his eyes pinching like a splayed fan on the edges. "See to it that you do."

"Yes, sir." Nathanael retrieved his hand and placed it back within his pocket once more to try to keep it as warm as possible.

"Do you know when you will ask her then? I know the misses will be pestering me to know when I tell her about our conversation." Mr. Summerfield placed his hat back upon his head and shrugged back into his coat, obviously not intending on staying for the upcoming service.

Nathanael did not move to rebuke him for he understood that the man had to labor many odd hours to meet the load of work pressed upon him. He knew from experience, that Mr. Summerfield would make up for it in the evening hours studying his Bible next to the fire or in reading it to his children, so it comforted Nathanael just a little that he did not need to chide the man too sternly for his absence here. "Would asking her by Pasha be too soon?"

"No, the sooner the better to my way of thinking. Not that I mind one more mouth to feed, but that girl has been pining over you something fierce ever since Christmas. It will be nice to see her happily married," he replied and began to make his way over to the door.

"That is good to know... I think," Nathanael answered and held the door open for him before turning back to cast a glance over at Elsie seated at the piano. The light of the bright Sunday morning sun was steadily casting a golden beam upon her auburn hair, making the various hues of brown and red strands shine under its glow.

I wonder what it would be like to touch her hair just once and feel the softness of its texture? Or to place my hand against her cheek and know that I will never need to hide anything about my desires ever again? He let that thought weigh itself out in the moment, then looked away and closed the back door once more. His parishioners would be arriving shortly, and with the cold breeze that had begun to blow even harder since sunup, he preferred to keep as much of the warmth inside the building as he could manage.

As the hour for the service drew nearer still, he made his way back to his study and spent the next half hour trying to pray and consider which sermon the Lord wanted him to preach upon, but his thoughts constantly went back to the conversation he had just had with Elsie's father, second-guessing his decision more than once when the seeds of doubt returned.

At the last, entirely frustrated now with his inability to focus as he should, he simply selected one of the prepared sermons from the top of the pile and left the room quickly to begin greeting the crowd, taking the time to shake each person's hand warmly before finding his place behind the pulpit.

As it turned out, it was the perfect sermon after all for the theme of it had dwelt heavily on waiting for God's direction. Something Nathanael was quite intimately acquainted with and today felt most keenly connected to. The familiar songs completed the service as they always had and when Elsie closed the lid of the piano to leave, Nathanael found himself asking her to join him on a picnic. The very one they had enjoyed just yesterday, in fact.

She had agreed, as he knew she would and when he picked her up mid-morning Wednesday, after her baking was complete, he had managed to concoct the perfect plan for his proposal. With the village offering very little in the way of diversion, it was always up to him to be constantly creative with their outings, enticing her with long strolls to watch the stars at night or a hike in the woods beyond the apothecary in search of edible mushrooms.

Yet today was something else entirely. Today he had arranged for a picnic by Miller's Pond, complete with a lovely lunch that he had persuaded the man at the tavern to procure for him. To his relief, it hadn't been overly difficult to do so as the proprietor knew from William's more colorful stories to the man, that Nathanael's skill in the kitchen was less than adequate for survival. But still, he appreciated his daily guidance all the same. Besides, the expense of the task would help Elsie's family, as well, as he knew Mrs. Summerfield often cooked various aspects of the meals for them.

"I'm sorry the day could not be sunnier for you. Try as I might, I couldn't convince God to change it, and so I think we will have to be content with a dreary day and hope in the end we are not rained out of the delightful outing that I have planned." Nathanael tried to be as encouraging as ever as he casually walked arm-in-arm with the woman beside him.

"I don't mind if you don't," she said sweetly, then allowed the hat on her head to slide down to her back, inviting the wind that had started to blow gently to play with her longer hair.

For the first time that he had remembered, she had chosen to leave it completely down, placing very little adornments to style it around her face. Most women in the village often chose to wear their hair tied up or in braids as Elsie had done on many other occasions, but today it was different. The thick piles of loose curls hung around her shoulders like a warm shawl, daring him to touch them.

Still, he resisted, yet only barely. Endeavoring to keep his eyes focused instead on the road ahead of them, they continued to stroll down the dirt lane past several other couples and children as they walked until they came upon a more secluded area on the opposite end of the pond—a small oval shaped patch of grass with tall green rushes of various varieties that showed off their brilliant hues. Satisfied with the moderate seclusion that the location provided, Nathanael set the basket down and unfurled the blanket Elsie had been carrying before helping her to take her seat upon it and joining her.

The weather, though threatening to storm at any minute, could not have been better suited for his needs if he had ordered it from the Lord himself. In fact, the entire sky was thickly overcast with foreboding grey clouds requiring not the least bit of a concern as to whether or not he would need to wear his dreadful brown cloak or any other extra pieces of clothing for protection. Better yet, though he had been struggling for the majority of the week with a terrible headache and shaking hands, today, the troubling symptoms had seemed to have disappeared altogether... miraculously so. It was almost as if the very thought of beginning a new life with Elsie had also changed who he was fundamentally at his core—though he was reluctant to believe so much could ever possibly be true.

"Would you care for something to eat, perhaps? I think there is enough in that basket to feed an army, maybe two," Nathanael joked with Elsie easily, lifting the lid to show her the various offerings that were carefully tucked within.

"Not just yet, thank you. I was mostly wanting to talk to you about the Pasha service coming up. Do you think our duet will be ready in time?" Elsie asked, curiously optimistic about how much the man beside her had been practicing after his lessons.

"I doubt I will ever be ready to enthusiastically display that particular talent publicly, but if you still wish to risk humiliation with my attempt, I will obediently comply." Nathanael sighed loudly, not interested in the least in making a bigger spectacle of himself than he already did.

"Oh, don't be so dramatic. You will be fine as long as you remember to breathe." Elsie rolled her eyes at the ridiculousness of his response and chided him on his lack of excitement.

Nathanael laughed. "Breathe? What is that?" He smiled again and took the opportunity to lay down upon his back to stare up at the clouds passing quickly by them overhead.

With little hesitation, Elsie moved the basket over onto the grass beside the blanket and did the same, her head resting fairly close to his own upon the blanket. "It really is quite lovely today, isn't it, Mr. Beckett?"

"Most definitely." Nathanael gave a quick glance over at her appreciatively, then returned his gaze back to the sky feeling a sense of calmness in the moment between them.

The two lay there for quite some time, pensively watching the sky above without the need of further conversation before Nathanael's hand brushed against Elsie's quite mistakenly and froze. Alarmed at the unexpected contact, his mind could not react quickly enough to form a plan to remove it, but instead chose to wait and see what Elsie might do. In a way, he half-expected her to at least chastise him for being so forward, but as the seconds ticked by, he began to relax once more when she did not.

Knowing what might possibly be going through his mind, or perhaps feeling the same way herself, Elsie wisely chose to say nothing... Nothing at all. It was almost as if he had not done anything of note whatsoever.

Then, when he thought he should pull his hand away and return it to his pocket once more, she closed her eyes contentedly, smiled and clasped his hand gently within her own before slightly wincing. "Goodness, Nathanael! You must have terrible circulation issues as your hands can be so warm sometimes, and as cold as ice in others."

Nathanael moved to release her, suddenly fearing his discovery more than his desire to be close to her, but she would not let him. Instead, she remained as she was on the blanket, perfectly composed and indifferent to the strange occurrence.

"Do you mind terribly?" He asked apprehensively, holding his breath until she gave her response.

Elsie shook her head nonchalantly. "Not in the slightest. It is what makes you, you." Her simple acceptance of the unusual surprised him once more as it always had.

He realized then that this endearing quality about her was the real reason why it had been so easy to accept her love from the very first time they had met and why he wanted to spend the rest of his life with her now. "Elsie?"

"Yes." She continued lying beside him, looking overly serene.

"Would you still be open to that discussion we talked about if I were to ask you?" He closed his eyes as well, not wanting to see her expression if it was not what he was hoping.

Elsie squeezed his hand reflexively and held it even tighter. "Only if you are truly ready."

Nathanael smiled once more and felt an incredible peace wash over him in the process. "Soon... I promise."

"Alright." Elsie released his hand and sat up, suddenly energetically inclined to do something else entirely. "What do you say about a trip across the pond together? I think I see a small boat over there we can use to do so."

"You want to go boating in March?" Nathanael sat up on his elbows and opened one eye to see if she were truly serious. "I know it is unseasonably warm for this time of year, but I shudder to think how cold that water might still be if either of us were to fall in."

"We aren't going to fall in, silly," Elsie declared positively and stood up. "Come with me."

"I'd rather not," Nathanael protested further.

"Suit yourself." She left him on the blanket and took two steps away from him towards the pond.

"Wait, Elsie! I am coming!" He reached out for her hand and clasped it, righting himself in the process. "You truly are a wonder sometimes."

"I am glad to hear it." She laughed lightly and the two of them made their way over to the small boat before pushing it into the water after much effort.

Then, waiting on the small dock for him to be seated first before helping her in, Elsie held his hand as he descended into it, watching in complete amusement at the many faces he made as he attempted to do so. "You have to sit down, or you are going to flip it for sure." She instructed him wisely.

"Sit?!" Nathanael's whole body quaked with the rocking motion the boat was demonstrating. "I think I prefer to abandon ship, miss."

"Not yet, Nathanael. You haven't even given it a fair try." Elsie tried to both steady him and hand him an oar to hold onto but that only made the situation worse.

With a sudden thrust of panic, Nathanael reached for the side of the dock for better balance, which only caused the vessel to dip dramatically towards it. Then, in what seemed to be mere seconds thereafter, the entire boat, Nathanael and all, flipped over completely, soaking him in the process as it provided the most delightful of entertainment for a very dry Miss Elsie Summerfield.

"You flipped me on purpose, didn't you?" Nathanael drug the front of the soggy vessel over to the side of the pond and shoved it higher up on shore before reaching out for the floating oar. His once neatly tied back hair now clung to his face and neck in a total state of disarray and his clothes were heavily drenched and soiled from the loose vegetation on top of the water and the sludge occupying the bottom below.

"Oh, Mr. Beckett!" Elsie shook her head at the sight of him but could not stop laughing at what had just happened.

"Mr. Beckett, indeed. I feel more like a bullfrog at the moment... or a fish," Nathanael grumbled as he tried more than once to successfully scale the slippery bank and join his companion, but in the end had resorted to crawling up on shore before righting himself once more next to her. "Your servant, *mademoiselle*." He gave a slight bow, that allowed a small plop of mud to fall from his shoulder almost onto her clean shoes.

Elsie placed her hand over her mouth to contain the giggle that followed. "Whatever am I going to do with you now, sir."

Feeling a flash of something akin to irritation, Nathanael tried to remain cross at his perceived humiliation, but he could not. In some small way he was grateful it had been him who had taken the undesired bath for it was probably best that he had been the one to have fallen in and not Elsie for he never felt the cold anymore and she would have most likely caught a chill. "I'm not sure, love me perhaps..." he said as if almost mumbling under his breath and tried his best to wring out at least some of the water from the bottom of his coat and vest.

"Well, that is a given, Nathanael, and not because I feel bad for you either." Elsie reached her clean hand towards his cheek and attempted to swipe some of the moisture from off his face.

Nathanael smiled weakly once more at the gesture. "That won't help for the rest of me, I am afraid." He chuckled, then added, "I'm sorry to say this, but I think our picnic has concluded for the present. Maybe we can reschedule it for another day when I am less... um, wet." He tried to be pleasant in his suggestion but wanted nothing more than to retreat to the apothecary and get out of his soggy attire as quickly as possible. Anything that would keep him from feeling even colder.

"Alright. Maybe you can come over for the meal my family is having for Pasha. I can even teach you how to cook if you like." Elsie waited patiently by the tree as he went back and reclaimed their belongings from the other side of the pond.

"I'd offer you my arm, but I fear you should most definitely refuse it under the circumstances, Miss Summerfield," he said politely, then watched as she wrapped the blanket they had been lying on around him instead.

"There, that will keep you warm until you get home." Elsie beamed and he could not help but join her.

"I love you, Miss Elsie Summerfield. You know that, right?" Nathanael declared easily as he finally gave in and reached forward to touch just one of her loose curls. In every way, it was indeed just as soft as he had imagined, unbearably so.

"I do, Mr. Beckett, and I love you, too." Elsie's face spoke only of her joyous contentment as they walked back to her home and tried to make some plausible explanation as to why they were back so early and why Nathanael was so very wet.

None of it truly mattered anyways.

Though no words of promise had ever been given, the shared knowledge of what they both felt seemed like enough.

~   ~   ~   ~   ~

Glancing down at his journal once more, Nathanael picked up his pen and dipped it deeply into the rich black ink before opening the book up again to the first blank page.

Journal Entry for March 8th
Day 16 of my fast

On Pasha, I think I will finally ask Miss Elsie Summerfield to marry me.
And despite how impossible it might be to even write this here...
I know she will say, "Yes".

Chapter Nineteen

March 15th, 1793

F eeling suddenly confused, William doubled the letter in half and placed it once again within the folds of his pocket, the way he had done at least three other times during his journey from London to Portsmouth that night. The address on the correspondence he had been sent was most certainly correct, yet the house before him appeared utterly devoid of life, and most definitely not where a family of three were supposed to be currently living.

With Sebastian gone, had they needed to leave? He scrutinized the dark windows on the second level as if checking for signs of life and narrowed them when he thought he made out the smallest glow of a flickering flame in the second one to the right. No, someone was most definitely home, which made the stillness of the house all the more worrisome to him. From what he had seen with his brother's children, two boys under eight should have been causing more than a little bit of noise, no matter what the time of day. Moreover, not a single animal was present in the rather large, gated pen and barn to the immediate right of the building. By all outward appearances, the home and its occupants were both alarmingly still and deathly quiet.

William tied his horse to the wooden column on the front porch and took the three necessary steps to the front door to knock firmly, hoping someone would answer before he had to resort to less conventional methods of fulfilling his called upon task. As a rule, he could not imagine himself to be as bold as to break down the front door to investigate further, but he was not opposed to slipping through a front or back window to discover if the person inside was not totally incapacitated, and therefore, unable to open the front door to allow him entry. In London, his father would have simply called for a magistrate to permit his entry, but in these lesser populated areas, Doctor Hadleigh had assured him that it was far simpler to ask forgiveness than permission, especially where health was concerned.

Hearing the unmistakable sound of soft footsteps descending a flight of stairs inside, his heart quickened its pace, causing him to focus more on the breathing exercises that he had perfected during the past three months to control it before his mind could fill with the more, darker thoughts of his existence. Though he had renewed his commitment at Señor Moretti's to spend his life healing others, that did not also necessarily mean that his body dutifully agreed with him—far from it, as he had seen with Mr. Morgan back in London. With every drop of blood that he consumed, he found himself drawn more and more to the necessity of it, despite what he might have desired otherwise. It was part of the motivation behind his writing so often to Sebastian about his struggles. For some unknown reason, simply putting the pain down on paper lessened its hold upon him as it freed him from the grip it steadily maintained, if only for a few moments.

Nevertheless, despite all of that, he <u>was</u> improving, and by the time that the handle of the door lifted slightly, he had gratefully found himself fully in control of his capacities once more. Or at least in that sense of the term for there always remained the usual nervousness that accompanied the meeting of new people.

"Can I help you, sir?" The woman, who looked shockingly beautiful even in her frazzled state, asked through a small crack in the door.

Clearing his throat to remove the last evidence of his anxiety, William reached in his pocket and retrieved the letter once more. "I'm sorry for the interruption so early in your morning, miss, but are you, Charlotte Fabbri?"

"Yes." The woman looked even less likely now to open the door to him than a moment earlier.

"I know that you don't know me, but a mutual acquaintance sent me to check on you and the boys, a Mr. Sebastian Fabbri."

The woman's eyes and mouth narrowed in increased scrutiny at the use of their family's lesser used name. "You must be mistaken, sir. There is no one here by that name." She turned to leave and attempted to close the door without waiting for William's reply.

"Please..." William placed one hand upon the door to forcefully stop her. "We were on the *Endeavour* together last fall. I met him there and formed an acquaintance with him thereafter. Here." He held up the letter that had arrived only yesterday morning imploring him to come as quickly as he could to check on them. "Do you recognize his handwriting?"

The woman behind the door opened it a little wider still so that she could take the offered correspondence from his hand and study it. "You say you know my Sebastian?"

"Most definitely. A blacksmith on his way to the America's who is also maybe a little too hard upon himself at times. Please, feel free to read what he sent to verify what I say is true." William folded his hands patiently in front of him and waited for her to check the validity of his words.

The woman, dressed only in a simple, cream nightgown and a long, richly colored lavender shawl that covered much of it, read the letter quickly, then wiped a tear that had escaped from the corner of her eye. "This is most definitely from my husband. And who are you again? My husband is not usually one to make friends so easily."

"I would have to agree with you on that point, as well, though I believe he has many other admirable qualities to offer. My name is William Wells by the way. I live in Wakefield but was in London visiting my parents last week when the epidemic struck. I would have returned back to my home sooner, but I have been so busy helping with the sick in London that I lost track of the time," William replied respectfully before pressing immediately towards the purpose of his journey. "His letter says that one of the boys may be ill, correct?"

Charlotte nodded and opened the door wider for the man to enter and follow her into the finely constructed home. "Yes, our youngest, Elijah. He took sick a little over a week ago. I thought he would improve as the rest of the others from his school have but he hasn't, and now I am worried. In fact, I was about to head into town this morning to fetch the doctor myself."

"Well, then you are in luck because I am also a very good doctor, or so my father is always telling me. May I examine the boy in your healer's place, or would you prefer to have me go for him instead?" William removed his hooded cloak and casually placed it over the back of the nearest chair as if the motion of it in this home was second nature to him already.

"At this point, I'd welcome any help offered, sir." Charlotte's eyes were now spilling over freely with grateful tears of relief. "You are undoubtedly the answer to my prayers and so much more." She led the way slowly up the short, wooden staircase to the upper floor and over to the second room on the left where the sick child lay before opening the door for him to enter first.

The room, which was still quite dark as he approached, held only a small halfway spent candle alight on the table near the young child and a single bed in the center of the room and nothing more. Not a single book or toy lay on the floor, but all were carefully removed as if in precaution for whatever might transpire.

Reaching down with one hand, William cautiously felt the forehead of the fitfully sleeping child and immediately flew into action at the touch. "Can you please fetch me a fresh basin of the coolest water you can find, and as many cut up rags as you can spare. We need to get his fever down and quickly."

Charlotte left out of the room obediently and returned just a short time later with the necessary items. "I've already done this twice since yesterday, but it has not seemed to help in the slightest."

"I am sure you did." William nodded as threw off the sheets and rubbed the boy's legs and arms to increase his circulation. "And you were very wise to do so." He pulled a small packet of white power out of his satchel and poured just a small portion of it into the metal cup beside the bed. "If you can add a little water to this and make the boy sip it slowly, that would help me tremendously." He set the woman to work as he listened to the boy's heart and examined him for other aspects of the illness he had been seeing back in London.

"What is it that he is suffering from?" Charlotte asked as she cradled the boy's head in her arms, sitting behind him on the bed to guide him in periodically drinking the bitter liquid.

"They call it the grippe for lack of a better term, though the symptoms vary from one individual to another. In my experience, the patient suffers from very high fevers, chills, headaches, a sore throat, and maybe even pain behind both of their eyes for a time. And if they survive all of that, there can sometimes be a racking cough that the patient suffers from for several weeks or until he is completely restored to health."

"Well, he has definitely had at least four of those symptoms already, though the slight cough did not start until this morning." Charlotte crossed her arms over the boy and held him close to her chest while placing her cheek beside his head. "Are we too late?"

William washed the boy's legs repeatedly, then laid the damp rags over any exposed skin to further cool the boy down. "I don't think so, though we will need to do this as often as we can until his fever breaks. Do you think you can help me with that?"

Charlotte nodded but did not let go of her protective grasp on her son.

"He is young, Mrs. Fabbri. And that means there are many things in his favor." William tried to comfort the woman the best way he knew how though he knew many such boys like him over the years had died from far less. "You mustn't lose hope just yet."

"Thank you for coming," she said quickly, then began humming a soft tune.

William paused for a moment in his work and watched the woman across from him, taking her in fully for the first time since his arrival. Sebastian had told him nothing in his letters of his wife's uncommonly stunning beauty, or of her indomitable strength which William could clearly see even from his brief encounter with her. Nor had the man expressed even once how very intelligent she seemed to be as she had kept pace with his every step he had taken whether he had given her a direction or not.

"Would it be alright if I were to stay until his fever has subsided?" He asked timidly, not wanting to overstep his welcome as the woman looked practically on the verge of collapsing herself from exhaustion. "I can even check on your other son when he awakens or perhaps bring you some nourishment. Have you eaten recently?" William tilted his head to study the woman more closely for there were already grey circles forming beneath her very tired looking eyes and a slight gauntness to her cheeks.

"Not recently, but I will be fine. I've just been a bit too preoccupied with Elijah to manage any of that myself. But if you have the time to spare to examine Jedidiah, too, that would be most welcome," she replied and the two of them fell into a collective silence once more as the sun began to rise in the sky just outside the window, filling the room and the bed within with its orange and red glow.

Reaching down, William picked up a wooden chair from out of the light's path and moved it more centrally against the wall at the foot of the bed and took a seat, content to spend the allotted time in silent reflection. Then, for several hours more, they repeated this same routine of bathing Elijah periodically and massaging his legs and arms and as they did, his concern for the boy's condition lessened along with his fever.

At last, when the sun had moved away from the window by at least 45 degrees, William moved closer to examine the boy's head and throat more accurately, judging whether their efforts were having any lasting effects at all. "I think we can safely say that his fever has subsided considerably for the present." William breathed a sigh of relief and lifted a silent praise of thanksgiving, grateful that the boy was at least improving though after what he had just endured back in London, he knew that it was far too early to think that the boy was completely out of danger yet.

"Mama? There's a horse out front. Has Papa returned?" A lean boy, not older than eight but definitely much taller than one should be, rushed into the room in search of his mother before stopping and almost falling over by the action when he saw the stranger sitting upon the bed next to his brother. "Who are you?" The boy scrunched his nose up in sharp judgment while protectively standing with his arms crossed firmly over his chest by the door.

"Now, that is a face I have seen before." William couldn't help the chuckle that escaped at the sight of the boy. "You most certainly resemble your father very much, remarkably so."

"That he does." Charlotte reached her one hand out to the boy and drew him closer to her on the bed. "Doctor Wells, this is Jedidiah, our oldest. Please mind your manners and say hello to the man, son," she chided him gently. "He came all the way from London to help us."

Still not convinced of the man's right to be present here, the boy skeptically held out just one hand to him formally. "I am pleased to make your acquaintance, sir."

"As am I." William took the offered hand, shook it twice, then stood up. "Speaking of horses, do you think you might show me where I might board my horse for the night?"

"Is he staying, Mama?" Jedidiah looked quickly up at the man as if reasoning out why this stranger had come instead of his beloved father.

"For the moment," Charlotte answered and moved the younger child's head from off her chest to a new position upon the pillow. "Now, can you please get dressed quickly and take Doctor Well's horse to the barn when you are finished?"

"Yes, ma'am." Jedidiah frowned, then left the room obediently to follow her instructions.

"Oh, I wouldn't want to impose on your resources here, Mrs. Fabbri. I can easily board him at the livery in town if you have one." William put his satchel back over his neck and replaced the sheet on top of the now sleeping Elijah so the boy would not catch a chill.

"Nonsense, there is plenty of room in the barn now that most of the livestock is no longer in it." Charlotte looked down at Elijah and kissed his forehead. "You can put your horse up there. By the time Jedidiah has gotten him settled, I should have some breakfast ready for all of us."

"Actually, I was thinking that I might head into town this morning and bring back a few things that I think will aid in Elijah's recovery. If you will accept them, that is." William tried his utmost to deflect some of the workload from her as he was not hungry in the least where that was concerned. "The last thing I want to do is cause you to trouble yourself more on my account."

"Are you the William Sebastian has been mentioning in his letters so frequently?" Charlotte looked at the doctor with a curious expression, realization finally dawning on her at last. "The one who currently lives with a preacher friend?"

It was William's turn to feel at a loss for words as he had no idea that his friend would even bother to mention him to his family. "Probably, though I hope he is still well or as well as a man can be away from his family." William followed his host out of the room and quietly closed the door behind him to allow the younger boy more time to sleep.

"Oh, I don't know. He seems to be doing fine without us so far," Charlotte answered apathetically as she tucked a loose strand of wavy hair behind her ear, then repented of it. "I'm sorry." She bit her lip anxiously before continuing. "That wasn't fair to him or to you. I am just tired, I suppose, and I miss my husband now more than ever... especially when one of our children is sick."

"I can imagine you do, and no offence was taken on my part whatsoever. In my profession, I often see people at their worst. So, I've learned to overlook what most others cannot." William tried to comfort the woman across from him as he could see plainly by the way that she held the wall next to her for support that she was just barely still standing. "Mrs. Fabbri, would it be alright if I take Jedidiah into town with me? Since I am new here, he can help guide me to where I should go. This way maybe you can enjoy a short rest while we are gone. I promise that no harm will come to him."

It was at that moment that Charlotte began to actually sob in front of him as the tenderness he displayed overtook her exhausted state. "I can't... I just don't.... how do I do this anymore?"

Without a moment of hesitation, William instinctively took the woman's arm and led her to the larger room across from the others. "As your husband's friend, I am going to do what Sebastian would do in this instance. Unless absolutely necessary, you are to rest for the remainder of the day. If Elijah is sleeping, so will you. It will be my pleasure to watch over Jedidiah and make sure he is well cared for in your absence. You have my word, on the honor of your husband, that there is nothing I would not do to protect the three of you in his place," he pledged to the woman faithfully in the hopes that he could convince her to accept his suggestions. In reality, it was not difficult to do for the stress of the boy's illness coupled with the sole responsibility of the family's care had already taken its toll upon her far more than she was willing to admit.

"Maybe just a few hours of sleep will help." She opened the door to her bedroom and went in to lie down. "Please send Jedidiah in once he is dressed,

232

and I will explain it all to him or he may not go with you otherwise as he makes it a point not to trust many people."

"Again, very much like his father." William smiled genuinely once more.

Reaching the side of her bed, Charlotte turned slowly back to him and gave the young doctor a funny look of approval. "You <u>do</u> know my Sebastian well, don't you..."

"He has become a most cherished friend," William admittedly honestly. "And trust me when I say that not being able to be here with you is also hurting him far more than he is telling you."

"I am sure you are right. Has he mentioned to <u>you</u> when he will return? All he talks about in his letters is meeting us in America."

"Unfortunately, that is a mystery to me, as well. Though I do know that he probably has a very good reason for not being here right now." William did his best to reassure her for the real reason for Sebastian's absence would be far too complicated to explain, nor was it his place to do so even if he could.

"He is always full of good reasons," Charlotte replied sadly and lay down on top of the quilt-covered bed without the energy to do anything else.

Unwilling to allow her to pass through the same illness as her son, William cautiously stepped into the room and picked up the quilt from the chair opposite the bed before asking her permission, "May I?"

Charlotte nodded, allowing him to respectfully unfold the blanket and lay it on top of her in one sweeping motion through the air. Clearly exhausted, she closed her eyes under its warmth and breathed out slowly just two words of gratitude, "Thank you."

"It is my pleasure, Mrs. Fabbri. I'll tell Jedidiah to come see you before we leave." William walked back out of the room and closed the door gently behind him, but when he turned around, he was taken aback with surprise to find a very firm, and scowling Jedidiah staring directly at him not more than two feet away.

"What are you doing in my mama's bedroom, sir?" Jedidiah accused in direct challenge to the man in front of him.

"I was merely putting a quilt on her, nothing more. You can ask her yourself if you like. She is very tired from taking care of your brother," William spoke slowly and calmly in a futile attempt to disarm the boy.

"She is always tired now, ever since papa left. Taking care of Elijah didn't make it no different," the boy stated plainly though William knew he was not meaning to be judgmental.

"Maybe so, but don't you think we could take care of her for a day? Like your papa would do if he were here?" William tried to reason with the boy so as to diffuse the situation further.

"Hmpff…" The boy huffed and squinted his eyes as he scrutinized the man. "I'll join you downstairs. I need to talk to Mama first."

"Of course, I will wait for you there." William stepped out of the way for the boy to enter the room behind him and descended the wooden staircase to the main floor. Feeling suddenly grateful that he had come so quickly after receiving Sebastian's letter, William took a seat by the now spent fire, crossing one leg over the other to await Jedidiah's final decision.

The boy did not take long, and in less than five minutes time he also came bounding down the stairs quickly and joined William in the larger room below. "Mama says I am to show you around the town."

"That would be nice if you are feeling up to it. Have you had any of the symptoms your brother Elijah has?" William leaned farther back in his chair to appear as relaxed and informal as possible so as to earn the boy's trust.

"I never get sick, Mister." The boy harshly scrunched his face up as if William had just asked him if he knew what horses were.

"My friends all call me William because Doctor Wells seems far too formal. Would you care to do the same?"

The boy stiffened slightly at the continued push of goodwill but remained respectful. "I think Doctor Wells is fine for now."

"As you wish." William nodded with calm understanding. "Are you ready to leave then?"

"Sure, but can we stop by the bakery and pick up something for Mama on the way back? I have a little money I have been saving up. I can use it to buy something for her." The boy walked over to the front door and opened it wide, letting in the fresh breeze of middle March.

"Absolutely, but it will be my treat entirely." William stood to follow the boy out to his waiting horse but paused when he noticed the change in the boy's expression for it had turned harder and more determined than ever.

"Papa said I was to be the man of the family while he is away, and that means I gotta take care of Mama… not you."

"I understand completely. Your papa would be very proud of you." William tried to encourage the boy, but just like his father, Sebastian, when they had first met, his kind efforts did not seem to be working. "Tell you what. You use your money to get something that you think your mama will really like and I will use mine to get something for you and Elijah. Does that seem like a fair compromise?"

Like a studious scholar contemplating a difficult question philosophically, Jedidiah rubbed his chin with the fingers of his right hand and thought deeply for several moments contemplating his offer. "I think that will be alright."

"Good. But we had better be off as I am sure the best breads have already been taken given the rather late hour to which you slept." William picked up his cloak from off the chair and tied it securely around his neck.

The boy only shrugged. "It's a Saturday, Mister. Mama lets me sleep in on Saturdays."

"Maybe she should be allowed to sleep in one day of the week, too." William untied his horse and lifted the boy easily up onto the saddle before sliding one foot into the stirrup and mounting the horse behind him. "Do you know of anything else your family might need while I am here?" William tried to discover any other way in which he could help.

"We need our papa to come home, sir," the boy said quietly before hanging his head just a little to hide whatever emotion he did not want the stranger to witness.

"I agree wholeheartedly, Jedidiah. You will see him again. I am sure of it."

"How do you know?"

William lifted the hood on his cloak and placed it over his head to protect him from the slightly overcast rays. "Let's just say I have faith that he will."

"That's what Mama says, too," the boy answered but did not seem any more convinced than he was before.

Not wanting the boy to mistakenly fall off by the jostling his horse might create, William hugged the boy closer to him and tightened the reins. "Well, as my friend Nathanael does every morning, I guess we will just need to pray that it will be soon, okay?"

"Okay." The boy sighed and held onto the hair of the horse's mane to steady himself. "William?" The boy asked quietly after several long moments of silence.

"Yes." William smiled both inwardly and out, knowing that he had finally earned the boy's trust, if only slightly.

"I am glad that you came today."

"Me, too, young man. Me, too." William guided the horse down the dirt road and into the already bustling town.

Chapter Twenty

*S*o much has transpired since my last entry that I dare not write it for fear that it might incriminate or at the very least discourage me at a later date.

William has written faithfully at last regarding the details of his most earnest search and troubling development, though regrettably his letter seems to have been delayed considerably by the post as it was dated well over a week ago. By all appearances it has been determined, most satisfactorily for all concerned, that our creator, Doctor Clarke, has flown the coop so to speak, in that William has heard from what he feels is a reliable source that the doctor has most likely been recently employed on a ship destined for a port somewhere near the current city of Baltimore. Sadly, he was not able to confirm this information further because the ship in question had already set sail, but he feels confident that the danger he envisioned for his family has been alleviated, if only for the present. As you might imagine, this was not the resolution either of us had hoped for as it still leaves a bit of a troubling thought regarding future encounters with the man in question, but for now, it will have to suffice and dare I say that I think William is the better for it. It is hard enough to want to protect your family, but doing so at the price of someone's life on your conscience would, in this most humble preacher's opinion, probably prove itself to be slightly more problematic than helpful, no matter what the justification or the reasoning.

Having succeeded in his mission of confirming the security of his family from that dreadful man, he writes that he has now chosen to undertake a brief journey farther south to visit the household of our good friend, Sebastian and with good reason. The last letter that Sebastian received from his dear Charlotte expressed concern over one of their son's recovery from the grippe. Since William has been dealing with the care of countless other patients suffering from the same in London, William felt justifiably compelled that he could not leave the area in good conscience without at least checking on the poor boy, if only to assure his friend of his son's continued health.

This was indeed prudent on all accounts, and I support his decision entirely, but I still cannot contain my selfish hope that William will return again soon so that we may continue in our previous nutritional arrangement. My last ten days of fasting have been... quite difficult to say the least. Why just last night while I was studying here at the church, I was met by one of the most intense trials, or rather temptations, of my physical and pastoral life.

During my hour of meditation and reflection in my private chambers that evening, I had chosen to focus on the passage in John chapter one, verses 43-51. There I discovered the story of my namesake, meeting his Lord for the very first time and becoming his disciple. Like myself, he was also astounded at the foreknowledge of our dear Savior in divulging his whereabouts before having ever met the man. Yet our Lord did not end his discussion in this mere form of familiarity, but rather went on to promise, the Nathanael listed here, that by following Him, he would be privileged to see many wonderful works and even angels ascending from the heavens. This image overwhelmed me then as it does now to mark it down for remembrance.

What a sight that would be even today!

This passage, among many others highlighted in this journal, will forever motivate me for years to come, I am certain. Yet, I digress. Admittedly, I found myself so engrossed in the text that I heard very little of what was transpiring in the church outside of my chambers proper. In fact, a thundering rainstorm could have occurred, and I most likely would have taken little notice of its passing, such was the state of my intense concentration.

And so it was, that it was not the sound of breaking glass that rang within my distracted ears, but rather the faintest smell of something altogether irresistibly familiar that pricked my senses and motivated me immediately to hurriedly close my Bible and rise to my feet in discovery.

Driven by a lust I knew only too well, I rushed headlong into the church sanctuary to discover the source of it, only to find Miss Summerfield very much in distress. Like a child, she was softly crying by the front pew just in front of the piano forte on which she had been dutifully practicing her hymns, her small hand cradled carefully in her lap.

By all other appearances, everything else in the chapel was entirely as it should be. Yet it was in that very singular of moments as I was walking up to the young woman that the metallic aroma stung my nostrils again with its fullest force and set my heart to a furious beating.

Afraid to come any closer until I had my senses fully in control once more, I held my breath and tried to speak politely through my gritted teeth, something which I am afraid, looking back on it now, probably sounded more like an angry outburst than a sympathetic inquiry. "What is the matter, my dear? Are you injured?"

What an utterly ridiculous question for me to have asked! I shake my head even now at my sheer stupidity. Clearly, something had occurred, or she would not have been sitting there weeping. Added to that fact was also the distinct odor of the blood that was almost certainly pooling somewhere close by.

I shudder to remember even now the sinister thoughts my mind expressed before I forced them back into captivity once more. As dark as they were, they were the worst of my existence thus far, and all of them involved taking much more than I nutritionally required. But there is one thing that I can say truthfully, now that it is over... that had I not been in the church itself, I do not know if I would have been as successful as I was in abstaining momentarily from this most singular of temptations. My acknowledgement of God's omniscience alone saved me once again for even though no other man might have seen me commit this most heinous of crimes, God surely would have and would have also most definitely held me accountable.

After all, why had I decided not to feed in the manner most others of our kind did in the first place? For one reason only, I could not bring myself for any reason, selfish or otherwise, to risk taking away someone's eternal life. To do so would be proclaiming presumptuously that I was more powerful than our Savior in controlling their eternal destiny, and that to me... would have been completely unacceptable.... even if that meant my own death.

And so, for several long moments, I remained at a respectful distance from Miss Summerfield and listened as she explained in a very broken conversation about how she had been practicing her hymns when she saw the small vase of flowers begin to fall from the top of the instrument. I had placed those flowers there that very afternoon to be something of a gift for her since I knew how much she loved purple and white violets. I had even thought it was a Divinely inspired opportunity when I noted a rather large patch of them just that morning. However, looking back at it now, I can see how the entire calamity which had befallen her was entirely of my own creation.

Feeling saddened by the loss of such a recently cherished gift, she had tried to pick up the tiny stems from amongst the glass shards, but in the end only managed to injure herself on the broken glass in doing so. It was then that I truly noticed from my vantage point the great quantity of scarlet that was now mixing with the tile at her feet. Her very small, but utterly beautiful feet, if I might be so bold as to write that here of all places, for I do not think I could ever express such a thing to her in person—maybe one day when our relationship is much different than it is at the present, but not now.

I know from her expression that she had probably thought I was upset with her since I did not move to give any comfort on the matter, but as kind as she always was, she did not say it. Instead, she tried multiple times to stifle the sniffles escaping while also placing her other, uninjured hand, across the angular cut just above her palm near the center of her hand, causing both to be coated with the same delightful liquid.

It was at that instant that I gratefully had a small moment of clarity as I remembered the very similar cut Señor Moretti had shown us back at his castle. Although admittedly, it was not an unpleasant memory, in and of itself, it did afford me a second to collect my raging desires once more and return to some sense of control.

With great care to exact the right amount of politeness towards her, I reached in and took out the slightly tattered handkerchief from my pocket and placed it upon her wound before instructing her to leave the mess for me to clean up. Though thinking about that article now, I do not believe I will ever want that handkerchief back, clean, or otherwise. It would hold too many unpleasant and yet altogether distracting memories within its fibers, at least for the present. Who knows if in time I will be able to do what William has done the past few months by exposing himself to this form of allurement daily by treating his patients.

How the man does not give in to temptation on every bloodletting visit I will never know. My only logical assumption is that he must be considerably stronger than I, or not as distractedly drawn to it. Either way, his restraint is most certainly something in the category of the miraculous to my mind.

In the end, despite the insignificant cost to myself, I instructed Miss Summerfield to see the village doctor immediately and allow him to tend to her wound. He could send me the bill for his labors thereafter, and I would happily pay it on her behalf. After all, it was the least I could do under the circumstances seeing as it was my fault entirely that the vase was placed in such a precarious position in the first place. If I had been thinking more clearly, I would have known that the repeated vibrations of her playing would cast it headlong onto the floor. But undoubtedly, when it comes to Miss Summerfield, my thoughts are always inexplicably scattered.

Still a bit out of sorts and whimpering softly from the pain in her hand, she thanked me most kindly, and I assured her that I would be happy to discuss it all at length with her again on Sunday next once she had some time to collect herself and heal. This was the most I could manage between us as I graciously ushered her out of the chapel as quickly as I dared possible while struggling all the while not to succumb to the very enticing pull of her blood behind me.

As the chapel door closed and was locked behind her, the expected relief within my tensed muscles did not commence even though I was most definitely alone again at last. Like a child about to steal a piece of candy from the counter of a store, I made sure to ascertain that no one would see what I was about to do first. Then, when I was assured beyond reasonable doubt of my solitude, I took one step after another towards the front of the chapel as I made my way over to where the broken glass lay on the earthen tiled floor. The magnificently painted red droplets between each of the squares drew me closer with every breath I inhaled like that of a tantalizing melody.

I could wait no longer, completely compelled, I partook in that sweet delight which had remained, small as it was and reveled in the delight of all that it offered. I freely admit that I am not sure if it was because of how long it has been since I last fed or if it was because the blood was from her, but the freshness of it was nothing compared to what I have enjoyed before. This small luxury, amidst my fast, was warm. It was vibrant. It was for lack of a better term, restorative. But it had a price to pay for it, as well. The shock of the pleasure it brought me when I should have been repulsed, pleased me as much as it frightened me to my very soul.

I dare not speak any more about this matter as I am already feeling the intense need for more of that particular form of nourishment, but I will not.

If Miss Summerfield and I are to ever marry, I must resolve more than ever to remain steadfast to my Lord and resist this abhorrent attraction that goes against His very nature, or at least until William returns. I truly hope I can wait that long, though I sincerely doubt it after that last experience. Then again, I may have to start thinking about alternate resources for my nutrition, but I sincerely hope not as hurting any of God's small creatures would sadden me.

This does put me to mind of a verse in Matthew that says, "The flesh is weak, but the spirit is willing"? Perhaps, I will search the Scriptures tonight for more verses on this topic of resisting temptation as it might prove to be an excellent sermon series one day or at the very least serve as a daily reminder to maintain my correct focus hereafter.

God speed, dear William. I pray you arrive soon.

~   ~   ~   ~   ~

Journal Entry for March 30th
Day 30 of my fast

Will the day ever come when my flesh will not cry out for that which it cannot have? In this mortal or immortal body, will I ever not yearn for the forbidden joy a few droplets of nectar will afford me?

Alas, I have not been as successful as I had hoped in this undertaking. From the very beginning, I have endeavored to keep this longing in its proper perspective, yet I have failed time and time again quite horribly. So much so, that I fear, in my present state, that no one, not even myself, may be safe from me.

Sebastian's family is still on the mend though William wrote days ago that he hopes to be on his way back, very soon. Yet, I fear if he ever does arrive, that it may be too late for me, at least. My resolve has been utterly spent and sadly I feel as though there is little left of the Nathanael that I once knew. He has instead been replaced with something more akin to the monsters in fairy tales than with anything seeking God's glory.

Elsie's father has invited me tomorrow for supper immediately following the service, and I have accepted, if for only the opportunity to see my Elsie once more. Perhaps, her presence alone will aid in my restoration, though I very much doubt it.

May the Lord help us all.

~   ~   ~   ~   ~

Journal Entry for April 2nd
Day 33 of my fast

Pasha Sunday, the 31st, started as any other Lord's Day with the silent preparations in my study followed by a greeting of every one of my faithful parishioners. It was the Sunday following Passover and to my recollection, the hymns were especially divine, given my current state of mind. Though thinking back on it today, they could have been on <u>any</u> given theme, and they still would have affected me the same for I was not particularly focusing on them, nor the words that they proclaimed.

For a minister, the Pasha is always an especially symbolic time both for him and for his church and so I had chosen to preach on a slightly different topic than the usual discourse about the Crucifixion which I had already elaborated on in depth the previous Sunday. Instead, I spoke about Peter's walking on the water with our

241

Lord as my main text. One that has always been my particular favorite and a comfort whenever I have felt overwhelmed in the ministry.

The sermon itself flowed methodically through me as I recounted Peter's eagerness to join his Lord upon the waves to prove his faithfulness and then concluded with his eventual demise upon taking his eyes off Him once the waves began to o'er take him. However, it was at that very moment of the sermon, in front all of my flock, that I began to see the increasing similarity that I now held with our dear Peter. In partaking this fast, I, myself, had been stepping out in faith upon the water, trusting beyond hope that my Savior would allow that surface to hold me.

Nevertheless, time and again, I had also looked around at my rather precarious situation and the waves had also threatened to swallow me back into their depths. Without a doubt, I was Peter.

In my desire to remain honest and transparent, I relayed to my flock my secret journey along my physical fast but left out the very unpleasant details that would have quite easily given me away. Their reaction was encouraging in their acceptance of my failure and understanding of the physical struggle it had necessitated. Some were even inspired to commit to a form of fast of their own. Yet, I wished for their sake that they would have more success in their endeavors than I.

After the closing of the service, I followed Elsie and her family to their home for a proper Pasha feast complete with a roasted lamb, potatoes, rolls, and various other desserts. The only thing remaining to be served that day was the salad—an insignificant, yet essential part of any meal. Though I wish now I had feigned an allergy to the vegetables and been done with it altogether for the grief it has caused me.

As you might have surmised, I eagerly volunteered my services in the kitchen and was in turn joined by Elsie herself to guide me along my path. I should have sent her back and allowed myself the opportunity to flounder away at my task, but I did not.

Upon seeing the ineptness in which I was tackling my work, she took control of the situation and instructed me to fetch all the necessary ingredients from the pantry. I was indeed grateful for her help and simply delighted to be in her presence once more. However, nothing in all the world could have sufficiently prepared me for what was to follow.

With great care, I set to work peeling the necessary vegetables and assembled each of them in a precise row for her to cut. Delighted by my progress, she looked up so innocently at me that I could scarcely contain the smile that was no doubt plastered awkwardly upon my face. Nor could I stop my heart from beating as fast as my thoughts.

Awkwardly, for there is no better word for the jumble of vocabulary that came out of my mouth that day, the words that I had long held back tumbled at her feet. Long-awaited platitudes and promises were given fervently, along with an overall dream-like explanation of a future life together. And all of it was shared over cut carrots and greens. In fact, before I had scarcely registered even saying anything at all, I found myself quite profoundly professing my love for her before subsequently asking for her hand in marriage.

Truthfully, I had not expected that she would accept me so readily for we had only known each other for a little over four months, but what joy filled my heart when she agreed unreservedly! For the first time in my life, I felt limitless hope—felt it, tasted it, dreamt it. And though I live to be as old as Señor Moretti or even Enoch, I think I will <u>never</u> have such a moment again. It was perfect, or as perfect a minute as anything on this Earth could be.

There will always be other moments in our lives where we keenly wish we had chosen another path for ourselves, or a time when we wish we had warned others of a danger we knew by divine revelation or otherwise would transpire.

This will forever be one of those moments for me.

A moment so sacredly secure, it has been branded into my consciousness to forever warn me of my failures for years to come.

Having secured her permission, I kissed her lightly on the cheek and promised to speak to her family directly the next day to announce our desire to wed as I did not wish to interrupt the true focus of our wonderful meal. She was as happy as I was, I believe, and kept looking up at me with great pleasure in between the cutting of the vegetables and the sporadic placement of them in the wooden bowl.

I should have warned her to stop.

I should have cut them for her.

I should have...

There are so many things in my life that have begun with such an introduction as this. Yet all remain with the same empty conclusive phrase thereafter.

The facts of the matter are this: she looked down at the carrots and then up at my eyes and smiled, her sweetness stealing my very breath away with its passing.

Like an idiot, I studied the slow movement of the blade upon the board as if time itself was slowing down just enough for me to watch it pass by in second after agonizing second. Then, I smelt the appealing scent all the way down my throat like a double-edged blade coated with acid—smooth on the way down, but destructive on the way out. At last, my worst fear in all the world became realized, or at least I think it did. The rest of what may or may not have occurred is sadly a confusing fog within my own mind for without the nourishment that it clearly needs, my usually acute reflections are now as broken as those shards of glass from Elsie's vase.

Did I make myself resist like I had so faithfully done on so many other occasions? I hope so. Though one thing is painfully certain, if I had stayed a moment longer, I know without a doubt that I would have absolutely killed her without a moment of hesitation. I would have been the one to take her life, and that would have destroyed me much more than anything Doctor Clarke could had ever accomplished for he only took my physical death; this would have taken my very soul.

And yet, if I cannot remember what has happened clearly, how do I know if I haven't failed already? I cannot simply go back to the Summerfield home to find out for fear of further discovery, and yet it is literally killing me inside not knowing if she is truly alive.

Is my love being laid to rest somewhere where I will never have the chance to see her again? Or worse... I cannot even speak of that possibility... now or ever.

I have absolutely no idea what to do next. As weak as I am, I cannot run and besides, there is nowhere to go. As it turns out, there truly is no place for people like me, there never was.

So, I must hide. Hide until William can return and discover my awful secret, my failure. Or die while I am waiting.

Either way, I will see my Elsie once more.

Chapter Twenty-One

April 1st, 1793

The young man with the disheveled dusty blonde hair from hours working out in the sun pushed the heavy, wooden wheelbarrow up the hill for hopefully the last time before lunch but stopped halfway to catch his breath. Working down at the docks was supposed to only be a temporary position to earn him enough money to afford a proper life with Hannah when he was of age but for the past few months the workload had been nothing short of tremendous. On any given day he found himself completing a myriad of unrelated tasks like delivering mail or taking goods from one business to another, not to mention hauling countless loads of materials that had arrived that day on the ships up to the blacksmith shop or the livery. Still, it was worth it if it brought him any closer to his goal. It would be a few more years before the two of them could marry according to Señor Moretti, but no matter how long it took, he would wait because despite what everyone else in town thought of the girl, he knew Hannah was worth it. From her infectious humor to her easy acceptance of him and everyone else around her, she was the perfect match for him in every way.

When he had approached her older guardian about possibly courting her last year, the man had been more than a little bit hesitant on the matter. Not that he claimed any ownership of the girl in any way or was her actual father, but given his long history of raising her, he was more than a little bit protective. And well he should be given the riffraff that Thomas saw pouring onto the streets on any given day. With new ships arriving on every tide, it seemed practically anyone could step onto these shores unannounced, and the citizens here would be none the wiser for it until something more sinister happened, like the day poor Rebecca had disappeared.

Though no one even bothered to look for the girl thereafter, Thomas had still wondered what had truly happened to her that night. Like on many other nights, he had seen her shortly after dinner sitting at the corner where she always liked to sleep, but by the next morning she was gone as if she had vanished with the wind itself. The whole experience did much to caution him about venturing out after dark and drew him to be even more protective about Hannah for he knew that she lived alone up the mountain, though thankfully, still within reach of Señor Moretti's watchful protection and now Sebastian's.

"Do you think you can get that load up here by yourself or will you be requiring my help, Thomas?" Sebastian called from deep within the structure of the forge to urge the boy on in his task more quickly.

"Coming." Thomas pulled his face into a tight grimace and pushed with all his might to achieve the necessary momentum now that he had stopped. It worked, for the brief rest had given him a sudden burst of energy, much more than what was needed to crest the hill for at the top he ran right into a wheel-sized divot of a hole and flipped the wheelbarrow, his load and himself head over heels onto the dirt at the summit. With a yelp and a crash, all landed in a horrible pile of man and materials sprawled out in various directions.

"Land's sake, Man!" Sebastian exclaimed as he rushed out to help the boy but stopped suddenly at the doorway. The sun this morning was intensely bright given that it was still a little before noon which meant that there was no way he could venture out to help him without his hooded cloak.

Snatching up the necessary nuisance, he threw it on over his head and shoulders and made his way over to the boy. "Are you injured?"

Thomas, though still slightly dazed and more than a little bit rumpled by the ordeal, looked more stunned than anything else and took a minute to check all his limbs before replying, "Thankfully, nothing broken but my pride, sir."

Sebastian couldn't help but chuckle at his humorous reply and wiped some of the dust from off the young man's shoulder. "You know what they say about you down at the docks, don't you?"

"What?" Thomas replied but was less than amused at the question for he knew that the rougher seamen had often teased him mercilessly most days to his face. There was no telling what they might be saying about him behind his back.

"That the workday hasn't truly started until Thomas has fallen down in some way?" Sebastian squinted one eye shut at him and smiled.

"Figures." Thomas stood up immediately and righted the tipped wheelbarrow before rubbing his head where he had connected with the ground. "It's not my fault that gravity literally hates me, Mr. Fabbri."

"I imagine not, Thomas." Feeling sorry for the boy who obviously tried so hard to please everyone but only ended up being an annoyance to most in the process, Sebastian helped him pick up the large pieces of wood that he needed for the forge and placed them onto the shelf within for close access next to his bellows. "You know, I used to feel like I couldn't do anything right either when I was your age. I probably even had funnier things said about me though most people were less kind than those sailors." He paused and pumped the bellows twice to stoke the fire brighter. "Still, I survived as I am sure so will you, if you can manage not to kill yourself before you reach twenty."

"If I live that long it will be a miracle indeed." Thomas placed the last of the load upon the pile within and plopped down onto a small stool in the corner to take another minute of rest.

"Oh, you'll manage." Sebastian laughed again as the conversation with the lad made him feel less frustrated than before he had arrived. It always had. Having Thomas around made him feel more like he was back home at his own forge again, and anything like that was far better than mindlessly working for hours on end each day by himself.

Overall, he had never been one who welcomed the company of others. Quite the opposite in fact, but those that he did, he felt the need to give of himself to wholeheartedly. Maybe that was why he liked his Charlotte so much when they had first met. In that quality of devotion, they were both very much cut from the same cloth so to speak. It was also something similar to what impressed him so much about William now that he thought of it. As much as the man truly wanted to help him by his repeated attempts to persuade him to come home to his family, William never crowded him or made him feel less worthy because of his choices one way or the other.

"Whatcha making today, Mr. Fabbri? More nails?" Thomas peered over the anvil in front of him and into the wooden bucket at the center of the room.

"More nails, I'm afraid." The corner of Sebastian's mouth curled upwards in mocked disdain as he hung up the light cloak behind him once more, grateful that he had not needed to wear it at all this week other than when rescuing Thomas. "Somedays I feel like I will go mad making them, but... they are necessary to support me just the same."

"Really? You?" Thomas squinted one eye in disbelief and tilted his head. "I wouldn't have thought you didn't enjoy your work. After all, you are <u>always</u> up here night and day it seems."

"Oh, don't get me wrong. I <u>am</u> grateful for the work, Thomas. But, after you've made several thousand of these tiny little demons, you start to think the work will never end. Either that or it might end you if you aren't careful."

Thomas nodded in understanding. "I feel like that sometimes when I am trying to run from one place to another all day. In the morning, everybody needs me all at once, but there is only one me to go around. Yet by the afternoon, things begin slowing down enough to catch my breath, even if just a little."

"And today?" Sebastian picked up his favorite pliers, drew a piece of thin metal out of the fire and began hammering it into shape methodically.

"Today is alright. The master down at port said I am to do whatever you need up here. Though to be honest, I think he was just needing a break from my constant calamity." The young man stood up from his seat and spent a minute walking slowly around the spacious shelter, taking his time to observe the many tools and items contained inside. "Hey, what are all of these!"

Thomas picked up one of the short blades that hung along the outer wall and examined it closely before releasing a shrill whistle through his lips. "This is incredible, Mr. Fabbri! Is it real Spanish steel?"

Unsure as to what the boy was referring to exactly, Sebastian looked up from his work and over at the boy before returning back to his work at the forge. "Yes, in a way, but be careful. They are all <u>very</u> sharp."

Sebastian could have been speaking to the wind for all that went into the young man's head at that moment for as soon as he had turned his back, Thomas began waving the blade in the air behind him that was much shorter than a proper sword, but longer than a dirk or a dagger. Like a seasoned fencer confronting his attacker, he parried and lunged with quick movements as he fought off imaginary foes and friends alike across the back of the shelter, drawing closer with each thrust to the man who was still working. "Take that! And that!" He swung around quickly once more and as he did, mistakenly collided into the wooden barrel that held the long pieces of nail rod that Sebastian used for his work.

"Oh, no! Aghhh!" Thomas shouted all at once.

With a shattering reverberation off all the walls of the forge, a horrible crash followed soon thereafter and the whole lot of it fell to the ground, along with the young man and his sword.

"What on earth?" Sebastian froze instantly as his senses picked up the very thing he had tried to avoid at all costs when he was in town—blood.

With deliberate but quick movements to avoid what he feared most would happen; he dropped his hammer immediately and grabbed the cloth that he normally used to protect his hands from the rod's heat. Then, swinging around to face the injured man on the ground, he immediately wrapped the cloth scraps around the upper part of the arm and held them there tightly to stave off the bright red flow.

"I'm sorry. I'm sorry." The young man kept professing repeatedly, obviously in shock from being cut by the masterfully created blade.

"I warned you that they were sharp, Thomas," Sebastian said calmly so as to not upset the boy further as he tried very hard to breathe shallowly and not succumb to its pull. *Was it safe to remain and help him or should I leave before something worse happens to the boy?* Sebastian pondered as he took a quick assessment of his faculties and his ability to withstand the temptation before him and decided to hold his ground. He couldn't deny that his heart was indeed racing, similar to that night in the alley with the others, but thankfully, it was not any more than it already would have been at any other surprise or accident, so that was at least progress. "Now I want you to go ahead and pick yourself up before you go on into town and make sure the doctor sees to that."

"But, but..." Thomas stammered, feeling a little embarrassed for causing so much trouble in the man's place of work. "I don't have the money to pay for all of that. Do you think it will just heal if I leave it?"

Like a stern father, Sebastian placed his hands upon his hips and cast him an uncertain expression, almost ready to refuse him outright, then changed his mind. "Let me look at it again in the light."

Feeling suddenly hopeful, Thomas stepped back into the covering of the forge and held out his arm for him to peruse.

Sebastian did not speak further but merely shook his head at the unwelcome imposition and lifted the rag slightly to examine the cut more closely now that the cloth had been given the chance to soak up the majority of the blood. "Alright... first, go and wash it off over there under the pump. Make sure it is the coldest water you can find. Then, after you've rinsed out my rags, bring them back to me. If we wrap it up tightly and keep it clean, you might be able to avoid the doc."

Without a word, the young man rushed out of the forge and over to the fresh spring that lay at the top of the hill, furiously splashing the cold water onto both his arm and the rags until the blood-stained water became clear once more.

"Give me strength, Lord." Sebastian wiped the stress-induced perspiration from off his brow and tried to distract himself once more from any possible further temptation by setting to work picking up his things that had spilled. About five minutes later, when he had almost finished hanging the last of his tools back up upon the wall, Thomas returned with the freshly cleaned rags, his face still as penitent as before for his carelessness.

"You will need to change the dressing and clean this wound at least twice a day until it heals. Do you understand me?"

Thomas nodded silently.

"And you must promise me that you will see the doctor if it gets red or hot to the touch in any way. Even the slightest bit, do you promise?" Sebastian instructed him firmly.

The young man nodded twice once again but still remained rigidly frozen as if still in shock.

"I mean it Thomas, don't test me on this. I'll even pay a portion of his fee if it comes down to it. Money isn't worth losing an arm or your life for any reason." Sebastian wrapped the cold rags securely around Thomas' upper arm before tying them with two small knots. "My wife would make you go anyways if she were here, but since it doesn't look that deep, I will allow you to wait. Just see that you show me your arm first thing in the morning and the morning thereafter and we will see how it goes, shall we?"

"I honestly did not mean to cause you so much trouble today," Thomas said quietly, though it reminded Sebastian once again of how Jedidiah would have reacted after he had been scolded as his oldest boy could be extremely hard on himself at times, just like Thomas.

"I know you didn't. You are a tremendous help to so many even if they do not say it to you directly. Accidents just happen, but we must learn from them as well, correct?" Sebastian stood up to his full height which was only a few inches taller than the young man and eyed the lad upon the stool beside him.

"Yes, sir."

"And I'll tell you what... if you can manage to not destroy my shop for ten minutes put together today, I will teach you how to make one of those swords for yourself."

"Really?" The young man's eyes grew almost as wide as his mouth in comparison, then in the same minute his whole countenance suddenly became more skeptical. "Oh, you are just teasing me again, aren't you? I never did believe you about the shipwreck, you know. No one can sail anywhere on a door." He shook his head and kept his gaze turned downward, his day sufficiently ruined.

Smiling again at the humorous story he had invented for the young man's benefit several months ago, Sebastian picked up the nicest of the blades from off the ground at Thomas's feet and handed it to the lad. "To prove to you that I am not. Here. It is yours until you make yourself another to match its quality."

"Wait! What!" Thomas took the weapon, but this time held it with the proper reverence that it justly deserved. "I can't make anything like this! I can barely lace my boots up somedays."

Sebastian chuckled at the man's blatant honesty. "Believe it or not, I couldn't either when I began my work in my master's shop, but I learned, and so will you."

"Did he teach you how to do this?" Thomas laid the blade across his lap, cleaned the blood from his ordeal off it and studied it carefully, admiring the scrollwork and etching that ran along the thin silver edge from the hilt on down towards the tip.

"No, actually my father gave me my first sword through a gift from another. He was an excellent bladesmith, or so I am told. Though I firmly believe from the quality of his work, that he was more talented in his rather short life here on Earth than I will ever aspire to be, even if I should work for a hundred years." Sebastian looked down at the ocean and paused. "The rest I learned by watching others, as you will see soon."

"When can I start?" Thomas looked up at the man, eagerly hopeful once more.

"As soon as you take this load of nails down to the harbor. I think I have made enough of the wretched things to keep the men busy until tomorrow morning at least. Besides, I think I need a break from all that monotony anyways." Sebastian picked up the heavy wooden barrel with both hands and placed it carefully within the wheelbarrow. "Now mind that you do not spill it as you go."

Without a moment of hesitation, Thomas jumped up from his seat and handed Sebastian his gifted sword carefully. "Will you hold this for me until I return? I wouldn't want to damage it."

Sebastian smiled and nodded. "Now, remember, not a nail spilled, or I will make you wait until tomorrow. As my master once told me, sometimes you have to go slow in order to go fast."

"That makes absolutely no sense at all, Mr. Fabbri, but I will walk more carefully all the same." Thomas cocked his head awkwardly at his logic and lifted the heavy handles of the load.

"See that you do." Sebastian walked back inside and hung the sword in its vacant place along the long wall of completed blades. How many similar weapons had he created in the past four months? Twenty or thirty? That was a lot of mental escape, even for him, and yet, he knew that every one of them was fundamentally essential to his daily sanity or rather mental stability.

Speaking of mental stability... He thought back again to the incident with the blade and the way he had been able to manage Thomas' injury. The cool and collected manner in which he had been able to treat his wound, despite the very real temptation, encouraged him greatly. For weeks he had been practicing the various techniques Señor Moretti had showed him to help with the unexpected occurrences among those he might be tempted to feast upon, and it seemed at least for the present that his work was paying off.

After all, if he could manage to do what he had just done, and then to spend hours teaching the young man daily to create a perfect sword, surely, he would be able to handle the chaotic life of his family back at home. Especially since his two sons were far more predictable and much less accident-prone than Thomas on any given day.

It was not the perfect solution by any means, but it was at least a start and at this point, he would try anything that would help him return to his family even sooner.

~   ~   ~   ~   ~

William sat farther back in the carriage as the wheels droned on in their rhythmic hum from London to Wakefield. Just the other night he was almost certain that he never wanted to leave the pleasant company Sebastian's family provided, but he knew it was more than time that he was to be heading home. After all, he had been gone far longer than he had planned already. Not to mention the fact that the tenor of Nathanael's letters had begun to worry him beyond that which he had thought possible given that the normally articulate, though slightly emotional, man had begun writing in manner more similar to Sebastian in his fatalistic musings and dismal conveyance of daily life. Still, the danger had seemed lesser to some degree than the treatment of Sebastian's son.

For almost four days, Elijah had weathered the worst of the influenza after William's arrival and in more than one moment of his illness the doctor had feared the debilitating cough would necessitate writing to Sebastian a letter that he had hoped never to write to the man. Though he knew it wasn't his place to summon the man like he was his authority or had a right to do so, he was also more certain beyond a shadow of a doubt that if it were his son who was dying and not Sebastian's, nothing here on this Earth, vampirism or not, would keep him from coming to be with him in his last moments. Thankfully for all concerned, the boy had improved quickly thereafter and both he and Charlotte had breathed a collective sigh of relief.

Moreover, Sebastian's wife had been a surprising godsend in every aspect of the word and William thanked Providence time and again for the way in which she had seemed to anticipate his thoughts in treating the boy. Many times, in his father's surgery he had often witnessed a few others who also maintained this most singular ability of forethought and even then, it had also astounded him to watch it in person. It was almost as if the two individuals working together had been using the same mind and not tandemly exercising their own abilities.

New as he was to the profession, he had thought that this had been a technique learned through a lengthy experience with a particular doctor, yet even after years of helping his father, William had not once been able to predict, nor provide necessary counsel a second before his father had needed it. It had been quite the opposite, in fact. In his case, years upon years had been spent in methodic imitation of his father's skills like a very obedient and convenient shadow of the man he thought so highly of and longed to emulate, just not in practice with him. That had felt far more denigrating at the time than he would have preferred, but now... not so much.

As anyone might expect, this had hurt his father's feelings at first, but true to his unfailingly understanding nature, he had instead encouraged William to be successful in whatever avenue he explored. It was partially the reason why it had not been overly difficult to convince his father to let him join the *Endeavour* last fall. That, and the fact that his mother and he had little in common when it came to marriage. It was true that William loved his mother deeply, and they were never openly hostile to each other in any way, but they simply wanted different things for his life and they both knew it, though neither would relent to the other on the subject.

Of course, William wanted to marry someday. But his idea of an ideal wife was someone who could work alongside him like Charlotte had and not a woman who needed him to fulfill her various social obligations. He wanted a marriage of minds where both partners could freely discuss whatever topic in which they were interested, like he could do with Señor Moretti and not nights spent in utter boredom at parties and balls he could care less about than he did some of Nathanael's sermons. Though, if he were to be completely honest concerning those, as tiresome as he found some of them to be, others were especially interesting, intriguing even. That and the fact that the man quite literally breathed his Bible even when he wasn't at church.

Yet notwithstanding his excellent ability to recollect any verse he ever read, living with the man these past five months was like living with one of Jesus' own disciples, if that were even possible. In truth, it had quickly developed a marked effect on him, but what that was precisely, he was still less certain.

Charlotte had said to William one night after the boys had gone to bed that her husband had also been an extremely religious man once, but over the years, many difficult events both in his life and in their marriage had hardened him towards a more personal reliance upon God. She had even gone as far as to say that although he was never in full opposition to the church, he had chosen rather to keep a careful distance from committing fully to it as if he were merely waiting for some divine explanation as to why God had made his life so difficult thus far.

Sebastian's wife had not seen fit to divulge her husband's confidence much more on the subject, and so William did not think it was appropriate to pry any further. But it did help to explain at least partially why the man was so protective of his family and why he was desperate to do whatever it took to keep them safe. William understood that, too. Having spent hours with each of them this week, he could clearly see that Sebastian was merely afraid of doing anything that would cause any of that to change.

In fact, on his last night with the family, the four of them had gathered together on Elijah's bed to read one of William's favorite books when he was their age, "Gulliver's Travels". He was supposed to leave early the next morning, and they had still not finished the last few chapters of the book he had started to read to them upon his arrival.

Like other boys their age, they had each been fascinated by the land of the giants and pirates alike, but when they had reached the portion where Gulliver had to learn how to speak like the horses they had jumped around the room and onto the bed pretending to be like those horses and he the great Gulliver who now had to learn their language.

Charlotte had laughed and laughed at their antics, and it took both of them the better part of an hour to quiet the boys down to a calmer state so as to not aggravate Elijah's cough into returning.

Still, when he had kissed each boy goodnight on the forehead as his father used to do for him, it was Jedidiah who had reached out to him and held his hand a moment longer, begging him to stay with them for a few days more if he could.

Oh, how he had wanted to stay with them forever... to be anything that the child needed him to be in that moment... but he knew that the boy, as intelligent as he was perceptive, was not longing for him personally. He was only missing the tangible presence of his real father. Someone William would never think of replacing on any given day—nor could he ever. Yet just witnessing their love firsthand had made him even more determined than before to find a way to reunite them all together. If for the boys' sakes alone. They needed their father and Charlotte needed her husband—vampire or otherwise.

There simply had to be a way, and he would find it, before it was too late.

Chapter Twenty-Two

April 7th, 1793

A single candle flickered in an upstairs window of the village tavern when William finally arrived back in Wakefield. In fact, it was the only sign of life the doctor could see in the otherwise eerily foggy atmosphere when the coach had dropped him off a little before supper near the center of town. Assuming his friend would be in his study busily preparing that evening for his mid-week service, William had gone over there immediately instead of dropping off his bag at their home first. Yet oddly enough, the sanctuary was empty. Despite the fact that it was just before sunset, and clearly time for the service, not a single candle lit the altar, nor a door secured. It was almost as if the Lord Himself, and not Nathanael, was running the service tonight and the angels or spirits were his willing congregants instead of people.

Chasing away the growing feeling of unease that had followed him all the way from the tavern beyond, William strode down the center aisle of the chapel and tried the door to Nathanael's study but found it was the only entryway he had encountered thus far that was securely locked. Confused but not the least bit surprised for Nathanael had often locked his door when he was in prayer, William banged on the door twice to possibly arouse the concentrating preacher but received no audible reply.

Was he at home instead? William's brow furrowed at the confusion he could not logically dissipate, then retrieved the hidden key that was tucked safely beneath the carefully stacked row of hymnals outside the door. A point which felt vaguely reassuring under the mysterious circumstances because it meant that someone had at least been there recently or that Nathanael had been alert enough to remember to hide the key for him afterwards.

"But when?" He whispered before trying the key in the lock and turning it slowly. With a click, the gears within rang out like loud bells against the granite walls on his left, causing the hair on both of his arms to elevate. All at once, he was unsure if he wanted to enter the room at all, not knowing what he might find therein. "Courage William," he said as he closed his eyes and braced himself for whatever he might see and pushed the door open slowly.

Nothing in all the world, fantastical or otherwise, could have properly prepared him for what he saw next. Nathanael's study within was nothing at all like it had been at Christmas, nor had it been so on any day thereafter. In its place was a room in utter disarray from the slightly askew desk, that normally sat perfectly placed in the center of the small room, to the littered floor in front of him. Books that were once neatly arranged in alphabetical order according to their topic and author, no longer sat on their shelves so purposefully. Instead, they were now strewn about with the rest of his belongings in various places on the furniture and floor. Some were even opened in precarious ways along their spines and pages professing lasting damage to both if they remained that way much longer. Moreover, loose parchments and music scores were scattered haphazardly across the floor as if they contained nothing more than the scribbles of a child.

Candles that were normally faithfully replaced at the end of every night were wastefully spent, with long dripping tails all the way down their brass candelabras allowing small yellow puddles of beeswax to pool on the tile below. It was something that would have driven the meticulous preacher mad if he had noticed it, and yet, here they lay. In fact, oddly enough, the only item remaining in its proper place amidst this cacophony of chaos was Nathanael's perfectly hung minister's robes, which stood silent vigil right behind his desk as if they had not been worn for quite some time.

Overwhelmed by what he saw all around him, William paused a moment to take it all in before stooping over and picking up a few of the parchments and books at his feet that restricted his entry but stopped when he went to place them back upon the desk for there, on top of everything else that shouldn't have been there, lay Nathanael's journal. The one that he almost never left unattended no matter what the reason, yet beyond all hope of understanding, here it lay... fully open upon its back, its yellowed pages relaxed and outstretched, inviting anyone who might enter therein to read its contents freely.

With fresh fear, William picked up the treasured manuscript with trembling fingers and noticed the distinct and hardly unmistakable traces of reddish-brown stains along the feathered edges, on one side. The remnants of some kind of blood no doubt, though whether or not it was Nathanael's or something or someone else's entirely, he was not sure.

"What on earth happened here?" William pondered aloud as he tilted his head to read the end of the last entry only as it was the only one with the handwriting so impaired that it was barely legible.

> *I have absolutely no idea what to do next.*
> *As weak as I am, I cannot run and besides, there is nowhere to go.*
> *As it turns out, there truly is no place for people like me, there never was.*
> *So, I must hide. Hide until William can return and discover*
> *my awful secret, my failure. Or die while I am waiting.*
> *Either way, I will see my Elsie once more.*

William's heart suddenly leapt in fear at the self-made prophecy and trembled, then sprang into action. Without a second of hesitation, he snapped the journal shut before hiding it within his medical satchel and took off almost at a run towards the apothecary on the other side of town.

He had been gone much longer than he had planned, delayed several times over for his own needs, Sebastian's family, and then there had been the uncharacteristically sunny weather that had prevented his travel on countless other occasions, not to mention the few seemingly pressing family matters his mother would not allow him escape from before he left. They had all been painfully important at the time and decisions that seemed justified when making them, though in light of what he had just read, all save his visit to Sebastian's home now felt most carelessly made. In the back of his mind, he should have at least considered the fact that his friend might be suffering, and yet he had still selfishly chosen excuse after irresponsible excuse about why he was not going to be returning that week.

"How utterly reckless have I been?" He chastised himself through gritted teeth as he ran but managed to reach his home without drawing the slightest bit of attention from anyone. This should have alarmed him most of all for there had always been at least some person stirring at any given hour in this sleepy town, and with it being the beginning of planting season, the inn and tavern should have been literally filled with patrons after a long day of plowing the fields. And yet, not a single person was in the street or standing outside any establishment deep in conversation with their neighbor.

Now gripped by an all-consuming guilt that would not relent, William tried the front door, yet it would not budge. Next, he sought entry by the windows out front but despite how hard he pulled up on the sash in the hope that he could gain entry in that way, they were also stuck fast.

Please let him be alright, God... William closed his eyes and steadied himself to calm his mounting anxiety at the certain discovery, but it did not work. With the added fear of failure, his mind only raced faster with all the possibilities that might lie within, much like the apparent disarray he had just witnessed in Nathanael's study.

Determined once again to enter his own home at last without destruction or by bringing undesired attention from the locals, he ran around to the back of the building by the river and managed to finally squeeze himself through the somewhat ajar door covering the cellar roof. He was in at last, but only barely. With a jolt of exultation at his triumph, he climbed up the small set of stairs that led to the main floor above but when he reached his apothecary, to his great surprise, his place of business looked exactly as he had left it a month ago. Not a single jar, crate or instrument had been moved in the slightest. In fact, absolutely nothing spoke of anyone living there at all, much less that a catastrophic event had occurred in his absence. Yet there also remained the bizarre fact that the doors and windows had all been bolted securely shut from within in protection. *But protection from what?*

William pondered that complicated thought, and as he did, fresh adrenaline filled his veins at the unnerving possibilities before him.

"Nathanael?" He finally called out tentatively to the man as he crept up the loudly creaking stairs knowing there was nowhere else his friend would choose to hide if he were in danger, which from what his journal had said, seemed entirely possible.

Nobody answered. Not a single spoken word, groan or whisper echoed back in the silence all around him. It was almost as if the dusty air hung warm and thick as it gathered up all the noise within.

"Nathanael Beckett..." He paused at the top of the stairs and took one step after another towards the shut bedroom door to his right. "It's William. William Wells, remember?" He added cautiously.

Still no answer.

Holding his breath, he clasped the cold metal doorknob in his right hand and turned it slowly, half-expecting it to be locked, as well, but to his great relief, the door opened quite easily as it groaned noisily on its hinges like something otherworldly in its shrill response.

Then there was silence—deathlike, uncomfortable, unnerving, silence.

Like the rest of the apothecary below, Nathanael's room lay unusually dark within, like that of an enclosed tomb, with the window curtains pulled tightly shut. In fact, by all outward appearances, every effort had been made on his part to keep out any other illumination to speak of that could possibly penetrate his quarters save one solitary candle that still stood vigil upon the table in the center of the room—its flame flickering brightly over Nathanael's cherished Bible though long tendrils of wax had already collected along its sides.

Peering in closer through the thick darkness, William allowed his eyes to adjust to the shadows even more, before he finally saw him on the other side of the room. There, only a few feet away from him, was Nathanael. Though he still did not seem to take notice of William's arrival in any way. Instead, he was rather lifelessly kneeling, or rather motionlessly leaning, as if in statuesque prayer upon his bed that had been moved into the corner of the room, as far away from the door behind him as humanly possible.

"Nathanael?" William's eyes grew wide in horror at the sight of his poor state and inwardly groaned. *Am I too late? Is this what happens to people like me when they do not feed? They solidify into stone.*

William shook his head, refusing to accept such an unconscionable fact and continued his measured steps apprehensively towards him, placing each one deliberately after the other until he was finally able to place his hand softly upon Nathanael's shoulder at last.

His friend was still alive, but only barely. By all observations, the man's chest still appeared to be rising up and down though only imperceptibly, much like it had when he had treated him on the *Endeavour*.

"I knew you would return, William," Nathanael's voice floated up to him, quiet as a whisper at first.

"I promised you, I would." William knelt down instantly next to his friend and placed his hand on top of the folded ones, willing some of his own strength into his ailing companion.

"I'm so glad... I can rest now." Nathanael tried to rise to his feet but could not. In his emaciated and weakened state, he crumpled hard upon the floor, while involuntarily folding his frame ever so carefully as to offer some form of protection from the impact.

"Nathanael!" William rushed to his side immediately and lifted the frail man onto the bed beside him as if he weighed no more than a child to him, which in a way, he probably did.

Seemingly pleased by his friend's return, Nathanael only smiled peacefully back at him for several moments before he whispered again, "I told Him you would come."

"Told who I would come?" William's brow furrowed as he feverishly retrieved several of the stored containers from within his bag.

Nathanael did not speak further but only pointed with one raised finger to the ceiling above in response.

William shook his head once more. "Here. You need to drink this." The young doctor held a flask up to Nathanael's lips and tried to help him drink the life-giving liquid—the blood he had secured while treating the sick in London with his father.

Nathanael did not have the strength to refuse though he very much wanted to do so. "I think it would be best to let me die, dear friend," Nathanael's voice tried to reassure him and dissuade his efforts. "You don't know what I've done."

"No, and neither do you it appears." William propped the man's head up slightly and began forcibly making the other accept all the liquid.

Obediently, for he could do nothing else otherwise to stop him, Nathanael swallowed twice and then a third time before the first of the containers was now empty. "But I am already dead, don't you see? Cursed beyond Heaven's admittance. An eternal vagabond on this Earthly shore to Hell. It can't be any worse."

William opened another flask and made his friend consume all its contents, too. "That's right, Preacher. Keep talking. You can talk all night about: Heaven, hell, my unworthy soul, our fallen state, just as long as you keep talking," he commanded him firmly.

Nathanael smiled again and tried to focus his gaze on his friend through almost closed eyes. "Your soul was never unworthy to God, William. You know that."

"So, you keep telling me." William patted the arm of the man but continued to revive him with dose after dose of the supply he had brought along with him just in case they had needed it.

For almost thirty minutes, time passed slowly between them, almost painfully so, but as it did, Nathanael's breathing gradually returned to its more even state, allowing William the chance to finally inhale an extended sigh of relief. In all, it had taken almost ten containers of blood to bring his friend back from the brink of death, but in his estimation, it had been worth every single drop.

"Only five more left for me." William shook his head in disappointment and reflected back to the strangeness of the empty town. "Where is everyone, Nathanael?"

"I don't know," Nathanael spoke the words slowly and softly without any recognition whatsoever as to what was transpiring in the world around him.

"Here. I found this in your study." William reached into his satchel and drew out Nathanael's forgotten journal before setting it next to his Bible on the table.

"Thank you. I must have forgotten it when I left." Nathanael watched William as he stood up and went back downstairs to unbolt the front door and the windows.

Once in the larger room below, however, William stopped to wind the clock on the wall and set it to the correct time, uncertain as to when it had been wound last for he knew that Nathanael hated the incessant chiming the clock made.

For William, it was a simple possession of his former life that meant very little to most people, but to him spoke volumes by its sheer presence. Even as a child, the rhythmic ticking of the gears had always seemed to calm him and since his transition it had grounded him even more. In this small token of the passage of life, it was almost as if he saw the world with great fascination within these cogs and springs, each person functioning with another to achieve an overall magnificent and useful product. Yet if one member of the community suffered, if one cog would cease to turn in the way it was meant to do, the whole struggled because of it. To his way of thinking, it was a perfect analogy for his and Nathanael's lives, even if it did irritate his friend to distraction.

His task completed, William hung the clock back upon the wall and opened the front door as he looked out and down the street before him. Not a single soul could be seen in either direction, nor heard for that matter—except perhaps maybe a dog barking at some stray cat off in the distance.

Determining there was more at play than what met his naked eye, his senses, both vampire and human alike, sent waves of warnings across his skin. "I'll be right back," he yelled up the stairs to his friend above, before locking the door safely behind him and began his brisk walk over to the other doctor in town, Josiah Hadleigh. If anyone knew what was amiss here, it was sure to be him for the man never missed a detail about anything, medical or otherwise.

The elder doctor's home behind the Summerfield's farm was only a short distance away from his own, yet the whole way there William couldn't help but notice that nearly every door he passed was securely shut, and every window held a single candle flickering wildly within. All that is except for the doctors. At his simple dwelling, both were open wide in welcome, inviting any to stop by for a chat or warm discussion around the fire.

"Hello!" William called as he unlatched the outer gate that protected Doctor Hadleigh's cherished herb garden and strode confidently inside. Row after row of columbine, feverfew, oregano, echinacea, lemon balm, peppermint, chamomile, turmeric, lavender and other plants he could scarcely remember their names greeted him in their neatly tended and labeled arrangements to avoid possible misdirection.

"Hello, William!" Doctor Hadleigh echoed back before meeting his unexpected guest at the front door. "My! If you aren't a sight for these sore eyes!" The older gentleman with the air of a man who was forever content in the world around him embraced him eagerly.

"I am almost afraid to ask, Josiah, but where is everyone tonight?" William followed the man into his humble home before taking an offered seat by the large fire already burning brightly within.

"Sick or hiding, I assume," the older man replied with the shake of his head and busied himself in brewing a fresh pot of tea. "Many of them caught the grippe just after Pasha from the looks of things. Terrible sore throats, fevers, catarrh and an unmistakable rash have been plaguing young and old alike, and it has not taken long for it to spread to nearly every household in some way or another." He stroked his neatly trimmed white beard and matching mustache, the perfect facial accessory, in William's assessment, to his sparkling blue eyes.

"They are calling it an influenza outbreak back in London." William took the cup of steaming liquid offered to him and blew carefully across the top to dispel the dissipating vapor. "My father has been quite busy this month with his own patients and with those from neighboring districts. Though I had hoped it had not spread this far north, or I would have sent word to warn you of it. I, myself, was treating the family of a friend down in Portsmouth as the villagers there have been hit fairly hard, as well."

"I was afraid as much. Comes and goes 'round this time every fifth year or so. You can almost set your calendar to it if'in you have a mind to." He picked up his favorite pipe and knocked out the old collection of tobacco hidden inside.

"Um-hmm." William sipped his tea politely. "Is there any way I can help now that I am back?" He asked while trying all the while to think of a way to ascertain if the fear Nathanael wrote about in his journal could possibly be true.

"Don't think for a minute I was going to let you out of my sight now that I know that you're finally back, William." The doctor chuckled in amusement and lit his pipe, the scent of cherry tobacco quickly filling the premises. "I need every man I can get and probably two more if we are to beat this thing."

"If it is as bad as it was in London, I agree. Incidentally, that has a very nice aroma to it. Is it new?" William asked curiously about the man's new choice of tobacco.

"Just invented this year actually, and only in England proper at the present, I might add," Doctor Hadleigh answered casually. "When old Josh Pennington suggested it to me the other day, I didn't think I would like it at first, but now I have to admit that it is growing on me a bit. In a way, I might even prefer it now over my old blend most days."

"Well, it's delightful." William smiled back, enjoying the camaraderie he always felt in the man's presence. In fact, in every conversation he had ever had with the man, it always felt more like he was speaking with a dear uncle instead of a man almost twice his age and his most definite superior medically. "And do you have any patient's tonight that I could check on for you? Maybe lighten your load just a tad."

"Well, I had a mind to pay a call on your friend tonight, actually."

"Oh, the preacher?" William felt instantly alarmed at his decision but maintained his calm expression, intent on dissuading the man entirely for Nathanael was in no state to entertain anyone other than his own kind at the present.

"I'm sorry to say, but no one has seen hide nor hair of him since after the service. Gabe said he left their family meal quite suddenly before it even started, and they had to eat without him. He thought the man looked slightly dazed when he left the house, too, though he said he could not be sure exactly as to his condition as they were trying to tend to a cut on his daughter's hand that she had received while preparing the food. Have you not gone home yet, son?"

"Yes, I checked on Preacher Beckett myself before coming over here tonight. He is still quite sick, but I think he will undoubtedly pull through. Thankfully for all involved, he has a very strong constitution," William lied effectively as he tried to convince him out of visiting altogether.

"I thought as much when I met him after he arrived last winter. A rather strange fellow I'll grant you, but far more robust than our last preacher. Still, I'm glad to know he is on the mend. Others have not been so lucky. Why we lost that very same sweet, young lady just a few days ago and another man only this morning."

"Who?" William took another sip of his tea and attempted to hide his growing alarm.

"Why our beautiful pianist, Elsie Summerfield, and the Dobson boy from over at the livery."

William's eyes opened wide at the news, fearing the worst. "I am sure her family is probably quite distraught over it. Was it the grippe that took her, too?"

"Most definitely. I saw her after the Pasha to treat her cut, and she was right as rain then. It wasn't until a day or two later that she was stricken with the fiercest of fevers that I have ever experienced and then, of course, the racking cough. You already know how the illness progresses after that."

"Yes, when the patient can no longer bring in sufficient air, they most often succumb rather quickly after that." William studied the fire in deep concentration, thinking back to his treatment of Elijah in Portsmouth and prayerfully thanked God for interceding on the young child's behalf for he was just as sick as Elsie had been it seemed.

"Yes, well, I would have called the preacher to officiate the funeral, but he was nowhere to be found, and the family had scarcely enough time to finish a proper burial for her before the rest of them were taken ill, as well. Sadly, every last one of them, from the father right on down to the littlest baby, has been struggling over there and unfortunately, there is only one of me, and I simply can't be everywhere."

"That is rather odd that it would affect so many in one house, don't you think?" William tried to puzzle out the possibility.

"Agreed, but that is how these things go sometimes. Elsie probably brought it back from one of her trips to the market, poor girl. And poor Summerfields for that matter, they have truly been suffering through this ordeal," he added with a shake of his head. "Well, as you have witnessed, it has the whole town up in arms thinking that the village is cursed or some other such nonsense since the preacher has been taken up ill with the rest of them. That is why most of them are in hiding, that and the fear of catching whatever it is to be caught." Hadleigh drew in another breath of his pipe and exhaled the smoke out slowly. "I tell you what William, the closer we come in our interpretation of the human body the farther we are from the understanding of the fragile mind."

"Agreed." William leaned back in his chair and watched the fire in reflection. "Would you like me to visit their family tonight, then?" He tried not to seem too eager to be off and investigating for himself whether or not Elsie had died of a human illness or a more devastating one for Nathanael's sake. Deep down, it was clear that his friend had obviously loved the girl very much, but how he had planned to make a marriage work with him being a vampire was beyond William's ability to reason it out.

Yet there was still one fact alone that bothered him much more than all of the others put together. If in his delirium, he had unconsciously changed the girl and her eternal destination, he knew beyond a reasonable doubt that it would ruin the man both mentally and spiritually far more than any fasting could ever have accomplished. Yes, he would undoubtedly have been given the blessing of Elsie's love for all of eternity, but in the unfortunate taking of her eternal soul, William was certain Nathanael would also have been crushed and utterly devastated beyond hopeful reparation thereafter.

"Aye, that would be a blessing for all if you are able, then the Thompsons and the Lewis family down by the glen might be the next stop along the way. But be sure to bring me word if anyone has passed so we can help try to stop the spread of this grippe to anyone else. And encourage Preacher Beckett to show his face as soon as he is able, or the village may never come out of hiding"

"I'll do that." William chuckled lightheartedly. "Well, if that is all for tonight, I had best be to it." He shook the man's hand but requested politely soon after. "Please sit, I've trespassed on your hospitality enough for one evening. I know how to see myself out."

"Oh, and be sure to take some of those herbs with you on the way, William. You know how to use them, and they will help with the catarrh, as will a warm mustard or onion poultice should the respiration be hindered."

"Understood." William waved to the doctor and selected several pieces of the echinacea before placing them carefully within his bag. As instructed, he went directly over to the Summerfield's home first and knocked on the door politely before leaning in to peer through one of the darkened windows, hopeful that he would not be disturbing anyone's slumber as of yet.

Thankfully, an obviously sick Susan Summerfield answered the door with a crying child upon her hip and another tucked safely behind her skirts, "May I help you, Doctor Wells?"

"Good evening, Mrs. Summerfield. Doctor Hadleigh sent me over to check on you. May I be of any assistance?" William asked quickly, not wanting to put any more pressure on the woman towards performing any kind of hospitality towards his arrival.

Almost crumpling into a chair beside her, the woman nearly burst into tears in relief at the sight of him. "I'd take any help offered tonight, Doctor Wells. I don't mind saying this, but I am about worn to the bone as it is."

"Then it would be my pleasure entirely." William caught the small child up within his capable arms instinctively and carried him over to the kitchen table within for a full examination. "Now what do we have here, little man?" He tried to distract the toddler from his sudden separation from his mother. "Are all your children as sick as he is or have some recovered?"

"I think four or five of them are on the other side of it, but Gabe and the youngest are the worst, next to Elsie, God rest her poor soul," Mrs. Summerfield explained to him wearily.

"I see. Well, I will check them all over then just to be sure." He repeated this routine with patient after patient throughout the house and in the end concluded that Mrs. Summerfield's assessment had indeed been correct. Gabe would need at least a few days more of bedrest, as would the toddler, but the rest, including the mother herself, would no doubt make a full recovery soon.

"If it would not be too much of an offence to ask it, might I inquire as to what happened to your daughter at Pasha?" William asked tentatively as he placed a thick quilt over the woman as she enjoyed a much-needed rest by the fire.

In her tired state, Mrs. Summerfield did not answer at first. Instead, her gaze remained entirely focused on the fire like someone almost lost in a trance for in a way she probably was as the weight of what was unfolding around her was absolutely debilitating.

"I'm sorry, if it is too soon to speak of it. We can talk later if you like." William picked up the toddler and held him close to him as he rocked the child back to sleep through his coughing.

"No," Mrs. Summerfield finally spoke. "It is not too soon, though I fear it never will be something any of us will want to remember for quite some time, as dear as she was to us all."

William nodded. "I can only imagine what a loss it is for you all. She was certainly a most endearing young woman. Mr. Beckett, I am sure, will be extremely affected once he is healed from his illness, as well."

"Mr. Beckett." She looked off into the fire once more. "Now, that would have been a true joy to have seen in my lifetime—his marriage to my Elsie and all, but sadly that is not to be. Doctor Wells, I have seen my fair share of illnesses in my time, but this one we are enduring now is like a thief in the night, stealing away bits and pieces of our lives without the least care as to the carnage it has left behind."

"I understand, truly I do. I helped my father with several losses during my time in London recently. There almost seems no rhyme or reason as to how it is acquired and even less certainty as to who will not be able to endure it." William shifted the child in his lap to a more comfortable position and patted his back.

"That is assuredly true here, Doctor, but to answer your question, the day or so after Pasha Elsie began with a very high fever that quickly spread to her lungs. For almost four days she suffered from a relentless cough that stole the very breath away from her until at last, she stopped her struggle altogether," she replied plainly without the least bit of emotion on her face. Not that she did not care for her eldest daughter in any way, it was rather almost as if the entire ordeal had not truly sunk in to her mental reality just yet. "The night before she passed, I kissed her goodnight like I always do for each and every one of my children before they retire for the night, and when I went to check on her the next morning she was gone. We buried her just a few days ago. Gabe was barely standing as it was, but we did what was right by her as best we could. Perhaps you can show Mr. Beckett her grave when he recovers."

"I will most certainly do that, and I am so very sorry for your loss, Mrs. Summerfield. We both are," William pledged on behalf of his absent friend.

"And I thank you for it, but God has a reason, though I'd like it very much if He would share it with me as I am going to miss that girl something terrible." A single tear coursed down the woman's right cheek and then dripped onto the collar of her nightdress.

The two sat for at least an hour thereafter by the fire before William was able to persuade her to lie down and left the now sleeping child in his sister, Alice's care.

At the Thompson's and the Lewis family home he encountered much the same as he did at the Summerfield's. Some family members he chose to bloodlet, given the severity of their symptoms, before carefully storing the refuse into a small, corked jug within his bag. While with others, he chose to follow the older doctor's instructions and applied steam breathing treatments, poultices for the collected phlegm and some tea to ease their sore throats.

When the morning sun had finally begun to respectfully peek its golden head above the horizon, William decided his work for the evening had been sufficiently concluded. Almost all his current patients were thankfully stable for the time being, provided they followed his direct instructions regarding rest and the increased need of fluids. Yet more excellent was the fact that despite the severity of the outbreak, he had not lost a single patient the entire night. As one might expect for someone in his position, he counted this a blessed triumph indeed and happily, but most assuredly exhausted, he entered the apothecary once more to rest, as well.

As he thankfully expected, the clock on the wall greeted him with its ticking in the continued silence before beginning its six successive chimes as he closed the front door behind him. Feeling the increasing weight of each of their vibrations he placed his coat upon the post and carried his bag up to the next level above.

"Is it still you, my friend?" Nathanael asked warmly, but still rather weak in volume from the room to his right.

"It is. Or what is left of him, I am afraid." William scrubbed his face with both hands to wipe away his exhaustion and took a seat in the chair at the side of Nathanael's bed. "Are you feeling a bit more like yourself now?" William instinctively felt his friend's wrist to test his pulse though he knew full well, nothing shockingly revealing would occur, yet the habitual action of checking it comforted him just the same.

"I would say that I was, but I am not sure how I am supposed to feel anymore as I have never felt fully alive since last November, I think," Nathanael answered him plainly.

With a brief prayer of thanksgiving at his friend's remarkably changed countenance, William closed his eyes and sighed, grateful once again that the man was improving little by little.

"Have you taken to praying now, William?" Nathanael tried to ask discreetly but was interrupted by a series of coughing fits thereafter. "It..." He took in a deep breath and then another. "...is none of my business really." He relaxed once more against his pillow, totally spent now by the ordeal.

"You really should just rest." William gave him another container of fresh blood this time to alleviate more of his symptoms since he knew from his experience with the man by the docks that the newer quality would restore the balance more quickly. "We can talk about all of this later today."

Nathanael drank the liquid willingly before handing it back to his friend when it was only half finished. "I know she is gone, William."

As tired as he was, William's head suddenly jerked back up at his friend's rather unusual revelation before he continued to finish the container that was handed to him, trying to ignore his statement altogether. "Who is gone, Nathanael?"

"My Elsie."

With a grimace that he could not hide, William shook his head, dreading the task that lay ahead of him at last. "It's not what you think happened, Nathanael." He tried to deflect the blame the man might be feeling on the matter though nothing he could ever say would assuage the guilt the man would no doubt carry thereafter for not being there in the first place.

"I almost killed her, William. Worse yet... I wanted to," Nathanael admitted seriously. "I loved her with all my being, but I wanted to kill her just as much. What kind of man does that?"

"But you didn't, Nathanael." William began to argue but stopped short. "Wait. How did you know that she had died?" He stared at the man in growing confusion as he assumed along with the other doctor that Nathanael had been locked up in here the entire time since before her passing.

Nathanael did not answer at first but chose instead to simply close his eyes as William watched him relax even further before a graceful smile lifted on his face at last. "I've seen her."

In sheer incredulity at what the man was saying, William shook his head at the impossibility of such a thing and stood up to take his leave, deciding that his friend was still not fully in his right mind just yet. "Rest, Nathanael. We will talk about it later. Goodnight... or rather good day."

"Goodnight. And thank you."

"For what?" William turned back at the doorway but did not move back into the room.

"For coming back."

"I should have come sooner, Nathanael. I am sorry I was late." He hung his head in shame, allowing the guilt he felt that was well-deserved to rebuke him further.

"At least... you kept... your promise." Nathanael drifted off to sleep once more.

"I always will," he pledged faithfully before leaving Nathanael's room to do the same.

Chapter Twenty-Three

April 21st, 1793

The entire city was aflame with indignation tonight it seemed as Emile walked casually along the river Seine enjoying his nightly stroll. It had been over two months since his conversation with Angelique, and now, tempers flared even brighter in the most casual of conversations, threatening to divide the very framework of his delicate society.

Still, no one among the elite wished to accept the change that was transpiring all around them, either that or they did not think it necessary to heed the danger of it at all. Either way, standing here in the midst of the two worlds tonight, Emile was not even sure where he stood on the matter anymore. Since meeting his Emma, he had discovered that his heart was now especially drawn to the unfortunate plight of the people within her world. People like Lucien and Michel, who, as destitute as they seemed, were not that much unlike himself at their age, minus the grand estate and servants to be sure. Nor did he particularly care for the cruel treatment those above the common citizens handed down so freely as if they were not worthy of anything better. Once upon a time he might not have noticed the circumstances at all, but now that he did, his mind could not possibly escape thinking of each one of them daily.

It wasn't his fault that his heritage and lifestyle had been handed down to him by generations before, but it <u>was</u> becoming clearer that the line between such classes in Paris was blurring rapidly. A change was definitely on the horizon, and he could feel it growing stronger with each passing day. Not to mention the fact that those in his inner circle were quickly disappearing in rapid fashion. If the trend continued, as he feared it might, it was only a matter of time before he could be next. And vampire or not, no ship to the Americas would protect him from the people's wrath or the dreaded guillotine thereafter.

Feeling increasingly guilty for dismissing Angelique's concern so flippantly at the party, he had endeavored for weeks to continue his efforts in securing information regarding the continued health of her family in the Bastille prison, but in each of the exchanges, he was met with only the same calloused affirmation of their eventual deaths. For as Michel had so wisely predicted, it seemed that the common man was utterly apathetic now regarding the fates of "some self-entitled aristocrat and his spoiled brat of a son".

To be truthful, so was he in a way. Despite all the circling rumors to the contrary, he had never cared a whit for the marchioness and her overly dramatic displays of emotion. His attention towards her in public settings had always been centered on a well-played ruse in an orchestrated diversion than anything personally sincere. Yet, notwithstanding his lack of personal interest in her, he did care very much about what happened to her brother, Jonathan.

Since the very first day that Emile had arrived in Paris years ago, Jonathan had been with him through thick and thin, almost as close as his own brother in some ways. Funny and charismatically inclined, the man had saved him from countless romantic entanglements that Emile would love to forget, and more than a few financial distresses to warrant his eternal loyalty. But on the night that he had disappeared, Emile had been far too concerned with finding his next snack than in escorting him back to his apartment. A fact which had shamefully plagued him often when he lay awake at night wondering what events had transpired on the way home and how he could have moved to prevent them.

Just thinking about his friend's predicament now, his mind replayed again a singular question that had been nagging at him no matter how hard he had tried to get away from it. *What if it were him in that prison and not Jonathan? He would probably already be dead by now or at the very least, starved, if they had not already discovered his darker identity and killed him outright.*

Emile shook his head in disappointment at the obvious answer. This game of his, in playing both sides of the saga, was becoming mentally exhausting. The whole concept of injustice in all its various factors of ugliness was taking on a whole new definition for him now as he saw both sides of the coin equally. However, for some reason unbeknownst to him, he felt the need to continue to wage the war within his mind for just a few days longer. Or at least until he had satisfied himself with the outcome for all involved, for nothing was worse than being forced into an action you never intended nor desired to do in the first place. Well, maybe one thing was worse. Choosing nothing at all.

If he had learned anything over the past five months, it was quite definitively that apathy was good for a party, but horrible for daily life. But then again, maybe that was the purpose of coming back to Paris after all. What he had initially thought would be an opportunity for yet another playful diversion, a return to his days of glory, had really only ended up being a temporary and wasteful escape from something he did not want to face in the first place—himself.

Emile had known for quite some time that the shallow life in which he lived for years was never meant to sustain him forever. Yet the alternative was equally daunting, and if he would dare to admit it, overwhelmingly frightening to contemplate. The one thing he remembered most of all when he lay awake at night, was his father speaking to him of his need to break out of the masterful actor he portrayed. But in his younger years, to become a man of integrity, seemed fantastically out of reach and frankly, not really worth his energy. Perhaps that was why he had refused but also respected the admonition of Señor Moretti at the castle, however misguided he felt it was at the time. Both men had been equally firm in their reproof of his character, but also patient in waiting for his acceptance, and that kind of deference against his stubbornness grated on his nerves as much as it inspired him.

"Still," Emile picked up a stone and skipped it as far as he could across the Seine to the other side. "If the common man can do such a thing, why can't I?" He decided at last and felt the rest of his pointless reservations fall away. Deep down, the crux of the matter was this, if he truly desired a complete and long-awaited reformation, he needed to change his entire perspective and not merely his situation alone for no matter if he were in England, Paris or the Americas, he would still be who he was, and no amount of charm would ever change that for him.

With a feeling of growing alarm, Emile cast a wary glance up the river and over to where several crowds of people were already beginning to gather near the inn. The citizens of Paris were especially fervent tonight as if something in their world had fundamentally changed. Yet, from all that he had heard down at the tavern recently, nothing of note had transpired whatsoever.

Moreover, none of his acquaintances would have ever dared to venture anywhere near this part of town where the rabble lived, nor would he be here either if he had not thought it especially important to be so. Emile was not a fool, or so careless in his actions as to allow himself to be in such a compromising situation, but danger aside, he simply could not leave Paris without at least trying to see to the safety of Angelique's family. After all, he was the only one left who could, and so he had to do what others could not, if only to be able to say to himself later that he tried.

With a sigh of resignation at last in regard to his forced upon task, he made his way up to the street level above and kept to the nearby shadows, traveling as inconspicuously as possible down to the inn that he was referred to on a previous visit. It was there, listening from across the street in the glow of several torches, that he heard from the rather boisterous speakers present that there was to be a trial of Angelique's father and many others that very next morning. The son, Jonathan, seemed of lesser concern to the crowd, but either way, both were in very grave danger.

The men and women of the new Assembly were now poised on the edge of a very great precipice of destruction, and like it or not, the gears of the upcoming revolution were now finally set in motion. Emile's world, and everyone in it, was about to be put on trial, and despite the threat to himself or anyone else in attendance, Emile knew he needed to be there.

Yet later that night, when he told Emma of his plans to attend, the girl could not stop for a moment in her pleading with him to reconsider, but he would not. Despite what she might fear would befall him, something in him compelled him to go and stand up for those who could not, if such an opportunity was given. To be honest, it was the first real argument the two of them had ever had during their brief time together, but one she reticently acquiesced to in the end for she knew he had already firmly made up his mind. For her sake, he would have done anything she had ever asked of him, given the whole of Paris to her if she had requested it, but in this he could not.

"Sweet, Emma." He closed his eyes and drank in the luxurious memory of their last rendezvous together to slow his racing heart from the contemplation of what was before him. Without hesitation, she had always given him everything he had ever desired, requesting nothing from him in return. *As if resisting him were even possible at this point.* He mused sarcastically but then felt the painful guilt once more because of it for the woman had done nothing to warrant such a careless remark on his behalf. On the contrary, her steady kindness steered him ever faithfully towards seeing the world around him in a different light altogether. A very rebuking, yet essential light he might add, if he was still truly sincere in his decision to change.

What's more, for some inexplicable reason he could not simply discard her like all the others. Those women had been absolutely expendable, a necessary distraction from the endless waves of apathy within him. Whereas she, on the other hand, was a healing balm, an anchor as deep as the roots of a tree, and vibrant and constant like the sun. Furthermore, the warmth of her inviting gentleness drew in all those around her and spread out its rays to everything it touched, especially himself.

Like a spoiled child, he had selfishly clung to those roots and continued their clandestine rendezvous much longer than he had ever planned or thought possible. And still, with an almost sacrificial devotion towards him that went far beyond his feeble attempt at comprehension, Emma had dutifully returned to his apartment every night only to leave the next morning after he empathetically soothed her tears over her incessant insecurities regarding his continued devotion.

For months, imploring invitations and endearing promises were made to her so delicately that she could not justifiably refuse any of them, and part of him regretted that terribly also... if only for a moment. The other half, the side of him he longed to be rid of completely, could not wait until he would be with her once more, to be with her forever—no matter what the emotional cost might be to her or him as Emma had become much more than a casual dalliance of his wayward eye. In her meek and quiet ways, she had quickly become the focus of his every thought and necessity it seemed.

Her fanciful light, which had drawn him to her initially in the street, had not been diminished in the slightest by his darkness, but had only grown brighter in his estimation against it. Like the angel that she was, she gave of herself to others as freely as a child gives their last crust of bread to a stray cat, with no expectation of ever receiving replenishment in return, and that hurt Emile's heart most of all. If her enduring love was indeed something he was seeking, he needed to do better by her or that hopeful strength she possessed might disappear entirely.

And so it was that he found himself in a shadowed corner beneath a bridge that very next morning as he stole into it to change into a half-open shirt and a pair of well-worn pants that showed a patch here and there where they had most obviously been mended. Accompanying them was a short, brown overcoat of some sorts with large black buttons that ran up the center. Though he had hated to do so, given her position on his required task, these tattered trappings of modest means that he now wore had been skillfully secured by her with the only provision being that he promise to have them back before nightfall or her younger brother would be sure to miss them—her very intimidating brother, even to a vampire, he might add.

To her credit, Emma assured him that it was the least she could do to assure his safety. If he were to succeed today in standing witness to all that transpired, she felt it was utterly imperative not to draw even the slightest bit of attention to himself as someone who should not be in attendance with the crowd, but rather on trial with the others.

He had even laughed at that when she said it, as arrogant as he always was in his abilities to take care of himself should a problem arise. This detail of self-preservation did not overly concern him as it would have anyone else in his position. In fact, if he had listened to even half of what she had tried to warn him of, he would have known that he should have been at the very least remotely terrified to attend where he himself could become their next target, but for some reason a strange force deep within him drew him towards it, instead of away. *No, that wasn't right, either.* Feeling the indignation and adrenaline build up within him like a secret boost of some kind of magic serum, he absolutely welcomed the danger today—embraced it even, like a long-lost friend.

As if sensing the need to distract him once again towards the inevitable that might befall him, the river beside Emile lapped upon the sidewalk where he stood under the bridge, almost wetting his boots as he waited for the sun to settle firmly behind the clouds before he left on his errand.

"If you knew what was best for you, you would stay far away from me, sir." Emile wrinkled his nose in disgust at the water's audacity to venture closer towards him and shifted his position along the stone wall where he leaned backwards upon it. He hated being wet. He always had. He always would. It reminded him too much of how cold he had been when he first lay on the beach next to William that night, utterly exhausted and too weak to move. The unrelenting rain that had pelted his face then was nothing in comparison to the raking tremors of ice that flowed across his skin and shook his whole body with convulsive force for days thereafter. Simply put, the whole ordeal was hell on Earth, if such a thing were possible, and something he felt he would never fully forget though he may live a millennium.

Everything from the hull imprisonment to the ocean voyage, the shipwreck and even the cave, had all been incredibly wet and unbearably cold even as a human. Yet it was equally staggering to realize how very frigid he always remained still. Nothing in all the world seemed to help to abate it in the slightest either: not the women, the money, or even the wine. It was almost as if his very transformation had sucked away both his soul and life force together in one all-consuming motion, leaving everything inside of him feeling utterly empty. And sadly, nothing on this Earth, save Emma alone, seemed to compensate for that lack of sensation he experienced every time he breathed. Maybe that was the real reason why he had needed her. She made him feel almost alive once more, or as close to it as he could possibly be at the present. And that one reason alone was enough to treasure every moment he spent with her.

Feeling more than a bit overwhelmed now by his reflections, he drew in several long breaths to steady his thoughts even more and exhaled them out slowly, drinking in the scent of Paris: the smell of the bakeries, the pungent oil on the artists' palettes down by the river, the murmur of people walking along on the street above him, the very hum of exquisite energy the city always possessed. It all revitalized and spurred him further on in his task. It was most definitely true that some of the people here may have been dreaming of a revolution, but he was more inclined towards the city's overall preservation, something he feared would be lost entirely amidst the bloodshed and hatred that was undoubtedly soon to follow.

Determined anew, he set his resolve firmly towards the task at hand and climbed the steps to the upper street before heading in the direction of the Rue de St Antoine. Through the thick layer of morning fog, the inn from the night before could still clearly be seen on the corner, though not a single passerby could have missed it whether it had been daylight or night for a large crowd had already gathered outside just like they had yesterday.

True to what they had said was the new judicial system of governance, it appeared that the awaiting prisoners were to at least be given a fair trial just inside the Bastille courtyard where the entire city could watch and participate, or so it was referred to as such though Emile suspected by the angry shouts for justice this morning that it would be anything but. To the naked eye, these people gathered here today were little more than very willing antagonists to what was about to unfold and not witnesses to the contrary. Moreover, as unfair as it seemed to Emile standing there, they were also about to become a makeshift jury of their peers. If the defendants were indeed found guilty, which it was becoming painfully certain they would be, then the sentence would most likely be carried out either that very day or the next, courtesy of *Madame* Guillotine to an all too willing and waiting throng of eager spectators.

Yet despite the uneasiness that accompanied the many people thronging along beside him on the street, Emile still followed the crowd, blending in with the merchants and farmers alike as they made their way to the Bastille, while all the while paying careful attention to remain cautiously towards the back of the horde should an escape become suddenly necessary.

Like the course of a river as it flowed, the mass of humanity passed within the outer battlements of the gated yard, just inside the fortified walls, and moved in a roughly semi-circle form until it quite easily surrounded all sides of the wooden platform at its center, leaving a small path for the prisoners to pass between. On the great stage sat: the current "magistrate", though most people knew him as the village coroner, two or three other men of professions unknown to Emile and then the most illustrious figure of them all, Robespierre himself.

The trials, in their official sense of the word, began very slowly at first as prisoner after prisoner passed in front of his or her judge and jury before each was given the same resounding verdict. "Guilty by means of rebellion to the National Assembly."

But what did that even mean anyways? He wondered each time it was handed down. *And what crime were they truly guilty of in the first place?* Surely a seamstress to the Marchioness of Bellamy had committed nowhere near as vile an offence as he had performed, why, just that morning, in fact. Something he had done probably countless times over since his transition and never once had he received any form of condemnation regarding it, except for maybe back on the island. And how could an elderly gardener well into his 70's, a faithful servant to the Viscount de Daumier, ever commit an evil so worthy of imprisonment, let alone death at the hands of a mob when he could barely ascend the two stairs up to his executioner's platform.

This was madness! His mind proclaimed loudly in absolute shock and repulsion at the scene.

Yet it was at the last, when both Angelique's father and her brother were brought to the platform and handed down their expected sentence, that the stark reality of his new Paris hit him full in the face. The ferocity of its newly formed callous disregard for life itself stunned him, leaving him reeling in shock and disillusionment at the intensity of the moment. What he was witnessing today was not justice at all like he had hoped. It was cold-blooded murder!

The disinterested judge, who, as tired as he was of the proceedings given the nearing approaching hour of his evening meal, condemned the two men without so much as listening to their defense, not that it would have mattered if he did for the crowd had not pardoned a single person present. Nor had anyone been allowed to speak on their behalf whatsoever.

Then as the trial seemed to be drawing to a close with the last verdict given, the leader of this great charade reached a step farther in proclaiming his authority over the entire proceedings and the people themselves as if feeling the need to add a further declaration of his own to the already ludicrous farce. "My fair citizens! It has been brought to my attention that there is yet one more member of this abhorrent family present here that has yet to be condemned this day."

Emile's blood froze at the unexpected declaration as he watched the crowd hush its volume out of respect for the man who clearly needed none in Emile's opinion.

"This man and his son are not the only ones worthy of your chastisement... your justice. There is yet one more to meet our fair lady of justice," Robespierre called out loud and strong above the display. "A Miss Angelique Toussaint also awaits your visit. You have condemned her father and her brother for their crimes against you. Should she not also join her accursed family in reserved punishment? Is she not guilty also of the same atrocities?"

To Emile's utter shock, the crowd agreed wholeheartedly and begged for more information about their prize, voicing their complete approval for all that had transpired around them, however horrific.

Then, as if suddenly trying to defend her unmerited execution, Angelique's brother fought bravely against those who held him on the platform, but in the end, was knocked entirely unconscious, incapacitated by a man not much older than himself who looked like he rather enjoyed the beating he gave him.

With every crushing blow his friend received from his tormentor, Emile's heart sunk, feeling each of them equally. Ashamed and very near the point of absolute horror for his friend, his hope drained from him as he watched Angelique's father lovingly stoop down next to his fallen child and cradle him in marked despair, sobbing openly in front of the crowd for mercy, both for his daughter and for his son's life.

The crowd, however, ignored his plight completely and only jeered even louder at the display, seizing this rather impromptu opportunity for action.

"We must finally purge our city of the refuse which pollutes its rivers, its parks, and its streets. They will hear us coming, and they will fear us!" Robespierre whipped the crowd to a frenzy even further.

Emile had heard all he needed to hear for one lifetime, maybe two. With the stealthy care of a thief in the night, he peeled himself away from the scene and clung to the shadows along the wall and out of the waiting gate ahead of those hell-bent on vigilante justice. From there he ran directly to the bridge over the Seine, scooped up his formal attire and set off at a dead sprint down the four miles to his apartment on the other side of town, grateful that the sun had still not made a visible appearance from behind the clouds. No doubt Angelique would be waiting for him there, and for once, he was grateful for it.

With fresh adrenaline coursing through his veins, his feet flew across the streets, down flights of stairs and up others, avoiding countless horses and people in the process. Immense gratitude filled his very being with every stride for a body that never seemed to tire no matter what the force placed upon it today.

In hindsight, he supposed it would have been far easier to simply hire a cab instead of running all the way home, but how could he have done so in his current attire or explain what he had been doing on this side of the city dressed as a peasant. Both instances would have drawn far too much attention from the driver or others on the street during his explanations, which at this moment, he was very eager to avoid.

At long last, he rounded the corner to his apartment and burst through the doors on the bottom floor, nearly knocking over his manservant in the process before closing the doors quickly behind him to avoid any further detection.

"*Monsieur!*" The man exclaimed as he fumbled for his footing once more, surprised more than offended at being assaulted in such a way.

"Has Angelique Toussaint arrived yet, Gustave?" Emile asked quickly after taking in a breath of air and helping the man steady himself properly.

The servant, who seemed utterly flustered still and far too shocked to reply properly, mumbled many things incoherently at first. So much so, that Emile felt understandably obligated to repeat it all once again, but this time, at a much slower rate of delivery. "Has Angelique Toussaint arrived?"

"Why... why... yes, *monsieur,*" the man stuttered a response, but Emile did not pause to wait for the rest of his answer. Without a second of hesitation, he charged up the stairs two at a time, away from the door, and up to the second floor of his lodgings. "She is waiting with Miss Larose," he called up after him quickly.

Hearing his intended warning, Emile stopped short in his journey at his report, pausing momentarily halfway up the stairs to take full stock of what may lay before him and considered his choices briefly. This unwelcome news of their meeting was both unexpected and a bit concerning all at the same time. "Please go on home now, Gustave. There's a storm brewing on the other side of town, and I would hate for you to be caught up in it tonight." Which was true, in a way, just not in terms of the weather. Neither did he wish any harm to befall the kind man on his account should the crowd turn on him next.

"Very good, sir." Without another word to the contrary, the man obediently picked up his hat from the rack by the door and walked out into the approaching night, closing the door softly behind him in the process.

Finally reaching the top landing, Emile stood for a moment outside the outer doors to his upper quarters before throwing them both open and striding in just as quickly as when he had arrived, intent on leaving as soon as he possibly could. Once inside, however, he found that he was once again met with the most curious of sights. The two women, both common and formal, were simply sitting politely at a table in the front room sharing a pot of tea as if nothing else in the world, good or otherwise, were possibly transpiring around them.

Shaking his head in frustration at the absurdity of the picture before him, Emile groaned inwardly. Here the world was melting down around them and the two women looked as if they were in total repose and completely unaffected by the world's events. It was peaceful even, if one could call it that, but from his brief experience with the woman, Emile could tell that Emma was not pleased in the slightest to be forced to entertain the other woman's company. Nor would she be happy to know just how close they <u>all</u> were to certain death.

Smiling nervously at the thoughts that might be going through her head at that very moment, Emile cleared his throat before composing himself as best as he could manage under the circumstances. "My dear ladies."

From their discreet position at the table, they both looked up in unison from their tea, but neither of them smiled nor offered a pleasureful greeting towards him of any kind. Emma alone cast him a genuinely worried expression as if considering the reasoning for the state in which he had returned. Since he had bid her farewell earlier that morning, she had been eagerly awaiting his return to hear each and every detail of his harrowing ordeal, cautiously hopeful that he would return at all for the stories she had overheard from her father had assured her quite terrifyingly that he may not.

Angelique, on the other hand, seemed classically irritated as if <u>he</u> were the one inconveniencing <u>her</u> with arriving at this late hour of the day and not the other way around.

Yet, it was at that very moment, at the conjunction of both of his worlds, that he clearly knew where his priorities finally lay. Like a coin that had been spinning incessantly in circles upon a table for months and had finally fallen to rest onto its correct side, Emile knew which side he was truly on.

"I will dispense with the pleasantries, ladies, as you have both quite obviously been given the chance to acquaint yourselves," he spoke quickly while on his way to collect the last of his things into a small overnight bag, not willing to waste a single second of the precious time that he had left. In truth, it took less time than he had supposed even though he had taken several extra moments to place: a few treasures he had seen Emma admiring during her stays, the leftover money from Señor Moretti, two changes of clothes for each of them, and the brown glass bottle that contained a liquid he had never once had the necessity to use until now, not to mention the need to secure at least one of his favorite hats for the journey.

After all, he might be dressed as a peasant now, but he very much hoped not to remain so for much longer.

"We must all leave... immediately even," he commanded as he strode into the room once more and lifted Emma protectively from her chair by taking one of her arms gingerly and guiding her towards the door, not bothering to explain anything else in the slightest.

Emma complied instantly for she had already felt poised to run all morning since he had left. "Oh, Emile, wait!" She freed herself from his grasp a few steps later and ran back to the table to snatch up the small purse she had left errantly behind before returning to him just as quickly.

From the moment she had awakened that morning, she was afraid something like this might occur. She had even thought about whether or not she would stay here without him but knew that was a pointless thought to even consider. Emile had never once made her feel any less valued than anything else in his world nor did he ever try to make her feel like she needed to change to fit into it. "His treasure" or something like that was how he always described her, but why he still thought that way she knew not. With everything that he possessed already, there was nothing she could ever give him that would ever hope to augment that in any way. But still, she was not ready to let him go and that meant that if he had to leave Paris, so would she. Yet she also knew that to leave behind what little possessions she still had left here in this world would be shockingly negligent, as well. And so, sensing in the pit of her stomach that something untoward might happen to him today, she had put what little savings she had managed to squirrel away inside of it, along with a few mementos of her past should flight become necessary and left a rather short note for her father under her pillow explaining her actions. He would no doubt find it someday when he eventually missed her, but at least she would have left him some kind of explanation for her flight.

"Where are we going?" Angelique looked mildly offended at his lack of physical care towards her, as well, but followed at a respectable distance close behind as he knew she would. "Did you see my father?"

"Your father and brother are lost to you, I am afraid." He used his other arm that was carrying the overnight bag to forcefully direct Angelique down the stairs with them to the lower level. "Please, we must hurry."

In the beginning, she complied quickly, but upon reaching the lower landing by the door, however, Angelique staggered on her feet at the sudden revelation. "They will be imprisoned for life then?"

"No, Angelique." Emile stopped abruptly and blurted out his news in the harshest way he could possibly deliver it so as to finally solicit a compliant response from the woman, "They will be dead. And so will you if you do not follow me, now."

In the end, it was all too much for her delicate nature. The false strength that she had always portrayed to everyone around her vanished instantly like the passing of a breath of air. Now incoherently dazed by his news, her eyes glazed over as if in a trance before she swayed in a near swoon and almost fell helplessly against the wall beside her.

"Angelique!" Emile abruptly caught her from falling and tried to steady her before turning to Emma. "You must help me with her," Emile pleaded, not wanting to lose another minute to this kind of frivolity. "It appears that she is not as strong as you or I."

Seeing nothing but fear and determination within his gaze, Emma nodded meekly and steered the other woman out onto the street after Emile. "You must try to come with us, miss."

"I believe there is a wagon that I can rent just down at the livery. Angelique, do you think you can make it to there or must you be carried?" He questioned the stumbling woman shortly, though he sincerely hoped he would not have to do so as it would draw further attention to the group as many people on the streets would notice a man carrying a woman and speculate if he needed their help. Which he most certainly did not.

"She'll manage. I'll make sure oft it. Just go, Emile... and hurry!" With Emma's continued, gentle prodding, Angelique snapped out of her confusion momentarily and followed him at a measured pace so as not to fall farther behind the rest and be abandoned.

Once at the livery, Emile quietly paid the daily rental fare for the wagon and pulled it around the corner to where the two women stood. "Step aboard, please," he commanded with the determination of a man who knew precisely what he was doing though Emile had never actually driven a wagon before in his life.

"Do you even know how to drive this?" Emma hastily climbed up into the back of the buckboard while Angelique required a great deal more assistance to navigate onto the hard boards behind him. In any other instance he might have laughed in utter amusement at the scene, but today, he was feeling only the raw energy of the moment as his body reacted to the increasing danger, both to himself and to the women.

"Not a clue, but to be on the safe side you should probably put the blankets over you until we are out of town," he advised as he hit the backs of the horses with both reins hard enough to motivate their response. "They aren't looking for me."

"Well, that makes me feel so much better," Emma's muffled, though sarcastic reply came from underneath the thick covering back to him.

Emile only smiled at her humor as the wagon lurched forward in response and took off at a comfortable pace through the thankfully, almost vacant streets and into the vast countryside beyond.

Almost an hour later, when they were out of the most imminent danger and farther along on their journey away from Paris proper, Emile finally called back to Emma playfully, "I'm afraid your brother will be cross with you come morning when he finds himself short a particularly favorite suit of clothing!"

Hearing his more light-hearted remark at last and not the stressed undertone with which he had arrived, Emma gratefully threw the stifling blanket from off her head and placed it in folded fashion behind her back for support. "No! Pierre will be angry at you, not me!' She yelled over the commotion of the horses.

"Fair enough! Then, I suppose it is a good thing I will be hundreds of miles away when he finally discovers it!" He chuckled and continued driving the wagon for several hours more, or at least until they had crossed more than half of the miles necessary to their destination of Le Havre, the only port close enough in distance for them to reach easily. After what he had witnessed today, everything inside of him warned him not to waste a single minute to rest, to drive as far as he could tonight without stopping, but though he knew that he had been graced with boundless energy, the horses had not. Driving them until they dropped seemed even less prudent if not reckless when he thought about it, and being selfishly reckless was just one of the many things about himself that he hoped he was leaving behind... forever.

Chapter Twenty-Four

April 22nd, 1793

W hen the wagon's wheels had finally ceased their spinning and the animals had been carefully unhooked to graze for the night, the three weary travelers finally breathed a collective sigh of relief despite the fact that they had not a scrap of food to eat nor anything on which to lay their heads. Yet they were safe, as if being in the middle of nowhere, with nothing but the clothes on their backs could be labeled as such.

Feeling more than a bit ill-mannered by his lack of provisions for the women, Emile set to work doing the only thing he could possibly think of to increase their comfort—building an admittedly rudimentary fire. A few sticks and a triumphant burst of flame later, the attitude around the encampment seemed vastly improved, jovial even under the circumstances. Well, at least for some. On the whole, Emile still felt utterly inhospitable after his ordeal and cold. The surging adrenaline that had been carrying him through the worst of his dreadful experience that day had worn off hours ago and with it the all-too-familiar ache he had once felt in a rowboat returned with a vengeance.

Taking his seat against a nearby oak, he closed his eyes to collect his thoughts and relax his aching muscles, wanting nothing more than to simply drift off to a welcomed unconsciousness and forget everything that had transpired back in Paris. *Maybe with a little rest*, he surmised gloomily, he could possibly make some sense out of what had just happened though he sincerely doubted it. It had been a long day already and tomorrow promised to be equally challenging if they could not find a ship that would take them to England. Still, he <u>had</u> managed to accomplish at least something of worth despite the heaviness placed upon him and that brought him at least a bit of satisfaction, even if it was destined to be terribly short-lived.

"Excuse me? *Monsieur* Deschamps?" Angelique's slightly tinging voice from across the flattened grass caused him to exhale slowly, releasing some of the stress he had been holding onto into the vastness surrounding them.

"Yes?" He replied, but still had not opened his eyes to address her, choosing rather to savor whatever peace yet remained within his position by the oak.

"I do not mean to sound ungrateful, but now that we have finally stopped, could you please tell me what exactly transpired this morning? And why you have brought us to this God-forsaken part of the country?" The woman with the normally pristine attire brushed off a few stray pieces of straw from her otherwise still perfectly intact hairstyle and waited impatiently for his response.

Blinking twice, Emile looked back seriously at the two women in front of him and judged just how much he should tell them about the trial. Emma, as he knew, was already fully aware of the new system of justice, but unfortunately, Angelique was not. For her, anything that he would reveal tonight would be shocking if not equally difficult for her to comprehend, ludicrous even, as if all of it were something out of a bad dream or horrible nightmare. Still, it was the truth, and as evil as it was, she deserved to know the extent of it, even if there was not a thing on this Earth she could do to change it.

"As per my original plan, I went to the trial this morning, Miss Toussaint. I started by following the crowd from the appointed tavern all the way to the Bastille where they judged the prisoners. I was there for everything—from your father's cries for mercy to Jonathan's failed attempt to save you both." Emile shook his head remembering the bloodthirsty scene and chose to look away from her to hide his true disgust at what had occurred. "But it was not what you or I would call a trial at all. It was a travesty," he condemned the judgment handed down through gritted teeth. "A 'civilized' massacre if you will, and nobody escaped their reach. Not a single soul was pardoned or imprisoned for their deeds. Everyone, from the young to the old was condemned like common criminals no matter their station or accused crimes."

"Why not?" Angelique asked quickly.

Emile sighed and glanced over at Emma before exhaling his reply, suddenly feeling incredibly tired by the struggle, "Because it simply didn't matter, Angelique."

"Then why am I escaping?" She replied in great confusion as if the full weight of the situation had still not entirely sunk in, yet. "You said earlier that I would be dead if I remained. Why?"

Emma moved a little closer to Angelique and placed a comforting arm around the woman, uncertain if she were strong enough yet for the revelation the man across from them was about to speak. "Are you sure you want to know?"

"Yes, of course!" Angelique defended, pulling away from her slightly as if she had felt it especially rude for the understated woman to be touching her in such a fashion. "I think I have a right to know why you have been so highhanded with me today, sir."

Emile tried his best not to show the distaste he truly felt in seeing her reaction to Emma's kindness and innocent support. His demure companion didn't have a mean bone in her whole body beyond her quick wit and sarcastic tongue and even those were far more tempered than his own on any day of the week. To watch her being treated like some kind of a pariah at the reception of that love made his skin quite literally crawl with irritation. It was akin to the very same abrasive annoyance he had felt that night at the gathering in his apartment when Angelique had condemned his opinion, and it rubbed him equally raw today. In fact, why he had once thought of himself as a part of her inner circle of friends was quickly becoming outside his feeble understanding now.

Resolved to put a stop to her impolite behavior once and for all, he began again, only this time with narrowed eyes that bore down on her with the full weight of his condemnation, mixed with a healthy dose of harsh reality. "Highhanded? You act as if what I did was for my own benefit. Which I assure you, it was not."

"Wasn't it? I see you brought Miss Larose with us, as well. Or was she in danger too? It seems by the looks of things that you are amassing quite a collection of women these days," Angelique taunted Emile mercilessly like a child poking at an angry animal.

At this point, Emile had been pushed beyond his desire for any further sense of decorum whatsoever. Incensed by the very reference that his deeds were in any way scheming or manipulative this time, he practically attacked the woman verbally. "When they had finished their display, Angelique," he said the word referencing the trial with acidic mockery. "Robespierre, their new leader, then denounced someone new, but not to their imprisonment like the others we have known. This last person he commended directly to their execution without any provocation or evidence to do so, and worse yet, the crowd agreed with him without reservation." He paused to clear his throat for it was already becoming far too constricted at the memory. "In fact, they were practically ecstatic to entrap them."

"Who?" Emma asked quietly, fearing the worst for Emile.

Emile flicked his eyebrows up once in Angelique's direction and pointed to the woman across from him flippantly. "You, Miss Toussaint."

"Me!" Angelique placed one hand upon her chest innocently and appeared to look just as stunned as he had been when he had heard it. "But I have done nothing wrong in all my life."

"Haven't you?" Emile and Angelique held each other's gaze for a moment longer before each eventually turned away, unable to continue, for both knew the lengths at which either of them would go to get their own way.

"Emile, please. This isn't helping anyone at all." Emma tried to keep the peace between the newly formed adversaries as no one could deny the intense animosity building behind every statement they uttered. "What *Monsieur* Deschamps is trying to explain to you is that all of this is because you are a member of the upper society, ma'am," Emma replied without the condemnation so obviously apparent in all her peers at the trial. "In the eyes of the citizens that is all you need to have done."

"And my father? My brother?" Angelique's voice finally held the concern it should have possessed from the very beginning. The same guilt that had begun to form a very raw scar on the inside of Emile's heart.

"It saddens me to say it, but they have probably already met their maker in Heaven as we speak. They were to be sent to the guillotine with the others shortly after I left. You would have been joining them, too, had I not found you when I did as the mob was on their way to your home when I reached the apartment." Emile threw a stick casually into the fire from his far position and spat back a frustrated accusation thereafter that was far less important than it was truthful. "This new Assembly cares nothing for civility and decorum, only violence."

Without meaning to do so, Emma chuckled lightly at his declaration, but not in a way that seemed hurtful to any of them by the fire. "As if any of your kind gave mine a moment's thought when we needed your help over the years. Some of the people you are judging are only acting out of desperation." She sighed, considering her words carefully before continuing, "The rest were probably monsters before it ever began. Either way, it appears as if the world has finally turned itself upside down and the rest of us are merely holding on for dear life."

Seeing the lingering hurt present within her eyes like a vast ocean of hidden moments of pain, Emile regretted his last statement very much. "I wasn't referring to you personally, Emma. You know that, right?"

"I know," Emma replied quietly but kept her eyes respectfully looking downward and into the fire in front of her, unwilling once more to see what she might find in his watchful gaze.

"So, where will we go next?" Angelique wiped a few freshly falling tears from the corners of her eyes, appearing to have been truly mourning her family's loss. Yet in the very next moment, she chose to add something further that proved her complete disconnection to the plight unfolding all around her. "If they have taken my home in Paris, then I have only one other inherited estate still remaining in my family's name. It was originally my great-grandfather's, but it is over in England."

"Well, at least you have something. My family probably won't care much more about me other than the loss of their needed income," Emma mumbled quietly and shook her head in disbelief at the woman who was complaining about something few of Emma's family could ever dream of owning, much less be related to someone who did. They were far more expected to clean the place rather than actually live in it.

"Who knows? With you gone, maybe your father will be forced to go back to work for once and stop depending on his children for his support," Emile commented offhandedly to her, still rather perturbed at the weight the man had place upon Emma's shoulders over the years.

"I doubt that very highly." Emma shook her head and snickered. "He much prefers a different sort of company over work at the present." She cast Emile a knowing glance and both of them smiled at the shared understanding. "It's a good thing she does not charge him what she does the rest of her admirers, or we might be all sent to the workhouses."

"Agreed," Emile huffed for he knew *Madame* Jeannette's prices were extremely high indeed, much more than Emma's father or even himself could afford though he had little desire of that kind of distraction from her today or any day hereafter.

"Yes, well, we can't always get what we want, can we?" Angelique tossed her curls in a childish huff and folded her arms to increase her perceived position of social class next to this woman of most definite poverty.

Glancing in her direction once more with a look of sheer incredulity, Emile recognized the exaggerated gesture all too well as one he had often made on several occasions to deflect others away from his own insecurities, though seeing it used on someone so undeserving of her denigration almost made his blood boil to witness it. "Honestly, Angelique... just stop talking," Emile said politely, but firmly and stood at last, taking great care to stretch out his stiffening muscles first before he walked over to Emma's side and offered her his outstretched hand. "Would you care to walk with me for a moment? I think I need some air."

"Of course." She obeyed without reservation, eagerly accepting his invitation as easily as if he had just asked her to join him for breakfast or to sit with him by the front window in his apartment. "I think a walk might do us both some good."

For several yards if not more, they meandered arm in arm contentedly in the silence far beyond the single ridge of trees that lined the meadow, enjoying the healing that it brought after such a stressful day. Never in all his life had Emile considered even once that he would ever be fleeing his beloved country, much less dragging two women along with him on that journey. But now that he was, he found that his mind was actively savoring each and every minute detail of the scenery around him like it was creating some kind of a mental memory of all that was good and beautiful about this land to possibly cover up all the more distasteful recollections from earlier.

The sun, which had thankfully remained hidden for the majority of the day, had set hours ago and with it a warm breeze that promised the arrival of the approaching spring had begun to gently surround their every step as it jealously trailed its fingers through Emma's long hair that now hung loose about her neck, far from its normally neatly arranged loops and braids. With the unexpected arrival of Angelique while he was gone, Emile assumed she had probably not been given sufficient time to fix it properly, but it was of no matter to him. He much preferred her hair exactly as it was, hanging down around her shoulders, to any other style she might have chosen. The peaceful motion of the swaths of strawberry sunshine as she moved always soothed him much more than he ever thought possible as it swept away with it the darker of his thoughts that held him captive and comforted him in its softness. In truth, it was the perfect antidote most days for his inner turmoil, if such a thing existed in this plane of reality, and one of the things he cherished most about her.

Glancing down at the beautiful woman beside him with renewed appreciation as they passed by a group of tall trees, Emile saw the briefest of glimpses as to what a possible life for the two of them might be somewhere beyond Paris. A respectable union perhaps, with an intelligent and caring woman that he had never chosen to contemplate, nor ever desired before. However, this time, it left him not feeling the expected eager anticipation as those facing such a complicated decision as one might expect from a suitor or chosen beau, but rather a deep sense of inadequacy at the very depth of his heart for even daring to consider it. And if he were to be completely honest, for the second time in his life, Emile felt an anxiousness within his soul that unnerved him so vastly that it broke down his very defenses against it, instead of bolstering him up with his usual air of self-confidence. Like on so many other occasions before, Emile found himself at a complete loss mentally as to how very much he needed this woman in front of him for his very survival.

"Is something the matter, Emile?" Emma glanced up at the man beside her and tilted her head a bit to see his face more clearly, sensing the change in his increasingly quiet demeanor

"I..." Emile started to speak but stopped and shook his head slightly as if reconsidering what he might have chosen to say, then began again more quickly, "Emma, I have decided that tomorrow we should try to find passage on a ship to England, if I can find such a vessel with room for all of us to board that is. If not, we can simply send Miss Toussaint on ahead first since her life is the most threatened here, and the two of us can wait for the next ship. From my last experience at port, there are usually a few vessels leaving every week delivering some form of cargo or passengers, so I expect it shouldn't prove itself to be too difficult to secure the berth we require or take too long."

"But, Emile, I don't understand why we have to leave at all? Certainly, you don't think what is happening in Paris will spread throughout the whole of France, do you? Couldn't we just find somewhere else to stay here? I am sure I can pick up work wherever we might decide to live." Emma's expression held only the necessary concern for their well-being and not the ill-placed condemnation of his hasty decisions by their other travel companion waiting by the fire.

"I'm afraid that from what I saw today at the Bastille, nowhere in France is safe at the present for people like me. Some kind of revolution is taking shape, and despite what you or I might hope, there is nothing we can personally do to stop it. The only thing left for me is to leave France while I still can. As much as I love my country, it is time I bid it *au revoir*," he admitted honestly. "I just wish you had more of a choice in the matter, too, but from what I saw this morning, you would also be condemned right along with me by the mere association, and that is something I cannot accept... not ever."

Emma nodded her head slowly, realizing the true immensity of the situation as it was laid out before them. "Then what will you do once you arrive in England?"

"Sadly, I have nothing like Miss Toussaint's connections there, of that I can assure you." Emile chuckled lightly at the thought. "But hopefully, I can find a few... um... friends, if they would still call me that. Though if you knew the whole story where they are concerned, you might choose to refer to them more as mere acquaintances of mine that I have lost along my journeys given the way that I have treated them." He closed his eyes momentarily, remembering his last, condemning conversation with Señor Moretti after his transformation and forced himself to speak slower as his words were now falling out of him before he could stop them. "Admittedly, I do not know if I can even find them, much less if they will welcome my presence any longer, but it is as good a place as any to start."

Emma gripped his arm tighter to encourage him in his path forward but almost threw her arms around him instead by what she felt. "Emile, what's wrong? You are positively shaking." Her mind reeled in alarm by the change in his usually collected countenance for never in their whole time together had he looked so completely unhinged and indecisive. In many ways, it was almost as if the whole experience of the day had sufficiently frightened him towards the making of countless decisions he had never fully contemplated.

"Am I?" Emile asked distractedly but seemed by all other accounts to be completely oblivious of the intense tremors that were now hitting him like waves. Taking a moment to cup his hands closer to his mouth, he blew on them several times before vigorously rubbing them together to stop their shaking. "There. Is that better?"

Emma shook her head at his incredibly futile attempt. "Not in the slightest."

Despite what he might have intended, the warmth he tried to procure did not travel past his hands. Yet as strange as that may be, Emma was not at all alarmed by that alone. When Emile had first touched her cheek in his apartment that first night, she had been keenly aware of how very different the temperature of his skin was compared to her own, but that in itself had not shocked her too greatly. She herself had often dealt with many similar issues from her hours of scrubbing floors to warrant such attention to something so trivial, but tonight the very arm that she was holding felt frigid and icelike as it repeatedly shivered beneath her slightly warmer touch. "What aren't you telling me, Emile? There must be something horribly important, or you wouldn't be so distant," Emma continued to pry but remained close enough to him to share a bit of the warmth she possessed and hopefully quell at least some of his inner trembling.

Unwilling to cause her any further hurt than that which he had already inflicted, he looked away from her gaze entirely and back towards the fire behind them in hesitant deliberation. "You always <u>were</u> extremely observant, Emma." Emile tried to smile at the thought of yet another of her endearing qualities but in the end, could not manage more than a slight grin that vanished just as quickly as it was produced.

"So, it would appear... so stop stalling already." She rubbed the top of his arm methodically back and forth to distract him further, diverting his nerves to another sensation entirely.

"Alright..." He gave in and cleared his throat twice to drive away the last of his reservations before compelling himself forward through them. "I think it is time that I finally tell you the whole truth about my life so that you can hopefully understand what all you are getting yourself into in England before it is too late."

"Too late for what? I'm already here, aren't I?" Emma said mockingly while also stating the blatantly obvious once more. "Whatever you are trying to say, Emile, I doubt it is as bad as you think. Besides, how much worse can it be compared to what you went through today already?"

"Oh, it can be much worse, I assure you." He rolled his eyes at her naivety before dropping his arm from hers and leaving her to pace nervously back and forth slowly in front of her. On any given day, he usually adored her sarcastic wit, but today it especially humored him to know how completely and wonderfully oblivious she was concerning his true nature. "Miss Larose, you and I both know that you wouldn't even be in this mess if I had not asked *Madame* Jeannette to find you that day. If I hadn't been so selfish, none of this might have ever..." He stopped his sentence midway, then uttered a more denigrating statement that seemed to be meant more for himself alone than the woman standing in confusion beside him. "I should have left you be."

"I'm listening." She reached forward and touched his hand to reassure him for his pacing was making her feel equally anxious to watch him suffer so. "Surely you must know by now that nothing you could ever say to me is going to make me run all the way back to Paris, so you might as well get it over with once and for all—take off the bandages so to speak and let the wound heal, Emile."

"You promise?" Emile's eyes pleaded with concentrated dependence, feeling as weak and vulnerable as the first night when he had envisioned her leaving.

Emma nodded sweetly; her unbridled kindness nearly stopping his speech entirely.

Scanning almost every inch of the woman in front of him from her delicate nose to her almost rose-pink fingernails, he knew at that moment that there was nothing else in all this world or beyond that he would ever need, and it was standing right here in front of him. A simple thing that cost him absolutely nothing to obtain in monetary value yet meant volumes more than anything else he had ever encountered.

Her love, as freely given as it always was, did not require his position in society or money to support himself in it nor did she grant him a stately home or fortune as her dowry. Emma and her love were simply enough, and as endearing as what she offered was, he realized it always would be. That was it—simplistic, eternal commitment without the necessary facade. The only thing he would ever require for the rest of his existence was <u>her</u> in his life, and the fear of possibly losing her because of his consistently self-gratifying actions terrified him now to the core to even consider it. From the very beginning, she had nothing but herself to offer him in exchange for his love and in this moment, that very fact alone was vastly more important than any monetary treasure he had ever possessed. Yet the thought of her expected rejection in time was also just as crushing for him to contemplate. Though if he were to think of it from another perspective, making her live in his complicated lie a moment longer would destroy her spirit even more so when she found out the truth on her own, and that was equally unacceptable.

"Emma," he began again slowly, deciding at last to place the absolute truth in front of her come what may. "Everything you have ever known about me since the very day we met has been a carefully constructed lie for your benefit. A well-rehearsed ruse, if you will, to deceive my closest of acquaintances of something that is simply not true." He swallowed hard, but his dry mouth would not be quenched no matter how hard he tried. "In essence, my family is not a wealthy one as you might suppose by my lifestyle. Nor am I what many would call 'a good man' by any stretch of the imagination. Yet believe it or not, I need <u>you</u>, most of all, to know the reality of what you are facing as ugly as it may be."

"I see..." Emma stared back at him, totally bewildered by what he was saying. "But you'll have to forgive me as I feel as though now you are talking in circles."

"You are probably right, as always." Emile felt the back of his neck with his hand beneath his long ponytail and began to rub it uneasily, feeling utterly flustered and at odds with himself again as he struggled in his confession. "My head is such a mess right now." In fact, it would have been far more accurate to say that every single synapse in his mind was screaming loudly for him to be silent, to forget all the reasons why she needed to know, but he simply could not. Just like at the Bastille this morning, he had finally reached a crossroads in his life, and like or not he needed to choose.

"To be honest, I am not exactly sure what I am trying to say either." He exhaled a long sigh and threw back his head in one quick motion to observe the delicate stars appearing above him in the sky. *How very insignificant a man can be compared to the vastness of the universe it seems.* He pondered the thought for a moment. In fact, everything about tonight was the exact opposite of the way

294

he had felt months ago when he thought he could have taken on the whole of the world after his transformation. That Emile Deschamps believed himself to be invincible to everyone and anything he might encounter, or so he assumed.

He was wrong. That man was arrogantly ignorant of the real worth of others and life in general. Something with which the Emile of today was becoming painfully aware.

Emma looked up, as well, but then turned her focus back to him quickly. "Then why don't we start with something easier, shall we? Like why you do not feel you are a good man. Is it because you seduced me?" She stated what he could not seem to utter without hurting her unnecessarily.

"Oh, sweet Emma..." Emile looked down at Emma expecting the deserved chastisement and naked condemnation to be staring back at him finally, but it was not there. In its place instead was a genuine care for what he was experiencing, not that which he had caused by his inconsiderate actions. Closing his eyes to hide from what he might see next, he released a long sigh of built-up regret and finally confessed openly. "Because I have seduced, for lack of a better term, many yous in my lifetime, love ... far too many."

"How many?" She raised her eyebrows, obviously teasing him a little, though she knew him always to be painfully direct and precise in everything that he did.

Emile opened his eyes then and couldn't help but laugh a little openly at her comment, grateful for a bit of needed humor. "Does it really matter?"

"It might to me." She smiled playfully with a glint of comedy in her eyes while trying to alleviate some of the tension developing between them.

"Honestly? I think I've lost count." He shook his head sadly. "But none of them were as unique as you, if that helps."

"I see, though if it makes you feel any better, I already knew that before I ever came to your apartment. It was part of the reason why I was so scared to stay in the first place. I understood even then that there was no way I could ever hope to measure up to any of those women, so why even try." She pulled her strawberry-blonde tresses back from her face and looked up into the wind to keep them from returning. "But seriously, none of that matters anymore, does it? As my mother always told me, things that we cannot change belong in the past where they should stay. There is no use punishing yourself repeatedly for things that have no hope of being remedied."

Surprised beyond words by her easy acceptance of his previous lifestyle, he shook his head in incredulous disbelief, unsure if the woman was truly understanding what he was telling her. "Your mother was very wise indeed, but you have no idea how I wish I could go back and meet you properly. Maybe even take you out to a fine dinner or spend countless days romancing you into an eventual acceptance of my proposal. That is what a true gentleman would have done. And trust me when I say this, Emma, I am <u>not</u>, nor have I ever <u>been</u> a true gentleman." He looked at her more ardently than before as if feeling the need to place the proper importance on this most singular of statements more than anything else he had just uttered. "The only regret I will ever have regarding you Miss Larose is that it is far too late for all of that between us, but what I can do from here on out is to vow that should you wish to remain with me hereafter, you will <u>never</u> be used like that again, not by me, nor anyone else for that matter."

For a moment, Emma's face became even more stunned than Angelique's had been back at the apartment. Living at the bottom of the lowest classes in France, she had never once been given this unique courtesy of honor by anyone, let alone granted the opportunity to curry the favor of someone as remarkable as he. By his confession alone, she knew she should have been angry or at the very least cross by all that had transpired between them, but she was not. On the contrary, standing here facing him tonight, she felt only an intense sense of being cherished and favored, and maybe even a little bit empathetic towards the process it had taken to bring him to this moment. "Emile, you speak as if you think you are the devil in all of this sad, but wonderful tale."

"Hmmm..." Despite how much he tried to hide it a second time, he couldn't help the little smirk that followed at the accuracy of her statement. "I <u>have</u> been at times." He exhaled slowly once more before adding in a tone he normally reserved for moments when it was just the two of them alone, "You might even run away now if you knew even one of the darker thoughts I have entertained about you over the course of the past four months."

"How dark?" Emma studied him intently from afar for she had long suspected that he was much more than he appeared, though she had never once felt that she was in any real kind of danger.

Emile's mouth watered once more reflexively, remembering the young woman he had feasted on shortly after Emma and he had met and how fulfilling that substitutive experience had been. "Shockingly lurid, I assure you." His eyes traced every one of the veins that ran down the side of her neck slowly in unconscious fixation.

Intrigued, Emma's eyebrows twitched upwards slightly at his focused attention, but not out of fear as any other girl in her rational mind might have reacted. Instead, she was more than a little keenly interested in anything that would explain the inner meaning to the many identical stares and intense deliberations that had transpired when he thought she wasn't looking. "I can see that you are trying to scare me away, Emile, but I fear I must warn you. In case you haven't noticed, I don't frighten easily."

"No, no you don't. But if you knew what was good for you, you would be truly terrified, Emma." He looked away from her at last, feeling justly vindicated in uttering this most sacred of warnings to her, but also not desiring for an instant to persuade her any closer to flight.

"Well, I'm not, so stop it." Emma eyed him seriously.

"If you insist." He half-smiled, enjoying immensely this side of her no matter the discomfort it caused him to bring it out.

Emma grinned widely back and pulled him closer to her, wanting to convey by the action alone her acceptance of who he was, no matter what he might think otherwise. "Emile, it doesn't matter to me what your family history is, or even how much money you might have. I never once expected a perfect life with you, nor would I particularly want one even if it was given. What matters most to me is that you and I have... an understanding, if you will... a way to move forward together."

Feeling perfectly content now to never leave her side ever again, Emile wrapped his one arm behind her back and fixed his eyes on hers alone, staring deeply into them at last. "Agreed, but I _would_ like to make you one promise though, if you will allow me."

Emma nodded slowly, providing him the space he needed to speak.

"Despite what all has transpired between us, I _will_ make it my goal to forever protect you hereafter if that is what you truly desire instead. You know I want you more than life itself, but I will not allow you to be condemned by my selfish actions any longer. I'm simply not worth it." He paused to slow down his racing thoughts and then continued more fervently, "Emma, I suppose I should have said this earlier, but you will always be the most important thing in my life, and as such, I will not allow _anyone_ to hurt you... ever."

Not even me. He pledged, mentally deciding once and for all the answer to the temptation that had often plagued him in his sleep—the bloodlust for the one thing that truly mattered to him

Overwhelmed by the devotion in his words, Emma did not answer at first. Instead, she returned his gaze as she studied him with growing admiration, her mouth slightly parted. The innocent reaction to his sudden declaration drew him in even closer with an almost intense intoxication as it had on so many nights before, only this time he firmly resisted touching her in any way that he would have deemed inappropriate to do so in front of others, though every last ounce of his being yearned for him to take her into his arms and claim her for his own forever.

Drinking in the palpable closeness that was increasing between them, as well, Emma closed her eyes for several long minutes, before almost whispering back to him in an almost childlike innocence, "That was a lot for <u>anyone</u> to take in, Emile."

"I am sure it was, and it should have been said long ago." Emile grinned at her straightforward reply but did not push her further.

"Can we wait to decide where we stand until we are safe in England?" She asked sincerely though he could already tell her mind was heavily weighing out everything he had just said.

"Yes, you can give me your answer in England, Scotland, Italy or in Spain." He rolled his eyes once more at the forced necessity of having to return to that God-forsaken island that he swore he would never set foot on again but ended with a small chuckle. "But most preferably, not in France, if you please."

Emma returned his playful laughter and countered. "This goes without saying, but you <u>will</u> owe my brother a new outfit, I'm afraid," she demanded before tugging at the large buttons that ran down the center of his chest. "Besides, these truly do not suit you, anyways."

"I will send him a full wardrobe if needed." Emile kissed her palms slowly in turn before cordially offering her his arm. "Shall we return to the other member of our delightful party before she becomes even more cross?"

"Do we have to?" Emma almost whined quietly in protest. "I much prefer the view and company over here. It's far less judgmental and increasingly more alluring."

"I can't say that I disagree with you, but it might be rude to abandon her completely for the night." Emile pursed his lips just once as he tried to hold back his appreciative smile.

"Fine. I'm sure you are right," she said with a dramatic sigh and took his arm graciously but when he started to walk away, she suddenly changed her mind and held him fast, not wanting him to leave just yet.

"Is there something more?" Emile turned around quickly to face her while also keeping his back to the fire behind him to block the view from the possible prying eyes and ears of their other companion by the fire.

Emma nodded, then reaching up to his cheek with her other hand she drew him down to her and kissed him discreetly, then deeper still, suddenly unwilling to part with him so quickly. For the past twenty-four hours she had been helplessly imagining her life without him in it should he be detected or worse yet, killed, and now that he was safe and only a few feet away from her, her heart ached even more to never let him go—at least not willingly.

Equally overcome by everything that had transpired today both in Paris and his confession here in the meadow, Emile wrapped his fingers in her hair in response and held her as close as possible until it was she, as always, who relented first. And yet... even in that, from the way neither of them shifted their position afterwards, both appeared equally moved by the closeness lingering between them.

"What was that for?" Emile's gaze focused deeply on her crystal blue eyes as he studied her reaction, unable to contain the growing hope that this woman in front of him might actually decide to pick him over the many other viable choices that would soon be available to her in England.

"Maybe I prefer a bit of the devil in the man." Emma's eyes twinkled as she raised her eyebrows impishly in silent confirmation of what they both knew they were thinking.

"Miss Larose..." He kissed her once more before eyeing her mischievously, obviously pleased with her response but needing no further encouragement in that direction.

"No, don't, Emile. Let it be always, your Emma," she stated firmly.

"Always." He allowed her to kiss him again lightly on the cheek, then smoothed out the hopeless wrinkles in his borrowed coat before walking her politely back to the fire.

With the hour growing progressively late, and with nothing else left to speak of regarding their journey the next day, the two women retired for the night under the length of the wagon for protection and warmth.

Emile, however, took his place over by the oak once more and laid down, too, but found that he was not the least bit tired physically other than the annoying stiffness in his arms and chest from driving the horses for the past five hours. The day's activities should have mentally exhausted him at the very least, but the events that had transpired had only heightened his already on-edge senses even more. Moreover, the whole conversation with Emma, though difficult at first to divulge, had left him with more hope than he could have ever imagined possible. But with it also came an absolute plethora of thoughts about what they might do together in England upon their arrival.

Insomnia and Emma aside, Emile thought of other things, too, as he lay awake well into the early morning hours, haunted by the faces of each of the condemned at their trial. When he had arrived this morning, he had known only two of the condemned prisoners personally. Yet after today he doubted, though he lived to be at least five hundred, he would ever forget even one of them.

Chapter Twenty-Five

April 23rd, 1793

"Trying to sleep here," Emile muttered grumpily at the nuzzling of one of the horse's snouts as it gently pushed against his hat while searching for fresh grass beneath it. Justifiably perturbed by the unwelcome interruption to his slumber, he rolled over onto his side and placed his hat in front of his face to block out the approaching dawn, taking great care to keep it as far away as possible from the area in which the animal was trying to graze.

It didn't help. The horse continued its search among the flattened greens beside him now, further jostling his neck and arm before eventually pushing back his shoulder violently as if making its intentions blatantly known.

"I understand. Enough already." Emile glanced over his shoulder at the animal and shook his head in disbelief. "I'm awake now, clearly. Are you happy?"

The horse snorted its hot breath upon him once, voicing his approval of the man's changed position, then continued grazing as if nothing was strange about the conversation between them in the least.

Feeling more than a bit worse for wear from sleeping on top of an equally uncomfortable maze of hidden tree roots, Emile rubbed the lack of sleep from off his face and set about attempting to arouse the others. Le Havre was still miles away at the present, and despite how much he would very much like to allow them the opportunity to sleep as long as they liked, there was still much land to cover and a great deal of uncertainty as to whether or not they had been followed. Despite what they all might wish to the contrary, the sooner they started their journey today the better if they were to hopefully set sail on the next tide.

From all appearances, the women who slept closer to the fire, had quite obviously fared no better than he, and with no breakfast amongst them to share, the three weary travelers put out the last of the embers of their smoldering fire, connected the reins and guides back to the waiting horses and climbed resignedly into their mode of transportation. The only thing on all of their minds that morning other than the obvious physical irritations that plagued them all, was the great distance that still existed in front of them and the equally difficult ordeal they had already all experienced.

Eager to be closer to certain safety in England, Emile kept the horses at a brisk pace for the majority of the long six-hour journey from the meadow until the busy city came into view at last, allowing him just a moment to exhale a sigh of much-needed relief. None of them would deny that they were all utterly exhausted by the constant jostling back and forth of the wagon along the uneven road that lead to the port of Le Havre, but thankfully as far as Emile could tell from the few conversations that he had overheard on his way to purchase their tickets, the news of the uprising in Paris had not yet reached this far away. This small fact in itself was the largest blessing of all, for it made it far less difficult to arrange their safe passage on the next ship out of France without raising any suspicions whatsoever as to their urgency in doing so.

As luck would have it, there were actually three ships ready to set sail on the tide, all bound for England, but only one of them that had room enough for all three passengers among its already stowed cargo. The older vessel, with the twin secondary masts on either side of the considerably larger center one, was not much to look at in terms of speed, still it appeared favorably more seaworthy than the Endeavor did during the hurricane last fall, which gave Emile at least a small bit of comfort in choosing her over the others for their journey.

Like most things in life, upon weighing the negatives and positives of the possible options, he determined that as seasoned a vessel as she clearly was, she was worth the risk involved for the convenience granted. And so, with little other options to speak of, Emile had found himself using half of his meager savings to book all their passages on it no matter what the fee the ship's quartermaster required, more than a bit anxious to be on their way immediately before anything in their surroundings changed dramatically for the worse.

The stout man with one leg creatively replaced with a carved wooden peg, greeted them once up on deck, looking not a day over thirty though his speech undoubtedly demonstrated a knowledge of one much older. From his neatly trimmed beard to his overly joyful demeanor, he was the perfect picture of what someone might come to expect from a first mate, if not the captain himself. Yet upon noticing the disheveled appearance of the two women as they boarded, he was only too gracious to show the group to their chambers below deck after first taking the time to offer them all a complimentary lunch from the galley seeing as Emile had so generously paid their fares plus a sizable tip. It mattered not to him where they were going or the reasons why, just as long as he was paid handsomely for it and more importantly, that they proved of little distraction to his men up on deck.

With every single muscle in his body now aching relentlessly from the past two days of regulated torture, Emile played with the vegetables on his plate distractedly, selecting only a few bites to consume before pushing the half-finished meal away from him at last. In any another situation, he would have simply eaten what was offered to him to avoid the scrutiny incurred by his actions otherwise, but today he could hardly force himself to consume any of the food he had been so freely offered.

"Not up to your standards, sir?" The cook, that very much resembled the belligerent quartermaster on his last voyage with his stern face and overly commanding ways, glanced over at him judgmentally from his position in the galley with a look of growing distrust.

"Not at all, I assure you." Emile tried to compliment the man. "I am just a bit tired from my journey, that is all." He deflected his apparent offense easily, not wishing to gain an enemy in the man so soon after their arrival.

"I see." The cook nodded in learned understanding. "Well, supper won't be served until after cast off and that won't be for several hours yet at least, so I would eat up while you can." The man attempted to be as hospital as possible under the circumstances.

"Noted." Emile wrinkled his nose at the necessity once more and drank the rest of his ale after chewing on one of the biscuits in the center of the table.

"Do you think it will take us long to get to England?" Angelique looked equally unimpressed with the meal she was provided but nibbled at the fresh beans and carrots that accompanied the rather dismal looking piece of chicken in the center of her plate.

"Probably less than two days at most, I would imagine," Emile answered her wearily, his body beginning to finally succumb to the stress of the journey they had all endured.

"I for one am looking forward to seeing the ocean," Emma excitedly replied as she finished her plate and returned it happily to the cook. "Thank you, sir. It was simply delicious."

With a smile, Emile watched her and attempted to imitate her happiness in consuming the meal but struggled instead to be merely content that it was edible. "Yes, thank you." He finished the food on his plate and bowed slightly in deep respect for the man's efforts when he also handed him his plate.

Angelique, on the other hand, was not the least bit inclined to eat another bite, let alone do more than sit dejectedly in the corner of the galley as she appeared to be clearly sulking within her own thoughts at the moment. "Would you like mine?" She offered the remnants of her plate finally to Emma by pushing it slightly away from her, deciding that she had endured enough torture for one day by the sheer choice to eat any of it at all.

"Gladly, miss." She cut the chicken up into smaller pieces and consumed it all rather quickly before returning the remaining dishes to the cook. "What is on the menu for supper, if it isn't too impolite to ask?"

"Salted pork and potatoes." He plunked the dishes into the waiting tub and placed both of his hands on his hips as if waiting for her disappointing reply. "Why?"

"Would you like some help?" Emma offered freely. "My father says I am terribly good at peeling potatoes."

From his seat opposite the exchange, Emile sat contentedly with one leg lazily draped over his other as he watched the way the woman managed to brighten every room that she entered and waited to see what the man in front of her would say next.

"That would be most welcome, miss, and thank you." The cook smiled and held out his hand to her cheerily. "Name's Curtis by the way."

"Emma Larose." She returned his handshake easily. "But first, if you don't mind, I think I'd like a short nap if I may. As you might expect of most travelers, I don't think I have slept very well for two nights put together already."

"Of course." He wiped his hands on the white linen towel that hung at his waist and directed the group down the long corridor to the left of the galley where their rooms lay. "This is where the quartermaster said to put you," the man directed as he opened the door to the first room and stepped back for them to inspect it.

"I believe that I will take this one as it only has the one hammock to speak of," Emile offered and opened the next door for the ladies to enter the other more spacious room with two more conventionally created beds firmly secured on the side wall.

"And it has a window, too!" Emma exclaimed upon seeing a large window on the opposite side of the room before practically skipping over to it and peering out of it like she was about to embark on some great adventure.

"Well, at least one of us is enjoying herself," Angelique muttered gloomily and fell into the bottom bunk attached to the wall, turning her back away from all the others gathered.

"Oh, Emile! You simply have to come and see this!" Emma called back to him from her position and pointed towards the ocean beyond. "Does the ocean always have so many shades of greens and blues?"

Emile couldn't help but chuckle at her increasingly endearing excitement and exuberant energy. "Yes, unless it is angry. Then, it turns a very dark black as if the entire sea has changed its mood to match the ferocity of the storm. Kind of like a woman, now that I think on it."

With sudden alarm at the unwelcome possibility for her very first voyage, Emma's eyebrows raised briefly at the disturbing picture he provided before she replied very quickly thereafter to counter its weight in positivity. "Then let us both hope she remains pleasantly inclined, shall we?" She continued on in his analogy, then walked back over to her bunk and inspected it before returning to Emile who was now standing close to the doorway next to it. "I know it might be a bit improper of me to ask this of you here, but do you think it would be alright if we were to step into your room for just a short while?" She whispered discreetly in his ear, yearning for just an hour or two alone with him finally to drink in the security of his warm embrace once more after so much time spent apart. "...just to talk, Emile, I promise."

As if seriously contemplating the acceptance of her very enticing offer, Emile placed his hand firmly around the back of her waist to draw her in closer but resisted steadfastly doing anything more. "We had better not. I meant what I said last night. I'll not open you to further ridicule by my actions if I can help it," he whispered softly back, endeavoring to keep their conversation away from the attention of Angelique. Though truth be told, as close as she was beside him, there was no way of knowing just how much she could overhear of their muted conversation in the doorway and how much she was simply ignoring.

"I understand." Emma nodded slightly and reached up on her toes to kiss him lightly on the cheek in the doorway. "... not even if it is me that chooses it?" She prodded quietly further.

Feeling almost tortured now by the pull that he always felt towards fulfilling her every desire asked of him, Emile groaned inwardly and led her farther out into the passageway so they could converse more freely. "If it was only me who would suffer the wagging tongues that would surely follow thereafter by our actions in doing so, I would not even think twice about giving you everything you could ever request of me, but I just can't, Emma. As strange as it may be to hear this coming from me, I want you to at least consider what other choices you might desire for your life once we set foot on English soil. After all, it's the least I can do after what I've put you through."

"Are... are you trying to say that you don't <u>want</u> me in that way anymore?" Emma's face looked momentarily hurt by the mere suggestion and the apparent confirmation of her greatest fear. After all, he wouldn't be the first person who had decided she was worth far less than she had imagined. On the contrary, up until now, not a single person in her life other than her long-departed mother had ever given her anything close in the way of actual, physical love in general, so to lose his favor now after everything they had been through together felt almost unbearable.

Emile's heart almost broke in two upon hearing her honest reply for that was the farthest thing from his mind ever, nor could he properly explain it all to her adequately in the middle of a passageway where any number of people might pass by and interrupt them easily. With little other recourse available to him than the one she had just suggested, he took her by the hand gently and guided her over to his room. Then, looking both ways down the long corridor before entering after her, he quietly closed the door behind them and turned to face it while placing both of his hands upon it to steady himself. "I will <u>always</u> want you in that way, Emma. Lord knows, I will want you until I draw my very last breath on this Earth, I think," he said with fervent finality. "But that isn't enough, and I know it. I want you to be mine because you choose to be and not because you feel you have to be or because I am the only option given to you. As self-serving as I might appear, I know that you deserve much better than that," he said slowly as he leaned his forehead upon the wood of the closed door in front of him, wishing if by some miracle it would fuse itself together with the rest of the ship and never be opened thereafter, thus sufficiently granting them their stolen moment of solitude without reproach.

For quite some time, the room remained completely silent behind him as if Emma had also needed just a minute to take in fully everything he had just confessed to her before he finally heard Emma take one hesitant step after the other closer to him and wrap her arms around his waist gently, her cheek resting comfortably upon his back. "You are one of the most incredible men I have ever met, Emile Bastien Deschamps, and I thank you for thinking I am worth even a portion of the consideration you are offering me."

"Oh, love..." Emile sighed in defeat and turned around to face her at last, holding her tightly within his embrace as he stroked her cheek next to his chest. "You are worth <u>every minute</u> of pain I have ever endured and every second of joy I have experienced in your presence," he pledged most faithfully, then felt the warmth of her falling tears upon his fingertips as he wiped them away.

"And so are you..." She replied simply.

Deep down, Emile was blissfully grateful for her ardent admission and easy acceptance of his genuine love for her, but true to his pessimistic nature, he remained equally skeptical as to its truth.

With nowhere else either of them wanted to be, the two remained there in the silence for quite some time before Emma eventually pulled away and looked up at him finally, her face now perfectly composed and ready to face her companion in the next room. "I <u>will</u> do as you ask, Emile. And though it pains me to even contemplate that kind of a future without you in it, I <u>will</u> properly consider everything that you have mentioned. But don't be surprised if nothing changes on my part."

"I won't." Emile smiled genuinely, opened the door, then checked the hallway first before escorting her back safely to her room and returned to his own yet again.

Sensing the growing irony in his life at the moment, he shook his head in disbelief as he opened the cabin door once more and flopped his long form into the swinging hammock of a bed before laying his cherished top hat next to him on the small wooden table. "This feels oddly familiar, doesn't it, *Monsieur* Deschamps?" He laughed to himself lightly at the ridiculousness of the situation both here and in Paris. The world had most certainly turned itself completely inside out for the moment. And he... well, he had uneasily discovered that as unaffected as he thought he was, he was still struggling to maintain his sense of purpose within it.

Still, at least something was comfortably familiar, and anything that spoke of normalcy right now was welcomed ten-fold, even if it came at the price of memories he would just as soon forget. The only blessed thing about his last sea voyage was the young doctor, William Wells, and even then, that also came at a cost, for the man had indelibly changed him in so many ways. Many more than he cared to admit.

As far as he was concerned, Emma notwithstanding, the only thing he truly lacked now were the proper directions as to where William's family might reside. Since he had chosen to leave well before anyone else had awakened at Señor Moretti's, he had no idea just where any of his last companions might have traveled afterwards, but it seemed only logical to begin in England and branch out from there. After all, hadn't William mentioned more than once that his father had a surgery in London? With even greater luck, the good doctor may have even written to his parents recently. If not, he would simply have to contact Señor Moretti and make the necessary, albeit awkward, inquiries as to their whereabouts. Though either way, he would be out of France. They all would.

Emile closed his eyes and tried to sleep as much as he could manage, certain that the rest would prove useful in the coming days or at the very least, numb his mind away from the more troubling thoughts he most certainly did not wish to entertain. The past few days had probably been the hardest he had ever experienced in his life other than the four he had spent during his transformation into becoming a vampire, and he for one was eager to put them all behind him for good.

~   ~   ~   ~   ~

Thankfully for all involved, their ship from La Havre made port just a day and a half later, and as it did, the three travelers disembarked quickly before standing upon the busy docks in London to judge their current situation better. Surprisingly enough, they were not the only ones doing so. Ship after arriving ship down the long pier beside them appeared to hold the same repeating story it seemed of a flight from France and the welcomed relief of safety at England's inviting shore. In fact, as far as the eye could see, the passengers and citizens alike were all buzzing feverishly in mutual conversation about the new National Assembly in France and the sorry plight of its people there. So much had transpired outside their shores that it was almost as if the street itself was a flowing river of compassionate humanity with its current being driven solely by a singular common theme.

"Will you be requiring my assistance in getting to your grandfather's estate, Miss Toussaint?" Emile asked distractedly, carrying the small travel bag on one side of him while also simultaneously focusing the majority of his attention on possible potential threats in the pressing crowd. For almost half a mile in every direction, thronging masses of people gathered and though everything around his party seemed perfectly normal and not the least bit troubling for an afternoon in late April, something about the others milling about here did not feel right to him either. Though to be truthful, nothing out of the ordinary stood out to him in particular except for the rather large amount of goods and wares that were being hauled to and from shore by the various ships behind them.

Yet, try as he might to uncover the source of his discomfort, he could not put his finger on exactly what it was that was particularly bothering him. *A presence possibly?* But that did not make much sense to him, also. With the sheer magnitude of the horde assembled, there could be a deranged maniac in the crowd today and he sincerely doubted he would have been able to spot him in time to react protectively or otherwise.

In the past five months, he had most certainly experienced many rougher encounters in the poorer end of Paris, but never once had he felt this singular way, not even close. Sure, he had perhaps been alarmed once or twice when something had taken him off guard completely, but never more than what might have caused anything greater than a mere nuisance of a chill. Yet this constant prickling energy that danced upon his skin incessantly was different, and frankly, it was almost unnerving to experience it and not react accordingly to it.

Maybe, as new as he was in his life as a vampire, the sensation was only a precursor of danger that his body involuntarily created when it registered something more than what his eyes could perceive on their own. This rare, but unique ripple of energy that it produced by its introduction of necessary information surged through his body all at once with a motion so strong that it caused the hairs on the back of his neck and arms to rise to attention and his eyes to narrow in their focus of every minute detail around him. In this state he could hear: the hum of the many insects passing by, the voices of the three children on the other side of the street as they pestered their exhausted mother for something sweet to eat and the soft whispers of the man saying farewell to his sweetheart by the coach almost thirty yards away. All of it was uncharacteristically loud as it forced his mind to absorb it simultaneously and most definitely unsettling.

Still, since he saw nothing that alarmed him enough to action, he tried his best to ignore it for the moment and pressed onward, yet not without taking the necessary precaution to draw just a little bit closer to Emma in a protective stance. Whatever it was that was casually amiss in the middle of all this chaos, it would have to go through him first as she was now and would forever be his first priority above all others, even beyond his own preservation.

"As kind as your offer is at the moment, I think I can find my way from here, *Monsieur* Deschamps," Angelique addressed him more formally to create the necessary distance between the two of them at last. "From what the ship's captain explained to me yesterday, my family home is not far from London proper. The estate lies just over in Kent, Sevenoaks to be precise. Though he says that the locals refer to it as The Knole. Or at least that is what he told me to tell the driver. You should not need to trouble yourself further on my account as I <u>do</u> have a few friends I can call upon here that can assist me should it become necessary." Angelique managed to sound more self-assured than she looked but her voice still betrayed a hint of a quiver near the end of her proclamation due to the enormous stress of the journey before her.

Compassion welling up inside of him at last as he witnessed her struggle anew, Emile leaned in closer and whispered in her ear something only loud enough for the two of them to hear, but also something few others of their acquaintance would understand, "Take heart, *mademoiselle*. This is but a brief interlude before your great triumph. We all need to play our parts in this great play, do we not?"

The stunningly beautiful woman, who was just as perfectly poised in the middle of a huge crowd as she was in the corner of his apartment, nodded and kissed him in friendly gesture upon the cheek. "You have my thanks, *Monsieur* Deschamps. Now, and always. And should you ever find yourself in my part of the world again, please do not hesitate to call upon me as I am truly in your debt."

"There is nothing to repay, *mademoiselle*. Your continued health and prosperity are payment enough." Emile smiled in immense satisfaction or in shared understanding. He was not sure which, nor did it truly matter. They were all fellow actors in a foreign land now, and though equally displaced out of necessity, both knew their past was as much a part of their future as the sun and the moon were to the sky above.

"Would you give me a moment with Emile, please?" Emma asked Angelique politely as if the two of them had already known each other for quite some time and not the shorter period of less than half a week.

Without a word, Angelique nodded politely, stoically moving out of her way before drawing closer to the main entrance of the inn directly across from their arrival platform, watching the many people pass her by with a look of disdainful annoyance at being forced to remain longer in such a location. Clearly England had a different way of doing things, and the woman, as insignificant as she was to everyone around her, appeared as though her status demanded that she should not have been left unattended in such a place as this.

Emile couldn't hold back his smile at the amusing expression upon her face, but then in the same moment became slightly concerned at the union unexpectedly forming between the two women. *Had they now secured some special sort of bond of attachment in their distress?* He doubted it. By all appearances, both earlier by the fire and also on board the ship, Angelique seemed to merely tolerate his companion. Yet her actions just now in the street spoke decidedly of a regulated kindness towards Emma that was most confusing, if not vaguely genuine.

Instantly skeptical once more, Emile's mind immediately raced with countless questions as to what her true motivation might be in doing so. After all, *what all did the women know about the other?* Or better still, *what did he want them to know?* Emile considered both thoughts equally with growing concern at the possible answers and frowned as the correct answer for both where he was concerned was simple. Just two resounding words were adequate to sum up all of his apprehension... <u>nothing, hopefully</u>.

Everyone who knew him back in Paris was also well-aware that he had never made any promises of faithfulness to Angelique or any other woman in his social circle for that matter, but that did not also mean that she believed the same. In his limited experience over the years with other intended recipients of his charm, he had discovered quite quickly that women often formed their own conclusions about a matter whether there was any truth to it or not. Adding to that the jealousy that Angelique had already shown towards him for taking Emma along with them in their flight, and there was no telling what might be going on in her mind regarding their relationship or what falsehoods she might choose to share to poison Emma against him. *Would Emma even believe her?* He hoped not.

Completely lost in his own thoughts and distracted deliberations now, Emile allowed Emma to draw him away from the crowded area and closer to one of the lesser occupied buildings that was being used for storing wares and other necessary cargo on the opposite side of the street. Working men waiting to load the many wooden crates and barrels onto departing ships were milling closely nearby, but none of them seemed to take notice whatsoever of the couple now occupying the shadows, nor did they seem to care. They were far too busy with their own affairs to bother themselves with two lovers hiding amongst the various bags of oats and flour. Or to state it more accurately, the scene was probably more commonplace to them than any other as most likely dozens of couples bid each other a fond farewell in similar fashion several times each month, if not more if the weather held out for a prosperous shipping season.

Suddenly content with finding a less conspicuous spot near the encroaching seawall, farther away from the distracting scene behind them, Emma stopped walking down the long pier and turned around to face Emile, her expression utterly changed from what it had held upon the ship. "There is so much that I need to say to you right now that I am afraid I will not be able to continue once more if I were to stop," she spoke her words so quickly at first that Emile was almost having trouble understanding them before she abruptly paused and forced herself to speak slower still as if stealing the last of her courage to do so, only this time with a look of pure love within her eyes. "You asked me to consider what choices I might desire now that I am no longer beholden to anyone in France, yet I fear that whatever I say to you today, it will never do justice to what is truly in my heart." Her voice caught as she held back a sea of emotion washing over her like the waves spilling occasionally over the seawall beside them. "In truth, there are so many important things that have been waiting to be shared between us, Emile. So many necessary things I <u>need</u> you to understand about myself that I am not sure how to even put them into words."

Hoping to instill some kind of peace to her in her struggle, Emile caressed her fingers within his hand several times for he was also feeling the unsteady importance of what she was undoubtedly going to say. For the past two days in fact, he had been laying in his bunk remembering the many meaningful conversations they had enjoyed together in France and the unpleasant moments of regret he had tried to help her forget. Both were an unbalanced scale of their love until now, and though he secretly hoped she would blissfully decide otherwise, inwardly he also knew the time of their separation was most likely close at hand.

"I think I have had sufficient time to make my peace with whatever you need to say to me, Emma, so please do not hesitate on my account." He tried his best to be reassuring, but the words came out almost as dead as they made him feel—maybe even more so given the fact that he was no longer one of the living in that regard. "After all, this is exactly what I asked you to do, and however you have decided... I vow to you that I will not react poorly, nor will I make a scene that would embarrass you here."

"I might..." She half-smiled and nervously chuckled. "But you promise?"

"I promise." Emile nodded seriously his pledge.

"Well..." Emma pursed her lips tightly as she measured the emotion looking back at her within his eyes then proceeded more timidly, feeling the heaviness of the weight she needed to let go. "You said the other night that you are not a good man, as if that were the only justification for me to refuse you outright, and for some women, I am sure that might be the case. But truthfully, if you knew the real reason behind why I stayed with you that first night, you might admit that it is I who has been the one who was unworthy in this relationship and not you."

"I'm sorry, but I wholeheartedly beg to differ, Emma," Emile laughingly protested, shaking his head from side to side in knowledgeable disbelief. "Compared to me, <u>you</u> are an angel."

"Oh, my love..." Emma took her right hand and ran her fingers through the side of his hair and down to the base of his neck before holding a handful of his soft dark locks above his ponytail, just the way she knew he loved her to do.

The motion of the simple act of affection between them sent the slightest stream of shivers across his skin and drew him in closer to her with wanting.

"When will you ever see that I am nowhere near a saint in this relationship any more than you are a devil." She shook her head slowly and painfully watched the minute changes in his expression soften under her touch. "Though it is most certainly true, as you say, that you may have invited me to your room that night with less than the purest of intentions, but it was I who willfully made the decision to return to you each night thereafter. Why do you think that was?"

"Probably due to my rather handsome good looks," Emile teased her lightly as he had on many other occasions before, seemingly drunk under her captivating spell.

"You always were a rogue, but that is not the reason, and you know it." Emma released his hair and tapped the tip of his nose in deserved punishment. "I returned because a part of me needed to live the lie that you offered me so freely. In that beautiful dream you provided, you were my noble knight who was rescuing me from the world I wanted so desperately to escape. My very dark version of reality, that you never saw from your polished apartment and expensive furnishings, was nothing like the world in which you lived. In my world I was the dutiful daughter who always did everything that was expected of her, no matter the personal cost it might entail. Yet, there was no one like you in that world, dark or otherwise. No one cared for me beyond my ability to perform my role as an expendable servant, a cast-aside sister or a neglected nuisance of a child. Essentially, I was invisible to practically everyone in my life and used like my rags that were washed so many times over they were only being held together by the thinnest of threads. They too would be eventually discarded, just like I feared I would be in time. But in your wonderful arms, I had choices, Emile. I had unconditional love. I was the beautiful mistress that was wanted..."

"Desired," Emile corrected her huskily, his heart filling with fresh admiration for the woman before him instead of the disdain she had thought he would offer.

"Okay, desired." She rolled her eyes at the interruption, then continued, "But all of it was only a lovely dream that we were both living to escape the sad reality of what we each could not face in our own lives. Our relationship, as beautiful as it was, soon became our own, personal means of salvation for both of us and that isn't true love, Emile, that is survival."

"Survival?" Emile set his bag down and turned his face away to hide his pained expression at her blunt assessment for she had seen the truth of the matter much more clearly than he had ever contemplated it before. Indeed, for several long moments, Emile remained that way, frozen in his place like a statue of intense introspection before he felt Emma place her soft hand upon his cheek and draw him back to her. Her gentle touch alone, though always meant out of pure love, broke his trance and caused him to inhale quickly as she did, giving way for the crushing emotions deep inside to almost overtake him by the simple gesture. "You're right…"

"I know… but you have no idea how much I wish I wasn't. From the moment I first saw you that day in your apartment, we have both been lying to ourselves in this dream, sheltering our true feelings about our own insecurities beneath the protection of the other as we used our love to hide from the harsh judgement of the world in which we lived. But love isn't supposed to be that way, not really. It certainly isn't meant to be simply a means of escape or a form of self-preservation if you will. Not a love that will last, anyways."

"Then what is it?" Emile stared blankly back at her, clueless as to the answer.

"It isn't living a lie. That much I know for sure, and so do you. You said the same the other night in the meadow. As much as we may wish desperately to do so, we simply cannot hide from the truth of our realities indefinitely or it will destroy us both in the process. And so, we must eventually find it within ourselves to face it, even if everything and everyone we hold dear may implore us not to." Emma pulled her cheeks in tighter still, obviously trying to control her emotions and remain strong in her decision.

"We can't continue protecting ourselves from ourselves, is that what you mean?" He added quietly.

"Yes." Her blue eyes, as rich and clear as the ocean behind him, implored as she stepped closer to him in the shadows. "Just like you, there is nothing else in all the world that I want other than you, Emile Bastien Deschamps. Nothing will ever change that for me, not even you." She looked out at the ocean over his shoulder briefly before reaching down to take his other hand in hers. "But deception is not who we truly are either… no matter how magnificent the dream is. Wouldn't you agree?"

Emile swallowed hard, nodded, but could not force himself to speak a single word in response, positive or otherwise.

"Then let us try something new, shall we?" Emma struggled valiantly to put on a smile, forcing herself to do whatever was necessary right now to hold back the tears threatening to spill over at any second into long sobs of grief that would never be quieted. "Let us attempt in this new world of ours here in England to live as ourselves for a time, without those means of protection for just a little while and see if our newfound perception can be fortified with the right kind of actions. Maybe then, we can know if living an honest life together thereafter is possible for both of us." She paused as she was interrupted by his gentle fingers as they wiped away her fresh tears that were now running in small rivers down both of her cheeks.

"Without question, what is best for me will always be you, Emma Larose," Emile implored genuinely. "And living a life apart from you will not change that for me, either."

"Thank you, and I love you for that. I just need a little time to be sure for myself if this dream of ours can become more than just an escape for me, as well." She smiled back and tried to sound as self-assured as she possibly could manage under the circumstances, yet her voice betrayed her at every word, "But first, I need to fix my own view of love before I can even hope to accept yours."

"I understand," Emile said quietly and stood there a moment longer, neither of them able to move any farther away from the other, before she drew in a deep breath and tried to change the subject altogether.

"On a slightly happier note, as a gesture of goodwill towards you for saving her life, Miss Toussaint has graciously offered to help me find a position with one of her friends or even at her own home in Kent if one is available when we arrive. It isn't what I would necessarily desire regarding employment as I think I have cleaned enough houses for a lifetime already, but it is a fair start here to be sure, with a stable income and housing included, even if that does require living under another man's leave. In addition, it is a position someone like me would never have been given so unreservedly back in France, so I will accept it happily and be grateful for it or at least for the time being."

"There is no one like you back in France, Emma. You know that, right?" Emile caressed her cheek with the back of his fingers, wanting so very much to be close to her right now for he could see how much the conversation was taking out of her both mentally and emotionally.

As if sensing his thoughts completely, she gratefully closed her eyes as he did so, then stopped his hand after a few moments by placing hers over his own, fearing that if he continued, she would never follow through with her decision. "Nor you, my love, but this can be a fresh beginning for both of us, and who knows what will come from our beginnings. Maybe even something wonderfully better than what we had before. It is possible, right?"

Emile nodded, then gave in to the overwhelming need to pull her close to himself once more in a shared embrace before picking up his bag and standing fully erect again in regained, polite, but albeit distant posture. "If that is what you truly want, I'll not stand in your way."

Seeing the marked transformation in his countenance towards her, Emma rebuked him sternly, slightly perturbed by the man he was currently displaying, for he had never once acted that way in her presence—with the servants, yes, but never with her. "Don't do that, Emile."

"Don't do what?" Emile replied flatly to hide the hurt that was now tearing him apart. Though everything she had said had undoubtedly been the necessary truth, that also did not mean that it made it any easier to bear. Try as he might, the very thought of being miles away from her right now made his heart ache just to consider it.

"I'm not rejecting you, Emile... far from it. I'm only asking you for a bit of time for both of us to sort this out first. That is all," Emma pleaded again more earnestly. "Can you do that? For me?"

"I can certainly try." He attempted to sound convincing but from the disparaged look upon her face in return he knew he had not been successful for she judged him with an expression that tore at him more than any of the ones she had given him previously.

"Good. We are not strangers, you and I," she said tersely in growing annoyance at his childish response, almost sounding indignantly agitated by the need to reprimand him for doing so. "I've seen how you act for Angelique and the others around you. Please don't hide from me like you do with everyone else. I can't bear it... not now."

Emile looked away to compose his emotions more fully, then swiftly leaned in so close to her that his breath tickled her ear when he spoke, "With you... never. With the world... always," he reaffirmed, then giving in to every emotion that had been kept captive within him since the moment they had set foot on the ship to England, he impulsively kissed her softly on the lips for a long moment before regaining his distant stature and formally offering her his arm. "Shall we return then, Miss Larose? Miss Toussaint will no doubt be missing us."

"Indeed." Emma shot him another disapproving glance but took his arm readily and countered just as formally, "*Monsieur* Deschamps."

"Alright, I see your point." Emile shook his head at the harsh use of his name and relented. "I'm sorry, Emma."

"You should be," she said tartly in rebuke, then smiled back at him with a look that assured him of her definite forgiveness.

With the conversation finalized, the couple reluctantly made their way back through the bustling crowd and over to their companion on the other side of the street who was more than ready to be moving forward towards her next step.

"Then it is all agreed, then?" Angelique replied happily when they were together once more.

"Quite and thank you for seeing to Miss Larose's care here in England. I sincerely appreciate the gesture," Emile countered aloofly and called a taxi for the two women. Not a single nerve inside of him desired any more discussion from anyone at that moment. As a gentleman, he would of course continue to play his part as he knew that he should, but his last reserve of decorum had truly been spent. All he wanted now was a quiet place to think and reflect. Perhaps somewhere where he could have a moment to collect himself and form some kind of plan as to how he was going to achieve the impossible it seemed.

When the next available carriage pulled up to the building beside them mere moments later, Emile opened the door politely and helped Angelique into it before retrieving a few articles of clothing from within his bag and the dreaded brown bottle. Satisfied at last with the selection of his meager possessions, he placed the small piece of travel luggage and the remainder of its contents, including the last of his funds, minus a bit for his travel fare, into Emma's awaiting hands. "You might need these in your journey."

Emma took the bag from him but hesitated when he held out his hand towards her to help her into the carriage, suddenly afraid to be parted from him now that the moment had finally arrived at last. "You will come back for me, won't you?"

"Oh, Emma..." Emile touched her cheek and almost lost all preservation of his self-control entirely, desiring more than anything else in the world to sweep her up into his arms and steal her away from here once and for all. He could do it so very discreetly that no one would scarcely notice. One long stare into her beautiful eyes and she would be his helpless captive once more and better still; she would be none the wiser for it. But he could not. As much as he wanted her for himself alone, he also knew that what she needed was infinitely far more important than his personal desire, or more appropriately put—his selfish need. "Yes, of course."

Emma bit the center of her lip in continued deliberation, then reached up to kiss his cheek impetuously. "You had better, Emile Deschamps. I'm not done with you, yet."

"Promises... promises..." He looked skyward and teased her lightly, the two of them easily smiling at their shared memories before she finally took his hand and allowed him to help her into the waiting carriage. Then, closing the door securely behind her, he gave her the most wicked smile he could manage in public and added more quietly still, "Until then, I'll see you every night in our dream."

"As will I." She blushed, then leaned back as the woman across from her cast them both a look of annoyance or jealousy. Emile couldn't tell which, nor did it truly matter anymore. His focus hereafter would forever be entirely on his Emma, and that was enough.

"Sevenoaks in Kent, if you please," Emile called up the address to the patient driver at last and tapped the side of the carriage to alert him that they were safely stowed.

Receiving his instructions, the carriage driver tipped his hat politely in Emile's direction and took off down the road to his final destination.

"Farewell... my Emma," Emile whispered sadly, then went directly into the nearest inn to change his awful attire. He had survived long enough as Emile the peasant. After what he had just experienced, today, he was especially eager to return to Emile the excellent.

Chapter Twenty-Six

April 27th, 1793

Almost three weeks had passed since the day of William's return to Wakefield, yet it felt like it had been only one with how busy the epidemic had regrettably kept him. Day after day, and night after sleepless night he and Doctor Hadleigh had gone from home to home, woman to child, and man to farmhand treating anyone experiencing symptoms whether they could pay or not. Together, they had devoted countless hours and resources sacrificially all in a coordinated effort to save every one of the villagers if at all possible. In truth, it was an incredible thing to witness by anyone's standards, but nothing less than what the citizens deserved, in William's humble opinion.

For the most part, their labor had been successful, but regrettably there were also moments that were filled with tears from both the two doctors and family members alike when a cherished loved one was lost to the dreadful disease. Yet on many other remarkable occasions, William experienced unspeakable joy when another poor soul rallied to renewed health from the brink of an almost certain death. Nathanael would have most definitely called it a miracle, but William was not ready to go that far just yet. He was simply happy that another one of his patients had survived, no matter the reason or deliverer.

Almost losing Nathanael that night <u>had</u> changed William irrevocably in so many ways. Most of them, he was not yet able to fully comprehend, nor could he remotely contemplate divulging them to Señor Moretti or even Sebastian for fear of their certain judgement at his utter carelessness. Yet every morning that he opened his eyes and heard his friend's quiet prayers in the room beside him, he remembered vividly the unmistakable fear that clutched his heart, both for his friend and for the village itself as if he were reading the last entry in the preacher's journal once more. With each fresh and equally unpleasant recollection, he was drawn closer still to a renewed responsibility concerning them both, as well as for their elder doctor in a way he could not explain to anyone if they had asked him. The boy down at the livery and the farmer on the other side of the mill were no longer simply his patients, but rather people that he would even now call his good friends.

Many years ago, his father had told him once that being a doctor was more than the actual medicine, but as young as he was at the time, he had never truly understood it. Yet he did now. Seeing the world around him in this new form of life, he not only grasped his father's explanation fully but had also formed a new appreciation for the patience he had displayed towards him during his apprenticeship. After this month of relentless trials, William knew in his heart that the man had been right, as he usually was, for there was an almost magnetic connection now between himself and the people around him that he had never experienced before in his life.

It was also true that he had come to Wakefield originally with the same selfish need that had carried him on board a ship bound for the Americas—an aspiration for excellence in his profession and to begin his own practice on his own terms. But now that he had been here working alongside Nathanael and others, simply making a difference in this world while he had the chance was beginning to feel a lot more like his own lifegoal than a childhood dream for adventure. In fact, standing here in his apothecary today, filling out the many orders for medicines he needed to deliver, he realized that he no longer desired the notoriety that came along with a placard placed prominently outside his door. In his simple existence here, he had grown far beyond all that he had ever imagined for his life and in doing so, deep down, he had also found his true purpose.

Serving others sacrificially made him far more fulfilled. It made him perfectly content, or as content as he possibly could be under the circumstances. So much so, that he would probably dare to say that he would be totally willing to do this kind of work for the rest of his existence if allowed, though he would most definitely have to change locations more than once as time passed or the people might start to grow concerned about why their young doctor did not age as much as his patients.

All things considered, he would be sad when that day arrived, but living his life dreading that moment now seemed utterly pointless, too. As unexpected as it was, living simply amongst those who found joy in the smallest of things made him see life in an entirely different way and caused him to experience a greater happiness than he had ever enjoyed in years. In a way, it made him even more grateful for his unfortunate transformation than to have cause to despise it for it had also brought him here and to people who made him a better person, even if some of them were far away in France or on an island on the edge of the Mediterranean.

Nathanael, on the other hand, now appeared totally lost mentally and practically despondent at times. Given the necessary nutrition, he had thankfully made a full, though emotionally guarded recovery physically, and even though he had agreed to accompany William on several of his visits in the past week, he did so almost in a trance-like state, shuffling from house to house like someone who was sleepwalking through the conversations rather than an active visitor.

As William might have expected of any other patient who had experienced such a traumatic ordeal, Nathanael was still not physically able to withstand long walks or taxing endeavors in the beginning. Nonetheless, any day that he accomplished anything beyond sitting at the desk in his darkened room or pacing the floors endlessly at night was a definite start in the right direction towards his complete restoration and return to the pulpit, or at least that was William's hope. Or rather perhaps, it was more of an overly optimistic expectation on his part that each day would only make Nathanael stronger, and that might also mean that just a small piece of the guilt William felt at abandoning him might also lessened by some degree.

Nathanael's distracted mental state aside, he was not the least bit idle in his recouperation, quite the opposite in fact. True to his determined nature and religious training, whenever the necessity arose, he had silently pushed himself past his weakened physical state many times over to feed the sick or pray over the dying and even mucked a few stalls when the laborers were too ill to do so for themselves. And though Nathanael had never once complained in doing so, William could tell that it exhausted him terribly each time he did it. But this was who Nathanael was at his core. Serving his flock was not only his job, but it was his passion. Or rather, it was the one thing that held him securely together beside his treasured text and that meant that nothing was above nor beneath him concerning their care.

It was yet another aspect of his friend that caused William to marvel more than once at the graciousness this man always displayed to those around him. And although he was not ready in any way close to a full conversion to Nathanael's way of thinking, he was at the very least a fraction more receptive to many of his philosophies than he was against them now. Though not surprisingly, it was the blind faith part that he struggled with the most, but even in that he was gradually accepting that not everything in his world could be easily reasoned out with science or with logical thinking. Maybe the belief that faith was all he needed in the end was a lot closer than he realized, or at least Nathanael liked to think so.

"A toddler learns to crawl before they walk, dear William," Nathanael had said to him last night after their supper as they were walking home from the tavern. Yet looking back on the conversation now, he understood what the man had been trying to explain in a whole new light.

The learned preacher was not at all insinuating that he was an infant in his understanding of his beliefs or in the Bible itself, but rather that William was simply exploring his boundaries within that realm of acceptance to find his own footing. This explanation seemed more logical to him than anything else he had heard lately, which meant that it was at least something he could accept, though maybe just a little more than some of the other disciplines he had read about when his friend had left his Bible unattended.

The weekly letters from Sebastian also came now like clockwork with constant news of his family and his busy forge on the island. From all appearances, it was almost as if the man had finally discovered a revitalization in his life, though he was still as pessimistic as ever regarding his transformation and recent temptations.

There was even a small note about his training of a new apprentice which gave William the slightest bit of hope that perhaps the man was moving in the right direction towards returning home soon. Still, to William's dismay, nothing was said by him or Señor Moretti regarding the whereabouts of a certain Frenchman with whom they had once been acquainted. This had worried Nathanael greatly, as he was more than certain that the man might be starting a coup over there in France at any minute or possibly creating his own legion of vampires to battle the revolutionaries taking over the government, but William doubted it very highly. Emile wasn't about seizing power and control. He was probably doing what Emile did best, charming his way through life without a care for the future or its momentary consequences.

From his brief experience with the man, he knew that if anyone was able to take care of himself, it was Emile Deschamps. The proud Frenchman had already managed to survive being kidnapped, a rogue hurricane, shipwrecked, being bitten by a vampire and chastised by a century old scholar. If he could do all of that and remain the same, independently austere gentleman that he was, then most certainly, he could survive a French rebellion.

Though part of William did also long to hear at least some news of the man if for no other reason than to quell the concern for him that grew with each passing day. Theirs had been a thrown together kind of friendship based on a need for survival and sheer necessity. But despite all of the man's deficits, William knew there was a sincere goodness at his core and a genuine desire to protect his friends no matter what the personal cost—even ones who apparently had no sailing knowledge whatsoever to speak of and were seemingly persistent in placing themselves in harm's way.

Among their other correspondence, William's father had also written to him recently about a stranger's visit to his surgery in London. This news, though in itself should have been uneventful and mundane in its presentation, caused more than a little concern for him as it worried and intrigued him all at the same time. Not many people were unknown to his father in his scope of the world. So, to say that someone of apparent social standing, that he did not immediately recognize, was seeking William out directly, gave him reason to pause momentarily.

The "rather foreign looking man", he had gone on to explain was quite obviously not from London proper by the look of his attire and casual air, but since the stranger had made only a basic inquiry as to William's exact whereabouts and nothing more, his father had, without reservation, given the nicely dressed man William and Nathanael's address in Wakefield.

However, the only thing slightly more distressing than an unknown guest was the fact that his father's letter was already half a week old. As delayed as it was in its arrival, he had half-expected a visitor any day now given the directions his father had bestowed upon his caller as London was only a three-day journey by carriage on any given route.

Had Señor Moretti decided to pay them a visit after all? Or was it Sebastian finally choosing to make an effort to join his family? Either would have been more than a welcome event for both Nathanael and him, but he doubted the unusual visitor was either of them. After all, they would have mentioned the upcoming trip in their letters, but since neither of them had, he was left to only vaguely speculate as to who it truly was that was coming.

To make matters worse, Nathanael had not seemed entirely himself this morning either while practicing his sermon. So much so, that William felt it would be more prudent to hold off telling him about the unsettling news for fear that it might deter the progress he had made so far this week. Still, he promised himself that he would do so promptly after their lunch that day, where hopefully, barring further interruptions, they could at the very least help to prepare a room for their guest before his arrival. Knowing that they only had two rooms between them to speak of at the apothecary, if their visitor wanted to stay the night, which he most likely would, they would definitely find a way to make the necessary accommodation for whoever it was, as Wakefield held no other inn to speak of at the moment. Nor would they turn anyone away as they had entertained very few visitors since their arrival last December.

For the most part, it had been an honest determination on William's behalf, or admittedly, a well-thought-out intention, but the completion thereof sadly never took place for just as he set the letter down upon the table in the main room below, he had been called away on an errand for Doctor Hadleigh and did not return until well after Nathanael had retired for the night.

And so it was, on the very next morning he soon learned who had paid a visit to his father's surgery in the most unexpected of fashions.

~   ~   ~   ~   ~

It was Sunday morning once again, and as such, he had decided, out of an abundance of caution, to attend the weekly service. Given the fact that it was Nathanael's first Sunday taking his place once more behind his beloved pulpit, he drew great concern for the mental stability and fortitude of his good friend. As everyone in the village knew, no pianist would be in attendance this time, and for that very reason alone he knew he needed to attend. If for no other excuse than to keep himself from going crazy conjuring up all sorts of possible scenarios for his friend's failure while sitting here alone at home waiting for him to return. Though attending the service also did not offer any promise whatsoever that it would also quell the rising anxiety he was feeling just watching Nathanael go through the necessary motions of his preparation, fully dedicated to his task at hand, but also lacking the inner fervor that normally burned behind his eyes.

Unfortunately for Nathanael, William could not have been more right about his attendance had he seen the event prophetically displayed for himself beforehand. Like witnessing the woeful procession of a funeral, every member of the congregation filed past him and dutifully took their seats without the usual merriment that the approaching service normally provided. And despite what he had done for practically every service since their arrival, Nathanael was not out at the door greeting his flock so jovially, nor was he anywhere to be seen whatsoever. Instead, one by one, each member entered the church of their own accord and shuffled down the center aisle slowly before they eventually slunk almost sleepily into this pew or that while obviously lost in thought over the changes in their usual routine.

Choosing a seat prominently in the third row, directly behind Doctor Hadleigh, William folded his hands respectfully in his lap as he had seen others do next to him and waited patiently for Nathanael's arrival.

They all waited, actually. Each person deciding to remain steadfastly lost in his or her own thoughts as they stared out a window, off into space or chose to whisper something softly to the neighbor beside them about whatever it was people talked about at funerals. What that was, William had no idea, neither did Doctor Hadleigh either, who seemed to be almost falling asleep at this point having probably been called out to some kind of sick call this morning or was recovering from the other day's events with William where they had been asked to assist in a rather difficult case of amputation. That man had lost the greater majority of his left leg, but at least he had managed to keep his life, or at least, so far.

And so it was that a few minutes after ten o'clock, when the congregation was beginning to sound a little more than restless by the hummed chatter he could clearly hear behind him, that William watched as Nathanael stepped slowly, but confidently out from his study and made his way up to the pulpit before inviting everyone to follow him in the first hymn.

Obediently, the people all stood in humble compliance and tried to sing along with him, though the pitch of the music was undoubtedly more than a little off key from stanza to following stanza. For Nathanael's sake, everyone was clearly trying their best to help him succeed by willing just a bit of their energy into their pastor, but in the end, the whole experience left William feeling a bit unbalanced and sad to witness it. After all the many joyous and uplifting services he had attended in Wakefield since they had arrived, this one was shockingly morose and totally uncharacteristic of anything Nathanael had ever orchestrated.

It was then, however, at the closing of the last chorus, that the most unusual of things occurred that William had not quite expected. From the back of the church to his left, he felt for the briefest of moments, an unmistakable breeze cross over his left shoulder as if a cold chill brushed his cheek from an open window, yet all the tall casements on both sides of the church were not functional in any way, nor could the wind be emanating from anywhere other than the doors in the back. Overwhelmed by the need to cast a quick glance at the door behind him, he studied it until he was certain beyond a doubt that it could not have originated from there either, as both large doors appeared to be securely fastened. Moreover, not a single soul at the back of the church seemed alarmed in the slightest or cognizant of any of the disturbance he was feeling across his skin.

Even more curious than before, William craned his neck in the opposite direction, scanning the parishioners to his right, looking for anything or anyone out of the ordinary, but saw nothing and no one of note. Whatever it was that was making the hair on the back of his neck stand to attention was clearly not visible, not yet anyway with everyone blocking his view of the rest of the chapel.

Satisfied at last, William shook his head to try to ignore his senses for the present and focused on the words of the hymn more closely, content that whatever it was, the danger he envisioned seemed minimal at best.

> *I sing the mighty power of God, that made the mountains rise,*
> *That spread the flowing seas abroad, and built the lofty skies.*
> *I sing the wisdom that ordained the sun to rule the day;*
> *The moon shines full at God's command, and all the stars obey.*
> *I sing the goodness of the Lord, Who filled the Earth with food,*
> *Who formed the creatures through his Word,*
> *And then pronounced them good.*
> *Lord, how Thy wonders are displayed, where'er I turn my eye,*
> *If I survey the ground I tread, or gaze upon the sky.*
> *There's not a plant or flower below, but makes Thy glories known,*
> *And clouds arise, and tempests blow, by order from Thy throne;*
> *While all that borrows life from Thee is ever in Thy care;*
> *And everywhere that man can be, Though God art present there.*

Nathanael motioned for the congregation to be seated and closed his hymnal softly before placing each of his hands deliberately on top of it. "What a wonderful consolation, is it not, that no matter what is happening in our lives, that our God is always with us?"

A few people around William nodded in agreement causing him to listen to his friend's words more intently, rather than anxiously focusing on the countenance of the man before him.

"It is very easy for us to believe, or at the very least accept as truth, that our God does not care about His subjects like He does the world on which we live, with all its complexity and changes. That His attentions are far more occupied at keeping the planets consistently on their paths around the Sun, than in listening to a young child's prayer. But I tell you in great honesty and truthfulness that I wholeheartedly do not believe that to be the case.

Over the past several weeks I have been more than privileged enough to hear many of those prayers spoken by His beloved children here in Wakefield, and though I am not their Heavenly Father, I know beyond a doubt that He is listening.

How do I know this to be true?

Because God says it is true to begin with. And yet if that is not reason enough, there is also a story I wish to relate to you today. It is a tale about a young man who was no longer content with what his earthly father had given him. Some may even choose to sit here and call this main entitled or spoiled, but I will not cast such a harsh judgement upon him. He simply had not grown up with the more basic needs and wants the rest of us have daily. Yet he did so, all the while, in a loving family. However, despite his most excellent upbringing, we are told that one day he made up his mind to leave the security of his home and chose this time in his life to step out into the world. He did so completely alone and with little regard for the certain consequences of that decision.

He asked... no, that is not correct. He <u>demanded</u> that his father give him his fair share of his earthly inheritance. I do not think that he was cognizant at that time, nor did he probably care about the very real stresses that this financial decision would probably place upon the rest of his family. From what we read, we can surmise that he was most certainly focused on just two things—what he wanted, and what he was willing to do to get it.

Does that sound very different than any of us?"

A few people around William nodded sadly in conviction, while others seemed entirely focused on every word that the young preacher was saying as if they had never heard the story before or at least not in the way he was telling it. Neither had William either, for that matter, and so it made the sermon all the more interesting to him.

Nathanael cleared his throat quietly and took a small sip of the water he had placed upon the edge of the pulpit earlier, his hand clearly shaking ever so slightly as he set it down, then continued. "I am certain that this hurtful decision saddened his father immensely, but because he loved his son, he did as he was requested and gave him everything that he would have received upon his father's death. A fortune in that time in history and in ours if we were to accurately measure the sum of it.

And what did the son choose to do with his exorbitant wealth? Build a home for himself? Finance a prosperous industry or occupation?

"<u>No,</u>" Nathanael said the word more forcefully to gain everyone's attention before continuing. "<u>He wasted every last shekel and talent on every imaginable pleasure life afforded him,</u>" he stated the sentence so profoundly that not a soul in the congregation did not feel the guilt resting behind his statement. So much so, that many hung their heads in shame, a few even whimpered a slight sob for the man or for themselves, yet no one seemed entirely unaffected, including William.

Nathanael began again, though this time a bit less condemning in his delivery, "The Bible does not go into all the particulars about his life thereafter because frankly, they are truly not necessary facts to know. However, I am confident that we can assume whatever it was he spent his money on, it was the very opposite of what he should have been doing. It was debaucherous. It was lewd, and it was most definitely everything that would satisfy the lusts of his flesh."

The room remained hushed as he drew in a long breath before exhaling it out again slowly. "I will not excuse what this young man did in quite literally throwing his life away into the very gutters of Roman society, but in the next part of our story we now find him eating in the feed trough along with a group of equally hungry pigs.

Pigs, I say to you. The most unclean of all animals in the Jewish world. One does not have to have a very vivid imagination to reflect on the most awful of situations he has now found himself in, nor should we think we ourselves have not also shared in that same trough of self-pity in our own lives, myself, as well."

"But friends..." Nathanael gave his flock an encouraging smile that seemed for the first time in quite a while to be genuinely filled with some small ounce of happiness. "The story does not end there, just as it does not end here for us, too. The ruined man eventually picks himself up from the refuse and self-created punishment and decides that he would rather work as a servant to his father than live in the way that he is doing now, for he knows from experience that even those of lowest degree in his father's home have food to spare, clean clothes to wear and are for the most part, well cared for.

He sets out immediately on his journey home, but before he is even a mile or so away, his father sees him walking up in the distance. Overjoyed, the ecstatic father runs to his lost child with abandon and embraces him as if he has never left.

We read that his child tearfully repents of his sin, but in truth, there is no need as the father has already forgiven him before he ever returned. Not only that, but the elder man showers him with all the care and affection that a loving parent demonstrates when his child has finally come home. The fatted calf is roasted, a feast prepared, new clothes ordered, and a general party-like atmosphere has commenced.

'Rejoice with me for my son is now returned!' The father exclaims. And they do. That is, everyone except one man. A brother who feels greatly slighted by this great show of affection towards someone he feels is so unworthy of it. He is understandably angry. He is hurt. But most of all, he is indignant at his father's senseless decision to forgive his brother for hadn't he <u>always</u> done exactly everything he had been told to do? Was he not <u>absolutely</u> faithful above all others? Did <u>he</u> not show by his actions every day that he loved his father more?

The father can clearly see the building turmoil and conflicting loyalties within his more dutiful son so he chooses to gently remind him that everything he currently owns will always be his, and his alone. More importantly, he should not waste the rest of his life building up bitterness and resentment towards others about things that he does not have the ability to change.

With overflowing love for both of his sons, he reminds the one before him to choose joy... choose happiness... choose acceptance of a brother who is now restored back to his family and his community.

Friends, our story in the Bible does end here, but it does not end here for each of us. We have also been asked to daily put ourselves into the places of the father, the faithful child or the prodigal son." Nathanael paused momentarily to look over at the empty pianoforte before continuing. "In losing those we love; we are constantly tempted to choose bitterness over acceptance... disappointment over peace. It is not an easy war to wage within us daily, but we must all fight against it all the same. We must choose in these times of trials to do as the father of the prodigal son chose to do. Embrace the blessings God has given us today. Embrace the happiness of each memory you have had with them. Embrace His love for the days to come. If we can do that, we will be truly joyful indeed." With a single tear falling down his left cheek, he ended his sermon and motioned for all to rise for the closing hymn.

The people sang more enthusiastically this time a song about giving to God praise for his repeated mercies before Nathanael closed the service in prayer.

"May you go in peace, my friends," Nathanael directed and laid his hymnal down on top of his Bible carefully.

The congregation all smiled in unison and began to disperse, though this time a bit more talkative and far less gloomy. William, however, remained in his pew and observed his friend who was watching his congregation leave from his position at the front of the chapel. From the way in which Nathanael's shoulders slumped ever so slightly as he leaned heavily on the pulpit, he could tell that the service had taken a lot out of him to do it, but William was still grateful to see the man try. Yet it was only a few minutes later, when the last parishioner was exiting out the door behind him, that he heard the audible and most unmistakably loud echo of a person clapping their hands once, then twice, followed by an elongated silence once more before the echoing third reverberated through the rafters above.

Instinctively, William swung around to face the back of the church and almost laughed out loud at who he saw sitting in the very last pew with his frame fully stretched out wide against the back of the wooden paneling.

"You!" Nathanael acknowledged from the platform, but not in a way that seemed overly upset in the least.

"What? Have you forgotten my name already?" The man jested cockily before he stood and began walking up the aisle to greet them like he was taking some leisurely stroll.

"As if that were even possible, Emile." William welcomed him heartily with a warm handshake before seizing the man in an equally viselike hug thereafter.

"I've missed you, too, William." Emile patted him twice on the back in response. "More than you could imagine, if you can believe it."

"I can." William practically beamed with delight.

"Did you know he was coming?" Nathanael met the men at the third pew with a questioning gaze at William but seemed genuinely happy that their friend had chosen to visit them at last.

William shrugged childishly. "Not really. I was going to tell you yesterday that someone had stopped by my father's surgery asking for our address, but since he did not say who it was, I was not even sure if it was something worth mentioning, yet."

"Ah, William, I am hurt." Emile feigned being wounded at his casual oversight.

"Not mortally, I assure you," William countered jovially as if the banter between the two of them had never ceased though it had been almost five months since they had last spoken.

The three men all laughed together in unison and smiled genuinely as they each exchanged warm embraces of pure joy before William excitedly inquired, "Where have you been, Emile? Tell us all the news!"

"Here?" Emile lifted his eyes and scanned the chapel from window to ceiling, admiring the beautifully crafted edifice as if it were something akin to the great beauty of his beloved Notre Dame.

"Of course, not here," Nathanael replied like a scolding father and left the two men to put away his vestments before departure.

"Still as dramatic as always, I see," Emile chided playfully and replaced the hat upon his head that he had respectfully removed for the service.

"Be gentle with him, please. He has been through a lot recently," William cautioned and picked up his leather satchel from beside him in the pew before swinging it over his neck as he was accustomed to doing.

This simple statement alone, though meant to be about Nathanael, caused Emile to suddenly reflect back on his time in Paris and the subsequent flight thereafter. "Haven't we all…" The Frenchman sighed briefly.

"Oh?" William's eyes lifted at the open-ended comment but waited patiently for his response.

"Perhaps it is one of the many stories we shall share over some lunch." Emile dodged his remark deftly and pretended to be not the least bit interested in divulging any of the details as of yet.

"Most definitely. I want to hear all about it. Starting with what you have been doing all this time."

William heard the familiar closing of the study door behind him and looked up as the two men were joined once more by Nathanael.

Ready to catch up on the past five months, the three of them stepped out into the generally overcast day, and it truly felt as if nothing had ever transpired without the other man's presence at all. The snow of winter had begun to melt weeks ago, being replaced instead by the promise of flourishing wildflowers and an absolute plethora of colorful plants that were eager to show off their newfound beauty all around them along the road.

"I must admit that it certainly looks a sight better here in the country than in your disgustingly, dirty capital of London." Emile wrinkled his nose at the memory of his recent experience. "The streets are quite literally overflowing on the edges with excrement of various degrees."

William laughed at his accuracy and unusual expression. "What? They don't empty their chamber pots into the streets over in your fair Paris?"

"They most certainly do not." Emile held his nose slightly aloft in obvious disgust.

Nathanael shook his head, calling his bluff. "I am sorry, but the whole of Europe has probably heard by now about how your King Louis would not even remain at his own castle of Versailles for a long period of time because his servants and visitors would relieve themselves in the hallways."

At his friend's revelation, William stopped walking briefly and hit Emile with the back of his hand upon the man's upper arm, incredulously surprised. "Have your people not heard about a privy?"

"A what?" Emile feigned stupidity then shook off the man's hand. "Of course we have, you idiot! We probably invented it as we have most other things that other countries like to take the credit for."

"No, that would be the Romans, Emile." William chuckled and resumed walking with the rest of them to the tavern in the center of town.

"And where do you think <u>they</u> got the idea from, hmmm? The Romans liked to steal everything from those they conquered and call it their own. But as for Versailles, I suppose we French simply do not choose to get our feet wet," he added while secretly acknowledging his hidden displeasure towards water though none of the other men picked up on it.

"Then you are in the wrong part of the world here for sure, dear friend." Nathanael held the tavern door open for the rest of the group. "This is farm country, and in England it rains almost every other day it seems."

"Indeed." Emile sniffed and wiped the now questionable mud from off his boots onto the scraper by the door. "That should make it infinitely easier for the three of us then."

"It does, though it's not all that bad as you will see. You are staying, aren't you?" William pulled up a chair and slung his bag over its back before taking his usual seat with his back to the front window.

Nathanael did the same, but not before offering to Emile the chair nearest to William out of politeness.

Emile, of course, was only too happy to take the available seat between the two of them and immediately leaned back nonchalantly. "If you will have me for a time, I'd be only too delighted."

"We have plenty of space at the apothecary if you do not mind sharing a room with one of us," Nathanael offered courteously before William could even suggest it.

"Well, then again, I don't know." Emile sized the two men up from top to bottom as if choosing which one of them would be the most preferable roommate, then quipped ruefully, "A raving madman or a questionable torturer? Ah the choices."

Nathanael and William both laughed together at his jibe.

"I had forgotten that you <u>do</u> have a rather colorful way of putting things, Emile." William signaled politely for the tavern's host so they could order their meals. "I won't ask you which one of us is the madman."

"It could really be either of us, honestly, though my money is on you being the torturer." Nathanael laughed lightly.

"Indeed." William chuckled. "Mad or otherwise, I do tend to torture people more than you do, unless you are referring to having to endure your countless lectures on the correct way in which to clean one's laundry."

"You still have no idea how it is done, do you?" Nathanael countered quite authoritatively, clearly freshly annoyed.

"Not a clue, but you do, and that is all that matters it seems." William smiled and shook his head slightly at the common disagreement they had encountered during their short time living together.

Nathanael, on the other hand, appeared almost irked momentarily by the very suggestion that he would ever force his opinion so callously upon his fellow man but chose to only roll his eyes at William's refusal to comply to the generally accepted order of things. "Just you wait and see, someday you will agree that I am right and do it properly."

"I doubt that very highly, my friend." William glanced back at him, staunchly unrelenting in his position but his eyes forever glistened with the merriment their opposing views created. "Still, you are welcome to continue to try to teach me if you like."

"No, thank you," Nathanael acquiesced and loosened the top button of his collar slightly as the air in the tavern was quickly becoming quite stuffy all of a sudden. "If you so choose to ruin your perfectly excellent clothing by your own wasteful ineptness, that is entirely on you."

Throughout it all, Emile only listened quietly with pleasure as he looked over his fingernails as if checking for some piece of dirt that was most obviously not present before suddenly interjecting another further qualification to stop the pair's civil bickering. "Yes, well, there is another way to truly decide this unfortunate dilemma of sleeping arrangements, laundry notwithstanding. Though if truth be told, I personally side with Nathanael on this issue. There is a correct way, William."

"Of course, there is," William mumbled and crossed his arms over his chest resolutely.

"William, please... What do you propose, Emile?" Nathanael looked up at him in surprise and picked up a roll from the center of the table intending to butter it as soon as the bowl of creamy goodness had arrived.

"Which one of you snores the most?" Emile's eyebrows lifted seriously with the delivery of the question.

They all laughed together this time at his suggestion.

"That would be me, I'm afraid," Nathanael admitted sheepishly. "And it appears, I talk, as well, though I have never heard it."

"How could you?" Emile smiled genuinely.

"We're bedfellows again, so it seems." William lifted one of the mugs that had been recently brought to their table and held it aloft to toast. "To new beginnings, gentlemen?"

"To new beginnings," they all replied in unison and clinked their cups together in the center of the table, though only Emile angled his head in response to the recent irony of William's statement. From all appearances, everything in Emile's world was about to change and for the first time in his life, he was not the least bit reluctant to embrace it.

Chapter Twenty-Seven

April 28th, 1793

At William's request, the host brought three heaping bowls of beef stew to their table and Nathanael, in turn, paid the man a generous amount for the fare.

"It always looks far better than it smells, does it not?" William sighed with resignation hoping this time it would be different, though he remained thoroughly unconvinced.

"Always," the two other men agreed in unison, but each still dutifully took several bites of the appetizing looking stew anyway.

"I shouldn't complain really as no doubt Mrs. Summerfield spent the better part of the day carefully preparing it." William stirred the stew with his spoon before tentatively selecting a few pieces of potato and a small chunk of beef. "And it does look absolutely delicious, but I just hate wasting good money on something I literally cannot taste," William said reluctantly, then placed the waiting stew into his mouth and swallowed reflexively, this time barely making a grimace with the necessary action. "Nothing... absolutely nothing." He shook his head in frustrated disapproval. "Not even a hint of spices, though I do taste a small amount of the salt."

"I wonder why that is?" Emile licked the back of his spoon to judge for himself. "Do you think it is the minerals in it?"

"Perhaps," William tried another bite and pondered on it once more, distracting his mind to another topic entirely. "I wonder..."

Nathanael on the other hand appeared totally disinterested in the science behind the odd phenomenon and chose instead to hold up another serving of carrots to his eyes before carefully examining them as if doing so would make them any more appetizing. "It is definitely far better than the food Sebastian and I ate on the island. My whole being still shudders every time I remember those awful snails." His upper body reacted involuntarily in a shiver as he put the spoon into his mouth and spoke with his mouth half-full. "Yes, much better any day than snails."

"It wouldn't take much." Emile wrinkled his nose at the man's obvious lack of manners and picked up a roll from the center plate before tearing it into smaller pieces as he spoke. "So... the prodigal son, eh, Nathanael? You wouldn't have been preaching about anybody we know, would you?"

"Be serious, Emile. He has been practicing that sermon for well over a week. Besides, he didn't even know you were going to be there today." William jabbed him playfully as he would have his older brother. "Why? Do you feel guilty?"

"You assume I think he was preaching about me." Emile looked down his nose at the doctor, feigning a lack of absolution on the topic.

"God knew who needed to hear it." Was Nathanael's practiced reply. "I make it a point to study several passages every week, but it is only just before the service that I truly know which it is He wants me to speak upon."

"Hmm." William leaned back in his chair feeling a little more than stunned about his revelation before admitting frankly. "Well, if I were to be honest, I did think you were referring to me at several points during the message."

"Does it really matter who it was intended for?" Nathanael folded his napkin before carefully placing it over his finished plate.

"Not in the slightest." William shrugged casually. "It was a good sermon, and one I had never heard before."

"Nor I." Emile agreed.

"Seriously? Never before?" Nathanael raised both his eyebrows in question.

"Not a single part of it," William admitted. "My grandmother must have missed that one."

Nathanael shook his head in disbelief. "Well, you should know that my sermons are as much for me as they are for any of you."

"You?" It was Emile's turn to look totally surprised. "You do not strike me as much of a prodigal."

"As far as you are aware, but I have been the other son on more than one occasion in my very brief life," Nathanael countered quietly.

The three men at the table nodded in silence, thinking back to the sermon and the various points he had made during it.

"Well, enough of this positive introspection, tell me all about what has been happening with you two." Emile waved his hand dismissively to change the subject to a much different tone and focus, feeling the same level of intense conviction he had experienced during the sermon attacking his soul once more.

The two other men next to him exchanged glances with each other warily, unsure just what details were important enough to share at the supper table and what should be avoided altogether.

"From the looks on both of your faces just now, it appears as though the entire world has been ending here, which I assure you, it has not. That particular prophesy can <u>only</u> be reserved for my fair Paris, but I'd rather not talk about all of that here. Mainly because it would be far too gruesome for polite dinner conversation. Now, out with it, you two," Emile demanded firmly.

"Well, for starters, the village and much of England has just finished dealing with a dreadful influenza. People from Portsmouth to even farther north than here have been battling and sometimes losing many members of their population for almost a month now." William leaned back in his chair and folded his arms across his chest, resting comfortably. "No doubt you saw the last stages of it back in London when you came through."

"Yes, I had very few choices of lodging along my route as most were either closed or deemed too infectious for tenants." Emile ate the last bit of his roll and wiped his mouth politely.

"I wish inadequate preferences for sleep was the only thing we had to deal with here," William quipped lightly but cast Emile a warning glance while Nathanael was otherwise occupied looking down.

Receiving the unspoken message, Emile nodded knowingly and respectfully changed the subject once more. "So, have either of you heard from Sebastian or Señor Moretti since we left?"

William smiled, grateful for the man's quick wit and attention. "Several times actually. Sebastian is living with Señor Moretti on the island still and working as a blacksmith down at their port."

"William even went so far as to visit his family last month. How many children did you say he had again?" Nathanael added.

"Two precocious boys. They look just like him, Emile. So much so that the youngest of them could probably be called his twin, though the eldest most definitely has his temper and demeanor," William countered. "You'd like them, Nathanael. His wife is pretty religious."

"I like all people, no matter their choice of denomination," Nathanael quickly defended, as if he had ever given the impression otherwise.

"Or lack thereof?" Emile lifted one eyebrow in questioned challenge.

"I am rooming with the two of you, aren't I?" The preacher smiled. "How much more pagan can it get?"

"True." William and Emile tilted their heads towards each other and said in unison.

"We are practically heathens compared to him." Emile laughed lightly as he took a sip of his drink and smiled back at William. "Pagan, indeed…"

"Speak for yourself," William huffed.

Emile glanced back at William with a questioned look across his otherwise emotionless face. "So, you've converted since we last met?"

"Not hardly, but let's just say I respect what Nathanael says a lot more than I do not." William placed his silverware inside his empty bowl and moved it to the center of the table. "But it's getting late, and I am sure you are probably tired after your long journey."

"I'll admit. It <u>has</u> been a long day," Emile conceded honestly and moved to stretch his limbs, feeling the same achiness he had experienced back in France. "Either that or I am simply getting too old to be travelling so long in confined spaces."

"Carriages are a brutal mode of transportation no matter your age or health," William admitted easily. "Though I suppose they are easier for us than being on horseback. And less inclined to necessitate delays due to the weather, I suppose."

"Quite," Emile agreed readily. "Shall we?"

The men all stood, pushed in their chairs, and gave the necessary pleasantries to the owner on their way out the door.

"Is it true what they are saying about Paris?" William asked as they walked along together down the road to the apothecary. "The newspapers from London proclaim dogmatically that the monarchy has been completely erased, and the people rule the nation now."

"A mob controls the country, I'm afraid," Emile replied with marked irritation while shading his eyes from the late afternoon sun that was barely breaking through the clouds here and there.

"Is that why you left?" Nathanael continued his friend's line of questioning.

"That and other reasons." Emile lowered his hand now that the sun had retreated but did not elaborate further. "And what have you two been doing in my absence? From the looks of how desolate this place is, I can't imagine you have been able to do much more than play cards or read books to pass the time."

"He's been working non-stop. I was preaching... and courting a woman," Nathanael mumbled the last part apathetically but continued walking without further explanation.

Emile's eyebrows lifted instinctively in surprise at the man's rather strange sounding confession. "Does she have a name, this mysterious woman?"

Nathanael stopped walking abruptly as if struck by an arrow with his words before quietly replying, "Her name was Elsie Summerfield," he said quickly but respectfully before looking down at his hands in concentration, wringing them twice with a painful sigh, then walking away from the two of them once more.

Suddenly sorry he had intruded on what appeared to be an equally uncomfortable subject, Emile cast William an utterly confused expression.

William only rolled his eyes towards the apothecary in response and jerked his head slightly to signal a later discussion.

Taking the hint, Emile nodded once and quickened his strides to keep up with Nathanael before sincerely apologizing, "I'm sorry. I should not have pried."

"It's alright, Emile, honestly. To tell you the truth. I think I am just feeling a little tired from preaching today, that's all," Nathanael explained slowly when the three of them were safely inside the shop and had closed the door behind them. "Perhaps I have not yet recovered as much as I had hoped."

"Some rest may do you good. You'll see. Emile and I will continue our conversation down here so that we will not disturb you." William touched the man on his upper arm and held his hand there a moment longer trying to offer him just a bit of encouragement for his friend had truly accomplished so much today, far more than William had ever thought possible.

"I'd appreciate that." Nathanael nodded solemnly but did not speak again as he shuffled up the stairs looking much older than he actually was.

A few moments later, the men below distinctly heard the closing of the door above, and only then did they know that they could speak more freely.

"I am assuming something happened to that poor girl. Did he...?" Emile left the sentence empty on purpose, fearing the worst for the man, though admittedly he did not seriously think that Nathanael could possibly be capable of doing such a thing.

"Oh, no." William waved the obvious assumption away just as quickly. "Nothing like that, I assure you. I have not seen him even so much as be tempted to transgress in that form of consumption when he has fed properly, though I myself have surely struggled not to partake on many occasions—full or otherwise. As you might imagine, being a doctor is most definitely fraught with far more difficulties in that area than I had originally expected. In fact, sometimes it takes all my willpower just to remain at a patient's bedside when all I want to do is run... Well, better that than eat them, I suppose." William smirked at the morbid humor but then sighed in inner chastisement of it again.

"I am sure. Though you two don't know what you are missing." Emile drew in a deep breath before exhaling. "The taste of it is..."

William raised his palm instantly to stop him short. "Please don't."

Emile turned his head inquisitively and narrowed his eyes to study the man a moment, wondering just how he had been able to withstand his most basic inner desires for as long as he had.

"Oh, I want it, Emile, very much, I'm afraid." William breathed in quickly and held it as he tried to steady his pulse that was already beginning to quicken at the very idea of feeding, before adding quietly to the man across from him, "Let me assure you that I'd love nothing more than to march right back to that tavern and feast upon something infinitely far more desirable than stew, but I can't. Despite what my body craves, I just cannot bring myself to hurt someone like that. I certainly do not abstain from a fresh conquest for the same reasons as Nathanael, but I am not naïve enough to say that I do not <u>want</u> it just as much as you do." He closed his eyes and inhaled and exhaled slowly to calm himself back to his original, even temper. "I know you mean well by it, but sharing all the delightful details will not help me either. Not unless there is something deliciously fulfilling to go along with it."

"A definite loss," Emile replied nonchalantly but it was evident to William that the man was once more carefully displaying his truest form of rehearsed indifference. Longstanding sincerity of character was always fleeting in Emile's conversations, but from his brief time with the man, William knew better than most that it was always just under the surface if you looked hard enough for it.

"No doubt." William shifted uncomfortably, wanting very much to go upstairs right then and help himself to some of the blood he had stored away just this morning. "And while we are on that particular subject, I think the two of us should have a discussion about your dietary needs while you are here."

"Go on." He motioned with his hand to indicate his openness on the subject.

"Emile, my responsibility will always lie with Nathanael. He is not like you or I and lacks both the stomach and the desire to do what is necessary to survive as we do," William explained simply.

"Is that why he is so weak?" Emile cast a wary glance towards the stairs.

"No." William plopped down on a backwards facing chair and rubbed his face with his hands roughly to rub away the burden of the past three weeks.

Even more concerned than before, Emile chose a seat across from him and politely crossed one leg over his other before placing his hands neatly in his lap while he waited for the man to speak.

"He is weak because the fool did not drink blood of any kind for over a month."

"A month!" Emile's eyes grew large in total shock. "How is that even possible?"

"I have no idea." William shook his head. "I've gone a week, maybe ten days at most when I had to, but never as long as that. To put it frankly, it almost killed him again so to speak."

"How so?" The man across from him grew in his interest of the topic.

William went on to thoroughly relay the whole awful history of his trip to London to find Doctor Clarke, his many delays along the way, including Sebastian's family, and the state in which he found Nathanael when he had returned. Not to mention the details regarding poor Elsie's death, and how it had affected them both.

"So, let me see if I understand this properly. He chose not to feed for almost the entire time that you were gone."

"Not a drop beyond our reserves and that, according to his journal, ran out a week after I left. Emile, I fully realize that this is not practical to ask this of you, but I can only manage discreetly the dietary needs of two vampires. I don't think I can arrange for three without drawing suspicion."

"You can rest your mind on that detail at least for I have already made plans to hunt... um, elsewhere for the time being." He paused while searching for the right words. "...far away from any of you. Should I need to find nourishment, it will never be traced back to anything you have established here."

"I am obliged." William breathed a sigh of relief. "If I am able to find another solution you might accept, I will let you know."

"William, I did not come here to be a burden on the two of you. Quite the opposite, in fact," Emile admitted honestly in a different tone altogether that William had never heard before from the man.

So much so, that it was his turn to look utterly perplexed. "Why are you here anyways, Emile? Did someone finally call your bluff?"

"No, I decided to finally fold, actually." Emile looked away from his friend and towards the floor at his feet.

"Hmm..." William nodded in understanding. "When I did not see you the next morning at Moretti's I was sure you had decided to live your life without regard to anyone else in it. Though to tell you the truth, I wasn't the only one who wished you had at least bidden us a final farewell. But then again, I suppose I understand a little why you did not."

"Would it have mattered?" Emile asked without daring to look up at the man, feeling a little more than guilty for neglecting to grant him the proper consideration before.

"I cannot speak for the others, but for myself, I have <u>truly</u> missed your company." William pursed his lips just once. "But you should also know that I wouldn't have stopped you, Emile."

"I know it." Emile nodded, then rose from his chair and began walking around the small shop anxiously, examining the various bottles and potions as if trying to delay the revelation of his true intentions. "As for why I am here, would it be too hard for you to believe that I am on a... a holiday of sorts?" He tried the first of his feeble excuses that he had contrived during his lengthy journey on the man.

"Highly doubtful." William smirked and shook his head back and forth, obviously not impressed.

"Research, maybe?" The second fell out equally flat at his feet.

"Definitely <u>not</u> truthful." William almost laughed at the mere suggestion.

"Searching for... companionship then?" Emile selected a reason a little closer to the actual truth.

"Getting warmer, Emile." William placed his hands upon the table and drummed his fingers there. "Look, I can tell you are stalling for some reason. Out with it already, or am I meant to play this game with you all night?"

As if debating inwardly for several long moments, his friend remained behind the counter and leaned back onto his palms behind him before he finally made a decision and blurted out the real reason in a great puff of expelled air like a child who had finally been cornered into telling the absolute truth. "Personal redemption, I suppose."

"Seriously? You? I am sorry, but that is not the Emile Deschamps I have come to know so fondly." William nearly burst out laughing at the revelation but seeing the serious look on the Frenchman's face, he held it back as best as he could with a very controlled smile.

"Hmm," Emile smiled and shook his head three times. "You'd be correct as always to say so. But I am trying something new for a change. Perhaps a bit of... oh I don't know... genuine honesty maybe."

"You?" William drew back once more, utterly stunned but also intrigued by the positive change in his friend. "I am not sure if that makes me feel better or worse."

"It's the same poison either way, I suppose." Emile looked almost bored now that he had finally admitted his insecurities. "Though between you and me, I am not sure what exactly I am even looking for in all of this? Maybe a new direction of some kind? Or a greater purpose? Perhaps even something along the lines of Nathanael possibly."

"What... a girl?" William offered flippantly, teasing him, for he knew the man never lacked for charm no matter what environment he was currently in.

Emile drew in a deep breath and held it before exhaling it out slowly once again. "Actually, no."

"Oh?" William's curiosity increased even more.

"I have one of those already... two in fact, though thankfully, only one is romantically inclined."

"Then where is she? Do we get to meet her?" William exclaimed excitedly. "I've simply got to meet the woman who can put up with the great Emile Bastien Deschamps."

"Honestly, William," Emile smiled ruefully but did not refute his accusations. "I really have made a terrible impression on you, haven't I?"

"You are all original, my friend, but I wouldn't have you any other way." William tilted his head to the side, then smiled back.

"Just so," Emile agreed with a wink. "But Miss Emma Larose will be staying in Kent for the time being. She..." He paused again and considered just how much information he was comfortable sharing, knowing that William was now the closest thing he had as a friend. "She has a position as a downstairs maid at an estate there for the present."

"Interesting. Well, I am sure you will tell me more about her in time. I need details, man, but for now, let us first decide what you will be doing tomorrow."

"Tomorrow?"

"You did say you wanted to try something new, correct? Well, how about doing what the rest of the people in the world do?" William folded his hands in front of him and took control of the conversation.

"And just what is it people like you do?"

"We work, Emile. Good old-fashioned, sweat-building, body-aching work, though I think in your case, it may take less work than the rest of us to get you to that point."

"We don't sweat, William. Not from that anyways." Emile rolled his eyes at the ludicrous reference.

"I know, though it <u>has</u> happened to me a few times when I have been under a tremendous physical stress," William countered. "Like a defense mechanism of some sorts, I think."

"Precisely, which I doubt anything you might prescribe will bring out that kind of a response, so what kind of job would you suggest?" Emile scoffed in mock offense.

"Well..." William thought for a long moment, considering more than a few adequate possibilities before suggesting. "It would be nice for someone to run the apothecary for me when I am out visiting my patients. I have been trying to do both, but I certainly cannot be in two places at once, and Nathanael is usually over at the chapel for the better part of the day, or at least he used to be. I am not sure what he will do now. As you might have noticed, he can be a little bit lost at times."

"I see." Emile nodded. "But I think I can manage that."

"And there is one more thing you can do. Something that would probably help Nathanael heal, as well," William added apprehensively.

Emile leaned down on one of his elbows, his fingers propping up the base of his chin before motioning with his other hand for William to continue. "And...?"

"Elsie's family has really been struggling since she passed away. She played a big role in helping her mother make baked goods for sale at the market, but with all the sickness and tending to the little ones, they have not had much to sell." William paused and pursed his lips before daring to ask such a large request of his friend. "How are you at baking bread?"

"How are you at playing whist?" Emile countered sarcastically back without missing a beat.

"Touché." William stood up from his chair, suddenly tired from the day's events. "But believe it or not, I am actually fairly good at it. I just don't enjoy playing it."

"You continue to surprise me, Doctor." Emile flashed him a genuine look of admiration.

"I'm glad to know it. Still, Elsie's mother or Nathanael can teach you what you need to know, and it will do you both good to be out helping others instead of letting Nathanael sulk up in his room. *D'accord*?" William offered him an outstretched hand with the familiar greeting the two of them had once shared upon the *Endeavour*.

"Agreed." Emile took it and smiled in remembrance. "Though thankfully this new opportunity of yours does not involve water of any kind."

"Or a storm threatening to sink us at any moment." The corners of William's mouth turned upwards before the two men laughed lightly at the distant memory.

With night quickly approaching, they started ascending the stairs one after the other, making various small talk about their time together on the ship. "But William, may I ask only one more thing, if you will?" Emile added.

"Name it," William agreed instantly near the top of the landing.

"Let us not take any more sea voyages together any time soon. I haven't fully recovered from the last one yet."

"Me neither," William replied over his shoulder.

They both laughed together quietly this time and retired to their room for the night. William would have to give the man his bed for the present but compared to the last time the two of them were together on the beach, sleeping on the floor would be absolute Heaven.

Chapter Twenty-Eight

May 1st, 1793

"That will be two shillings, *s'il vous plaît*." Emile placed the small envelope on the counter in front of his very first customer of the day, a rather old looking woman who could barely walk, much less count out the change that was required.

Never one to wait for anything, much less on paying customers, Emile tapped his foot silently, trying to contain his impatience as she took one thing after another out of her small purse and placed them ever so slowly but judiciously onto the counter in front of him.

"I'm sorry to be such a bother, young man." She fingered the bottom of the bag carefully. "But I know there is another shilling in here somewhere."

Emile's eyes widened as he plastered on the best smile he could manage under the circumstances, but he still waited several more seconds for her to search before offering. "Would you like me to help you?"

"Oh, that would be so nice." She smiled gratefully and handed the small purse over to him. "And from such a handsome young man, too."

Smiling dutifully, he pulled the material as much as he could this way and that to view the entire contents of the bag as instructed. The purse was indeed empty, as he had already suspected.

"I'll tell you what? Why don't you just go ahead and take this powder for now and you can settle up with Doctor Wells later? How does that sound?" He tried his best to be as empathetic as possible given her current situation for he knew William had told him at breakfast that it was imperative that she receive this medication today, even if that meant taking it to her himself.

"Well, I don't know." The older woman appeared quite nervous. "It doesn't seem right not to pay what is due, him being a doctor and all. I wouldn't want him to go hungry."

Emile rolled his eyes at the absolute irony of her statement before helping the woman return all the items into her bag and handing the envelope back to her from across the counter. "Then why don't we make a trade of sorts."

"A trade?" She looked up at him sideways, suddenly hopeful. "You could do that?"

"Why yes. Doctor Wells often accepts other forms of compensation when the need arises. Surely there must be something that would be of fair value that you might be willing to part with," Emile reasoned with her cautiously. "Something simple perhaps."

The woman nodded her head many times, deep in thought, before offering what appeared to her to be a comparable trade. "Come to think of it, I could send him over a dozen of my best eggs. Do you think that will suffice?"

"Most definitely." Emile smiled warmly and handed her the envelope, seizing upon any opportunity to be done with such an already tiresome client. "That will work nicely. I'll send Mr. Beckett over to pick them up tomorrow, if that is most convenient."

"Oh, the preacher!" Her entire face lit up with delight at the mere mention of his name. "That would be so nice. He always has the best things to say when he comes, he does." She began her shuffling walk to the door before calling back her thanks to the man at the counter and shutting it quietly behind her.

"Give me strength…" Emile threw his head upwards and sighed, letting all his frustration out at once. He had spent nearly six hours behind this counter already today, and all he could show for it was a lousy dozen eggs and a shilling. "My father would be proud of me indeed." He flipped the shilling once in the air before dropping it into the drawer intended for petty cash. Frowning, he shut it once more just as the door across the room from him opened and closed, instantly attracting his undivided attention. "Welcome… oh, you're back." Emile tried to hide his sudden excitement at being rescued from his boredom, but William had already seen it.

"I just passed Mrs. Harris out front. Did she get the envelope I left for her this morning?" William asked pleasantly. The look on his face and casual demeanor demonstrated that he was obviously having a far more agreeable day than his new clerk, or so it would seem.

"Yes, you just missed her actually." Emile looked down at the counter and noticed the envelope he had selected for her was still waiting there. "Um, I could have sworn I handed her this envelope directly, William." Emile held up the small white packet and waved it in the air. "Yet here it is just the same."

"Really? She had an ivory one in her hand when she left." William took the offered packet and left quickly out the door to exchange the medicines before the woman would travel much farther on her way.

"Excellent," Emile muttered as he rolled his eyes and picked up the broom to sweep... again. "My only customer and I just poisoned the old woman."

It wasn't long before William returned in short order with the ivory envelope and handed it back to Emile without any chastisement for the error whatsoever. "You will probably be needing this back."

"My sincerest apologies, William. I most certainly handed her the correct one, but after returning all the contents of her life back into that small bag of hers they must have gotten mixed up." Emile tried to deflect the blame in the matter.

"Relax." William waved his hand dismissively. "It's your first day, Emile. If you only knew how many mistakes I made during my first year alone as an understudy for my father, you would be shocked."

"So, what did I give her anyways?" Emile opened the packet William had handed him and peered inside as if doing so would reveal his answer.

"Well, this one was meant for a different client in the next village over. But be careful not to breathe any of it in. It is arsenic."

"And what pray tell does that treat?" Emile asked curiously.

"Primarily syphilis, so I am most certain Mrs. Harris would have no need of such a medication at her age." William chuckled.

Knowing precisely what that particular ailment was, Emile stiffened and placed the envelope behind the counter more carefully than he had placed anything before in his life. "I should hope not."

William laughed again and hung up his medical satchel on the peg by the door. "It's not going to bite you, Emile."

"Still..." Emile dusted off his hands in front of him to rid him of any possible contamination anyways before smoothing out his precisely ironed apron. "What did she require then?

"Oh, just some willow bark powder for a headache. She has some bad ones from time to time. Though at her age there is not much else I can give her other than that to remedy it." William picked the clock off the wall and wound it like he did every day about that time.

"There are stronger medications, I am assuming?" Emile watched him curiously for several minutes, studying his repetitive habit while waiting for his answer.

"A friend of my father's prefers cocaine in some of his more painful cases, but in that instance the remedy can be much worse than the ailment."

"I see." Emile pursed his lips slightly. "Obviously there is much I do not know about the world of medicine."

"Same here as it changes almost daily." William hung the clock back up on the wall and turned around before inquiring. "Did Nathanael return yet?"

Emile shrugged and pointed to the stairs. "He came home shortly after ten this morning. I thought he was practicing one of his sermons by all the talking up there, but now I am not so sure. He has been saying something about love for the better part of half an hour. Love this... love that... It hasn't made much sense from down here. Is he always like this?"

"No..." William's brow furrowed. "I'd best go check on him." He climbed up the stairs quickly but paused in hesitation before opening the door a crack when he heard Nathanael speaking like Emile had described.

"Love is patient, love is kind. It does not envy, it does not boast, it is not proud. It does not dishonor others, it is not self-seeking, it is not easily angered, it keeps no record of wrongs. It does not delight in evil. It rejoices in the truth. It protects, it trusts, it hopes, it perseveres. In short, it never ever fails.

Has not God shown us plainly the depth of His love over and over again throughout the ages, starting at the very beginning when He made man in His own image? He loved Adam as His creation and when He saw that he was incomplete, He made for him a helpmeet. We all know her as Eve. Yet His love did not stop there either.

Time and time again He has displayed that love to us, has He not? And yet, what does He now request of His children here? Matthew clearly directs that we should love the Lord, our God with all our heart and with all our soul and with all our minds. Is that truly too much to ask? I think not."

The talking ceased for several long moments as delayed footsteps paced the floor of the room before they were replaced with several audible sobs thereafter, each more difficult to hear than the next.

Imagining all sorts of things from the opposite side of the door, William's heart began to ache even more for his struggling friend. Then, deciding he had heard enough, he lifted one hand and knocked just twice on the wooden door between them to announce his presence. "May I come in?"

"Most certainly, William," Nathanael replied, but William waited a tad bit longer to give him a few moments to collect himself before opening the door fully.

"Seems like you have a very good sermon for Sunday by the sound of it." William sat on the edge of his bed and folded his hands, trying to be encouraging.

"It is getting there, yes." Nathanael busied himself in tidying up his loose notes and written verses that were littered across the center table before placing them carefully within the folds of his journal once more. "I am not sure if this is the one our Lord will be asking me to preach just yet, but it doesn't hurt to be prepared just the same."

"That makes sense." William folded his arms behind his head and leaned back onto his bed to relax. "Did I bother you leaving as early as I did this morning?"

"Oh, no." Nathanael waved at him indifferently. "I don't think I was asleep when you got up anyways."

"Hmmm." William looked at the ceiling and sighed. "I wonder why that is...."

With a frustrated groan, Nathanael sat down finally onto his own bed and looked at the door to the other room. "Probably for the same reason why the two of you think I need a babysitter," he grumbled darkly for just a few nights after Emile's unexpected arrival, William had asked if he could move his bed into the room with Nathanael and borrowed another bed from the Dobson family for Emile. He had explained to Nathanael that he was simply trying to allow Emile some space to adjust, to which Nathanael had readily accepted the awkward excuse, but deep down, both men knew the real reason for the change.

"What?" William stared back at him, feigning confusion. "Have you not heard Emile snore? Hungry animals are quieter than that man."

"I can't say that I have noticed. Sorry, I didn't mean to accuse falsely." Nathanael looked as if he had aged almost ten years just by the expression on his face today as a greyish form of gauntness had begun to form beneath his eyes, much like the way it had been when William found him a month ago. If Nathanael had been one of William's patients, William would have recommended fresh air, sunshine and some more fruits and vegetables to restore his normal balance, but none of those would help him in in this form.

As such, William ignored the apology altogether, grateful once again that his friend had relinquished so easily and continued on in his mocking of their new guest. "Now if you can think of a medical treatment for him that wouldn't kill him outright before I do, I am open to any suggestions on the matter." William chuckled at the fleetingly morbid thought of suffocating the man in his sleep with his goose down pillow to quiet him.

Nathanael smiled, too, and attempted to laugh, but not much of his mouth moved except for the corners. "Maybe it is time I considered some of that medicine myself," he admitted timidly.

Relieved that Nathanael was at least talking about his struggles, William closed his eyes and thought very carefully about how to proceed with the man. Overall, the most troubling part of Nathanael's recovery so far was the fact that his friend appeared not to be sleeping anymore in the slightest. In fact, on the nights he had attempted to do so at William's urging, he had only found himself waking up in a cold sweat shortly thereafter. Either that or pacing the floor in the apothecary below for hours on end to ease his sleep deprived symptoms.

"What do you think is keeping you awake, Nathanael?" William asked his friend thoughtfully instead of his usual manner of symptom-driven diagnosing.

Nathanael hesitated, clearly unwilling to delve into the subject any deeper. "I am afraid to say it for fear that you will think I have finally gone mad."

"Try me." William rolled onto his side to face him and propped his head up with his hand. "You never know. You might surprise me."

Nathanael sighed, then started once or twice to tell him but could not manage to say anything at all.

"Nathanael, what is it that you are afraid to tell me?" William encouraged him further. "I promise, whatever it is, we will find a way through it. I meant what I said back on the island. You are not alone in this."

Nathanael nodded solemnly but still looked just as conflicted as he was before. "And I told you then that I never was alone, but now, I think I might prefer a night of solitude."

William's eyebrows lifted in response. "Do you want me to sleep downstairs? It's not ideal, but I wouldn't mind if it will help."

"No. I don't mean solitude from you." Nathanael licked his chapped lips and began to speak very clearly and slowly as if measuring each of his words out with the others. "Every time I close my eyes, whether I am awake or I am sleeping, I see her, William. She is alive and well and doing all the things that I loved so much about her."

"Who? Elsie?" William asked carefully.

Nathanael nodded and closed his eyes for just a moment before abruptly opening them back up quickly, slightly startled.

"How can that be bad, Nathanael? I would think that having her close in thought would be a comfort to you, like a brief reminder that she is always with you in some way."

"You would think…" He trailed off. "But when I see her, it's like I'm not really dreaming at all. It feels more like she is actually there standing in front of me in real life. Truthfully, she is as present as I can see you lying over there." He closed his eyes and continued to speak as if he were vividly describing everything behind his lids. "I can smell the scent of her hair, and almost touch the very softness of her cheek, William. It's so real, in fact, that I often cannot tell when the dream has actually ended or if she has never left me in death at all." He stood up and walked over to the window before opening it to let in the warm breeze and clear away the staleness of the air around them. Like lifting up the opening of a dam, it rushed in happily, pushing his light brown hair back from his face to reveal to the world the dark circles under each of his eyes. "Are you certain they buried her?"

"Quite sure. We went to her grave together, remember?" William raised his eyebrows at the man across from him, judging whether his memory of recent events was still lucid.

"I remember," Nathanael said without any hint of emotion as he continued to stare out the window. "It's just so vivid that it makes me wonder, that's all."

"I understand." William pursed his lips at the troubling revelation, then sat up and took off his coat and vest before neatly folding them upon the bed. "Well, I think I have a much better remedy than medicine in this case. Something we both need from time to time, especially on days like today."

"What is that?" Nathanael looked back at him, but the question did not seem to have been intended for William at all. Rather, it was almost as if he were momentarily answering someone else in the room entirely.

"Nathanael?" William watched him for a few minutes more, studying the way his eyes traced the room behind him and felt a shiver run up his spine. "I think we have had enough confession for the present." William shrugged off the eerie feeling that was washing over him and sprang into action. "Come with me downstairs."

"Where are we going?" Nathanael glanced back at him, suddenly confused as if he had missed part of the conversation entirely.

"Just trust me and come." William grabbed the linen towel from off the peg behind the door and went back down the main stairs before proclaiming to Emile. "I hope you don't mind, but we are closing up shop for the rest of the day!"

"Fantastic! But why?" Emile stopped in his hopeless attempt to sweep the sand away from the front doorway.

"We, my friend," William looked over his shoulder towards the stairs behind him to make sure that Nathanael had followed him. "Are all going swimming."

"Swimming?" Emile appeared positively shocked now. "In May?"

"That's right... in May." William went over to the closet by the counter and retrieved several more linen towels before turning back to his friends who still stood utterly dumbfounded where they remained.

Undeterred by their lack of enthusiasm, William commanded them both firmly into action as he held open the front door and waited until they complied, "Now, come on you two. Let's get a move on."

Emile shook his head in definite displeasure but dutifully hung up his apron and unbuttoned his formal outer coat to hang it up beside it. "Do we even have a choice?"

"Nope," William replied with a shake of his head and kept his eyes turned downward while he waited patiently.

Nathanael did not bother to comment at all but simply followed behind the others as if he were sleepwalking, which in a way, perhaps he was for he did not seem wholly interactive with anyone these days, much less his two roommates.

"I am assuming you know how to swim, given your prowess on the ship, Emile," William said confidently, leading the way to the local pond behind the livery across town.

"Just because one knows <u>how</u> to do a thing, does not mean one enjoys it," Emile stated proudly but found himself liking the balmy weather of their excursion just the same. After all, he had been cooped up all day in that stuffy shop and the fresh air seemed to be the perfect remedy for his building anxiety.

"Cheer up, both of you. It will be fun. You'll see." William tried to be overly energetic for the three of them to entice the others to join him in his positive attitude on the subject. "You've been over to Miller's Pond before, haven't you, Nathanael?"

Nathanael only nodded silently, his feet continuing to move automatically as he walked beside them as the last time he had ventured near this particular body of water was the day that Elsie and he had held their picnic.

"Hello?" William tapped the man on his shoulder lightly. "Are you still with us?

"Of course." Nathanael nodded his head again quietly, but just kept walking, content to dwell upon reliving his memories once more.

Equally concerned, Emile raised his eyebrows at William and took the man's other flank to make sure he did not stray too far from the path as they passed by the Summerfield's home along the way. "I see that Mrs. Summerfield has finally put Simon and Levi to work cleaning out those pans." Emile nodded at the boys gathered in the yard, a pile of blackened bread pans next to each.

"It's about high time she did. She has enough to do already," Nathanael agreed and lifted his hand slightly to wave at the red-haired boys who were hard at work scrubbing while their father was off in the distance helping to tow the wagon into the barn.

"Where ya headed, Preacher?" The younger of the freckled-faced brothers called after them.

"Swimming, I believe, Levi," he replied politely as if instantly awakening from his reverie. "Know any good spots down by the pond?"

The boys both shook their heads in unison before Simon suddenly spoke up, "Pa says that pond's mostly good for fishing, but I suppose you could swim there just as well. Frightful full of bullfrogs at the present though."

"Huh, on that point, I can wholeheartedly concur." Nathanael chuckled lightly at the memory. "But I don't recommend catching them like I did."

"Sounds disgusting." Emile wrinkled his nose at the very idea, most definitely not interested in the least in that kind of activity, however it was done.

"Well, you might have to show me where to fish someday," William invited them openly and continued down the path without pausing further to chat. "How's next Saturday sound?" He called over his shoulder behind him.

"Sounds about near perfect. Thank you most kindly, sir." The older boy nodded and began to discuss excitedly with his brother all the places they would take him to fish.

"You might regret that decision next week." Nathanael warned him as they came to a stop in front of the large pond with tall, green grasses lining the edges. "I've never seen either of those boys fish a day in my life. So, I'm not sure they would be qualified to teach you much of anything on the subject to be successful."

"It's no matter. I've gone fishing with my grandfather hundreds of times. I think I know the gist of things." William sat down and took off both of his boots before throwing them casually by the large oak beside him.

"Then why, pray tell, did you ask them to show you?" Emile shook his head in obvious perturbance.

For a moment, William stopped unbuttoning his outer shirt, then and looked over at the two men who seemed completely ill at ease for such an activity. "Because my grandfather also told me that men just need to know that you are interested in them." William looked away once more and continued undressing.

"I think he is talking about us now, Emile," Nathanael said quietly to Emile, then looked down to play with the soft earth at his feet with the front toe of his boot.

"I don't particularly care." Emile raised one eyebrow up and scoffed back at the young doctor, "I am <u>not</u> swimming, today or any day. Just being here without my suitcoat is indecent enough in my opinion."

"Suit yourself, but you will miss out on a tolerable good time, I can assure you of that." William slid out of his outer pants and laid them next to his heavier shirt before plunging headfirst into the rippling water in only his white undershirt and inner breeches.

"He is trying awfully hard, isn't he?" Nathanael sighed as he watched William surface and splash water playfully towards the embankment where they were standing.

"It would appear so." Emile narrowed his eyes slightly at his friend's immature actions but did not remove a single article of clothing. "Are <u>you</u> going to swim? It looks awfully cold." His body reflexively shivered in remembrance of his earlier encounter in the cave.

"I don't see why not. I haven't felt anything for weeks, cold or otherwise," he said despondently and removed his outer clothing one piece at a time before jumping into the water with an audacious splash.

"Children..." Emile muttered and walked a few steps closer to the pond to look at a flower he had just noticed near the water's edge—something he might be able to press and send to Emma later perhaps. Yet, it was at that very moment that he realized his most horrible miscalculation, or at least where his footing was concerned, for as his left boot pressed down firmly onto the soaked soil near the edge of the tall grass, his right foot took the bold opportunity to slide quickly to the other side, sufficiently throwing him off balance entirely.

"Argh! No!" Emile cried out, still struggling to remain upright, but as he tried to compensate for the unexpected motion and swing hard to his left and upwards his feet went entirely out from underneath him instead, dropping him squarely onto the muddy shore in a horrible sploosh. "Fantastic." He frowned as he picked up one mud-caked hand after another and tried to shake off the gooey muck.

"No sense putting it off now, Emile. You might as well jump in clothes and all if you want that sludge to come off," William taunted as he moved his arms back and forth to stay afloat. "That's good, old, English black mud and it sticks to your clothing forever unless you wash it properly."

Emile ignored him completely and tried to stand once more but only managed to slip and fall again twice. "*C'est fini! Je déteste être mouillé,*" he spat out angrily at the slime at his feet, suddenly feeling very hot and agitated with the whole situation.

355

"What was that?" William asked.

"I hate being wet!" Emile growled back. "It is like standing in the rain like a dog!"

William and Nathanael both turned to look at each other and laughed raucously together at his analogy before Nathanael added teasingly to William, "He kind of looks like a wet dog right now?"

"He certainly sounds like one." William mockingly showed Emile a copy of his face.

Emile laughed, too, at the revelation of what he must obviously look like. "C'est la vie... such is life." He gave in, crawling back to higher ground and managing to remove, with much effort, both of his tall boots before diving athletically into the water, fully attired. "It truly is freezing still!" Emile complained at last when he resurfaced.

"It puts a whole new definition to washing your clothes though, does it not?" Nathanael stated as he floated on his back while looking up at the thickly clouded sky.

"Indeed," Emile agreed, though he most definitely did not prefer this way of cleaning whatsoever.

For the greater part of the lazy afternoon, the men all swam and laughed together under a sunless sky while talking of nothing important at all for several hours as they thoroughly enjoyed themselves for one brief moment in time. Yet when the afternoon had passed, and the cows had started making their way in from the fields to be milked, the three men decided it was finally time to end their frivolity and return to their world of duty once more.

Completely at ease now in their semi-dry clothes and uplifted spirits, they walked back to their home laughing at shared stories and experiences and spoke of little else but the weather and the beautiful countryside all around them. For just one afternoon, it was nice to have forgotten all the drama of who they truly were and how complicated their lives could be.

And in the end, both Emile and Nathanael were forced to admit for many days to come, that as it turned out, William had been right after all. Today was a good day for a swim, and despite it being May, it felt nice to remember once more how great it could be to just be alive.

Chapter Thirty

May 24th, 1793

"The effects of the transfusion lasted almost twelve hours this time." Sebastian relayed the good news to Señor Moretti when he returned from working down at the docks. "Enough to make it almost all the way back home without the need to wear that dreadful cloak in the afternoon sun."

"That is excellent news, my friend!" Señor Moretti replied enthusiastically. "Almost a full four hours more than the last time we tried, and with only a fraction of the amount of blood required, too. That is true progress and something to celebrate!"

"I'll admit. I was highly skeptical at first." The light in Sebastian's eyes had joyfully returned, clearly inspired now by the success of the day. "But I think this may be proof of a real breakthrough."

"I'm sure you were, but I had faith." Señor Moretti picked up a few of the books he was studying while Sebastian was away and set them once again upon the bookshelves.

"So, how exactly does it all work again?" Sebastian studied his mentor from across the room.

"Well, for the most part, I've built upon the principles established by Denyshas in his study of blood transfusions." Señor Moretti placed another log upon the fire in the great hearth, then turned around to continue the conversation while rubbing the excess dust from off his hands.

"Alright..." Sebastian accepted easily the information given him, cast him a troubling glance. "Wait, I'm not sure I follow."

"Let me see if I can explain it more simply." Señor Moretti drummed his fingers upon the mantle of the fireplace for a moment. "We have learned that a human may receive blood from another human, and on many occasions this mixing of the two blood forms allows that human to regain their necessary nutrients, much in the same way our own systems regenerate slightly when we partake in human blood. Only for us, we do so orally, and not intravenously."

"So, by us injecting this human blood into our veins directly, we are sort of replacing the bad blood that is already currently in our systems, right?" Sebastian rubbed his stubbled chin and stared deep into the fire beside him with intense concentration.

"Precisely!" Señor Moretti exclaimed excitedly. "When a vampire is bitten, his blood begins to change in every way possible. But as we have seen with yourself and many of the others I have met, that change does not complete itself for several days. It is only then, when this process is finished, that the blood of a vampire can no longer regenerate itself and is, in itself, dead. Yet in all other regards it is still moving freely within the veins like the way in which a fountain of water functions—always flowing but never regenerating new water of its own accord. So, in essence; by exchanging our blood for new blood, we are only delaying temporarily the ill effects of the bad blood."

"Then, why does the new blood not last longer than it does?" Sebastian took a seat in his favorite chair next to the fire and tried to comprehend the entirety of everything he was being told.

"That is an excellent question, and one I am still studying, but suffice it to say, it appears by our recent experiments that if someone were to replace a certain amount of this blood in their system to counteract their vampiristic malignancies, then the effects of that blood transference, would be different as well. I expect the end result would all simply depend on the quantity used and how many times it was used, much like a solute and compound solution. Or, hypothetically speaking, the more concentration of good blood over the bad, the longer the effect should last."

It was then, in the midst of all the complicated jargon being shared, that a sudden realization struck Sebastian fully as if he had been cruelly slapped back from unconsciousness. "Then why can't we merely exchange out all our blood. Would that not change a man back into what he was before—back into being a human that is?"

"One would assume so as a logical assumption, but sadly, through my other experiments I have not found that to be the case. Simply put, our vampire blood acts less like normal blood that heals and sustains a human body and more like a parasitic disease that is bent on destroying anything it encounters." He paced about the room with his hands clasped firmly behind his back. "Extracting the blood found within our veins alone would never be enough to cure us, as no matter how much of it you might choose to remove, there would still be small vestiges remaining. Think of it like a single droplet of color on an otherwise purely white paper. Adding a little water to it causes that droplet of paint, though diluted, to spread out until the greater majority of the paper is no longer white. Or to give a very practical example from the kitchen, a little leaven raises a whole loaf of bread, does it not?"

"And drinking enough blood beyond what would normally sustain us does not change a vampire back either," Sebastian added sullenly.

"Correct. That singular system of digestion functions entirely different from that of the circulatory, for no blood is ever exchanged for another in that process. As such, it is only natural that no transformation would take place. It is rather... um... processed for lack of a better description into a nutrient for the vampire, much like food is for a human."

"I see." Sebastian sighed, feeling slightly defeated once again for he had secretly hoped that his success today would have been the answer he had dreamt of for months.

Lifting his head in response, Señor Moretti couldn't help but notice the change in his countenance and moved to prevent the downward spiral he was certain would follow. "But why oh, why must you always look so glum when you should be rejoicing, Man! All of this is revolutionary! With what we have just discovered, we could very well be on the brink of changing everything for our kind, given the right treatment and resources. Why, to even erase an hour of our desires is a clear triumph, let alone removing eleven of those hours like you experienced today. Is that not reason enough to cause joy?"

"I suppose, but I fear that to get enough blood to make a long-term difference it might just require the life of an innocent person to do so." Sebastian shook his head in final resolution. "And I am not certain my happiness alone is worth such a price."

"Nor would I ever ask it." Señor Moretti placed one hand on his shoulder. "The transfusion lasted much longer this time, and definitely longer than the time before that. Perhaps, you are, in essence, building up some form of immunity each time you try it. If that is so, maybe we are managing to trick the body, if for only a moment or as needed. Be patient, Sebastian, there is still time to discover many things."

"Actually, there is not." Disheartened once again, Sebastian handed the man the most recent letter he had received from the lawyer in the America's. Per his description, the sale of the home and property had been finalized, and everything was finally prepared for his purposes. It would remain so until he arrived but knowing that his goal had finally been achieved, brought with it not the happiness he had half-expected, but a deep feeling of longing that had clung to every one of his steps since he had read it this morning.

"So, does this mean that you have finally chosen to be with your family, after all?" Señor Moretti asked cautiously.

"I had hoped so." Sebastian pursed his lips and exhaled quickly, allowing some of the dull ache to slip away from him in the process like pieces of his inner soul slowly seeping out of him a little at a time. "That was actually why I have been pushing myself to interact with Thomas so much of late. And honestly, things have been going very well, but I think it might be best for now if my family were to go on without me for the time being. I will simply have to make up some excuse as to why I cannot come and hope to join them in the future, whenever that may be."

"But that is quite obviously not what you desire, is it?" Señor Moretti leaned his head to view the man's face completely and scrutinized him further. Despite what he wanted; he knew the hardest part of his relationship with the man had finally arrived. For months he had respectfully kept his distance on the topic, praying that Sebastian would eventually come to the right decision on his own and prevent him from having to say anything at all, but it appeared his discomfort would not be spared.

Moreover, he was also aware that William had made several attempts to persuade him on the subject, as well, but to no avail. He knew, along with Señor Moretti, that if the man's family were to go on ahead of him to Philadelphia, their friend would probably never leave the island again.

"Hmpf... what I want is immaterial, sir." Sebastian folded the letter and placed it neatly into his vest pocket once more alongside the newest letter from William. "I gave up my dreams the day I found out I was a vampire."

Señor Moretti's heart literally hurt to watch his friend struggle so. He knew from experience that it was the same pain he had felt the day he realized that everyone he had ever known was no longer living. The day from his far distant past where he forced himself to consider the answer to his own question that he had so often offered to others. Only at that time, his answer was much more apathetic in its reasoning than it might be today. "I can only speculate an empathy with your situation as I myself have never been married, Sebastian. Nor do I have any offspring to speak of besides the adoption of my ward, Hannah. Certainly, I would think that you do not need me to convince you that you have indeed made strides towards asserting control, if that is what you are worrying about. If not, then what is it precisely that holds you back from returning to the America's with your family?"

Sebastian shook his head and grimaced. "Life is never about what you want once you become a husband or a father. On the day that I married Charlotte, my vow before God and man was to love, protect and care for all of her needs, no matter what may occur in my own life. Then, when our first child arrived, I thought there was nothing I would ever do that was more important than being that child's father." Sebastian wiped a stray tear from the corner of his eye and rubbed his hands anxiously.

Seeing the obvious distress on Sebastian's face, Señor Moretti took a seat in the large chair directly across from him and folded his hands. "Well, then if the true reason is merely monetary provision, you can most certainly do all of that from afar, but that's not it either, is it?"

"No." Sebastian tried to steady the quiver in his voice, but it still came out strained like a man on the verge of tears. "All I have ever wanted to do... all I have always focused every ounce of my energy into, is the desire to give my family the life that I never had. A life with a father and a mother. A life where people cared about: your present, your past, and your future. A home where no one took you for granted or cast you aside just because of where you came from or who your parents might be. My entire purpose in life has always been to provide for them a place where they could always belong... a place to be truly loved."

"Hmm..." Señor Moretti smiled empathetically. "Are you speaking like a philosopher tonight, or did you not have those things yourself?"

"Ha!" Sebastian chuckled as he rubbed at a line of soot on the back of his hand and shook his head. "I certainly never had any of this, that's for sure." He waved his hand dismissively towards the highly decorated room all around him. "To most people from my world, I am living like royalty here. Though please do not misunderstand me, I am very grateful for everything you have given me to be sure."

"What did you have?"

"As far back as I can remember, I never really had a home to speak of, but I was certainly one of the lucky ones. You see, in my village we had a monk who looked after those of us who had no parents, no prospects, no power to do anything beyond being dependent on another's generosity. It was he that helped me when my parents died. I was but four then, and truthfully, I don't remember much about either my father or my mother or the life we had before to miss it. I only have glimpses really, but not a solid memory to hold onto."

"Do you know at least what your father did for a living before he passed?" Señor Moretti leaned back in his chair and studied him intently, thoroughly invested in his story tonight.

Sebastian raised his eyebrows and shook his head slightly. "Probably a trade similar to mine own, I suppose. My first master told me that he was quite a talented sword maker in his time, but all I know is that whatever talent he had, it was never bequeathed upon me before his passing. Yet, I was given one of his swords several years into my first apprenticeship, however. It was a miraculous chance encounter to be sure, but an old friend of my father came into the shop one day and gave it to me freely out of respect for my father. It is a stunning piece of craftsmanship that now hangs above my mantle back at home, but the knowledge to create another just like it came much later, and by another master."

"So, was it your first master who raised you and taught you your trade then?" He added curiously.

"Yes, and yet no. He taught me how to smith, that much is true, but in regard to anything else, I was most definitely left to fend for myself. To the world, I was simply one of the lost ones, from a family that few knew or even cared of their existence. And like other orphans before me, I was given only a rudimentary education to speak of. However, there was one thing I did have, a person that cared enough about me to provide an opportunity. That monk, as poor as he was, paid for my initial apprenticeship, but even in that blessing beyond blessings I was still alone in many ways for the master's family did not wish to be associated with a foreigner's child.

Oh, they accepted my sponsor's money right enough and the free labor that came along with it. After all, I was young and could handle the larger bulk of the menial tasks needing to be done but offering me any kind of love in return was not part of the contract. So, I slept in a cold barn in the winter, using the sheep around me for warmth, and sweated in a dusty hayloft in the summer. I ate whatever scraps were allotted to the servants most days, but I was never part of anyone's family, much less loved." He ran his fingers through his longer curls to pull back the loosened strands behind his ear and attempted to collect himself once more as the retelling of the tale had made him suddenly more emotional.

"I'm so sorry. I had no idea your life had been so very hard." Señor Moretti placed one hand upon his knee to comfort him. "It seems that my struggles pale greatly in comparison to yours my friend."

Sebastian smiled at the action, grateful once again for all of the man's wisdom and encouragement in their many conversations. "We all have our own burdens to bear, and I am not telling you all of this to complain in any way. Frankly, I have far more to be thankful for than many others in this world." He stood up and walked over to where his favorite guitar lay, then sat down on the tall wooden stool beside it to tune it. "It's true that my life was difficult in many ways, but it also made me strong. It forced me at an early age to appreciate the importance of those things which I lacked. It is also why I cannot return to my family now, no matter how much it is killing me not to be there."

"Why? Is the risk you imagine still truly that great?"

Sebastian closed his eyes, and his cheeks flexed with the gritting of his teeth inside before he spoke again, "I simply don't know. But as God is my witness, I will not be the reason why any of that world which I have constructed for them changes. My children will not grow up without a mother because I could not control myself, nor my wife without a child because of a moment of indiscretion."

Señor Moretti had heard enough. "Oh, Sebastian. You sincerely think so little of yourself that you consider it even a possibility? Be reasonable, Man!"

"I am. Though I would like to think that I am still myself and would never even contemplate such an abhorrent action, I am also not naïve enough to ignore what I have become—a vampire. Despite how much easier it has been to control that side of me of late, how do I know for certain now which side is stronger—the man or the monster?"

"So, in answering my question, it would seem you have chosen to abandon your life with them and live instead as a martyr then." Señor Moretti nodded in understanding but not in any way towards an acceptance of Sebastian's many excuses. Rather he finally understood the man's greatest lie—even if it was the one he was telling himself alone.

"I suppose so, if you look at it that way." Sebastian shook his head dejectedly. "Or as I said before, like in every other horrible event that has befallen me throughout my entire life, someone else has already made this decision for me."

"No." His mentor refused staunchly, rebuffing him yet again, only this time more firmly. "That is not how martyrdom works, Sebastian."

"What?" It was Sebastian's turn to look confounded.

"A martyr chooses his fate, Sebastian, and he does so for the greater good with no thought to his own life or safety. And though yes, you are admitting that in some regard, you are doing it for reasons far less noble and worthy than you portray."

"I'm sorry, but I cannot think of a more noble reason than not killing my family," Sebastian defended but refused to move an inch in his position.

"Correct, but that is not the true reason why you are not returning home, is it? Consider it honestly, sir. Deep down, what is the only thing keeping you here?"

Sebastian thought for a long while before exhaling out a drawn-out sigh and closing his eyes as he realized his mentor was completely right. "Fear."

"Yes. And fear is the most formidable enemy of all—much more powerful than any vampire could ever be." Señor Moretti stood and walked over to the other side of the room, as well, hoping that in doing so he would lessen the great distance between them, both physically and mentally.

"Then I suppose there really is no hope for me, is there?" Sebastian's face fell once more.

"Far from it!" Señor Moretti practically hit his fist upon the top of the piano beside him with his passionate remark. The jolt of its echo surprised Sebastian and himself for it had not been what he had intended whatsoever. "I'm sorry, please forgive my exuberance," he apologized sincerely, then pleaded heavily with him further, hoping to reach him with every ounce of his motivational power. "Sebastian, you must find the courage within yourself to do as I have, and as William and Nathanael are still struggling to do each and every day. Life is not easy for them either. You have read their letters. Do they not speak of the very same things you are fighting against? Yet you alone must decide if you, too, can face those fears one by one and determine once and for all who, or rather what, controls Sebastian Fabbri's future. Despite your unfortunate past, you must make the decision not to be a victim of your circumstances any longer. Or have you finally chosen to give up altogether?"

"Now who has become the philosopher?" Sebastian raised his eyebrows, the corner of his mouth turning upwards at the edges into a slight grin.

"I guess I have a bit, haven't I?" Señor Moretti admitted sheepishly as he eyed the man hoping he had not pushed him too far. "I can get very emotional about these things, I know."

A moment of contemplative silence followed between them before he began again, only this time in a tone Sebastian was more accustomed to hearing. "Look, I am not saying that I have not also strained under the weight of many similar thoughts as yourself. Yet perhaps the reason why I can give you a small morsel of assurance tonight is because I have had many centuries of painful perspective to allow a clearer picture on these topics."

"Perhaps." Sebastian played a few chords on the guitar aimlessly, then wrinkled his nose. "I'm sorry. I know you love your piano, but I still prefer my guitar over that clanging instrument any day."

Señor Moretti smiled back at him genuinely. "And I enjoy your playing, as well. Your company has been one of the greatest blessings of my very long life."

"I would also agree wholeheartedly." Sebastian returned the gesture in shared understanding. "Well, not to make you think that I am trying to change the subject, but I <u>have</u> received another letter from William just today." Sebastian pulled the ivory-colored correspondence from his pocket and held it aloft in front of him. "Would you care for me to read it tonight, or wait for breakfast tomorrow? Either way, I can weed out all the more tiresome parts so as not to burden you unnecessarily."

"Tonight, of course." Señor Moretti walked over and took a seat on the other side of the room. "Come join me by the fire. The night grows colder, and it is always warmer over here."

Sebastian nodded and moved to sit down in the large chair opposite him. "As you know, the majority of his letters usually only relay bits and pieces of information about his many patients, but sometimes there are a few other pieces of news you always find amusing. My favorite thus far was his very vivid description of his first time being called by a midwife. I've never heard of anyone so stunned as he was."

"Really? Why was that?" Señor Moretti inquired casually.

"William thought he was being asked to deliver a baby, but what they had really needed him to do was help deliver a pair of twin calves." Sebastian laughed. "The man was arm deep inside a cow's insides and covered in muck and blood by the end of the ordeal, but thankfully, from what his letter said, they all survived—including William."

"A veterinarian and a doctor it would appear." His mentor lifted his head in humor.

"Yes, but I don't think William ever intends a repeat event." Sebastian chuckled lightly at his friend's expense. "I'll begin reading and you can tell me to pause as necessary." He picked up the letter and moved it into the light to see it better.

"Most certainly, and please feel free to omit those few portions you must keep to yourself, as always." Señor Moretti motioned for him to begin reading as if he had not just uttered the most shocking of phrases imaginable.

"I don't hide anything from you, do I?" Sebastian grinned for he truly was enjoying the relationship growing between them. In many ways, Señor Moretti may have been his benefactor financially, but with each passing day, he was also quickly becoming one of his closest friends, if not more of a father figure than he was ready to admit. Or at least, certainly as close to one as he had ever experienced before.

"You are an open book, my friend, but you are welcome to try." Señor Moretti closed his eyes contentedly.

Sebastian only smirked at the open challenge, opened the letter and began reading it aloud.

Dear Sebastian,

I hope this letter finds both you and Señor Moretti well. Have you finally adjusted fully to life on the island? How are Charlotte and the boys? Will they be leaving for the Americas soon? Some part of me misses the chance they will have to experience life there, but the other half of me is grateful to remain here in England on solid land. I do envy now those people who can withstand such voyages with little to no effect from the waves, but as I know I should, I have accepted my deficiency as it is and must move forward despite of it.

How is my life here lately, you might ask? Well, I will not bore you with the many mundane details of life in rural Wakefield this time, but suffice it to say, I am glad that Nathanael chose this place in the world to settle down. For the most part, it is not a very big town compared to the one in which I grew up, but I am finding that I much prefer the slower pace of life here in the more pastoral part of the country over the busyness of city life. Thankfully, our time is not set in this area by a great clock that rules over the very minutes of our day, but rather, life moves in the more rhythmic flow of nature's breathing. It is partly why I feel so at peace here, and that is a true blessing.

I even think you would like it here, given the chance to visit, which I very much hope you will one day. Though unsurprisingly, our lives do begin quite early each day, which is still a marvel to me why we are not more tired. On any given morning, we are normally up with the milking of the cows and the day ends fairly early with that very same milking of the cows once more. Have I mentioned that there are cows here, my friend? Well, there are a lot of them, herds upon herds, but I do not mind them in the least just as long as I am viewing them and not aiding them. To tell you the truth, they are actually quite fascinating creatures to study when my time has allowed. Now that I think on it more tonight, it is quite possible that this daily cycle of constancy has been what has calmed and directed me, no matter what the weather or conditions.

But enough of that nonsense. You will be glad to know that Nathanael is doing much better physically and barring any new desires on his part towards starvation, I am certain that he will make a full recovery in that regard. However, I cannot attest to his current mental state for that most certainly has taken quite a turn in the most troubling of directions. So much so that I have taken to sleeping in the same room as him due to his reoccurring night terrors that appear to be strengthening in their intensity instead of my desired abatement.

The subject of these dreams, as you can no doubt imagine, is the death of his beloved, Elsie. It is my understanding that their official engagement was to be announced on the very day after he had left the family meal. According to Nathanael, there was a small mishap in the kitchen during the preparation, and not trusting his increasing nutritional desires, he not only fled to his sanctuary at my shop but also boarded all the doors and windows to safeguard himself against taking any possible action. Sadly, he did not see the young lady again in this lifetime.

It was in this state of delirium between life and death that I discovered him upon my arrival, the details to which I have already previously relayed, as well as the facts concerning her thereafter demise by the influenza. Yet what I have not disclosed to you or anyone else besides one other man is the fact that Nathanael has entered a slightly catatonic state at times even during the daylight hours, or at least I can only attribute it to that as I have no other evidence to explain otherwise.

What does all that mean? Simply put, Nathanael has disclosed freely to me that he believes he is seeing Elsie in his dreams, his very vivid dreams I might add. She speaks to him and even plays her piano forte at times. In this he is both comforted and tormented by her presence as you might expect. He even refers to her as his angel when he is awake, though admittedly, it is usually said very quietly under his breath, and usually when no one else is currently in the same room.

On the surface this all seems innocent enough for a man who is grieving someone he loved but given his attachment to the poor girl and his already sensitive nature regarding his immortal state, I fear the direction these dreams might take him. I also worry about the day I may come home and find him either utterly out of his mind or unable to be the man we all know and love if they do not cease and soon.

And ... there is another rather important piece of information that I feel I must divulge, or perhaps I should have stated so in the beginning and not at the end of this rather lengthy correspondence. Do you remember a certain self-important Frenchman? Of course you do. Well, he has since chosen to re-join our happy company here in Wakefield and despite my initial reservations about his intentions, he has become quite a useful asset to our little group.

I would not go so far as to say that he has made a complete transformation from the man we all know and love. That would be impossible for any man, much less Emile. But I am sure you will discover, as I am certain we shall meet again, that he is at the very least, a markedly, changed man.

I will write more on that subject later but wanted to get this note off on the evening post. Please do ask Señor Moretti about his thoughts on the matter of Nathanael. I welcome his advice and possible remedies. I would petition my father's opinion, as well, but I do not think he would be able to recommend anything more than what I have already done. Especially so, given the special parameters of this particular patient. I know Nathanael would simply ask for your prayers, and so on his behalf, I will do the same.

Your devoted friend,
William

P.S. Emile says to tell Señor Moretti that he was right. It was said a bit begrudgingly as he walked by and saw me writing this to you, but since he made the deliberate effort to pass on his regards, I am writing them here. I hope it makes more sense to our benefactor than it does to me.

Sebastian handed the letter over to Señor Moretti for his further perusal. "Emile in England? I wonder what made him leave France."

"Gone are the days of the Sun King and the beautiful gardens at Versailles, dear Sebastian. Now is the time of revolutions and Assemblies. I'm afraid."

The two men nodded.

"Do you know how to help Nathanael?" Sebastian asked, cautiously hopeful.

"Possibly." Señor Moretti tapped his fingers upon his lips thoughtfully then spoke, "If Nathanael has indeed had a form of psychotic break, it will take much more attention than dear William can afford to give him. But I will speak to my friend that is over his bishops. Perhaps, they can start by directing Nathanael towards a period of respite. Many scholars believe that a good relaxation of the mind is the best medicine of all, that or a necessary change of scenery to avoid all stressors that might trigger the very same episodes Nathanael is experiencing."

"Do you think he will ever recover fully?" Sebastian leaned in with his forearms resting comfortably on top of his knees.

"With time, perhaps. Given the right care and direction. The most important thing now is coming to terms with his grief, and not letting it control him. It is all about perspective, remember?" Señor Moretti handed the letter back to him. "But it <u>was</u> nice of Emile to send his salutations."

"I'll try to keep that in mind." Sebastian put it back in its envelope and excused himself to retire for the night.

Chapter Twenty-Nine

May 10th, 1793

My Emma,

You will see by his letter that I am still living with my friends here in Wakefield. Though admittedly, I am not sure that I am helping them at all by staying here, or if I am being a bigger nuisance than I was to you back in Paris. In fact, just today I burnt four loaves of bread that I had spent quite literally the whole morning making. As you can imagine, it was a disaster of epic proportions. And when I say epic, I mean that nothing in all the world could have saved those four briquettes from the fire, as carefully as they had been crafted.

The perfectly risen circle breads even had a few decorative additions to the top which would have made them quite delightful to behold had they survived the fires of hell. Instead, not even the Summerfield's dogs would touch them. Ah well... c'est la vie.

Who are the Summerfield's you might ask? Well, to shorten an incredibly long story, they are the family I am helping as they recover from a recent illness. Or rather it is more like a trade of services if you will. For the most part, Mrs. Summerfield, the lady of the house, teaches me how to cook and I... well, I try to make a valiant attempt at doing some of the farm chores along with the help of her nine children for I haven't the foggiest notion as to what I am doing in milking the cows and bringing in the hay for the animals either. Sadly, they'd probably all starve to death if their care was left entirely up to me alone, which thankfully for them it is not.

There were ten children in the family as of last month, all with bright red hair and freckles, ranging in ages from eighteen to a baby boy that could not be older than half a year. Sadly, however, the eldest has recently passed on from this world to the next. As you might expect, this unhappy fact has brought a great melancholy upon this household, but through it, they are teaching me daily what it means to weep with those who mourn. It turns out, I don't like weeping much. In the past, it always seemed so self-satisfying. But watching others mourn, and trying to offer them comfort in return, now that is another matter entirely.

I would ask you how things are faring with your duties, but I would not want to cause you any more unnecessary grief. Though I am equally certain you will laugh quite uncontrollably at the next thing I am about to share. Believe it or not, I am working, too. William, one of my friends here, told me that I also needed to learn an honest trade if I am to remain useful, and so when I am not baking or assaulting cows, I have been attempting to run his apothecary shop while he is seeing to his patients.

I'm not sure I am very good at that either, as you might already expect. In fact, I almost poisoned an old woman there just last week. She was well into her nineties already, but still, I do not wish to be the author of her untimely demise by my own negligence. So, perhaps being a shopkeeper is not my forte either. For now, it might be best for the population at large if I can manage to find something constructive to do that has the least potential of killing people when I am too bored to pay attention properly. I'm not saying that I am giving it up altogether mind you, but maybe it might be safer for the citizens of Wakefield if I stick to professions that do not result in me hurting anyone but myself—livestock exempted.

One never knows though what they will excel in so, we shall see if I can make it through the rest of this week without murdering half of the village either by my new baking abilities or my careless actions. Though on the plus side, I <u>am</u> getting very good at making my own butter, so at least I can claim that one redemptive skill above all the other more dramatic failures.

Yet sitting here writing this now, I do wish I could see the light in your beautiful eyes tonight, if for only a moment. You have no idea how many times this week I have turned around thinking I have heard you say my name or thought of something I wanted to tell you only to realize I could not. Your presence is everywhere here, haunting me daily by its absence. Moreover, just thinking of you again in this moment tonight, has brought tears of loneliness to my eyes as I remember fondly the softness of your cheek... the smell of the freshly crushed lavender oil in your hair... or the way you always could make me smile at my failures. There is not one single aspect about you that I would ever change.

In truth, I miss you beyond words of expression, Emma.

All my love,

He folded the letter up and placed it carefully within its outer covering next to the five or six others he had written since their separation. Each one, in and of itself, was a virtual diary of his activities and thoughts in this new life without her, though he had no intention just yet of ever mailing a single one of them—maybe one day perhaps, but not for some time, if he could stand it. He had meant what he said when he promised to give her the space that she required to sort things out and part of that vow also meant guarding her from him, as well. Or at least his every waking-minute desire to run back to her and take her into his arms forever. If he truly loved her as much as he said that he did, he needed to give her the chance to succeed in whatever endeavor she had chosen with or without him. As such, she needed to do that without his constant distractions, good or otherwise.

"Writing to that girl again, Emile?" William asked from the other side of the room, deeply engrossed in a large medical publication of some kind that had arrived from his father just that morning.

"Only just, why?" Emile looked up from his stack of letters and tried to appear less affected by what he had just written than he truly was.

"Oh, merely curious, that's all." He kept on reading without further comment on the man's unusual habit.

With a slight huff, Emile ignored the intrusion and tucked the packet of letters back under his mattress carefully. Then, as if his muscles had been tightly woven together for far too long, he stood up from his bed, stretched his arms to the ceiling, and looked out his window for several long minutes at the moonlit fields beyond before asking in an almost wistful tone, "Do you ever miss it, William?"

"Hmm? ... miss what?" William appeared entirely engrossed once more within his text but still attempted to placate him with his somewhat distracted conversation.

"The lights of the city at night. The way people are always walking to cafés and taverns no matter what time of the day it is. The sheer undercurrent hum of civilization all around you—like the city itself has its own kind of pulse beneath the surface." Emile sighed, realizing there was so much of his past life that he missed very much right now, including a very special young woman.

"Oh, that..." William flipped a page, not truly listening to his musings. "I don't suppose so, no. I rather like the quiet here." He turned yet another page. "It feels... I don't know... calming, I guess."

Emile pursed his lips and shook his head in disagreement. "I would have to protest on that point most vehemently, sir. My skin actually feels like it is crawling doing nothing like this all the time."

"Why don't you try eating something then," William mumbled and moved to study the length of another page. "That seems to help most people I am told."

Emile cast him a dark look and scoffed mentally. *Easy for him to say. He has a ready supply of what he wants while I have to...*

"I'm sorry, did you say something?" William looked up at him in confusion, finally alert to his conversation at last.

Emile was almost too stunned to answer him at all. Looking over at William, he stood pinned like a deer trying to ascertain if the man had recently discovered in that journal how to be able to read his mind.

"Truly, I'm sorry, Emile. Was there something you were saying about feeling poorly?" William gave him his full attention, feeling ashamed for ignoring his friend for so long.

Emile shook his head and waved him off. "I'm fine... truly. Go back to your book. Though I think I <u>will</u> step out for a minute to clear my head."

"That's fine," William replied, quickly distracted once more within his text. "If you see Nathanael on your way, can you tell him it's time to come home?"

"Why?" Emile wrapped his simpler overcoat around his shoulders before affixing the metal clasps in dismay at the necessary responsibility. "I'm <u>not</u> the man's father, and he is not a <u>child</u>, William. You should try not treating him so."

"I know." William finally laid the book down on the table in front of him, ready to explain his reasoning. "I understand. Really, I do, and it <u>is</u> a bother to ask it of you, but we need to at least try to keep the man focused on life right now, Emile. You can see he is still struggling, can't you?"

"I suppose so." Emile rolled his eyes though part of him did feel slightly empathetic for the man with whom he was lodging. If it had been Emma and not Nathanael's Elsie who had died, he was not sure if he would be in an even sorrier state than his friend. "I'll walk over to the church instead of to the pond and send him home directly." Emile placed his favorite hat upon his head for he never went anywhere outside without it, night or day, partly because it shaded him from a great majority of the sun's harmful rays and also because it reminded him very much of the hat he had lost just before his unfortunate voyage. The one that had regrettably, belonged to his father, God rest his soul.

"Thank you, Emile. You're a good man." William smiled at his friend as he studied him from afar. "You believe that, right?"

"So, you keep telling me." Emile tried to answer him politely, but it sounded more like a drawn-out sigh from a rebellious teen that was required to do extra chores. Lately, he had heard many such replies from the Summerfield boys around milking time and unbeknownst to him, he had started to copy some of their more, surly tones.

"Only until you believe it, friend.... only until you believe it." William went back to his reading again without adding further.

Emile only shook his head in opposition to the man's errant opinion, went down the stairs and out the front door before the young doctor could impose on him more. All he had wanted to do for hours was to get out of that stifling house and into the crisp evening air where he could think of something, anything but what he really wanted. The two things he always wanted—blood and Emma.

How did William do it every day? Pretend that it didn't bother him in the slightest if his patient was cut and needed his help? What heroic strength kept the man from feeding like every other normal vampire in his existence? Were there other vampires in their existence? Would Emma want to be a vampire to exist with him? Did Nathanael have these thoughts about his Elsie? How did Nathanael not die from his fast? Could he himself continue the fast that he had begun upon arriving in England? Would it make a difference? How can I be different? His thoughts tumbled out of him one right after the other as he made his way down the street, past the tavern, and over to the stone chapel in the distance. Yet repeatedly, one by one they always fell back to one all-encompassing topic of comfort—Emma.

Like a man being chased by his own demons, he continued on along the path, focusing on it instead of her until he happened upon a stray cat who was startled by his presence. In a streak of panic, the poor creature darted across his path and into the thicket near the garden steps—afraid he would be some animal's next meal.

"Stupid animal," Emile muttered in irritation taking the steps two at a time up to the courtyard level before opening the heavy door at the back of the church. "He is lucky I did not step on him... or eat him." The tempting thought held its place within his mind a moment longer than he would have liked. Though he had certainly been in more than a few hunger-deprived states in the past, he had never once contemplated feasting on animals, let alone one as harmless as a barn cat, but this new change in his diet was forcing him to reconsider many of his previous inhibitions—some of which he was most definitely certain he would not enjoy.

Shaking his head in disbelief at how far he was now willing to go to avoid slipping back into the man he had once been back in Paris, Emile stepped inside the building and was more than surprised to find it completely dark and silent as if no one was there at all, instead of the expected, illuminated chapel. William had seemed quite certain that Nathanael would still be here studying tonight, and from his limited experience, his friend rarely erred in his assumptions. He was uncanny like that—almost annoyingly so to a fault, but at least this quality he could deal with. Nathanael's unrelenting night terrors were another story altogether.

Since the day that he had arrived, Nathanael had passed nearly every evening awake until some odd hour of the night, either in pacing the floors or in praying. Something that appeared innocent and maybe even helpful on the surface. Yet when he did sleep, if you could even call it sleeping, he did so in such a way that left little to the imagination as to what he was dreaming about.

William had told him that this was more or less normal for someone who had gone through a traumatic experience like he did, but Emile wasn't so sure. William had not heard the conversation he had overhead Nathanael having yesterday just after lunch—a conversation that included surprisingly enough, no one but Nathanael in the room above him.

"Nathanael?" Emile took off his hat and called out in a clear voice for the man as he listened raptly to the fine acoustics the chapel afforded. *Excellent. Amazingly so.* "Are you still here?" He said once more, only this time a bit louder still, hoping beyond words that whoever Nathanael had been talking to earlier, he or she was a figment of the man's overactive imagination.

No one replied. Thankfully, there was not a single sound other than the reverberating echo of his perfectly pitched, tenor voice spoke out in the silence.

Looking from one side of the sanctuary to the other, his eyes stopped to scrutinize the smaller instrument that stood silent vigil at the front of the church and rubbed his right thumb across his lips in deliberation. The piano, as simple as it was, playfully beckoned to him to draw closer. Though why, he did not know. Without a doubt the instrument was much tinier than any of the pianos he had been accustomed to playing in the past, but still... his mind drifted off his newest distraction in the chapel and back to his last day with Emma at the docks, the softness of her cheek when he held her, the lilting composition of her voice as she bid him farewell, the sound of her heart beating when she kissed him...

"Enough!" Emile's intensely vibrant command echoed back to him across the rafters, scattering away a few errant birds that had chosen unwisely to nest there within. Determined to put a stop to this mental torture at last, he took stride after deliberate stride towards the piano as he made his way resolutely across the neatly laid, brown flagstone floor to the front of the church.

Yet upon reaching the silent siren, he hesitantly paused as he gingerly pressed just one of the keys and then another as if to timidly test its accurate tuning.

"Absolutely perfect," Emile whispered almost reverently and took his seat upon the bench, feeling in control for the first time in days and yet also uncharacteristically self-conscious all at the same time.

"Let's see what you are made of, shall we?" He asked the instrument politely before closing his eyes and beginning energetically with the first full-shifting chords of Toccata and Fugue in D Minor by Johann Sebastian Bach—a German composer, but one of his utmost favorites to play any time he was given the opportunity.

Like releasing the storm of emotions within him at long last, he leaned this way and that through the melodic strains that then punctuated like hail upon the keys of the staccato notes. With little else holding him back, he played on as if rising to the crest of a great ocean wave before crashing back down again upon a wasteland shore in measure after satisfying measure. The fantastical score, as beautifully written as it was, tore at his very soul and exposed him nakedly—flaws and all, just like it always had.

Then, as the music's echoes continued to fill the farthest recesses of the chapel beyond, a silent figure entered from behind the platform and watched Emile's every movement from the shadows. Just like everything else in the room, the man did not dare utter a sound to disrupt the intensity of the music or the weight of the energy before him but instead slunk slowly into the large chair by the pulpit and merely watched it all unfold; a voiceless participant to the raging sea next to him.

Without remorse, the composition itself dramatically surged upwards past him through a series of overlapping strains, dragging Emile along with it, as it finally climbed to the peak of its greatest passion and finality, begging its player to pour the remainder of his anxiety out onto the keys with such voraciousness that Emile feared the instrument might buckle beneath him, yet it did not. The smooth keys held onto him in the fight against the elements al as much as he clung to them.

And then, with a lingering chord that almost made Nathanael cry, the piece ended. In sheer distress from the ordeal it had just witnessed, the instrument fell silent once more as if catching its breath at last from near drowning.

The battle was finally over. In the ensuing silence that followed thereafter, nothing whatsoever remained of the torment and the ocean that had been so vividly portrayed but the ringing vibrations that came back in soft murmurs from the lead-paned windows lining the walls.

Overwhelmed beyond measure, Nathanael clapped slowly, looking more physically and emotionally shocked by Emile's performance than pleased.

"I'm sorry." Emile immediately stood up and apologized, feeling instantly inadequate for taking such liberties in Nathanael's obvious place of solitude. "I should have asked first."

"Oh, no." Nathanael shook his head from side to side but did so with an almost reverent admiration for the man. "An instrument in any form of the word is meant to be used, is it not?"

"I'm sorry, what?" Emile looked up at him, suddenly confused by the analogy.

"I was just listening to you play and thinking what a waste it has been to not have anyone play that instrument since Elsie died."

"I am assuming she also liked to play?" He closed the cover over the keys in front of him to protect them and laid his elbows on top of it before offering a compliment. "She must have played very well for you to have regarded her so."

"Yes," Nathanael said, though his voice had lost some of its intensity. "She played like no one I have ever heard. Not like you, of course. You are a master, but she... well, I cannot accurately describe it tonight in the proper words."

Emile nodded but did not speak.

"It was nice to hear you play though, Emile, truly." Nathanael stared at him in appreciation. "You have a real talent. You know that right?"

"My mother used to think so. Even when I was a child, I found that it was always something I could do to help me think."

"Me, too," Nathanael admitted. "The music helps me think that is. I personally cannot play more than a simple tune if required and even then, only after much practice."

"If you will excuse my directness, what did you mean by 'any instrument is meant to be used, *mon amie*?" Emile looked up at his friend with great curiosity.

"Oh, it is just something Elsie used to say to me when I was too afraid to do something. She was good about things like that—encouraging others on to greatness." He wiped a small tear from his cheek at the memory. "I remember how she would stand up as tall as she could and defiantly remind me, 'any instrument is meant to be used, dear sir.' I thought she was talking about me at the time, but now, thinking on it more, I am not so sure."

"I'm sorry. It must be the language, because I am still so ... how do you say it correctly?... totally lost?" Emile admitted honestly.

Nathanael stood up slowly and made his way over to the pianoforte before placing his hand on top of its smooth lid. "This instrument was made by a man to be used to create music, correct?"

"Yes." Emile nodded slowly.

"Now, if the purchaser does not play it, the instrument will merely become a decoration, if you will, as it cannot fulfill its true purpose otherwise. Just as you or I cannot fulfill our purpose unless we are willing and open to be used like this piano."

"<u>Who</u> is going to use <u>us</u>?" Emile's brow furrowed.

"God, another person here on Earth, really anyone we allow to do so, I suppose. The point is not <u>who</u> is using us, but rather our willingness and openness to <u>be</u> used. Our personal piano is merely a pile of rubble if we refuse to allow someone: to play our keys, to direct our steps, to display our talents to the world around us, not for ourselves, but for <u>His</u> glory."

"I see." Emile leaned around the piano's stand to see Nathanael's face more clearly in the moonlight. "And your Elsie encouraged you in this?"

"Yes." Nathanael nodded. "Many times... She was actually trying to teach me how to play, too."

"She sounds like she was a very wise young lady for someone so young."

"She was, thank you. Are you finished practicing, then? I think I am ready to lock up for the night if you are."

Emile nodded and stood up from the piano before placing his hand on top of Nathanael's for a brief moment. "We shall take your Elsie's advice, shall we not, and not let ourselves collect dust in the corners of our world out of fear of disappointing others."

Nathanael smiled. "We shall certainly try."

Emile put his father's hat on once more and motioned for Nathanael to lead the way.

In the silence of the night gathering all around them, the two men walked side by side down the center aisle towards the back before Nathanael spoke up once more. "By the way, of all the selections you could have chosen from Vivaldi to Handel, what made you pick that particular song. It sounds rather dark and foreboding, don't you think?"

"Oh, I don't know." Emile shrugged and held the door open for Nathanael before waiting for him thereafter to lock it behind them. "It sort of suits the way I feel somedays, other times not so much."

"Dramatic and forlorn?" Nathanael's eyebrows raised in great concern for his new friend.

"Alright." Emile smiled and tried to stifle a small chuckle. "I guess it does sound like that a bit, too, if one were to hear it in passing."

"A bit?" Nathanael laughed lightly, too, at the obvious understatement. "My chapel sounded like something out of a scary story, Emile."

"Okay, a lot," Emile admitted with another laugh. "But for some reason it makes me feel more focused after playing it, as if somehow the music is a kind of cathartic means to releasing a part of that drama that has been building up within me."

Nathanael nodded as they walked for several moments while deep in thought before adding, "Well, you are welcome to play it any time it suits you, if it helps."

Emile looked over at him and realized how very much he had underestimated the value of his counsel before for he was certainly more impressed now by the care displayed by the man beside him. "That is a very kind gesture, and in light of that, maybe I can offer you one in return."

"Hmm, really?" Nathanael looked back, focusing on the new understanding growing between them. "Did you have something in mind?"

"What would you say about me playing for a service or two until I can teach you how to play it properly for yourself."

"Seriously? You know how to play hymns, too?"

"No...." Emile's eyes grew wide as he looked to the heavens and laughed. "Not in the slightest, but as you say, perhaps we should learn to use our instruments together."

Nathanael nodded. "I'll try to remember that. And thank you for the kind gesture. I'll consider it."

Emile smiled and glanced over at the man to judge his reaction fully. "No, thank you."

"For what?" Nathanael asked in confusion.

"For reminding me that I still have a purpose."

Nathanael nodded again. "Good. Now, you will just have to help me find mine."

"Oh, Mr. Beckett," Emile shook his head at his friend's growing disillusionment. "I know you may not think so right now, but from what I can see, you haven't truly lost it."

"Really?" Nathanael continued walking towards their home, past the fields filled with sleeping cows. "How are you so certain?"

"Because I heard someone say once that God has a purpose for everyone, even those who have lost their way."

"Hmm... who said that?" Nathanael swiped at a small stone in front of him, sufficiently kicking it out into the field next to him.

"You did. Or rather something like that in the service after I arrived?"

Nathanael shook his head and smiled at his sudden forgetfulness. "So, I did, Emile. So, I did. Maybe I should be paying more attention to the things I am preaching."

"Maybe you should," Emile said quietly, but not in judgement in the slightest. "Maybe we all should."

Nathanael smiled warmly back at him, then opened the door politely for Emile to enter the apothecary.

Chapter Thirty-One

May 24th, 1793

F eeling exhausted in more ways than one from his day at the forge and
the rather intense revelations he had just experienced while talking with
Señor Moretti tonight, all Sebastian wanted to do now was close his eyes and
forget everything—the nails of the new shipping project yet to be completed,
his attentive actions to avoid Thomas's many catastrophes, William's unsettling
dilemma with Nathanael, the reason for Emile's presence in England, the whole
lot of it.

"When did my life become so very complicated?" Sebastian muttered while
rubbing the back of his neck as he mounted the steps to his room and closed the
heavy door behind him, eager for some peace and quiet and maybe even some
uninterrupted sleep. Though the latter he doubted very highly would ever occur
short of a miracle as he had not slept a full night completely since he had left his
home in Portsmouth back in November.

Even before his life as a vampire, he had <u>never</u> truly been able to sleep very
well without the presence of his wife next to him each night. Since the day that
he had married her, she had physically compensated for an emptiness inside of
him that he had never fully realized existed before. In short, she was his constant
comfort here on Earth against every evil that threatened to overwhelm him each
night when his melancholy thoughts overpowered his ability to sleep. Her love
alone was a silent beacon of protection in the darkness, that had been absent for
far too long. And suddenly, finding himself hundreds of miles away from her

with no hope of an imminent reunion, did little to change his inability to rest in the slightest. On the contrary, it only made it more impossible to accept.

To make matters worse, his whole being felt inexplicably frigid tonight as if his entire body was slowly shutting down one system at a time. Whether that was from the stress of his day or the fear of what was to come, he knew not. The only thing that <u>was</u> for certain was as far away from the warmth of the fire below as his room was, the stone walls of his chosen sanctuary felt as cold as he did right now as if they were encasing him in some kind of uncomfortable tomb.

Sebastian stood up and began to build a fire in the small hearth next to his desk and thought back to the time he did so for the men in the cave.

When he had awakened on the beach that dreary morning, he had not the faintest idea what had happened to him at all. In fact, the only thing that had registered in his mind when he opened his eyes was how inexplicably cold he felt and how strange it was that he was staring up at an almost grey-black sky. By all accounts, he should have still been on the Endeavor, but he was not.

In front of him, the turbulent ocean with its rich hues of blues and greys, mixed with the rough caps of white along the tops of the waves, had stretched out as far as the eye could see, repeatedly crashing upon the sand at the edge of his feet as it dragged everything within its grasp back out to sea. An artist could have almost called it poetically beautiful and picked up his brushes to create a stunning masterpiece if he had been there, but sadly, he was not. Not a single soul other than the three men that lay next to him was present and little more than a rather rough-looking rowboat littered the beach. There was not even a bit of land on the horizon beyond the vast ocean, which made Sebastian keenly certain that wherever he was, he was most definitely somewhere far away from home.

The young preacher, who looked as frail as he did young, had been lying on his side on the sand to his left, mumbling something about God through a strange sort of verbiage that Sebastian now recognized as being a verse of some kind from his treasured Bible, but for the most part he had remained as he was. Yet despite the fact that he was becoming almost alert enough for conversation, the man had barely moved an inch in almost half an hour, choosing rather to allow the rain from above to pelt him incessantly in his semi-conscious state.

Panicked now remembering the feeling of abandonment he had felt that day, Sebastian focused instead on the baser details of the experience. The fleeting memories, as painful as they were, were now as much a part of his future as they were his past.

Out of a desire to get his bearings once more, he had remembered standing up and spinning around in all directions, thinking that perhaps he had been wrong in his initial assumption and that he had been brought back to England by some horrible mistake, but soon realized it was nothing of the sort. By some strange occurrence, or by some God ordained reason, he had been deposited there, wherever there may be, and short of a miracle, he had no earthy idea how he would ever make it back home again.

It was only then that he had finally noticed the deteriorating condition of the doctor and Emile lying on the beach in a definitely sadder state than either he or Nathanael. The rain that had been steadily increasing in its ferocity since he had awakened was pouring now, thoroughly soaking every inch of him from head to boots. No doubt, the two men, who were shivering uncontrollably where they lay, were experiencing the blows even more so, and that was at least something he could remedy easily.

"Sir? Are you stable enough to help me?" He remembered calling out to Nathanael, in an attempt to solicit his help.

The look on the man's face when he turned over was priceless. In fact, Sebastian still laughed when he remembered it, even today. "Nathanael probably thought he was looking at a ghost that day... or a demon." He chuckled again and shook his head. "Well, at least he got part of it right," he mused darkly then returned to his mental story.

Thankfully, for all involved, Nathanael did recover from his shock enough to help him carry the men into the cave and for the most part, Emile, the closest within reach of his other two companions, had been completely incoherent and regrettably awkward to carry given his taller build and rather slippery attire in the rain. While William, on the other hand, was infinitely far more vocal in his delirium but was equally as confusing in his conversation.

If he had known then what he knew now, would he have still worked to help them that day? Sebastian contemplated thoughtfully as he placed the necessary smaller kindling and mid-sized logs into the fireplace and blew on the embers from the previous fire to catch them. *For William, most definitely... for Emile...* He stopped and thought about Nathanael's struggles and what William had said about Emile's possible transformation and narrowed his eyes. "I highly doubt that man has changed that much," Sebastian grumbled sarcastically and held his hands closer to the growing flames to try to warm them even slightly.

Sadly, not much changed. As bright as the flames were becoming, he still felt absolutely nothing. Not even the slightest bit of residual heat reached its way beneath the layers of his clothing to his waiting skin, and that fact alone bothered him more than the mundane work he was required to complete each and every day. Still, Sebastian knew the room would be warm soon enough, and it <u>was</u>

steady work, after all. Something he should, of course, be grateful for, even if it was something he hated.

And yet what am I doing here still?

He remembered once again Señor Moretti's accusation that he had essentially abandoned his family by his decision to remain and that shamed him more than anything else his mentor could have said.

Sebastian also knew from experience that it was one thing to force himself to accept something he hated doing every day without complaint as if it were a blessing to do so. Yet, it was quite another action entirely to resign himself unconsciously to a truth that was utterly false. A truth that had essentially stolen away whatever time he had left with his family like it meant nothing to him or that it was so inconsequential in its importance to his survival in the first place.

How in the world did I not see it sooner? Sebastian looked skyward and shook his head.

Feeling isolated and more than a little annoyed with himself at his lack of observation, he made his way back over to the walnut chair by the desk and sat down. The all-too-familiar stack of paper and feather quill were exactly where he had left them yesterday as they dutifully stood ready to be his sole connection to the life he desired most of all.

Dear William,

I received your letter today. Despite the constant arrival of ship after ship this week, it took almost two weeks for yours to arrive, but I was grateful to receive it just the same. Señor Moretti sends his regards and will no doubt mail you a follow-up correspondence regarding his suggestions for Nathanael himself.

Sebastian paused and set the quill down, thinking about the many things William had shared with him recently regarding his stay with his family. The funny stories about the antics of his sons, and the extremely positive comments about the intelligence of his wife had been wonderful to relive through William's memories, but they were also equally overwhelming at the time to read. And if he were to be completely honest, he had also been extremely jealous over the love his family had so freely shared with his friend despite his gratitude for his son's restored health and William's assistance.

He would even go as far as to say that he had been angry at William for several days, but not for the reasons that anyone else might expect. His misplaced ire had been more centered on the fact that a part of him had hated that it had been William and not him helping them in the first place. Or better still, the irritating truth plagued him that they would not have needed his friend's help at all if he had returned to England like the others did last December.

After all, the young doctor did not deserve his chastising irritation whatsoever, nor would he ever reveal to him that he did. To his knowledge, William had not done a single thing wrong since he had met the man, quite the opposite in fact. But just hearing Señor Moretti say to him tonight that he himself had chosen his life here out of deference to his own fear had been enough to sufficiently slap him back into reality—a very sobering reality to be sure. And that had only made him feel worse about everything else that had transpired.

Sebastian removed his elbows from the table in front of him and ran his fingers through his hair, holding the ends of his curls along the base of his neck under his callous hands. "Enough is enough already. It's time to go home, Sebastian," Sebastian relented and picked up his quill once more, attacking the parchment with fervor like any other of his projects at the forge.

In one of your previous letters, you wrote that a man cannot live his life in isolation from the world. I know now that you were not speaking to me directly when you wrote it, but I confess that I doubted that statement many times over and even rebuffed your wisdom in the heat of the moment after reading it. In fact, I am sorry to say that I almost burned that letter outright, but rest assured, I did not. Strangely enough, it has actually become the one I have read most often on nights like tonight.

Yet upon further reflection and most recent admonition, you will be happy to hear that I have decided that it is time I started living my life again, whatever that may entail. It's true, that although I made my decision long ago to protect my family from whatever might befall them, I have just discovered today that the reason I gave to remain here was not a worthy reason after all. In staying here, I am not protecting them... I am really just protecting myself.

My fear of losing my family has become so great an idol in my life that I willingly chose to isolate myself from them entirely. Though if I were to be more truthful, I would also have to say that if I do not return home soon, I will have lost them already by my sheer absence. In essence, I will have essentially orphaned them without ever actually doing so, and that is not the kind of life that I want for my sons. I am ashamed to admit that I should have realized this sooner.

I, of all people, should have known that a child simply cannot become the man he should be without his father's physical influence, and you cannot do that in letters. Nor am I willing to forever be a victim of my circumstances. For far too many years, I have lived my life under the shadow of that lie, as well, and I for one, am tired of it. As you will no doubt agree, it is high time I stepped away from my dependence on those excuses and fears that have directed my past and command control of my life once and for all.

And so, it appears at last, that I must choose an answer to that question we were asked so many nights ago. And regrettably, as you must know, no answer is still an answer, William.

What was it that he asked us again?

No, I have never ceased to forget it. How could I?

That singular question, more than any other in my life, has been burned permanently into my memory like a brand upon a piece of leather. With every stroke of my hammer and quench of steam, I have been reminded of it again and again as its need for an answer has tormented me.

Do I want to live <u>forever</u>?

Do I <u>want</u> to live forever?

Do <u>I</u>?

Not if it means spending the rest of my days alone as I am. That will come in time, as we are both painfully aware, but how careless I have been to waste a single second of the time I have left with them. Inexcusable even.

So, I must finally decide on a different route than the one I have charted.

I must choose life, William.

I must choose my family above all else.

No longer satisfied to be a prisoner of my fate,

Sebastian

P.S. I realize after reading this that you might mistakenly conclude that I have been completely ignoring your counsel for the past five months and that your letters and advice were not welcomed. But let me reassure you that this errant assumption is farthest from the case. Your friendship and continued wisdom on my behalf has been essential to my recent revelation and I count you now as one of my closest companions. Thank you for being so patient with this stubborn man.

~   ~   ~   ~   ~

The next day Sebastian made his way down into the village after sunup and waited his turn in line at the harbormaster's office. The wait to see the ticket master was already at least ten men long, with women and children waiting outside under the shade of the covered porch. No matter the time of day, it never ceased to amaze him how incredibly busy this port was given the remoteness of the island on which he lived.

Half an hour passed, and a few people shifted forward in line in front of him. Now bored and entirely eager to exit and begin his work farther up the hill, he tried to occupy himself by counting the nails in the wooden floorboards that spread out all around them—186. *Huh, I wonder why so many?*

Finally, when he feared he might have to return later that day, it was his turn at the window.

"Ah, Sebastian!" The clerk behind the small counter smiled happily to see a familiar face. "How is Hannah?"

"She is doing tolerably well, thank you. I'm sure she passes on her good wishes to you this morning, Thomas. They have you doing a bit of everything down here at the port today, don't they?"

"I try to make myself useful where I can. Every bit helps when you are saving up for something special, right?" The young man grinned from ear to ear.

"Right." He continued to make small talk with the clerk. "Are you planning a visit soon?"

"This Friday night, as always. But how can I be of service to you today? Surely you aren't planning on leaving us?" Thomas asked respectfully, remembering the warning he had been given this morning to officiate his duties with precision and decorum.

"Actually, how would I go about purchasing tickets for a berth out of Portsmouth?" Sebastian tightened his lips to contain the nervous energy flowing over him at the mere mention of the upcoming trip.

"Well, in most cases you'd have to buy them in Portsmouth directly from the company itself, but I could send a message over to the harbormaster and see if he could arrange the purchase for me," Thomas replied eagerly.

"Would that cause you much difficulty?"

"Not particularly." The man shuffled the stack of thick cards in front of him. "Though it might take a bit more time. Can you afford to wait? I know you have many things that you have to do this week, as always."

"I can wait," Sebastian said politely.

"How many tickets will you be needing?" Thomas took out a small sheet of parchment and began scribbling some notes.

"Two adults and two children."

"Are they under the age of 12?" He scribbled some more.

"Yes, for both boys."

"That is lucky, as most ships do not charge for children if there is an adult travelling with them. As if you would send a child on a ship alone." The young man laughed at the absurdity. "And the destination?" He continued his copious notes for the Portsmouth manager.

"Philadelphia."

The clerk's eyes widened instantly at the news as he whistled. "All the way to the Americas will cost you almost 5 pounds sterling, Sebastian. Can you afford it?"

"I've got a little money saved up. When will I know the date of departure so I can tell my family to pick up the tickets in port?"

"I'll send the request over directly. I should think we will hear back within a fortnight. Can you manage at least half of the payment, now?"

"I can pay it all, actually." Sebastian retrieved the money from out of his leather pouch and carefully counted each coin out to the man behind the counter.

"Always a pleasure, Sebastian. I will let you know any information as soon as I have it." Thomas placed the coins into the waiting till and slid the note into the side pile for the next correspondence.

"I am obliged to you." Sebastian shook the man's hand and turned to leave before returning back to the window. "Oh, one more thing, where is the new ship we are building heading when she is completed?"

"Why? Are you thinking about joining her on her maiden voyage, Mr. Fabbri?" Thomas tried not to look as hurt as he felt at his mentor's unexpected trip.

"Possibly, but I haven't made any plans, as of yet. And the ship, Thomas?" He attempted to redirect the young man back to his previous question.

"Not precisely sure they have decided on an exact location as of yet, but I did hear talk that it would most definitely be heading to England to test her out first before they try a longer run." The man in front of him looked more worried by the second.

"Thomas, relax. I promise I won't leave without a proper goodbye. Besides, I still need to finish the nails to build her first." Sebastian tried to cheer the clerk up. "She can't float without them."

"Understood," he replied and tried his best to brush aside his emotion on the matter, preparing himself for the next customer. "Please say hello to Hannah for me then."

"I will," he called back as he made his way over to his shop to stoke the fire and begin his work on another order of barrel rims.

With renewed determination filling his steps, he knew that today was most definitely going to be a wonderful day.

Chapter Thirty-Two

June 6th, 1793

"That is not how you milk a cow, Mr. Emile." The young girl that could not have been much older than ten remarked from the open door of the barn, her hair tightly woven into two long braids that hung on either side of her head.

Perturbed and feeling hot in every way other than in temperature, Emile pulled harder on all the teats in front of him once more before finally throwing up his hands in defeat. "I suppose you could do better, Alice?"

The shy girl did not hesitate to respond but walked aimlessly over to the cow and leaned down in front of him to demonstrate. "You have to be gentle with her, like this." She showed him the correct method without pretense or rebuke as if she were exhibiting something that came to her naturally. Just as she had expected, under her firm but gentle touch, milk flowed freely from the cow's udder and down into the metal pail beneath it like magic.

Frustrated by the ease with which the child had accomplished something that had eluded him for almost an hour, Emile tried once more with equally dissatisfying results. "What am I doing wrong!" He fumed and tossed the linen towel he had hung over his shoulder onto the hard-packed earth at his feet in great exasperation at his ineptness to complete such an obviously simple task.

The cow in front of him mooed lowly in protest of his actions before Emile mimicked her right back with squinted eyes, daring her to continue further.

"You sure are funny when you're angry, Mr. Emile." The little girl laughed, and the sound of her giggle softened just a small bit of his lingering displeasure.

"I have been trying to milk this cow for over an hour, and I have not been able to get anything from her at all. Are you sure she has any more milk left?" Emile tried to offer a sincere smile for her sake but did not feel the least inclined to entertain her at the moment.

"Oh, I am sure." She put a piece of hay between her lips and played with it as she talked. "Just try again, only this time much nicer. Pull down on it slowly... like this." She showed him again by taking his hand in hers as she performed the necessary action. "Papa always says you can spend hours doing something the wrong way, or one minute doing it the right way."

"A wise man, your father." Emile pursed his lips and concentrated intently on copying the action as he tried it once more. To his great relief, creamy milk poured out in a torrent this time causing him to brim over in giddy excitement. "I did it!" He tossed his head backward and sighed in exultant relief. "Finally!"

The cow mooed in congratulations of his efforts, too.

"I'll thank you kindly not to laugh at me, madame," Emile spoke to the cow as he worked steadily to repeat the action and fill his pail completely.

"Do you often talk to Matilda when you milk her?" Alice asked politely with one eye shut and the other looking out through a hole in the barn's wall.

"Don't you?" Emile challenged her as if the notion was the most common in all the world.

"Nooooo, of course not." The girl giggled once again at the absurdity of such a question.

"Then who do you talk to?"

"Myself mostly." The girl turned around and walked over to the face of the cow to stroke her soft ears and nose. "Now that Elsie is gone, nobody has time to listen to me anymore."

"I see." Emile kept on milking, not wanting to upset the child any further by dwelling on such a sensitive topic as her sister's death. "Well, I probably won't be as good as your sister, but you could talk to me if you like? After all, I do have two ears to listen if you wish to use them."

"Really?" The girl stopped petting the cow, looking over at him as if she were suddenly ready to cry.

The expression alone was enough to instantly frighten him. It was one thing to comfort a child with his words when it was needed, it was quite another to console one who was weeping. "Yes, though you might have to forgive my ignorance on many subjects as I can't say that I know much more than Matilda it seems." Emile winked. "But I do believe her to be quite intelligent on most other matters."

The girl's face relaxed casually back to its more normal expression before she mumbled, "It's okay. Most people think what I have to say is dumb anyways."

"Not a cow," Emile stated plainly. "I talk to her all the time."

"What about?" The girl tilted her head in curiosity, suddenly interested.

Emile contemplated for a moment the most mundane of his conversations that she would find acceptable. "Sometimes I talk to her when I am hungry, and I can't find anything I like to eat. Or when I am lonely, and I miss my lady friend back in Kent."

"You have a girl? Oh, what is she like, *monsieur*?" The girl asked excitedly while clasping her hands together in front of her.

"Well, she has hair much like yours, but it has more blonde to it than red."

Alice smiled broadly at the comparison.

"And just as beautiful," he added with a wink.

Ducking her head sheepishly at the compliment, the young girl blushed a bright pink on her cheeks and went to hide from him on the other side of the cow. "Will she ever come to visit you here do you think?" Alice said as she re-emerged and offered a fresh handful of hay to Matilda with both of her cupped hands.

Hungry as she was since Emile's task had delayed her dinner, the cow gratefully accepted it, pulling several of long green strands from her hand as she folded them over with her long tongue.

Emile shook his head slightly in response to her question but kept on milking. "I doubt it, but I still miss her all the same."

"Will you ever marry her?"

Emile stopped milking mid-pull and contemplated the complicated question before answering her again simply, "I hope so... one day." He started milking once more before adding more confidently, "Now that you mention it, yes, I think I will, but not for quite some time, I am sure."

"What are you waiting for? Elsie waited and now she cannot marry anyone. You don't want that to happen to you, do you?" The child's simple logic stuck to him like a pin through his heart, pegging him solidly to the wooden stool and to the earth below it.

"No, no I don't," he said quietly. "But I don't even know if she will accept me. I am a bit rough around the edges, don't you agree?" He tried to be as delicate on the subject as he possibly could.

"Well, since you learned how to bake bread without burning it with mama and now you can milk a cow, I would think that given enough practice, you could learn pretty much anything if you tried hard enough, sir. Maybe even how to get her to accept you," she stated plainly as she walked back over to the barn doorway.

"You know, Alice... you are much wiser than Matilda any day," Emile complimented the girl freely, enjoying their conversation immensely.

"I know." She smiled to show a few missing front teeth. "Elsie used to say that, too, though not about Matilda."

"I know precisely what you mean." He grinned back at Alice.

The girl giggled again and played with the dirt at her feet with the toe of her shoe, seeming to be lost in thought for a brief moment. "Anyways, I gotta be getting back to help Mama with the laundry. Do you think you would mind talking again sometime?" The child asked him timidly, unsure if he was truly sincere with his previous offer.

"You know where to find me," Emile said almost despairingly as if he were the one being punished by the assignment and not the other way around.

The girl smiled. "Talking to Matilda?"

"Talking to Matilda. Now, please tell your mother I will be in with the milk directly. With how terribly long this has taken me, she has probably assumed that I most likely died out here." Emile patted the cow in front of him and moved the milk to the side to protect it from spilling.

"I will." The girl laughed and skipped quickly through the small yard and up to the house beyond.

With a sigh that carried with it the weight of the decision he had just made, Emile stood up and hung the wooden milking stool back onto the wall of the barn. "So, what do you think Matilda? Have we made a friend today?"

The cow lifted its head in approval and mooed loudly.

"I quite agree." Emile beamed with great satisfaction and lifted the pail while paying the necessary attention not to lose any of the precious cargo on his journey back to the kitchen.

Once inside, he poured half of the pail's contents into the butter churn that was waiting just outside on the front porch. The rest of it was carefully dispersed into the other two large, glazed pitchers on the mud room counter for later consumption.

"Alice said you were having some trouble getting the milk. I hope Matilda cooperated in the end. She is getting old, but we have had her for years." Mrs. Summerfield busied herself in plunging shirt after dirty shirt into the warm water before dragging them ferociously across the washboard ribbing in the yard out front. "Hate to think about when it will be time to put her down. It will be like losing one of mine own family when we do."

Emile nodded his head respectfully, though he had never once in his past considered an animal as anything more than something that he ate, much less as a pet. "I was wondering one thing though, were Alice and Elsie quite close?"

Mrs. Summerfield smiled quickly then wiped the sweat off her brow with the back of her wrist that had been accumulating there. "Thick as thieves most of the time though there was a good ten years between them almost."

"Why do you think that is, their closeness, I mean?" He took one of the finished shirts and began helping her by placing each of them on the waiting clothesline next to him.

"Oh, mostly because of all of them boys, I suppose. They liked to torment the girls something fierce. It's not their fault that the Lord gave us more of them than gals, but it has made my husband quite happy to know that he will have a ready crew to help him at the mill in his later years." She willingly handed him another piece of clothing to hang up.

"I can certainly see the wisdom in that." Emile clipped the shirt on the line and stared appreciatively at the crispness of the material and the fine stitching along all of the seams. "Did you make this?"

Mrs. Summerfield stopped washing for a minute to examine her eager helper. "You are an odd one to be sure, but yes, most people in these parts do sew their clothing if they are able. Why?"

Emile felt suddenly embarrassed by his prying questions into her personal life. "Because it is very good workmanship. Have you ever thought about selling some of your pieces to a local store, perhaps, or at the fairs nearby? I've seen items of lesser quality sell for high prices indeed, and they were nowhere near as nicely constructed as this shirt is."

"That so? ... Hmmm..." She picked up a pair of breeches and examined them before dousing them into the water and rubbing the material with lye soap upon the board. "Well, by the way my boys are going through clothing these days, I will be a pauper long before I can ever hope to be wealthy selling shirts."

Emile chuckled at the thought. "They are an energetic bunch of boys to be sure, but they are also the most kind of my acquaintance."

It was Mrs. Summerfield's turn to laugh at the understatement of his compliment. "The wildness they get one hundred percent from their father. He was always traipsing from one end of this county to the next in his youth after some kind of animal. The rest, I am not so sure."

"Well, I think the kindness is from you." Emile looked over at the house and smiled in admiration. Their home was, indeed, exceedingly busy, that much was true, but first and foremost it was one that was always filled with love. He himself could not imagine his life with one, let alone nine children running about the place, but Mrs. Summerfield handled the brood with a care he had not seen since before his own dear mother had passed several years ago.

"So, your husband likes to hunt also?" Emile raised his eyebrows, instantly intrigued at the possibility. "I didn't realize he enjoyed that kind of hobby."

"Just ask him to take you sometime. He would jump at the chance to escape that mill any day of the week."

"Regrettably, I'm afraid I lack a gun at the present," Emile said politely but added further mentally, *or probably the ability to hit anything at which I am aiming but...* He trailed off in inner humor.

"Oh, I wouldn't let that hold you back if you have a mind to go. He can simply borrow one from the neighbors," she answered encouragingly.

The corners of Emile's mouth turned upwards once again as he nodded in appreciation. "I'd like that very much. My father rather enjoyed hunting when I was younger. We did not go very often, but I do remember there were a few times that my brother and I went with him when he was hunting pheasants. Unfortunately, I don't recall being any good at it, but that never stopped him from trying to teach me, poor man."

"I wish you had said something to Gabe earlier. Come to think of it, why don't you go over to the mill to arrange a time now. He won't mind. Even as late as it is in the day, I am sure you will find him still grinding away there. He's got a big order that is supposed to be sent to the next town over this Friday if he can finish it in time, plus a bonus to boot if he isn't late, which will certainly come in handy this month."

"Thank you, I will." Emile hung the last item on his side of the line and left her to walk briskly over to the mill. For the better part of ten minutes, he strolled through the tall grasses of the field that climbed well over his waist in some places and noticed how they skirted the river in a more southerly course as they flowed past the Summerfield's barn and in the same direction as the stream.

In his trek, he thought back distractedly to his recent decision concerning Emma and what he might say to her when they finally saw each other again. It was the same conversation actually that had been replaying itself incessantly in his mind almost every night when he tried to fall asleep, minus the part where he actually built up enough courage to propose to her properly. That part would probably be created tonight and every night thereafter until it was ready to drive him mad.

So much had happened in just the short time that they had been apart that he could scarcely believe that it had been almost two months already. Time enough to create countless questions that could never be answered as he was waited on customers in the apothecary or baked in the kitchen with Mrs. Summerfield. Questions like: Was she safe with Angelique or had she accepted a position elsewhere? Did she even remain in England at all, or had she chosen to return back home to France? Better yet, would she still even want to speak to him after everything that had transpired in Paris?

His brow furrowed at the very definite possibility of her ultimate refusal and continued aimlessly onward until he finally paused in the middle of a great field, suddenly confused as to his proper bearings for though he had been in this pasture many times before, he now felt suddenly disorientated regarding which direction he should eventually choose.

Instantly alarmed at his utter carelessness, he scanned his surroundings slowly as he took in the view in all directions for some kind of clue, but nothing stood out to him in any way. Thick forests lined the edges of the river that he knew flowed down to the village to his right, and behind that was also the apothecary if he followed it far enough. So, at least in that he was not totally lost. But for acres upon acres all around him, the only thing he could see now were the endless green waves of grass blowing gently in rhythm like a rolling sea. Not a single landmark that he was accustomed to using was visible now through the tall vegetation, nor a living soul present except for the meandering cows off in the distance.

Feeling even more famished than usual by the exertion both physically and mentally, his head began throbbing for several minutes before he was able to finally calm it back down to a low hum. It had been simply ages since the last time he had fed properly and even then, the small amount of blood that he had consumed was not at all what he had become accustomed to since his transition.

William and Nathanael had made it their practice to use only what William had acquired through his research façade and treatments, but Emile had not the opportunity for such a thing, nor did he feel particularly drawn anymore to the way in which he had once feasted either, despite what he had told William otherwise.

On two occasions already, William had compelled him to drink one of his stored vials when he had almost stumbled in front of him. And although it had not been anything too dramatic by any means, William's keen eyes of observation had not missed a single detail of his battle. As a doctor or otherwise, William could plainly see that his friend was in trouble and as faithful as his character always showed, he tried to offer whatever assistance he could manage, even if it was only temporary.

Nevertheless, despite the fact that the scant nourishment had abated the worst of his symptoms momentarily, he still felt the overwhelming compulsion to abstain fully from any temptation that would bring him back to the man he was in Paris. That man, who cared very little for the well-being of others, needed to be silenced, or at least tempered if he were to be truly worthy of Emma. But as conflicted as he already was on the topic, he had no way of explaining all of that to his friend.

William had enough on his plate already in keeping everyone in this village alive, he didn't need to worry about the nutrition of another vampire. Nor did Emile wish him to do so. Besides, the stored blood just wasn't the same, anyways. In truth, it lacked energy, vitality, and warmth. Like drinking a glass of water that had been left to sit out on the counter all night, it quenched the thirst when needed but sincerely left you wanting, just like the other meals he was forced to consume to avoid detection. Each one served its purpose in keeping up the careful charade for the other humans around him, but since their digestion worked entirely different now than before, it never really satisfied him physically, nor would it sustain him indefinitely, as Nathanael had so clearly demonstrated.

Six long weeks ago, Emma had asked him in London to try living a new form of reality and for all that it was worth he was trying, truly he was, but this new kind of lifestyle only frustrated him at every turn, leaving him feeling even more debilitated in the attempt rather than strong. In fact, every single day that he put on his less formal attire and convinced himself to copy the actions of the day before, he was painfully reminded that everything in his new life brought him only struggle, not pleasure. From having to clean the dishes each time that he ate to washing his own clothes in the river each Saturday, all of it felt insanely foreign to him now and definitely almost not worth the energy he was putting into it. Not to mention the immense difficulty he was experiencing today with his newfound diet, or lack thereof. And yet, all of this couldn't be helped. Change had to begin somewhere, so it might as well begin with the most basic of his urges towards selfishness and work his way up to the other vices in time.

Was the child right? Emile thought back to his conversation with Alice earlier in the day. *Had he merely been practicing his life in all the wrong ways all these years, pretending to be trying, while all the while living beyond his means and above the expectations of others? Was the change he was seeking truly as easy as simply deciding to live his life the right way? But then again, what _was_ the right way for any of them?* He doubted even Señor Moretti knew the answer to <u>that</u> or he would not have chosen such a ridiculous question to ask them when they had first met.

"Do you want to live forever, indeed," Emile scoffed and frowned at what that decision would mean for him or more importantly how much more work still remained for him to accomplish anything of worth.

Overwhelmed by the prospect facing him yet again, Emile felt the need to sit down and rest for a minute, taking a moment to glance casually over once more across the field before his eye picked up the presence of a nearby cow grazing at the forest edge. From what he could see, it was one of the brown jerseys that was often kept in the pasture solely to fatten up for the winter slaughtering and not one Emile would be required to milk any time soon.

"And yet...I wonder..." Emile's mouth watered at the errant thought as he eyed the cow a few yards away and pursed his lips, considering the distasteful possibility before him with even greater determination. *Despite what I may want otherwise, I will have to eat something eventually or I will go mad like Nathanael and I'd rather it be the cow that suffers than one of the men down at the mill.* Emile reasoned decisively.

Blissfully ignorant of the dangers all around him, the cow only munched on the lush grass, enjoying its life out in the open field with little regard to the man in it or of the darker thoughts within his mind. The lumbering beast appeared to have a good five months more before anything untoward might occur but from the look of its bulging haunches, it was already well on its way to achieving mammoth proportions. As large as it was, it would surely bring in a high payment at the market come Christmas and that, no doubt, would be a nice bonus to the Summerfields.

Like a man who was dreading the inevitable, Emile narrowed his eyes in reluctant resignation and calmly walked over to the animal before rubbing the top of its head as Alice had done earlier, admiring the stance and posture the animal possessed.

The cow responded in kind to his gentle touch and lifted his head up to greet him as if revealing purposefully a large vein that pulsated wildly an invitation that only Emile could see.

Hesitantly checking all areas of the field to see if he was indeed most definitely alone, Emile cast a quick glance around him once more and knelt on one knee next to the animal to attempt something that felt utterly abhorrent to his very nature but also welcomed all at the same time. Then, with a speed that felt as slow to the naked eye as he felt in doing it, he took out the narrow pen knife from his pocket and nicked the cow's skin just below a secondary vein to allow the smallest amount of access—not large enough to drain the animal by cutting it outright, but enough to cause a small line of blood to trickle out from its rather tough hide.

Suddenly, intensely ravenous by the powerful aroma, he struggled to remain still as the red liquid began slowly pooling up in his hand below the cut, the warmth coating it as it called up to him like nothing he had ever experienced before. Oh, he had enjoyed many a delightful rendezvous on his journey back to France that had provided him with the freshest fulfillment he had ever experienced, but each one had also carried with them a tinge of something more. He knew now that feeling was possibly regret or guilt at the ending of a life, but as selfish as he was at the time, he had chosen to block out those emotions entirely—taking what he wanted, when he wanted it with little thought about who it was or the sadness his actions might bring about for others.

Yet, this blood was different in so many ways, too. Like any other meal he might consume down at the tavern, it had no strings of insecurity or scrutiny attached to it as it was simply there to be enjoyed. Simply put, it was food, nothing more, nothing less.

Restraining himself a moment longer to make certain he could digest it, he leaned down and smelled the blood nervously then tentatively put the red liquid up to his lips and drank... and then he drank some more, savoring the herby richness of it as it coated his parched throat. The throbbing in his head that had been present for weeks instantly ceased, being replaced instead by the delicious euphoria he had always enjoyed thereafter. Admittedly, it was not the same at all as human blood. No, it was far better in some ways, others not so much as it did also carry with it a bitter aftertaste, that was not as much unpleasant as it was unusual in the beginning.

Excited beyond expectation at this welcomed discovery and what it might mean for his future, he filled another palm and consumed it gratefully before picking up some of the mud from the ground and carefully worked to rub it into the now barely open wound to stop any residual flow. The last thing he wanted to do was injure the animal who had bestowed such a blessing on him by providing just the right amount of hope that he needed today.

"I'm sorry for the intrusion, friend." Emile stroked the animal fondly, who did not seem the least bit fazed by what had just transpired. "But you have no idea how much I needed that."

Feeling much like a cat who was ready for a pleasant afternoon nap, Emile made his way over to the river and washed the remainder of the blood off his hands before checking his attire for any other lasting evidence. "Now that wasn't so bad, was it?" Emile said more to himself than to the cow, feeling exuberantly satisfied, then laughed so loud that the cow looked back at him in confusion.

"Well, that settles it. Alice was right. Maybe I <u>have</u> gone completely insane. What do <u>you</u> say?" Emile asked the cow before he started once more to make his way through the tall grasses in the direction in which he hoped to find Mr. Summerfield.

The cow only mooed back his low and long reply as if wishing him well on his journey, madness aside.

"Most definitely, dear friend..." Emile called back to him feeling wonderfully alive at last. "Most definitely. And many thanks, once again."

He continued on through the field and over the hill to where he was certain that the mill lay just beyond, each step feeling like yet another step closer to certain victory.

Chapter Thirty-Three

June 8th, 1793

Nathanael closed his eyes once more, attempting to ignore the incessant ticking of the clock at the bottom of the stairs. For some odd reason, William liked the infernal contraption and its religious clanging every quarter of the hour, but lately it just made him more anxious. In fact, just listening to it click persistently without relent made him feel almost like it was generating some kind of horrible countdown to an event that would take place with or without his permission, exactly like the night when Elsie was injured. He had wanted to stop the gears that time, too, but thankfully for William's sake, the clock had run out of tension long before he had been motivated to smash the grating device of impending doom. Though that last description sounded a bit dramatic thinking it, even for him. Yet, all of it was the truth, however theatrical it might have been to his way of thinking at the time.

Hour after hour passed by him tonight in the deafening silence collecting all around, just like the night before, and with it the loud ringing of the chimes within announced once again that he was still awake and not sleeping like the other two men in the apothecary. The stillness of the night that used to give him the greatest sense of peace with its enveloping darkness now chafed on his nerves more than the clock itself, sending him into irritating spirals of frustration when yet another clang of the hour sounded, and he still found himself staring up at the blank ceiling above, farther away from the rest he desired than he had imagined. Lying here this way, in total aggravation, he felt more like his insides were constantly poised to spring outward beyond him in a great explosion into the room, surrounding it completely with pent-up emotions and nerves. The very same nerves he wished to be rid of once and for all if he could ever manage it.

Oh, how he wished it would be as easy as simply closing his eyes and drifting off to a peaceful slumber like it used to be. In the past, he had never even given falling asleep much thought as it was simply one of those things he quite naturally took for granted because it was something as automatic as breathing. But when that system also fails and you are left grappling with its absence, it was crippling to experience, utterly and frustratingly debilitating.

Oh, he <u>wanted</u> to sleep. He had even tried countless remedies in the hopes that something would work, but none of them had. On the contrary, every avenue he had skeptically explored had only left him feeling more hopeless and helpless than the night before. And so, as a healthier alternative to dwelling on his more negative thoughts concerning the matter, he had resorted to using the time in a more profitable way by praying. Whether in his bed or in pacing the floor below, he had tried his best to allow the other two men above the opportunity to sleep undisturbed by his whispered pleas, or at least that had been his intention in the beginning, but sadly, they could not. What he thought would be his more noble attempt at providing William some much needed peace and quiet, had only resulted in him causing the man even more concern in regard to his motives.

The doctor <u>was</u> a good friend, that he would never deny, but even though he obviously had a brotherly affection towards the man, William still had no earthly idea just how difficult his life had become since Elsie had passed. How every day and every moment brought with it the same uncertainty as the one before, despite his focus otherwise.

Troubling questions that he never once contemplated, now became his focused obsessions like tiny pebbles that entered his shoes as he walked back home from his study. And every breath he took in now held with it a poised energy that threatened to either topple him over as the air rushed into his lungs or the power to suck him deeper into a realm of apathy that he was not accustomed to as he exhaled that unwanted desire out again.

As a trained physician, William was far more familiar with the quick solutions that his university studies had prepared him for, and not the more complicated treatment of mental instability, if that was what it was called for there was no other explanation Nathanael could give for it. The realm of the mind was supposed to be <u>his</u> world as a spiritual advisor for his flock. The one instance where he was expected to excel above <u>all</u> others, and yet, just thinking about wasting another hour in pointless pursuit of something so absolutely unattainable now created more questions of its own.

If I can't find a way to fight my own demons with God's help, how can I expect others to do so? Nathanael contemplated seriously and blinked his eyes twice to see the lines in the ceiling above him more clearly, his mind drifting back once again to the letter safely stored beneath William's pillow. Earlier that week, William had placed it there after both of their mentor's letters had arrived merely days apart from each other, but despite the fact that he had chosen to openly share one of them, Nathanael could not help but wonder what the other contained.

To date, William had always been entirely honest and open about all his endeavors, but though Nathanael knew his mentors' thoughts on his condition, the oddness of William's chosen secrecy now unnerved him with the volumes that his actions spoke in doing so. Whatever the letter contained, whether good or otherwise, William either did not feel Nathanael should hear it, or he knew that the man would eventually not require it. Or at least that was what Nathanael had hoped it held. The alternative would be far less acceptable for all of them if he did not conquer this period of grief once and for all.

Which was yet another question that kept him awake tonight. *What would his friend be compelled to do if he eventually succumbed to the waking dreams which he had been experiencing for weeks?* There were asylums for people like him, but none were equipped to handle anyone of their kind specifically. And yet, even lying here contemplating this dilemma yet again for probably the third time this week, he did not feel as though he was actually losing his mind, but rather that he was simply struggling with the intense difficulty of letting Elsie go.

He supposed it might have been much easier to do, had he actually been there when she had passed, or had even been given the opportunity to place her in the grave, but to not have seen with his own eyes that moment of earthly finality rubbed against him like rough wool upon his skin. The garment of grief and longing that he was now forced to wear as every day dawned anew was a comfortable warmth as it was placed upon his shoulders once more, but an irritating sensation all at the same time.

"Clang... clang... clang... clang..." In the muffled hush, the clock on the wall below chimed four long times before its echoes ceased and retreated to the corner from whence it came, jolting Nathanael into an upright position instantly in mounting aggravation.

"You alright?" William opened his eyes and stared back at him from across the room, quickly aware of Nathanael's alert state.

"I'm sorry I woke you, William. Please, try to go back to sleep." Nathanael rubbed away the cold sweat that had collected across the back of his neck before shaking his nightshirt to unstick it from where it had gathered down its center.

"Are you sure?" William yawned then pulled the covers up closer around him.

"No, but I suppose I will fall asleep eventually." Nathanael tried to reply in a tone that sounded vaguely reassuring, but the frustration that he felt at that moment only made him sound more perturbed than anything else.

"Is there anything I can do to help?" William's voice came back barely more than a whisper as he tried not to waken their other companion across the hall.

"You could stop worrying about me all the time," Nathanael grumbled but then repented of it when he saw the hurt flash across his friend's face. "I'm sorry, William. You didn't deserve that."

"It's okay. I only wish I could help you more. I hate seeing you this way."

"I know you do, and I am grateful that you care enough to try. Just go back to bed. I promise I won't do anything drastic while you are sleeping." Nathanael laid back down and turned to face the wall, thus hoping to end the concern aimed at him from across the room.

"You better not do anything drastic at any time, Nathanael. I'm not ready to lose you, too," William warned sternly, but Nathanael knew he was not upset with him directly. He was just voicing the inner fears within his own heart.

With a sigh that spoke a language all its own, Nathanael answered, "I'm not going anywhere... remember, we cannot die no matter how much we may want to do so."

"We can, though you had better not!" William's commanding voice was now taking on a more fatherly tone in its vehemence, much like that of Sebastian or even Señor Moretti.

"William, it has been my experience, that people who talk about it, rarely do it, friend," Nathanael mumbled but remained in his position facing away from his friend and waited for the rhythmic breathing of the young doctor to return before rolling back over to face the ceiling.

Giving up his desire to do anything else but breathe at this point, he closed his eyes once more, only this time when he opened them again, he was no longer in the dark room where he had been trying to fall asleep for hours. Instead, he was in the large meadow by the pond which was now abundantly filled with thick wildflowers that had grown almost as tall as the grasses. Hints of white, orange, pink and purple dotted the thick strands of various shades of brown and green along the water's edge, stretching as far and away to the horizon before him as he could possibly see. Even the sun was brilliantly shining above which clued him in instantly that he must be dreaming for he finally felt the warmth of it as it permeated through his shirt and vest, and not the burning fire that he almost welcomed at this point.

Blissfully content to have arrived at last, he laid there in the meadow upon the quilted blanket, drinking in the wonderful sensation for he had longed for just a taste of what he was experiencing for the past seven months. Anything really would have been welcomed over the cold emptiness that now gripped him every time he closed his eyes. In truth, feeling the wind blow across his skin just enough to cool the impact of the sun's warm rays brought with it a healing energy that both revitalized and calmed him in the same action.

The grasses that swayed beside him, did so with an energy all their own, moving in time with his breathing as they brought along with them the faint rustling sound of someone who was passing through them. Someone familiar was approaching, and as they stepped closer, they did so not in a hurried or deliberate manner, but as one who was merely parting the green curtain in front of them as they passed.

Thinking that he had heard his name being called, Nathanael looked up and shaded his eyes but was still completely blinded by the rays, so he closed them once more, content to merely drink in the energy the experience provided.

"Wake up, Nathanael." The noiseless visitor knelt down and leaned over him as they placed one delicate hand against his cheek, trying to awaken him gently.

Without needing any confirmation whatsoever now as to who it was, Nathanael turned his head instinctively towards the voice and smiled sweetly. "If it's you, I'd rather not."

The wind picked up slightly and blew through his loose hair, causing him to shift ever so slightly so that there was room for Elsie to lay down next to him on the blanket, her head placed comfortably upon his chest. "Do you remember our picnic here last March?" She asked him as her fingers played with one of the buttons that ran down the center of his brown vest.

"Yes." Nathanael sighed and stroked her long red hair that had been let down in loose ringlets just like it had on the day of their outing. "How could I forget? You purposely tried to drown me because I couldn't figure out how to sit down in that boat."

"I did not!" Elsie laughed lightly at the lie. "Though now that I think on it, you probably deserved it."

Nathanael chuckled, too, and the feeling it created within him made his chest hurt to experience it. "I probably did. Though I knew from there on out not to go boating with you any day. That water was frigid, and disgusting. I never could get that black mud out of my favorite shirt after that ordeal."

"I'm so sorry, but at least it was a profitable lesson, after all." She grinned and looked up at him with such an endearing expression that it tore his heart away along with it. "Why <u>aren't</u> you sleeping, Nathanael? You know William is going to think you are crazy pretty soon, right?"

"Hmmpf… no doubt he already does," Nathanael muttered sarcastically and looked up at the clouds, ignoring her question entirely for he simply did not care what William thought in this moment of sweetness and perfection. Nor did it particularly matter how he would ever cope with the dream he was having now after he returned to his own form of reality thereafter.

"I wish you didn't have to grieve so. If you need to see me in order to heal, you know I will always be here in your dreams when you want me," Elsie promised him faithfully and watched his expression to see if he were truly listening.

"But that's just it. I will always need you," Nathanael vowed. "And not just here in my dreams."

"Yes, but as you know, need and want are two different things. What you need is sleep, but <u>that</u> is not what you want is it?" Elsie tried to reason with him carefully.

"Nobody ever asks me what I want anymore." Nathanael started to close his eyes again as his body relaxed even more within the dream but stopped himself, fearing that the moment between them would completely disappear if he did. "I suppose I am just tired of constantly feeling like I'm broken, Elsie. Or rather, I am tired of being forced to go through my life as half a man, and half a monster. Is that not reason enough to never want to never wake up again?"

"Maybe, if you choose to look at yourself in that way, but the only person who sees you as a monster is you, Nathanael." Elsie reached her hand over and took one of Nathanael's within her own and squeezed it tightly. "All I ever saw was a man who had a great capacity for love. Even if that person was undeserving of that love."

"But that's the problem, too, isn't it? I never felt like I deserved your love, Elsie." Nathanael tightened his other arm that was wrapped against her. "Maybe that is why I cannot let you go now. Why I may not ever be ready to do so. Despite what you might think, you were the <u>one</u> thing that was holding me together most days beyond God."

"But you <u>need</u> to be ready soon, my love. You have to let me go in order to live," Elsie said sadly.

"That is what everyone keeps telling me." Nathanael sighed once more and shook his head slowly. "Please, can we talk about something else… anything else really?"

"Alright," Elsie said politely. "I'd say we could talk about the weather, but you and I both know none of this is real, so why don't we talk about what you just said to William."

Nathanael almost groaned as he looked over at Elsie and watched her intently as she sat up. "You mean about doing something drastic, don't you?" He joined her and leaned onto his right arm to face her.

Elsie nodded. "You know that is never the answer, right?"

Nathanael nodded. "Of course, but I have already died once and yet here we are. Who's to say what will happen when I eventually do die. Does being a vampire mean that I will simply cease to exist entirely, or will I even have a chance at an immortal destination? Like any other good preacher, I instruct my flock of their need to repent. That there are only two choices after death—Heaven or hell. That they need to choose Christ and his sacrifice for admittance to Heaven or they will spend an eternity in hell. Yet, what am I doing here every day? Like it or not, I am living in an earthly hell. I exist. I eat. I breathe. I use up valuable resources on this planet, but for what? What purpose do I still possess in all of this that can count for anything?"

Elsie listened quietly, allowing him the chance to voice all of his many insecurities, then placed her hand over his when he had finished. "It sounds like you need me to flip you in that rowboat again."

Nathanael grimaced, his brow furrowing up in several places. "I'm being serious, Elsie."

"So am I!" Elsie smirked playfully but then turned more sincere. "And I think I know now why you aren't sleeping anymore."

"Really? Why?"

"You are afraid you won't ever see me again in the afterlife, so you are trying to make this created time with me last for as long as you can," Elsie said the very truth that had been hiding within himself for months. "Am I close?"

Nathanael looked away and over to the pond just beyond them, ignoring the words she had just spoken as if they meant nothing to him. "Do you know what I always envied about you during our time together, Miss Summerfield?"

"What?" Elsie replied quietly, not wanting to press him towards a decision one way or the other.

"How simply you always looked at life." He shook his head. "In truth, life was never as complicated <u>with</u> you as it is now without you."

"Life isn't really that hard, Nathanael. You know that. You just need to learn how to view it from the right perspective again." She tried to give him the encouragement he needed to make the right decision.

Nathanael smiled and huffed at her wisdom. "It's exhausting to view it the right way and you know it."

"It can be..." Elsie nodded but did not rebuke him. "But it can also be joyful and fulfilling again if you let it."

"Elsie Mae Summerfield," Nathanael looked over at the woman by his side who had given him just as much in life as she was now seeming to give him in death. "You were always joyful and fulfilling to me every single day that I knew you."

Elsie blushed. "You know I would have loved nothing more than to marry you and stay with you forever, right?"

Nathanael glanced down at their hands and nodded. "I do."

"Then as hard as this might be to accept right now, you need to know that we were never meant to have more than a few months of happiness."

"Meant to have? You speak as if me losing you was all part of something that was good. I'm sorry, but I cannot see anything good coming from all of this. All I see is pain and emptiness." His eyes began filling with the tears which for weeks, had not been able to be shed.

"Oh, love." Elsie took his face in both of her hands and leaned in closer. "'No good thing will He withhold from him who walks uprightly.' That was what you told me the day when we made the snowman with Michael. And 'every good gift and perfect gift comes from above and is handed down by the Father of life.' That was what you said when you proposed. You were my gift, Nathanael... my precious, considerate and loving gift. And I would not trade a minute of the time I had with you for anything in the world."

The tears fell from both of them now in the silence that followed.

"But I still don't think I can do it... I don't know how."

"Why not?"

"Because I fear that when I do, all the happiness that you gave me will vanish along with you, and all I will be left with is that same emptiness I felt back on the island. The one that was so vast that I feared it would swallow me whole if I let it." Nathanael held his breath, remembering the moment Emile had told him of his fateful transformation. '*we have all become that which is typically destroyed by most of your kind...*'

"Let it all go, Nathanael..." Elsie wiped away one of his tears with her fingers and kissed him gently where it had been on his cheek. "You will see me again, I promise you. Nothing about God's eternal plan has changed regarding that, despite what you have become. It will just take you a little longer than others to get here, that's all. Just maybe don't take as long as Enoch, alright?"

"You have no idea how much I <u>wish</u> I could believe that." He pulled her in closer and held her tightly.

"Then trust the One who walks on water, Nathanael. He will lead you out of that dark valley you are lost in if you let Him," she spoke softly the words he had already known in his heart all along. The ones he had memorized from the twenty-third Psalm long ago. The very same chapter in fact, that he had read to William when he also was on the edge of a very deep valley in the cave.

"I'll try... for you."

"No, Nathanael... do it for Him. There is so much more you are meant to do still." She pulled away and stood up. "I need to go."

Nathanael rose immediately and reached for her hand to stop her from leaving, but his hand passed right through the image of hers, solidifying the façade of this alternate reality. "No! Wait!"

"But I must." She looked back at him as she continued to walk away.

"Wait, Elsie! No!"

"Good-bye, my love! I'll see you soon." She blew him a kiss and walked into the sunbeams that blinded him once more and kept him from seeing her clearly.

"Stop!" Nathanael yelled and fought against the grasses that were now tripping his feet and causing him to fall every time he tried to walk closer. "Come back!" He shouted and tore at the weeds that held his feet within their grasp pulling him closer and closer to the darkness now enveloping him. The warmth of the dream he had been enjoying vanished just as quickly as it had appeared, leaving him physically trembling as his world around him swiftly shifted violently back into one of ice.

"Wake up, Nathanael!" William shook the man who was thoroughly drenched in sweat from his ordeal and was now thrashing within his sheets violently upon his bed.

"You might have to slap him this time," Emile advised groggily from the doorway and rubbed the sides of his face with both of his hands, not the least bit certain any of their efforts were doing any good.

"I'm <u>not</u> hitting him, Emile." William shot him a frighteningly intense glare, incredulous at the very suggestion.

"Suit yourself." Emile yawned in response but otherwise did not enter the room. "But it seems to work with everyone else I know."

"Elsie! Come back!" Nathael now sobbed, completely still oblivious to the conversations taking place around him.

"Emile, some assistance would be nice," William grunted as it was taking every muscle he possessed to hold his friend down firmly from leaping from the bed. "I don't think I have seen him this bad. Not ever."

"Fine, I'll help." Emile trudged over sleepily and took his place on the bed, allowing William the opportunity to fetch some form of a sedative.

For the most part, the laudanum William had acquired had not worked the same on Nathanael as it had on William's other patients, but it did at least make the worst of the violence abate considerably for a time. Something that had proved itself to be most useful on at least two other previous occasions.

Beyond tired at this point and having finally endured enough of whatever it was they were calling this, Emile lifted the man beside him into a sitting position and grabbed his face within both of his hands, forcing Nathanael to focus all of his attention on him alone and nothing else. "Nathanael! You <u>have</u> to wake up! Now! Elsie is dead, and you need to accept that!"

"Emile... stop." William poured some liquid onto a spoon and waited for the right moment to draw nearer and administer it. "Yelling at him isn't helpful to either of you."

"You sure?" Emile rolled his eyes darkly. "I feel much better already actually."

"No, you don't. You and I both know you will feel terrible about it later." William shook his head tiredly.

"You're probably right." Emile tilted his head, then snapped his fingers in front of Nathanael's eyes. "Nathanael?"

"What?" Nathanael's eyes suddenly opened wide in obedience and stared directly at the Frenchman who was mere inches away from his face. "Where am I?"

Emile wagged his head slightly in William's direction to indicate the fact that Nathanael was becoming less violent and therefore, no longer in need of medical intervention. The last thing they needed now was to have Nathanael think they were overstepping his ability to decide these matters for himself and thus, draw his ire for using it. "You are in Wakefield, Nathanael."

"And Elsie...?" Nathanael asked Emile seriously.

"In Heaven, as you are well aware. She died two months ago," Emile stated the fact flatly with no hint of emotion whatsoever.

"She's really gone then, isn't she?" Nathanael's whole body then began to shake in response as if a terrible tremor was beginning to overtake him.

"Yes," both William and Emile said in unison, extremely tired of reminding him of this depressing fact night after following night when he awoke.

Compassion finally overwhelming him to see Nathanael as broken as he was, Emile wrapped one arm around the trembling man and held him there as he shook and sobbed uncontrollably.

"I'd best go fix us some coffee," William suggested quietly, feeling at a loss for what else to do under the circumstances.

Emile nodded without saying a word and simply held the man stoically instead, knowing that a complete purging was probably what Nathanael needed most. After all, no one was going to be getting anymore rest tonight anyways, so he might as well make himself useful for once. William, as intelligent as he was, would have coddled the man for all of eternity if he had felt it would have been helpful in the least, but Emile knew it was time for more direct measures for all of their survival. As difficult as the situation may be, Nathanael needed to face the truth of what had happened and come to terms with her death as this disguise of living without living was growing tiresome to those around him and in reality, detrimentally fatal to his overall health.

"Nathanael, you know Elsie is never coming back, don't you?" Emile asked his friend seriously when the man had finally pulled away from him at last.

"I know," Nathanael said quietly through a long-exhaled sigh of acceptance, then stood up.

"And you know you can't keep doing this to yourself every night, too, right?" Emile stated the obvious as plainly as he had his first statement.

"I do." Nathanael walked over to the window and stared out at the approaching sunrise that was beginning to light up the room slowly.

A few moments later, William returned and inclined his head respectfully towards the apothecary below. "It's ready. Are you coming?"

"We will be down shortly." Emile stood and motioned for the doctor to go down without them. "I know it is not what you want, but some refreshment will do you good."

"Alright. I'll just be a minute. I'd like to change out of this shirt first." Nathanael hesitated and began taking off his moist garment.

After what they had just been through, Emile couldn't help but cast him an uncertain glance, debating whether or not to leave the man alone so soon after his ordeal. "Nathanael, please, don't make me..."

"Please... I'll be fine." Nathanael cut him off quickly, trying to assure him of his promise and slid out of the remainder of his loose attire and into a clean linen shirt before buttoning it up. "See. Perfectly composed now, or at least most of me is."

"Hmmm... We shall see." Shaking his head at the ridiculousness of his friend's statement, Emile left him alone at the window as he walked wearily down the stairs one after the other while giving a final warning. "Five minutes only, Nathanael, or I am coming back up there and carrying you down myself."

"Now that I would love to see." William grinned in humor at the obviously hilarious image in his head and took a sip of the steaming cup before him. "Might be something all of us would remember for years to come."

"No doubt." Emile looked less than pleased at the idea then added, "We are going to have to do something different, William," he commanded resolutely to the doctor and took his seat at the single table in the main room. "Neither of us can go on much longer like this and you know it."

"I do." William took the other mug that he had filled and placed it on the table in front of him. "Got any bright ideas?"

Emile shook his head and took a tentative sip then smiled. "Cider in June, William?"

"Yup." William picked up his mug, toasted him slightly with it and smiled right back. "At least it tastes better than what I served you back on the *Endeavour*."

"Ha! I think anything would be better than that swill." Emile took another sip. "But in June?"

"In June... though at this point I can't say that I know what day of the week it is, let alone the actual date." William shook his head in disappointment. "But I do I agree with you that I would absolutely love a cup of coffee right about now. However, as luck would have it, I am afraid we ran out of the last of it yesterday. In my sleep deprived state, I simply haven't had the cognizant ability to buy any yet."

Emile stopped for a moment to smell the rich aroma of the cinnamon and apples and breathed it in deeply to properly appreciate it. "I do have to admit this is not a wholly bad alternative under the circumstances. It just won't have anything to aid in keeping us awake all day."

"Most definitely not." William's reply was muffled as he took another sip and tilted his head back in utter exhaustion.

"Would you like me to make us some breakfast?" Nathanael descended the stairs then, neatly dressed and ready for the day that had been planned in helping at the Summerfield's kitchen.

"Breakfast?" Emile and William's eyes both lifted together in unison, though neither of them was sure they trusted the man to make them anything of edible quality this morning.

"Is it that time already?" Emile added quietly and closed his eyes for a moment to try to refocus himself for the day. Something he had made a practice of doing every morning as of late.

"We were actually just talking about grabbing a cup of coffee down at the tavern when we were all ready," William offered quickly, welcoming Emile's grateful nod from across the table.

"Why? Are we out of coffee here?" Nathanael peered into the empty canister that normally held the grounds and frowned.

"Only just," William replied slowly, his mind still half-asleep and not fully engaging in the current conversation.

"Oh, and did you move the furniture around in here yesterday?" Nathanael said distractedly as if he had just noticed many of the things around him.

William glanced over at Emile with a look that said he totally agreed with the man about a change of plans and shook his head. "Last week actually."

"Huh," Nathanael eyed the different counter position and various other misplaced items. "I'm sorry that I didn't notice it sooner. I could have helped you to..."

"Actually, you know what would really help both of us?" Emile cut him off abruptly but stopped when William tapped his foot against his under the table in gentle warning to be kind.

"I already know the answer to that one." Nathanael glanced up at the two men who looked quite obviously worse for wear. "Me sleeping at night?"

"Yes." William and Emile each focused on the preacher and nodded repeatedly.

"I'm trying, gentlemen, truly I am."

"How can we help?" William offered seriously though he had already exhausted all his efforts save one to do so. The last one would require a great deal more laudanum than they had tried previously, which made him hesitant to do so as he had no idea just how much was too much for a vampire. Or to put it more succinctly, their last resort would help them all sleep, but it also might kill Nathanael, as well, which kind of made the whole idea seem ludicrous to even consider it.

"I don't think you can." Nathanael peered out the window blankly, then sighed. "It is just something I have to battle for myself." He shook his head once and then walked resolutely across the room and grabbed his hooded cloak in resigned frustration. "I'm going over to the cemetery for a little bit, but I'll meet you at the Summerfield's in an hour, Emile."

"You promise?" Emile leaned back in his chair and called over his shoulder to the man behind him as if he needed a firm word of affirmation on the subject.

"I promise," Nathanael replied, then walked out the door before closing it quietly behind him.

"Are you worried about him doing something drastic, too?" William asked while he watched Nathanael walk down the street through the window in front of him.

"Aren't you?" Emile finished his drink and stood up to place his mug on the back counter for washing later.

"Always, but Señor Moretti said in his letter that I have to give him space to sort all of this out for himself. We cannot force him to accept her death any more than I can force you to do anything you do not wish to do."

"I might be tempted to disagree with you if I wasn't so exhausted, but still... Señor Moretti has been around a bit longer than the rest of us, so I will give him the deference this morning." Emile folded his arms across his chest and studied his friend at the table. "I guess the real question is, do you think you or I will survive this?"

William chuckled, but both of them felt the weariness it brought along with it. "If Nathanael can survive losing someone he cared about more than life itself, I think I can lose a few more nights of sleep. Can you?"

"I suppose so, but with the way that things are now, I am starting to miss the revolution..." Emile rolled his eyes but then smiled patiently. "I can manage if you can. Who's on duty tonight?"

"That would be you. I had tonight." William placed his half-finished mug on the counter and turned around to trudge back upstairs.

"Lovely."

"Do you think anyone will notice if I don't visit them until closer to lunch?" William asked quietly.

Emile huffed, "I doubt anyone will notice anything in this sleepy little town of yours, but please, by all means sleep when you can. I'll man the store down here later today."

"Alright... just wake me if something urgent runs through that door." William yawned at the top of the stairs back to the man who was ascending them towards him.

"I'll only wake you if it's an emergency or if someone is actually bleeding. A bump, bruise or headache can wait." Emile headed towards his room to get dressed.

"Thank you, Emile." William stepped through his bedroom door and tried not to sound as drained as he felt.

"I'll lock the door behind me when I go to the Summerfield's and put a sign up to reach me there if someone needs to pick anything up." Emile changed his shirt and glanced through the doorway at the doctor across the hall but did not comment further. As fatigued as he was, the man had collapsed upon his bed and from the sound of his heavy breathing was already sound asleep. "Sleep well, William."

Emile walked over and closed the door to his friend's room and quietly descended the stairs before locking the outer door firmly behind him.

Chapter Thirty-Four

June 12th, 1793

S even long weeks had passed since Emile had initially arrived in Wakefield, traded in his reputation as a French socialite and exchanged it for that of the common man. And to be honest, though it <u>had been</u> extremely difficult at first for him to let go of the familiar comfortability of all that world had provided, he had quickly discovered that after a time of adjustment, he did not miss anything about his previous lifestyle whatsoever—save Emma alone.

Gone were the nights of parties, wine and an occasional dalliance with a woman on the side. Something that many men of his acquaintance might have missed greatly if they had tried to do the same. And yet, there was also a rare blessing he had not expected that had come hand-in-hand with that change. By applying himself to his work every day, gone also were his days of constant regret and mundane boredom that often led to his self-destructive behavior. Something he was most definitely ready to rid his character of completely. In his new life in Wakefield, his days were now filled instead with long hours kneading and baking dough, milking the cows, churning that cream into butter, and then collapsing into bed each night before another day's work would begin again.

William had also been more than correct in his initial assertion that Emile had probably never worked a day in his life, but he would never have let the man have the joy of knowing it. After all, as a gentleman, he had been born for greater things than menial labor and hard work. Those were jobs specifically reserved for people beneath his status, people like those with whom he was now finding he had much more in common with than before. Yet now that he had given the opportunity a fair attempt, he had discovered something else about himself that was quite profound and equally surprising.

Despite his initial misgivings regarding his ability to succeed at <u>anything</u> he might attempt to do, he had quickly excelled in becoming an excellent baker, remarkably so according to Susan Summerfield's compliment yesterday morning. What's more, he absolutely loved doing it. Given the time and space to explore his personal creativity without the fear of failure or meeting anyone else's limiting expectations, he had wonderfully flourished under her tutelage to the point that he could see himself doing nothing else for the rest of eternity.

"But of course, *mon cherie*, did you not know that all good bakers are French?" He had jested with Mrs. Summerfield just this morning when she had doubted his decision to possibly begin a bakery of his own one day. "After all, who else could have invented the croissant? And did not French nuns only recently create the macron that is now famous across all of Europe?"

With that piece of audacious bragging, she had laughed along with him in his proud assumptions, but still found the need to lovingly correct his many, many mistakes in the kitchen daily, like using corn instead of wheat flour and allowing the bread to rise long enough to completely spill over onto the counter, not to mention the various scorched or burnt items he had created while learning how long to bake bread over her open-hearth fire. In the beginning, as in today, all of those were "happy little mistakes" as she would always lovingly call them before trying to cut off and salvage whatever she could of his failures. And in truth, her whole attitude towards life in general amidst her trials made <u>him</u> happy, too. Without comment or opinion of any kind, she had unconditionally accepted him for who he was, faults and all, and made him a better person because of it, much like his Emma had done back in Paris.

Yet for all her redeeming qualities, Mrs. Summerfield was not always the most observant of women either which served Emile's purposes excellently on multiple occasions. With the added income from their increasing sales at the market in town and in several other taverns, and markets locally, Emile had been able to purchase a few things that the family lacked without her knowledge. Things like a new broom and some much-needed fabric that had magically been discovered one week lying just inside the mudroom door as if Saint Nicholas himself had stopped by unannounced one night, while a freshly planted rose and a pitchfork had materialized in the barn and front garden on another—each a silent testimony to someone's creative generosity.

To Emile's delight, no one either here or in the village had suspected the new Frenchman in the slightest of being their loving benefactor and that suited him just fine. For the moment, he was perfectly content to play his part in the background of the play here in Wakefield, choosing rather to enjoy watching the performance of others for a change than in causing drama all his own. Besides, it was much less exhausting this way to do so and far kinder to his pocketbook overall.

As for Nathanael, life for him had continued on as it had the week before with only one exception—the tenor of his dreams, which had kept them all awake for months, had thankfully ceased in their more violent nature for a time. This fact alone should have brought with it a great relief to everyone involved as some kind of harbinger of healing, but it did not. Instead, the emotionally driven dreams that replaced the previously tormented ones were almost worse. Neither did the extra sleep they received in-between periods of comforting him through them help to bolster William or Emile's confidence as they watched their friend fade farther and farther away from them with each passing day.

On the surface, Nathanael appeared entirely normal and physically present to the world at large around him as he methodically spent his days studying his Bible at the chapel in preparation for his weekly services or in visiting members of his congregation around the village. Yet beneath the disguise that had now become a part of his normal expression, his mind was still often apathetically elsewhere, or distantly distracted by things William and Emile could not prevent him from seeing, nor could they even hope to circumvent them if they did.

This inner struggle was certainly difficult for everyone else in the village, as well, as many of those he had helped selflessly during the influenza now yearned to console him with their encouragement. Nathanael was their preacher after all and although he might have been the youngest minister they had ever encountered, his flock thought the world of him and his open transparency. In fact, not a day had gone by since his initial recovery that some man, woman or child, had not knocked on their door with something special intended for their spiritual advisor. Whether it was a small token of their affection, a note, or just a reassuring smile and embracing hug to wish him well on his day, everyone gave something of what little they had to aid in his recuperation.

Mrs. Summerfield had also made it a point to stop by on several occasions to give Nathanael a memento she had discovered in Elsie's belongings or to drop off a basket of treats she had reserved solely for them alone. Both of which were instantly treasured by everyone, no matter their dietary requirements, but not more so than the wise counsel they received from her each time before she left.

"The preacher just needs some time to sort things out, like we all do. Give him the love and space he needs, and he will heal." She had said simply without the least bit of concern as to whether or not Nathanael would ever reach such a goal, but Emile was not so certain she was correct. To begin with, she had not heard the many conversations of memories the man had spoken when he was asleep. Emile's favorites being the time when the two of them spent the day sledding down one of the hills by the pond or the one this past week where he said that it was she who had flipped over their rowboat—a fact which assured Emile more than ever that had fate not intervened, he would have liked this Elsie Summerfield very much. Nor had Mrs. Summerfield been the one each morning to see Nathanael open his eyes, looking more ragged than the day before, with yet another sliver of hope faded away from his previously bright expression.

But it was this listening to the joyous, yet albeit sad list of memories night after night and having the woeful task of constantly reminding Nathanael of the disappointing reality of her death every morning that wore Emile and William's resolve to the breaking point. Their noble intention of supporting their friend through thick and thin felt more like the systematic torture of everyone involved now than actual help for the man in the way in which it was performed. And short of a definite intervention, it was becoming painfully clear that nothing was going to change for the better if they did not also stop their constant appeasement to his desire to let him sort this out for himself.

Yet, it was another week at least before William finally summoned up the courage to attack the problem of Nathanael's nightmares head on by declaring what he felt was the most excellent of suggestions at dinner one evening. "Nathanael, my friend, I'd like to make an announcement," William said after he finished his last bite of shepherd's pie at the village tavern and set down his fork beside his finished plate.

"An announcement?" Nathanael's raised one eyebrow in responsive attention, suddenly alert to the conversation his friends had been enjoying all throughout supper. "What kind of announcement?"

"Oh, just something that I think will benefit all of us. After all of the work that we have been doing for the past several months and the stress we have been under most recently, Emile and I have decided that it is high time that we all take a much-needed holiday." William folded his napkin resolutely and set it next to his plate on the table in front of him. "Isn't that right, Emile?"

"What?" Emile almost choked on his water at the sudden inclusion in William's apparent scheme but managed to swallow it in the end.

"Are you okay?" Nathanael turned his head and looked over at Emile with great concern etched across his face.

"Ahem... quite." Emile coughed once or twice more before wiping the water away from his chin with his napkin and politely replacing it back onto his lap. "A holiday? Yes... um, I believe that is exactly what we had talked about at breakfast." He played right along with him though he had absolutely no idea what the doctor was referring to as neither he nor William had discussed anything close to this sort of thing in the past.

Certainly, William had mentioned the vague possibility of visiting his family soon, but nothing definite had been planned between either of them nor had that spoken desire included Nathanael or himself. Moreover, Emile had rather hoped that he would have been chosen to be left behind for such an adventure if it came down to it or at the very least tasked with the assignment of nannying their struggling friend should a trip back to London be absolutely necessary to undertake. Yet, from William's brief announcement just now, it was blatantly apparent that he had obviously decided otherwise.

"Really? That sounds nice, but where did you have in mind?" Nathanael seemed slightly perplexed at being left out of such an important decision, but did not complain as this wasn't the first time he had felt lost.

"Definitely not to France," Emile said ruefully under his breath as he took another sip of his water. "I've had quite my fill of that kind of adventure for a lifetime, I'm afraid."

"No, not to France." William shook his head and sighed dramatically at the man, then began to relay his plan slowly and deliberately to entice both of them further. "I thought we might all go to London for a few days so that you could finally meet my family and maybe while we are there, we could also do a little sightseeing. Then, if the weather holds, perhaps we may even venture down to Portsmouth to see Charlotte and the boys or spend a day at the ocean. What do you think?" He eyed the two men in turn for signs of their acceptance.

"I've seen the ocean already, William... four times in the last year alone, in fact. Let me assure you, it's wet," Emile mumbled his reply aimed at William in particular, while also not amused in the slightest at his disappointing suggestions. "I'd much rather stay right where I am for the present."

"Not helping, Emile," William whispered quietly out of the side of his mouth and leaned in closer to him from across the table to solicit his further assistance in convincing Nathanael.

"What I meant to say is, that would be a lovely idea, William." Emile rolled his eyes quite heavily at the exchange and unwelcome inclusion, clearly somewhat annoyed at the direction the conversation was suddenly taking.

"I suppose it would be nice to see Sebastian's wife and children if we are able. With everything that has happened since you visited them last, I was wondering if I would ever get the opportunity to meet them before they left for the Americas," Nathanael replied almost wistfully.

"Do you think you will be able to find someone to preach for you in your absence?" Emile questioned Nathanael politely, genuinely interested in the man's care and determination to serve his flock under the current circumstances.

With a sigh of frustration, William practically kicked Emile's foot out from beneath him under the table and shot him thereafter an equally frustrated look.

"*What?*" Emile motioned with his mouth and hands silently, growing more irritated by the moment at the fallacious conversation and the audacious authority being displayed by the man next to him.

"*Stop giving him excuses,*" William said silently with his mouth. His face a perfect picture of conflicted annoyance under pressure.

Nathanael, however, did not notice either the conversation between the two men or the thud from under the table at all as he was already looking down at his meal, keenly focused on not eating a single morsel of it, but rather making a practice to spread out the food to all areas on the plate in a vain attempt to make it appear as if he had. "Well... actually... to answer your question, Emile, I suppose since we are sharing our news, I have a confession to make, as well."

"Hmm." William crossed one leg over the other and leaned back in his chair, suddenly curious as to what his friend might say next for he had a general idea of at least one possibility.

"Wait, a confession? You?" Emile asked incredulously. "I doubt you have done anything so heinous as to require any of that."

"As I said before, nothing that you know of." Nathanael smirked playfully but continued on. "It seems that my leadership has heard about our little epidemic here and my subsequent...um, illness. They have even gone so far as to say that they think it would be in my best interest if I were to take a brief furlough of sorts to recover my health properly." He paused before continuing in a different tone, "I suppose to their way of thinking, it is better to let me have a few weeks of rest than to have to find a replacement for me when I become unfit to continue."

"That sounds like a logical request under the circumstances." Emile pushed his plate away and exhaled, deeply satisfied. "Will you accept their suggestion?"

"I don't know if I have a choice at this point. I hate to admit to them that I cannot do my job, but..." Nathanael placed both of his silverware on top of his plate and closed his eyes. "I am just so tired all the time that I can barely think coherently enough to form a sensible sentence, much less write a whole sermon right now."

"Probably because you are not eating or sleeping properly," Emile said matter-of-factly as he reached over and picked up Nathanael's plate before helping himself to the discarded meal. "Mrs. Summerfield's shepherd's pie is famous all over the village and probably even the county by now."

"Oh?" Nathanael seemed to perk up slightly at the news. "Is it hers?"

Emile finished the last bite on the plate satisfactorily and set it down on top of his own. "No, it was hers, and I made the crust for it."

William chuckled at the exchange, then asked again hopefully. "So... is it decided then?"

"It would be nice to take a trip back to civilization once more provided we can make an extra stop or two along the way." Emile tapped his lips with one of his long fingers, considering the possibilities before him.

"Are you thinking about finally visiting that girl you are always writing to, Emile?" William inquired, but did not divulge anything else.

"Perhaps. Though I don't know if I will allow either of you two cads to meet her." He smirked but kept the rest of his opinion to himself.

"What? Us?" William looked as if he were heartily offended momentarily but recovered just in time to tease him mercilessly. "Are you frightened that I may scoop her up and save her from the likes of you?"

"Hardly, William. I doubt Miss Larose would be interested in a life as a doctor's wife, but I'd be happy to send Miss Toussaint your way if you are interested." Emile returned to his previous state of aloofness.

"'The debutante with an attitude'? Wasn't that how you referred to her when you came?" William asked with a shake of his head. "No, thank you. I've got enough drama to deal with all on my own without adding that into the mix."

"Suit yourself." Emile inclined his head in the opposite direction. "But Miss Larose is most definitely spoken for."

"So, you say..." William prodded the man further towards a reaction but stopped when he saw the flash of darkness cover his eyes once more. "Alright, I relent... enough is enough already."

"Quite." Emile staked his territory firmly but politely, then cast a glance over at their silent companion.

As always, Nathanael appeared not to be listening to a single word that was being spoken around him, focusing instead on something just outside the tavern window along the road. Something that had drawn his attention on more than one occasion this week alone.

Noticing his silence once more, Emile and William both stared at their friend before Emile finally snapped his fingers twice in front of Nathanael's face to awaken him from his trance.

"I'm sorry. Was I doing it again?" Nathanael's face showed his true shock at being so distracted.

The two men shook their heads slightly and lied once more. Though sadly, as often as they had been doing it of late, the lie was becoming more and more like the truth by the minute.

"Do you think leaving this Sunday would be too soon?" William questioned before checking the contents of his leather satchel for something, then closing it up tightly once more.

"I don't see why not." Nathanael shook his head without objection, then glanced over at Emile. "You?"

"I'll try to send a letter ahead of us to my friend in Kent to make a few inquiries on our behalf. With the number of letters that woman has sent me since I arrived, I am sure she wouldn't mind putting us up for a few days if we wished to visit." Emile offered, though part of him dreaded the thought of seeing Angelique once more. Still, it would be nice to at least find out something about Emma's current whereabouts and that information alone would be well worth whatever torture Angelique had in store for him.

"Wonderful, I can't wait to meet her. Now, if you will excuse me, I think I would like to go pray for a little while at the church," Nathanael added graciously and stood up, pushing in his chair before the others could protest.

"Alright, goodnight, Nathanael." Emile bade him farewell as he watched the man walk behind him and out the door, then turned his attention fully on William alone. "Do you really think a change of scenery is the best idea, William? For the most part, we have been able to manage his nightmares here well enough, but I shudder to think how we will cope when we are at your parent's house or even at Angelique's estate." Emile let his head fall back slowly against his neck out of habit and closed his eyes for just a moment to contemplate the whole scenario. "I mean, maybe he is getting better." He shrugged. "After all, it <u>has</u> been almost a week since the last true nightmare."

"That's just wishful thinking, Emile, and you know it." William dismissed his easy assumption outright for he knew that patients who were very ill often rallied back to normalcy physically before finally perishing. "But I do see your point about the danger of taking him anywhere in this state."

"Then what will we do? Tie him up?" Emile opened one eye and smirked at the errant thought that probably should have been kept safely within his own mind.

"Of course not, though now that you've said it, that is not a wholly bad idea." William sighed heavily once again at how far he was now willing to go in protecting his friend. "But we have to at least try something new—for his sake and for ours."

"You are probably right." Emile collected the plates and silverware from the table and brought them over to the man behind the counter. "Please give my regards to the cook." He winked playfully, paid the man for their meal and motioned for William to follow.

With the day drawing to a close, the two men stood outside on the hard-packed earthen street and quietly took in the view in front of them. The summer heat that had normally started in the middle of May had not yet appeared in force, leaving every field around them a bit soggy and smelling of pungent vegetation. Some of the farmers had said it was because of the late frost last winter, but the fireflies did not seem to take notice. As if they were right on schedule, they had dutifully arrived and played in the meadow beyond at sunset through twilight every night, making the fields look almost magical with their fairy green bursts here and there against the dark mud.

From where he stood, Emile took in the view happily while winding the watch on his chain before he placed it again, moments later, into his lower vest pocket. The watch itself had been a cheaper replacement to the one he had given Michel back in Paris. Just something he had traded for at the market last week on a whim. And although it was new to him in every way, the memory of the poignant exchange from his past had been carried over to the new piece of his apparel with great affection. "Living in this town kind of makes you forget just how upside down the outside world really is, doesn't it, William?"

"I suppose so," William answered distractedly as he was only half-listening to him while placing more of his interest in watching the progress of a certain preacher as he shuffled over to his church ahead of them.

Hearing his distant tone, Emile glanced over at him and studied his expression thoroughly before inquiring of him further. "What is on your mind, really, William? And don't say it is something medical because you and I both know there is only one thing on your mind right now and medicine is not it."

"Oh, it's just something Señor Moretti said." William shook his head, but did not look at Emile directly.

"Really? When did you hear from him?" Emile crossed his arms over his chest casually and waited for his reply.

"Just the other day, actually. I sent Sebastian a letter after you arrived asking for Señor Moretti's advice on Nathanael. That was all before the dreams took a more violent turn, of course. Now, I am not so sure if what he said even applies anymore."

Emile shaded his eyes from the setting sun, allowing them to adjust better to the approaching twilight. "I would say 300 years of wisdom is most definitely much more than you or I possess, so I am sure whatever the man might have said will be useful to some degree."

"Well, he writes that he cannot say for certain, but that many times a person with night terrors has to find out what is truly making them afraid and then face it if they wish to overcome them, either that or avoid the triggers altogether to be free of them."

"So... since Nathanael cannot avoid the fact that Elsie died, what do you think he is afraid of then?" Emile picked the more logical choice of the two offered.

"To be honest, I haven't the foggiest notion, truly." William kicked a stone at his feet towards the field. "Only Nathanael knows that. But according to his journal at the time, he might possibly still blame himself in some way for Elsie's death. Though I haven't read anything the man has written in it since. I wouldn't have even known that much except for the fact that it was open on his desk when I arrived."

"Relax, William. No one is accusing you of snooping." Emile jibbed, then stopped when William looked at him with the same tired expression he had already seen twice that evening already.

"Can you be serious for once in your life, please?" He almost begged.

"Of course." Emile nodded in sober compliance, then added, "What you say may be true to some extent. I know Susan Summerfield has spoken many times of how hard it has been on the family since Elsie died. Elsie was her oldest child, and I know that type of pain is different, but I cannot imagine the depth of despair one might experience when it is someone you were hoping would be your wife... or more importantly for us, your future."

"Have you ever had someone that close to you die, Emile?" William looked out at the fairy fields and pondered deeply how he would feel if his mother or father had died in the epidemic or worse, one of his siblings.

"Both of my parents, actually. My brother, Gabriel, still lives somewhere over in Austria, I believe, but I haven't spoken to him in years."

"Were you close? To your brother, I mean."

"When we were younger, I suppose so. Now, not so much." Emile picked up a small pebble from beside his foot and threw it as far as he could manage into the field, startling the fireflies as they flew upwards where it landed and danced towards the small flecks of white light appearing above. "I haven't written because I think he may blame me for many things I simply cannot change. Some are justly deserved, I assure you, while others... I will simply need to let time heal in its own way. Still, I do miss his companionship sometimes, or at least I did until I met you."

"That is most certainly hard, Emile. I can't imagine not being able to talk with one of my siblings because of a rift of some kind... but speaking of wives...." William turned back to Emile and leaned in closer so that only he could hear him. "Have you told Miss Larose that you are a ...."

"Of course not! I'm not a complete idiot." Emile shrank back instantly in repulsion, cutting him off before he could proceed further.

"Emile... though I do understand the complexity of our lifestyle and the necessity for caution that accompanies it, you <u>will</u> have to tell her someday, or you may end up like Nathanael, and I cannot handle two of you like this. I know my limits." William's nervous laughter sounded genuine, but also very apprehensive.

Nodding his head in agreement, Emile took a deep breath in slowly before exhaling it out again, knowing his friend was merely trying to help him see reason. "I do not disagree with you on that point but in this particular situation, nothing may ever come of our relationship as it is. As such, there is nothing truly to tell her. Wouldn't <u>you</u> wait until there is something far more substantial between two people before telling the lady things that might upset her? Especially when doing so might mean having to ostracize yourself from everyone you know because of the knowledge they have now received."

"You'd probably have to leave the country... again." William sighed. "Being a vampire <u>does</u> have its very delicate limitations, and this is definitely one of them. But face it, Emile, you are going to have to choose someday. Either wait until she has grown to love you before telling her or make her choose between living forever and loving you?" William replied flatly. "I'm sorry to be so blunt, but neither of those options seem fair to you nor her."

"You never know, she may choose to do both," Emile offered quickly, apparently still holding onto that small sliver of hope he had been clinging to since Paris.

"She might." William agreed, then smirked. "Though she may also change her mind altogether if I tell her just how much of a scoundrel you really are."

"Not a chance." Emile cast him a wicked grin and then scoffed, "The lady is already well-informed in that area; I can assure you."

"And she still wants you?" William looked at him wide-eyed and leaned back, laughing easily though also pleasantly surprised. In truth, it was the first time either of them had truly enjoyed such spontaneous humor in quite some time and it felt marvelous to experience it. "Well, now I really have to meet her."

"In due time, William, in due time. Come, it is getting late, milking begins at five tomorrow morning, and I, for one, am tired."

"I'm sorry, but every time I see you half-huddled under one of those milking cows it just makes me laugh." William tried to hold back his growing merriment but could not manage to hide his smile.

"I dare say that I have learned to do many tasks others would find humorous for a gentleman to perform." Emile held his nose up proudly. "And I will be happily obliged to continue doing them as long as I am living with the two of you."

"Why?" William asked but was grateful to see the genuine change that had come over his friend.

"Because someone has to learn how to cook or the three of us will starve. Or at least appear to do so." Emile laughed along with him.

"Changing you mind about the diet then?"

"Certainly not, but that does not mean I have to be especially eager to torture myself unnecessarily either," Emile replied defensively hoping to divert William from the subject entirely for he was not certain that he was ready to share those kinds of details with him just yet.

"Progress indeed. Well, I'll be home presently. I just want to check on Nathanael first." William patted Emile on the back before jogging up the road to the chapel. "Don't wait up for me."

"I won't." Emile yawned and turned in the opposite direction towards home. It was his night to help should Nathanael require it, and as tired as he was already, he wanted to get every precious minute of sleep possible before the man next awoke.

Chapter Thirty-Five

June 12th, 1793

William continued on in his trek down the road and through the garden gate, pausing momentarily to take in the distorted shape of his friend sitting just behind the tall-leaded windows in front of him. Even at a distance, he could tell by the shadows the sunset cast that its rich hues of golden yellow, warm amber, and vibrant orange covered all of the walls and floor within like a blanket of honey poured upon the pews all around him. Majestic God beams traced the edges of the landscape along the horizon and danced wildly upon the roof as they reached their fingers across the entire length of the chapel to the stone walls just beyond, as if beckoning him closer with their enticement.

Lifting the hood of his cape once more to shield him from harm, he thought back to that day at the castle when he had experimented with the light in his room and was grateful once again for the protection that the thicker quality of the old glass provided. In this near twilight of the day, the departing rays of the sun would probably do less damage to his skin than a slight irritation if he removed his hood, but the action of lifting it whenever he was outside had now become so second nature to him that he had found himself doing it even when it was no longer needed.

Not wanting to disturb his friend's prayers within, William slowed his pace down considerably to a respectful walk and quietly opened the heavy door, allowing himself just enough room to slide silently into the empty foyer, unnoticed. Without even thinking, he glanced immediately to his left and waited for his eyes to adjust to the lighting within, as he scanned the chapel for his friend.

There, in the center pew, directly facing the wooden cross that hung high behind the front altar, Nathanael dutifully sat as attentive as any of his flock ever was in attendance.

Grateful once again for God's hand of protection, William released a sigh of relief and removed his cape before carefully hanging it up quietly on the peg by the door next to Nathanael's.

When he had decided to come here tonight, he had done so with the intention of gaining some form of insight into what his friend might be facing. Or rather, anything that might aid him in understanding how he could help him. Yet as he listened intently to the words of his friend's prayers echoing back to him in the empty church, what he heard instead sounded more like the conversation of a broken man than the rhythmic repetition he had half-expected all clerics to recite.

"God, was there <u>ever</u> really a remote possibility of a happy life for us... for Elsie... for me?" Nathanael looked up at the cross and questioned respectfully, though William could plainly see the true humility and insecurity it took for the man to ask it at all.

Nothing happened. Only a long pause that echoed back from the vastness all around him.

Feeling defeated, Nathanael cast his face downwards and let out a soft whimper of a sob as he spoke more to himself than to anyone else present, "Oh, why did I ever think a life with Elsie would be attainable when everything else in my life is so uncertain?"

He drew in a steadying breath as if needing to steal up the remainder of his courage, then continued, only this time with even greater conviction. "I don't believe in fate, God. I never have. I believe in Your Word, and in it You say that it is the Truth. That You are my light. And I trust that You always have a purpose for everything You have asked me to do. You <u>always</u> have. But please... tell me why?" He fought back another sob, unable to control the emotions that were flooding over him with every sentence he uttered. "Did You <u>intend</u> for all of this to happen?" The last word came out fairly garbled as his voice was now filled with the anguish and sorrow he had been experiencing for weeks. "And if so, what are You trying to teach me in this? Help me to see it, I beg You."

Another long length of time passed in the ensuing stillness before the man began again, only this time much louder and more forcefully than his original question as he beseeched, in mournful examination, a God who seemed as if He was not truly paying attention to his plight at all. "Is this all I am ever to expect in this world?" He reached his arms forward in despair before placing his forehead on the pew in front of him, pleading further, "<u>Nothing</u> but loneliness and guilt set aside for people like me. A life intended for pain and nothing else at all?"

Yet even in this, there was no audible answer from anyone in response.

William's heart almost broke. From his vantage point in the back of the room, Nathanael appeared in his struggle as if he were naked and afraid before his Maker though the man was fully attired. Furthermore, just having to watch it all unfold in front of him felt absolutely crushing to experience firsthand because he too was captivated in waiting and listening intently, as if he also very much expected an audible reply, given the intensity of the emotion he was seeing displayed. But nothing came.

For almost ten minutes, Nathanael remained in that position of abject submission as he waited for the wisdom his soul craved before he sat up and inhaled deeply, only this time his face did not show the depth of grief it had portrayed earlier. In the faint light that illuminated it, William could see that it was now covered instead by an almost resolute anger—something William had never seen the man <u>ever</u> express towards anyone, let alone God.

"Why would anyone ever want to live forever when everyone they could ever love will <u>die</u>!" He practically spat the last word out in disgust though William was certain that this accusation was not intended towards God in any way. He was merely voicing his regret towards the decision he had made back on the island.

William knew then beyond a doubt that this conversation was the very reason why he had felt so compelled to come here tonight. Why Nathanael's God had quite obviously sent him. With great compassion filling his heart, he walked slowly up the aisle to his friend, before placing his left hand upon his shoulder as he imagined Nathanael's loving Jesus might have done for him were He to have been here physically instead.

"William..." The broken preacher looked up at him, his face streaming with fresh tears that flowed freely down his face in long streaks and onto his shirt below. "It isn't fair." Then, with gritted teeth he added further, "God isn't fair!"

Nathanael's face immediately fell upon his folded hands in front of him as if feeling inwardly rebuked by his childish statement. "Oh, why did God not take me instead!" He sobbed with his head down for quite some time before tapering off to a more controlled pattern of breathing.

Unable to do anything more than he already was, William remained where he stood and did not remove his hand. Neither did the two men move to speak, but rather the comforting action alone allowed Nathanael the time he needed to process and purge all the emotions that had been building up within him.

When at long last he finally drew in a shuddering breath and sat back upright, William removed his hand and retrieved a small, silver keepsake from within his coat pocket and paused momentarily before offering it to him. "This is for you. I have been waiting for just the right time to give it to you, but I think tonight is the night."

"What is it?" Nathanael tried to wipe the blurriness from out of his vision to see it more clearly.

"An heirloom. A remembrance. Call it what you will, as it is both. It isn't much, though I fear what it contains may make you feel even worse tonight, but you deserve to have it anyways. When you open it, you will understand why I have waited so long to give it to you."

Nathanael took the offered gift and fingered the smooth, filigree etched surface of the silver frame and the heaviness of it. Then, seeing the gap on the side of the small rectangular object that fit into the palm of his hand, he used his right thumbnail to pry the two sides apart revealing a stunning black and white portrait of his beloved Elsie drawn to perfect likeness on one side and a thickly circled lock of her curly red hair on the other.

"Where did you get this?" Nathanael asked incredulously as he rubbed one of his fingers along the delicate edge of the picture before retrieving the lock of hair and placing it gently against his cheek in awe.

"Susan Summerfield gave it to me weeks ago, but in the state that you were in at the time I was afraid something might cause it to come to harm." William fumbled for the right words to describe his hesitation. "The drawing is just another little hidden talent of mine."

"I... I don't know what to say," Nathanael's voice sounded hoarse and distant, completely overwhelmed once more by the intimacy of such a gift.

"Say it is finally time to let her go, Nathanael," William almost whispered back his simple reply.

"I don't know how." He shuddered just once and tried to hide his new tears with the back of the hand that was holding the lock of hair.

"You <u>have</u> to and not just because I am telling you to do it, but because both you and I know Elsie would not have wanted you to live this way—a mere shadow of the man that she loved so well."

Knowing he was right, Nathanael gripped the portrait case within his palm tightly and hid his face behind his folded hands. "Why did he take her instead, William? What kind of purpose can I possibly have like <u>this</u> that would make me such a better choice than her?"

"What does the Bible say?" William said the only thing he could think of at that moment to redirect him.

For a long time Nathanael remained silent, stubbornly unwilling or too emotionally affected to engage.

Taking a seat beside him, William lifted the lovingly worn Bible Nathanael had placed there and offered it to his friend, compelling him to answer. "Nathanael... try."

"They shall walk and not be weary. They shall run and not faint." Nathanael repeated dutifully, though the hollow words barely touched the emotions that should have been delivered with them like someone reciting them while half-asleep. "For my burden is easy and my yoke is light... Think it not strange concerning the fiery trial, which is to try you, as though some strange thing happened unto you." He let out a longer sigh that seemed like a falling away of some kind of weight and took the offered Bible as he continued. "But rejoice in as much as ye are partakers of Christ's sufferings that, when his glory shall be revealed, ye may be glad, with exceeding joy, First Peter."

"You have to remember that Jesus felt the pain of loss, too, Nathanael. Didn't his close friend die?"

"Yes, it says that Jesus wept—the shortest verse in the whole Bible, in fact." Nathanael nodded his head and placed the loose ribbon Elsie had given him in his Bible carefully between the pages at Psalm 23, his favorite chapter in all the Bible, and one he had read almost every night since Elsie's passing. "Two very short words for such a moment of immense grief."

"And yet, they are included in the Bible just the same. Do you think that's an accident?"

"Nothing is an accident to God, William," Nathanael affirmed quietly then raised his eyebrows as if realizing at that moment that this was something of an answer to one of his questions earlier.

"Then it stands to reason that nothing that has happened to either of us is an accident, too," William reaffirmed, hoping that he was not pressing the man too hard.

"What man meant for bad, God meant for good? Is that what you are implying?" Nathanael looked over at William and studied him closely.

"Something like that, maybe." He shrugged.

"You do know that his brothers sold that man as a slave before he was unjustly imprisoned, lied about on many occasions, overlooked, and then had countless other calamities befall him, right?"

"It is one of the few stories I <u>do</u> know, given that my father was named after him. My grandmother made sure of that." William leaned back in the pew and looked up at the cross before adding, "Just because I do not believe as strongly about everything as you do does not mean that I do not also trust that God has a purpose in all of this. He has to or what are we all doing here on this Earth, anyways? Or at least that is what you have been preaching to me this past year, correct?"

"Yes, but I didn't know if anyone was really listening."

"Oh, we have <u>all</u> been listening, even Emile. Some of us have just been too proud to admit it until now. Logic will only get a man so far, or at least that was what you told me back on the island, and you were right." William smirked and looked at his friend out of the corner of his eye, then shifted the subject. "Do you know what you are going to do?"

"Truthfully? I don't know what I want anymore, but I do know what I <u>need</u> to do."

William nodded silently before asking, "Would you like me to leave?"

"No." Nathanael shook his head while rubbing the worn leather cover of his cherished text with his palms. "But I do want to know one thing."

"Hmm... what?" William answered easily.

"Why <u>did</u> you come here tonight, William?"

Feeling instantly introspective, William's eyes darted out the window behind Nathanael as if searching for the right words to explain everything to him and then back to his grieving friend. "Because a wise man once taught me that no matter what is transpiring in a person's life, no one should have to carry that burden alone. He most certainly didn't." William pointed at the cross then turned back to Nathanael. "His disciples were with him when his friend died, were they not?"

"Hmmpf... they couldn't stay awake while He cried in the garden," Nathanael countered curtly. "He was alone then."

"No, He wasn't," William quickly replied with a look of sheer surprise at Nathanael's oversight.

"What?" Nathanael looked up at William, suddenly perplexed.

William could hardly contain the dramatic roll of his eyes at the necessity of being the one to point out something as plain as the nose on his face. Something Emile most definitely would have done had he been here in his place. "I've been listening downstairs to you practicing your sermons for the past six months, Nathanael. Didn't you teach just a short time ago that there was someone else in the garden while He cried... while He prayed."

"His Heavenly Father," Nathanael whispered in final acceptance.

"You are not alone, my friend." William placed his hand on top of Nathanael's for a moment then let go as he folded his own in his lap. "As you have so often reminded me, you never were. None of us are it seems."

"Yes." Nathanael nodded in acceptance and smiled slightly as another thought struck him in its beautiful revelation. "But William, if your acceptance of God as more than the great clockmaker you once thought Him to be was the purpose in me becoming a vampire, it was worth it—100% worth every part of it," Nathanael stated honestly as he looked over at his friend.

"Then Elsie's death must have a greater purpose, as well. One that I am certain God will show you in time." William pursed his lips to hold back the emotion he was trying not to share as the moment of admission tonight was more than he had ever expected or intended to experience.

"True." Nathanael nodded in silence and the two of them simply sat in the chapel, not speaking, until the sunset hues were long exchanged for moonlit shadows.

"Do you think you are finally ready to go home?" William asked when he could see the brilliance of the stars beginning to shine in the sky outside the chapel windows.

"I am now." Nathanael placed the lock of hair back inside the silver case and slipped the keepsake into his pocket before patting it affectionately. "Let's go home, William."

William nodded and the two of them walked along in silence all the way home and up to their bedroom upstairs. As both of them had expected, Emile was already quietly snoring in the room opposite of theirs, and the sound of it through the closed door was such that the two men finally let out a lighthearted chuckle of relieved stress.

"And he asked <u>us</u> which one of us snored the most." Nathanael tried his best to laugh quietly, but Emile's snores still stopped abruptly at the interruption like a snort from a pig before beginning again once more, only this time even louder.

"Now, you've done it. We'll never get any sleep if he keeps that up," William chided him ruefully. "I just can't believe you haven't noticed it at all over the past two months. He can be louder than a thunderstorm at times."

"It seems I have missed many things haven't I, William? Missed life." Nathanael shook his head in displeasure but felt grateful for the first time in a great while.

"Well, not any longer," William assured him and held open the door for him to pass inside first.

"Agreed," Nathanael replied as the two men smiled in unison and dropped into their beds without even bothering to change out of their daily clothes.

"Goodnight, Nathanael." William almost sighed happily to have his friend back once more.

"Goodnight, my friend." Nathanael smiled and closed his eyes, instantly drifting off to sleep.

And with the clock on the wall faithfully chiming the quarter of the hour below them, it was the first night in months that everyone in the house slept well.

Chapter Thirty-Six

June 20th, 1793

"The vacation from hell," as they would all sarcastically refer to it for years to follow began as most trips do, with carefully laid out plans, well intentions and an overall optimism towards an achieved goal. But sadly, the reality that occurred was the farthest thing from what they desired than what they could have ever envisioned at the time for though William had promised Emile and Nathanael, in the most convincing of terms, an absolutely "wonderful time of respite and relaxation", the journey from Wakefield to London proved itself to be much more difficult. From mud-filled roads that jostled the carriage and threw them against the sides every twenty-five to fifty feet, to beds so filled with fleas that they covered their arms and legs thickly like a moving garment as they slept, understandably refusing to drink from the vampires they were offered. Every single mile that they put behind them was fraught with confounding difficulty and far more disgust than any of them had ever imagined possible.

The only thing that <u>had</u> worked in their favor as they travelled were the overcast skies, but even in that smallest of blessings, nature was still working against them. From the very morning that they left, the ominous clouds overhead followed their progress steadily across the land as they dominated their journey, just as dark and as gloomy as the increasingly downcast moods of the travelers beneath them. And night after following night a hard-driving rain, that never ceased to let up, accompanied their movements like an unpleasant shadow, efficiently soaking everything and anything within its reach, including the three of them. At every single step of the way the three men could hardly deny the weight that they felt from nature itself as it raged its violent battle against them, refusing to allow any of the travelers within its grasp to escape.

And so it was that the weary group was especially grateful for just a bit of sanctuary when they finally knocked on the door of the residence of Doctor Joseph Wells in London, England, eager for some dry clothes and a much-needed bath. The tumultuous journey, and all the other horrible aspects of their travail was finally over for the present, though unfortunately, every inch of them still also carried with it some kind of remembrance of its dreadful passing.

"Welcome, welcome! Oh, dear William, I am so glad you are finally home. I thought you might never make it back again before Christmas after the calamity of your last visit," William's mother greeted each of her visitors politely while grinning from ear to ear, obviously excited to see her visitors at last. "Won't you all come in, please?" She stepped back away from the doorway and waited for all of them to enter.

"Thank you for having us, ma'am," Nathanael tried his best to answer as cordially as possible while taking great pains to wipe off the mud from the edge of his boots before entering the magnificent house.

"Yes, thank you," Emile answered in turn and attempted not to appear as disheveled as he felt under the circumstances as he carried his small bag of luggage in one arm but chose to remain rather awkwardly in the front foyer once inside. As filthy as they all had become from the various pitfalls along their way, it seemed almost mandatory to remain where he stood near the outside wall of the foyer to avoid soiling the very prominently placed white and blue woven rug just inside.

"I am so excited to finally meet you all." William's mother moved to the room beside them without pausing to examine them closely and busied herself around the room with moving pillows and newspapers this way and that so the men would find ample room to sit on the available furniture and chairs. "As you might expect, your father is still away at his surgery at the present, William, but I am sure he will be home sometime before supper if he is able. Though with how busy his practice has been of late, one never knows when he will arrive home on any given day, so I would try not be too disappointed if you do not see him until morning."

"Yes, I remember Mamá, but..." William cast a nervous glance at both of his companions who looked more than exhausted and shrugged helplessly. As determined as she was talkative, it was almost impossible to stop his mother from her chosen path once she had begun focusing on something, which at the moment, was quite obviously her attempt to display hospitality.

"But what? I am sure you must be ready for something to eat or drink after that long ride from Wakefield. Come and sit for a minute and tell me all about it. I'm sure it was simply marvelous to take in all that scenery," she said over her shoulder while urging them to join her in the small sitting room, clearly still oblivious to the men's overall condition.

"Um, we would, Mamá, but I think it might be best if we freshened up a little first. As you might expect, we've carried half of the English countryside home with us, I am afraid." William grimaced at the detestable accuracy of his statement and hoped to appeal to her more sensible side as he did not wish to upset her unnecessarily if he could avoid it.

Finally noticing the concern in his tone as he spoke, William's mother turned around slowly to see the truth of the matter for herself and audibly gasped when she registered completely the state in which they were in. "Oh, that won't do at all. Here, let me show you all to your rooms at once. Then, we can enjoy a lovely pot of tea and chat about your news. Would that be acceptable, gentlemen?"

"That would be wonderful, Mamá. Thank you," William replied politely and kissed her cheek in welcome before motioning for the two other men to follow him up the narrow, wooden staircase to the second floor and after that, the third.

"I feel I must apologize, son, for the change of plans concerning your stay but I'm afraid that your friends will need to share a room up here for the time being if that is acceptable as unfortunately, the lower rooms are being cleaned at the moment," William's mother explained as she lifted the front of her skirt with one hand and held onto the railing with her other as she climbed the second flight of stairs to the last floor above.

"Of course, but is everything alright?" William inquired curiously, slightly alarmed by the sudden need to clean all the rooms on one floor. And especially so when she had been expecting their imminent arrival any day.

"Oh, nothing too catastrophic, I assure you, dear. It seems that one of the chimneys backed up horribly yesterday morning when the maids were lighting the fires and sent smoke and soot everywhere. As you might imagine, the cataclysmic cloud that poured inside my beautiful home covered every inch of the two guest rooms I had reserved for your friends on the second floor and made them quite uninhabitable at the present." She stopped when she reached the third floor and motioned to the door at the end of the hall to her left for Emile and Nathanael. "William, if you are still amenable to it, you can sleep in your old room at the other end if that suits you. I would hope that you still remember where it is."

"Certainly, Mamá. The last thing we want to do is be a burden to you," William replied obediently and turned the corner at the top of the stairs as he walked down the short, ornately decorated hallway to his room, completely abandoning them to her care.

"It was most generous of you to host us despite your unfortunate circumstances, Mrs. Wells," Nathanael thanked his host respectfully, then entered the offered room without further comment, feeling as if they had all been horribly cursed in this endeavor from the very beginning.

"It was most generous, indeed," Emile agreed and stepped to the side to allow William's mother the space she required to pass back down the stairs behind him.

"I am sorry for the inconvenience this is causing you both, truly. But as unaccommodating as sharing a room may be, I pray that it is just a little hiccup in your otherwise splendid rest here, and that nothing further will derail the enjoyment of your stay in any way. If you require anything else at all, please do ring the bell by the fireplace and someone will attend you directly," William's mother called back to them from the second-floor landing and waited for both men to disappear out of sight before going back down to the sitting room below.

"I am certain it will be fine," Emile reassured her and walked into the room, as well, eyeing Nathanael as he passed, who appeared to be shaking his head in disappointment as he stared into his small bag on the bed.

"I don't know about you, but I personally cannot <u>wait</u> to get out of these wet pants!" Nathanael exclaimed with great agitation when the door was firmly shut behind them at last before beginning the laborious process of peeling off the half-soaked brown trousers and similarly moist matching suitcoat. "Do you think they have someone who can possibly clean them here for us, or must they be sent out?"

"Clean them?" Emile wrinkled his nose at the very idea as he removed both of his boots and smelled just one of his own putrid socks before jerking back. "At this point, I think I prefer to burn... <u>everything</u>." He dropped one offending article after the other into a nearby metal pail that was normally reserved for removing ashes from the fireplace, then contemplated what other pieces of his formally immaculate attire he would not miss in the slightest should they also require immediate incineration.

"Oh stop. If you do that, you won't have any clothing left to wear at that rate," Nathanael chided him glibly but felt equally inclined to follow his example.

"Huh, in the state that I am in, Nathanael, I may just need to be scrubbed from top to bottom like Susan Summerfield's floor after a long week of baking... either that... or boiled alive." Emile flipped his black felt top hat from off his head and carefully set it on top of a nearby bookcase. Ironically, it was the <u>only</u> piece of his attire that had managed to survive in perfectly pristine condition.

"Whatever doesn't kill you makes you stronger, eh, Emile," Nathanael shot back the age-old adage and continued on in his search, desperate now to find anything that still remained even remotely dry at this point but found none. With a huff of final frustration at his inability to see, Nathanael gave up his fruitless search completely and dumped the entire contents of his bag onto the wooden floor of the room before scanning the scant assembly of fabrics for something suitable to wear. "You would think that there has to be at least one dry shirt in here, right?" He proclaimed incredulously as he removed one of the darker colored shirts from off the top of the pile and placed it onto the chair beside him to hang up later.

"I wouldn't count on it. As hard as it has been raining thus far, we might have fared better if we had chosen an ark for our transportation." Emile shook his head at the humorous image and picked up one of the linen towels stored on the rack by the window to wash his face and neck.

"That might have worked for Noah, but I don't think it would have helped us, my friend." Nathanael cast another long look down at the pile lamentably and watched in horror as a rather large bug scurried its way out from beneath his clothing towards him, resulting in a rather unflatteringly high pitch shriek from his lungs.

"Seriously, Nathanael? What now?" Emile set down the towel and turned around in time to see his friend dodge out of the bug's vindictive path towards the closed door behind him. "No, you don't, you vile pest." Emile gritted his teeth and flew at the bug from across the way, stomping him out of existence as if taking his turn at exacting his own form of revenge against just one of the things that had tormented him. "*Tu es morte!*" He proclaimed happily and double-checked the still corpse once more just to be sure.

"Is he dead?" Nathanael's eyes widened at his sudden reaction but also breathed a sigh of relief and gratitude for his quick thinking.

"Most... definitely." Emile raised his head triumphantly and returned to the pitcher and wash basin once again to thoroughly clean off his foot now instead.

"After what we have just been through, I am starting to think William took us through the ten plagues of Egypt on the way down here, Emile." Nathanael hesitantly lifted the edges of a few more articles of clothing to check for any more of the bug's comrades-in-arms, then decided the clothes were fine where they lay.

"Um, didn't a great many people die during those plagues?" Emile put his arms into a freshly picked shirt from his bag and took the greatest of care in buttoning each and every one of the delicate circles in turn.

"Only the Egyptians." Nathanael changed into a new pair of pants and frowned for they were probably not much drier that the pants he had arrived in. And if he were to be totally honest, possibly nothing in his bag that he had encountered thus far had managed to escape the incessant moisture of their trip.

"Then it is a good thing that we are not Egyptians," Emile continued by putting on a pair of black, stiffly ironed slacks that fastened neatly on the side of each knee.

In growing dismay, Nathanael looked over at the man and frowned while holding up a very wrinkled white dress shirt. "Why is it that your clothes look utterly untouched, while mine appear to have been rolled up under someone's mattress or stomped on by the horses?"

"I don't know." Emile looked into the mottled mirror on the wall to arrange his cravat about his neck into a loose knot and smiled wistfully at him. "Did you place them under your mattress last night? That last inn we stayed at did not even give me a pillow—terrible manners in this country."

"At least your room didn't have mice. I was probably up half the night listening to them gnawing on something under the dresser." Nathanael buttoned up his shirt and tucked it into his faded trousers. "Not a chance I was putting anything on that floor."

"Indeed," Emile agreed and delayed fastening his matching vest as their conversation was abruptly interrupted by three soft knocks sounding on the door behind them, followed by a polite pause.

Glancing back to check on the completion of Nathanael's attire, Emile opened it graciously and was greeted in turn by a young woman around the same age as Emma, who was quite obviously an upstairs maid.

"Beggin' your pardon, sir, but the lady of the house asked if you would be able to join her in ten minutes time as the tea is now ready?" She curtsied before waiting patiently for his reply.

"Please tell Mother we will be down presently, Cassandra," William answered authoritatively from behind her, already fully changed into an outfit none of the rest of them had ever seen for he was dressed as that of a gentleman of high society, complete with an embroidered cravat, overlapped, cuffed jacket with lace-edged sleeves peeking out of it on both sides and two smartly polished black shoes that even sported a keenly placed and highly decorative brass buckle on top.

Shocked beyond expression at the image of his friend in front of him, Emile whistled at the sight of him while Nathanael on the other hand just stood fixed to the floor, totally stunned.

"What?" William held his hands out in confusion as if nothing about himself had changed in the slightest.

"He actually makes you look plain, Emile, and that is saying something." Nathanael reached behind him for his own brocade vest and put it on. In truth, it was quite easily the fanciest thing that he owned and yet it still paled in comparison to the attire of either of his companions.

"Bravo, man! Well played." Emile clapped unceremoniously four times at William. "And all this time you made me think I was the only one with social obligations."

"Oh, stop." William waved the two of them off dismissively with one hand and started down the stairs to the sitting room without them.

Unable to recover from their shock, Emile and Nathanael both exchanged a shared look of total amazement before closing the bedroom door shut tightly behind them.

"Did you know that his family was rich?" Emile looked around curiously for several moments at the many statues, vases and paintings adorning the upper floor's walls and tables that he had not fully appreciated upon their arrival.

"I knew of his father's profession, but nothing could have properly prepared me for any of this." Nathanael tried to smooth out a few of the wrinkles in his vest, feeling slightly more embarrassed by the minute given both of his friend's austere attire.

"Same here." Emile turned around and with a brief scan noticed his friend's obvious distress. "Don't worry about anything today, Nathanael. We will get your clothes sorted out first thing in the morning, I assure you. Let's just get through supper without any more catastrophe, shall we?"

"Well, I suppose that I can't look any worse than I already do." Nathanael shrugged and descended the stairs after him, walking in the man's shadow into the pale-blue tinted room near the front of the house.

"Well now, don't you both look much improved." William's mother motioned for Emile and Nathanael to join her in the heavily decorated room. "Though I feel as though I know you both so well already from the way my son has described you in his letters."

She took Nathanael's hand and squeezed it warmly. "You would be the preacher if I am not much mistaken, correct? Are you feeling much better now?"

"Yes, I am and thank you for asking. It is most kind." He nodded politely and took a seat opposite William on a silver-toned upholstered chair with a rich cherry finished wood supporting its frame.

William's mother then turned her full attention to Emile, the last of the group to enter. "And you are the debonaire Frenchman who has just escaped that awful episode over in France, are you not?"

"Guilty as charged." Emile took her hand in his, brought it up to his lips and with a kiss, bowed slightly. "I am honored to make your acquaintance, *madame*."

William shook his head at his overly graceful display and flexed the muscles in his jaw for he had seen it all before, only this time from a much less appreciative view. "Emile, please do come in and sit down with the rest of us or at least stop flirting with my mother already," he almost grumbled disdainfully in judgement from his seat by the window and crossed his arms tiredly.

Surprised by the ill manners her son had acquired in his absence; William's mother shushed him quietly then returned her focus back to his charming companion. "Please forgive my son, sir, but I must admit that you do have a way with you. William was entirely accurate when he said that ladies must simply fall in love with you just by your speech alone."

"Did he now..." Emile squinted his eyes slightly in irritation in William's direction, then recovered his poise without missing a beat. "As you know, a man's looks may fade with time, dear lady, but your beauty has not." He flirted respectfully but casually with his host with the skill of someone who was well-versed in such an area, then looked over at his friend to judge his reaction.

"Oh, my... you are good. Careful, dear sir, or my husband will most definitely think he has competition." She placed one hand over his and blushed. "Now, William is right, please do come and sit down and tell me all about your travels. I'm simply dying to hear all the delightful details."

Nodding his head, Emile made his way across the room and took his seat quite formally next to Nathanael before choosing to cross one leg over the other. "Yes, dear William. Tell her all about our travels." He tried to hide his sarcasm with a smile but could not help himself chuckling just a little at his expense. It had been ages since he had played this kind of part in a play and doing so now felt oddly amusing and thoroughly entertaining to be on the other side of it for a change.

"Well, there is not much to speak of besides the incessant rain that seems to have followed us all the way from Wakefield." William began casually and ignored his friend's sarcastic tone.

Emile and Nathanael both rolled their eyes this time and shook their heads slightly at the overstated lie from across the room, but did not move to correct him in front of his mother for his assessment had indeed been true. In fact, it was pouring incessantly even now outside the windows as they spoke, yet this time they were in no way forced to endure its attack. Nor would they be required to make any excuses of any kind regarding their need to stay out of the sun's rays should it continue.

Appearing completely at ease now in his family home, William nodded as Cassandra came to his rescue just in time by entering the small room with a tray fully-ladened with their tea and some small cakes.

"Thank you, my dear." William's mother motioned for the girl to place the contents on the table next to her and depart. "Milk and sugar, Mr. Beckett?" She looked at Nathanael in question first and waited for his response.

"Both, if you please," he answered gratefully and took the offered cup as carefully as he could manage given its delicate nature. Never before in all his life had he been given anything as fragile as this piece of porcelain, which only made his hands jostle the teacup all the more as he carried it over to his lap where it finally ceased its chattering and stabilized on top of his knee.

"And you, Mr. Deschamps?" She looked over at the other man respectfully and paused, her hand perfectly poised above the sugar and cream.

"Sugar only, *S'il vous plaît.*" Emile stood up and took the cup with consummate grace before taking his seat once more and pouring a small amount of the liquid into his saucer carefully to cool it.

Not wishing to offend his host in any way so soon into their visit, Nathanael watched him from the side earnestly and tried to copy his actions, though in the end, they were nowhere near as smoothly done as his friend had openly demonstrated.

"Will you take tea today, son. I know it is not a favorite of yours." She touched the cheek of her favorite child lovingly for just a moment and waited for his reply.

"Thank you, but no. It still keeps me up at night." He took her hand in his and gave it squeeze just once before letting it go, feeling a bit awkward at receiving her unexpected attention in front of his gathered friends.

"That is what it is supposed to do, William," Emile mumbled under his breath quietly while taking a small sip of his tea to hide his muffled comment and smiled when William's eyes warned him to stop. From the way in which the doctor angled his head in his direction, his expression most definitely looked more tired than angry, but it also reminded him very much of Emma's when he had decidedly pushed her too far.

"So, Mamá," William continued to ignore him. "I know when I wrote to you about our trip, I said that we would try to stay for possibly a week at least, but I am afraid we cannot stay that long as we have also promised to visit the family of another friend further south before we return."

"The one you went to see last time?" His mother sipped her tea while skillfully slipping past his all of his planned explanation.

"Yes, the very same, and possibly one other in Kent." William tried his best to remain pleasant and reserved.

"I told your father I had hoped that you would remain for at least a fortnight, but he surmised that you might say as much." She waved him off with her handkerchief. "Children are always quite occupied with their own lives once they are fully grown, are they not?"

Emile and Nathanael nodded in agreement to her assertion but said nothing as neither of them still had their parents living at this time.

"I am sorry, truly I am." William tried to appease his mother further. "But we <u>have</u> planned to stay here for at least a few days if that suits you and father. And I think I can promise that I will try to come back around the fall of this year, barring any other medical entanglements."

"Really?" William's mother's face lightened considerably with the news. "That would be splendid, of course. Now, have you made any plans here yet? I hear the Theatre Royal is fairly popular with many young people this time of year, or you could visit Covent Gardens perhaps, if you were looking to purchase anything in particular in way of a gift. With all the merchants and wares for sale along the street, you can find whatever you might like there with very little difficulty most days."

"Actually, I was kind of hoping to get a chance to see the dissecting room of Mr. John Hunter this time." William crossed one leg over the other and leaned back comfortably in his chair.

"That indecent place?" William's mother closed her eyes and covered her mouth with her hand in swoon-like horror. "Why would you want to spend your only holiday <u>there</u> of all places!"

"Probably because Father spoke so highly about it the last time I was here. I've also read since that many surgeons throughout the country have taken the opportunity to assist Mr. Hunter in his daily dissections to increase their knowledge of the human anatomy. I think at this point, it would be a crime to my profession if I were to miss it altogether."

Nathanael watched William speaking and felt the room suddenly spin as he thought about what all that might entail. "Would you please excuse me for a moment?" He asked politely and walked out of the room and down the hall to the front door for some much-needed fresh air.

"Is he quite alright?" William's mother inquired before sipping more of her tea.

"A weak constitution only," William reassured her dismissively as if he were addressing the parent of a patient, knowing all the while that all Nathanael probably required was a bit of nutrition as he most likely had not consumed any blood since they left Wakefield almost three days ago. "I'm afraid that my profession causes him a bit of distress at times."

"I would imagine that it distresses a great many people, dear William." She took a small bite of the dessert she had picked up from off the tray before offering one to William.

"Would there be anywhere one might purchase some new clothing close by?" Emile skillfully changed the subject for his friend while picking a small piece of lint from off his tailored vest. "After the journey we just had, I may have need to replace a few things that were damaged along the way."

"I am sure there are many places over on Bond Street or perhaps Piccadilly that might suit your needs quite nicely. It isn't the same as the fashions you are probably accustomed to over in France, but I believe you will find that the milliners there are quite famous for their laces, silks and other essential adornments. Why Ms. Pearson just purchased the most fetching little fascinator at their store last week. Though I myself would have no need for such frivolity, they do say it is a must for any woman in society these days. Most likely due to the increasing popularity of Mrs. Woolstencroft and her forward opinions as of late, but let's not discuss that subject in front of your father again, William. He may be openminded on most subjects, but you know how he feels about the rights of women."

"Indeed, Mamá," William agreed with her suggestion.

"What do you think about going over there the day after next, Mr. Beckett? To the milliners that is?" Emile asked Nathanael who had re-entered the room and took his seat next to him as if he had never left the conversation at all.

"A new suit of clothing would be nice, I suppose," Nathanael agreed and took another sip of his tea. "And I do have a bit of savings set aside for a special occasion such as this."

"Splendid." Emile's whole countenance seemed to light up like a child at Christmas as he rubbed his hands together with growing excitement at their upcoming excursion.

"Careful, you two, don't get too carried away or we will never be allowed back in Wakefield." William finished the last bite of his small dessert and laughed.

"Why? Do they not wear the proper attire where you live?" His mother looked back at him in great consternation, suddenly alarmed at how her youngest son might be presenting himself in public.

"Wakefield is a very simple village, mostly comprised of farmers, and a few other necessary businesses." William patted her hand lovingly and tried to explain more. "Given the very small population, we rarely have the occasion to wear anything extravagant more than on holidays or maybe at a special dinner or two."

"There is always the occasion," she declared, completely undeterred in her position on the matter.

"I quite agree, dear *madame*." Emile saluted her with his teacup and finished his drink before a thud from the other room sounded at the front door closing.

"Good evening, Lavinia. I hope I haven't kept you from your supper again," a voice interrupted their conversation as it called from the foyer just beyond before the butler had time to address it.

"In the sitting room, my dear. Our guests have arrived early," William's mother replied cheerily and stood up to greet him with a peck on the cheek as he subsequently strode into the room and smiled widely.

"William! What a joy it is to see you once more!" The man's presence as he entered was almost as large as he was for he quite easily stood over six feet tall, was broad shouldered and had a thick head of silver-white hair that matched William's perfectly in cut and style.

"Father." William stood and embraced his father warmly before the two men laughed with immense happiness and began talking wildly about the senior doctor's day.

Amused and more than a little bit enamored by the exchange, Emile leaned his head over to Nathanael and spoke quietly, "It is like watching a stranger's life, is it not?"

"I agree. Though I think I haven't heard him talk this much the entire time that I have known him." Nathanael finished his cup of tea and nodded his head in agreement.

"Nor I," Emile added as they both smiled together, enjoying the scene of merriment created by their amiable hosts.

"Would you introduce me to your friends, son?" Doctor Joseph Wells finally stopped conversing and offered his outstretched hand first to Nathanael.

"Most definitely. This is Nathanael Beckett, the vicar of Wakefield." William used the playful name he had once discovered on the book cover last Christmas as he eagerly presented him.

"Indeed," Nathanael replied, unamused. "Though most definitely not as infamous as the first. Still, it is a delight to meet you finally, Doctor Wells."

"And this is Emile Bastien Deschamps, most recently of Paris, France." William motioned to the next man in introduction.

"A pleasure, I am sure, sir." The senior Doctor Wells grasped his hand firmly and shook it.

"And mine, as well." Emile received him courteously.

"I am glad to see that you escaped unharmed from that horrible situation unfolding over there." Doctor Wells shook his head and grimaced. "A rather messy affair, or so the papers say. Were you there when it began?"

"Only just." Emile tried to smile politely but had no intention of going into further details on the matter. Thankfully for him, he did not have to, because almost as soon as he had replied, the head butler entered the room and interrupted their discussion formally from the doorway.

"Dinner is served, ma'am... sir." He nodded in both of his employer's directions.

"Shall we?" William's father motioned for everyone to proceed ahead of him into the dining room. "Come William, tell me all about your patients and what is new in that part of the world. I am dying to hear all about it. Have you had any interesting cases?"

"A few, though none that would have taken you very long to diagnose. Well... come to think of it, there was one man who had this thorn stuck in his leg..."

"William, please," William's mother interrupted him quickly with a raised hand. "Could we save that conversation for after dinner?"

"Agreed," Emile and Nathanael both said in unison.

"If I remember correctly, that case was rather disgusting." Emile wrinkled his nose in her defense.

"You didn't even have to clean it, Emile." William laughed lightly.

"I saw it, that was enough." Emile shivered in response. "Trust me, *madame*, that is one conversation you will wish to miss."

"William..." His mother was beginning to sound more insistent on the matter, her tone more direct in its challenge.

"I think we shall have to oblige them just this once, mustn't we, son?" William's father said politely, but the two men seemed just as eager to begin again right where they had left off just as soon as the others had left the room.

"Another time, perhaps." William shot Emile a dark look for ruining his fun so soon but then lightened once again considerably.

Undeterred in the least, Emile only cast away his glance entirely from the man with a smirk as if he personally did not care what his friend thought on the matter. In his experience, formal dinners were no place for talk of shop or anything more gruesome than the meat in which they were going to be served.

The group followed their hosts and continued to make their way into the large dining room beyond without further comment but stopped once more at Nathanael's audible gasp when they entered as the rather large chandelier that hung brilliantly over the table quite literally took his breath away with all its opulence and grandeur. On the whole, this was not merely a light fixture in any form of the definition, neither had Nathanael seen its equal though he had frequented many a home during his days at seminary. No, this was a magnum opus of illumination, incomparable to all others, as each of the tall candles reflected stunningly against the crystals, casting beautiful prisms across the ceiling and upper moldings above.

"Oh, that old thing?" William's father pointed at the chandelier as if it were nothing more than a brass candelabra and went on to proudly explain its origins to all. "This was a gift from Thomas Cranmer, the Archbishop of Canterbury back in 1543 when he served as an advisor to both King Henry VIII and Edward the VI."

"It is simply breathtaking, sir." Nathanael shook his head in awe. "With something that precious, I am sure you know a great deal about English history."

"We should. Our family has lived in this home for well over four hundred years," the senior Doctor Wells replied easily, obviously pleased by William's friend's admiration.

"Father, I beg you. Please don't brag," William chided him uncomfortably, feeling slightly embarrassed by the focus on their obvious display of wealth.

"Whyever not! It is your heritage, man," his father corrected but did so warmly. "It's not every man in England that can boast that his family helped shape the monarchy or at least aided it in some degree."

"Just because our family started out as document copiers for King Henry the VIII, doesn't mean we shaped the monarchy. With all his wives, he simply had a great need for paperwork." William shook his head, regretting the necessity of having to remind his father once more of the baser truth of the matter.

"Yes, but your ancestors were soon recognized for their advice and exactness concerning the laws and English history thereafter. So much so, that they were then elevated to the status of noblemen during Queen Elizabeth's reign," his father added further.

With a sigh of defeat, William looked to the ceiling above him in mortification and offered a more accurate explanation for his friends, "So, essentially, all of that just means that in the end, they were glorified librarians."

"In the beginning that may have been true but look at us now." His father acquiesced finally.

"Yes, look at us now." William smiled in admiration of his father, but not in true appreciation of his inherited position, rather in learned understanding of his father's achievements in his profession—something he hoped to share with him in the years to come.

"The dinner is growing quite cold, dear," William's mother reminded him again and motioned for the serving staff to enter with the food.

Without further discussion, the men were each directed to different chairs around the large oval table and stood politely behind them until their hosts had been properly seated before seating themselves opposite of each other, as well.

Two male servants then arrived in short order with several silver platters in hand, beautifully arranged with fish and other assorted cheeses followed by a tomato-based soup before the main course of roast lamb was presented, complete with steamed, green vegetables and carrots.

For the rest of the meal and well into the later hours of the evening, the conversation was lively and entertaining with plenty of facts about London proper mixed in with more than enough humorous stories about William and his brother and sisters to provide Emile and Nathanael with playful ammunition for his future humiliation.

Indeed, it was an incredibly delightful evening with William's family and one all of them hoped to look back on fondly for many months to follow.

Chapter Thirty-Seven

June 22nd, 1793

"**I** am telling you. This is the one to purchase if you are going to buy anything, *monsieur*," Emile advised Nathanael who was trying on a completely new outfit from head to toe. Regrettably, the overall tone of the ensemble was most definitely still his favorite shade of brown as most of his clothes normally were, but this one had almost four layers total in its composition. From its inner white blouse, speckled quail egg styled vest with olive trim, to the high-waisted suitcoat that hung all the way down to the back of his knees behind him, everything complemented the lighter beige breeches and his multi-hued brown hair.

"The only thing it is lacking is that which every man must decide is his own personal style, his signature so to speak." Emile ran his fingers down the long row of tatted laces and silk fabrics that would eventually be quite skillfully used to create a stylish cravat or knot. "You must choose only <u>one</u>. The rest, are immaterial as only one defines the man he is to portray."

"Portray?" Nathanael lifted a few of them awkwardly and held them up to the light. "I wouldn't know the first thing about fashion, Emile. I never have. You'll simply have to choose one for me, or we will be here forever."

"No." Emile wagged a chastising finger in front of his face. "A man does not simply choose another man's wife. It is *Impossible*. Or how do you say it in English?" His face scrunched up in deep concentration as if trying to remember the correct word all of a sudden.

"Impossible," Nathanael answered shortly and shook his head, still fidgeting with the length of the vest.

With a drawn-out exhale that sounded more like a sigh, Emile paused and looked heavenward, praying for patience once again as he was not certain if the man was correcting him or simply complaining. This whole idea of shopping was supposed to have been a fun excursion for the two of them, but it appeared that the preacher had less focus on fashion than anyone he had ever met. "Pick... one... please," he spoke slowly and tolerantly while tapping his fingers together and annunciating each word like strings on a guitar, hoping to motivate Nathanael further without any other inducement.

"Fine, I'll... just pick this one," Nathanael replied in a huff and chose one of the more ornately created fabric, hoping for his friend's instant approval.

Emile shook his head at the choice. "Not that one."

"Okay, this one, then?" He held up a shiny silken fabric quizzically and leaned his head towards his friend once again.

Emile could only purse his lips for a moment to hold in what he wanted to say, then covered his eyes with one hand in disbelief. "Only if you want to look utterly ridiculous."

Nathanael sighed again, then truly took the time to study the lot in front of him for several long moments before selecting one fabric in particular with a satisfied smile. Emile was right. It was perfect. Created with a handmade cotton fabric that had a finely pattern embroidery on, it very much resembled the stitching on the dress Elsie had worn on Pasha. In fact, it was the first thing that had felt right to him in this shop today.

"Excellent." Emile nodded in approval and stood back upright from his leaning position against the wall. "Now, we will just have to settle up the bill, and we can be off. They can wrap up your old rags and other purchases and have them delivered to William's home if you so wish, or at least that is how it is done back in France."

The clerk who was standing quietly, but attentively, nearby nodded in agreement and whispered the total discreetly in Nathanael's ear.

"Why that is exorbitant!" Nathanael shrank back in horror and almost choked at the sum.

"Fashion usually is," Emile replied with not the least bit of concern as to whatever the total may be.

The clerk wholeheartedly agreed but waited politely for Nathanael's confirmation of his purchase while also not pressing him to do so either.

"Fine." Nathanael nodded in agreement, more out of defeat than out of joy at spending so much money on himself. Never in all his life would he have ever contemplated buying one, let alone two new outfits, but William had said that he would need at least that many for the dinner parties at the Knole and so it seemed frivolity, on this one occasion alone, could not be helped.

On any other given day, he would have much rather stayed at home and discussed <u>any</u> topic with William's mother than socialize with strangers, but he was also extremely curious to see the great estate. After all he had heard over the years, it was supposed to be one of the finest exhibits of art in the country with over ten gardens to tour and an incredibly well-stocked library.

"Please send the clothes and the other items to the home of Doctor Joseph Wells. I will settle up with you directly."

"Very good, sir." The clerk departed immediately and left the men admiring his new purchase in the tall mirrors of the store.

"It's a pity that fashion comes at such a high a price, my friend. Can you afford it?" Emile inquired politely.

Nathanael merely rolled his eyes at the sheer absurdity of the question this far in the process. "It's a little late to ask that, don't you agree?"

Emile tilted his head towards the mirror in front of him to admire his friend in its reflection. "Perhaps, but despite what you might think, you cannot put a price on quality. Besides, this ensemble will most definitely make you look like less of a peasant and more like a gentleman at Angelique's dinner party tonight. But are you sure you wouldn't want to try something with a bit more color? Perhaps something in a deep red or even blue?"

"No, I think I am at the edge of my comfort zone as it is, Emile. Though if truth be told, you two are the ones taking the biggest risk at the party. I'm just hoping that when all is said and done, I won't embarrass you with my lack of etiquette."

"From what I have seen, you certainly have all the manners you will require, Nathanael, so stop worrying." Emile smiled affectionately and shook his head, clearly pleased by their growing friendship.

"Do you really think so?" Nathanael checked the length of the sleeves in the mirror in front of him.

"I know so," Emile said while pretending not to show any true emotion on the matter and cleared his throat. "Furthermore, you never know who you might meet there. Maybe even... dare I hope for you... another young lady perhaps?"

"Emile, I don't want to meet anyone right now." He tugged at the tightness of the new collar as if the room suddenly seemed extremely stuffy to him. "I am only going because you and William both insisted that I <u>must</u> go."

"Hmmm…" Seeing his distress mounting but also knowing it had nothing to do with his collar, Emile moved to loosen the starched band slightly for him from behind. "Dear sir, there are always more fish in the ocean. And as difficult as it may seem to be at the present, you must at least try to get out of your stone chapel and open up your mind towards the many prospects available to you."

"Emile," Nathanael sighed tiredly. "I don't feel like fish, in women or in the ocean," he added more firmly, hoping his friend would change the subject altogether.

"Ahem, a man is <u>always</u> interested in fish, sir. He just may not feel like fishing, that is all." Emile turned his nose up in definite reproval.

"True, and to answer your other question. Yes, I have enough funds for the clothing. I have not touched even a farthing of the money Señor Moretti gave us, so this seems as good a time as any to enjoy a little bit of it."

"A worthy investment indeed." Emile set down a vest he had been eyeing since they had arrived, choosing instead to save the little funds he had left for something special for Emma. Despite what he hoped, he wasn't exactly sure if he would even see her there at the Knole given Angelique's silence on the topic. But maybe, if he could inquire at the other neighboring estates while he was in the general vicinity, he could at least find her and have a brief conversation before he left. If she was still interested in doing so, that is.

Then again, after all of this time that has passed between us, she may have found someone else entirely and moved on. He thought morosely and weighed out the true possibility of it.

Ready to be on his way at last to something far more agreeable, Nathanael called the clerk over with the wave of his fingers and whispered something in his ear while Emile was otherwise engaged in his thoughts.

"Very good, sir," the clerk responded in kind and the two men left to continue their shopping at Covent Gardens as Lavinia Wells had suggested.

To their great surprise, they soon discovered that William's mother had indeed been most certainly correct in her assumption of what they might find there, as well, for by the time that they had turned the corner onto the busy street, the market was quite literally packed with vendors of many shapes and kinds butted right up to the next for almost a mile. Fresh fruits and vegetables, flowers, books and nicknacks of every description drew their attention from shelves and carts that were lined up along the street—their merchants standing readily nearby to peddle their worth at the top of their lungs. In truth, it was an absolute mass of commerce and customers everywhere, but it was also a plethora of visual temptation for them both.

"I'm going to look in this shop over here by the taxidermist. Can you meet me there after you are done with the bookseller?" Emile questioned before leaving Nathanael who was still eyeing a rather old, two-volume set of Pilgrims Progress.

"Of course, go," Nathanael agreed readily and waved his hand to push him onward. For the first time today, he was most assuredly in Heaven and nothing short of a turbulent rainstorm would move him.

Emile couldn't help but smile at his friend's excitement but did not judge him as he made his way over to the end of a long row of carts near the store to his right. "Every man has his own vices, I suppose." He chuckled to himself and stopped at the edge of one of the carts to peruse the various trinkets, snuff boxes and the one thing that had caught his eye from afar—a simple ribbon necklace with a very small rose charm at its center.

"It's perfect," Emile whispered to himself and held it up closer to his eyes to judge its quality better for himself. With a tilt of his hand to make sure it was genuine, he moved the small charm to the left and then the right and realized that he was most definitely wrong about this treasure, and yet also undeniably right. The necklace with the black velvet ribbon that made the silver charm it held stand out even more was more than perfect in every single overlapping petal of the carved center rose and intricately lined outer leaves, it was enchanting and delicate, just like his Emma.

"How much?" He slid the thin black ribbon between his fingertips carefully and felt the smoothness of the material against his skin.

"Three shillings, six pence, if you please," the man replied gruffly, obviously prepared to haggle a bit on the agreed upon price.

"Hmmm, that might be a little high for me." Emile casually reached into his pocket and mentally counted his change once more before counteroffering. "Would you take two with the knowledge that it is going to a very worthy young lady?"

"Done. And done." The man reached out, shook Emile's hand and retrieved the necklace to package it up for him. "Picking something out for your wife, sir?"

"Something like that." Emile paid the man the two coins and thanked him heartily as he was handed the small bag in which held his gift. "I am much obliged."

"The same to you, sir," he replied almost out of repetitive habit and moved on to bartering with the next customer behind him, a bald man who was eyeing a very large hairbrush.

Emile smiled once more and tried not to laugh at the irony of the image as he passed. In another life, he might have stopped to tease the stranger or at the very least recommended something a bit more appropriate for him under the circumstances, but today he was doing his utmost to remain on his best behavior for Nathanael's sake, if for no one else.

"Spent your last farthing, Emile?" William joked from the street when his friend finally exited the aisle between the carts and stepped closer to them. The young physician, who had quite obviously returned early from his day with Mr. John Hunter, had seemingly already collected Nathanael along his way and was now standing in the center of the large, circled area of benches.

"Not hardly." Emile deposited his small gift discreetly into the inner pocket of his coat without delay and replied, "I still have enough for the ride home if need be.

"Home?" Nathanael raised his eyebrows suddenly at the choice of words and patted the side of William's upper arm with the back of his hand to get his attention. "Did you hear that, William? We are home to him, now."

Fearing where this sudden turn in the conversation might take him, Emile started to say something rather sarcastic and witty to deflect any display of emotion on his part from being misused against him but stopped himself and grinned innocently instead. "You two have been as close to a real home for me as I have had in a long time, that is certain. But more importantly, I do plan on staying for as long as you will have me."

"Forever, my friend, forever." William clapped him on the back twice with his free hand as if needing to reassure him of his eternal security without reservation. "Don't think we are letting our only chance at an edible, square meal run away so easily."

"No." Emile chuckled lightly and ducked his head at the compliment. "Thankfully not."

"And you had better not sneak out in the middle of the night again, either," Nathanael added before he pulled a rather vintage-looking top hat out from behind his back and presented it proudly to his friend, seeking to garner his approval of the impromptu purchase. "Oh, and just look at what I found for you at that shop over there!"

"Hopefully, not a book," Emile said sarcastically as he was still looking down, then froze when he finally glanced up and saw what he was holding. Suddenly, unable to breathe or even think a conscious thought otherwise, Emile swallowed hard to contain his emotions at seeing the piece of presented apparel and almost cried.

I don't believe it! Emile's mind shouted in incredulity at the discovery but in every possible way, he was still unable to move a single muscle towards him or away for fear that the moment would cause the vision in front of him to disappear fully, and he would reawaken.

"What? Is there something wrong?" Nathanael noticed the marked change in the man's countenance and brought the hat closer to his eyes to see if perhaps he had missed something when purchasing it. "I could never pull off wearing something as audacious as this back in Wakefield, but when I saw it hanging there on the cart, it quite literally leapt into my hands and begged me to purchase it for you. Do you not like it at all?" Nathanael appeared more than a little bit worried at the possible offence he was quite obviously causing him after all of his help and looked to William in confusion.

William could only shrug for he had not the least idea either as to why Emile might be reacting this way.

For the first time in all his life, Emile was entirely at a loss for words—utterly and incomprehensibly silent. In fact, for several long minutes, he struggled to even make sense of what he was seeing and reply, but he simply could not make his brain send to his mouth a single intelligible word.

"Emile?" William's voice came from a distance back to him, the worry and concern evident with every syllable of his name, but still he remained fused in place where he stood.

"Wh-where did you find this again?" Emile's voice came out just above a whisper at last as he finally managed to reach forward a trembling hand and move his fingers along the rim of the hat in front of him while caressing the top of it with the other.

"Are you feeling alright?" William touched the man's shoulder and examined him closely, looking for signs of actual shock.

"Most... definitely... not..." Emile shook his head slowly three times in pace with his reply, still incomprehensibly stunned.

"Um, the hat was over there across the street. The man said something about it being sold to him last fall for some quick cash. Why? Is there something wrong with it?" Nathanael looked at William, then back to Emile quickly. "I can probably return it there if you don't want it."

"Yes, I want it. A million times over, yes, Nathanael." Emile turned the hat over and inspected the inner binding around the base to verify his assumptions. "William, this is the hat that I lost that day when you and I met on the Endeavor."

"The day you were conscripted? Emile, be serious. That is not possible. Your hat is probably halfway across the globe by now or in the rubbish bin." William shook his head in disbelief as the possibility of such a thing was too staggering to comprehend.

"Really? Then, look here." Emile pointed to the three carefully sewn initials within the inner lining and proclaimed definitively, "Those are my father's initials. I know it because I watched my mother sew them there myself since he was always leaving his hat places and couldn't remember where."

"Well, then I am so glad that you have it back." Nathanael looked up at the man across from him and contemplated the deep emotion such an article of apparel would hold for him.

"Here. You can wear this one for now. I'll collect it later when we get back to William's." Emile took his previous hat from off his head and placed it upon Nathanael's, but the less ornate chapeau did not fit him in the slightest. Instead, it fell all the way down over his ears and touched the very top of his eyebrows humorously.

Not willing to cause a scene in the middle of somewhere so public, William was forced to cover his mouth instantly to stifle the guffaw that threatened to escape at his expense. "I am sorry, but hats do not suit you at all, Nathanael."

"Quite." Nathanael grinned and the expression only made him look even more ridiculous than before.

Emile ignored their antics entirely and placed his father's hat slowly upon his head once more before closing his eyes in satisfaction—contentedly transported to another world all his own. "It still fits me perfectly. Though I would like to believe that the man who wears it today is far different from the one who lost it last November."

"There is no comparison, Emile." William placed a reassuring hand upon the back of his coat for support once more.

"Agreed," Nathanael added before taking the rather outrageous looking hat from off his own head. "Though I think I will stick to letting you wear all the hats you desire, Emile."

The three men all laughed and enjoyed watching Emile beam with delight as they made their way back to William's family home.

Feeling suddenly much more like himself than he had felt in months, Emile stepped around a puddle in the middle of their path and walked briskly down the street. "Does the sun never shine in this city of yours?"

"Sometimes, though <u>my</u> theory is that it chooses to match the mood of the people under it instead." William looked up at the grey clouds that most definitely warned of rain.

"Well, while I am grateful for the dismal weather in regard to our safety, for summer, it <u>can be</u> rather dreary to experience it every day." Emile turned the collar up on the back of his neck to protect it from the spitting precipitation that had seemingly chosen to commence in adherence to William's judgmental remark.

"Speaking of dreary, how did you find the dissection room?" Nathanael asked out of courtesy, though he was not truly wanting a detailed reply. "Didn't you find it difficult to be there? I know I would."

"Not at all. It was entirely enlightening. There are so many things one can learn from a doctor such as him. And to answer your other question, no, it was not a problem at all in that way. The chemicals used to preserve the bodies do deter that kind of temptation, or I would never have gone in the first place."

"I see, but are you thinking about becoming a surgeon like your father someday?" He countered, cautiously reticent to push his friend in any direction whatsoever.

"Not hardly. I much prefer treating the <u>outside</u> of my patients for the time being, but I did find everything that I have learned today to be quite useful in that, too."

"That is good to hear because I am not sure I can do more than help in the apothecary should you decide to go in <u>that</u> direction." Emile stepped closer to the group to avoid a passing wagon. "Our current diet would make your patients a bit too appetizing in that regard and with little need of healing thereafter."

"Agreed," the other men said in unison and laughed lightly.

"On a happier subject, I did find something else that was quite interesting at the booksellers before I found your hat. Did you know that there were actually two installments of The Pilgrims Progress when it was first published and not the one copy currently sold today?"

"No." William shook his head but kept right on walking. "But then again, I only remember my nanny reading it to me before bed as a child. I always loved the part where Christian finally puts down his heavy load, but not so much the part when his only friend dies."

"That part <u>was</u> sad; I will grant you. Well, the seller had both copies in his possession," Nathanael explained further but frowned when both of his friends simply shrugged at the lack of importance. "It is quite rare to find one, if not both of them in one place. Not that I am going to buy them for the sum that they are worth, but it did make for a very interesting find among other things a bit more precious and sentimental." Nathanael dodged several people who walked between them and continued on as if nothing had transpired.

"I am sure." William agreed. "And I see that you got your apparel all sorted out by the looks of things."

"Paid a king's ransom for it, too. But the way I see it, it will be as Emile said, 'a worthy investment' as the last suit I purchased was probably five years ago and even that was secondhand. The majority of what I have in my bags has been given to me by members of my flock in some way or another over the years. You know as they say, beggars cannot be choosers."

"Huh, on that point I would like to respectfully disagree." Emile pulled on his own shirt cuffs one by one.

"You would." William leaned forward to tease Emile on the other side of Nathanael. "For most of my life, I have never been one to be overly focused on the accumulation of things, but I do understand more the plight of those who lack them now."

"I will concede on that point alone, friend." Emile inclined his head towards him and nodded slightly as he walked. "But nothing more."

"You wouldn't be you, if you did not." William chuckled to himself and felt wonderfully warmed by the delight of his companions' friendship once again more than any amount of sunshine ever did.

"Indeed, and as William so often likes to remind us... you are all original, my friend, and I am grateful that you are. You make our lives far more colorful by your sheer presence," Nathanael added as he crossed the last street in front of them and stopped when the three men had arrived at William's front door.

"Your purchases have been delivered by the milliner and are waiting for you upstairs, Mr. Beckett," The family butler cordially greeted by them just inside and waited to attend to their needs.

"Thank you, most kindly," Nathanael acknowledged.

"And a letter has arrived for you, Mr. Deschamps." The Butler handed the correspondence over to Emile and shut the door behind them ceremoniously.

Instantly curious, Emile opened the wax seal and read it silently before also reading just some of its contents aloud to the others. "It appears that our dinner party invitation at the home of Miss Toussaint has been extended to include staying the night at the Knole for at least two days. Something about delaying one of the events due to an illness with the servants, but not to worry about the household as they are wholly removed from the those who are ill."

"That should not be a problem. We were already planning on looking for room and board on the way to Portsmouth afterwards. This way we will simply stay at the Knole instead, then continue on after the party." William handed his cloak to the butler who took it and left. "I wonder what ailment has befallen them to make them change their plans?"

"We are on a holiday, William. Please try to remember that." Emile raised his eyebrows in admonition.

"Yes, if I have to rest, so do you." Nathanael agreed, then looked at Emile. "I've heard that the Knole is a fairly large estate. Is that true?"

"I actually couldn't say for certain as I have never been. Have you, William?"

"Not that I recall, why?" William cast him a puzzled glance.

"Just making sure that this time we can be fairly confident that our rooms will be mouse free," Nathanael quipped lightly.

"One would hope, especially given its position in the county for social gatherings, or so Miss Toussaint has told me in her last correspondence," Emile responded. "Though she does advise here that it would be best to arrive by six o'clock this evening if we can. Do you think that will be possible given our late arrival, gentlemen?"

The others nodded and began ascending the stairs promptly.

"I, myself, cannot wait to meet this, Miss Toussaint. You said you knew her from France?" Nathanael turned on the first landing and headed up the second flight of steps ahead of them.

"Actually, we have been acquainted for many years, but always in Paris, yes." Emile followed him but stopped outside his door to politely allow Nathanael the opportunity to enter first.

"Splendid! I have always wanted to visit the Knole. My friends in seminary used to say it was like visiting a great museum with the artwork, sculptured ceilings and tapestries there." Nathanael opened the door, then reached down to his bed and picked up one of the smaller, carefully wrapped brown paper packages. "This one is for you, I believe."

"*Pour moi?*" Emile motioned to himself with his right hand and took the offered package with the other. "They must be mistaken. I did not order anything there."

"No, I did," Nathanael said nonchalantly while packing up his meager belongings for the trip.

More than a little surprised at his generosity now twice in one day, Emile untied the string on the thin package to reveal the expensive vest he had been admiring at the tailors. The rich garment that had seemed fit for a king had been skillfully crafted from a cream linen material that fell slightly around the hip region in its length. And adding to the stylish cut and overall presentation was a delicate, but detailed gold trim that lined all the edges including the left and right pocket which was finished by a line of brightly polished brass buttons down the center. The price for which had been far above what he had deemed responsible for him to spend at any time, but it had not deterred him from regarding it favorably just the same.

"Will it do?" Nathanael eyed the man from across the room to view Emile's expression better.

Unable to accurately express himself once again, Emile pursed his lips to hide his overwhelming emotions and managed to say hoarsely. "It will do rather nicely, thank you."

"It was well-deserved." Nathanael moved to complete his packing.

"Oh, I don't know about that." Emile tried the garment on once more with great satisfaction. "But then again, not everyone can turn a pauper into a prince for a night."

"Only in fairy tales I am afraid." Nathanael smiled, grateful that he had made the impulse decision to buy it, especially at seeing how much Emile liked it. "Besides, at least one of us needs to be able to outdress William, and as we both know, that will never be me."

Emile laughed lightly. "He really is a different man here in London, isn't he?"

"Maybe." Nathanael shut his bag and laid it casually next to his other parcels. "But deep down he is still the same man I have always known, just enhanced by the atmosphere here, I suspect."

"Perhaps." Emile took off the now-cherished garment and placed it neatly with the rest of his things into his luggage before turning back to Nathanael. "I am very grateful for both of my gifts today, Nathanael."

"Good, that pleases me greatly to know it," he replied nonchalantly and took his two bags out of the room and down the steps without him in preparation for their departure.

Feeling more than a little bit grateful today that God had seen fit to capture and imprison him on the Endeavor last fall, Emile remained where he was and watched him go, simply nodding once more at his friend's characteristically humble reply. In all of his life, he had never felt so incredibly blessed nor cherished for doing so little to deserve such kindness, care and attention. Yet, knowing that he could do nothing more but thank God for His divine intervention, Emile merely smiled at the meaningful exchange with Nathanael and the many other gifts beyond the more tangible ones that the man had so unknowingly given him over the past few months.

"It is enough, God," Emile said in deep satisfaction as he picked up his father's hat from on top of the bookcase and put it on once more. "And I will not waste this opportunity again," he replied even more fervently and closed the door behind him to depart.

Chapter Thirty-Eight

June 22nd, 1793

O n the whole, the short, three-hour carriage ride to the Knole was absolute heaven compared to their last journey together from Wakefield. So much so, that the men had hardly finished their discussion of the recently established Republican state in Germany and the new £5 note than they had noticed their arrival just outside the town where the stately home lay. Having never been exposed to politics in any way back in France, Emile had never once considered the life of a politician beyond that of his various social duties, but listening to the two other men debate the two rather complex subjects had surprisingly intrigued him or at the very least, had distracted him enough from the many anxious thoughts racing through his mind as they travelled.

"Do you think that your friend has had a hard time fitting in with English society since her arrival?" William asked while looking out the window at the passing scenery leading up to the estate.

"I highly doubt it. It has been my experience that Miss Toussaint knows her way around a room no matter what country she may be in." Emile participated briefly in the conversation but seemed otherwise, momentarily preoccupied with something deep within the folds of his inner pocket, patting the area repeatedly from time to time to make sure the object was still safely inside.

"By the way, you might want to stop holding your breath every five minutes when you get there, Emile. Right now, you look more anxious than I do and that is saying something," Nathanael said quietly to the man who was seated next to him. "Is something the matter?"

"Hmm?" Emile looked up briefly but had not really heard what the man had been saying to him. "What?"

"He said that you looked a tad uncomfortable, Emile. Something you care to share?" William leaned forward and rested his arms across his knees, waiting to hear what was troubling his friend enough to cause him to fidget so excessively for over an hour. "I haven't seen you this unhinged since the day you arrived in Wakefield."

"It's nothing, I assure you, gentlemen. Just thinking, that's all," Emile deflected their alarm and clasped his hands together firmly to steady himself once more, his whole body becoming painfully rigid in obedient response from doing so.

"So, it would seem." William pursed his lips, but the worried expression his face carried did not change in the slightest. "Maybe you should try a little less of that at the moment or at least until you and I can talk properly."

Unwilling to say more, Emile shifted in his seat uncomfortably and crossed his leg over one knee as he tried his best not to look at his friend directly, fearing that if he did, the man would know all. "Please just let it be for now, William," Emile pleaded more earnestly and flicked his eyes upwards just once to mark his expression.

William only narrowed his eyes as he examined him further and then cocked his head ever so slightly as if he were forming a question of his own with the gesture that was only meant for the man across from him.

Lifting his chin in response to his question, Emile raised his eyebrows just once and exhaled almost as quickly, releasing just a bit of the anxiety he had been feeling since their carriage ride had begun but also attempting to answer discreetly William's inquiry further in doing so

"That bad?" William whispered almost inaudibly while staring out of his window as a ploy to hide his muted comment from Nathanael.

"Immeasurably so." Emile's head moved just barely in the shadows from side to side twice as he closed his eyes to focus on the gait of the carriage horses once again to distract him.

"Soon..." William promised him quietly, knowing that nothing he could say at that moment would help the man prepare for his possible encounter with his old love. Nor did he even have the words to encourage him later in it as he himself was as conflicted on the matter as Emile obviously was it seemed.

When he left Charlotte's home back in April, for the first time in his life, he had started to envision a future for himself with someone else mentally his equal.

Yet after Nathanael's recent experience with Elsie, he had most definitely decided to close the book on that dream firmly shut and lock it away securely.

Helplessly watching him suffer night after night with very little to offer him in means of comfort, made it hard enough to believe that any of them might have a soulmate somewhere in this world that would fit into their current lifestyle and restrictions, let alone dream that she would also be willing to accept the most demanding parameters of their diet. But it was even worse to contemplate what he would do if he were to also put himself into a situation where he would be forced to choose between having to live a life steeped in secrecy as they endeavored together as man and wife over a lifetime of solitude without her which was clearly not helping Sebastian and Charlotte. Either way, in his more logically inclined mind, there really was little choice but to let that dream go.

... or was there a way... William's mind pondered once more on the possibilities of that kind of reality then shut the book once more out of necessity. *Maybe it is just best for <u>all</u> of us to remain bachelors, after all.* William reminded himself seriously once again and nearly jumped when Nathanael's suddenly, exuberant statement startled him.

"Look! There it is!" He proclaimed as he drew all of the men's gaze back towards the view on their right, obviously the only one enjoying the short time of silence and reflection.

The carriage, which had finally turned off the main thoroughfare from town, was now steadily making its way directly through the arched outer wall and up to an almost castle-like building that stretched out in the formation of a perfect square with its various wings and walled gardens. Intrigued, the men all strained to see the great estate from their positions inside the carriage and watched as a line of servants and underbutlers stepped out of the inner doorway and formed two rows on either side of the front entrance. The next to exit the large doors was the family of the estate and Miss Angelique Toussaint who passed through their center easily in joyful anticipation of her arriving guests.

"Shall we?" Emile drew in a breath and held it as he stepped out of the carriage first, powerless to delay the inevitable any longer, followed by an equally affected William and Nathanael. The latter looking rather awkward given the formality of the reception and all it involved and his restrained excitement.

"Welcome to the Knole. We are very pleased to have you *Monsieur* Deschamps, Doctor Wells and Bishop Beckett," the 3rd Duke of Dorset greeted them cordially as if <u>they</u> were the ones in the higher position of importance and not the hosts themselves.

"This is quite a welcoming party for three men of little regard such as us," William acknowledged his host's hospitality with a slight bow and a handshake thereafter.

"On the contrary, Doctor Wells, we have heard nothing but the most wonderful praise from your father concerning your practice in Wakefield. Not to mention the heroic exploits of *Monsieur* Deschamps in saving at least one of our fair relations in France," Lady Arabella graciously added while motioning one hand in Angelique's direction.

"It was my duty, *madame*." Emile bent forward and kissed Lady Arabella's hand. "Any man would have done the same given the opportunity."

"Indeed," Anglique said quietly yet did her best to bat her eyes in obvious flirtation in Emile's direction.

Surprised beyond expression at the action, William and Nathanael each looked back at the other and then to Emile, clearly confused by the display for they had heard little of this woman in Emile's life to warrant such an interaction, quite the opposite in fact. As far as either of them were aware, Emma Larose was the only person Emile was interested in at the present, which only made his next words and actions towards her all the more interesting.

True to his previous nature, Emile fell instantly back into his rehearsed persona easily, smiling ever so politely in response to her compliment and gave one back in return. "A pleasure as always, my dear." He kissed her hand courteously as she curtsied in response.

"I am sorry that we had to delay the more formal dinner party until tomorrow night, but I hope you will all join us for some sherry and cards this evening, and maybe if everyone is amiable to it, we can petition a few of the local boys for a game of cricket while you are here tomorrow afternoon," the duke offered hopefully.

"Cricket? I thank you for the inclusion, but though I am sure that would no doubt be quite lovely to experience, I wouldn't know where to even begin in playing such a game." Emile offered his arm to Angelique who took it quite readily. "I'm sorry to say, but I don't think that particular diversion has caught on in France as of yet."

"Nor for myself either, and I have lived here all of my life," William replied. "I suppose you will have to settle for a couple of spectators here, I am afraid."

"A true shame, but no matter. It doesn't hurt to be optimistic when guests arrive." The duke motioned for the group to follow him inside. "Still, I am sure we might be able to do some other form of diversion. What about hunting?"

"Now, hunting I know." Emile cast both William and Nathanael a side glance and grinned mildly at the ironic humor of the moment.

"A lovely idea, sir." William chuckled lightly. "In fact, from what I hear, Emile is quite good at catching his prey no matter what continent he is on."

"Is that so, Doctor Wells. Well, that fact aside, I believe the duke is referring to the local fox hunt, sir," Angelique chided her consort openly in an almost annoyed tone. "But I can assure you there will be plenty to tempt you and your friends tomorrow night if you are still interested in that sort of prey."

"Why you astonish me, *mademoiselle*." Emile looked casually surprised, but not the least bit interested in her suggested sport. "I thought my invitation to your lovely gathering was from a friend, and not the county matchmaker, but perhaps I was mistaken."

Angelique rolled her eyes at his sarcastic repartee but smiled sweetly instead so that the rest of the group gathered would hopefully not comment further on their inner jest. "And so it was, *monsieur*. Now, if you will follow me inside, I am sure you would all like a moment to view the many treasures the Knole has to offer and maybe we can tempt you with some refreshments afterwards. I have heard that the journey from London <u>can</u> be a bit tedious this time of year."

"Only somewhat," Nathanael agreed excitedly and followed the group as they passed on through a very large, ornately carved, walnut door before stepping into a long hallway with intricately cast plaster ceiling tiles.

In the large, inner foyer where they paused to wait for further instructions, stood a marble fireplace that reached from the floor to the ceiling, complete with a painted oval mural of a quaint country scene and multiple copies of Italian statues that were also tucked carefully between large paintings of Charles I and other dignitaries or distant relations. From every corner all around them, the finest of objects were displayed like hidden riches, begging to be appreciated and noticed for the obvious value they possessed.

Clearly overwhelmed by the stateliness of the room in which he now stood and all that it contained, Nathanael took but a few steps inside before he stopped and stood fixed to the floor, too in awe to continue onward. "This is truly the most agreeable home I have ever personally encountered."

"Thank you." The duke shone his great approval of his guest's compliment and began taking Nathanael and William on a tour instantly of the many rooms and treasures in his great estate, being careful to also regale them with the brief history behind each and every one of them as they passed.

"I will see that the servants bring your things up to your room directly. You will be staying in the east wing along with the family, if that suits you *Monsieur* Deschamps," Lady Arabella explained courteously.

"I am sure whatever you decide will be lovely. We are very grateful for the opportunity to stay on such short notice." Emile charmed his host and watched her carefully as she left the remaining pair in the Great Hall to speak more freely.

Alone at last, Angelique quickly drew in closer to Emile's shoulder trying her best to entice the man with her more direct attention towards a renewal of their most recent romantic acquaintance. "Have you missed me?"

"Miss Toussaint...?" Emile cleared his throat and stepped away from her respectfully to allow a very definite space between the two of them to form. "I am sure it must be very exciting living in a museum like this. Or what I mean to say is," he kept the conversation as mundane as possible to discourage future advances on her part. "That I am curious what it must be like to own your own castle in some regards." He tried clumsily to divert her further as he cast his gaze on several of the various artifacts around him.

"A mausoleum more like it." Angelique tossed her head back cheekily and began pacing about the room while fingering the many fragile objects as she passed without paying them the care they deserved for their magnificent creation. "As beautiful as the estate may be, there is practically nothing to do here but watch the paint dry on these old relics and listen to the many, many conversations about the duke's cricket matches."

"I gather he is a bit of a player, then?" He studied the foreign antiquity on his right with increasing interest as to the origin of its craftsmanship.

"I'll say. He has already had one affair with the Countess of Derby and even Lady Elizabeth Foster, but I am sure you will meet a few of them tomorrow."

"He keeps in close relations with his mistresses? That seems very... um, French." Emile gawked in astonishment.

"Oh, it's quite the scandal here, but yes. Lord Derby has received him quite politely given the circumstances, though I cannot say the same for his poor wife. Despite the duke's many connections, the countess has not been accepted back into high society since her unfortunate dalliance."

"A pity for her." Emile rubbed the back of his neck guiltily, remembering with fresh shame how he had first eyed Emma back in Paris. "But, to go back to my original question, I was referring to the game of cricket, my dear, Miss Toussaint... not women. Or would you still prefer m*ademoiselle*?"

"Miss is sufficient for now. We are in England, after all." She waved her hand dismissively at the necessary redirection, already entirely bored by the new path of the conversation. "As I am sure he will be happy to tell you, Sir John Sackville has been part of the leading cricket club in Hampshire for simply ages. He has even been reported on in the Morning Chronicle and the Whitehall Evening Post."

"Our host does seem like a very energetic fellow." Emile crossed his hands behind his back as he walked aimlessly down the hall, taking great pains to stop at each painting in turn, all in an effort to put a visual distance between himself and his past association.

Still undeterred in the least, Angelique caught up with him easily and impetuously reached out one hand to take his in hers. "Emile, wait."

"*Mademoiselle*?" Emile stopped abruptly and turned to face her; surprise clearly written across all of his features.

"You <u>must</u> know why I wrote to you so many times since we arrived?" Angelique batted her eyes while biting just the front edge of her lower lip, an action she no doubt thought would make her seem even more irresistible and tempting.

Emile was not impressed, nor was he attracted to her in the slightest, no matter what she may choose to do. "Actually, I do not. I assumed your repeated request for a visit was merely a meeting of old friends, nothing more," he replied while trying to convey an attitude of aloofness to her and close off any false ideas to the contrary.

"Old friends? Is that what we have become here now?" Angelique leaned in closer and fingered the crease of his suitcoat lapel looking entirely hurt by his outright dismissal. "I thought that we have always been much more than that. Or at least we were back in Paris, that is. Has England truly changed you that much already?"

"Actually, it has changed me more than I ever thought possible." Emile coughed nervously at the unwanted attention and shook his head slowly before unwinding her fingers gently from his clothing. "No one would doubt that I have admired your charm <u>and</u> your beauty for many years, Miss Toussaint, but you and I are both well-aware that we were <u>never</u> romantically inclined, at least not in the way that you think."

"Not romantically inclined?" Angelique looked positively hurt now by his statement but held her head high. "I can remember many a time where you couldn't help yourself but to draw close to me back in Paris. Even Jonathan thought so," she added the final remark to persuade him further on her behalf but regretted it afterward when she saw a glint of coldness overshadow his eyes.

"Miss Toussaint, I truly have no idea to what you are referring, but I beg you to leave Jonathan out of whatever fantasy you have created and not embarrass yourself further on the matter as my mind has not changed in that regard, nor do I expect that it ever will." He took another decidedly deliberate step back but tried to maintain a sense of decorum between them, not wanting to hurt her feelings callously as she was his host after all, or at least one of them.

"Hmm..." Angelique's eyes narrowed instantly at his request, obviously perturbed by his response to her advances, but in the end, remained not the least bit discouraged. "We shall see, Mr. Deschamps. We shall see..." She turned around just in time for the other men to re-enter the room from their brief tour and rejoin their party.

"Emile, the duke says that they own the oldest organ in all of England. Isn't that absolutely fascinating!" Nathanael chimed in eagerly, his youthful exuberance on the subject clearly bubbling over.

"I am told by your friend, Mr. Beckett, that you can play very well. Perhaps you can do so for us this evening if you are so disposed," the duke invited him openly.

"No!" Nathanael and William immediately stepped in to divert what most likely would occur, but did so almost a bit too loudly, requiring William to add politely thereafter, "What we mean to say is, it might be best if you tell him what you wish him to play first as he has a very wide palate of interest when it comes to music, sir."

With a look of almost annoyance, Emile eyed the two men sarcastically from across the room but did not engage verbally as the three of them were already well-acquainted with his musical library and his obvious preferences.

"Ah, do you have a current favorite, *Monsieur* Deschamps?" The duke petitioned him closer, completely unaware of what was transpiring.

With a shake of their heads, William and Nathanael both hung their heads in defeat as they knew exactly what piece of music Emile would choose to play—something loud, something dramatic, something dark. Something he loved to play in the chapel whenever Nathanael offered him the chance.

"Why yes!" Emile smiled widely at the invitation, ignoring the judgement of his two friends and walked over to his very amiable host. "I've recently begun a small study of Mr. Johann Sebastian Bach these past four months. I am sure you have heard of him."

"Most definitely, a favorite to all musicians, I should think. Please follow me." The duke led Emile through a series of side rooms and corridors to one whose entire wall contained the largest pipe organ he had ever seen.

"It is magnificent, sir!" Emile stood with his mouth slightly open in astonishment. "May I?"

"But of course, I'd love nothing more," the duke encouraged and pointed to several small red and gold benches along the opposite wall for the others gathered to sit and enjoy his impromptu performance.

Feeling slightly intimidated by the sheer size of the instrument before him compared to Nathanael's practically miniscule one in the chapel, Emile pulled out the tall wooden bench and took his seat anxiously before placing each of his hands delicately along the length of the many sleek keys to get his bearings. Then, with the skill of someone who had spent hours practicing the same piece of music every day of their life, he began the first notes of Bach's most famous and yet foreboding composition. The one he loved most out of all of them.

Like a brilliant burst of light, the rich scales the organ bellowed out from its gleaming pipes surged and pulled in their intensity as his hands played several of them in succession, allowing each mesmerizing note after the other to feel cool to his touch and yet electrifying all in the same motion. From every corner of the room, the melody spun as he swayed deftly through the legatos, the sequences, and the crescendos until he finally reached the very definite merging of all before a great and glorious silence ensued—the moment of anticipatory cessation just before the climatic lead-up to the grand finale.

With the full support of the added lower-pedaled tones near the end, the small room shook with the organ's power and command before the echoes of its singing all ceased. After nine long minutes of pure joy from the wonderful experience the organ had provided, Emile bowed his head in great satisfaction like a man who had just completed a masterpiece of epic proportions... again.

"Bravo, sir!" The duke exclaimed in admiration as the applause from all who attended erupted. "You play simply marvelously!"

"Stunning, as always *Monsieur* Deschamps," Angelique also complimented him freely, clearly enamored by the man she had chosen as her favorite.

"Indeed," William remarked quietly in a bit more disparaging tone as he watched with great curiosity the over-exuberant response from the young lady. By all that he had seen since his arrival of her definite infatuation with the man, Emile had some explaining to do, and whether he liked it or not, William had questions.

"You will most definitely need to play for our guests tomorrow," the duke decreed excitedly. "Though I do agree with your learned friends here, that perhaps another of Mr. Bach's selections might be more appropriate for our smaller gathering. We cannot touch the heavens twice in one week, can we?"

Emile nodded with a smile of great satisfaction at the duke's obvious appreciation and stood up to bow to his host. "It would be an honor. The

Bourree in E minor might be a tad more suitable given the intimate occasion and it also lends itself to dancing should the party be so inclined."

"Agreed. Now, I think we have imposed on your courtesy long enough, *monsieur*. After such a long drive from London, the three of you would probably like a time of respite." The duke played the consummate host once again.

"Maybe an hour at most, if that is acceptable." Emile inclined his head politely, controlling the scene unfolding around him.

"Excellent, let me have our underbutler show you to your rooms."

The duke rang the bell for the necessary servant and within moments a young man, smartly dressed, arrived and escorted the three guests up the main stairway and down the hall towards the east wing.

Chapter Thirty-Nine

June 22nd, 1793

"This will be your room, Bishop Beckett," the servant directed as he opened the door to the red room and waited politely for him to enter.

"Just Mr. Nathanael Beckett will be sufficient, thank you. I have not achieved such a position as a bishop as of yet, but I felt it rude to correct our host upon our arrival." Nathanael tried courteously to correct the error without offense.

"Very well, sir," the man acknowledged. "I will make the necessary adjustments for the future. And if the two of you will follow me across the hall, I will show you to your room Doctor Wells and *Monsieur* Deschamps."

The other men both followed behind him obediently and entered the room directly across from Nathanael's, a room more than big enough for an entire family to enjoy back in Wakefield yet this was intended for just one man here in Kent.

"This specific room has a door connecting to the suite on the other side of this wall. The duke thought you might appreciate the convenience of conversation above the others available as this one also includes a shared sitting room." The man opened the door between the rooms and motioned for Emile to enter. "This will be your room if you please, *Monsieur* Deschamps. You may lock this center door at your pleasure when you require privacy. The lock is on your side alone."

Emile followed and smiled at the clearly French-inspired motif in the chosen tapestries and linens. "The duke quite obviously has good taste."

"I'll be sure to tell him so. Will there be anything else you gentlemen require?" The underbutler inquired dutifully.

"Did the duke ever live in France by any chance?" Emile fingered the satin on the pillowcases and admired the *fleur de lis* embroidered bedspread.

"Why, yes. He was the English ambassador there until just last year."

"Ah, that explains a great deal. Thank you, um... I am afraid I did not catch your name," Emile addressed the man as his equal and not as the servant in which he was.

"Peter, sir. Just Peter. You will find a bell next to the fireplace on your left. Please ring it if you find yourself in any difficulty. The family has explained that they will receive you for drinks around eight o'clock sharp," the man instructed him politely, clearly pleased with his personable question.

"Thank you, Peter." Emile turned to gaze out the window at his view of one of the gardens just beyond. With the patience he had worked very hard to garner for the past two months, he waited for his nerves that had been on edge since his arrival to settle and took in the moment fully. As hard as he tried to deny it, he still could not get away from the fact that something in the back of his mind was still bothering him. Something more than the irritating attention of Miss Toussaint and definitely far greater than his growing anxiety about possibly seeing Emma again if he could manage to locate her, but what that was he had no idea.

Since the very first moment that he had stepped into this house, there was a distinctly unsettling feeling that was unusually triggering about its inhabitants. However, as strange as that may be to think it, there was also not a single tangible reason he could contemplate as to the exact cause or he would have investigated it already... or at least nothing visible that is.

Was it all just a feeling of insecurity, maybe? And if so, why? Hadn't he already proven definitively that he had changed for the better, or at least as much as humanly possible for the time being? The rest, he was certain, would no doubt come in time, and after much continued attention to those areas of his life that were still lacking.

On the other hand, if the prospect of seeing Emma once more was the reason for his growing anxiety, he knew precisely why he felt so inadequate, but he sincerely doubted that it had anything to do with it.

Looking out the window to distract his thoughts from that possibility, the same sinking sensation and prickling of his skin that he had felt at the port upon his arrival months ago washed over him yet again drawing his attention immediately back to the hallway from whence he had just come as if his mind were measuring the danger lurking there. As far as he was aware, they certainly had nothing to fear from the servants, nor Angelique for that matter, for as annoying as her presence might be, he knew she was completely harmless.

Then what was it?

Nevertheless, the sensation persisted on the back of his neck like an irritating buzzing phenomenon that seemed to move up and down with his breathing as if warning him repeatedly. Still, he tried to ignore it, choosing to remind himself yet again that there was not a single item here that might elicit that kind of response. Perhaps later, when everyone else had gone to bed, he might investigate a little for himself just to end his incessant curiosity on the matter. But for the moment, he decided it was probably best to remain where he was.

Shaking his head once again at his seemingly senseless paranoia, he sat down on the edge of the bed and stretched out his tall frame completely upon it, grateful at last for such opulent comfort. The bed itself felt simply incredible compared to the much shorter one to which he had grown accustomed to at William's home, though he would never complain to his friend about it. Why, just being given the opportunity to sleep for even one night to the fullest of his stature was going to be divine and most welcomed after months of hitting his ankles accidentally on the foot of his bed in his sleep.

Intensely satisfied within his thoughts at last, he closed his eyes for a moment to drink in the wonderful experience afforded him but opened them instantly a short while later when a young maid entered his room unannounced while carrying a rather large stack of freshly pressed linens for the bath.

Entirely focused on her task at hand and completely buried beneath a mountain of supplies, she made her way into the room without pausing to announce her presence but stopped abruptly in her humming when she finally saw the still form of a man on the bed while peeking over the top of her towels, noticing all too late that the room was currently occupied.

"Oh, dear me! Excuse me, sir," the demure girl began to apologize profusely to cover up the flustered frustration her actions had created by her impromptu interruption and moved to prevent his chastisement. "I wasn't aware these rooms were being assigned tonight. Please accept my apologies." The young woman, who never made eye contact with Emile curtsied but kept her face inclined respectfully downward before turning on her heels abruptly thereafter as she attempted to retreat as quickly as possible without completing her called upon task.

"Please do not feel uneasy. You may come in and continue your delivery if you must." Emile sat up and angled his head sideways to see her face more clearly, suddenly keenly interested about who it was behind all the towels.

"Sir?" The girl froze and turned back around. The sound of the man's familiar voice drawing her even closer as she lifted her head ever so slowly in response above the towels. So slowly, in fact, that time itself seemed to almost stop between them in its passing. "Emile Deschamps, is that really you?"

"Emma?" Emile stood up instantly and rushed across the room to her side, forgetting all the many wonderful things he had planned to say when they had next met.

"Oh! It is you, Emile!" The girl's face practically beamed as she ran to him instinctively, as well, almost colliding in the middle of the room from the excitement at the unexpected surprise. "What are you doing here?" Emma held Emile's hand unashamedly, rubbing his fingers casually between her own over and over again as if it were the only means afforded her to reestablish their previous connection.

"Me? What about you?" Emile's heart swelled instantly with obvious delight at the familiar action for it had been one she had done on so many nights as he held her in his arms and read to her on the large settee by the window, waiting for her to fall asleep. "Miss Toussaint invited us to stay for a few days during our holiday, but I had no idea you were here. I mean, I had hoped so, but when I did not see you out front with the others, I thought perhaps she might have found you work elsewhere."

"I'm not that high enough of a servant to greet guests, yet, Emile, but a holiday? What I'd give for a holiday, Emile. Or even a night off every once in a while, to walk around town would be nice. You know, just like we used to do back in Paris." Emma wiped her brow that was slightly wet with sweat with the back of her sleeve. "Please don't misunderstand me. They treat the servants here quite well. In fact, I can assure you that it is most definitely far better here than any job I have ever had back in Paris, but still... a holiday... that would be wonderful."

"The duke and his wife do seem quite amiable." Emile clasped her hand firmly and kissed it just once before holding it close to his chest, as if afraid to sever their connection so soon should she suddenly need to leave.

"Oh, they are! And they just had the most precious little baby. You cannot help but smile when you look at it," Emma gushed over with admiration and joy at the little bundle he had yet to see.

"Emma, love, you have no idea how happy it makes me to find you so well after all this time." Emile touched her cheek with the back of his fingers then drew them away quickly so as to not embarrass her when William unexpectedly interrupted them by entering through their adjoining door unannounced.

"Emile, what time did the underbutler say we were to meet the duke for..." William started to ask but stopped abruptly when he saw the young girl standing so close to Emile.

"Beggin' your pardon for the disruption, sir." Emma curtsied formally to William showing him the proper respect for one in her position.

"Please... you do not need to bow to <u>him</u>." Emile shook his head and laughed lightly at the very idea. "I certainly don't."

William ignored his comment completely as his eyes lit up instantly in recognition. "Are you the elusive Emma Larose I have heard so much about?"

Emma blushed at the man's obvious foreknowledge and nodded twice with a smile. "Guilty as charged, I am afraid."

"I am so glad to finally make your acquaintance," he said excitedly as he walked quickly over to her and shook her hand vigorously under the folded towels. "Here, let me help you with those." He tried to relieve her of the heavy load, but she refused.

"Oh, no, sir. It wouldn't be fitting. As kind of a gesture as that may be, if someone were to see you, I'd lose my position for sure."

Emile and William grimaced at the forced realization that they were in a much higher position in this estate than with someone they would normally converse openly with back home.

"Perhaps, we can talk more freely when you are done with your chores. Maybe somewhere a bit less... um, problematic for you?" Emile eyed the open door to the hallway.

"I'll have to clear it first with the housekeeper, Mrs. Berry, but I might be able to meet you in the gardens after the party tomorrow night if that is soon enough." Her blue eyes sparkled at the possibility. "As you might expect, things are a bit busy downstairs at the moment, preparing for all of their guests or I would offer to go with you anywhere... right now, in fact."

"I can only imagine. Shall we say nine o'clock then? Will that give you enough time?" Emile could not diminish the smile now plastered across his face, nor the butterflies dancing about his insides from one edge of his being to the other.

"Plenty to be sure." She curtsied and dutifully walked around the bed and over to the bathroom behind with her load to complete her required delivery before anything further prevented her from doing so.

Able to speak somewhat freely now in her absence, William motioned with his eyes and hands at least five questions all at once, then stopped immediately and folded his hands quite gentlemanly afterwards when she returned as if he had said nothing at all while she was away.

"I bid you a good evening, gentlemen," Emma said kindly before casting a slight glance back at Emile filled with hopeful anticipation on her way back out of the room.

"And you, as well, Miss Larose," William countered cordially and looked over at his friend to judge his reaction. It was exactly what he had expected to see: fear, longing, desperation, and joy. Not a single emotion overpowered by the other before it in his expression, but all mixed themselves equally in various ways across his conflicted face. Yet, it was the first that stood out the most in the end after being compelled to watch her leave once more after so much time spent apart. In fact, William could tell from the way that Emile almost didn't breathe, that his friend was barely keeping himself from rushing after her. Something the man might possibly have done had others not also been in the room with them. Either that or not let her leave in the first place.

And as kind as she appeared to be, Emma probably would not have rebuked him too harshly for doing so, that much was certain by the way in which she held his stare, but it would have most definitely made a scene and possibly hurt her future employment at the Knole. Neither of which were obviously desired by either of them it seemed, though both appeared desperate to talk.

The complicated interaction between the two former paramours intrigued William immensely while witnessing it, making him infinitely more curious as to what had actually happened back in France. To date, Emile had told him next to nothing about his life with her beyond a romantic connection when he arrived in Wakefield, as if the secret was too sacred to share, but William knew there was more to it—something Emile was ashamed of maybe, for the man rarely hid anything else from him of late.

And yet, despite how very much Emile struggled to do so, he politely kept his place by the bed and flexed his fingers in and out as she passed, taking in her slender form once more until she was almost to the doorway when Nathanael also walked unceremoniously through it at the same time, colliding with her without noticing their unexpected visitor.

"Have you seen the paintings in the hallway, Emile... Opppf, my apologies, Miss!" His face turned a bright shade of pink to red with embarrassment at his complete lack of observation in the matter.

"It was my fault entirely, sir. If you will excuse me, please." Emma exited the room without any further comment and had almost closed the door completely but not totally behind her before the three men heard a distant voice calling out her name from the end of the hall.

Alarmed for the girl, Emile and William walked closer to the door and listened through the crack.

"Miss Larose, I hope you have not been disturbing our guests," Angelique chided her most sharply, thick disdain evident in her tone. "As you are well aware, you do not even belong in this part of the house, let alone upstairs."

"Yes, ma'am." Emma kept her head turned downward, folding her hands respectfully in front of her. "Mrs. Berry just asked me to deliver some of the linens to the rooms in this wing since Tracey, the upstairs maid, has been sick since yesterday."

"Well, see to it that you send one of the underbutlers next time. You are not in France anymore, miss." Angelique looked down her nose at her and replied in a manner which seemed less convinced of her sincerity.

Emile's blood began to rise in temperature as he narrowed his eyes at the obvious slight to the young woman's character, but he managed to hold his tongue for Emma's sake.

"Yes, ma'am," came the obedient reply and distant quick footsteps down the stairs, signaling to all listening that the conversation had effectively ended.

Shaking their heads in unison, the two older men closed the door quietly thereafter before turning back to a very confused Nathanael waiting behind them.

"Who was that?" Nathanael asked, still not completely recovered from his recent misstep.

"That was Miss Larose." William smiled and nodded with definite approval.

"I'm so sorry, Emile, I didn't realize. Should I go and apologize to her again?"

"No!" The two men stopped him firmly, knowing that saying more would only get Emma into further trouble.

"I'd say it was a pleasure to meet her, but I do not think that attacking the poor lady qualifies," Nathanael apologized profusely.

"Don't trouble yourself too much about it, Nathanael," William assured him and watched as Emile tapped his tallest finger on both of his lips while pacing the room deep in thought, distractedly ignoring the conversation from the men around him.

His two companions, however, watched him pace in silence for several long seconds more before William finally spoke up and asked, "Did you know she was going to be here, Emile?"

"Not really. I only knew that she could have accepted a position here or at another estate nearby. Given the details when we parted, I could not properly petition for her correspondence." Emile looked out the window and tried to distract himself once more from his racing thoughts concerning her.

For the past two months he had thought of nothing else but this very conversation with Emma, and now that it had happened, he had discovered he was feeling even more unbalanced in his feelings than he had ever anticipated—insufficiently adequate financially, socially, and eternally, but the last one bothered him much more now than it ever had before.

Perhaps Nathanael was making more of an impression on him, after all.

He hoped so as it was becoming increasingly evident to him that he was going to need a bit more of his religion if he was going to survive any of this without regression.

"Well, she seems lovely. Will we get to ever properly meet her?" Nathanael looked over at Emile curiously.

"Tomorrow. I've arranged to see her in the garden later that evening."

"No doubt she will have chores to complete first," Nathanael again stated the obvious, while attempting to make encouraging conversation, having missed the bulk of the encounter previously.

"No doubt." Emile rolled his eyes at the accurate annoyance of the statement and grabbed his father's hat from off the bed in mounting frustration. "Now, gentlemen, if you will excuse me, I think I wish to go for a walk."

"A walk? But it's already quite late?" Nathanael protested. "Aren't we supposed to be meeting the duke and his wife for drinks in half an hour?"

Humored by the man's panicked expression, Emile patted him on the shoulder lightly as he passed by, though not at all with the same rude intentions as he had once done so in the cave. "Take heart, dear preacher. I will not send thee into the lion's den alone as I shan't go far this time."

"Huh, I've heard that before..." Nathanael relaxed slightly but was not overly convinced on the matter. "Lion's den indeed... I never know what to say to these people."

With Emile gone, William directed Nathanael back through to the adjoining sitting room and towards the waiting table therein before motioning him to sit. "Whyever not? You talk to me every day without any difficulty."

"Yes, but you are not a duke." Nathanael smiled halfway in mock-grimace.

"True," William took his seat, inclined his head for a moment then righted it as he nodded. "We are fairly close enough to it, but thankfully for my sake, we maintain a slightly different title."

"What?" Nathanael selected a chair at the small table in the room and sat down next to him.

"My father alluded to it when you first arrived. Though it is true that we did start out as document procurers, without going through all the lengthy particulars, it might be easier to say that the position developed into much more than that later. In the ensuing years, my family has achieved a societal status most people of our acquaintance envy, though I have never seen the need for it much myself." William sat down easily across from him, somewhat enjoying this moment of toying with the man's intelligence.

"So, what <u>would</u> your title be then?" Nathanael asked curiously.

"A duke, a lord, a viscount, why does it matter? I much prefer being William Wells the doctor and so does my father despite his delight in bragging about the family antiquities." He waved his hand dismissively in the air. "The game of tit for tat and mindless verbal banter drives me crazy. So much so, that I quite literally jumped on the first ship out of London to escape it all the last time my mother had intentions of marrying me off to a well-bred lady of culture."

"Marrying you off? You speak as though you were some kind of ware to be sold to the highest bidder, William." Nathanael shook his head, not believing a single disparaging word his friend had uttered.

"It does rather feel like that at times. Oh, there were dozens of ladies last year vying to be the wife of the very eligible, well-to-do, Junior Apprentice Surgeon in London. No doubt they would have loved the society and amenities such a position would have provided them, too, but I would have been in hell... literal hell, Nathanael, and I don't mind saying so. My father knew it and moved to prevent it by securing for me an apprenticeship position on the *Endeavour* instead, which is where I met the two of you."

It was Nathanael's turn now to sarcastically roll his eyes at the overly dramatic way William described his privileged life. "You make courting seem like a dreary affair, but it can also have its definite perks."

William laughed lightly at his very simplistic view. "Now that is something we can both agree on. But the affections of a lady are not what truly troubles me, Nathanael."

"Then what is it?"

"I'd love to find the right kind of wife." He looked directly at his friend to judge his reaction before continuing. "Maybe even someone like Elsie or hopefully for Emile, Miss Larose. But those are the kind of women who love you for who you are, not for what you can give them. A wife should be someone who accepts you in your current state of imperfection, not as a bartering chip to accelerate her own ideals. That was what I was running away from—a form of indentured hypocrisy as many men of my acquaintance would call it."

"Ah, I see." He nodded in final understanding. "Well then, that is all there is to it."

481

"What do you mean?" William replied, suddenly confused by his easy acceptance.

"We shall simply have to find you a well-bred woman who has no need for your title or £500 per anum."

"Um-hmm..." William fingered the brocade on the tablecloth in front of him without expression, judging whether or not to reveal his true identity at last. "Maybe try close to three times that amount, and you would be a little nearer to the actual sum."

"What?" Nathanael's mouth instantly dropped open at the admission. "Per anum?"

"Per anum until my father dies, and then the entire estate falls directly to my brother through the heredity laws. Though he would still be required to uphold the previously established arrangement, or at least until his death where the lordship would then fall upon me, which it undoubtedly will, seeing as I will be here much longer than either of them."

With nothing else left to say, Nathanael shook his head in total astonishment. "I am never paying for dinner again, William."

"Nor do I ever expect you to." William smiled sheepishly and laughed, grateful once again for his friend's jovial candor and blind approval where matters of possible conflict might arise.

"Come. Let's head down a bit early. It will give me a chance to view those paintings in the hall you were mentioning earlier when you bumped into Emma." William stood and motioned with his hand towards the door.

"They are stunning. Or perhaps you could even buy one for the apothecary," Nathanael teased him openly.

"No, thank you, Nathanael." William shook his head in amusement. "I prefer my obscurity just the way it is. No Rembrandt will ever be necessary to fulfill my happiness."

"Oh, I don't know. I've heard that _A Painting of St Peter's Ship_ is quite a beautiful piece to behold in person." Nathanael pushed in his chair and followed after him.

"And also currently housed in the Netherlands, if I am not much mistaken. I doubt Mr. Hinloopen is disposed to part with it as of yet," William countered.

"But someday he might. And after all, William," Nathanael paused at the door before opening it for him. "We have time to wait. Though honestly, the very fact that you know all that information means you have at least considered it."

William shook his head once more. "And I thought the women were bad."

"Seriously?" Nathanael appeared suddenly offended, but not at all deterred. "You have to admit you have at least thought about things like this at least once in your life, William."

"In the profession that I am in, I choose to think about today only, Nathanael. The Lord will have to work out the rest." He closed the door behind them securely and the two men continued on their way as they walked down the hallway and towards the grand staircase that led to the sitting room off the Great Hall.

~   ~   ~   ~   ~

Emile felt the small pebbles crunch beneath his feet as he strolled along deep in thought through the walled garden just below his bedroom window. The sun, which had started to peek out from behind the clouds during their carriage ride, had eventually set during their discussion inside, allowing the moon to make an appearance between the otherwise twilight hued sky before it retreated once again into hiding behind some clouds high above. Watching it as it slunk away discreetly back into obscurity, he couldn't help but smile once more at the quite obvious, visual analogy to the way he was currently feeling.

Two months ago, Emma had asked him to live honestly for a time, and true to his intentions, he had done his best to do so. William had also been entirely correct in his assessment of him at Señor Moretti's and before. He had been rather self-focused and admittedly pompous... lazy even, but that was not the man he was becoming now. And if he were to be fair, he rather enjoyed his new life with William and Nathanael, even if it was in the desolately unsociable North. On the whole, it was infinitely far more interesting than anything he had ever experienced in the past, even with his failures, and it continued to fill him with even more satisfaction with each passing day. Moreover, it was becoming more and more acceptable to him that though their simple existence lacked the flair and color of Paris, it also held a much deeper treasure—lasting friendships that were open and uplifting to experience. Something that infinitely made him a better person because of them, not by merely using them.

Emile had also not realized fully how accustomed he had grown to living alone as a solitary bachelor. Or to put it more accurately, how sad his life had truly become while choosing to live as a person that did not require anyone but himself for survival. Before meeting Emma, he had not properly contemplated what an honest relationship could bring to his life. Or the immense pleasure he might have as he watched it flourish and grow. The uniqueness of that kind of relationship was built on choices and a genuine trust. Neither of which should be compelled or forced, but rather both were essential in order for it to be enjoyed and open to possibilities. Something which was completely foreign to him before, but not now.

In Nathanael, the most unexpected of his friendships, he had discovered a meeting of the minds with his deep discussions about morality and eternal purpose, whereas William added the very practical tools he lacked for daily interactions. They were the perfect balance of opposing viewpoints in their instruction as his mentors, and both were as essential to him now as breathing on this new journey of transformation, this life of renewed purpose.

Yet perhaps this was the very thing that had shocked him most of all. In helping others in Wakefield, he had quickly learned that he was no longer content to live his days aimlessly in pointless pursuits. Through his daily tasks of baking or helping the Summerfield's prepare the meals for the tavern, he had also discovered a hidden talent he had not known he ever possessed. In fact, the whole experience had opened his mind to the expansion of opportunities that kept him up at night... not with the dread of his failures, but in the hopeful consideration of the next step in his journey.

Still, that was not the only thing that kept him awake most nights.

Was William also right about Emma? Was it truly necessary to give her the option to let him go now before she formed an even more definite attachment, one that would cause her lasting grief should she, in turn, refuse him? Or was he right to wait until he was certain of her love before risking the loss of it when she discovered his immortality?

His mind, as always, spun in many different directions around the subject but returned each time to the same question over and over again.

"How does a man tell the woman he loves that he is a vampire?" Emile shook his head and sighed at the impossibility.

Life was so much simpler when I didn't have to care what happened to the girl I was seducing. He let the errant thought go and rebuked himself once more for the cavalier way in which he had treated her back then.

With renewed resolution, Emile nodded as he finally decided what he must do. If he were to have any hope at all for a future with Emma, he simply had to give her the chance to choose between a life of uncertainty with him, or a whole life without him. Though as complicated and convoluted as his eternal existence might be at the present, he might forgo telling her all the more colorful details about his current temptations and focus instead on the most basic of facts concerning their possible future.

And yet, if in the end, naked honesty was what Emma needed most from him... then that was what he would give her, no matter what it might cost him to give it. Despite what he truly wanted otherwise, he was finally ready to let go of their beautiful dream if he must, no matter the pain it might cause him for centuries thereafter to do so. Or to put it more accurately, it was high time he put her needs before his own as they should have been all along.

His only thought now was whether or not to let his heart dare to hope she would choose him after all.

Chapter Forty

June 24th, 1793

I t had taken Nathanael the better part of the day to tour the greater majority of the ten gardens the estate afforded its guests, but in each new one he entered, he had discovered something beyond his expectations. Reveling in the many varieties of flora and fauna while also dutifully taking copious notes in his journal about them, he delighted in the way in which each walled off area displayed a unique and inviting theme. In his short time on this Earth, he had been privileged enough to see many fine estates and even a royal garden in his youth, but nothing compared to what he was experiencing today for never had he been so abundantly surrounded by such order and beauty that it felt almost as if the Garden of Eden itself had come alive for him, minus the foreboding angels at the gates and a very untouchable tree at its center. From the tall wisteria to even the tiniest of daisies, they all reached out their vines and blossoms towards him as they sang out their melodious symphony. In short, it was more than he could have ever imagined possible as he allowed it to fill his entire being with a renewed sense of peace and calm that had long been absent.

William, on the other hand, had spent his day entirely sequestered indoors, choosing rather to enjoy the rare opportunity afforded him to peruse the Knole's vast library before selecting a few volumes to read quietly in one of the smaller corners of the large room. As busy as he had been in the past few months, it had felt oddly satisfying to selfishly devote a few hours to personal entertainment without the fear of neglecting his patients. Not to mention finally paying heed to the true reason for their vacation of sorts—rest. Even when he was younger,

William had never been one to sit idly by as there was always something that could be done for someone, but today, not a single soul required his attention. None that is except for those fictional characters found within his chosen books, which felt far more comforting to revisit than the many medical journals he had been pouring himself over.

Only Emile seemed to be anxiously awaiting the party that evening as if his whole being stood poised like a twig, ready to snap with the slightest movement in either direction. For hours he had paced the length of his room, rehearsing various alternatives of his speech for Emma that night before giving up entirely in a huff and collapsing onto his bed in utter defeat. No words in all the world seemed entirely adequate for the task in front of him just now but find them he must if he were to have any hope at all of persuading Emma to change her mind about him and marry him.

And so it was that as the evening approached, it could not have come soon enough for Emile as the men all gathered together once more with the twenty or so other guests in the ballroom as was customary after dinner for drinks and discussion. From all vantage points around the great chamber, standing groups of guests chatted about the newest gossip and current events while the duke's closest friends gathered closely around his life-sized portrait that was painted by the esteemed artist, Sir Joshua Reynolds only a decade earlier. The whole atmosphere from the wine that was served, to the discreetly playing violin and cello ensemble, all spoke only of the best that society had to offer, seeking to provide something far removed from the quieter nights the three men usually enjoyed at the tavern or apothecary back home.

"I'm afraid to touch anything in here, William," Nathanael spoke just above a whisper to his friend while still fidgeting with the length of his sleeves and matching coat at the opposite end of the red room, far away from most of the guests assembled. "From what I can see, every piece of furniture here appears to be either made from or gilded with gold. Is this normal?"

"Yes, I'm afraid so." William smiled, enjoying his friend's honest assessment and obvious attention to detail. "But now that you mention it, it does look a bit like the Great room in Buckingham House. Not exactly, mind you, but definitely very close."

Shocked once again at his friend's intimate experience with that of the royal household, Nathanael's eyes suddenly grew wide at the disclosure. "You've been in the house of the King?"

"A time or two over the years. Though it has been probably at least a year since the last time I went." William took a sip of his drink, then replied without the least bit of importance, "Kings get sick, too, Nathanael."

"Indeed." His friend only shook his head in utter amazement once more at how much the simple doctor had kept carefully hidden away from all of them. "We will have much to discuss when we return home, I should think."

"Quite." William swallowed another sip but appeared totally disinterested in the upcoming discussion that Nathanael seemed so eager to have. "Besides, you wouldn't like it there, anyway, but Emile might."

"Oh?" Upon hearing his name, Emile stepped nearer from the next group over and rejoined the two men waiting on the far side. "I'd like what?"

"Buckingham House or rather the Queen's House as they call it now. It has a very French influence in its architecture and furnishings," William explained easily as if the information was common news to everyone gathered.

"Of course it does. Everyone copies the French," Emile proclaimed proudly.

"Everyone copies who?" Angelique leaned in closer from his side to hear more clearly what the three men were saying by a large gold family crest that hung on the south wall.

"The French, my dear, the French." Emile sipped his drink, enjoying the rich flavor of the wine his host had provided. "You will have to pass my compliments on to our host, Miss Toussaint, as this is a very good red."

"It ought to be for the price he paid. Ever since they started that awful taxation of the wine back in '89 the French government has made it particularly difficult to acquire virtually anything of quality." Angelique moved her head slightly to bring her long curls to the front of her body.

"Well, this is most definitely a higher quality." Emile swirled his glass in a circular pattern slowly before smelling the rich bouquet of the liquid once again. "Simply excellent in every way."

"And you, Mr. Beckett... Do you drink?" Angelique tried to continue the pleasant conversation, noticing the lack of participation on his part.

"Only on Sundays, my dear," Emile interrupted mischievously before Nathanael could answer as a personal tease to his abstinent friend.

"On Sundays?" Angelique's face turned into one of utter confusion, completely unaware that a reason existed where one might only drink on that specific day of the week.

"An inside jest, Miss Toussaint, nothing more." William grinned at Emile and tried to hold back his polite chuckle with his cupped fist.

Desperate to end the merriment at his expense, Nathanael ignored their antics like a patient saint, choosing rather to allow his expression to carry with it only a slight amount of annoyance instead of the true irritation he felt inside. "I hardly view communion as drinking, gentlemen. That would be a definite sacrilege, but to answer the young lady's question, no, I try not to partake unless it is for medicinal purposes only."

"Oh." Angelique seemed at a loss for what to say next as the entire room around them was enjoying some form of spirits or another. "I beg your pardon then for my careless inquiry. I had no idea. Would you like me to ask one of the servants to bring your something more suitable? Water perhaps or even tea?"

Noticing her increasing discomfort and equally awkward suggestions, William whispered a piece of advice quietly next to Nathanael's ear as discreetly as he could manage without drawing her or anyone else's attention, "If you don't want to stand out tonight, you might want to consider medicinal drinking just for the evening or at least appear to be doing so." He handed him a half-full glass of wine from the server who was passing by. "You don't have to actually drink it."

"Fine." Nathanael smelled the liquid and tentatively took a very small sip, then struggled to maintain a polite expression thereafter. "It is without doubt an acquired taste, I am sure." He winced at the strength of the offered wine before respectfully refusing to drink any more.

"Most definitely." Emile finished his current glass and swapped it with the half-empty one that Nathanael had been handed. "No sense letting excellent wine go to waste, gentlemen. Now come with me Angelique. You have still to present me to your many wonderful friends." He offered her his arm and winked back over his shoulder at Nathanael—obviously rescuing his friend from further torture on the matter.

Overjoyed at last to have Emile's undivided attention, the woman at his side readily accepted his offer and toured the room quite proudly while introducing him to several of the ladies and men of her acquaintance. Most of them, William had met at least once in his life at some sort of gathering or another. While others were new additions through marriage or rising stars from another country or station. Yet, whoever they were, it mattered little to him anymore, at least not in the way that they would think was important. Every one of them would be talking about the same thing tonight and yet, nothing of consequence at all. In fact, just watching the recently joined pair enigmatically control the crowd, William was more certain than ever that he much preferred his corner of the room with Nathanael any night to the center of the room like Emile and Angelique enjoyed.

"Do you see anyone you know?" Nathanael inquired politely, studying William's expression so as to judge his thoughts more clearly.

"A few. And you?" William replied casually and finished his glass of wine.

"None in here to speak of, though I did meet a rather interesting gentleman in the garden earlier today. On the whole, he looked vaguely familiar when I first saw him, and I told him so, but after we spoke, he assured me repeatedly that we had never met." Nathanael paused and shook his head in frustration. "And William, even if I felt so disposed to do so, I couldn't argue with him for his name is a complete mystery to me even now just as much as it was then. And yet, there was also something else in his overall demeanor and presence that made me intensely cautious, too," Nathanael explained his experience at length, hoping that in doing so William might aid him in putting together the confusing pieces and help him in placing the stranger.

"Hmmm. I wonder who he was." William's whole forehead scrunched up tightly in concentration before he cocked his head slightly in Nathanael's direction. "Did he say why he was at the estate, perhaps?"

"Actually, I never had the chance to ask." Nathanael shrugged. "I thought I heard someone walking down the path behind me after I had spoken with him, so I turned around, thinking it was one of you fetching me for lunch. Yet, by the time I turned back to continue our conversation, he was already gone."

"Maybe it was someone you met in your ministry once upon a time." William tried to give him the best reason he could think of to abate his concern.

"Perhaps," Nathanael agreed easily, then clasped his hands firmly behind his back enjoying the light violin music being played. "Well, strange men in the garden aside, Emile is obviously in his element tonight, isn't he, William?"

"Most certainly, though I think the lady has much more intended for him than Emile is aware of, at least for the present." William set his empty glass on the silver serving tray to his left then scanned the room again, searching for Nathanael's mystery guest.

"Really?" Nathanael watched the pair in action. "I see nothing amiss."

"You wouldn't. Though I mean no disrespect by it at all, Nathanael." William tried to deflect any criticism that might have been intended by his remark. "You have but to merely observe her movements to know the cues she is sending out to everyone in this room."

"How so?"

"Look here." William leaned in closer and spoke softly so as not to offend anyone else listening nearby, "Notice the way in which she holds his arm like that. She does this so that there is no space left between herself and Emile. An otherwise inconsequential thing on the surface mostly, but in doing so she is saying to any other lady present in this room that Emile is most definitely her property, so to speak. And then there are the smiles, the overly gracious laughter at his remarks. It is all part of the great performance she is playing to exude dominance over Emile, or rather, to mark her current conquest."

Nathanael watched the many interactions more closely with renewed interest, analyzing them intently to learn their patterns, then shook his head doubtfully. "I'm sorry, but I still don't see it."

William could only laugh lightly at his friend's naivety and patted Nathanael on the back. "Let's just determine that I will watch out for <u>you</u> this evening should anyone else form a special attachment to a certain preacher friend of mine."

"You won't have to try very hard as I have no intention of fraternizing with anyone other than the two of you, if I can help it." Nathanael waved him off, certain that he would have little need of his protection

"Well… you might want to hold that thought…" William trailed off as he put on a diplomatic smile for the two women who were now slowly walking their way.

"Lovely," Nathanael grimaced at the intrusion but displayed his best smile to address them anyway.

"Good evening, ladies," William greeted them cordially without missing a beat.

"Good evening," the taller of the two women acknowledged him. "We were told by Mr. Deschamps over there that you are a doctor."

"Yes." William nodded in agreement. "Mr. Deschamps is correct, as always."

"And you are a man of the cloth?" The shorter of the two women spoke kindly to Nathanael, displaying the extent of her knowledge on the subject, "That seems so exciting!"

"Really? Yes, well, I do have a small congregation up in Wakefield, but I am not certain that anyone I know would call my job exciting," Nathanael dismissed her assumption easily.

"That far north!" The taller woman exclaimed. "How do you bear the lack of society there or are there other distractions to speak of?"

"The people in the town are pleasant enough. Many are in fact, quite charming when you get to know them." Nathanael watched the two ladies before him and began to finally comprehend the direction the conversation was taking him. "And my fiancé even played the pianoforte for our services when the occasion called for it."

"Your fiancé! Oh, I didn't know that you were already spoken for, my apologies for the oversight. Still, she is a lucky lady to be sure," the taller woman replied.

"Angelic," William added cautiously, while also judging his friend's reaction to his veiled comment.

The corners of Nathanael's mouth lifted slightly at the hinted humor, allowing for the first time in months a long-missed sparkle to reach his eyes. "From the heavens to be sure."

"Truer words could not have been better spoken." William nodded, distractedly fingering the chain of the watch in his pocket before pulling it out to check the time. It was nearly 8:45 already, meaning that they had but a mere fifteen minutes more of obligational purgatory.

"And you, dear doctor, are you kept fairly busy in your part of the country?" The taller woman shifted her attention to the smartly dressed man in a predominantly blue ensemble by the preacher's side.

"Immensely so, though I am afraid you would find that many of my profession usually are," William answered her politely but showed only the necessary interest in the conversation so as to diffuse it as quickly as possible.

"Then perhaps you can help us figure out the mystery surrounding the servants in Kent while you are here." The younger lady's eyes lit up with increased excitement at the unexpected prospect.

"Oh?" William's curiosity suddenly piqued considerably. "Is there a problem?"

"Well simply every estate in Kent has had at least one servant die over the past three months if not more," the taller woman explained as she looked down her nose at him at his lack of knowledge.

"That many?" Nathanael questioned the accuracy of her statement.

"Well, to be truthful, there aren't many prominent estates in this part of England to begin with, but if one were to put a number on it there would have to be perhaps fifteen or so," she answered him directly.

"At first many of the owners attributed the illnesses to poor constitutions or even the lingering effects of the influenza, but all of that passed months ago and the deaths are still occurring." The younger lady finished the tale started by the other as if the two of them were part of a perfectly choreographed chorus of stored gossip.

"Surprising to be sure." Nathanael and William each cast the other an inquisitive glance but only William continued further in his line of questioning. "And it is only at the higher residences that this is happening? What I mean to say is, have there been any other deaths to speak of among those in the town?"

The two ladies looked at each other and shook their heads.

"Not that we are aware of, though we do not often make it our business to know what is going on in the daily affairs of the lower classes to know for sure," the older woman answered quite plainly and giggled behind a gloved hand at the absurdity that she should be pressed upon enough to care about their welfare.

"I am sure you don't." Nathanael tried to smile genuinely, but every word of the conversation was making his skin crawl just listening to their condescension and flippant disregard to those who suffered beneath them.

"Has a doctor been called?" William continued on in his interrogation.

The women both laughed giddily once again. "I simply have no idea, sir. We only arrived here just yesterday ourselves, but the unusual tattle has been spreading like wildfire among the guests tonight."

"I see. Now that you mention it, I do remember receiving word about the illness back in London when we received our initial invitation." William nodded. "Perhaps I should find out more information directly from the source while I am here."

"Yes, do," Nathanael encouraged him. "And speaking of that, would you please excuse us, ladies."

"But of course." The young women smiled and allowed the two men to pass by them and walk over to the other side of the room where Emile and Angelique were now casually standing alone while chatting by the tall windows.

"Have you heard what they are saying about the servants?" William tensely blurted out his alarm to Emile without bothering with the necessary pleasantries of formal conversation, especially with Miss Toussaint present.

"No." Emile shook his head in confusion but otherwise appeared vastly unfazed about the discussion being presented, choosing rather to hide his true concern behind another sip of his wine before answering calmly. "Should I?"

More than a little perturbed now at his callous dismissal, William's eyes narrowed just a little, certain that he was not ready for the old Emile to be returning any time soon, no matter what the occasion. "It concerns the roommate of Miss Larose, Emile."

"Ah, I see. Have _you_ heard anything, Angelique?" Emile raised his eyebrows just once in reaction to his friend's changed expression and obvious annoyance before slightly rolling his eyes towards the woman at his side.

"Yes, well, he is probably referring to the sickness that has been occurring among the servants. It started sometime around the middle of March with the undergardener just one house over dying from severe dehydration from what the duchess has told me, but it has spread quickly to many of the other prominent households since." Angelique fanned herself slowly, causing the many curls framing her face to sway with the breeze.

"Have they all had the same symptoms?" William inquired respectfully.

"I am not entirely sure as I only arrived near the middle of April myself. Isn't that correct, Mr. Deschamps?" She leaned in closer to Emile and stroked his arm like she was petting a favorite cat or dog.

"Quite so. We came to England on the same ship." His lips pursed together once in dissatisfaction of her increasingly intimate advances but attempted to ignore them for moment, much like he had been doing for the bulk of the evening.

"Huh, you make it sound as if we had a choice." Her eyes started to moisten only slightly at the shared memory of her father and brother, yet Emile could see clearly that everything about the display was a well-practiced facade used for nothing more than the continued garnering of sympathy for her benefit.

Her brother, Jonathan, would have been furious if he had seen it tonight, or at the very least disgusted by the repeated defamation of his memory. After all, he had never much cared for the overly elegant life Emile led or the parties he was forced to attend. He would have much rather been out working in the garden any day than listening to the annoying whispers and polite laughter events like this specialized in.

Nevertheless, there was a reason why he had been one of Emile's closest friends before William and Nathanael. For almost six years, he was the one person who could tell Emile the truth concerning his failures without fear of retaliation, but also, he was the only one who was the most loyal when Emile needed him. As such, watching Angelique's senseless deception about her grief concerning his death only made Emile's stomach churn even more remembering Jonathan's face on the platform once again. His friend had fought for her until his dying breath and yet she could not even bother to mourn him properly when it mattered.

Well, so be it. Emile thought darkly and accepted the challenge placed before him at last. If she would not honor Jonathan in death, he would do it for her by ending this game of hers once and for all.

"I do not think tonight is the proper time to go into all of that, wouldn't you agree, my dear?" Emile patted her arm in mock comfort and removed it from his own delicately but firmly, knowing better than most that two could play at this game of charades.

The woman beside him pretended not to notice his action at all. Instead, she only sniffed and dabbed at her barely shed tears with her handkerchief before adding further, "Perhaps you're right. But to answer your question, Doctor Wells, one of our staff told me just last night that the upstairs maid, a Miss Tracey, is now ill. Maybe you could speak with her concerning the matter directly. As you might imagine, it has been terribly inconvenient finding a replacement for her at such short notice."

Emile rolled his eyes and felt another wave of disgust wash over him, as fresh as the one he felt the day before. After months of quietness in Wakefield he had been looking forward to this social gathering very much. But after listening to the pointless conversations and vain presentations by Angelique, they all made him realize fairly quickly that he no longer belonged to any of this world anymore.

Though his life in Wakefield may not be his ideal home either in the end, at least it was a great deal more genuine than a single second of time spent socializing here with her. Well, almost everything was pointless about tonight. There was a certain young lady that would be waiting for him in the garden shortly, and despite what she may think otherwise, she was most definitely worth the wait.

"Do you believe the duke would mind me examining her when she is clearly not my patient? I wouldn't want to offend our host," William interrupted Emile's mental deliberations as he motioned to the duke across the room, soliciting him silently for a possible conversation later.

"Mind? I should think not. He has already employed the services of an out-of-town doctor several times actually with little improvement after his visits. In fact, come to think of it... I don't think any of the servants have improved at all no matter what the man has advised." She tapped her fan in concentration onto her free hand before adding saucily, "But then again, they could also be just faking it for an extra day of rest."

It was Nathanael's turn then to feel the raw indignation surge within him at her blatant rudeness and struggled thereafter to put his sharply intended remarks into more satisfactory words. "Do you really think your servants would do such a dishonorable thing?" His eyes betrayed the true irritation he held at the mere suggestion.

Standing just to his right, Emile watched his friend carefully with the same growing resentment they both shared at the very idea but chose to remain silent for the moment. As much as he wanted to say something more, it appeared by all accounts that Nathanael was doing a fine job all on his own.

"Oh, you know the rabble. They can be quite a lazy lot, but given the right inducement..." She said casually, as if what she was saying meant absolutely nothing in the world, which it probably did in her regard.

Having finally heard enough, Emile stared at her incredulously and corrected her firmly in French before his friend said something he would no doubt regret, *"Angelique, it would be wise of you to know your audience a little better."* He motioned with his eyes to the two men by his side before returning back to English. "None of us standing here believes any servant in your employ to be lazy, let alone bold enough to take advantage of their employer in such a fashion. So, hold your tongue... please."

"Indeed. Well, your Miss Larose certainly has a few things to learn then," she replied tartly at his open criticism of her while staring him down. "You might as well know; she has been quite the disappointment since the very beginning. I should have sacked her long ago, but I didn't because I knew it would upset you."

Emile closed his eyes briefly and tried to tame the fire building within him to a civilized response but could not manage to utter a single, polite word to the woman who used to be his romantic focus once upon a time.

"Miss Toussaint," William placed a supportive hand deliberately behind the small of Emile's back to steady him as he watched his friend struggle, then rescued him in the only way he knew how. "I am sure it has been hard for all of you to adjust to another country's way of doing things, isn't that right Nathanael?"

"Absolutely. Miss Larose seemed extremely polite and well-mannered when I met her yesterday." Nathanael picked up on his cues perfectly. "A definite asset to any employer."

"Quite," she stated unapologetically. "If you will excuse me please, gentlemen. This conversation has grown tiresome." She turned on her heels and left the three men to go find more amiable discourse.

"Yes... most definitely go, m*ademoiselle*!" Emile growled under his breath. "Far a-way."

"I am sure she is only trying to get a reaction out of you, Emile," William advised, though he himself could not hide his equal offence at her comments and lack of compassion.

"Well, it worked. Yet, despite all my French the only thing I can think of right now is one very excellent English word."

"Really? What is that?" Nathanael asked curiously.

"Ingratitude."

"Yes." His companions all nodded in unison with his assessment.

"Should we surmise that she already knows Miss Larose from your time in France?" William stroked his freshly shaved chin while still contemplating the problem with the servants and not the story he had been waiting to hear unfolding before him.

"Yes, she met her just before we left, the very day in fact. I was at the trial of Miss Toussaint's father and brother when the people announced her death sentence, as well." Emile's temper decreased gradually with the continued discussion

"And you succeeded in bringing her all the way here despite all of that?" Nathanael appeared shocked. "How <u>did</u> you manage to escape?"

"Would you believe dressed as a peasant?" Emile laughed lightly at the memory and felt the remainder of his anger dissipate entirely with the added humor Nathanael always managed to encourage from him.

"This is truly a story worth telling, Emile, but can we save it for later?" William urged gently. "I'd like to go back to something that she mentioned just now. The doctor that has come has not been able to help them, but they have instead gotten worse. That would not raise my suspicions if it happened once, but almost fifteen times? He is either the worst doctor I have ever met, or something is not right here."

"Agreed." Emile nodded. "I am supposed to see Emma shortly as it is almost nine now. Would you care to join us? I am certain she would be happy to answer any of your questions with far more care than Miss Toussaint over there... Rest indeed," Emile repeated once more Angelique's accusation through gritted teeth. "The audacity of the woman. Part of me wishes I had left her in Paris..."

"No, you don't, Emile," Nathanael reminded him kindly. "You just wish things would have turned out differently."

"True."

"Well, as harsh as she may appear, it was not too long ago that a certain man of my very recent acquaintance would have acted in the same fashion, maybe even worse if given the right provocation," William huffed back at him with a smile.

"*Qui? Moi?*" Emile smiled and easily slipped back into his former self.

"Yes, you. I remember quite well a most belligerent Frenchman standing up to our quartermaster with those very same words."

"I was quite vile then, wasn't I?" Emile raised his eyebrows impishly with a delighted smirk.

"Quite," William replied, humorously smiling, as well.

"It was fun then. Now... not so much." Emile chuckled lightly. "I suppose I have the two of you to thank for that side of my reformation."

"Us?" William and Nathanael each stared at the other in confusion.

"I didn't do anything. Did you?" William protested firmly, pointing at his chest with his hand before turning to accuse Nathanael.

"Though I would love to take the credit for <u>any</u> growth this man has accomplished, I simply cannot," Nathanael added more genuinely.

"Face it, Emile. You might just have yourself to thank this time... or should we be issuing our gratitude to someone of the fairer disposition for the motivation?" William teased lightly though all of them knew the truth.

"Most definitely a woman, but <u>not that</u> one." Emile's eyes flashed in anger once more towards the woman across the room as he finished the last sip of his wine and made the necessary excuses to his host for their departure. At long last, the garden awaited them, and he could not seem to get there fast enough.

Chapter Forty-One

June 24th, 1793

"Fifteen people and not a one of them ever recovered?" William paced back and forth along the pathway beside the garden, the moonlight casting long shadows from the walls and over the plants and bushes just beyond. "Think of it in terms of numbers, gentlemen. Would you not notice if fifteen people died among say... I don't know, a hundred people?"

"I'd be more concerned if it was contagious." Emile took his hat off and flipped it around in his hands aimlessly while he waited.

"Precisely. So, why are people not more concerned about it?" William shook his head, fighting with the facts presented to him. "Nothing about this makes any sense."

"Does it normally?" Nathanael questioned, trying to be helpful in his friend's deliberations.

"Science always makes sense, Nathanael, except well, when it doesn't." William chuckled lightly. "I'm sorry. I know that does not help at all."

"It makes sense when you think of <u>who</u> is sick." Emile stopped playing with his hat and turned around slightly to glance back down the lane behind them, thinking he had heard a strange noise coming from the garden directly to his right.

"What?" William noticed his abrupt action, but did not understand it.

"Oh, nothing... it's just... Well, it felt like someone was behind me just then." Emile rubbed his chin in concentration, then tried to brush off the feeling as best as he could but just like before in his room, it would not dissipate.

"Did you actually see something?" Nathanael leaned his head over to peer around Emile.

"No, but I thought I heard..." He paused to listen more closely as his intuitive sixth sense caused the hair on the back of his neck to stand to attention once more. On the whole, it had been something he had been able to remotely ignore since yesterday evening, but ever since he stepped into the gardens tonight, the uncomfortable sensation that followed him more than unnerved him now as it caused his heartrate to quicken involuntarily and his mouth to frequently water.

"I heard it, too, that time." William took a few steps closer to the sound to investigate, but when he did, it stopped altogether, allowing the atmosphere to fall incredibly still around them as if nature itself was being forced to hold its breath in response.

"What do you think it is?" Nathanael asked.

"I'm not sure," Emile said with great hesitation, still uncertain if he should go investigate or simply let it go. "The last time I felt this particular feeling was when Emma and I arrived from France. A coincidence?" He raised one eyebrow with his question to William.

"Depends on where you were at the time," William added as he examined the shadows beside them.

"Down by the shipping warehouses in London. There was nothing there then either, just random men loading the waiting ships, but still..." He cast another look behind him, then shook his head. "It's odd that I feel it here, too. In fact, I have felt it the entire time we have been here, William."

"I know what you mean. I felt something like it a few months ago, but thankfully the intensity of it passed with time. Either that or I've become more accustomed to it since, like when you arrived Emile," William admitted but narrowed his eyes once more on the bushes just behind him and to his left.

"Was the other time while you were in Wakefield, too?" Nathanael asked, starting to feel more unsettled by the minute by whatever it was that was lurking in the darkness close to them, unseen by their naked eyes.

"No, it was in London when I went to check on my family," William replied, then shook his head. "Truthfully, I have to admit that I didn't give it much thought at the time. It disappeared just as quickly as it came so it didn't draw too much of my attention. Do you think it is signaling some kind of danger, Emile?"

"Danger?" Nathanael's eyes grew wider still at the possibility.

"Relax, Nathanael. I am sure it is probably some rodent hiding amongst the hedges. Weren't you ever told those tales as a lad that made you go jump in the night?" Emile smirked as he tried to comfort the man.

"Most definitely not!" Nathanael turned up the collar on his suitcoat to block the chill creeping up his spine since the mere mention of anything spectral.

For Nathanael's sake, William tried his best to hold back a chuckle, but some laughter still managed to escape. "We shall have to indulge him with a few someday, Emile. Just so that he can temper that over-active imagination of his."

"What! And risk those night terrors all over again?" Emile shrank back in horror slightly. "<u>No</u>, thank you." He shook his head most resolutely and flashed his attention immediately in the opposite direction towards the sound of approaching footsteps coming from the house. By all appearances, a small figure was moving toward them quite rapidly, but thankfully, this person did not also bring with it the same sense of uneasiness as whatever it was that lingered in the shadows behind them.

"I thought I would never finish with all of those dishes," Emma said cheerily, though notably out of breath from her brisk walk from the house.

Grateful once again for the welcomed distraction, William pulled his attention from off the bushes momentarily and onto more pleasant things. "I'm so sorry. Is that your official job here at the Knole?"

"That among many others." She smiled and the pink flush in her cheeks from the exercise only added to the light of her countenance. "I help with the cooking too, mostly the desserts, but I do also fill in here and there with the chores downstairs like cleaning out the fires or dusting the paintings. There are a lot of them and boy do they collect dirt."

Sensing the moment for his sincerest of apologies was finally at hand, Nathanael cleared his throat. "I feel I must beg your forgiveness for my clumsiness the other night. You should be quite cross with me for running into you the way that I did."

"Oh, don't give it a second thought, sir. I am sure I didn't. I found it kind of funny actually." Emma's eyes twinkled at the humor of the recent memory.

"You would," Emile teased the girl easily, falling right into the casual banter they had always enjoyed before.

With a slight nod that seemed adorably demure, she waved him off. "Are these the friends that you spoke of before?" Emma pointed to Nathanael and William in turn. "The ones you were looking for when we arrived? I'm so glad to know you have not been alone all this time."

"My apologies." Emile stepped closer to her side and held out his hand, palm up, to formally introduce his friends. "This is Doctor William Wells. He owns an apothecary in Wakefield, but his main job has been to rescue me from peril on at least two separate occasions in our short history together."

501

"Oh, my! So, this getting in and out of trouble has been a reoccurring habit of yours lately." Emma feigned surprise for she would absolutely believe anything of her paramour at this point.

"A very bad habit, I'm afraid." William cradled her extended hand in both of his and held it affectionately for a moment. "Though I feel like I already know you by the many wonderful things Emile has shared."

"I am honored, I think." She curtsied out of habit before also adding a hint of concern, unsure what Emile might have shared about their recent history together.

"Only good things, I assure you, Miss Larose." Emile smiled genuinely before proceeding, "And this young man over here is Mr. Nathanael Beckett. He is the one trying to save all our poor lost souls for the kingdom beyond." Emile placed one hand on the man's shoulder tenderly, clearly acknowledging their newfound friendship.

"And I attack unsuspecting women at strange homes apparently, too." Nathanael chuckled and kissed the back of her hand with great chivalry. "Your most humble servant, miss."

Emma giggled. "You are both so sweet. It's not every day that a woman is practically swept off her feet by a handsome gentleman, Mr. Beckett."

"Handsome would be debatable, miss." Nathanael blushed at the compliment. "But inherently clumsy would not be too far of a stretch."

"Emile, I just realized now that you had better be more careful around Nathanael. With the new way that he meets women, you might just have to worry more about him than me," William taunted him mercilessly.

"Hardly." Emile rebuffed him with a sarcastic grin, yet he did also move to place a protective arm around Emma and felt her entire body shiver ever so slightly in response. "I'm sorry, I didn't realize how cold it was becoming. Here, take my jacket. I shan't be needing it at the present." He removed his formal overcoat and wrapped it around her thin frame, the bulk of it practically swallowing her up easily into it.

"That is very thoughtful of you, of all of you really. But I must be careful just the same. If I get much more of this noble treatment, it will be hard to return to the servant's quarters. They'll think I've put on airs, as they say here."

"Not possible." Emile stood directly behind her and wrapped his arms around her to block the wind more, despite the scandalous nature of the gesture.

"Thank you. That helps tremendously, Emile." She looked up at him and smiled most gratefully. "Are these all of your friends?"

"Mostly." Emile considered her question thoughtfully for several seconds, then moved his head from side to side as if contemplating the correct response under the circumstances. "There is one more, um... but I don't know if he would call me a friend, as of yet. Who knows... maybe someday, perhaps."

"Why?" Emma could only furrow her brow at the rather confusing description he provided. "Did you offend him in some way?"

William took the opportunity then to sit down on one of the grey stone benches in front of them and crossed one leg over the other before trying to explain the origins of their complicated friendship for him. "As you probably already know, Emile has a way with people. Wouldn't you agree, Nathanael?"

Nathanael smiled in agreement but did not fully engage. "I think we have teased the man enough for one evening. We wouldn't want to be rude in front of his guest, William."

"My apologies, of course then... on behalf of Miss Larose only, if I caused any offense." William exuded politeness. "Besides, I am sure Sebastain will join us all in our appreciation of Emile's many talents and courtesies when he finally sees him again."

"Why not now? Does he not live in England?" She continued her questions innocently.

"He hails from Portsmouth originally. But no, he does not live there at the present," William replied quickly.

"Oh?"

"The three of us met him on a ship that was sailing to the Americas last fall," Nathanael explained further.

"I was just visiting, remember?" Emile protested, as he always did whenever the subject was brought up.

"How could we ever forget?" William replied but paused to cast yet another glance over his shoulder into the garden behind.

Seeing his concern drawn in the same direction once again, Emile tightened his arms around Emma protectively at the gesture. "You feel it, too?"

"Like a cat watching its mouse." William adjusted the top of his suitcoat collar twice to dispel the feeling as he saw nothing of consequence besides the hardy purple geraniums clinging close to the shadows, some white Erigeron that crawled along the raised beds and stony formations and potentilla lining the hedged walls with their pink blossoms. "Perhaps, it's the wine playing tricks."

"No, it's most definitely something..." Emile shrugged as the sensation began to slowly dissipate until it was little more than an irritation. "I just don't know what."

"Anyways, as I was saying... " William continued on with his explanation as if he had never stopped in the first place. "After our, uh, shipwreck, Sebastian chose to remain on the island where we were marooned."

"That is so sad. Did he not have family here?" Emma placed one of her hands on top of Emile's, appearing not the least bit apprehensive.

"A wife named Charlotte and two sons, in fact. They still reside in Portsmouth, but they will be leaving for the Americas soon, or at least that is what his letters say. He has purchased tickets of berth for the beginning of next month if everything can be arranged in time," Nathanael interjected, excited to be an integral part of the conversation at last.

"That sounds like an exciting opportunity for all of them," she replied and relaxed fully as she leaned her head back casually upon Emile's chest as if the action were something completely natural between them. "Do you think he will ever return?"

"Not likely," William responded morosely. "It would take something monumental now to move that man from his island given his current convictions or something desperate."

"Convictions?" Emma looked puzzled once again.

"A story for another time, perhaps." Emile changed the subject quickly and leaned down further to speak softly next to her ear. "Love, there is another matter in which they need to speak with you directly before the two of them can retire for the night. Something of far greater importance."

"Really?" She lifted her head from off his chest, suddenly fully attentive. "How can I possibly be of help?"

"Could you tell me a little bit about the symptoms of a Miss Tracey, the upstairs maid? I understand she has been very ill." William asked cautiously.

"Yes, for two or three days now at least. The second servant in just a fortnight to have the same illness. Fevers, restless sleep, delirium, tremors... oh, the chattering tremors she has had today." Emma reached up and nervously tucked a few of the loose strands of hair that had escaped behind her ear once more. "The last servant, a Mr. Graham, died in less than a week's time."

"Emma, what's wrong? You're positively shaking now?" Emile remarked anxiously, instantly alarmed at the sudden change in her usually collected demeanor.

Unable to stop them, the woman in front of him crossed her arms about her body and held them there for a few moments to steady the increasing tremors, but her voice still waivered just a little when she finally spoke, "It's silly of me, I know, but Tracey has been my roommate since the day I first arrived—a nice girl, in fact, all the way from Ireland, or so she says. She has a kid brother and a mum and a dad who love her very much. She came all the way here to help them last year, and every single farthing she earns, she sends it back to them because the family is struggling with the poor conditions there and all."

"Then what is frightening you so?" Emile placed his hands protectively upon her arms and felt the fear radiating up from her.

"I shouldn't say." Emma shook her head quickly, then bit her lip in building anxiety. "Emile, I know you may not understand this, but people in my position do as they are told, especially when it comes to someone in authority." She looked away and said dejectedly, "It's not my job to question things."

From his position across from him, William watched as the anger Emile had been keeping at bay since he first heard Angelique's harsh condemnation of the young woman yesterday began to rise once more. "Emma, I don't know what you think is not acceptable to share, but I assure you that you can tell us anything you feel is important without fearing any reprisals from your current employer, or his familiar relations. We only want to help, but we can't do that properly if we do not know all the particulars?" William prodded her gently. "Has someone hurt her? Is that why she is ill?" He cleared his throat and paused to watch Emile's expression before adding more delicately, "Has something also happened to you, too, possibly?"

Emma stared blankly back at him as if he had struck the target square in the center, then shook her head once more in refusal. "At this point, I cannot say for certain about anything really. People come and go so quickly around this place that anyone could have brought the illness you are curious about." She paused, then furrowed her brow considerably. "The only thing that truly stands out to me as strange is the doctor that keeps visiting."

"Why him?" William asked carefully.

"He, um, frightens me, actually," she finally admitted.

"Frightens you?" Emile's heart literally raced at the revelation as he imagined all sorts of scenarios that might have triggered such a response.

Once upon a time he had threatened to divulge much more about his true self to her in the hopes of motivating some kind of logical response from her in return, but even in that she had extinguished whatever fear he might have held in doing so by her simple reply that she was not easily frightened... and he believed her, for how could he not. On that same night, she had also freely admitted that she had remained with him even though she had sensed that he was more than what he appeared. So, stating this now, almost made it doubly relevant.

"How so?" Nathanael asked quietly, equally as concerned as Emile obviously was.

"It's something I just can't put my finger on exactly, or maybe it's more about the way he looks at me all the time. I don't know!" Overwhelmed now by the tears spilling over at last, she put both hands over her face and hid behind them to compose herself. "I've seen that look before, Emile. I dare say that most women have at some point in their lives, and I know enough to stay away from people like him, but I can't do that as a servant here. Besides, no one would believe me even if I tried."

"Oh, Emma..." Emile's heart poured out through his voice as he held her close, knowing there was no possible way now that he would be leaving here without her again, even if that meant finding her suitable employment back home in Wakefield.

"I'm so sorry." William reached his hand forward and placed it on top of hers, his own heart filling with a growing compassion for the struggling girl in front of him. From what he had seen so far, he could clearly understand why Emile had chosen her above all others. So much in fact, that in the short time he had spent with her, he could not imagine his friend with anyone else, human or otherwise. She was his match in every way—undeniably strong in character should she need to stand up to him, compassionate of heart as she had already displayed many times over both in her actions and conversations since they had met, and yet also touched with an inner humor that the man needed in a mate. Standing here right in front of him tonight was living proof that hope for them yet remained in finding a suitable spouse—remained for all of them possibly.

"But if I might ask one more question, <u>how</u> does he look at you, Emma?" William inquired thoughtfully.

"Oh, you'll just think it's silly if I told you," Emma replied, releasing a somewhat anxious giggle while wiping away her tears.

"Try me," William coaxed, entirely enamored by the girl's transparent reply.

"Like how my younger brother looks at an almond croissant that is fresh out of the oven." She laughed again lightly and covered her mouth with the back of her hand to contain it. "I told you it was silly. Besides, the duke says he is not from around here actually and is only coming as a favor to him. Perhaps a second doctor will be called for in the future if another member of the staff falls ill."

William drew in a quick breath and held it before blowing it out slowly, hoping he was totally wrong in his next assumption. "Do you think this doctor is hurting her possibly? Or what I mean is, could he be taking advantage of her in some way?"

Emile caressed the hand he held even more, wishing beyond anything that in doing so it would alleviate some of her fear.

Emma shook her head. "I don't think so as he has only been here three times since it all began. The other servants think she contracted the illness from her relationship with Mr. Graham, but I don't know."

"Were they lovers?" Emile whispered quietly; his voice far too constricted to say more.

"Yes." She nodded her head quickly in admission. "Though no one else was supposed to know."

"Well, I do not believe you are being silly, Emma." William ignored the confidential information and comforted her seriously by speaking in very firm, but slow terms. "If studying medicine has taught me anything, it is to always trust your intuition. So, you should trust your own in this matter, as well. If the doctor makes you feel uncomfortable, allow us to help remedy that situation for you and remove him from the equation if we can."

Emma nodded several times quickly and brushed away her tears with the back of her hands until her face was dry once more. "That would be wonderful, but how?"

"When you go back tonight, do you think you could arrange to sleep in another room, perhaps? Just for the time being. I will let the duke know that I requested it myself if that helps," William suggested carefully.

"Of course. I'll have to ask Mrs. Berry, the housekeeper, first but there is a spare room downstairs by the pantry that we save for the delivery man when he needs to spend the night. She might allow me to sleep there, especially given the severity of Tracey's illness and all."

"Excellent, the last thing we want to do is cause more trouble for you." He rubbed his hands together. "If you can manage to do that, then that should keep you from having to be alone with the new doctor, should he need to treat your roommate again. Do you think that can all be arranged?"

"I'll certainly try, though I'll have to think of some excuse should he ask for me directly. He has been making it a point to check on the health of all the servants each time that he comes," she replied, though quite understandably a little stunned by the intensity of the conversation. "He visited the staff just this morning, in fact, but left a little before I came out here to meet the three of you. You might have even seen him as he passed."

Emile and William looked at each other and shook their heads. "No one has come this way except you."

"That is odd as he left not more than five minutes before I did." Emma wrinkled her brow in concentration. "Strange, as I was sure I overheard him telling Mrs. Berry that he would leave out the side door."

"Where is that exactly?" Emile scanned the walls of the estate beside him, looking for the doorway.

"Just over there on the other side of the garden." Emma pointed in the general direction in which the rest of the group had heard the strange noise earlier.

Emile's interest peeked considerably.

"Our mysterious noise, perhaps?"

"Hmm, maybe, but I wish we <u>had</u> seen him. I could have at least discussed his treatments with him in person instead of all this guesswork." William eyed the area where they had felt uneasy before and tried to shake off the sensation it generated just remembering it. "Well, I'll most certainly speak to the duke directly on your behalf before I retire tonight, Miss Larose. Perhaps I can put a stop to his care altogether since nothing he is doing is producing any benefit whatsoever," William encouraged. "Granted, if Miss Tracey's illness is indeed contagious as one might expect, limiting your exposure should have been the first logical course of action for all involved."

"Do you really think I am in danger of catching it?" Emma bit her lip nervously, considering the possibility.

"No, but I'm surprised he did not mention it himself." William tried to reassure her carefully, for he still had no idea what this mystery ailment might possibly be.

"That's reassuring, and would it be too much to ask if you could check on my roommate yourself?" The concern for the girl was clearly evident on Emma's innocent face. "It would mean so much to me to know what <u>you</u> think. You must be a very good doctor, or Emile would not think so highly of you."

"She's right." Emile nodded to his friends in agreement. "...on both accounts."

William smiled at the compliment, knowing his friend did not give them out freely.

"Be assured, dear lady. We will make the time." Nathanael placed his hand on William's shoulder.

"I will go now, in fact. It shouldn't take me long, and maybe I can even give you a positive report before you retire for the evening," William promised as he stood up.

Emma's countenance lightened slightly. "That would be more than I could hope for. Thank you."

"Not at all." Nathanael kissed her hand in farewell and the two men walked briskly back to the main house, mission in hand.

Chapter Forty-Two

June 24th, 1793

Alone at last, Emile finally felt his body begin to relax as he pulled Emma still closer and allowed his head to fall comfortably next to her own, enjoying the sudden quietness of the scenery around them after the chaotic scene of the party back at the house. "You have no idea how many times I have dreamt of this very moment in time. Every single second of it, in fact." He sighed happily and rubbed his cheek against her soft hair with pleasure.

Emma smiled at the familiar action, enjoying the same closeness of his embrace. "Would it be improper of me to say the same?"

"Not in the least." He lightly chuckled but his head swam with the intoxicating scent of lavender coming from her long tresses. The ones she had quite obviously let down in preparation for their talk this evening. Just as before, the calming sway of her hair was the most comforting thing he had ever experienced, filling him with a deep sense of peace by its very existence alone.

In her presence at last, his entire being finally felt the freedom to relax, allowing itself to become absolutely numb to all the emotions that had been raging within him for months and utterly freeing himself from the constraints of his nutritional deficiencies and distractions for the moment. From her blue eyes, like the color of bright glass in the sunlight, to her tiny feet that seemed entirely too small to belong to anyone that walked this Earth, everything about her soothed him beyond expression. Even the very sound of her rhythmic breathing matching his own calmed him far more than any blood had ever done, animal or human alike.

Doing little else but revel in the pureness the moment provided, Emile shut his eyes and held her close in the moonlight for what seemed like ages before he finally felt her begin to pull away. "Oh, please don't go, Emma... not yet," Emile's voice pleaded with her softly with the first signs of true vulnerability that Emma had always known lay just beneath the surface.

"Emile..." was all she could manage to say and even that seemed choked and strained as she turned around reluctantly to face him with a sadness to her expression that almost broke him completely to see it for it was the exact opposite of the serenity he was currently experiencing.

"What's wrong, love?" He reached out his left hand as if he knew it would pass right through the vision in front of him and touched the side of her cheek as he held it there, smiling contentedly when his fingers felt the slight warmth of her skin and not the expected mirage of his dreams.

"I can't tell you how much I have missed that." Emma sighed as she closed her eyes, drinking in the coolness of his touch once more, then said the very thing he had longed most to hear from her lips. "I don't <u>want</u> you to leave again, Emile. I never really did, but..."

"Then I never will," he interrupted her as he pledged decisively with no reserve whatsoever behind it. In truth, it was the simplest promise he could have ever offered to her given the intensity of the sincere love he now felt for her. Yet, as powerful as he might think he had become in his new form; he also knew it would take much more strength than he currently possessed to leave her once more should she send him away like before.

Hearing his almost too easy reply, Emma's lips released a sigh that sounded far more painful than accepting before she almost whispered back, "Oh, how I wish it were that simple, Emile, but it's not."

"But it <u>is</u> that simple, Emma." His eyes lit up with hopeful anticipation as the energy surged within him at the prospect. "Come with me tomorrow. We can go back to Wakefield together and set up a home there if you like or travel the whole of Europe if you are so disposed. I'll take you wherever you wish to go, no questions asked."

Emma looked up at him tentatively and studied him, daring to capture just a fraction of his promising picture. "But what about our honest beginnings? Wouldn't we just be falling back into our old habits of destruction again? And if so, what was the point then of everything we have just endured apart?"

"If you are worried about what people might say, I happen to know a very good preacher who might be easily convinced to perform an impromptu wedding first," Emile teased her lightly but then turned very serious instantly when he saw her changed countenance. "What?"

"It's not just that and you know it." Emma frowned. "What I am more concerned about is whether or not you would be marrying me for the right reasons."

"Fair enough, and you are right as always. But all joking aside, I meant every word of what I said to you in France. I will protect you with every ounce of my being, even if your decision is to not be with me in that way anymore." He paused before continuing with even more sincerity, "If we take another path together, it will forever be your choice as to where we stand as I will never coerce you into something you do not want ever again. Nor will I errantly assume that just because you want to be with me, that it also bestows upon me certain privileges by default." Emile took a step closer to her and reached for her hand, feeling the need to slow down his racing speech into a more controlled state. "Emma, you mean much more to me now than you ever did back in Paris, and if I were to marry you, it would be because I desperately love you and you alone, and not because you are my only means of salvation."

"Are you sure?" Emma asked hesitantly.

"Am I sure? What kind of question is that?" Emile looked away from her incredulously for a moment before chuckling to himself. "I have never been more sure of anything in my entire life, Emma Larose. Like it or not, you have quite definitely become an integral part of my being now, and one I have no intention of being without ever again. It would be like trying to exist without one of my arms for you are just as essential to me."

"And if I decide to choose all of you?" She looked down at the hand that held hers, certain that if she were even a fraction of an inch away from him, she might forget how to breathe.

"Then I will never let you go." He lifted her chin and kissed her passionately, refusing to hold a single piece of himself back from her any longer. Almost three months had passed since the last time he had been given the privilege of holding her in his arms once more, and not a single morning had arrived thereafter where he had awakened without the intense desire to do so again. To waste even a single second of the immense pleasure the closeness of her love provided tonight felt almost criminal. "I love you, Emma. And I will keep telling you that every day until I take my final breath." The words came out so effortlessly at last that he was surprised he had not said them to her many times before.

"I love you, too, Emile Deschamps." The woman in his arms sighed happily as she eventually turned her face away, breathing deeply several times to steady herself on her feet once more and regain her composure. "I suppose I always have, though I did wonder a time or two about your true motivations when I was forced to have tea with Miss Toussaint that last day in Paris."

"Please..." Emile grumbled at the disturbing memory, wishing he had never even met the woman in question. "That woman likes to create drama wherever she goes."

"And you don't?" Emma's eyes glinted with sudden humor as she looked up at him and laughed lightly.

"Yes, well, I think you will find that side of me to be greatly tempered at the present. Or at least I hope so." Emile chuckled, too, before turning a bit more serious. "Emma, I know you may not believe this, but you are worth my very life just the way you are, and no one else will ever hope to compare, not ever."

"And so are you," she said quietly and rested her head upon his chest at last.

Elated now beyond expression at what all the future might hold for them; he held her tightly in his arms feeling the completeness the action brought him before stepping away when he felt her body finally relax.

"Would you care to take a tour of the gardens with me, *mademoiselle*." He offered her his arm respectfully, allowing his elegant poise to further charm her.

She nodded, and just as she did, he thought he saw the moonlight glisten against a single tear before she quickly wiped it away.

"Now, that won't do at all." Emile reached inside his outer coat pocket that she wore and retrieved his embroidered handkerchief before handing it over to her. "In case you should have need of it."

Emma couldn't help but laugh again lightly at the gesture and waved him off. "You always did know the perfect thing to say." She took the offered keepsake gratefully before casually drying the corner of each eye in turn. "These are happy tears, I assure you."

"Indeed." Emile smiled at her innocent reply, then frowned as another thought struck him. "I'm afraid to ask this, but after what I overheard in the hall yesterday, has Angelique been horrible to you the whole time while I have been gone?" He asked her seriously, fearing that from his recent exchange at the party, his *la petite amie* had been less than kind.

"To be honest, I hardly see her, or maybe she makes it so that I do not see her, but either way it is of no matter to me really. It has been a good job, and I have been thankful for it. I've even been able to send a little money back home along the way."

"I'm sure your father appreciated the gesture," Emile added politely knowing that the man probably used her hard-earned money on anything but something of lasting value.

"I'm sure he did, though he has never written back to inquire as to my health or anything else of consequence." The corner of Emma's mouth contorted slightly at the admission. "But my brother does thank you for his clothes. I gather you sent him something in the way of compensation?"

"Enough for two replacements actually since he was so gracious in loaning it to me in the first place." Emile stopped walking then and waited for her to look up at him. "Emma, I know you don't need me to tell you this, but whatever you sent was a kind deed no matter the reason or reception."

"Thank you." Emma nodded and the two continued to walk together along the garden pathway, stopping to admire this plant or that beside the way.

"But to get back to our other conversation, you mean to tell me that your world here does not simply revolve around the happiness of the fair *mademoiselle* Angelique Toussaint like she thinks it does?" Emile teased.

"Hardly. I am most definitely far too busy to care about anything in her world, much less seek out ways to annoy her. Though truthfully, I'd have much rather received a letter or two from you. Oh, why did you not write, Emile? I thought perhaps you were angry at me for sending you away when you did not."

"Angry? Never. But I did write actually, three times every week at least, sometimes more." Emile looked away nervously and cleared his throat, waiting for the rebuke he so justly deserved... again.

"What?" Emma stopped walking immediately and stepped directly in front of his path, utterly shocked by his revelation. "But I never received even one of your letters? Were they not delivered by mistake?"

"Well, not exactly." Emile shook his head and grimaced like a child suddenly caught within a lie but unable to justify his actions in doing so. "They were not delivered at all, I am afraid."

"But..." She furrowed her brow in great consternation. "I don't understand."

"They were not delivered because I did not mail a single one of them, dear Emma." He rolled his eyes and sighed at the end in total embarrassment.

Suddenly humored by his honest confession, she began walking again. "Whyever not, Silly?"

For several moments Emile tried to think of a very excellent excuse that would defend his reasoning in doing so but gave up the occupation entirely when he could not. "Because I wanted to give you the chance to breathe in England, I suppose. Or rather, I thought I should provide you the space to see what your life could possibly be like without me in it. Maybe even offer you the opportunity to find someone more suitable if that was your desire or live your life on your own terms instead. Isn't that what we agreed?"

"I have no intention of finding anyone else, Emile. Either then or now." It was her turn to sigh dramatically and look at him with great disappointment. "But my life is still controlled here, Emile. Just in a different way."

"That may be so." He stopped by the opening on the far end of the garden that led back to the house. The one that was half-covered with climbing green ivy. "Just not by me this time."

She nodded in agreement. "And not like in Paris."

"Not like in Paris." His face bore only guilt for his abhorrent actions there.

"And you?" She looked up into his eyes imploring. "Have you found a new reality that suits you here in England?"

"Actually, I think I have, and please don't laugh, but it is something I never thought I would ever do." He leaned his back against the brick doorway and took his hat off once more to rub the brim of it in his hands.

"I would never laugh at you, you know that." She picked a blueish-colored daisy with dainty petals from the side of the opening and held it between her fingertips.

Still unconvinced of her faithful sincerity, he raised one eyebrow up at her in further test.

"I promise." She tucked the flower into the side of her hair. "Truly."

Uncertain he was ready to share something he himself was still deliberating greatly upon, he pursed his lips and waited just a moment longer before plunging ahead anyways. "I have been helping a family run a bakery of sorts back in Wakefield—breads and hearty pies mostly, but I am thinking about opening up a full establishment of some kind or another when I have enough capital to do so."

"Now, why would I ever laugh at you over something like that?" Emma smiled genuinely.

"Well, maybe I am the one still trying to accept it. Most people do not think the son of a gentleman would be in trade someday. It is usually the other way around." He stopped playing with the brim of his hat and looked up at her nervously.

"The world cannot be filled with estate owners indefinitely, Emile. Someone has to work an honest trade, or the country will never grow."

"I quite agree." He stood again erect. "Anyways, William thought it would be good, while I lived there, to give back to others, and he was right. I have thoroughly enjoyed my life there. Much more than I had ever dreamt possible."

"I am so glad to hear it." She started to make her way back to the house, but with a burst of indecision, Emile took hold of her hand tightly to stop her.

"What?" She looked over her shoulder, suddenly surprised by the action.

"I wanted to give you something I bought for you back in London." He took out the satin bag that held the necklace from his vest pocket and handed it over to her tentatively.

Intrigued, as he had never given her a present before, she untied the small cords one by one and drew out the thin ribbon necklace with its small, silver charm. "Emile! It's beautiful!"

"I know, it isn't much, but it reminded me of you the moment I saw it."

"Would you help me put it on?" She took off his coat and handed it and the necklace back to him before turning around and lifting the hair that covered her neck.

Like a warm breeze that brought with it something far more than the wind itself, Emile instantly felt the rush of something much deeper than emotion or physical attraction. He felt the one thing that he now knew he would never ever act upon where she was concerned, even if it meant death itself—bloodlust.

God, help me, please... Emile prayed and tried to calm his shaking hands as they reached over her head and downward to place the ribbon gently about her neck, resisting steadfastly every urge within him to lean in any closer.

On the first night he met her in his apartment, the desire to be near her physically was undoubtedly one of the easiest things to control compared to what he experienced thereafter. The racking tremors that had often plagued his every dream and waking moment for almost a week afterwards were quite another thing entirely. Nor were they easy to forget as they increased exponentially the longer he was with her, until he was sure they would overwhelm him completely. Yet in the end, he had managed to resist then, and he would do so again. He just needed a little time to adjust to her presence once more, much like he had then.

"Is the clasp too difficult?" Emma asked curiously, waiting patiently for him to finish, while also unknowingly providing the very necessary mental distraction he needed to regain control.

"Just a bit," Emile lied as he breathed in and out slowly to steady himself once more, then deftly secured the small metal clasp easily before allowing himself just a brief opportunity to play with the small wisps of strawberry curls at the base of her neck beneath it. "That should do it, I think."

Wanting the closeness almost as much as he did at that moment, she hesitantly stepped slightly away and let her hair fall back into place in one beautiful, smooth waterfall motion upon his hands before turning back around to face him. "Thank you. I doubt I shall ever take it off."

Emile half-smiled, feeling immensely pleased with her response, but even more grateful that the temptation was finally abating. "I'm so very glad you like it, but it is getting late. We should probably be heading back before you are missed or chastised for breaking curfew." Emile slid both of his arms back into his suitcoat and offered her his arm.

"Um-hmmm," she agreed slowly while fingering the smoothness of the charm between her fingertips as they walked back up the gravel pathway side by side, only this time in silence, too deep in their own thoughts to converse any further.

Yet, when they had reached a mere ten feet from the servant's entrance of the estate, Emma finally spoke up again quietly, only this time she did so with the same insecurity Emile had been feeling earlier, "Emile, do you truly think there will be enough room for a servant girl in your world in Wakefield—the daughter of no one of consequence, but the mistress of some Frenchman simply everyone on the street talks about?" She attempted to describe her insecurities in the plainest of ways, giving him one last chance to walk away.

Emile swallowed hard at the question, stopping in his tracks abruptly as she finished speaking and slightly dug the toe of his recently polished boot into the loose pebbles at his feet before looking up at the windows high above them, noticing casually how the glow from the party illuminated the two of them perfectly in the pathway below. "I don't know, really. I suppose it all depends."

"Depends on what?" Her reply came back barely more audible than a whisper as his response had clearly not been what she had expected at all after his recent proposal in the garden.

Surprised more now by the tone in her voice than in the actual words she had spoken, he chanced another quick look back at her and his heart almost melted completely as he took in the quivering pout her lower lip made against the top. The pitiful action, though miniscule in nature, caused his whole being to ache in response when he saw it and lowered whatever defenses were still remaining within him. So much so that he realized then that the moment to tell her of his darker side had finally arrived, and yet, now that it had, he could not form a single word to explain any of it, nor did he especially want to, given how wonderfully the evening had progressed already.

Unable to set his emotions aside any longer, he leaned in close enough to almost feel his lips upon her cheek before whispering to her softly the words he knew would comfort her the most, "What I meant to say is that I thought we left that woman back in Paris." He paused before pulling away and adding more resolutely the truth he now felt was far more accurate, "I know I left the man there, left all of him there. Well, maybe only the bad parts. The rest you are regrettably going to have to tame in time, love."

Relieved at last, she smiled up at him, suddenly grateful for the welcome challenge. "I think I can handle that. To our respectable beginnings then?"

Emile's gaze scanned every inch of the beautiful woman before him, knowing that now was not the time for any more revelations. William was right. He would need to tell her before they wed, that much was certain, but for just one night longer, he wanted... no, he needed this moment to be as perfect as it was. If for no other reason than to preserve what may end up being the only thing he had left when she eventually walked away, which he was fairly certain was still quite possible.

"To respectable beginnings." He leaned down slowly and kissed her once more, then paused and pulled her closer to him in a tight embrace, his fingers clutching at clumps of her wavy curls. "You are my whole world, Emma Larose. Don't ever forget that for a minute."

Emma nodded and sighed happily. "I won't."

He held her a moment longer before releasing her unwillingly and opened the door for her to pass into the house. Then, with a heavy but jubilant heart, he watched as it closed once again on his very new future. Only this time, he felt assured that when it opened once more, she would be his alone, and he would never be without her ever again.

Chapter Forty-Three

June 24th, 1793

B eyond anything he could have ever imagined, elation filled his every step as Emile charged through the front doors of the estate quite unceremoniously and flew directly up the Grand Staircase in front of him, taking the steps two at a time to find William and Nathanael. It had been a long time since he had ever felt this much joy and news like this simply had to be shared. Things were about to change in a big way for him, and right now, he couldn't think of anyone else with whom he would want to share it.

When he reached the long hallway to their rooms, however, Emile was surprised to find that Nathanael's room was still, strangely empty. Thinking that the man may be simply conversing with William, he continued across the hall only to discover that William's room was also unoccupied. Yet as he walked towards the door to his own suite to change out of his formal attire and wait for their return, the two men he was seeking rushed through the open doorway behind him like two assassins in the night and not the calm men he had left not more than an hour earlier in the garden.

"How is Emma's roommate?" Emile asked, genuinely interested in the young servant's fate and whatever information William might have been able to learn.

Without missing a beat, Nathanael and William closed the door firmly behind them and seized Emile by both of his arms in their passage to the adjoining room. Neither willing to converse freely with him until they had both half-dragged Emile through the adjoining doorway and closed it securely behind them without saying a single word of explanation for their sudden assault.

"What in the world? What is wrong with the two of you? Unhand me!" Emile protested strongly against their actions, attempting to release himself from their hold, but made no headway at all against them.

"Shut up you fool! We have a problem." William covered his mouth instead with one hand and sat him down forcefully in a chair at the farthest end of the room, away from any door or window of any kind before almost hissing out his command.

"A problem?" Emile's hands went up defensively to deflect the physical attack from his friends. "Have the French invaded England already? You'd think so by the look on both of your faces just now."

"Much, much worse, Emile, as if that is even possible." William's eyes were filled with a fire Emile had never seen before in the doctor and a determination that would frighten even the most stoic of gentlemen.

"Honestly, you two look as if you are about to start a war." Emile tried his best to regain his footing in the unfolding drama before him, while still also remaining completely clueless as to what it was he was supposed to be fighting.

"That is exactly what is happening, Emile, and you are right in the thick of it, I'm afraid." William fell into the chair across from him, allowing Nathanael the necessary space to lean on the sturdy back behind him.

"Be reasonable. I see no danger, gentlemen. Except maybe from the two of you." He attempted to straighten his attire that had become askew in the melee.

"Oh, you will. Just be quiet and listen for a minute," William warned him sternly. "Let me put the pieces together for you that I have been too stupid to realize for myself!"

"You are being incredibly too hard..." Emile tried to reassure him but was cut off by William's hand placed tightly across his mouth once more when he heard some individual passing by just outside their rooms in the hallway. The heavy footsteps that sounded as if someone were shuffling along the rug came all the way up to a room near their own, paused, then continued on without further interruption.

"It must be one of the servants, I suppose." Nathanael breathed a sigh of relief and began to relax somewhat once more.

"What is going on with you two?" Emile gritted his teeth, starting to feel an irritation he did not like coming over him.

"Fifteen people dead in a little over two months' time, that was what we were told, correct?" William gripped the arms of his own chair to steady his anger further.

"Yes." Emile tried to follow his explanation but saw nothing suspicious as of yet. After all, every detail William had just uttered had all been perfectly repeated almost verbatim to what they had all been discussing earlier.

"That is close to two deaths a week give or take if we started counting a little before your arrival from Paris." Then, giving the next statement as quietly as he could manage though the force of each word was still clearly evident, William restated the information more accurately, "Two <u>kills</u> a week, Emile."

"Two kills?" Emile looked back at him, still struggling to comprehend the full gravity of the situation.

"We saw Miss Tracey, Emile," Nathanael admitted carefully. "She looked positively dreadful. Deathly so."

Emile's concern only grew stronger. "Could you tell what is wrong with her, William?"

"Yes, but I'll put it to you, instead, and see what you make of it. Fevers that are not fevers... an unrelenting restlessness of spirit... hallucinations... chills that cannot be warmed... no remedy to speak of... and she is a victim that someone would not be thoroughly investigating... a nobody among nobodies here. And to get rid of the um, evidence thereafter... as with all the rest of the patients, they <u>always</u> die in less than four days' time. Which means from her current rate of decline, I believe she has a little less than a day left to live. Sound familiar yet?"

"A vampire," Emile whispered, finally understanding the danger they were facing.

"A vampire," William replied in horrified mimic.

Stunned at the realization, the three men sat together in the ensuing silence thereafter, too affected by the news to move or to speak until Nathanael timidly asked aloud the one question that was on all their minds. "What should we do? Should we let her transition into one of us and help her or give her a painless death before all of that happens?"

William groaned at his lack of intellect on the matter. "I had not even thought about <u>that</u> ramification. Seriously, Nathanael, I don't know if my mind is utterly failing me lately, or if I am just plain ignorant at this point."

"William, please. In the first place, we don't even know who it is that bit her, and even if we did, who else do we protect? We can't be everywhere, helping everyone," Emile finally spoke, rattling off just some of the obvious thoughts pouring through his brain.

"How would we protect them?" Nathanael added. "Should we protect them?"

"We most definitely should." William felt instantly incensed at the mere possibility of passivity. "I mean no disrespect to those who chose that kind of lifestyle. That is their choice, of course, but my vow to my fellow man is first to heal, not to harm, and though I cannot guarantee that others will do the same, I also cannot condone the systematic murder of those who simply cannot defend themselves. No matter how many times I have been tempted to do the same."

Trying his best to remain outside of the discussion at hand and the subsequent judgement that was sure to follow, Emile folded his hands in front of him, wondering if his friend was speaking about him, as well. "You know I have not done so in months, William. Not since I set foot in Wakefield actually," he truthfully admitted while turning a blind eye to William's accusations towards his previous lifestyle.

"I know." William looked back at him quickly, then down at the floor once more without the least bit of rebuke or chastisement. "I can tell when you haven't."

"Really?" Emile cast him a disbelieving glance. "How so?"

"You get cranky when you are hungry, Emile," Nathanael quipped as he sat down on the edge of the bed and subsequently fell backwards onto it. The immense coverlet enveloping him instantly. "Land's sake, Man! How do you sleep in all of this?" He laughed lightly, giving a much-needed break to the growing tension in the room.

"Like sleeping on a cloud, I assure you." Emile smiled at the childish exchange between them.

"We will have to discuss your actual nutrition later, as I would be very interested in finding out all of the particulars, but right now we have more important things to decide tonight." William sat back in his chair; his arms now firmly crossed over his body.

"Do you think it is one of the servants?" Emile formed his fingers into a triangle and tapped them against his lips as he leaned on the table between them.

"Too problematic for discovery, I should think. Besides, the victims have been from multiple estates in the area. The odds of it being one particular servant here feasting upon them all would be simply astronomical," William replied.

"A delivery person then, perhaps," Nathanael offered while blowing a loose feather high into the air above him. "That would give him access and the anonymity to feed as he preferred."

"A very good idea, and one I had not thought of. But who?" William rubbed his chin. "There are probably a dozen people who make deliveries or do some form of business with an estate of this size every week at least. No, it <u>has</u> to be someone more central who provides services for all of the estates in the area."

"We could start by asking Mrs. Berry who that might be and interview each in turn. At this point it could be literally anyone." Emile shrugged his shoulders before leaning back in his chair. "I'll try to make some excuse to Angelique in the morning about us needing to stay a day or two longer to do so."

"Yes, that might be best, given the late hour tonight there is little we can do at the present. Whoever it was, I haven't felt anything since we left the garden, so I don't think they are still here. For the present, I suggest the three of us get some rest if we can. I have a feeling that tomorrow is going to be a long day." William stood up from his chair and turned to leave. "As for me, I am going to start by talking to that doctor Emma told us about first thing in the morning. Something about him doesn't feel right, especially given her distrust and Tracey's condition."

"Yes, well, speaking of Emma... there was something I came up here wanting to tell the two of you before you both so rudely accosted me." Emile pushed himself out of the stuffed chair and looked from one man to the other nervously. "Something that might change some of our arrangements when we get back to Wakefield."

"You're not leaving us so soon, are you Emile?" Nathanael propped himself up on his elbows on the bed, suddenly disappointed. "I thought you said you liked it in Wakefield."

"Don't be so daft man. I'm not going anywhere anytime soon." Emile shook his head and nodded in the direction of the adjoining door. "Now, get off my bed, if you please."

"Alright." Nathanael tried to obey but struggled to extricate himself from the many loose layers of down and fabric. "Um, a little help would be nice, please."

Emile laughed and reached down a hand to provide the needed leverage, lifting the man easily up and off in one pull.

"Much obliged." Nathanael straightened his vest and hair making sure no errant feathers still remained present.

"Then what is it?" William's eyes betrayed a hint of concern behind them.

"What would you say to an addition to our little company?" Emile pursed his lips anxiously. "A very much feminine addition."

"Huzzah!" William embraced his friend out of pure joy. "Will Emma be joining us then when we return?"

"She will be joining us when we leave for Portsmouth if she can, or whenever you both agree is most prudent. Though I doubt I will be leaving her here at this estate after what you just disclosed."

"That is truly wonderful news, Emile." Nathanael tried his best to put on the happiest of expressions for his friend even though the news still stung slightly.

"Thank you, gentlemen." Emile rubbed the carpet with his foot just once, embarrassed by his growing feeling of affection towards them, as well. "And I might have also promised her a small wedding, Nathanael. Think you are up to it?"

"Up to it. I wouldn't dream of having it any other way." Nathanael smiled genuinely. "Or maybe I should try to talk her out of it before it is too late."

"What?" Emile's face turned suddenly darker at the mere suggestion. "You wouldn't dare."

"You'd be actually doing the poor woman an incredible service, Nathanael," William quipped. "She probably has no idea how loud he snores."

Emile shook his head at his friends' banter at his expense. "Just wait until the two of you marry one day. I'll make your lives miserable if you try anything with Emma."

"Is that a challenge?" Nathanael looked positively eager to begin his newest assignment.

"You better not, Nathanael. I don't know if I can defend you from a vengeful madman," William advised.

"Well, you know, the ether worked well before..." Nathanael teased again lightly, then hid behind William for protection just in case.

Emile could only shake his head before holding it higher in total aloofness at the shared memory back on the island. "You have no idea how humiliating that was, gentlemen."

"Ok, ok, enough. Should I ring for some champagne, or have you had enough port for the entire castle tonight, Emile?" William accused.

"It was good wine," Emile replied, feeling completely unashamed on this particular subject alone.

"*Vive la France,*" William said with a playful chuckle.

"*Vive l'amitié.*" Emile placed one hand on each of the men's shoulders affectionately. "Now, goodnight you two. And don't break down my door before ten if you please. I'll need to sleep this off just a tad."

"Goodnight," each man called as he left the room and closed the door behind him.

"Vive l'amour, Emma." Emile unbuttoned the six buttons on his gifted vest and lay down before closing his eyes in immense satisfaction.

Chapter Forty-Four

June 25th, 1793

A pounding that would not cease awakened Emile just barely after nine o'clock in the morning, though he could not say for certain as to the exact time as the curtains of his windows were still carefully drawn to strategically block out the possible rays that always threatened to burn him if the weather had finally decided to stop in its incessantly depressing presentment. Yet for all of that, the German clock on the mantle had most definitely echoed a time somewhere after seven earlier this morning as that was the last chime he had heard faintly deep within his dreams, or at least he had thought it had been seven. It could have been eight for all he knew, for it was a very good dream—one he had every intention of continuing once his visitor left.

"*Assez, assez, arrêtez,*" he grumbled crankily and sat up in bed.

Yet despite what he had preferred, the pounding continued on without relent, like the hammering of some annoying blacksmith upon his door.

"*Arrêtez*, you foul person." He felt his head spin violently with his new position and muttered an admonition for the future, "Perhaps less wine next time, eh, Emile." He shook his head to clear away some of the fog and the pounding thankfully ceased, if only for a moment, before it then started up again once more as he stood up and walked slowly across the room before opening his door just a crack.

"No, I will not stop, *monsieur.*" Angelique stood just outside his door in the long hall, clearly incensed about something. And yet, he was fairly certain already, that it would be nothing he would care much about in the least.

"What is the matter now, woman? And why must we be discussing it at this ungodly hour." He tried to brush back his hair into some semblance of order, as he could feel by the coolness on the back of his neck that it must be in a horrible disarray.

"As if that matters." She placed one hand upon her hip. "From the state that you are in, I am sure you were up all night enjoying yourself." She clucked her tongue against her cheek saucily with great certainty.

"Enjoying myself?" Emile asked in total confusion as he squinted at her and rubbed his face with both of his hands to force himself to awaken further. "I must still be intoxicated as I haven't the foggiest notion as to what you are talking about, *mademoiselle,* nor do I probably care."

"Don't you?" She flashed him a look like a woman who had already been put to scorn. "I know she is in there somewhere, sir."

"Who is in here?" Emile looked down at his thoroughly rumpled and untucked shirt, feeling slightly embarrassed at the apparent indecency he was displaying and tried to push it back into his pants more appropriately.

"Miss Larose, of course. I saw the two of you kissing last night."

"I see." Emile rolled his eyes and sighed heavily at the accusation. "So, was it you who was spying on us in the garden?"

"I do not know what you mean, but the entire dinner party could have seen you both plainly through the ballroom windows if they had cared to look. With all that moonlight, you might as well have been standing in the sun. Either that, or you didn't exactly try to make your affections a secret."

"They have never been a secret." He exhaled loudly in growing irritation. "You, of all people, should know that."

"I do." She sniffed proudly. "But we are not in Paris anymore, Emile. Servants in England do not carry on with those of our class. Nor do they sleep with them whenever they are asked," she said the last sentence more quietly through her teeth, but still loud enough to make her point quite clear.

"You're embarrassing yourself, Angelique." Emile looked at her with fresh loathing and released his hold upon the door, intent on shutting it just as soon as she was finished. "Don't make me regret more about you than I already do."

"Really?" Seizing her opportunity, she pushed her way past him and threw open the curtains to let in the bright sunlight, allowing it to fully illuminate the now, empty bed.

"Satisfied." Emile crossed his arms casually across his chest as he leaned back upon the open door, paying careful attention to remain safely within the shadows just beyond the sunlit carpet in front of him. "You obviously know me so little to think so highly of me."

"I'm sorry, but I was so certain she would be here." Angelique counterfeited an apologetic expression, but it was already too late.

"Did you now?" Emile felt increasing annoyance with every word the woman was uttering. "And why are you looking for Miss Larose anyways?"

Hearing the commotion taking place on the other side, the door to his adjoining room opened then and a fully dressed and presentable William entered thereafter. "What is the matter? Have the French attacked already?" He continued their jest from the previous evening before noticing a slightly stunned Miss Toussaint on the other side of the room.

"It appears so." Emile waved a dismissive hand towards Angelique. "And well before our agreed upon ten o'clock, too."

"Did you invite her here?" William raised one eyebrow in his direction, not the least bit impressed.

"Certainly not." Emile yawned and shook his head from side to side with a look that showed he was just as confused about her presence as William quite obviously was.

Attempting to regain an ounce of her dignity back from her display of apparent jealousy, Angelique held her nose proudly aloft and tried to defend her actions, "When I overheard this morning that Miss Larose did not report for chores as expected, I naturally thought ..."

"You thought what again?" He challenged her openly once more in front of William, wanting very much in all of his pettiness to humiliate her sufficiently. "Actually, never mind, why don't you start with what precisely you heard that warranted such a conclusion?" Emile glanced back at William, beginning to show the first inclination of true worry.

"I wasn't being a gossip, if that was what you were thinking." She stood her ground proudly in front of him. "Since one of her staff was missing, the housekeeper was forced to ask the duke at breakfast if the girl had been dismissed without consulting her," Angelique explained insolently in a huff.

William and Emile both looked at each other quickly once more, carrying on an unspoken conversation with their eyes.

"Have they checked the room downstairs? The one reserved for the delivery man?" William inquired immediately after.

Angelique shrugged. "Now that you mention it, Mrs. Berry did say something about giving her the courtesy of sleeping elsewhere considering the illness of her roommate, though she did not mention where that might be precisely. But, from what I gather from the butler's comments afterwards, the bed she had been assigned had not been slept in, as well."

Instantly alert, Emile suddenly grabbed his vest and suitcoat from off the floor and began buttoning them up quickly. "And so, you automatically assumed she would be with me."

"Why, yes," Angelique admitted unashamedly. "It seemed only logical."

"*Ça semble tout à fait logique*," he repeated her mockingly in French and went to an available mirror to tie his cravat into a quick knot.

"I'll get Nathanael," William said with urgency and quickly left the room, ignoring Angelique completely.

"Why is everyone in such a bother over one lost servant girl?" Angelique tossed both her hands up in disbelief as she began walking towards the open doorway on the other side of the room. "There are ten more who would be willing to take her place that are far more qualified than she is."

Having heard enough irritating nonsense for one lifetime already from the woman he hoped to never converse with ever again, Emile spun around and stared her down darkly. So intensely, in fact, that Angelique took several steps backwards towards the open door beside her should she need to retreat. "Miss Larose is more than a servant, and you dear woman, are <u>nothing</u> to me," he spat the words out as harshly as he felt them, holding nothing back.

Clearly insulted at last, she flashed him the same look of resentment she had shone him in his apartments that night at the party when he refused to acknowledge her concern about her family. "We shall see, *Monsieur* Deschamps. We shall see." She left the room in a huff and strode down the stairs as if on some mission of certain destruction.

At this point, he didn't care one bit what the woman did. After pulling on his tall, leather boots, he shut the door behind him and met an already dressed Nathanael and William in the hall.

"That was fast," Emile remarked as he buttoned his cuffs and followed them quickly down the main stairs.

"You are the only one of us that likes to sleep late, Emile," Nathanael added politely up to him.

"What on earth do you do with all of that time?" Emile quipped back as he walked, easily overtaking Nathanael on the stairs until he was now leading the group.

"Pray for your soul mostly." He tossed a humorous remark back at him on the stairs.

"Well, then keep praying, friend, for I feel like I am on the verge on doing something appallingly evil today." Emile gritted his teeth so tightly that he thought a few of them might break under the strain.

"Steady, Emile. Steady," William cautioned him when they reached the lower landing before making their way over to the kitchen below where the staff remained. "We don't even know if what she said is true, do we?"

The others followed after him, then stopped when they reached the outer doorway to the servant's dining room, waiting patiently to be noticed as none of them wanted to interrupt their well-earned meal.

"Can we help you, Gentlemen." The head butler and housekeeper stood out of respect and half-bowed as he folded his napkin before setting it politely on the table next to him.

"I'm sorry for disturbing all of you, but could you tell me if you have seen Miss Larose this morning?" William inquired politely.

The housekeeper and butler both exchanged a knowing glance before the head of staff motioned silently with his hand for the men to follow him discreetly down the shorter passageway to the room Emma had been given.

"I am assuming one of you gentlemen is her suitor from France?" The butler asked, but did not elaborate further as to how he knew such information.

"Yes," Emile answered quietly. "I only just proposed last night."

"I see. Well then, we did check her upstairs chamber this morning shortly before breakfast since she had not come down to prepare the morning meal, but we were sad to discover that all her things were now missing. Naturally, our housekeeper followed up thereafter by seeking her out down here, as well. This room was also empty, as you can see." He motioned with his hand to the vacant room, inviting their careful perusal.

"Then no one has seen her this morning at all?" Nathanael asked cautiously as he watched Emile, who was still clearly reeling in shock.

"Not since she spoke with Mrs. Berry a little after ten last night. From what I understand, she was quite excitedly discussing plans for her upcoming departure with your friend today. So, as you might expect, we mistakenly assumed that the lady might have changed her mind and left sooner than expected, nothing more."

"Since the three of us are all still present, quite obviously, she did not leave with us," William added politely. "Can I speak with the upstairs maid this morning, if she is feeling up to it? Maybe she has some idea as to where she might have gone."

"Again, I am sad to report that the young lady passed away sometime during the night, though we cannot be sure when. Her family has been notified, but I expect there will be a simple burial here in Kent, given their financial position." The butler's face turned suddenly solemn and grave at his petition.

"Yes, Ireland would be a great distance to transport a body on such short notice," William replied with a forlorn expression. "And you are quite certain she has passed?"

"Most definitely, sir." The butler looked at William as if the man had insulted him openly. "Our doctor confirmed it earlier this morning, in fact."

"I am sorry, I meant no disrespect by it." William tried to apologize. "Please give our condolences to her family and your staff. We will not trespass on your time any longer."

"Very good, sir." The butler bowed again slightly and allowed Emile and William to pass by in front of him before waiting on Nathanael, who had bent down near the doorway to pick up something from off the floor before placing the small object into his pocket.

"Did you find something, sir?" He inquired curiously.

"Oh, just a pebble of some kind. It probably came off the pathway out front. You know how those things stick in your boots," Nathanael lied awkwardly. "I'll see that it is put back where it belongs."

"Quite. Now if you will please excuse me?" He motioned for Nathanael to follow his companions and left them to rejoin the staff at breakfast.

"Does this look familiar to any of you?" Nathanael retrieved the item he had hidden in his pocket and showed it to the rest of them once they had reached the front entryway. The delicate metal charm that was much smaller than a shilling appeared as if someone had stepped on it or at the very least scuffed the back of it against their shoe and the unrelenting stone floor.

Suddenly unable to breathe, Emile grasped it tightly within his palm and held it close. "It was my gift to Emma last night. She said she would never take it off." The hand that clasped the small charm now physically shook with the rage that had been threatening to spill over since he was awakened. "We led the monster right to her, William."

"Be calm... reposed," William soothed. "You cannot help her if you lose control."

"Agreed." Nathanael eyed him with even greater concern.

Emile closed his eyes and tried to steady himself even more for Emma's sake.

Nevertheless, it was at that most inopportune of moments that Angelique strode back into the room behind them with a small, folded packet in hand looking rather confident and triumphant in her task of delivery. "So, I was correct? The bird has flown the coop?"

At the sound of her voice, the men all stiffened in response to her cavalier assessment and obvious joy at Emma's expense, but only two turned around to face her.

"This is not a good time, Miss Toussaint," William warned but remained quite formal in his reply to his host.

"I am sorry. Truly, I am, but these things do happen." She rolled her eyes towards Emile. "And really what do you expect from..."

With a look that would freeze the speech of anyone instantly, Emile swung around and cut her off curtly, "I beg you to stop..." He breathed in deeply several times to control himself, knowing she was most definitely not worth the price he would pay to end her here and now.

Finally, sensing the caution she should have held since the very beginning; Angelique did not continue further but instead walked directly up to William as if the climate in the room had instantly shifted entirely. "This was left for you. The staff found it on the breakfast table this morning. An admirer from the party, perhaps, or maybe even a final farewell from your dear Emma?" She smirked at him playfully, obviously delighting in her final torture of Emile at last, then turned around and walked out of the room without a second glance at the rest of them. With confirmation that her rival was indeed gone, her day was obviously looking infinitely better.

"Detestable woman," Emile spat back at her.

"For once, I wholeheartedly concur," Nathanael replied. "Though it pains me to say it about anyone of the fairer sex."

Intensely curious now as to what the correspondence might contain, William flipped the carefully folded parchment over in his hands and picked up the silver letter opener from off the plated tray in front of him as he slid it seamlessly under the wax seal in one swift motion. Though in truth, he had half-expected a letter from Emma of some kind detailing why she had left, the small, packaged paper appeared to hold very little. Lifting it higher up to peruse its contents, he pulled out the singular calling card from within and held it up to the light. On it, in very thick brush strokes from a quill pen was a singular name only written in bold scrawl and nothing more.

"Charlotte?" William mumbled and turned the card over, then dropped it suddenly onto the floor in shock. With just three printed words, he knew precisely what it meant and what had befallen Emma.

Alarmed at his uncommon carelessness, Nathanael rushed to pick it up, then passed it over to Emile with an equally stunned expression.

On the other side of the card, in neatly stamped font, was the answer. Three words that needed no further explanation as to what had been happening to the servants in Kent and just who the vampire truly was that had killed the others.

"Doctor Malcom Clarke," Emile hissed tersely.

"He's here," William said, as if in a trance. "He didn't leave England after all."

"He has Emma!" Emile threw the card down vehemently onto the table next to him.

"He is going for Charlotte," Nathanael stated what should have been equally as important to the rest of them. "But how?" Nathanael asked, suddenly confused. "He knows nothing about Sebastian's family."

"He knows enough now. Like the fools that we are, we told him all about them in the garden last night. Remember that feeling we both had... the same that I felt back at the port in London... that must have been him, and we stupidly made it only too easy for him to pick us off one by one. Just like he tried to do on the *Endeavour,*" Emile fumed in anger.

Suddenly motivated into action, William snapped out of his trance and flew up the stairs like lightning, hellbent on wasting no more time. "We stopped him then. We will have to stop him now, before he has the chance to kill anyone else!"

Without a second thought or discussion otherwise, the others all followed his lead and threw their belongings hastily into their bags before rushing back down to the foyer. Yet, upon reaching the main door, the underbutler unexpectedly met them coming in looking visibly stunned by the determined look on all their faces. "Can I help you, sir?"

"Yes." William grabbed the folded paper and card from the table that had been cast aside in his haste. "If I were to draft a letter, could the duke send it express for me?"

"But of course," the servant replied. "I can arrange it easily, should you wish it."

"Good." William grabbed a fresh sheet of parchment from out of his leather satchel that he always kept hung around his neck and quickly scribbled a note before placing it and the physician's card into the previous package and wrote out the name and address on the front. "This has to go out now. Immediately even, if at all possible," he urged him most fervently. "It is a matter of life and death."

"Certainly, sir." The servant took the note and left at a quick pace towards the servant's kitchen and hopefully towards the available express.

"We will need to borrow three horses if they can spare them, Nathanael," William advised, then checked the weather outside. "At least the clouds are in our favor."

"When aren't they in England?" Emile chuckled sarcastically, not the least bit inclined to his usual form of merriment.

"I'll go ask the stablemaster about the horses." Without further delay, Nathanael hurried out the front door and over to the adjoining stables to arrange their transportation.

Entirely preoccupied within his thoughts once more, Emile began to pace with his hands tightly clasped behind his back, his fury mixing dangerously with his steadily increasing fear. "Where do you think he will take her?"

"Emma? To Portsmouth most likely, seeing as that is where Charlotte lives." William tied the flap tightly shut once more on his bag. "I doubt he will dispose of her while it still serves his purposes to use her as bait for you."

Emile's eyes darkened once more as he envisioned what all might have transpired last night concerning Emma. "Mark my words, I'll kill him myself when I find him," he expelled his promise out like venom.

"That is exactly what I am afraid of. Listen to me, Emile." William grabbed the upper arms of his friend and forced him to look directly into his eyes. "We know this villain better than anyone else. We have even seen firsthand how he works. We know his pattern and for some reason, he has taken it upon himself to settle some kind of vendetta with the four of us. One that started on that ship long ago. As much as I want to do exactly what you do, we <u>have</u> to think rationally in order to beat him and trust that he won't kill the others as long as he can use them. So, that means that we must make sure he thinks they are still necessary. Do you understand?"

Emile focused all his attention on listening to the more rational words of his friend and not the emotion that begged him towards revenge. "Yes. We need to get to Charlotte first to do that and protect her family until Sebastian arrives. Then, we can finish this once and for all," he said the last sentence with great determination and finality.

"Agreed. This isn't going to stop until he does. But we need to buy our friend some time and hopefully find Emma in the process before something else happens to her," William vowed resolutely.

"Then we will need to hurry, William. From the look of things, the man is already several hours ahead of us." Emile urged as the two of them went out the front door after Nathanael and hopefully to the awaiting horses.

~   ~   ~   ~   ~

Sebastian sat down lazily into a chair by the fireplace after his long day of work. Given the June heat, and the Mediterranean climate, the sun had been especially brutal today, forcing him to spend the better part of the afternoon hiding far into the shadows of his shop.

Paying customers came and went steadily all day, but the excitement at receiving a letter once again from his Charlotte far outweighed the turmoil of the relentless work at the forge. Horse after horse needed to be shod and since he was the only farrier in a hundred-mile radius, he had to do it. Oh, he could have refused them, of course. Or he might have possibly asked the customer to return on a much cloudier day, but money was money and every bit of it would help his family, both now and in the future. So, he did as he must, as he always had. He stayed in the shadows, hammered the nails, and worked the job. It was long. It was hard. It was cathartically necessary.

He closed his eyes and tried to remember with fondness the way his wife had looked the last time they had seen each other but was instead rudely interrupted by the most incessant knocking on the large wooden front door behind him. Alarmed, he immediately made his way over to the door and started unbolting it. No one from the village dared to venture this far up the mountain after dark on account of their deeply rooted superstitions. So, whoever it was, they were probably either up to no good, or in desperate need of Señor Moretti's help.

Maybe someone like him, once upon a time. He thought appreciatively and unbolted the lock, but the knocking continued relentlessly, waiting for his acknowledgement.

With one arm, he opened the door and peered into the darkness awaiting him just beyond. "Yes, may I help you?"

There stood an express messenger, completely covered in a dark hooded cloak with only his long, stringy ink-like hair poking out of the opening here and there. "Are you Sebastian Fabbri?"

"I am..." He answered hesitantly, unsure now if he wanted whatever the man was carrying for him.

Without a word, the man thrust a slightly damp letter in his direction and waited for him to accept it.

"Who is it from?" Sebastian inquired hesitantly as he took it from him.

"Doctor Wells of London, England." With his task completed, the man spun around and mounted his horse before taking off into the distance and out of view moments later, leaving Sebastian confused and cautiously concerned as he stood in the open doorway.

Feeling the all-too-familiar now sickening feeling building up deep within his gut, Sebastian re-bolted the door and quickly opened the letter that bore the unmistakable handwriting of his friend. Once opened, the card enclosed fell to the floor instantly but did not go unnoticed. With a quick raise of his eyebrows at the included item, he retrieved it but chose to read the folded paper first instead.

"Charlotte in danger. Come home immediately." The hastily written note declared and nothing else save the man's signature on the bottom near the corner.

Stunned, Sebastian turned over the other card immediately and read the foreboding name printed on the back. "Doctor Malcom Clarke." Sheer panic now filled his body, mind and soul as he read the letter once more, as if making sure he was not living within some kind of a horrible nightmare. "Charlotte in danger." The words jumped out at him and clasped his throat tightly. With a surge of fresh adrenaline, he crumpled up the paper into his palm and took off at a run up the stairs and to his room to pack.

"What is the matter, Sebastian? Has something happened in the village?" Señor Moretti asked as he saw him fly by his study and immediately followed the man up the spiral steps in alarm.

Sebastian, however, did not hear a single word. As if in a world entirely his own, he threw item after item of clothing into a small leather drawstring bag that he had made to be a gift for one of his sons for their trip to the Americas.

"Sebastian? Is everything alright?" Señor Moretti pleaded calmly.

"My queen is in danger, sir! I have to go. I need to leave now!" He snatched the box that contained the remaining funds from Señor Moretti's gift and tossed it into the bag, as well.

"Why is she in danger?" Señor Moretti watched the scene unfolding before him, powerless to do anything whatsoever to help.

"Remember that ship we all came from?" Sebastian grabbed his thick cloak from behind the door and threw it over his shoulders before tying it securely.

"The one that wrecked in the storm, yes." He turned to follow him down the stairs.

"Well, the man that changed us all was on that ship," Sebastian said in a huff of an explanation.

"But didn't William say that he was washed overboard when it sank?" Señor Moretti tried desperately to put all the pieces together quickly, hoping that if he could do so, he could prevent whatever dangers lay within the rash plan Sebastian was quite obviously hatching.

"From the letter I have just received, it appears not. Worse yet. He is going after my family." Sebastian stopped at the bottom of the stairs and quickly turned around to embrace his friend. "I don't expect you to understand all of this right now. There is too much to tell, but I have to do what I can to save them. And I have to go now!"

535

"But of course! Of course!" He urged. "Only let me send something with you before you go." He hurriedly left Sebastian waiting near the door and retrieved a small bag that clinked when he handed it to him. "Use this only as necessary and it will suffice until you reach home."

"Alright." Sebastian tucked the small parcel safely into his drawstring bag. "But what is it?"

"Something that will prove most useful to you on your trip," he replied.

Sebastian nodded. "I will forever be grateful for everything, sir."

"This is not good-bye, my friend." He put a reassuring hand upon his shoulder. "Just promise me that you will return if you can when this is all over."

"I will," he pledged most faithfully and set off at a run down the well-worn mountain path.

"God speed," Señor Moretti said sadly. "And God protect."

Chapter Forty-Five

June 26th, 1793

"Hurry up Elijah or we are going to be late." Jedidiah helped his younger brother tie his shoes before picking up the leather strap that held the primers the boys shared for their school.

"I'm trying." The boy whined impatiently but stopped when he saw the stern look on his mother's face. "I'm sorry, Mama."

"You know how fortunate you both are to be able to attend Father Benedict's school. Lots of boys your age would be thrilled for the opportunity to sit under his teaching, so I will not hear of my sons casting a long face about it."

"Yes, ma'am," the two said in unison, each grabbing their brown uniformed jacket and putting them on.

"Thank you." She smiled, adoring the way both of them favored their father before leaning over and wiping some dirt off the older boy's forehead with her wet fingertip.

"Awww, Mama." The boy winced as he pulled away. "I hate it when you do that."

"And yet, you still love me." She kissed his forehead where the mark of dirt had been. "Now off to school with the both of you." She smiled and handed each their lunch and late afternoon snack in a carefully packed metal pail, covered with a tan muslin napkin.

"Thank you," the boys proclaimed in unison before scrambling out the front doorway and down the dusty street towards the monastery-styled school on the other side of town.

"And mind your manners!" She yelled after them.

"We will, Mama!" They each echoed back over their shoulders as they skipped and played along the path without the least bit of concern towards their prompt arrival.

"Just like their father, I'm afraid. Late, but always with a diverting reason." She shook her head and drew in a deep breath of the salty sea air coming in from the port while thinking of her husband once more. It wasn't the first time that she had missed his strong arms holding her tightly these past eight months, but with each passing day adding to his increased absence, the ache only grew deeper and rawer still, making it unbearable on most days, and on others like today, tolerant at best.

Like everything else in her world, the kettle over the fire behind her called to her, demanding her attention just as much as the wash waiting to be hung on the line and the dishes left soaking in the small wash tub on the kitchen counter. Every single moment of her day before she had even awakened had already been judiciously allotted towards making the necessary preparations for their upcoming trip as there was little time for anything else. Certainly not a spare minute for pointless daydreaming about a husband who was not coming to help her today or any other day this week for that matter. Nor was there ever a minute for the rest her body so craved or the will to do more than merely survive at this point. Still, it all had to be done one way or another, so she might as well get to it.

Charlotte let out a long sigh and summoned the courage to continue another day more without her husband, finally resolving that today was most definitely going to be one of those trying days. As a rule, the boys would be away at school until at least mid-afternoon, which meant she had a solid four hours to complete all her chores. Another hour would be spent in the preparation of their supper, and maybe if she was lucky, a half hour could be spared to entertain a quiet moment to herself before she would be needed to help with the boys' homework.

After supper her activity would thankfully slow down considerably. Despite the fact that there would be at least half of the packing necessary for Elijah's room to be completed, she still thought she would have enough time to follow that with a little mending here and there of some of Sebastian's old shirts before the three of them all gathered together once more in the main room to read by the fire the latest book William had sent before bed. In all, a rather packed day by the looks of it, just like the one before.

And yet, there was at least one ray of sunshine in her otherwise melancholy view today that she could cling to. When the post had arrived earlier this morning, it had carried with it yet another letter from her husband. In fact, almost three letters had arrived for them this month alone, which was infinitely more than most people could boast with their family in faraway places.

Even more surprising, was the fact that his last letter had been completely different than all of the ones that had arrived before it as this one was filled with a hopeful optimism that had flowed without pretense into promises of their imminent reunion. This highly anticipated news in itself should have at the very least thrilled her to read it, but it did not. At long last, he was finally coming home to her. Yet even seeing the words on the paper as she read them this morning while eating a small bowl of cold porridge, still could not move her to fully accept them.

Though she knew Sebastian to devoutly keep his word no matter what the personal consequence to himself might be, she also still couldn't help but feel the dark foreboding of the events which had thus far continued to torment their lives together—first with the death of their little daughter Sarah two years ago and now with the recent shipwreck. Life, in all its cruelty, seemed endlessly stacked against them ever succeeding, and his prolonged absence now only caused her to doubt they ever would.

But in spite of all of that, she would never let Sebastian know of her doubts, her fears, her intense agony at their loss of their daughter or the tears shed during the many lonely nights without him. After over a decade of marriage, she knew exactly what her husband needed for his survival—hope. Something for which she was happy to give in daily doses to him for as long as he needed it. After all, she had much to be thankful for. He had given her two beautiful boys and a wonderful home, and in every respect, he had been a very attentive father and a steady provider.

Yet, all of that came at a very high price, too. True to his inherited temperament, he always felt the immensity of everything around him much more profoundly than others, even though he tried his best to hide it. And when you added to that the burden of an emotionally traumatic childhood beyond most men's comprehension, you then had Sebastian Fabbri-Smith, hardworking blacksmith, loving husband and dedicated father.

She picked up his last letter from the table and read the bottom portion again as she lifted the kettle from the fire to quiet it, then read the whole of it once more.

Dear Charlotte,
I have arranged passage to the Americas for you and the boys. In fact, the tickets are waiting for you with the ticket master at port even now. And unless there is an

unexpected delay, the ship will leave in the middle of July. So, that means you will most likely arrive well before fall.

From what I have read, I think you will find this new country of ours to be most welcoming if you give it the chance. I know you would much rather stay on familiar soil than traverse the whole of the Earth in pursuit of your husband's dreams, however misguided they may seem at the present.

I feel that I must also convey to you how very sorry I am, Charlotte, for putting you through all of this. With all the extra time I have had recently to think, I have come to the realization that there are many decisions I would change, if I were given a second chance, the first being leaving you all behind in England. Though on that point alone, I thank the Lord that you did not come, as the thought of losing any of you on that voyage would have been incomprehensible. Yet most of all, I realize now that it was wrong of me to ask this journey of you in the first place.

Still, if this time apart has taught me anything, it is that you cannot change the past no matter how much you might want to do so. You must only push forward and make sure not to repeat the errors you learned from once again.

You will see by the enclosed letter from the clerk of court that the house has all been arranged for us in Philadelphia. He will give us the deed upon our arrival and also direct you as to where the boys can attend school as I would not want them to fall behind in their studies. There are many fine schools there, and I am cautiously optimistic about the heights of their future achievements in that area.

I do fully comprehend that this is a tremendous burden to ask you to undertake as you prepare, but also not entirely beyond our original plans. Please be patient with me, my darling. I will be with you soon and drawing you into my arms once more, right where you belong.

Through a miraculous gift, everything from the ship's fare to the house and land has been paid for and much more. And though I know that things have not transpired how either of us had wished, I _have_ kept my promise to provide for you, and rest assured, I have not abandoned my family entirely. Lord willing, this is but a season of trial, and we will all be together as a family again soon. Or at least that is my current prayer.

A hopeful reunion before you sail, maybe? Please tell me you will still want this foolish husband of yours as I most definitely still adore you.

Give the boys a kiss for me and tell them I miss their laughter daily.

Forever Yours,

Sebastian

Soon. What a terribly small word that covers an immense sea of emptiness, Bash. She thought as she shook her head to dispel the waves of overwhelming emotion she felt and placed the letter back inside the box he made for her last Christmas. His latest correspondence had only arrived shortly after his last that had brought along with it several other gifts for each of the boys, but the blessing of its arrival only intensified the loss of its maker even more.

With an equally heavy heart today, the same as the day that he left, she caressed the carving on top with her two fingers, tracing the swirls and patterns he had created so skillfully. "Soon, you stubborn man," she whispered and went back to her work scrubbing the laundry for their upcoming trip.

The ticket master had indeed sent her notice just this morning that arrangements would need to be made today regarding their luggage, but she was far from ready for their departure in just a little under three weeks' time. Tools had yet to be crated, all the furnishings would eventually be sold, and goodbyes still needed to be said to their life in Portsmouth, and to their daughter buried in the church graveyard behind the great live oak.

She wiped another tear away with the back of her hand. Charlotte had known since last November that the day would come when she would have to leave her precious daughter behind, but the knowledge of that fact did nothing to soften the acceptance. Her little Sarah resided in heaven. She never doubted that for a moment, but a piece of her heart would be always buried alongside her here on Earth. Or rather, a little bit of Charlotte Fabbri-Smith would forever be buried in Portsmouth, England, no matter how much of her went to the Americas.

She poured another cup of tea and sipped the hot drink as she looked out the kitchen window and down the street towards the many ships docked at port. Each was a visual reminder of the constancy of change in her world and an irritating remembrance of how close her world nearly came to crumbling when she heard about the shipwreck and her husband's possible death.

Portsmouth was a bustling metropolis of a city, owing much of its industry to the trades necessary for transportation. As such, it provided, by default, a decent livelihood for the young blacksmith and his wife. And yet, she was also keenly sensitive to the prejudice they had also experienced here as well. Which was probably why she allowed her husband to persuade her of his idea to move all the way to the Americas in the first place.

Watching the excitement grow on his face for the first time in years, had made it all too easy to be swept up in the charisma of the idea that a place could exist where people focused more on what you did than who you were or what you looked like. From what the papers said, America was becoming a great nation, entirely independent of their King here in England. A country where someone could supposedly stand up for what they believed and be passionate without the fear of reprisals.

"A place of possibilities," or something like that, Sebastian had said to her convincingly one night after he had brought home the recent flyer from town telling of a ship that was sailing that month to Philadelphia. And because she loved him, she could not say no. If Sebastian Fabbri wanted his sons to live on the other end of the Earth or beyond, she would go with him happily... or at least most of her would.

But there was only one thing, however, that she had not been able to bring herself to do. Something that had begun as a wonderful surprise but had grown to become a burdening secret. A secret she had kept from her husband initially out of fear, then out of dreaded necessity.

In late November, when his ship had sailed, she had not the faintest idea of the possibility that she could have been pregnant, but by December when his Christmas gifts had arrived, she was fairly convinced. Given the harrowing details of her previous births and the time it had taken for them to conceive, the doctor in Portsmouth had reminded her of the necessity for rest and caution as the pregnancy progressed. Yet taking care of two energetic boys on her own was anything but restful, nor did she seem to have any other choice.

Sebastian had only just survived the shipwreck and was miles away on some island at that time. Nor did she want to make him desperate where he was or cause him to feel more pain than was absolutely necessary about his absence if she told him the wonderful truth. Yet despite all of that, as much as she wanted her husband home with every breath she inhaled, she also knew that she could not suffer the thought of how he would accept yet another grave behind the great oak should this child also not survive.

Or maybe... She bit her lip nervously, contemplating his reaction once more. Maybe she did not tell him because she was not sure if she could either.

It was one thing to bury a child and grieve over its passing. It was quite another to relive it day after day while looking into the despairing eyes of someone you loved. Besides what she hoped, there were no guarantees that this baby would be any different, so why take the chance of crushing her husband all over again? If she said nothing at all, it was only her heart that would be breaking, and not his multiple times over every time he looked at her. In his ignorance and safety elsewhere, he would be none the wiser, and as sad as that fact may be to even think it, she almost preferred it that way. Or at least until she could find the right moment to tell him sometime in the distant future when things were more stable.

And so, for months she waited. She hoped. She rejoiced daily in the miraculous gift God had given them growing inside of her, and she dared to believe that God would make it all possible yet again. She prayed to have the right words in the end to explain it all to Sebastian. She pleaded with God that her husband would mercifully understand. She begged beyond measure that her heavenly Father would allow the baby to survive, to be healthy and whole. In short, she prayed nonstop for her own little form of a miracle, if God would so allow it to be.

Yet, when the influenza came through in March, she had been so mad with worry over Elijah's health that she almost couldn't manage to hide the truth of her pregnancy from Sebastian's friend, Doctor Wells, when he arrived. Admittedly, looking back on the whole time they had spent together, it would have made things so much easier today if she <u>had</u> just told him. Maybe then he could have helped to accustom Sebastian to the news, but she did not. Instead, she hid it from him, too. Though through it all, she still had no idea how she had managed to pull it off as William was uncannily perceptive and had diligently scrutinized her every move like she watched those of her children.

The week before his arrival and the week following were a blur to her even now, but she did remember vividly how relieved she had been when he had eventually left. The day when she could finally remove the many layers she had worn to prevent his detection felt glorious. In truth, she felt guilty even now remembering her deception, but in her mind, it couldn't have been helped at the time.

Month after following month thereafter, Sebastian's letters came like clockwork, and each time she wrote a reply, her heart yearned to tell her husband the blessed news. Yet as they passed, each day also made it harder to do so. What had started out as her empathetic desire to wait until she knew if the baby would endure had now been replaced by a desperate fear of whether or not Sebastian would be cross with her for not telling him sooner. By not offering him the chance to be a part of this special gift with which God had mercifully blessed them, she had essentially stolen this happiness from him, as well. Or perhaps, <u>she</u> was the one now that had just added more foreboding things to heap upon the pile already accumulating around them, like a towering pyre only waiting to be lit.

Overwhelmed yet again by the immensity of the challenges ahead of them, Charlotte sighed and smiled as she felt the baby kick once more. "You are going to be strong like your father, aren't you?" She rubbed her hand lovingly across the side of her apron. "Do you think it is finally time to tell him? Maybe he would tell us that we could postpone this silly trip of his and stay here. What do you think about that little one?"

The baby responded in kind with another strong tap against her fingertips, clearly voicing its opinion on the topic.

"Yes, he would probably agree with you. As much as I would like to think otherwise, America is our new home, now, right?"

She turned back to fire and placed another log onto it to keep it from going out entirely but jumped slightly when a knock at the door behind her half-startled her upright. Visitors rarely came to the house now that Sebastian had closed his shop altogether. So, this unusual disturbance in her normally busy, but otherwise peaceful day was more than surprising, it was concerning. Her last unexpected visitor had been William months ago, but his most recent letter had said that he and his friends would not be arriving for another two days at least.

Could he have changed his mind and come sooner?

Part of her hoped so as she could most certainly use their help in packing. The other half dreaded the truth finally coming out and the subsequently awkward series of questions that would no doubt follow for there was no way she could hide the baby now, layers or no layers. Her time was almost upon her, and come what may, she was most definitely ready.

"Coming," she called sweetly, hoping for the best, as she untied her washing apron and unlatched the front door, expecting to see the kind face of the man she had grown to love as one of her own family.

To her surprise, however, a stocky man, about the same age and build as her husband with dark hair, a matching thick beard and a neatly trimmed mustache stood just off the front porch by a waiting wagon. "I'm sorry to disturb you ma'am, but is your husband at home?"

"No, I am sorry, he is not. Can I help you?" Charlotte fought back the nagging feeling about the man's uncertain intentions and chalked it up to her growing list of errant concerns that Sebastian always joked she tended to collect.

"I was sent by the shipping office to arrange your luggage at the warehouse," he said plainly but maintained his position at a distance out of respect.

"Ah yes, I received his letter today, in fact. But... I am not sure I am ready with all of our things just yet. Can I arrange for you to come back for them in a weeks' time?" She tried to be as convincing as she possibly could as she was far from ready to hand over anything, let alone deliver it to the shipyard in her condition.

The man shook his head apologetically. "I am afraid you will need to speak with him directly to arrange those details, ma'am, as I am but the messenger. Can you come now if I drive you?" He persisted further.

"Um, certainly, if it is absolutely necessary." She nodded, then pursed her lips, feeling a slight tinge of pain cross the small of her back—her almost daily reminder for well over a week now to be mindful of not overdoing things. "I'll be with you directly, sir." She went back inside and wrote a simple note for her children before wrapping her knitted shawl around her to protect her dress from the dust of the journey.

"It won't take but a half hour at most, ma'am," he reassured her before helping her carefully up into the buckboard. "I'll be sure to drive slowly as I doubt the shipping company knew you were expecting, or they probably wouldn't have imposed."

"I am much obliged." She steadied herself on the seat and tried to lessen the jostling the roads created as they passed over them.

"You are leaving for the Americas soon I hear." He tried to make amiable conversation as the wagon rattled its way down the rutted street from the recent rains. "I myself have served on many ships over the years. It is a wonderful journey: the open ocean, the sails blowing in the wind, the interesting people you will meet. You will see."

"I am sure it will be lovely." Charlotte half-smiled and tried to place where his accent originated but was forced to concentrate the majority of her attention instead on quelling the nausea the trip was creating more than on her examination.

Before long, the wagon turned the corner softly and pulled up next to the last shipping warehouse at the end of the busy docks, far from the departing and arriving passengers.

"Is this where I am to meet him?" Charlotte shielded her eyes from the noonday sun as she peered up hesitantly at the tall building before her.

"Yes, he is waiting just inside. Do you have any other children than the one you are carrying?" The man tied off the horses and looked up at her and though he was making perfectly cordial conversation, Charlotte was hesitant to give him more than the most basic of information as she still did not trust him for some reason.

"Yes, but they are at school right now. Does the manager need to see them, as well?" She asked politely while taking hold of the side of the wagon and stepping down backwards without his help, for he was still on the other side of the wagon, busily collecting something from out of the back.

With a jolt that brought her up short, her stomach tightened instantly at the reaching movement as it yanked away whatever breath remained in her lungs momentarily. "Lordy be, little one, behave," Charlotte stifled a quiet groan and tried to get her bearings once more through it.

"I suppose you are hoping to deliver before you sail." The man continued on in his rambling without noticing her distress. "I can't imagine how difficult it would be to do so once at sea, though I <u>have</u> seen a delivery or two during my time. Still, you'll have to trust me when I say that a ship is not exactly the best place for a birth."

"Yes, I am due well before, prayerfully." A sharp gasp escaped her lips once more as she held onto the sideboard of the wagon with a grip so tight it made her fingers look white and bony.

"Say, are you alright, ma'am?" The man asked, and for the first time since he had set foot on her doorstep, his voice sounded genuinely concerned, carrying with it none of the falseness she had sensed earlier.

"I will be in a minute or two." She straightened up and breathed in and out slowly to temper the pain and calm whatever it was that was transpiring within her. "This has happened before."

Though not as bad as this to be sure, Charlotte added mentally thereafter.

"Perhaps, you should come inside and sit a spell first." He directed with his hand towards the door of the warehouse, prodding her to step inside.

"Yes, thank you. That might be best, all things considered." Charlotte nodded and opened the door, expecting to find a room busily flowing with people and cargo. Yet once inside, the arm of the man reached around her suddenly from the shadows and placed something vaguely soft and pungent directly over her mouth and nose, partially restricting her breathing.

With her worst fears in all the world realized, panic consumed her very being as she struggled against him, but in the end, fell as limp as a used rag against his chest as he laid her clumsily into the nearest chair. Truthfully speaking, it was the last thing she remembered before waking up next to another woman who was still very much unconscious and shivering uncontrollably.

Instantly frightened and more than a bit disorientated, she felt around herself carefully in the darkness on her hands and knees for any kind of light but found none. The room itself was completely dark in every direction save that of a tiny sliver of light that had managed to peak itself in through a small crack in the ceiling about eight feet off the hard-packed clay floor.

Where was she? In the warehouse?

No, that didn't make sense, and yet how could she not be. The man couldn't have possibly carried her any farther in her condition without someone else noticing.

But why? What did he want with her anyways that he would keep her a captive here?

"Hello?" She called and stood up to feel the walls of her prison. From what she could tell, they were smooth and moist like the stone of Sebastian's forge after it rained, strangely so, and not at all like the wooden walls that lined the building she had seen up above.

With a sigh of defeat that pulled at the edges of her very soul, she placed one ear on the wall closest to her and thought she could make out the echoing sounds of the crashing waves beyond, but as muted as they were, she could not be completely certain.

"Is there anyone out there?" Her breathing sped up once more and her throat became constricted unconsciously as she tried to calm it.

No response came back to her, though the girl on the floor behind her did moan just a little.

Feeling fresh concern for the woman who was obviously struggling more than she was at the moment, she bent over and felt her forehead. To her relief, no fever was present, even though her entire body did appear to be covered in a cold sweat that ran down the sides of her temples and back into the locks of her hair. In the dampness of the room around them, she could also tell that the woman trembled from head to toe far more from the strange fever-like state she was in than from the actual temperature around her for though it was most definitely slightly chilly below, the air also contained a warm breeze from time to time that slipped through the trap door above.

"Can you tell me your name, miss?" She took a seat next to her in the dirt and put the girl's head onto her lap to support her as best as she could. Or rather what was left of it, as the baby had been managing to take up far more room as it had descended lower since last week.

"Em-ma," the girl chattered uncontrollably. "Wh-where are we?"

"I'm not sure. It feels like a cave of some kind, or maybe even a root cellar. Do you remember how you got here?" She wiped the damp strands from Emma's face and tried to soothe her further.

The young lady turned her head from side to side, but the shaking only intensified with her response. "I'm s-s-so c-cold. Please help-p-p m-m-me."

"I'll try my best." Charlotte removed her shawl and placed it over her, tucking it in around the edges of the woman's body. "My name is Charlotte, and this will help a little, but we will need to find a way to get you out of here. Do you think you can walk if I do?"

The girl did not respond. She had unfortunately fallen back unconscious, though the intense shivering continued on.

With little else she could do to alleviate the poor girl's suffering; Charlotte held her as close as she could manage and began humming the tune she always sang to her own children when they were little. Something that was born out of an old Irish melody that was foreign to most, but one that she had always remembered fondly as something her grandfather had sung to her on those nights when she was afraid. The monsters then were quite imaginary and mostly contained in those bedtime tales that always frightened her so. Still, as scary as they were, they were a far cry from the human-like monster who had kidnapped them both earlier today.

She thought back again to her boys, who would be arriving home from school shortly, and prayed that there would be no one waiting for them inside. As careful as they were, she knew that they would no doubt be frightened by her absence, but that was a much better thing to contemplate than the thoughts that made her own mind race with dread.

Would Jedidiah know what to do if she never returned? Would he remember the letter in the box she had told him about? The one only to be opened in an emergency? Would Sebastian's friend, William, be able to care for them until Sebastian arrived? Or if he did not?

Oh, how she wished now that she had told her husband about her pregnancy. Perhaps then he would have been here so her children would not be alone right now. Or at the very least, not in harm's way.

If only...

She felt her stomach contract again, only this time with much more force behind it and a great deal more pain.

Please God, not here. Not now.

She hummed a little louder, but the tune did not echo off the walls as she had expected. Instead, it was swallowed up like the rest of them, deep into the earth below, just like a grave.

Chapter Forty-Six

June 26th, 1793

"Mama said we should stay put, Elijah," Jedidiah, the older of the two brothers, instructed after he read the note his mother had left on the table for at least the second time before answering his younger brother yet again. "See. Read this right here."

Elijah picked up the scrap of paper and began to read it laboriously, "I've g-gone to the ship-ping ware-house. Be b-back soon. Take care of each o-th..o-th." The boy tried again and again to say the last word.

"Take care of each other and that means staying put. Do you hear me?" Jedidiah commanded authoritatively. "Papa made me the man of the house when he left, and I mean to do as he said."

"But where is Mama?" The little boy frowned anxiously.

"You read what it says. She went down to the warehouse to get things ready for our trip. She will be back soon."

"But I'm hungry, now," Elijah pouted, unconvinced of his brother's more simplistic answer to the situation.

With a huff, Jedidiah rolled his eyes at him and put the note safely back into his mother's box. "You are always hungry, Elijah." He walked over to the counter and picked up a ripe red apple from the wooden bowl near the sink. "Here. Now eat this and let's work on our homework until she gets here."

"Thank you, Jed." Elijah's eyes gleamed at the unexpected treat and eagerly plunked himself down onto the wooden bench next to the table before taking out his slate. For more than two full hours the two boys worked steadily together without pausing until Jedidiah felt the need to light the candle on the table in front of them.

"I'm worried, Jed. Mama has never missed dinner before." Elijah's lip quivered as his brother lit the candle's wick and then another.

"Is that all you can ever think of?" He sighed. "Your stomach?"

"No." The young boy shook his head back and forth in denial but fearfully plunked it down on top of his little folded arms anyways. "I'm scared."

As if right on cue with an answer to his concern, the handle of the large front door jostled behind them, shaking the wood just a little on its metal hinges by someone who was pounding on it several times thereafter.

Without uttering a sound, both boys froze instantly at the interruption before Jedidiah held one finger up to his lips and moved stealthily to pick up the axe that was always kept by the fire.

The same deliberate pounding sounded again, only this time it was followed soon after by a voice, a vaguely familiar voice. "Charlotte? Are you home?"

Elijah's face lit up instantly as he whispered as quietly as he could from across the room to his brother on the other side, "It's William, Jedidiah! Maybe he has brought us food again like last time!"

"Hush, Eli," Jedidiah commanded as he held his ground and motioned with his hand to Elijah. "Maybe he has brought trouble. Now git over here and stay behind me."

"Alright." The little boy moved slowly to obey him, while still not entirely understanding the reason for his brother's alarm. "But Mama said he was coming this week, didn't she? Please... he said he would bring another book, Jed."

The latch on the door jostled up and down once more as if the person outside was trying to open it, but the door still remained securely fastened from within.

"Jedidiah? Elijah? Are you both in there?" The voice called again tentatively.

"It is William, Jed!" The little boy pushed past his brother's guarded arm at last and rushed to the door before throwing it open before his brother could move to stop him.

"My! What a greeting, little man!" Doctor Wells caught up the boy in his able arms and smiled from ear to ear. "And so much stronger than when last we met. Have you been eating your vegetables like I instructed?"

"Nah. You're just puny, that's all." The boy scrunched his face up playfully. "You're not like Papa at all. He has muscles everywhere." Elijah hugged him once more around his neck, relief clearly painted across all his features. "We've missed you."

"I've missed you too, Elijah." William clasped him tightly to him and peered over his shoulder before taking in his brother's stance fully. As if still afraid to move any closer, Jedidiah stood at attention on the other side of the room near the wide fireplace with his axe raised over his shoulder in protection. "It's okay, Jedidiah. I am not here to hurt you. You know that. Is your mother home?" He spoke slowly and gently as he tried to calm the boy's nerves just like he had done on their first encounter.

It worked for as the sound of his words reached the boy's ears, Jedidiah's resolve melted along with his strength. Assured now that his protective measures were no longer needed, he set the axe down carefully and left it by the fire. Then, taking several steps quickly together, he fell into William at his waist as emotions overwhelmed him in choked sobs. "Mama hasn't come home like she said, William. She told me to take care of Elijah, but I don't know what else to do."

"It's alright, Jedidiah. I am here now." William held the two children tightly and motioned with his head for Nathanael and Emile to enter the cabin behind him and close the door. "You both have been very courageous, just like Gulliver was, but it is my turn to be brave for you now, okay, Jed?"

The boy nodded and wiped away the tears he was once again too embarrassed to show. "Papa said I was to take care of Mama and Elijah while he was away."

William nodded and ruffled his hair. "And so, you have. Have you heard from your Papa yet?"

"Yes." The boy's face began to lighten just a little with the redirecting question. "He says he is coming with us to America soon. Mama said he might even be on the ship when we sail."

William knelt down at Jedidiah's level to look him seriously in the eyes and inquired carefully so as not to upset the boy further. "Can you tell me where your mother is then?"

The boy shook his head.

"Has she been gone long?" Nathanael asked cautiously next, looking over at Emile to judge his reaction to the news.

"I'm not sure. She was here this morning before school." Jedidiah seemed to be growing more nervous by the new visitors William had brought and the countless questions that he could not answer than he was with anything else. "But she has never missed dinner like this before, sir."

"It's okay. We'll sort it out soon," William encouraged him. "May I introduce you to two of your father's other friends from the ship? I assure you that they are as safe as your Papa and I. Do you trust me in that?"

The boy jerked his head up and down quickly but the look on his face told another story altogether.

With a smile at the remembrance of his father, William set Elijah down so that he could stand higher than Jedidiah upon the wooden bench before waving his hand to his right in introduction. "This here is the Mr. Beckett I told you both about last spring, but you can call him Nathanael like I do. He much prefers that over preacher but don't tell him that I told you so."

Nathanael rolled his eyes at William's jest in front of the children and offered his hand to Jedidiah first, who pumped the man's hand up and down twice formally.

"I'm pleased to make your acquaintance, sir," the young boy acknowledged him more formally.

"Thank you." Nathanael couldn't help but smile before adding truthfully, "You look like your father, young man."

Jedidiah shrugged. "That's what Doctor Wells thinks, too, but Momma said Eli is more like him than me."

"Perhaps they are both right." Nathanael nodded and took off his cloak before folding it up and setting it carefully on the chair next to the stairs beside him.

"And this is Mr. Deschamps..." William began to introduce but was quickly interrupted by an inquisitive Elijah.

"Dah-what?" Elijah squinted up at the man whose head, complete with added hat, almost reached the top of the ceiling in their somewhat modest home.

"_You_ may call me Mr. Emile." Emile reached forward and tapped the tip of his nose like he had done to Mrs. Summerfield's son, Joshua, when he asked him impertinent questions.

"Ohhhhh." The little boy smiled in understanding. "You're the one Mama calls the naughty Frenchman in Papa's letters, aren't you?"

Emile smiled back at the boy, clearly amused. "Yes, the naughty Frenchman." He made a playful face at the boys.

William and Nathanael each tried to hold back their laughter at the lighthearted exchange, but it was good to see the boys bonding so well with all of them at last.

"Is Papa really coming home, William?" Jedidiah inquired; concern plainly written across his forehead. "If you say it's true, then I'll believe it."

"Yes." He walked over to him and placed a hand on his shoulder. "What would you say if I told you that I was absolutely certain he was on his way here right now, in fact?"

The two boys both screamed with delight and danced around the room like they were horses once more and not young boys who were, at this very moment, in very grave danger. "We can be a family again! Just Papa and Mama, us and the baby."

"The baby?" William's eyebrows shot up instantly at the news. "Is your mother expecting."

"Oh yes!" Jedidiah exclaimed. "She says the baby will be here hopefully before we leave, maybe even sooner. Papa doesn't know about it yet though, but he will soon. It's our little surprise, Momma says."

"It certainly is." William and the others exchanged a deeply concerned look. The situation was clearly complicated enough without adding in the complexity of a woman about to give birth.

"I best see if I can make them some supper," Emile offered and went into the small pantry to find ingredients for their meal.

"You know how to cook?" Elijah scrunched up his nose, distracted from his antics around the room. "But you're a man?"

Emile nodded just once at the boy when he turned around with several containers, some vegetables and a bag of flour in his arms. "Well then, since my honor is clearly in question, you must tell me how I do once it is finished. I'll let you be the judge if I can cook or not," he challenged.

"Alright." The boy approved and from that moment on he sat religiously watching every single thing that Emile did in the small kitchen.

Smiling contentedly at his raptured attention, Emile put him immediately to work, handing the young boy a carrot and a very small metal blade. "Drag this gently across the sides for me, please."

"Mama doesn't let me play with knives, Mr. Emile." The boy turned the carrot over again and again in his hands but would not pick up the knife.

"Then we had best not play." Emile put the bowl he was mixing the flour in down and took the boy's hand in his own to demonstrate exactly what he wanted him to do.

"Ahhhhh," the boy said and held his tongue on the side of his mouth in careful concentration on his task. "This is kind of fun."

Emile nodded. "Yes, it is."

With the younger child now sufficiently distracted, William sat down at the table with Jedidiah and Nathanael to sort out as many details as he possibly could to aid them in finding their mother. Though Doctor Clarke was possibly several hours ahead of them, there was no reason to believe just yet that her absence was in any way related to Emma's earlier disappearance. Charlotte could have been merely visiting a doctor or had gone to make the necessary plans at the shipping office before being unfortunately delayed. Though equally not ideal, he also had to consider the distinct possibility that she could have also gone into labor somewhere along the way. In fact, if one were to be totally honest, there could be at least a dozen logical reasons for her not returning home as planned, though he hoped for all their sakes, at least one of them was plausibly true compared to the dreadful alternative. "Now, did your mother leave you a note perhaps? Or said something to let you know where she might have gone?"

Without missing a beat, Jedidiah respectfully opened the small box on the table and took out the half-ripped scrap she had left for them before handing it over to William. "This was the only thing on the table when we came home from school."

William read the note carefully and frowned.

"What?" The boy's voice became instantly tense. "Mama and the baby are going to be alright, aren't they?

"Of course they are." William placed his hand on the boy's shoulder to reassure him before offering the message to Nathanael to read. "Is there anything else you can think of that might be helpful?"

Considering his request seriously, the boy thought long and hard for several moments before his eyes lit up with excitement at the realization. "Mama told me once that I was to give something to Papa if anything were to ever happen." He dug into the box and took out a tightly rolled-up piece of paper that was tied with a simple green ribbon. The same type of ribbon William had seen the woman use on her brown braids each day when he had last visited.

"May I see it?" William asked politely, his hand poised in the air slightly between them.

"Mama said it is only for Papa." The boy's eyes narrowed as his face shifted to one of intense protection once again.

"Of course." William nodded in understanding and relented quickly so as to regain his trust. "Then you can be sure to give it to him when he comes, okay?"

"Okay." The boy put the parchment securely back into the box and slammed it shut accidentally.

"Opps, sorry. I didn't mean to shut it that hard," the boy apologized quickly like it was something he did more out of habit.

"I know you didn't, son." William smiled warmly up at him.

Hearing the familiar reply, the boy's positive countenance returned once more. "That's what Papa used to always say."

"Mine, too, Jedidiah. Maybe that is what all papas say." William's eyes sparkled warmly at the exchange.

"I doubt it." Jedidiah played with the lock on the wooden box as his mind wandered. "You gonna stay longer this time around?"

"Yes, until your papa comes at least, maybe a little longer. I promise you that we will be here to help in whatever way we can," William answered him honestly.

"Speaking of help, I'll go see about bringing in more wood for the fire. The pile here is almost spent," Nathanael offered awkwardly and stepped out of the cabin and into the warm air on the front porch desperate for a breath of fresh air. Despite how much he wanted to be of use to Sebastian's family, he felt totally out of place in this house and almost immaterial. The boys, most understandably, had already formed a distinct attachment to William, given their recent history together, and Emile could not help charming his way into anyone's affection, but he... He thought back to his conversation with Elsie once more and frowned. He had been grateful beyond words when she had said that she did not want any children of her own to speak of. As for himself, he had never been very good with other people's children, let alone desire to have one of his own. It just wasn't in him. It was one of the consequences of being an only child, he supposed, and Elsie had understood that. William did too in some regards, but it still didn't make Nathanael feel any better in situations such as these.

Yet, he could help to ease the burden on others wherever it was needed most, even if that was always in the background. It wasn't as flashy as Emile, or as elegant as William, but it was still useful.

He picked up a full armload of wood and entered the cabin before placing it dutifully by the warm fire without comment.

"Dinner is served," Emile stated shortly afterwards as he laid a heaping bowl of stew in front of each of the boys.

Utterly famished, given the approaching late hour, the two eagerly grabbed their forks and dug in, wasting no time at all to consume every bite.

"I made the carrots," Elijah proclaimed proudly to his brother in-between mouthfuls.

"So, I heard." Jedidiah tried to ignore his triumphant remarks and focused more of his attention instead on eating.

Taking advantage of their suddenly distracted state, William adeptly removed the box from the table and carefully carried it over to the window by the sink before discreetly turning around to peer at its contents. The scroll with the ribbon still lay diagonally directly on top of a stack of letters that, judging by the handwriting on the front, were obviously written by Sebastian.

With great care then, he lifted the corner of each one of them in turn as he sifted through them quietly before another letter near the bottom of the pile caught his eye, one with his name written boldly on the front and nothing more. Curious, he pulled it out and held it up to the candlelight on the counter to make sure he had read the inscription correctly.

"Oh, I almost forgot, that one is for you. Mama put it in there after you left. She said you would know what to do with it." Jedidiah exclaimed with his mouth half-full of food when he saw him from across the room.

"She wrote this back then?" William's interest piqued considerably more.

"Um-hmm." The boy swallowed another gulp of food.

"This sure is good, Mr. Emile. You certain you are definitely a guy? I mean... you got long hair and all." Elijah scrutinized him with one eye closed and the other one squinted as Emile sat leaning back in his chair with his arms folded comfortably across his chest, perfectly amused by Sebastian's youngest son.

"Mind your manners, Eli," Jedidiah corrected him sternly at his overly rude comments.

"Most definitely a man, Master Elijah." Emile smiled and playfully batted his apprentice with the towel that had been resting on his leg, resulting in a small puff of remaining flour flying upwards and into the boy's face.

"Hey!" The boy giggled and shied away from his playful attack.

"On guard, my little apprentice." Emile winked at him in growing affection and prepared himself for another assault.

Nathanael smiled, too. "My Elsie did that to me once."

Emile's eyebrows lifted slightly at the comment and dropped the towel back onto his lap, grateful once again that Nathanael was choosing more and more often to share his stories about the dear woman.

"We made a horrible mess though. Completely covered her mother's kitchen with it, in fact." Nathanael chuckled at the distant memory.

"Who is Elsie?" Elijah interjected innocently, his spoon scraping the bottom surface of his bowl at last.

"A very special young lady," Emile answered him quickly before the boy could say something that might derail the progress Nathanael was making.

"Ohhh." Elijah ate another mouthful of food, then spoke simply once more, "She sounds awfully nice."

"She was, thank you." Nathanael nodded and leaned back in his chair to watch carefully out the front windows for anyone approaching. Emile, for all his charm and debonair ways, might have appeared calm and collected in front of the children, but Nathanael could tell from the constant drumming the man did with his fingers upon the table's surface while he waited for them to finish that he was concentrating all his strength to remain so. In fact, if they weren't in the middle of this tense situation, Nathanael could have almost made out a distinct rhythmical pattern—much like that awful song he loved to play.

William, on the other hand, was focusing his attention instead on the letter in his hands, turning it over once or twice again before finally deciding to pick up the knife from the counter and carefully pried back the wax seal on the other side of the paper. In truth, he had no earthly idea just what it might contain, but nothing in all the world could have properly prepared him for what had been written therein.

Dear William,

Sebastian told me last February that if there was anyone else in this world he could trust other than me, it would be you. He has said many times that you are a good man, and since I know his character, I also know it to be true of you.

Life is entirely uncertain, as both of us surely know from even the most recent of events. So, I feel it would be wrong of me to not try to do the smallest of things to at least secure a future for my children if something were to happen to either of us.

Neither Sebastian nor I have discussed this arrangement, nor do we have any living relatives to speak of. This means that the boys would naturally be taken to a public establishment upon our deaths. You know as well as I that it would be entirely the farthest action from our wishes to do such a thing. And yet, to ask this of you seems equally monumental.

If you, or anyone else, is reading this letter, it is my desire that you raise the boys as your own and try to at least comfort them through to their apprenticeship year. Which hopefully, should only be a short time for Jedidiah. I am not expecting you in any way to take the place of their father, but at least in having a mentor, the boys will have someone in their lives that cares for them as I know you do.

How do I know this? How does a mother know anything? By simply watching your face tonight as you stroked Elijah's hair and read to him assures me of this fact. You have the heart of a father, William; and I know Sebastian would approve of this solemnest of decisions that I make on his behalf.

Father Benedict, at their school, has another parcel for you and the boys should you have need of it. He is a very trusted man of the cloth, and the documents and money inside will allow the boys to get a start in this world, though admittedly, a very meager start.

My prayer is that it never shall come to this. Or that you will never even see this letter, but I simply cannot leave this decision left unspoken.

Remind the boys daily of my love for them, especially Jedidiah. He is too much like his father in that regard and will need daily encouragement.
In this, you will have my forever gratitude.
Charlotte

Overwhelmed, William wiped a tear from the corner of his eye and tried to compose himself as he placed the letter and its covering paper deep within his left-hand pocket.

"What's the matter, William?" Elijah's face was full of worry once more.

"Nothing, Elijah." William put on a cheerful expression and tried to speak without wavering. "Nothing, truly."

"But you're crying." The boy scrunched up his nose once more as he peered across the room at him.

"Happy tears, I assure you Eli. Now, please finish eating before the supper gets cold." William cleared his throat and shut the lid of the carved box on the counter securely.

Without another word, the boy obediently turned back to his food and finished the stew completely in a few more large bites before proclaiming triumphantly, "Done."

"Do I pass your inspection, young Master?" Emile inquired while removing his finished bowl aloofly like a seasoned waiter.

"Well..." The boy closed his eyes and tapped his chin several times in deliberation. "It is not as good as mama's, but you will do."

Emile smiled. "Then I will take that as the best compliment I have ever received."

"You shouldn't," Jedidiah remarked sarcastically before handing him his finished bowl, as well. "He'll eat anything."

The room then erupted into polite laughter before Nathanael ushered the boys upstairs to get them ready for bed.

"Does the letter say anything about Emma?" Emile asked optimistically at the sink while washing the dishes once the boys were out of earshot. "My skin is literally crawling over here doing nothing to find her."

"I'm afraid not. Quite the opposite, in fact," William replied and helped to dry one of the bowls.

"How so?" Emile's face betrayed just a hint of his inner turmoil. It was similar to what he had been struggling to do since they arrived. For everyone around him he kept on a collected exterior, but William saw over and over again the brief flashes of his pain that slipped out here and there in his quick glances out the window and false smiles after humorous remarks.

"She left me her last will and testament, Emile," William said quietly and braced himself for what might follow next.

Stunned just as much as William had been when he had read it, Emile stopped washing the bowls and stared blankly out the window for several moments without saying a word before adding resolutely, "Then we had better make sure we never need it."

"Agreed." William sighed but his mind only continued to race with the millions of questions and possible contingencies.

"The boys want a bedtime story, William," Nathanael called down from the upper railing to his friend below. "I'm afraid all I know are biblical ones, but they say they want something about horses?"

William sighed and shook his head. "I'm so torn. We need to be out there looking for Charlotte and Emma, but someone needs to be here with the boys until Sebastian arrives. We can't leave them defenseless either and as much as I may want to be, I'm simply not able to be in two places at once."

"What did you read to the boys the last time you came?" Emile placed the last wet dish on the counter and took the towel away from William to dry it.

"Gulliver's Travels, but I don't think I have the patience for any of that tonight, so I'll probably just make something up," William answered Emile but began making his way dutifully over to the stairs to advise Nathanael. "Tell them I will be up in a minute if they get in their beds and wait for me there."

"If you wish." Nathanael shrugged and turned around to relay the message like a dutiful errand boy.

"William, please..." Emile's voice betrayed just how much he was truly restraining himself in remaining there.

"I know." William looked back at him, his eyes displaying the conflict within him, as well.

"I need to be doing something... anything. I can't just sit here knowing she is out there and in danger. Do you think you can manage the boys if I were to go into town and take a look around?" Emile slid his dark cloak over his shoulders and affixed the clasp in case he needed it, not truly waiting for anyone's permission on the matter.

"And what if you find him without us?" William's normally guarded demeanor displayed his true emotion concerning his friend. "I don't want to lose you either, Emile."

"The feeling is mutual, I assure you, Brother." Emile pursed his lips but held back the rest of what their eyes said in its absence, acknowledging him in a way he had never done so in the past. "How's this? What if I promise not to act on anything I find unless it is a matter of life or death? Would that suffice?"

William nodded. "We <u>have</u> been like brothers since the very beginning, haven't we?"

"Yes, but who is older <u>and</u> wiser? That is the most important," Emile taunted him, needing the release of some of his pent-up stress.

"Mentally or physically?" William teased him right back and smiled. The answer didn't matter. They both already knew the truth. "On second thought, you had better take Nathanael with you when you go."

"Why?" Emile looked back at him quickly, uncertain as to how the man who refused to harm a fly could be of any assistance to him at all.

"Right now, I think he is more afraid of those boys than Doctor Clarke," William replied honestly as he began climbing the stairs. "Besides, it would make me feel better if I knew you were not out there hunting for her alone."

Emile only chuckled lightly at his remark, then added, "You are probably right. Tell him I'll be waiting for him by the horses and to hurry." Emile walked out the front door and latched it securely behind him allowing his eyes to adjust fully to the night all around him. With all the adrenaline that had been building up on their journey from Kent, he had half-expected some kind of confrontation with their nemesis when they had finally arrived in Portsmouth. Yet to find nothing but a sleepy port and two scared children waiting for them, concerned him more than he cared to admit and only filled his mind with even more troubling questions.

Had they made a mistake in coming here in the first place? Or did Doctor Clarke only leave the cryptic note to throw them off his trail so he could continue to feed as he wished while in Kent? And beyond that, what did he want with Emma anyways, or even Charlotte for that matter? Were they simply his next meal, or was this truly only about the four of them? And if so, why?

Emile waited for his sixth sense to rise like it had in the garden, but it did not. Nothing in the slightest seemed casually amiss in the silent countryside, which made him think that perhaps one of his earlier assumptions might have been correct. If Doctor Clarke had indeed come to Portsmouth for Charlotte, he was sadly, no longer close enough nearby to trigger it.

"Are you thinking about Emma?" Nathanael asked when he rejoined his friend once more on the porch, grateful once again for any assignment that allowed him some room to exist outside of that cabin.

"Doctor Clarke, actually." Emile scanned the horizon and focused his attention yet again on several lights off in the distance before mounting his horse.

"I don't understand why he would be so angry at any of us as to want revenge like this. William seems to think it is because all of us are some kind of witness to what he has been doing all along or that he is afraid of what we might do to stop him. Accessories to his crimes so to speak, if you look at it that way, but we are nobody, Emile. And I certainly have no plans to say anything about what Doctor Clarke might choose to do. Who would believe me if I did?" Nathanael untied his horse's reins from the porch railing and stepped over to the side of the animal to mount it.

"Speak for yourself. I've never exactly found it easy to hide anywhere." Emile smirked audaciously. "Though I do understand what you are getting at. I don't personally care how the man chooses to feed, but I draw the line when it is someone that I love."

"Everyone is loved by somebody, Emile. You just don't know them at the time," Nathanael remarked quietly, fearing that he might be causing offence to his friend in his open opinion.

"Rest easy, Nathanael. I do understand the gravity of that now. Still, everything inside of me is compelling me to search every single house in this town tonight if it will help us find Emma." Emile turned his horse around to face the town beyond and urged him forward.

"Well, I don't think we can search every home, but we can start with the ships and the warehouses down at the docks. That was where he was hiding the last time someone was after him, and with any luck at all, he will be there again."

"That is an excellent idea, Nathanael." Emile nudged his horse more and the two of them took off at a quick pace down the road, towards the docks.

Chapter Forty-Seven

June 28th, 1793

A little over thirty-six hours had passed since the moment Sebastian had been handed the express forewarning a change to his very existence and yet every one of them had been more agonizing than the next. As it turned out, securing the necessary passage on a ship bound for Portsmouth that night had probably been the easiest part of his journey thus far as providentially there had already been one leaving on the tide, fully laden with Genoan wine and textiles. Yet this stroke of unusual luck was of little comfort to him when it did not also provide him with something constructive to do during that voyage.

Before his current transformation with its irritating limitations, he had always thought of himself as a fairly patient man, no matter the difficulty placed before him. But as the wind pushed the sails to their fullest extent and the waves cut through the front of the ship's bow with no hope of land on the horizon, he soon discovered that he was not. For when a man has nothing to do but lie helplessly in his bunk creating terrifying realities in his very vivid imagination, or the only option of occupation afforded to him is to stare out into a vast ocean of absolute nothingness, a man's mind can become a dangerous place indeed. Something he would not wish on his worst enemy... Well maybe on one of them, but right now that thought had to be tamed completely, too.

If truth be told, the whole experience was a little maddening to endure as not a single day of his life to date had ever been spent in idle pursuits of any kind. Nor was there any task available to him as a paying passenger other than merely strolling aimlessly on the deck above or watching the currents from his bunk inside his cabin. Which only meant one thing, there was no earthly way to make time pass any faster other than maybe the many prayers he had sent up since throwing his leather bag upon the swaying hammock below.

In an effort to quell that frustration and the fear that threatened to overwhelm him, Sebastian had tried repeatedly throughout the voyage to temper his growing anxiety much like he had learned to do with his bloodlust, by distracting his thoughts towards more pleasant things like his mentor had shown him. Events like the day that he had married Charlotte. Or the look in her eyes every morning as she stared after him on his way over to the forge. The calmness of spirit she always passed on to him as he hugged her each night and the joy of the laughter from his two sons as they greeted him at the door. All of these were wonderful alternatives to the darker contemplations his mind fought to conjure up about what might be befalling his family in his absence. Each of them was as powerful as the next as they eagerly gnawed at his insides like a hundred hungry rats, threatening to break through at any gruesome moment.

Why was Charlotte in danger in the first place? Were the boys safe? What if I arrive too late? Why was William the one writing to him? Was he there with them already? And if so, why?

Again, and again, the questions played themselves out in his head with no acceptable conclusion until he finally heard the most wonderful thing he had ever remembered hearing next to the cry of his firstborn child. The two holiest of words that jolted him into action from his bunk below and thrust him towards the railing of the ship's deck with motivating expectation.

"Land Ho!" The man shouted from the crow's nest high above the vessel, his voice echoing down to the sailors working at their posts and to the others resting farther beneath the ship's deck.

Without hesitation, Sebastian rushed from his sparsely decorated cabin down below and up to the edge of the ship's port side, straining his eyes to see it, too. Yet despite how hard he tried; he could barely make out anything beyond a brown line of distortion along the horizon beneath an equally black blur of a sky. The ship's captain had said something at supper about how they had made excellent time due to a headwind or some other kind of sailing jargon similar to that. And truthfully, he <u>had</u> tried to listen to everything he was saying at the time but sadly, he still had not the foggiest idea as to how that had helped them to arrive well over ten hours ahead of schedule. Quite honestly, he didn't care. He was just glad they did, for it also meant that he was even closer to his family and their possible rescue.

After what had seemed like an eternity of waiting thereafter, Sebastian held his breath as the ship drew closer to port, and within less than an hour's time, familiar buildings and scenery came into view. Unable to contain himself any longer, he impulsively grabbed his leather bag and threw it over his shoulder, intent on jumping overboard, if need be, to accelerate his arrival but because he could not do so without raising the unwelcome admonitions from the crew, he forced himself to be patient just a little while longer, or at least until they were a bit closer to the waiting docks. He was finally home! Or as close enough to it as he had been in months.

Then, like a cry in the night, the ship's whistle sounded from the quartermaster behind him, notifying the other sailors gathering on land of their imminent arrival. Grateful to be here shortly after midnight, Sebastian climbed up onto the railing and steadied himself with the large rope hanging from the main sail, preparing himself to disembark.

"Ho, there, Sebastian!" The quartermaster called from behind him authoritatively. "Wait for the gangplank at least. What's your hurry?"

"Sorry, sir." Sebastian tried to look more embarrassed than panicked when he cast a glance back at him. "Haven't seen my family in almost nine months."

"Well, then..." The man laughed, then slid a long, makeshift plank out from the ship down to the wooden walkway below. "Off with you now, Sebastian! But be sure to collect your things with the ticket master tomorrow if you have any."

"I will." Sebastian leapt easily onto it and took off at a run down the street and past the tavern, the church, the mercantile, the old forge of his former master and finally to the well-worn pathway that led directly up the hill to his small wooden house beyond.

From what he could see from a distance, a light line of smoke faithfully spiraled out from the stone chimney above the all-too-familiar building, casting a spectral mist through the warm glow of light that spilled out onto the porch from the kitchen within. The warmth of its anticipated welcome drew him in closer with an almost mesmerizing quality and made him feel the love he had so long desired as it beckoned to his very soul with its arms of invitation. Yet the silence that also accompanied it halted him dead in his tracks, making his blood run colder still. In all directions, the night around him had seemingly grown uncharacteristically still as he approached closer to the house, deathly so, if he were to describe it more accurately.

In fact, not a single soul, living or otherwise, was lingering outside to acknowledge his presence or greet him warmly along his way home. Which was, in itself, unusual as there should have been at least some men working down by the pier or even possibly a rogue cow by the back of the small barn next to the house. Why even the absence of their favorite barn cat that loved to sleep on the seat of the front porch chair every night stood out as strange to him.

Feeling completely alone in his home country now, as well, Sebastian realized with a start that it was almost as if nature itself was skeptically watching his every mover rather, maybe it was selectively choosing to hide from this stranger's arrival and his, no doubt, darker purpose.

Where were the horses? Sebastian pondered as confusion washed over him once more. Undoubtedly, something was definitely amiss beyond the fact that everyone in the village and countryside that he passed by was clearly, already fast asleep. Possibly all the occupants in the house, too, by the looks of things. But that wasn't the source of his discomfort either. In every other tangible way, the tiny world of Portsmouth looked exactly as it should, and yet it also didn't. Something beyond description was undeniably off, but what it was, he could not say, nor could he even hope to put it into words accurate enough to comprehend it fully.

Yet upon hearing the unmistakable, low moo of their milking cow off in the barn in front of him, Sebastian felt his body relax momentarily, thinking perhaps all the pent-up worry he had been experiencing since the arrival of William's letter had been ill-placed before he suddenly saw it. A solitary figure, and nothing more, appeared just inside one of his home's two front-facing windows and began pacing back and forth systematically directly behind them—a very unfamiliar looking figure, he might add.

Determined to reach his home at last and discover for himself what had truly become of his wife and children, his eyes followed the shadowed form intently as he watched it stop, peer out the first window by the kitchen, then walk over to the next before doing the same action again towards the kitchen once more. As anticipated as he had hoped that his arrival would be, he was still hesitantly cautious that his movements were being watched or at the very least, he had to consider the fact that by lying in wait in the shadows tonight he looked more like the possible intruder than the absent owner of this home.

There was only one way to find out which was the truth. Taking every precaution to keep safely out of sight, he crouched instinctively behind the empty wagon that had been left at the edge of the yard and peered around it to see what the shadow within would do next.

As he expected, the silhouette in the window also stopped, as if patiently waiting for his quarry to change its position once more before it continued on in its logical pattern across the room as if nothing out of the ordinary had transpired.

Sebastian studied the stranger more carefully from his hidden position, trying to ascertain quickly just who it might be inside. Neither of his boys would cast that tall of a shadow any day, even standing on a chair, nor could it possibly be his wife, as the individual appeared to be of a much broader stance and longer stride. So, that meant that whoever it was that stood silent vigil within the very safety of his own home, they were most definitely <u>not</u> a member of his inner family, and thus, became an alarming anomaly amidst a plethora of other considerations.

Was William's letter, correct? Had Doctor Clarke arrived before him? And if so, was that who was waiting for him inside now?

Suddenly motivated into action, Sebastian stole stealthily to the back of the house where the side door to his home lay, paying special attention to keep to the darkest of the shadows along his way as he crept closer to the corner of the building. Then, as he peered in through the back window and to the kitchen beyond, he could tell from his new vantage point that the tall figure from the front window was no longer visible, nor could he make out much more than a few darker shapes associated with the various furniture within through the equally blurry panes of glass.

Where was he hiding now? Sebastian's brow furrowed in deliberation as to the stranger's whereabouts. *Could the man have gone out the front door in search of him when he had retreated behind? Possibly...*

With deliberate movements, he felt for the handle of the door in the moonless night and tried the small latch. To his surprise and equally great dismay, it lifted quite easily with a loud chunk as the wooden gears moved behind the door to allow him entry. Unable to do otherwise, Sebastian's mind froze as he pulled the door towards him, too overwhelmed to take it all in as the hairs on the back of his neck stood immediately at attention. The simple truth of the unlocked door spoke terrifying volumes all in itself as Charlotte would never have left this door unbolted for any reason, and especially not with the boys at home. As she had told him before, she was too afraid of opportunistic bandits or marauding pirates from arriving ships to be so careless. Nor would she have left it open purposefully in expectation of his possible arrival either. No, something far worse must have befallen her. Yet despite how much it pained him to consider it, either way, he simply had to press onward and find out more. At this point, any information would be infinitely more helpful to his next course of action than the endless speculations running amuck in his overactive mind.

Daring to take two steps carefully inside the threshold at last, he held his breath as he surveyed the room around him, expecting to see signs of a struggle or anything else that spoke of mischief, but every single item in the house looked exactly as it should, just like the way it had been on the day that he left last fall. So much so in fact, that it appeared as if the last eight months had never occurred at all.

Had all that had befallen them only been part of a terrible dream or an alternate reality of some kind? He pondered distractedly, unsure if the scene before him was a mere figment of his overactive imagination or a wonderfully welcomed mirage.

Hesitating, Sebastian reached for the shelf to his left where they always kept the extra candles and paused as he studied the depths of the darkness first, allowing his eyes to adjust fully to the inner shadows. The room before him was still only sporadically illuminated by the large fire that was left burning in the great hearth. All that is, except for the area that contained a very tall shadow leaning towards the front doorway from the fireplace across from it. A distinctly human shaped shadow that stretched out in a long line slightly around the corner to his left.

In a blur of indecision, Sebastian's mind raced while searching out possible scenarios for overtaking the intruder without injury, but not a single one of them solidified into a useful plan. For the second time in his very short span of existence, he was regrettably at a loss for as to what to do next. Yet try as he might, he needed to devise some way to get the upper hand against this person before it was too late, something impulsively effective, for all of their sakes.

Closing his eyes, he shook his head at the sheer stupidity of the only choice that made any sense whatsoever to him and regrettably embraced the option afforded to most attackers, spontaneity. Without pausing to contemplate further any of the fatal ramifications for his impetuous decision should he fail, he courageously charged headlong into the darkened area in front of him, hoping to catch the trespasser by surprise, or at the very least on the defensive entirely.

It worked. As Sebastion was enveloped instantly by the sporadic darkness, he gripped his would-be attacker from behind in a great constraining motion and knocked him against the wall. The man who stood almost half a foot taller than himself, responded in kind by striking back against him and almost flipping him sideways as each man then clung desperately thereafter to the other in horrific defense. In many ways, the ensuing battle resembled very much a carefully choreographed dance of ferocious quality as the two, now-entwined figures tumbled hard onto the floor and wrestled across it. Chairs and benches fell almost out of fear of being attacked themselves and objects normally kept secure on top of the table toppled helplessly next to them as both men fought desperately against the other this way and that, neither willing to relent even for a moment an inch of the ground they had seized in the struggle.

Echoing exclamations and ensuing footfalls on the floor above them sounded shortly after the fight had begun: some louder, others lighter, before the light of several candles filled the room from various locations, bringing with it a much-needed brilliance to the otherwise dimly lit room. Yet despite all of the added illumination, Sebastian still could not see his attacker's face clearly through both of their unruly and completely tousled-about hair, nor could he possibly stop fighting long enough to observe adequately who had just come down the stairs towards them. The adrenaline surging throughout his body at that moment sufficiently prevented him from doing anything more than what he was currently doing, just as his attacker was equally focused on accomplishing the same.

"Sebastian, stop!" Someone called out in the distance but for several tumultuous minutes more, the pair continued to thrash back and forth together on the floor as they knocked over the small table by the fireplace in their struggle. Then, through a moment of sheer luck, Sebastian managed to restrain the intruder securely beneath his grasp but was still continuously fighting to maintain that hold every second for the taller man was undoubtedly almost stronger than he was in many ways, though he was scared to admit it.

"Papa!" A familiar voice called from the stairs excitedly, causing him to loosen his grip for just a moment as he dared to look up in jubilant surprise at his young son.

Regrettably, the unexpected distraction was all his opponent needed. In an instant, Sebastian was tossed completely over with a loud thud onto his back, his arms pinned down sufficiently along the wooden floorboards next to the fire like the weight of the world had suddenly come crashing down on him at last.

"*Arrête... arrête!* Stop, I say!" Emile shouted at Sebastian while straining to catch his breath and contain the man securely on the floor underneath him.

"Emile?" Sebastian threw his loose hair back out of his face and looked up in wide astonishment at the man hovering over him.

"Of course, you idiot! Who else did you think I was?" Emile climbed off the man clumsily and attempted to fix his appalling disheveled ensemble while still gasping intermittently. "Though truth be told, you are a bit stronger than the last time we did this."

"You were calling me a demon back then if I remember correctly." Sebastian sat up on the floor, bringing his knees upright while dusting off the dirt and ash from off his shirt but otherwise appeared to be equally as winded.

"You fight like a demon." Emile looked up at the ceiling and drew in a steadying breath before falling into his favored chair by the table, somewhat grateful for the altercation, as it had allowed him to release just a portion of the anger he had been holding onto for days.

"I think I would prefer to think of it more like Jacob wrestling with the angel." Sebastion grinned, but his body still remained quite rigid from the force of the confrontation and his equally necessary expenditure of rage. "It's less demoralizing that way when you lose."

"Touché," Emile saluted him tiredly. "Wait... who's the angel?"

Without waiting for permission, Elijah and Jedidiah ignored everyone else in the room entirely and instead ran up to their no longer absent father, tackling him almost back down to the floor in their excitement. "Oh, Papa, Papa! You came home to us! William told us that you would."

"Boys!" Sebastian closed his eyes to drink in the scene and held them both as tightly as humanly possible in his arms, afraid that the very moment would disappear once more if he opened them again. "I'm here. I'm here. Now, where's your mama?" He kissed each of his sons in turn repeatedly.

In an instant, Jedidiah's face fell, allowing his whole countenance to turn very solemn as the tears of his certain failure filled his eyes. "I tried to take care of her, Papa, just like you said." The boy began to sob uncontrollably, fearing that he had disappointed his father in his task.

"It's okay, son. It's not your fault. It's mine. It wasn't fair to ask it of you, and I should never have left you alone for so long." Sebastian drew him closer to him. "It was my responsibility to protect her, not yours. And it is my job as your papa to protect you now."

He remained on the floor cradling his two sons until their tears turned into echoes of laughter at the joy of their reunion once again. "You've grown into quite the little man, Jedidiah!" He pulled himself upright and ruffled the older boy's hair.

"Mama said I have grown a whole two inches since you left. Isn't that right Jed?" Elijah proclaimed as he vied for more attention than his older brother.

"Two inches! That is impressive! It seems I have missed much while I was away," Sebastian admitted in earnest.

"Why were you away so long, Papa?" Elijah asked innocently. "Didn't you love us anymore?"

"Oh, son…" Sebastian's heart stopped beating for a very long moment before he looked down at both of his sons with deep affection and replied sadly, "The reason no longer matters. What matters most is that I am here now, and that I will never leave you again. I can promise you that."

The boys hugged their father tightly once more, both unwilling to let go of him so soon.

"Now, you have school in the morning, don't you? You wouldn't want Father Benedict to be disappointed when you fall asleep in Latin class again," Sebastian instructed them firmly, attempting to maintain as serious of an expression as he could possibly manage on the surface.

"Aw, Papa! But you only just got here!" The two whined in unison.

"Boys… I'm serious. It's time to be going back to bed." Undeterred in his decision, he gave them both a stern glance which stopped the noise immediately.

"C'mon, Eli. Let's go." Jedidiah took his hand, and half-dragged the younger boy up the stairs who was still protesting loudly. "Jedidiah is the one who always falls asleep in school, Papa… I don't <u>want</u> to go to bed yet, Jed. I want Papa."

"I'll be up shortly to tuck you in," Sebastian promised while watching their progress up the stairs and waited until the tiny footsteps no longer sounded on the wood ceiling above him before he turned his attention to the three men who were rearranging the various displaced furniture in the room all around him.

"<u>Where</u> is my wife, gentlemen?" Sebastian demanded bluntly as if he cared very little for manners at the moment. Nor was his patience great enough for more than the most basic of conversations after what he had just been through on the ship.

"You had better tell him, William." Nathanael looked down at the table before setting the candle and its holder back on top securely. "I am in no condition for a fight like Emile just experienced, angel or not."

"I am most definitely the angel, and I shan't be doing all of that again for quite some time." Emile leaned back in his chair, crossed his outstretched legs and motioned with his hand for William to continue in his place.

"Please…" Sebastian looked at him unimpressed and unengaged. "I have had nothing but six words written in a letter to keep me company for the past thirty-six hours, so suffice it to say, I am in no mood for this playful banter between all of you. Now out with it. Where is she?" Sebastian stated firmly.

"Certainly, a demon," Emile mumbled under his breath, taunting him even further, but stopped when William placed his hand on Sebastian quickly before he could react again in anger.

"Charlotte is not here, obviously. We think Doctor Clarke has already taken her, but he did so, thankfully, when your sons were both away at school." William did his best to explain the situation briefly to him at last.

"Then what have the three of you been doing for the past two days? Playing house?" Sebastian fumed though he was not really angry in the least with any of them. He was more upset with himself for putting his family in this kind of a situation in the first place. "She could be dying somewhere, or worse, William."

Already tired of the way in which the man across from him always liked to control the room, Emile's eyes narrowed but remained steadfastly temperate in his subsequent response, deciding now was not the time to be starting an all-out war between any of them. He had already seen firsthand just what Sebastian was truly capable of and despite what the man might think, Emile did feel sincerely sorry for him, even if his comments appeared otherwise. "You are not the only one suffering in this situation, sir, and Charlotte is not the only one missing. You say you got six words. Well, count that a blessing because I got none," he said the last sentence with such unintended, raw finality that it literally stung his heart to utter it aloud.

Expecting another explosion like the one they had witnessed moments earlier, Nathanael moved to take his place between the two men, deciding once and for all that a dose of passivity was definitely in order. "Let's just take a minute to calm down and let Sebastian absorb the facts, shall we? I am sure we can all formulate a plan of action thereafter, now that we are all together."

Without waiting for his approval one way or the other, William picked up the carved box from the counter behind him and brought it over to the center table before setting it down in front of Sebastian unceremoniously. "I am assuming you recognize this?"

"Yes." Sebastian placed one calloused hand across the top. The size of it almost completely engulfed the delicate carvings underneath. "It was a Christmas present. Why?"

"Open it," William stated firmly, knowing that Sebastian appreciated directness more than lengthy explanations any day.

With trembling fingers and an uncertain heart, he obediently did as he commanded and pried open the lid, afraid of what it might hold just as much as he was frightened to leave it closed.

"Jedidiah said the parchment on top should be only opened by you alone, Sebastian," William instructed but did not divulge the information about the second letter for himself. At this point, he felt no need for him to ever know of its contents then or in the future since Charlotte was not going to die, nor was he ever going to need to raise their children without them.

"I see." Like a man hesitant to take in a full breath, Sebastian picked up the parchment, untied the green ribbon slowly and read it before collapsing into sobs on top of his thickly muscled arms. "I am such a fool. I should never have left them unprotected, William."

Feeling like it was finally time that he contributed something of spiritual value, Nathanael sat down immediately next to him and placed his arm around his shoulders, his heart full of compassion at his pain. "We sorrow, but not as those who have not hope, Sebastian. I know it is speaking about salvation here, but I think it can also be applied to your situation, as well. Do not lose your hope for her recovery so easily."

Sebastian nodded, wiped his tears with the cuff of his sleeve and explained plainly what everyone in the room had already expected, "The letter describes her pregnancy. Or more importantly, how she was afraid of telling me with me being so far away and all." He paused then looked up accusingly at William. "Did you know?"

"No." William shook his head apologetically. "It seems you were not the only one exceptionally good at keeping secrets, my friend."

"Secrets... I am starting to hate everything about them. I feel ashamed, numb, frightened. Yet most of all, I'm uncertain if I should feel elated at the idea of having another child or entirely scorned." He paused before he cast a glance over at Emile that was not inviting, nor friendly in the least, causing Emile's hands to go up instantly in obvious protection.

"I was most assuredly in France, *monsieur*."

"Stop this! Both of you!" William sat down across from Sebastian and rebuked him strongly. "Do you really think so little of your wife to believe this child is from another man?"

"No." Sebastian returned his gaze to the letter in his hands and felt the sickening possibility grip him all over again. "But eight months is a long time to be alone, William. Trust me, I should know."

"Well, if you believe that, you are more of a fool than I realized," William chided him, his face as stern as any his father had ever displayed to him.

"Trust your wife," Nathanael advised encouragingly. "Satan would love nothing more than to steal our joy with his lies. Have faith in the truth that no matter how incredible it may seem, it is possible."

Sebastian nodded. "So, what do we do now?"

"I've been asking that same question for days," Emile replied in frustration as he began pacing the room behind the group making animated hand gestures much like Sebastian had done when they had first met Señor Moretti at the castle. "So far, we have searched all the warehouses down by the docks, climbed down into countless holds, examined dozens of cellars and still we have not found any trace of them anywhere."

William shot Emile another worried glance then continued where the other man had left off, "We know she has to be somewhere in town because some of the people there saw her riding in a wagon with a strange man the day we arrived."

"We think that man was Doctor Clarke, but no one here knows him by that name, and the description they gave of the gentleman riding with Charlotte did not completely match the man we all know. So, there is that, too." Nathanael tried to be helpfully direct with his explanation.

"More importantly, not a single person has seen Emma or her since," Emile said through gritted teeth.

"Wait. Who is Emma?" Sebastian asked curiously, suddenly unclear as to who it was Emile was searching for.

"The young lady from France that I told you about," William said quickly, hoping Emile would not be cross with him for divulging his friend's personal business to others. "She is Emile's betrothed now."

"As if any of that matters when the Earth has picked them both up and swallowed them whole, it seems." Emile's usually calm exterior was beginning to crack under the strain.

"He's right," Sebastian said slowly aloud while clearly deep in thought. "Maybe it has..."

"That doesn't make any sense at all!" Emile blurted out, his palms slamming hard onto the wooden table between them in utter frustration.

"Wait a minute, Emile. What do you mean that he is right, Sebastian? How has it swallowed them whole?" William prodded patiently.

"You said you checked all the warehouses down by the dock, right?" Sebastian asked Emile sharply with as much patience as the man was giving him.

"Yes, every crate, barrel, and container, both up and down." Emile shook his head in irritation. "Twice!"

"Are you sure you looked everywhere?" Sebastian ignored his antics like he would those of one of his children, refusing to engage with him further.

"There is something we missed, isn't there?" William's eyes narrowed in concentration like he was trying to ascertain the solution to a very difficult puzzle. "What didn't we see?"

"Something you did not know was there in the first place, I suppose. A place I dare say not many people <u>do</u> know about. But I could be wrong." Sebastian shook his head in guilt.

"Where should we look?" William asked more earnestly.

"Years ago, I built a rather strange compartment of sorts at the request of a visiting seaman. For months, he had been working down at the shipyard and said he had need of a room that the other sailors would not be able to access. I thought it was for the security of some personal goods when he was away or for his protection as several seasoned deckhands had gone missing during that summer with no one ever knowing their whereabouts thereafter. Yet despite the oddness of the request, it was good money at a time when little was there to come by. So, I built it anyways as I could not see the harm in such a secretive room, but looking back at it now, it all makes perfect sense."

"Hold on. I thought you were a blacksmith?" Nathanael asked, looking rather perplexed by his explanation.

"Certainly, but I've built many a project to make ends meet over the years, like this house you are standing in for example." Sebastian began the process of rolling up each of his sleeves to his elbows.

Suddenly tired of the man's seemingly never-ending explanation, Emile placed both hands impatiently on the table and said every word as an accusation towards the only person he felt held the answer to Emma's rescue. "<u>What did you build, man</u>!"

"I think I built his lair," Sebastian's voice sounded empty at the realization.

"Then it is time to find the devil," Emile replied resolutely, grabbing his cloak from the back of the door and slipping it on easily, ready to depart.

"And Jedidiah and Elijah?" Nathanael questioned immediately while stating the obvious. "You just promised them you would never leave them again. What happens when they wake up and find you are gone once more."

Sebastian stood and picked up one of the green ribbons from off the floor that had fallen errantly during their conversation before declaring resolutely his unspoken opinion. "Promises <u>are</u> meant to be kept, sir, but not at the expense of their mother's life. One of us will need to stay here to protect them."

The four men each looked around the room at the others gathered before all eyes save his own fell on one man.

"Someone they, no doubt, trust," Sebastian encouraged without reservation.

"Someone who can fight back, if need be," William added in agreement.

"Someone who is far braver than he portrays," Emile admitted honestly.

"Me." Nathanael sighed in resignation, knowing full-well who they were all talking about. "I am no one's hero, gentlemen. Neither am I any braver than the next man. You don't know what you are asking of me."

"But you <u>are</u> brave, Nathanael," William affirmed encouragingly. "And it is high time you stopped being content to merely watch the divine timelines of others. Seize your life back and be who you were meant to be. Step out of the shadows for just a moment."

With great hesitation, Nathanael picked up the axe that still lay carefully stored by the side of the fireplace and pursed his lips once in deliberation, though in truth, he looked undeniably ridiculous holding it. "Are you sure this will work?"

"Maybe we should get you a gun, instead." Emile tried not to laugh at the absurdity of his stance and implausibility that his friend would have the strength to wield such a weapon, let alone attack someone with it should the need arise.

"Better make it two." Sebastian decided and left to retrieve his pistols from the back room where he hoped they were still stored under the floorboards.

"How are you with a sword?" William grabbed the beautifully crafted blade from its mount above the fire and held it out to him.

"As good as you are at preaching sermons, I would imagine." Nathanael took it awkwardly with a wink and parried with it just once in the air in front of him, surprisingly adept for a man who never carried a weapon of any kind. "I had a few lessons when I was a lad, but much like your grandmother's stories, the instruction was a bit sporadic at best, and certainly not intended for defense."

"*Vive la revolution,*" Emile quipped sarcastically, though the man appeared outwardly to be utterly enjoying this stolen moment of spontaneity much more than any of his friends.

"Indeed." Nathanael's brow wrinkled in disbelief at where this day had suddenly taken him. "Though I doubt even the National Assembly would contemplate taking on a centuries old vampire in order to achieve their independence."

As if hearing a spoken truth that carried the weight of the most profound importance imaginable, the three other men all stopped what they were doing around him and suddenly glanced back at him in shock.

"What?" Nathanael looked up in surprise. "What did I say?"

"That is <u>exactly</u> what we are doing, Nathanael," William stated as if he was finally realizing that everything in the past eight months had been steadily leading up to this very moment in time. "We have all just been fighting for our independence amidst this tragedy that has befallen us as if we needed to find some kind of justifiable acceptance for what we have become."

"Precisely," Sebastian added. "And I'll not waste another minute of my life without my family, nor spend the next two hundred years constantly looking over my shoulder for someone who thinks it is his right to end us. That would be worse than living on that secluded island."

"For once, you and I are in total agreement." Emile's face had turned to one of hardened determination as he eyed the man across the room from him like a comrade-in-arms.

"Please, I wasn't trying to start a mutiny, friends." Nathanael appeared more frightened now than he was before at being the motivating cause for their actions. Actions that could possibly lead to the untimely end of one or all of their lives.

"Mutinies are for people without a just cause, Nathanael. I think we are all in agreement that this game of his has to stop here and now. We are the only ones who can do it, so we must stand up for those who cannot." William tried to convince his friend of the very real necessity of their actions.

"Don't you think Doctor Clarke has created enough destruction for one lifetime, let alone several?" Sebastian placed the two loaded pistols on the table in front of Nathanael and the powder horn to reload them if need be.

"You know that I cannot support killing someone, no matter what the cause, William." Nathanael laid the sword down on the table, its blade reflecting the looks from the rest of the men as they feared the man before them would abandon their cause entirely. "But I will do as you ask and defend the innocent, whatever it may take for me to do so."

"Thank you." Sebastian placed his hand firmly on Nathanael's shoulder at last and squeezed it once gently. "They are my very life, Nathanael."

Nathanael looked directly into his eyes and finally understood completely the deep love this man held for his family. "And so is Charlotte. So, go find her before it's too late."

Sebastian nodded in gratitude for Nathanael's sacrifice and left with the others out the front door.

Suddenly alone, Nathanael bolted the door securely behind them and lifted up a silent prayer.

Protect them, Lord. May they reach the women in time. He sighed as he sought the peace he so greatly needed. *And give me the strength to do what must be done.*

Chapter Forty-Eight

June 28th, 1793

T he hours upon hours in the unrelenting darkness of their enclosure had ticked by slower than any that Charlotte had ever experienced before in her life. In the beginning, she had tried counting her breaths and those of the girl beside her to pass the time and distract her mind from the ever-building anxiety at being trapped there, but after several hundred of them had passed by her into the oblivion beyond, she had given up on the occupation entirely. Day had obviously turned into night at least once, maybe twice, but their captor had returned only a few times with meager rations for each of them and a gruff command to be silent. She had obeyed at first out of fear, not knowing just what the man had intended with her or the poor girl cowering on the floor, but as the dark reality of her hopeless situation finally set in, she had turned in desperation to a much different course of action, possible escape.

Climbing the set of wooden steps that led up to the trapdoor covering just above them, she had hesitantly placed her ear as close to the opening as possible and listened for something, anything that would give her some clue as to where she was and how she might be able to draw someone's attention towards their plight. At first, the room above had sounded only hollow, but as the hours passed by, muted voices could also occasionally be heard over the soft ocean waves and the shrilling whistles from the deckhands announcing cast off and docking. From the bustling activity around her overhead, it was clear that she was most definitely still near the docks as she had suspected, but where? She could have been underneath any of a dozen buildings for there were a long line of them around the pier. And if that was truly where she was, could any of the sailors really hear her screams if she could barely make out their conversations?

Exhausted by the effort required to stand on her tiptoes in order to reach the small opening above, she climbed back down the few stairs and took a seat once more by the young woman. Even in the darkness of their enclosure she could tell that she was probably a little more than half her age and very beautiful though in an understated sort of way for her clothing was the only thing on her that diminished it, simple as it was.

"I'm sorry I cannot do more for you, Emma. I wish I could." She stroked her long hair back from her face and braided the sweat laden strands to one side to keep them from tangling further.

Yet it was not until quite early in the morning on the next day, that the older man from the wagon returned once more and opened the door at the top of their enclosure allowing a brief rush of fresh air to fill the cellar below. "An early breakfast time for the captives." He announced callously and threw two hardened loaves of bread, a flask of water and two apples at her with no more care than if he were feeding the animals on a farm.

Startled by the sudden burst of light upon their surroundings, Charlotte shielded her eyes against the harsh adjustment and spoke up in earnest, "Please, sir." She caught the flask and apples with both hands and tried to concentrate on as much of the upper world around him to aid her in her future plans of escape. "What do you want with us? If it's money you are seeking, I don't have much, but you are welcome to it."

"Ha! You don't have enough money in all of the world for what I want, dear lady," the man sneered at the insinuation that his motives were monetarily driven. Without giving her question a moment of attention more, the man clumsily reached back to grasp the wooden door with both hands to close it again before Charlotte interrupted him desperately.

"I beg you! Please have mercy on the girl at least. She is very sick and needs a doctor, or maybe even a blanket if you can spare one," she begged her tormentor as politely as she could manage, appealing to the only thing she thought he still possessed... his very decency as a human.

She should have saved her breath.

"What she is suffering from, no doctor can heal," he scoffed back at her, his eyes filled with fresh disdain and loathing. "So no, I will be fetching no doctor. But here..." He tossed her down a piece of rough woolen fabric that was normally used to cushion belongings in the crates of the ships. "You can have this until your husband arrives."

What? Sebastian was coming here? Her heart gripped suddenly with the terror and joy of the revelation, unsure if he was telling her the truth or simply looking for some kind of emotional reaction from her in some way.

"My husband? I'm sorry, but if you are talking about Mr. Smith, I fear you are mistaken. I haven't seen him in over eight months. In fact, his last letter said he is already on his way to the Americas," she lied to her captor as convincingly as possible, hoping he would release them both now that his intended quarry had fled from his grasp.

"Really? Then, tell me this. Why do people leave their loved ones so unprotected?" He stared her down incredulously then added in a rather satisfy tone another piece of information that he thought would torment her further, "Your husband arrived a few hours ago, madame." He shook his head and sighed as he paced at the top of the ladder. "Though I have to admit, that his arrival only makes everything I have planned so much easier…"

"Everything you have planned? I don't understand, sir," Charlotte asked innocently.

"All of you are like puppets on a string really, letting me pull you this way and that at my every command." He waved with his hands in such a way as to display his use of some imaginary marionette puppet of some kind. "And how, might you ask, can I accomplish this so easily? Fear, madame. Unadulterated, controlling fear. And as you can see, it works quite nicely indeed, don't you agree?"

Charlotte placed her hand over her mouth to hide the expression she was no doubt showing and tried to control her mind as it raced for something helpful to divert his dark intentions but thought of nothing productive that might persuade him otherwise. "Is there something you want from me, sir? Something I might be able to help you accomplish? If my husband is truly here, I can… "

"Oh, shut up, will you!" The man commanded in irritation and the sound of his harsh instruction chilled Charlotte more than his previous declaration or even the wet cellar around her. "There is nothing I desire from you that you would be willing to part with, my dear, but I'll see to that later, when I am done with the four of them. Oh, and while we are on the subject, have you heard from your precious William lately?" The man above her probed, searching for more information it seemed.

"Doctor Wells?" Charlotte played dumb.

"Is there another?" He tossed his head back in another sick sounding raucous burst of merriment.

"Um… yes… well, he wrote from London just this week asking us about our plans to leave on the next ship, sir," she deflected the truth once more, for though it was true that William <u>had</u> written to her, his letter had been dated over a month ago. As far as she was aware, he knew nothing of Sebastian's plans for her and the boys, or of the trip her husband had recently purchased.

"Ah, that would be my apprentice, Doctor Wells. Ever trying to be the savior to everyone. He is always thinking he is one step ahead of the world's evil, correct?" He trailed off and the hideous grin returned... the one that was half-twisted up in a sneer and half-disdainfully warped into showing his full set of crooked and yellowed teeth.

"I'm sure I don't know what you mean. I've only met the man once when he came to help my son last spring." She tried to make excuses nervously.

"This conversation is growing tiresome, woman," he interrupted her at last as he callously gave what felt like a final command. "It's no matter really where he might be, if I can't take care of William here, I'll simply have to settle up with him later. Being in another part of the country or even on another continent altogether will not protect him from what is coming for him. It is high time I dealt with the rest of his friends, then maybe save him for last. Besides, they've been a thorn in my flesh long enough."

"Long enough... but why? What has my husband done to merit your anger?" She looked up at him, confusion filling her eyes as she clung protectively to the stone walls of the cellar as far away from the man as she could possibly manage under the circumstances.

"Oh, my dear, it's nothing personal, I assure you. But none of them were ever supposed to leave my ship in the first place. Now be quiet before I change my mind about you, too, and end the both of you right now instead of later." He paused momentarily as if a thought suddenly struck him and studied her darkly with a look that made her blood run colder still. "Then again, now that I think on it, I haven't had a proper consort for almost a century at least. Maybe one of you will prove yourself useful to me in the end, though I doubt you'd be the one so inclined. Not without the proper motivation, that is. After all, you wouldn't want those precious boys of yours to meet a stranger coming home from Father Benedict's school, would you?" He threatened, but his face gave no assurance that he meant to do otherwise.

"Please, they are just children." With rising horror, she watched as the man closed the door in front of her and heard a new, albeit dreadful, sound coming from the room above. A clanging like that of a much heavier object being dragged across the wooden hatch before the deafening click of the old lock securing it.

"Well, that finishes that plan. There is no way we can break a chained lock from down here." Charlotte sighed in defeat.

"*Mon Dieu, aidez moi,*" Emma moaned in pain next to her, begging God for His help.

Filled with fresh compassion, Charlotte snatched up the piece of discarded wool and wrapped the girl up in it. "There now, this should help. It won't be long now, Emma. You'll see." She tried to be encouraging though her heart pounded frantically just thinking about what the man might do to her children if she could not manage to get out of here in time.

Why would anyone want to kidnap the wife of a Spanish blacksmith anyway? She had no money to ransom, no virtue to tempt, especially not in her condition. Not a single part of this whole awful ordeal made any sense at all. *And why did the man want to kill any of them? Had Sebastian wronged him in some way on board that fateful voyage? Could he?*

Though she knew her husband was not the type of man who made friends easily, he had never once brought a man to violence of any kind. Irritation, maybe, but never to the point of actually coming to blows. Nevertheless, everything the man had said just now had made it almost too impossible to deny. And yet, why had Sebastian not mentioned any of this in his letters. *Was his guilt so great that he was too afraid to tell her about the man? Or about the events that had truly transpired on the Endeavor?*

She would never have thought so before, but ever since last fall his letters had been so different, more guarded in their descriptions and lacking any true details as to their future together. *Was he trying to protect her from something. From the man perhaps?* From her recent exchange with the kidnapper, she wasn't sure what to believe. She trusted William as Sebastian's friend, but *had he inadvertently roped her husband into some kind of trouble upon their ship to America?* After what she just heard, she wasn't sure.

However, as confusing as all of this was at the present, there was only one thing that was most definitely for certain in her mind. If the man thought Sebastian might come for her, he was probably already on his way. She just had to remain calm until he arrived and, more importantly, alive. "Stay focused, Charlotte Fabbri. Survive," she instructed herself quietly and reached down to lift Emma's head before trying to make her take a sip of the water the man had given them.

As weak as she was, the girl drank a small amount eagerly then coughed the rest of the liquid in her mouth back out onto the dirt floor. "It tastes, horrible, ma'am." Emma rolled weakly onto her side but remained curled up next to her.

Concerned that the man might have chosen to poison them instead, Charlotte smelled the drink cautiously. The water <u>did</u> have a slight hint of rum to it that must have been added some time ago, but nothing else out of the ordinary stood out to her. Equally perplexed, she picked up the loaf of bread and pulled off a small piece before putting it to the girl's lips. "Try to at least eat something then. Just a few morsels will help you build your strength back up."

The girl obeyed and ate at least four pieces of the bread before moaning in pain once more.

"Is there anything I can do for you?" Charlotte's heart ached for the young woman.

Emma did not respond initially. Her eyes were too tightly squinted as her face contorted in obvious pain. "Could you distract me?"

"Alright. The man who captured us says that my husband is close by, but I am not sure how long it will take him to find us." Charlotte picked up both of the apples and took a large bite of one, grateful that at least the fruit the man had chosen for his victims was delicious. She could not say the same for the bread for though she had not tried it as of yet, it did have the familiar fragrance of fruity mold upon its outer crust.

"That is comforting, I think," Emma finally whispered softly, her pale cheek resting awkwardly upon the dampened clay of their cell. "What is the last thing you remember?"

"A wagon ride from my husband's shop." She took another bite and chewed it more slowly, savoring the juice and sweet pectin the summer fruit had provided. "You?"

"Same, but from my employer. A doctor there asked me to come with him to meet my..." The girl hesitated for several moments as she closed her eyes and then opened them once more with a jolt.

"Your what?" Charlotte gave Emma a small piece of the apple to try.

Still shaking profusely from whatever was attacking her system, her tiny fingers trembled as she tried to nibble at the pulp slowly. "I just realized I don't know what to even call him now. I would say my fiancé, but Lord knows we have been much more than that in the past." Emma sighed slowly, her voice trailing off here and there throughout the reply.

Charlotte chuckled. "Oh, my dear, I am the last person you need worry about giving a confessional to. Despite what you might believe, I've been lying to my husband for months." She rubbed the top of her belly, thankful that the stronger of the contractions had finally slowed down to softer aches near her lower back.

Sensing his or her mother's attention, the baby kicked at her fingers playfully like it was continuing a game with her, then calmed down considerably, completely oblivious to the precarious situation it was now a part of.

"What does your husband do for a living?" Emma rolled over onto her back to face the ceiling, but the close proximity of the woman next to her did nothing to stop the incessant tremors that seized her body almost every five minutes.

"He is a blacksmith by trade. Has been all his life, I suppose." Charlotte gave her another piece of the apple. "And your beau?"

"A French baker." She ate the apple piece tentatively as if the fruit did not agree with her either. "Or at least that is what he wants to be now. He was a more of a socialite in the past."

"I'm sorry, did you say French?" Charlotte asked again curiously.

"Yes, we met in Paris, but that seems ages ago now." Emma sighed quietly as if the whole conversation was taking up the last of her strength.

"I don't believe it." Charlotte shook her head and smiled though nothing about their current situation was humorous in a way. "This beau of yours wouldn't happen to be friends with a man named Doctor William Wells, would he?"

As if giving the girl a much-need burst of hope, the girl's eyes lit up instantly, but she lacked the energy to move in the slightest. "How did you know?"

"That naughty Frenchman," Charlotte muttered, then chuckled at her pet name for the man. "Well, at least he has finally chosen to do something honorable for a change."

"Who?" Emma asked.

"Would it help if I told you my husband's name is Sebastian?"

The girl smiled and relaxed once more. "Emile said he used to live in Portsmouth. Is that where we are?"

Charlotte nodded. "Yes, or at least I hope so."

"But why would Doctor Clarke bring both of us here?"

"Is that his name? It's hard to believe someone as terrible as that could possibly be a doctor to anyone," Charlotte scoffed openly.

"Yes, William warned me before I was taken that I was not to go anywhere alone with anyone, but when he said that Emile needed me..." The girl trailed off as a tear slid down her cheek. "Emile has no idea where I am does he?"

"I'm afraid not. Though I think he may be safer than us at the moment. From what I can tell, we are merely a lure of some kind, a pawn in a much larger chess game if you want to think of it that way. And yet, from the look on Doctor Clarke's face just now, something is clearly not working like he planned. Which makes me cautiously hopeful."

"I see." Emma began coughing so violently then that the conversation ended for quite some time as she recovered, gasping weakly for air as if her lungs would not draw it in. "I'm so sorry I am not more help. I am just so tired... and cold... s-s-so very c-cold, Charlotte."

"No, I'm sorry for asking you so many questions. You should rest while you can. You may need your strength later."

The girl nodded slightly. "Maybe I will just close my eyes... for a few minutes."

"I'll be here when you wake up, dear," Charlotte reassured her and felt the tension in the young lady's body finally ease before she looked up to what she felt was the ceiling and prayed.

Please hurry, Bash. We need you.

~   ~   ~   ~   ~

The faint stream of light that had filtered through the crack before the man left with his lantern had been crippling to lose when it had happened but as Charlotte sat with her back against the wall counting the frequent kicks her baby made, the many times Emma held her breath in her fitful sleep, and the scurryings across the floor in the darkness, the shadows all around her felt alive. Without a doubt, she could have been in this tomb for minutes, hours or even days; she had no way to know for sure as time felt endless here in this dark abyss, as if it was also cautiously holding its breath as it waited to be rescued.

Yet when Emma had finally ceased being able to converse at all about thirty contractions ago, Charlotte let her head fall back upon the stone wall behind her, permitting her thoughts to wander aimlessly back to the day on the dock when Sebastian departed. That November morning had been the coldest she had ever experienced since her childhood. And from what she remembered, a light frost had even collected on the window sashes that morning, bringing with it a crisp aroma that coated the air with the faintest scent of apples from some mill pressing them into cider.

Sebastian had informed her that he had to leave then. That his ship needed to depart before the snow had the chance to move in behind them but try as she might she simply couldn't imagine it arriving that early and begged him to postpone his departure just a little while longer, or at least until the next ship left in the spring perhaps. Or really, any excuse that could have delayed their inevitable separation would have been preferred, but he could not be persuaded.

A snow-covered Christmas in America, he had promised her again and again to appease her worries, complete with all the things she had ever desired. Things he could not provide for them here in England.

"As if those things even matter now, darling." She sighed but caught her breath suddenly at a noise scooting across the floor directly above her head. From the vibrations that echoed down to her below, someone was moving something very heavy up there, make no mistake, and the thought of the man's return to 'finish the job' caused her whole body to shiver and bear down against the fear that followed. *Would this new life growing inside of her never have the chance to be born after all? Or more importantly, could she do anything in this condition to help Emma against such a man if he tried?*

Unfortunately for them, however, the noises ceased almost as quickly as they had begun, leaving only a deafening silence in their absence.

Rubbing her cold hands together to stop her own trembling that had commenced at the stronger pains that now crossed the top of her belly, she pushed back her hopeless thoughts and hugged her arms tightly about her chest for warmth before she forced herself to fall back to her memories in the shadows.

The look in her husband's eyes as he waved back at them from the ship flitted through them again and again like the sails behind him. Against the backdrop of a grey sky, his eyes had been the perfect shade of rich chocolate brown and so filled with promise and hope, a hope she had longed to see in them since a little after they had married. Well before the harshness of the world had stolen his pride away from him along with his dreams.

It was that singular expression that had carried her through the news of the shipwreck, also. It encouraged her each time she cried herself to sleep reading his letters. Motivated her in every step that she took with this new gift from God. And in sheer desperation, she had clung helplessly to that hope and had also managed to keep Sebastian's memory alive inside of her and in the lives of his children in the process.

Opening her eyes once more and watching the woman sleep fitfully next to her, she pondered again on the three names she had reserved for when the momentous day might arrive and selected one decisively as her final choice.

Sebastian had proudly named the first of his sons after King Solomon of the Bible. A man who was known for his wisdom and was well-beloved of the Lord. The second was most definitely in honor of his father's namesake. Sarah had been her decision after the Lord had answered her prayers for a daughter just like God had fulfilled Sarah's prayers for Isaac. But this child would have a name that meant much more than any of the names they had previously selected for it had been created with it, nurtured by it and if she was not rescued soon, it might just be delivered in it. It was perfect, just like she knew the baby would be.

With a loud clang, the heavy chain rattled across the door once more, announcing their unwanted visitor's return but Charlotte barely heard it over the sound of her gasp and subsequent groan. The contractions she had been feeling for the past few days had suddenly chosen to overtake her at last, capturing her every thought with their intense pain. Out of sheer desperation now, she clasped Emma's frigid hand beside her through it, as she stole the last of her courage, feeling certain that this was the awful moment of finality. Not finding what he wanted, the man had obviously changed his mind and was now coming for the two of them. What he would do in his anger she did not know, but if there was one thing she learned from Sebastian it was this, to stand tall, no matter how high the odds were stacked against you.

Just like before, the heavy door above them opened with a thud, but the light she expected to blind her did not flood the prison below. Instead, the world all around her still remained utterly dark except for one solitary lantern that shone in the darkness above.

"Hello," Charlotte said firmly, then held her breath through another terrifyingly strong contraction.

Boots thudded loudly on the steps of the ladder near the wall, momentarily blocking out the light and caused her to shrink back from what she imagined they brought with them—a painful death and eternal separation from her boys and Sebastian.

"Please... don't!" She anxiously begged as a brush of wind passed by her next and strong arms wrapped themselves around her body, pinning her tightly. Thinking it was their captor; she struggled helplessly against his hold, then stopped when she realized that the person was not hurting her as she had expected. Instead, he had been only trying to help her to her feet.

It was at that very moment that she knew her prayers had been answered, for no other person in all the world smelled like the man supporting her in her dungeon... a mix of creosol, pine and salt. "Sebastian..." She placed two hands on either side of his face and felt the features she would know in the darkness of eternity, or even if a thousand lanterns had been lit.

"I've got Emma," a shadow of a man said breathlessly as he bent down and scooped up the frail, young girl into his capable arms.

"Charlotte, my love," the man's voice said just in front of her now.

"Bash." She clasped him tighter still, gripping his shirt through the pain. "I was so afraid for you."

"Come. We have to hurry!" William called from above. "Someone could be here any minute."

"I am not sure I can manage the top of the stairs without help, Sebastian," she admitted honestly, feeling another contraction come upon her once more in her upright position.

"Why? What's wrong? Are you hurt?" Sebastian moved a strong arm around her back to support her.

Charlotte didn't answer, but rather focused all her remaining attention on climbing the steep steps hurriedly before another contraction could strike her immobile.

"Give me your hand, Charlotte. I'll help you." Ready arms from another familiar face reached down from above and assisted her near the top before taking Emma from the other man so he could also climb out. "Lay her over here, Emile," William commanded quickly as he moved out of Sebastian and Charlotte's way.

The tall man she had never met, released his possession reluctantly before his voice choked in panic, "William... I don't think she is breathing."

"Let me see her." William set to work diligently, examining the young woman closely for signs of life, just as he would have done with any other patient. With steady hands, he methodically felt her forehead, her pulse, and listened to her chest before confirming accurately. "She is still alive, Emile, but just barely."

"Merci a Diou!" Emile lifted her limp body up onto his lap and held her close as he praised God for sparing her life thus far, feeling true fear for the first time in his life.

It was at that moment that Emma's eyes fluttered open slightly upon hearing his voice, but she was not focusing on anyone in the room save the man in front of her. "You came for me." She touched his cheek just once with two weakened fingers before letting her hand fall limply back to her side, unable to say more.

"Emma, no... not yet." Emile held her hand within his own and tried not to show how much he was struggling to keep himself together.

"What is wrong with her, William?" Sebastian whispered quietly.

"Bash..." Charlotte touched his arm out of respect and tried to explain it all for him, "The man who took us said no doctor could help her."

Without taking in another breath, Emile looked up at William both in horror and in veiled hope at the discovery. "He has bitten her, hasn't he?"

William nodded. "It has a similar presentation, yes."

"Bitten her?" Charlotte asked, then gritted her teeth for a moment before breathing out through another wave of tightness that now spread all the way down her stomach and below.

"It is the same as what he did to all of us, Charlotte. It's the reason why I have been away all these months. Something he did changed us."

"Changed you how?" She took his face in hers and stared into the rich brown eyes once more, pleading with him to finally divulge everything.

587

Tears immediately began to fall from Sebastian's eyes, but even though he tried several times to answer her, he simply could not speak the words she needed to hear.

"If you will allow me, I'll explain everything to you later when you are safe, I promise," William said plainly what Sebastian could not.

"Fine." Charlotte's eyes closed tightly as she groaned, unable to hide any longer the intensity of what was transpiring within her.

"Please, Charlotte, not here," Sebastian pleaded with her as he held her hand through the pain. "Anywhere but here."

"As if I get a choice in these things." Charlotte huffed and tried to breathe slowly and deeply for several seconds more through the pain.

"We need to get them both out of here," William advised. "If Doctor Clarke were to come back..."

"He... is not... coming back. At least not... right away," Charlotte interrupted him as she moved to her knees, attempting to draw enough strength to stand before Sebastian reached over and supported her with his help. "He left probably an hour ago, looking for you, Bash. He knew that you had arrived and that you were close enough to kill."

"Did he say where he might go?" Emile asked quietly.

"I don't know. He seemed like he was looking for all of you actually. I assume he might try back at the house first as he suspected William was on his way to visit us. Something about saving him for last or whatever that means."

"I am starting to truly hate that man." William's reply came out more like a curse upon his lips.

"The feeling is mutual, I assure you," Sebastian agreed. "Only I wish right now that I had never gotten on that dreadful ship in the first place."

"We all do," Emile said quietly then looked up at William with a smile. "But then again, I wouldn't have met the three of you."

"Oh, just like that miraculous hat of yours, you would have managed to cross my path at some point in my life. There is no doubt in my mind about that." William smiled back and shook his head at the distinct possibility.

Finally upright, Charlotte breathed slowly and deeply for several seconds focusing on allowing the contracting sensations to pass. "Sebastian, where are the boys? Tell me they are somewhere safe." She swayed on her feet, though beads of sweat had already started to form across her brow.

In fearful realization of where Doctor Clarke was most likely arriving at that very moment, Sebastian's heart sank like a stone. "We left them with a friend just twenty minutes ago."

"Where?" Charlotte pleaded as she exhaled.

"At the house," he groaned and almost shook in his anger at his certain failure.

William understood it, too, and grabbed the lantern reflexively and handed it over to Emile before heading for the door. "We need to get back there and help Nathanael if he is to have any chance at all against him, Sebastian."

"But what about them, William?" Emile motioned with his head to Charlotte who was clearly in no condition to travel anywhere, nor was Emma, and he was most certainly not leaving her again. "We can't abandon them here."

"You'll have to stay with them, I'm afraid. Can you manage things here without me?" William asked quickly.

Incredulous at the mere suggestion, Emile's eyes filled with a panic William had never seen before as he struggled to remain civilly compliant. "I know you think I am much more than I am, but seriously man, I've never delivered a baby before."

"Well, that makes two of us." William threw Emile his satchel from the doorway. "You'll find anything you might need in there. Be sure to tie the cord off securely and keep the baby as warm as possible until I return."

"We'll be fine. You have to go! Now!" Charlotte demanded and pushed her husband towards the doorway. "Save our sons, Bash!"

Still uncertain if he was choosing the correct course of action, Sebastian looked back at her for a long moment and breathed in and out quickly, clearly conflicted.

"I mean it. It's not like I haven't done this before, three times actually. I should be an expert by now." Charlotte chuckled nervously then commanded him firmly with all the love and determination he needed behind her eyes, "Go! Please!" A contraction caused her to double over once more and push hard with it.

"I love you." He rushed back and kissed her quickly on the forehead.

"I know," Charlotte whispered back. "Now go!"

Chapter Forty-Nine

June 28th, 1793

For a little less than half an hour, Nathanael sat nervously with his back against the fire, holding a pistol in one hand and the silver cutlass in the other. "Ridiculous," he muttered before placing the sword on the table beside him in dissatisfaction. "I would probably kill myself if I tried to use this thing, much less be very effective against a marauding vampire."

The flames of the fire danced wildly off the beveled edge of the perfectly crafted instrument once more, illuminating the bench in front of it with their flickering shadows. Unable to do otherwise, he admired the delicate craftsmanship once more and marveled at the narrow, sculpted lines which swirled this way and that along the blade down to the hilt below like ink spilt onto a piece of pristine paper.

I wonder who he made this for? Nathanael thought, appreciating the angled lines of the Toledo steel that must have been created and etched by a master and not the simple blacksmith Sebastian had always professed to be.

The tilted blade in its new position caught his reflection dimly through a distortion in its matte finish. Suddenly intrigued, he stared at it deeply, trying to see the man with whom the others had put so much confidence. The man they were willing to entrust with the lives of two people, two innocent children in fact. He wouldn't. He knew nothing about defending anything other than a Biblical thesis, much less... people.

At primary and at seminary, all his fellow classmates had teased him mercilessly into adulthood about his lack of agility and strength, thinking that in some way it would affect him. Quite the opposite was true. Because what they felt were criticisms were also somewhat true, he hadn't paid much heed to all their taunts and ridicules at the time. Probably because he had always thought of his clumsiness as more of an endearing nuisance than a true deficit. Yet today, just a fraction of that elusive strength would have been most helpful, welcomed even as he sat here waiting for whatever or whoever might walk through the front door next.

"God, what am I even doing here? I'm not a soldier. I've never been trained by anyone in how to fight. Not really." The man in the reflection looked back at him, terror now spreading it's etch into the very lines of his face.

Was that what he truly was inside, a frightened man who had not been strong enough to battle against his own nature to be with the one he loved more than life itself, let alone be able to fight now when he was needed most?

He thought back to his last day at the castle so long ago. The very night that he and William had told Señor Moretti of their plans to leave. Emile, of course, had already departed days earlier without saying a single goodbye to anyone, but Sebastian, on the other hand, had decided to remain for the sake of his family.

A wise decision at the time, Nathanael had surmised, but in the harsh light of their reality today, perhaps he had been wrong about that, too. After all, he had been wrong about a great many things lately it had seemed. Why not everything else?

Oh, how he had wished many times over this past summer that he had stayed with Sebastian in the safety and solitude of that castle. Maybe then he would not have this gaping hole inside of him that never seemed to heal no matter how hard he tried to fill it.

Though it was true that the sharpness of Elsie's death had abated somewhat with the passage of time, the ache of that loss had always remained. As painful as it was to bear, it was almost as if it would forever be a constant scar upon his soul of his catastrophic failure and a daily reminder of her absence.

Had he been wrong about Elsie too?

He had not thought so at the time, but then again, maybe he had been just swept up in his emotions for the woman to see in all his naivety how utterly hopeless such a union like theirs would have been. In that light, her death could have been a blessing in disguise because if the influenza had not taken her, they would probably have been wed by now. Or at least, that had been his hope. But what kind of life would that have provided for her really, trapped in a brief existence while married to a vampire who never aged? Or worse yet, forced to live a life espoused to a man who always needed blood and struggled against a daily attraction for danger, despite his desire to think otherwise.

Would she have been happy with that kind of life? Would he?

"Dangerous," Nathanael said the one word that made his skin crawl every time he thought about the honest truth of his transition.

Is that what he was now? A man who would forever attract the vilest of evils by his mere existence. Or did God have something more for him in all of this, something greater that he still could not see?

William and Emile seemed to think so, but since last November he had felt more like a charlatan in his position at the church than a true leader of his flock. 'A Judas among God's faithful disciples' he often likened it to in his journal, or rather someone at constant war with who he was and what was expected of him. Yet how could he possibly continue to do the Lord's work, when he himself felt like he was fighting against his darker side more than for what was right.

Was he still good? Señor Moretti was, undeniably so. Their mentor had even made it his life mission to help those who could not help themselves. *Was that his calling now, too? Or was the creature that he had become merely the means to make amends for everything he arrogantly thought he was capable of doing in his own strength before he became a vampire?*

Since he was a boy, he had never once desired any other path for his life. Undoubtably, there were other opportunities and noble professions to choose from with his scholarly background, but none were so nearly as attractive to him as that of the clergy. And God's work had sincerely been enough for him. It still was. *But could he still do as God had commanded him as a vampire? And if so, had he finally found an answer to Señor Moretti's question after all? Did he want to live forever, even if that meant living a celibate life, solely dedicated to the Lord's service and nothing more?*

"Perhaps." He looked away from the reflection in the sword to the window, thinking he had heard someone walking up the long pathway from town. At nearly three o'clock in the morning, no one but his friends, and possibly the man they were all waiting for, would be out at this hour. But still, from off in the distance, he could have sworn that he had picked up something more than the sound of the barn cat on the porch or the swishing of the tree branches against themselves behind the house. He was almost positive that the sound he had heard was the unmistakable crunching of pebbles down the path from someone or something that had trodden them under foot. Yet upon examining the area from his position, the moonlight revealed absolutely nothing for miles and miles through the front windows. Certainly, not the danger he was expecting to arrive.

This task has made me paranoid it seems, he thought with a shake of his head before he stood up and placed the treasured weapon back upon the mantel. Enough was enough. He had spent a sufficient amount of time on self-reflection for one evening, maybe many more. And yet, he also could not remove the nagging fear that stole at the very center of his chest now, or the dread that crept up the back of his neck with its icy tendrils as it grew in the silence.

Something was off. Something he could not put his finger on just yet. Something that felt vaguely the same as that night back in the garden.

"Have not I commanded thee. Be strong and of a good courage. Be not afraid. Neither be thou dismayed. For the Lord thy God is with thee withersoever thou goest," a small voice reminded him in his head of memorized Scripture.

Had not the Lord told Joshua those words when he had to lead the new nation of Israel into the promise land? And just like Nathanael, he was called to do it all by himself, too, without the help of his mentor and friend, Moses. That task had been equally as daunting and possibly even more terrifying to contemplate. Yet from what Nathanael had remembered reading; he did not falter in the slightest. Obedient to the last, he had charged up to Jericho and saw His God tear down a daunting city to rubble and dust with his mighty yell.

Could he be as bold if called upon tonight?

Several horses whinnied in the stable next to the house alerting him further of a new presence.

Someone was most definitely approaching. The animals knew it. He knew it. He could sense it, like a thousand charged particles flying through his veins all at once. With every hair on the back of his neck and arms, he could tell that someone was most definitely watching him—someone, quite obviously, not invited.

With deliberate movements, so as not to alert whoever it was who might be watching him, he shifted the chair he was sitting in carefully to the side of the fireplace, choosing to face the door head-on for whatever might pass through it shortly.

Then, as if moving of its own accord, the handle lifted slowly and stopped when it found resistance, then dropped before someone threw themselves against the front door, sufficiently breaking the board across its back as it allowed the heavy obstacle to fall backwards upon its hinges with a loud thud on the inner wall.

"It's you," Doctor Clarke said mockingly but stopped within the wooden framework of the door, as if judging the man's stoic reaction to his unannounced presence.

Nathanael, on the other hand, did not change his position whatsoever, even though every muscle in his body was now poised to jump like a very uncomfortable spring. Only his eyes managed to narrow just a little with a determined form of greeting. "So, it would seem." He recognized instantly the man he had met in the garden.

"To tell you the truth, I was rather half-expecting William might have come to the aid of his dear friend, like the protector he always demonstrates himself to be, but I see he sent along the preacher instead. Rather convenient for me, don't you agree?" He chuckled darkly, clearly amused by his entry and the drama that would most likely be unfolding soon.

"How so?" Nathanael lifted his chin defiantly in response but not enough to move the rest of his body in the slightest.

As if dismissing the man's bravado entirely, Doctor Clarke waved him off like he was having a perfectly normal conversation with him and leaned against the wooden frame of the door with one hand. "William has been such a disappointment since the day that we first met. The son of London's most prominent surgeon and the top of his class at the university, and he still cannot figure out the tiniest of problems it seems. 'Why are all these people dying? What is happening to them?'" The man across from him mimicked his apprentice's medical deliberations from the garden. "C'mon man! Does he seriously lack intelligence or is he simply that ignorant all the time?"

"I don't know, you tell me," Nathanael demanded coolly, refusing to engage whatsoever with his repartee.

Doctor Clarke laughed quietly once more at Nathanael's defiance and *laissez-faire* attitude but continued. "Oh, Preacher, you really made finding the four of you incredibly easy for me. You know that, right?" He paused and glanced to his left and then to his right as if needing to check for the possible presence of the other men but still did not move to enter the house. "You let yourselves talk so freely back in Kent, ignoring everything your bodies were telling you and why? Because you are fools, sir. Compared to me, you are all children. Why, I would not have even known of your existence if I had not happened upon you all there. As far as I was aware, the rest of you perished in the wreck like all the others... well, most of them," he admitted sarcastically with a definite smirk.

"In a way, we did," Nathanael said disdainfully and felt his hand clench the weapon by his side in disgust at their thoughtless negligence and the man's quite obvious pride at what he had accomplished.

Delighted to have finally gotten a response out of him at last, Doctor Clarke's face twitched slightly at the movement, then his whole countenance shifted back to one of congenial apathy. "It's not my fault really that your friends were turned into vampires. It's his. William was always saving people who were never intended to survive in the first place. Like yourself for example and that sniveling Frenchman. Now he was a true disappointment. I thought if anyone was going to make a splendid vampire, he would. I even contemplated keeping him as a pet of sorts during that voyage. Well, that was until William intervened that day and stopped me."

Doctor Clarke looked slightly above Nathanael, as if he were considering something poetic and profound, though what he could have determined to be noble in anything he had just said was completely beyond Nathanael's means of comprehension.

"Oh, he would have been magnificent, too, sir. I could tell, even as a human, that he had the raw desire for our existence, the self-preservation skills, the cold-blooded lack of emotion to do whatever needed to be done in order to survive—to feed on whoever, whenever, however. But you all ruined him, didn't you? Turned him into a fragile excuse of a man. Disgusting, really."

Doctor Clarke moved through the doorway brazenly then and took several steps towards the kitchen to Nathanael's right, as if inviting himself into the home as a guest. "If only William had left you alone in the cabin that day. Maybe then, I could have finished your sorry existence as it should have been all along. But no, he was always thinking he was so clever... always getting in my way. Why that spoiled Spaniard also wouldn't be a vampire either, if it wasn't for him. Does the man never sleep?"

"Not that I am aware." Nathanael stood up finally and countered his adversary's movements exactly, drawing his body closer to the stairs instead, to place himself between Doctor Clarke's path and the boys. "But is that why you hate William so much? Because he stopped you from killing people on the ship? That seems rather self-condemning all on its own, sir."

"Ah, Preacher, as intelligent as I am sure you may be, you have missed the point of our existence entirely, but then again, you are new." He picked up an apple and took a large bite of it, chewing it most dramatically, as if he appeared in no rush whatsoever to complete his task. In fact, by all outward appearances, he was clearly savoring every minute of his certain victory and Nathanael knew it... knew it and dreaded it all at the same time.

"Then why don't you enlighten me, please." Nathanael's fingers flexed on the pistol in his right hand feeling the weight of the weapon balance itself against his chest.

Utterly delighted now by his captive audience, Doctor Clarke laughed at his feeble attempts of valor, and the sound of it made Nathanael's skin crawl. "Oh, if you only knew the truth of the situation you have no doubt turned your back on, you might find it humorous yourself."

"I highly doubt that entirely." Nathanael shook his head incredulously, no longer interested in anything the man was going to say next.

"I wasn't killing people... No, no, no." He wagged one finger at him in time with his words. "You were merely... my lunch."

Nathanael felt his stomach churn and the uncomfortable acid within him rise to the top of his throat in response.

"Is Papa still here, Mr. Nathanael? He forgot to hug us goodnight," a small voice suddenly called from the stairs high above him, sufficiently interrupting their tense conversation and drawing Doctor Clarke's greedy examination of the young boy from his position, as if contemplating his next victim.

Nathanael's heart leapt instantly in fear at the man's obvious intentions as if reading his lurid thoughts, but he did not dare to remove his gaze from him for even a second to address the boy properly. "Go back to bed, Elijah... instantly please," he commanded firmly without any emotion whatsoever, desiring only to get the boy out of sight and farther away from the monster in front of him.

"But... but..." the little boy tried to protest further but was stopped immediately by Nathanael's increasingly strict reply.

"Do as I say," he spoke slowly, but firmly enough to motivate an obedient response from the boy. "And I want you to stay with your brother, no matter what. Do you hear me?" He added for good measure, hoping that he would be safer with him than where he was for the present.

"Yes, sir." The boy tearfully pattered back to his room, sniffling; his feelings obviously hurt by his new friend, but thankfully for him, it was nothing that could not be mended in time.

"So, you do have a backbone after all. A pity it is only for small children." Doctor Clarke swallowed his last bite of the apple and tossed the half-finished core casually to the floor somewhere beyond the kitchen itself. "Still, it is nice to see it, even if it is too late."

"Too late for what?" Nathanael watched him like a mouse watching a snake stalk its prey. This game of his was growing increasingly wearisome and his conversation irritating, if not outright offensive.

"Oh, Preacher, I haven't lived this long as a vampire without knowing the number one rule for all. Perhaps, you can guess it," he taunted him like he was rather enjoying this exchange of tit for tat.

"Really, pray tell, what is that?" Nathanael's voice came back hard and sarcastic, completely uncharacteristic of his normally careful remarks.

"You never... leave... loose... ends. They are a risk, a parasite, a canker if you will." Doctor Clarke took three deliberate steps towards Nathanael with each derogatory expression he uttered and smiled at him cruelly. "For the past 300 years, I have <u>never</u> left things unfinished... until the four of you. Well, then again..." He paused and looked up at the ceiling once more as if deep in thought. "There was that one book I sent to a bunch of dogmatic monks over in Italy. For months, they had foiled my attempts at feeding in their village, but that gift was merely an ill-humored joke on my behalf. With all their dusty volumes of theology, I doubt anyone has even stumbled upon that hidden vial as of yet or I am sure I would have heard about it. We may be immortal, sir, but I do love a taste of petty vengeance from time to time." He smiled and chuckled at his clever prank.

Nathanael thought of Señor Moretti's unfortunate transformation instantly and raised his pistol up chest high, aiming true for Doctor Clarke's head. What an incredible irony it was that their mentor on the island had done only good with the immortality he was unfortunately given, whereas the man in front of him had made it his mission to cause so much pain. "I will not tell you again, sir. Stay where you are. This is my last warning."

Doctor Clarke couldn't help but smirk in response but stopped in his progress across the room momentarily as if contemplating his next move. "Would you really shoot me, Mr. Beckett? The man who created you? Oh, I doubt it." Doctor Clarke clicked his tongue then smiled, but the sadistic grin once again set Nathanael's nerves on edge.

"You may have transformed me, sir, but you did **<u>not</u>** create me." Nathanael glared at him darkly.

"Dear preacher, if your God truly existed like you think, why would He have allowed me to make a monster out of you, out of all of you." He laughed at him like how Goliath must have mocked David. "I am god here and your future has always been mine to control since the moment you stepped on that boat, not some silly person out of an old forgotten text."

Completely incensed now with a righteous indignation, Nathanael shook his head slowly back and forth in response, enraged at the man's audacity and utter irreverence. Yet it was at that moment that the most unusual thing happened. A peace, unlike anything he had ever felt before, filled him from his head all the way down to his toes and spread out through the very room around him.

"I am with you, too, Nathanael." He felt the Holy Spirit say to him personally and he believed it, for how could he not.

"What?" Doctor Clarke taunted him further. "Are you so incapable of being a true vampire that you cannot even fight me when it matters? Or were you always destined to die at my hands?"

Nathanael sighed in total repose and felt the power of the peace he now contained, as if it had given him the strength he needed to do what he must. "If my God let me live so I can stand here against you today, then this was always my fate, sir. As God is my witness, I will not let you hurt these boys."

"Have it your way then," he muttered and lunged at him like a bear attacking his kill, releasing all the fury that normally went with such an attack.

Standing his ground, Nathanael braced himself for the impact while closing his eyes briefly, and squeezed the trigger of the gun reflexively, but nothing happened. Nothing but an audible, sickening click from the loaded weapon.

"How pathetic! You can't even defend yourself, it seems." Doctor Clarke reached forward and wrenched the pistol easily from his hands in one swift motion before throwing it across the room towards the open door.

Desperate now to find any weapon at all that would suffice to defend himself against Doctor Clarke's subsequent attack, Nathanael dove for the axe Jedidiah had there left there days earlier, but the man stopped him just before it was within reach, wrestling him against the stone wall of the fireplace with the force of ten men and not the one exceptional being before him. The subsequent collision that followed knocked the wind out of him completely and forced him to redirect his efforts in yet another direction... delay. From the strength he had just experienced, Nathanael knew beyond a shadow of a doubt that there was no way on earth that he would ever be able to stop the obviously stronger man by himself. Yet, there <u>was</u> one thing he <u>could</u> do. He just needed to hold out long enough to keep him occupied until more help arrived.

"For all the bravery you just showed with your words, Preacher, you should at least try to fight me," the older vampire mocked him mercilessly as he raised Nathanael up off the ground and threw him towards the front door like a limp puppet before following after him and seizing him around the chest in a tight hold, the action of which almost restricted Nathanael's movements completely.

Instinctively focused now on self-preservation amidst certain defeat, Nathanael swung his head backwards in desperation, managing to strike Doctor Clarke hard in the face with a deafening crack as the man went reeling backwards away from him, wounded, but otherwise still vertical. Yet, stunned as he was, he didn't remain motionless for long. Furious and clearly bleeding down onto his white shirt below, the man wiped the blood that was now flowing freely from his nose away with the back of his sleeve and growled as he lunged back towards him once more with even more anger than before.

From the kitchen to the fireplace and even almost to the stairs themselves, the two adversaries fought dramatically with neither man giving an inch until Nathanael felt two hands firmly tightening around his neck at last, though try as he might, he still could not find sufficient strength to wrench them even a fraction of an inch away from his throat, or at the very least, loosen them enough to draw in a single gasp of a breath. In their viselike grip, the room spun viciously around him as the last of his oxygen left his lungs and weakened fully his already feeble defenses.

It was only then, at the brink of total unconsciousness, that a single gunshot exploded next to his ear. So close, in fact, that he felt the distinct fire of the powder flash upon his left temple and cheek. The first vestiges of warmth that he had felt in months actually. And yet, as completely frightening as the prospect of being shot might be, it also felt bizarrely comforting to sense that heat once more, as it was almost like stepping out into the bright sunshine from an otherwise cloudy and overcast day. Throughout their struggle, Doctor Clarke must have found the other pistol that Sebastian had left for Nathanael on the center of the table and used it, for how could he have felt the burn of the weapon otherwise?

Suddenly overwhelmed by the experience, everything within his vision went black in the silence that followed, allowing a deathly stillness to creep over him from the various corners of the room. Nothing else in all the world registered in his mind whatsoever except for the sound of the soft wind that was being expelled as he steadied his breathing back to its usual rhythm of exhaling and inhaling in and out slowly.

And then... as always... he was so very cold again.

"He's gone..." He thought he heard William whisper softly beside him in the distance, though he could not be sure exactly what else he was saying as everything around him appeared to be muted and muffled now like he was in some kind of watery existence or under a very thick blanket.

Drinking in the feeling of inner peace that washed over him once more like the day he had dreamed about Elsie by the lake, he felt his muscles relax as he waited for death to take him.

At least this way he would see her again.

And as tired as his body was steadily becoming lying here, he couldn't wait.

"I'm coming, love." Nathanael sighed happily at last and closed his eyes.

Chapter Fifty

July 16th, 1793

B eautiful guitar music filtered through the morning rays unexpectedly as Señor Moretti opened his eyes that warm July morning, sufficiently interrupting his extended slumber. Well over two weeks had passed already since Sebastian had abruptly left the castle in a desperate attempt to save his wife and family, and not a day had gone by that Giacomo had not thought about the danger the young father had placed himself in, or whether or not he had been ultimately successful in his most worthy endeavor.

And to make matters even more concerning was the alarming fact that not a single piece of news had arrived describing any unusual events transpiring in England at all. Nor had there been word mentioned by anyone in port about the Blacksmith's quite sudden disappearance, save Thomas' frequent visits to the castle to pester Hannah as to his whereabouts. Moreover, not a solitary correspondence had been delivered from anyone for weeks—not a normally detailed letter from William describing what was happening in his part of the world with Nathanael and Emile, or even a short note from Sebastian about whether or not he had made it safely to England at all. In every way, it was almost as if all of their lives had suddenly vanished along with Sebastian, just as quickly as they had all appeared on his island months ago.

At one time, this lack of frequent contact might not have overly concerned him as he had rarely grown close to any of his visitors over the years, but this group of men was different for some reason. Not that they were extraordinary in any way on their own or were more keenly matched to his particular interests in general. But rather, it was especially intriguing to him to see how each one of them had been the perfect complement to the others and to himself, as if they had all maintained an integral part to an overall whole. Moreover, from what he had witnessed in the past nine months, each man clearly lived his own life in oblivious display of his own talents and deficits which the other men then moved in turn to balance out with small actions and gestures to either sharpen or encourage the other towards an even better man overall. Something, even <u>he</u> had found himself subconsciously striving to do, also, on occasion.

Señor Moretti sighed as he considered the many possible reasons for their silence and closed his eyes to listen to the unmistakable chords being played from a particularly cherished Spanish guitar, as they echoed off the walls to his room above. *Was he still dreaming?* He did not think so, and yet, how could he deny it?

As if needing a few moments more to contemplate that remote possibility and drink in the peaceful melody, he rolled over and waited as the familiar song played on for several stanzas more before allowing himself to hope or even imagine that the probable was indeed possible. The stoic Sebastian <u>must</u> have returned, *but for how long and why?*

Good, bad or otherwise, he was simply going to have to go downstairs and find out for himself. Though if he were to be totally honest, never before in all his life had he ever been so filled with increasing trepidation that he could hardly draw in a breath to face it. Mainly, of course, because of the possible darker outcome that went along with this arrival, for if Sebastian had indeed been successful, he would have most certainly stayed in England or even gone on to America with his family.

If not... he let that thought linger a bit too long in his mind as he threw back the heavy covers and put on his thick, grey cotton blouse and dark breeches from the back of his door before bracing himself for what he hoped he might encounter below.

The stone beneath his feet as he dressed this morning mimicked his own temperature, cold and steadfast. But then again, it always did. In truth, it was just one of the many things he enjoyed about his home, its ability to provide constancy and security amidst outward change. Right now, it was the one thing that was keeping him grounded when the world around him was apparently shifting once more.

Still, despite his growing apprehension about what he might find, the music played on as it lured him down the long, arched corridor, serenading him with a greeting as familiar and as sweet as anything he had heard in all of his existence.

Yet in many ways it was different, as well, as there was a hopeful lightness to its timbre and cadence now that far exceeded the typically somber tunes Sebastian was more accustomed to playing each evening.

Nevertheless, it was at the top of the stairs that he heard a change to the piece entirely, as it was now surprisingly joined by a diverse accompaniment on the grand piano. A complex and yet also wonderfully pleasant arrangement was now being playfully supplemented to his solo by someone of incredible talent, as both instruments were now harmoniously entwining their notes beautifully together to create a satisfyingly, peaceful duet with neither one owning the melody in its entirety nor hiding beneath the multiple harmonies.

Equally distinct, and yet also perfectly matched, the musicians exchanged the perplexity of the moving notes so seamlessly in fact, that it appeared as if one of them was inhaling throughout one measure, while the other was exhaling right through and onto the next. In essence, though he had never heard this particular piece of music before, it was still hypnotically mesmerizing to listen to it being played. Like a dizzying duet of two opposing viewpoints, each performer worked to complement as well as challenge the other in measure after following measure.

Filled with an ever-increasing awe and curiosity as he listened, he stepped down the short flight of stairs carefully towards the orchestration that beckoned to him and prayed for the outcome he most desired—that Sebastian and his family were safe and sound, no matter the loneliness he was sure would follow for him thereafter. After all, it would be selfish of him now to encourage his friend in anything that would disrupt his goal of wholeness with his family. Time itself was precious, and not a minute of it should be wasted. Yet even believing this, it still did not mean that he would not mourn the possible loss of his friend all the same.

Life, in all its complexities, was moving incredibly quickly these days, much faster than it had ever moved before, and soon he would be completely alone again in his castle once more, just like what he had experienced during the first century of his existence. And yet thankfully, his life had not always been full of solitude and isolation. By God's gracious gift, Hannah had also entered his life most unexpectedly and for the past twenty years she had been more than his ward and cook at his home. She had been a tremendous blessing in his life, filling his days with a hopeful expectation of conversation and a warm delight in her mentorship. But even she would also soon be moving on in marriage to Thomas, as she should. And just like all the others who had come to him for help before her, their lives would also move at pace with the ever-changing tides of time. Yet, as an immortal being, he would not. His life would remain forever fixed and immovable as the stones upon the rocky shore of this island... unable to deviate from his allotted course, and yet also helplessly exposed to whatever weather might erode him next.

"Perhaps it is time the rock moved, if only just a little. Either that or risk being buried beneath the shifting sands all around me like everything else," he pondered as he stopped at the base of the stairs and sighed. "When Hannah marries, maybe it will finally be time to step out of my sanctuary and explore those lands I always dreamt of seeing? Create some maps of mine own, perhaps."

As if wanting to answer his question for him, the music grew suddenly louder, sufficiently distracting him away from his deliberations and welcoming him with raptured attention to the Great Hall just beyond. With a large crescendo of delight, the legato rose dramatically as he approached until it finally reached a lingering chord that left him as speechless with its splendor as he was to its origins. In the room before him sat not one but two minstrel figures, who, like the instruments they played, could not have been more contrary in their attire, personality or overall approach to life, yet both seemed completely at ease with their surroundings, each other, and their chosen task.

"I don't believe my eyes, gentlemen!" Señor Moretti gasped in deep satisfaction as the formally dressed man on the bench turned towards him slowly and politely nodded, then waited hesitantly in the ensuing silence for his justly deserved admonishment. Sebastian, on the other hand, carefully set down his guitar by the piano and beamed widely at his mentor, almost unable to contain his joy from the other side of the room.

Delighted, Señor Moretti rushed to each of them in turn, forgetting everything he had been worrying about all the way there. "Emile! I had no idea you would ever return!" He laid a warm hand of welcome upon his shoulder, then walked over to Sebastian and embraced him heartily like a father welcoming home his lost son. "My friend! You are alive!" Señor Moretti grasped the sides of his face within his hands emotionally, and the two men laughed and cried together all at once. "My prayers have truly been answered."

"Yes! But only barely," Sebastian admitted and patted his mentor on the back twice. "It is good to see you so well."

"Well, I am now! And what is this? You've even brought me a guest!" Señor Moretti tried to wipe the tears of happiness from off his cheeks, but they continued to flow freely.

"I've actually brought a whole house full this time," Sebastian proclaimed proudly. "Boys..." He waved his hand to get his family's attention from across the room as the children were already perusing the vast assortment of books and curious antiquities located on the shelves behind him. "This is Señor Moretti. The man I have been telling you all about."

Both boys obeyed immediately and came rushing over to him at his invitation, each hugging the sides of his body in eager anticipation. "Is this our new gran papi?"

Señor Moretti's eyes twinkled with obvious joy at the newly granted title. "I would be honored to be so, if you will allow me that blessing." He patted each of their heads in turn.

"This is Jedidiah, my oldest, and the younger one is his brother, Elijah." Sebastian paused then moved to the side slowly to reveal his wife casually resting in the great chair that used to be his sanctuary on so many nights after a long day at the forge.

"And you would be his dear Charlotte. My, how I have longed to meet you!" Señor Moretti stepped around the boys to greet her. "You are most definitely welcome. But oh! Who is this little one?" He gasped as he pointed to the squirming bundle in her arms. "I don't recall you mentioning anything about a baby, Sebastian?"

"A surprise for both of us, sir." Sebastian smiled unapologetically, as he picked up the newborn adoringly before placing her in Señor Moretti's uncertain arms. "Señor Moretti, I'd like you to meet Hope Rose Fabbri, my daughter."

"Aww," Señor Moretti sighed at the beauty of the little bundle. "What a truly prophetic name given your most recent ordeal."

"Her name was my wife's idea, but I do agree that it is quite perfect, indeed," Sebastian explained as Charlotte glanced up at her husband with love and renewed understanding.

"An angelic blessing to behold any day!" He touched her tiny pink nose with his finger and leaned in to kiss her forehead lightly. "It has been so long since I have held a little one like this. I may never give her back."

"You can keep her." Jedidiah wrinkled his nose up in definite displeasure.

"Yeah," Elijah agreed readily. "She cries a lot."

The three adults laughed together in unison at their honest opinion.

"Most babies do, I'm afraid." Señor Moretti felt the softness of her tiny hand as she gripped his finger tightly. "But you will cherish her soon enough."

Still unconvinced, the two boys looked at each other, raised their eyebrows and shook their heads in unison. "Nah..."

"Alright, enough picking on your sister." Sebastian ruffled their hair playfully. "Go along now and see what Miss Hannah has for you in the kitchen. It is just through that door on the left. The one I showed you earlier. And mind that you do not touch anything without being asked."

"Can we, Mama?" They asked eagerly, making sure it was definitely okay to leave.

"Of course." She nodded and took the baby back from Señor Moretti.

"What a blessing it is to have you all here. Though I must admit that never in all my life have I been so pleasantly surprised," he exclaimed before turning back to Emile who was still seated at the piano fingering the keys aimlessly but not creating a sound from them in the slightest. "And Emile, too. Does this mean you have finally decided upon a path for yourself? The last I heard from William you were thinking about a bakery of some kind."

"Perhaps," Emile tilted his head slightly towards the piano. "Though I do still have a few details to work out first before I do."

"A few details?" Señor Moretti's face displayed confusion. "Are you not thinking about starting it in Wakefield where you can be close to the others?"

"I was leaning more towards a place called Charleston, actually. It's near the coast in the Carolinas. Since I heard that there are still a great many <u>adjustments</u> being made since the revolution farther north, I decided maybe not there for the time being." He tried to be as polite as possible in his explanation. "Besides, this place boasts quite unashamedly an environment of culture and cuisine, and so understandably, I am merely curious as to why." Emile leaned one elbow on the frame above the keyboard itself and lifted his eyebrow to add mockingly. "The British are coming! The British are coming!"

Señor Moretti laughed lightly at his playful reference to the recent revolution and replied, "They did indeed. Though I fear you may find the change in society a bit challenging at first. The newspapers claim they are still quite provincial in the outer regions of the Colonies."

"I don't know that I would mind the quiet so much now." Emile shrugged. "I guess I've grown used to a different set of actors at the moment."

"Really?" Señor Moretti's eyebrows lifted, as well. "Will miracles never cease today!"

"Emile, do you want any tea? Hannah says she may have some Dammann Frères, if you do," a woman's lilting voice spoke sweetly from just outside the room as she walked through the kitchen door and towards the man at the piano as easy in this home as she was in any other.

"And who is <u>this</u> stunning young lady?" He clasped his hands together before his eyes lit up at seeing the petite woman take her seat next to Emile on the piano's bench.

"Well... Señor Moretti, may I be the first to introduce to you my wife, Mrs. Emma Deschamps." Emile put his arm around her waist proudly and held her as close as politely possible given the current company.

Overwhelmed by the emotions flooding over him once more, Señor Moretti reached down and took her hand in his in most definite welcome before casting a glance at both of them in turn, as if suddenly contemplating a very real, but dark possibility. "You came of your own will, did you not, dear lady?" He narrowed his eyes at Emile with a look that was filled more with warning and judgement than in actual approval.

"Yes." Emile laughed lightly at his suggestion, then beamed back the same smile that had not left his face for weeks. "I assure you that my wife has a will completely her own on the matter."

"And a mouth, too, I'm afraid." Emma jabbed Emile playfully in his stomach at his intended tease. "I'm delighted to make your acquaintance finally, sir."

"And she's a ..." Señor Moretti turned his back to Charlotte and insinuated a word to Emile that was too sacred to speak in front of all gathered.

"Yes." Emile nodded, feeling completely content by her side. "She is."

Suddenly even more concerned than before, Señor Moretti looked down at him once more like a scornful schoolmaster, much like the way he had done when Emile had challenged him before about Hannah. "Do I need to have a talk with you about this matter in private first?"

Watching his interrogation, Emma couldn't help but giggle at the manner in which he was now making her husband squirm. "I like him a lot."

"I told you, you would," Emile agreed, albeit still a tad bit nervously. "And no, suffice it to say, I had no hand in her transformation. Rather, we have the same, misguided creator."

"Good." Señor Moretti nodded in approval, clasping his hands firmly behind his back at last before turning back to Sebastian with a look of deepening melancholy.

"What?" Sebastian prodded, noticing the change in his usually happy demeanor.

"It's nothing really?" Señor Moretti half-smiled and tried to wave off his concern just as quickly as it had appeared.

Unconvinced, Sebastian set down the book he had been showing Charlotte on the table next to him and prodded him further, "You can't fool me. I can tell by that look on your face that something is definitely bothering you."

Señor Moretti only shook his head as he walked over to the fire. "I was simply remembering the last time you both were here, that's all."

"I was very different then, and for that I beg your forgiveness," Emile said quietly, knowing full-well just how much he had to atone for where their mentor was concerned.

"We all were, Emile," Sebastian agreed.

"No forgiveness is necessary but freely given, dear friends." Señor Moretti looked back at the newly married pair by the piano and smiled. "Life has certainly changed many things for all of us this past year. Why Emile, you practically called me a hermit of my own castle. Which upon much reflection afterwards, I suppose I must admit to you that at times I have been. Mostly because it has been easier to live unnoticed here than in the open elsewhere. Yet it was Sebastian's presence those many months that helped me truly see today how much I was missing in my life by desiring that kind of solitude."

"But surely you know that you do much more than you realize." Sebastian tried to appeal to the man honestly, hoping to distract him from that familiar line of destructive thinking, for he knew well enough where that path led, no matter what the intentions might be otherwise.

Señor Moretti waved a dismissive hand towards him. "Oh, I doubt that, but that was not what I was sad about actually. I was merely feeling the slight loss of the rest of your company, as well."

Sebastian and Emile each took turns looking down at the floor solemnly or nodding in agreement afterwards to what the man had just said.

"I'm sorry, but has something happened?" Señor Moretti asked as if sensing the perceived tension building in the room all around him.

Neither of the men spoke for several long minutes before Sebastian replied bluntly, "Oh, sorry. When we arrived, William offered to tend to the horses in the stable. In fact, I think that is him coming in now."

As if perfectly timed to his explanation, the door to the front of the castle closed loudly behind them. "Sebastian? Emile?" William called as he hung up his light cloak respectfully on the peg by the door.

"Over here," Emile directed but his voice carried through the room much louder than he had originally intended, sending multiple echoes of his response off the stone walls and back to him once more.

"That was a little creepy." William laughed as he entered the room. "I bet you didn't realize you had a haunted castle, Señor Moretti?"

"Oh, I assure you that there is nothing so fantastical here, friend." Señor Moretti warmly embraced the man with whom he held a great sense of camaraderie. "I've missed your letters this month."

"Really? I'm sorry, but as you can probably guess, things have been a bit busy recently. By the way, how is your research coming along?" William asked excitedly, not bothering to pause with formalities with his fellow scholar. "Anything new?"

"Actually, you will never believe what I have just learned!" Señor Moretti exclaimed as he pulled William aside to his study to view some of his recent discoveries.

Sebastian and Emile only chuckled together.

"We travel well over a thousand miles and still the man has nothing else on his mind than science," Emile rebuked sarcastically.

"Well, I don't know about you, but I am personally grateful he decided to come along. Half the time I have no idea what Señor Moretti is talking about," Sebastian added as he tended to the fire to lessen the flames just a little when he saw Charlotte wipe the sweat from her brow.

"Aren't you hot, Bash?" Charlotte asked as she fanned herself with the small cloth she kept for the baby.

Sebastian and Emile only smiled at each other, then said in unison, "Never."

"That is definitely something I am going to have to get used to." Charlotte rolled her eyes and continued to fan.

Feeling equally concerned about her overheating; Sebastian apologized, "I'm sorry, dear. Maybe I can help you move farther away from the fire."

"I will be fine, honestly. Besides, I should think that it is a small price to pay to have you with me." Charlotte took his hand and held it close to her shoulder, suddenly unwilling to let him go.

Sebastian smiled at the gesture, then asked her hesitantly, "Should we interrupt those two? I mean, at this rate, they could be in there for hours."

"Give them their minute. William needs to be able to talk to someone." Emile motioned politely to Emma to allow him some space at the piano to play once more.

"I suppose you are right." Sebastian sat down and watched his daughter sleep.

This dissertation of ideas and findings went on between the two colleagues in the other room for almost a full twenty minutes as the two men discussed, without stopping, medical advances and recent publications that affected their work, while Emile played compositions alone and with Emma as she mimicked his notes humorously on the upper register of the keys. In reality, she was not a skilled musician in any way, but it did bring her great joy to try to distract the man playing beside her.

Sebastian's boys also returned several times, delivering fresh batches of cookies from Hannah's oven to the waiting couples before contenting themselves with a game their father had laid out for them on the large rug by the fire. The reunion could not have been sweeter nor the company more at peace had they spent a hundred years together and not the fractured and emotionally unbalanced one. With the laughter and companionship displayed in many forms, every corner of the room seemed filled with their love for one another. In tiny ways here and there, it spread out its warmth in their laughter, pulsed with the playful banter and pushed back at the shadows of the past. In truth, it was a long-awaited respite from the drama that had filled their lives both before and after their trip on the *Endeavour*.

"It's perfect." Emile rested his chin upon Emma's shoulder at last, taking a pause from his repertoire for just a moment before placing both his arms around his wife once more. "In a way, it's kind of like what I always imagined Christmas would be like growing up." He watched the scene unfold around him with increasing awe and gratitude.

"Really? What was yours like?" Emma asked carefully, not wanting to say anything that would spoil the moment for him.

"Not like this." Emile sighed contentedly, then smiled as he breathed in the fresh lavender scent of her hair once more. "Not like this." He drew her in closer still and closed his eyes in expectant pleasure.

"Would you like to hold her, Emma?" Sebastian looked up at them from across the room and offered, unable to help the feeling of friendship that he was steadily building towards the man who was once his greatest irritation.

"Oh, may I?" Emma answered him eagerly, instantly hopeful at the prospect.

"Definitely." Taking care so as to not upset the pieces on the rug, he stepped over the game the boys were playing and placed the child safely into Emma's awaiting arms. "I don't see why not. She wouldn't even be here if it wasn't for your husband."

Suddenly at a loss for words, Emile shook his head quietly before replying with the least bit of sarcasm he could manage, "That is one memory I would most definitely like to forget, *Mon amie*."

"Agreed," Charlotte answered from across the room. "Though all things considered, if your bakery fails, you might make a fantastic midwife, Emile."

"Hardly," Emma chuckled lightly at the prospect as she rubbed her nose against the soft tip of Hope's. "I think this is the closest thing he will ever get to a child of his own, Charlotte, and that suits him just fine for now."

"Most definitely. I'll leave the nappies and such to you, and your most excellent wife, Sebastian." He held his nose slightly aloof before adding with a downward glance, "Speaking of which, I'm sorry, love but..."

"Oh," Charlotte took the veiled hint and stood up to retrieve her daughter. "Bash, if you could show me to a room, I can take care of her there?" She asked Sebastian politely. "I promise to return her to you after, Emma."

"Of course." He motioned for her to follow him up the stairway behind them.

"She is beautiful, isn't she?" Emma folded her now-empty hands in front of her and looked up at her husband wistfully.

"Not as beautiful as you." He kissed her quickly on the cheek, while also being painfully aware of the ache both of them now felt holding Sebastian's newborn daughter, or rather, the loss of that kind of possibility for their own lives.

"Ewww, yuck!" The two boys exclaimed loudly at the display.

"What is ewww?" Señor Moretti re-entered the large room with William trailing close behind.

"They are always kissing." Elijah stuck out his tongue to make a contorted face at Emile.

Like the petulant child that he oft times could be, Emile mimicked him right back playfully and both fell into a light laughter of sorts at the picture of it.

"Stop encouraging him, Elijah, or you know he will never stop." Emma giggled at the antics between them but reveled in the more spirited side of her husband, something she had never expected when they had first met.

"And you, William? What will you do now? Continue on with your apothecary?" Señor Moretti questioned, as if the conversation with the larger group gathered had not ceased.

"Probably not." William pursed his lips just once in hesitation as he paused for a few minutes before continuing, "I don't think I could do it there anymore."

"Whyever not?" Señor Moretti asked quickly, suddenly confused as to why he would leave his already established place of business.

"It wouldn't be the same without Nathanael, I suppose," William admitted while he fingered the smoothness of the wooden column beside him.

"I see." Señor Moretti placed his hand upon his shoulder. "Sometimes Providence chooses the path for us, does it not?"

"Something like that." William breathed in deeply then cleared his throat and tried to perk back up. "Nathanael told me once to trust that God always has a plan, so I think I shall rest in that for the time being."

"Wise counsel indeed." Señor Moretti nodded, then twisted his head back to look at him. "Is someone going to tell me just what happened exactly, or am I meant to be tortured about the details for all of eternity? Which by the looks of things, might just happen with the three of you."

"Right..." Emma took her cue then and stood up, calling to the boys happily, "Jedidiah... Elijah, why don't you come explore this castle with me."

"Really? Do we have to?" The boys groaned in disapproval, not wanting to leave their father's side so soon.

"Uncle William just said that it might be haunted," she teased further and watched as both boys jumped up from their game, suddenly more scared than actually intrigued.

"Haunted? You mean like ghosts and such?" Jedidiah asked more cautiously, unsure if he truly wanted to know the answer.

"You never know. At the very least you can both help me make sure there are no monsters under our beds."

"I can never tell when you are fibbing, Auntie Emma." Elijah closed one eye and scrutinized her greatly, like he had the day when Emile had first told him he knew how to cook.

"Neither can I, little man," Emile agreed with his chief apprentice with a knowing nod of understanding. "So, it might be best to see if she is, just to be on the safe side. I'm scared of monsters."

"... monsters, indeed..." Emma scoffed, then muttered under her breath sarcastically, "I'm more afraid of you before breakfast than any phantom I might find in the night around here."

"Touché." Emile kissed the back of her hand lightly before she left the room with both boys in tow.

With a drawn-out sigh of exhaustion from their recent trip, William plopped down finally on a small bench opposite Emile before folding his hands restlessly. "I'm assuming that you were referring to the whole affair in Portsmouth?"

"Yes." Señor Moretti took a seat in the wooden chair in front of them and leaned forward in intense interest. "And why no one has communicated with me since. I was going out of my mind with worry waiting here for news."

"Well..." Emile drummed his fingers very slowly upon the lacquered piano top, avoiding the subject altogether before adding seriously, "I'm afraid it is a rather long story to tell, sir."

"Then tell me only what you feel is absolutely necessary, chiefly being whether or not any of you are still in danger."

"Doctor Clarke has been removed from the equation entirely," Sebastian stated curtly as he strode back into the room and cast a dark look of pleasure mixed with just the slightest hint of satisfaction towards Emile. "I made sure of that."

Emile only raised his one eyebrow and smirked in most definite agreement for the man's actions, then replied, "Yes, thankfully, he will be causing no further disturbances in this plane of reality." Emile translated smoothly.

"And your wife?" Señor Moretti's forehead furrowed upwards. "Does she finally know?"

Sebastian nodded. "Yes, but the boys do not. We thought it best to keep it between the two of us for the time being."

"Rightly so." Señor Moretti nodded in agreement. "But they may have to be told someday. After all, one of them is bound to wonder why you no longer age."

"That is true, but I hope to have selected an appropriate reason by the time that day finally arrives. No sense worrying about that now when we have years to create a convincing excuse."

"True." Señor Moretti sat pondering the dilemma for several long moments before finally adding with great curiosity, "And how will you manage your diet?"

"I have a few ideas on the matter thanks to Emile, but suffice it to say, my wife has decided we are better suited tackling this life together than apart. It's high time to put away our secrets." Sebastian looked up in earnest before adding, "At least from each other."

Señor Moretti nodded. "That seems very wise. And Nathanael..." He began to ask but stopped when he saw William suddenly look towards the front door as if lost in thought.

Noticing it too, Emile quickly picked up where Sebastian had left off and went on to explain the rest of the story in a detailed burst. "On the day Sebastian arrived, we left Nathanael at Sebastian's house to protect the boys while the three of us went in search for Emma and Charlotte. We had no idea, at the time, that Doctor Clarke was on his way back to the house, nor did we know his darker intentions towards who he would find there when he arrived."

"And what were those intentions?"

"To end the line he created on the *Endeavour*," William added flatly without any emotion whatsoever. "To kill Nathanael, Emile, Sebastian, or to put it more bluntly, to kill all of us who escaped his grasp... me most of all."

"But why would he single you out above so many others? What did you do to this man to cause him such disdain?"

"Simply put... I stole his prize," William admitted honestly. "Once upon a time I kept him from being who he was, and he simply could not tolerate the insult."

"I see. So, it was merely retaliatory vengeance."

"More or less... though it all seems rather pointless, but it is what it is," William added.

The room fell silent once more except for the crackling of the fire in the hearth and the sounds of the giggling children running along the corridor above them.

"Well, thankfully he did not succeed, otherwise you would not all be blessing me here today." The corner of Señor Moretti's eye teared up slightly. "And a true joy it has been."

"Absolutely." William nodded his head before another loud voice echoed back to them from just beyond the hallway.

"Hallo?" Nathanael yelled from the front door. "Did you all forget about me?"

William smiled and leaned back towards the hall behind him. "Speaking of prizes."

"Thank the Lord..." Señor Moretti's eyes closed in noticeable and appreciative relief.

With the mirth and exuberance that the man always seemed to possess, Nathanael made his way down the hall towards them, entirely encumbered by wrapped parcels and boxes of various shapes and sizes. "A little help would be nice, please."

"Certainly." Emile jumped up from his seat at the piano instinctively and took several of the packages from the top of his pile before laughing so hard that the corners of his eyes wrinkled to match his smile. "Land's sake, Man! You probably scared Señor Moretti half to death coming in here like Père Noël just now."

"Who? Oh, Father Christmas?" Nathanael laughed, too. "Now that would be an idea! Though I do love Christmas. It was the first time I knew Elsie would be the one I would forever love." He paused, not in sadness anymore, but rather in affectionate remembrance. "But none of that now. Sebastion, will you please take the rest of these and place them over by Señor Moretti? In truth, they are getting a bit heavy."

"Of course, but what took you so long?" Sebastian complied happily and soon there were well over a dozen presents gathered around the master of the castle, filling the space at his feet entirely.

"Oh, I was just simply paying my respects to Rebecca before coming in and praying for a minute. Why? Did I really take that long?" Nathanael admitted sheepishly.

"A bit..." William grinned widely at his friend's casual demeanor.

"Please don't be troubled in the least on my account. But I'll freely admit that when William said he was not returning to Wakefield because of you, Nathanael, it did give me pause for concern." Señor Moretti held his hands closely to his chest. "But what is all this?"

"I'm so very sorry. I only meant that Nathanael's elders have finally given him a commission in the Americas. He is to report to Philadelphia just after the new year," William apologized before adding. "And these..." He motioned to the gifts. "Are just a few tokens of our appreciation."

"For me? But why? I have done nothing to warrant any of this," he defended honestly.

"No?" Sebastian let his hand rest upon his mentor's shoulder. "I told you once that I thought of all of us were merely pieces in a great game of chess, and in many ways, I was right. Yet in hindsight, I also forgot one other important piece of information that really should have been included with the rest... your guidance as the board itself. We all might have been the various pieces with which to play such a complicated game, but you provided the actual board, and without it, there would have been no game to be played at all. Your inexhaustible counsel, support, and overall generosity has been guided only by a genuine desire to help us all succeed, and for that we are all eternally grateful."

"My dear Sebastian, I am just a man, and certainly no one worthy of any fuss such as this, I dare say," Señor Moretti said honestly.

"Well, you have done more than most men would have in your position," Sebastian said solemnly then picked up a gift and handed it to him in the same manner in which he had once been handed a very beautifully carved wooden box. "You gave me a home when I had none and wanted no one."

"Provided direction when I felt lost and afraid." Nathanael also placed a small parcel into his lap and tightened the corners of his mouth to hold back his building emotion.

"Bestowed a listening ear without judgement, even when I refused and most definitely rebuked you." Emile smiled apologetically and gave him another gift that matched his own style perfectly.

"And granted us all a chance for a future after we had been sentenced to death." William placed one hand upon his other shoulder before handing him a very carefully wrapped parcel. "In short, none of us would even be here if it was not for you, and we want to honor you for that."

Overwhelmed beyond words at last, Señor Moretti glanced at the gifts before him and tried to compose himself, his voice coming out barely above a whisper as he tried to answer, "I... I don't know what to say."

"Then I will say what you once asked us," Emile stated boldly with a tilt of his head towards their host.

"Really? What was that?" Señor Moretti inquired, deeply intrigued.

"Do you want to live forever?" Emile asked him seriously without any further pretense or explanation.

Looking at each of the men in turn, Señor Moretti pursed his lips to hold back the true feelings he felt for each of them and said fervently, "I have never wanted to do so more in my life than in this very moment."

Equally pleased, the men all smiled broadly in mutual appreciation.

"Then there truly is a place for us after all... for all of us," Nathanael added satisfactorily and took his seat to watch his mentor open their gifts.

"Ajaccio." *Wikipedia*, Wikimedia Foundation, 17 Sept. 2024, en.wikipedia.org/wiki/. Accessed 7 Oct. 2024.

Allthatsinteresting.com/vampires

"Great Storm of 1703." *Wikipedia*, Wikimedia Foundation, 16 Sept. 2024, en.wikipedia.org/wiki/Great_storm_of_1703. Accessed 7 Oct. 2024.

"Jean-Baptiste Denys." *Wikipedia*, Wikimedia Foundation, 15 Sept. 2024, en.wikipedia.org/wiki/Jean-Baptiste Denys. Accessed 7 Oct. 2024.

Memon, Nazneen BHMS. "What Medicines Were Used in the 1800s?" *MedicineNet*, www.medicinenet.com/what_medicines_were_used_in_the_1800s/article. htm & https://www.webmd.com/a-to-z-guides/features/look-back-old-time-medicines. Accessed 7 Oct. 2024.

"Piano Sonata No. 11 (Mozart)." *Wikipedia*, Wikimedia Foundation, 19 Nov. 2024, Piano Sonata No. 11 (Mozart). Accessed 19 Nov. 2024.

Pierce, R.V. M.D., "The People's Common Sense Medical Adviser In Plain English, 1888, World's Dispensary Printing Office and Bindery.

"Planning a Visit to Knole." *National Trust Registered Charity*, www.nationaltrust.org.uk/visit/kent/knole. Accessed 7 Oct. 2024.

Sackville-West, Robert. "Inside Knole, Home to the Same Family for over 400 Years." *House and Garden*, 17 Oct. 2023, www.houseandgarden.co.uk/gallery/knole-park-house-national-trust. Accessed 7 Oct. 2024.

"The Hierarchy Of Servants." *Donna Hatch*, 31 Aug. 2018, donnahatch.com/the-hierarchy-of-servants/. Accessed 7 Oct. 2024.

Watts, Isaac. "Joy To The World." Open Hymnal Project, 1719, 1836, 2005.

Watts, Isaac. "I Sing The Mighty Power Of God." Divine and Moral Songs For Children, 1715.

Wesley, Charles. "Hark The Herald Angels Sing." George Whitfield altered. 1739. en.wikipedia.org/wiki/List_of_ships_of_the_line_of_the_Royal_Navy

"Who Wants To Live Forever." The Tenors. www.tenorsmusic.com. https://youtu.be/IbYG30ucL7Q?si=fqj4UoCIByjv_WYt .

www.historyhit.com/locations/simpsons-tavern/